DRAGON SHIFTER'S VENGEANCE

DANIELLE MOSHER

The Reading Glass Books
1-888-420-3050
www.readingglassbooks.com
fulfillment@readingglassbooks.com

Table of Contents

DRAGON SHIFTER'S VENGEANCE

Chapter 1

"Maggie, sweetie are you listening to me?" I blink several times and come back to reality, no I was *not* listening.

"No, sorry." Ms. Hamper -my therapist - smiled wanly; this was the third therapy session I had zoned out on. She wasn't happy with me.

"I said you've done well these last few weeks. Your temper control has improved greatly." I smiled. I was proud of myself, I hadn't snapped at anyone, hadn't thrown anything, and hadn't beat the shit outta anyone or thing in three weeks. Though somehow I didn't think it was 'cause my control had gotten better, but because people had learned to not piss me off and to leave me alone. Also my being a dragon shifter helped.

I had only just celebrated my 16th Birthday. I know most kids would be psyched at the possibility of getting a car, new or otherwise in some cases, but me; I was just glad to be alive. I know that makes it sound like I've been suicidal, thankfully that's not the case. There had been seven people in my family six months ago, now there was only two.

"Did you consider my questions from our last session?" Our last talk was three days ago, I was required to see her every three days for sanity purposes. Her questions had been, will I start talking to anyone but her and Mr. Hydell? Will I go to prom? Or will I transfer to the shifter school I had recently been given a scholarship to?

"To answer the first one, no. I don't feel I'm ready for any kind of social interaction with anyone my own age yet." My friends had all abandoned me after my family had been murdered. There was a damn good reason for it though, which is why I wasn't mad at them or felt betrayed by them. They distanced themselves at my request, for their own safety. The man who had killed my family and been after me had gotten away and was still missing. Six months had passed since the murders and the police still had no clue where he was hiding.

"And to the second and third?" She prompted.

"Before that, has the scholarship expired?" I asked.

"No, it's still open. It doesn't expire until next year, they wanted you to take as much time as you needed. Since it will be the first time you'll be interacting with your own kind."

I nodded knowingly at that; my father, siblings, and one friend were the only other shifters I had ever been in contact with. His parents had died before he even graduated high school. Now I knew some semblance of how he felt. My mother had been a wiccan high priestess, a highly respected one too. My older brother Reggie was about halfway through college, working towards a degree in astronomy. He wanted to work at NASA. Go for it bro, that would be the coolest thing ever. He had been on a field trip to the Atacama Desert, visiting the Cerro Paranal hotel with his class. So he had been safe from attack. For safety reasons, I had no idea where he was, and he was equally in the dark about my location. We had mutually agreed to temporarily end contact until the murderer had been caught, but we were both hoping he'd fight and be killed in the aftermath. Our sister on the other hand -older than me but younger than him – had died with our parents and maternal grandparents.

"As for number two. Hell no, I hate the idea of buying a dress your only gonna wear once and can't even return it. That and I have no interest in prom or homecoming at any time in my high school career. I feel that it's a waste of time and money." My school did things differently. Prom was held at the end of the year as a kind of celebration.

"That's understandable. And question three?"

"I wish I could give you an answer now, but…"

"Your still unsure." I nod.

"I would like to finish this year at my school, - there's only a few weeks left – then maybe spend the summer somewhere quiet. Give me time to try and come to terms with everything fully."

"Okay." She said in an excited tone, like she knew I would say something like that and had planned for it. "My uncle owns an absolutely beautiful estate in Scotland." I looked at her with wide eyes and felt myself give a real smile for the first time in weeks.

"Scotland!" She nodded.

I had been on a roster to visit Scotland with my history class earlier in the year, the trip was set for this summer, obviously the injuries I'd acquired during the attack had meant a few weeks in the hospital. As a dragon shifter I heal quicker than most shifters, but that doesn't apply to a shattered femur bone. So for those reasons my place had been given to someone else. That didn't mean I wasn't highly disappointed.

I had wanted to visit Scotland since I was little and seeing 'Brave' only made it stronger. "My uncle is willing to let you spend the summer at the estate with the year round staff. He went through something similar that you did and understands the need for time and distraction."

"How big is the estate?"

"300 acres, and most of it is thick forest, there's even a small lake, and a few mountains within hiking distance."

"Anything else?" I asked trying to contain my excitement.

"The building is actually a fully restored castle, with a view of the sea." I clapped my hands like a super excited little girl. This couldn't be happening.

"You're serious about all this?" I asked.

"100%" I leaned back in the chair, covering my face in astonishment. Three months in Scotland. Yes, please. Oh wait I was forgetting. I sat up.

"Rules?" She raised her eyebrows, not quite understanding. "About staying."

"Oh, okay. Well… I haven't discussed that with him as of yet, but I will definitely bring it up when I call him later." She smiled; she had never seen me this animated. The only thing she could do now was make sure I stayed that way. She glanced at the clock. "Oops, we've gone five minutes over." That hadn't happened before. "Don't worry, my next appointment isn't for an hour. Dang it." The last bit was because she had trouble getting out of her chair. I immediately stood, walked around the desk, and helped her.

She was eight months pregnant; her chair wasn't exactly conducive for a pregnant woman. It was comfortable sure, just not easy to get out of with a big belly. "Thank you sweetheart." I made sure she was steady before I let go.

"You're welcome." She grabbed her bag while I grabbed my coat.

"Your guardian should be here by now. You head home and make whatever preparations you need. I'll call my uncle and set everything up, okay."

"Okay." I held the door for her before walking out myself, I was suffering from depression, but that didn't mean I had to stop behaving how I was raised.

Mr. Hydell was waiting at the elevator, on his phone as usual. He was my official guardian; I had no other family besides my brother, and he was somewhere safe. I gently kicked Mr. Hydell's leg. He looked up, "Oh, you're done. I thought the session was going long."

"Just a little bit." He led me into the elevator. Not a big talker Mr. Hydell. That was fine with me, I didn't always like to do a lot of talking. I like to keep to myself, mostly. We got in his fancy Cadillac after leaving the elevator. It was only as we were leaving the underground parking lot and entering the streets of Los Angeles that I realized that I had forgotten to ask where this new school I might be attending was.

I didn't bring it up though, I knew Mr. Hydell had a date tonight and I didn't want to bother him. I like having the apartment where we live to myself. He knows that so he's gone most of the time, and since I'm not under 12 it's fine for me to be alone. The door is locked, he's a licensed gun owner, I know where the gun is kept as well as the ammo, and my father taught all three of us how to use a gun, so I was safe from intruders. There are days though that I wish my sister hadn't been such a pacifist, not liking violence is fine, but refusing to pick up a gun even to save your own life was stupid. I thought back to that night. Again.

It had been like that 2008 movie Prom Night. A teacher from school becomes obsessed with a student, murders her family, and is arrested. There were a few differences though. Mr. Kepner had taken one look at me as I had entered my physics class and decided he wanted me. I was the youngest student in the class, that right there was proof of how smart I was. With an IQ of 179, you'd think I would have seen how he looked at me, but like a true Brainiac, I had been too focused on the next test to see clearly. My teacher had kept his desires well hidden. No one had known what he was planning, not even his wife. Mrs. Kepner had been found dead in her car in an apparent suicide, along with their three-month-old daughter. He had feigned grief well, even taking time off from work to mourn. It wasn't until the investigation team who had been studying the deaths had found evidence of foul play that anyone got suspicious. Although the only reason their deaths had been investigated in the first place was because the mother-in-law knew her daughter well enough to listen when Mrs. Kepner told about her husband's odd behavior. Mr. Kepner apparently vanished for two weeks after that.

Police looking into what was now a double murder looked back over several weeks and followed him via cameras across the city. That was how they had found he'd been following me home since the first day of school, hence getting home late. Had spent the time off 'mourning' following me across town when I wasn't at school or home. I had noticed a shadowy figure one week into school and had mentioned it to my parents. My sister said I was being paranoid, but my parents and grandparents listened. I had started martial arts training at 9, it was upped after he started stalking me, and a good thing too. Just not good enough.

After he disappeared I started randomizing my schedule, making it so no one would know where I was and when. I started distancing myself from my friends so that they wouldn't get hurt. I couldn't exactly do that with my family though. Finally five weeks after he disappeared, he cracked. I had gone to a movie by myself to try and calm my frazzled nerves. It was a decision I'll always regret, maybe if I had been home I could have saved them. Every detail of that day was permanently etched in my brain.

I smelled the blood from a block away. My grandpa had had cancer, so I knew it was his blood that had been spilled. I pulled my hood over my head, and while calling the cops ran to my house. They had told me to stay away, what good would that do? If I could somehow save my family I would do it. I entered through the kitchen, making no noise. The smell of blood was over powering. My grandma lay on the tiled floor, her throat slit wide open. She had been on blood thinners; she never stood a chance. Grandpa's body was a few feet away. He'd been stabbed. I could see from my angle that the blade had gone through his aorta, his death was at least instantaneous. Avoiding their bodies and blood pools, I made my way upstairs. I heard whimpering. Slowly I made my way toward them. They were coming from across my sister's room. I looked in; she was barely alive.

I quietly rushed to her, one of our dad's guns was within reach. She had never even reached for it. I lifted her head off the floor. She'd been stabbed in the abdomen seven times, right in the small intestines. There would be no saving her. I started to cry.

"I'm gonna die. Aren't I?" She asked, I didn't want to, but I nodded. "My own damn fault, I should've grabbed the gun."

"Yes you should have." We laughed. There was a thump a few doors down. She grabbed my arm.

"He's looking for you."

"Mr. Kepner."

She nodded, "You have to get out Maggie, now before it's too late."

"I'm not leaving you Amanda." I said with anger.

"I Love You."

"I Love You Too." She died in my arms a few seconds later. I cried harder, still never making a sound. I heard another thump. Now I was only angry. This man had come into my life and started to destroy it; I would not let him finish it. He was in my room at the end of the hall. I would kill him. My anger was my undoing.

I left my sister's body and started making my way down the hall. I felt myself begin to shift as I creeped. Fingers became claws, teeth became fangs, my legs extended, and my hearing sharpened; too late. I caught the ticking just before the bomb went off. He had set it up in our grandparent's room, expecting that my parents would look there last and be taken out that way. He was wrong.

The resulting explosion shook the whole house, blowing me backwards into the bathroom across from their room. I was stunned, my ears were ringing, and there was an odd, pungent odor filling my nose. Because of this I didn't hear the floor give way beneath me and the old-fashioned cast iron bath tub. I landed on grandma's vintage car, bouncing off after, and ending up on my back, only to land in the tub's path. The bathroom was directly above the garage, her car was parked on the left side, while the tub was on the right side of the bathroom. I had fallen through the floor above the car, my bounce planting me just to right of the front bumper. The whole floor was too weak to take the tubs weight. It fell through, the front pulling off to the left toward the car, before skidding off of it. A femur can at times withstand over 2000 pounds of force before breaking. Not a human femur, that only takes 624 pounds. The bathtub landed with much more. I never felt any pain, the sudden shock of it landing on my leg, and shattering my left femur overloaded the pain receptors in my brain and I lost consciousness immediately.

I awoke to the smell of blood being much stronger than before. I was still in the garage and despite the amount of debris piled up after my fall and the collapse of the floor from the tub, I had a clear line of sight outside. I could see Mr. Kepner, straddling my mother, demanding to know where I was. He was hysterical and somehow hadn't noticed me in the rubble. I wasn't until later that I learned why. The explosion had left a lot of debris behind; my face was dirty and the rubble I was trapped in was piled well enough that my face was in shadow.

My mom noticed me though. She never said a word. No matter how many times he stabbed her, nothing left her mouth. The only thing she said was done telepathically and it was at me. *"Stay quiet, don't make a sound. Your father will be here soon"* I did as I was told.

Even if it killed me to do it. I knew there was nothing I could do, I was wounded, pinned, and in no fighting condition whatsoever. I was forced to watch as he tortured my mom to death, and when my dad did finally show, it was too late. She was dead. I was hyperventilating from frustration, unable to move and destroy that bastard. I had never seen my dad shift before that night, we were supposed to be a secret, but sometimes things need a response. I heard his roar just over the tubs movement. I gasped. The back-right leg was partially supported by floor and roof remnants, but not well enough. If it didn't get more support, it would finish its path. I moved my arm. Got a good grip on the lips edge and using my dragon strength without changing my skin or the ends of my fingers, I pushed just enough to support the tub. Injured, I wouldn't be able to hold it forever. Time to take a note from 'Daylight'. Just like Stallone's character, I pushed a pressure point in my arm which locked the muscles in place. I was now the leverage holding the tub in place. I hoped I was conscious enough to undo it when the paramedics showed.

I don't know how, but Mr. Kepner won the fight against my dad, I suspect it had to do with that odd smell that had suddenly become stronger. All I saw was him standing over my dad, getting ready to finish him off. A 12-gauge pump-action shotgun in his hands. I heard him say, "Tell me where she is, and I'll let you live."

"No you won't. You messed up Fuck!" The gun went off, severing my dad's leg at the knee.

"Tell me. Now!"

"Go Fuck yourself. You'll never find her, and even if you do, she'll rip you limb from limb."

Mr. Kepner crouched, still pointing the gun at dad. "No she won't. She loves me."

My dad laughed, "Your more messed up than we thought." I saw Mr. Kepner's grip tighten.

"She despises you, and she will avenge us." I could hear the sirens, "All of us."

Mr. Kepner pulled the trigger. My dad's chest was torn to shreds. It took every ounce of my will to not scream. He stood and moved up to my dad's head, intending to make sure he was dead. He wasn't. Like lightning my dad swiped at his legs, shredding the muscles on his thighs. He had shifted his right arm when it was hidden behind him. Mr. Kepner- in his surprise- dropped the shotgun. My dad grabbed it, and not knowing how many shots were left, returned the favor. Mr. Kepner lost his leg too. I heard rather than saw him hobble to a car and drive away. My dad dragged himself to my mom's body. I heard him apologize for getting there too late.

I couldn't take it any longer. "Daddy." It wasn't very loud but with his dragon hearing, he knew where I was. Using the last of his strength, he crawled to where I was hidden. His face lit up when he saw I was alive, then changed to devastated when he realized I had seen everything. He touched my face.

"Are you all right?"

"My leg is broken, and I'm pretty sure I've got a concussion. Other than that I'm peachy." We laughed.

"Your sister, your grandparents?" I shook my head. "All of them?" He asked. I nodded.

"I'm so sorry sweetie."

"It's not your fault dad."

"It is because I wasn't here, I might have stopped him."

"I don't blame you."

"You find him, and you make him pay for what he has done to us. All of us."

"I will dad, I promise." I saw the light in his eyes begin to fade, just as the cops and ambulance arrived.

"I Love You Maggie."

"I Love You too Daddy." His eyes closed and his heart stopped. He had put up a valiant fight. Shame it was all for nothing.

I lost consciousness again as the medical crew reached him. I woke up in the hospital. It had taken them three hours to release me from the damned rubble. It didn't help another bomb had been found and had to be disposed of before they could proceed. The cops told me that the escape car had been found two towns away and no sign of Mr. Kepner. I gave them every detail, leaving out how I'd tried to kill him and had partially shifted. Their autopsys only confirmed what I already knew.

Reggie came home after that. At 22 he had the only authority on what to do about burials. Cremation had been what mom, dad, and our grandparents had wanted. Then their ashes turned into trees. Amanda was more of a problem. She'd been 19 and about to start college when she died. She had no funerary plans. Obviously. In the end, it was decided her body would be given the same funeral as everyone else. Despite the objections of her boyfriend. It's not like the trees wouldn't be labeled in some way. We both decided that they'd each be turned into their favorite trees. Grandma and grandpa would be birch trees, Amanda a weeping willow, and Mom & Dad as oak trees. Planted in a circle on the family grounds in Michigan.

Getting this done was a problem in a half. I had to get special permission just to leave the hospital for the funeral. Reggie and I planned out the whole thing. Full burial rights and ceremony under wiccan tradition as they all wanted. Amanda's boyfriend wanted hers done as a Christian. Uh hello she's our sister, she gets buried how she would have wanted it. He held his own funeral for her after that. We didn't care. Neither of us had liked him to begin with. We did let him plant a cross at her grave though. We knew she would have been okay with that.

We never saw her boyfriend after that. It made no nevermind to us what he did afterwards. So we all moved on. Or we tried to. Reggie went back to school, of course. He'd wanted to take me with him, but I knew I would only be a distraction to him. And not the kind he needed. So I stayed, my things were removed from the house and brought to Mr. Hydell's apartment. Mr. Hydell oversaw the attempted selling of our house, then the demolition of it. Everything that had survived was put into storage and put on hold for when Reggie and I could finally go through it and split it between us.

We had come to our no contact agreement after the funeral. Neither one of us had felt safe together with Kepner still on the loose. It was an easy decision to come to, since I had told him all the details of that night. The last we had heard from each other; he was at school in New York. He transferred elsewhere for safety reasons.

"Earth to Maggie." Once again I came back to reality. "We're back kiddo."

"Sorry." He didn't press, he knew the story. "Aren't you gonna be late?"

"Naw, I've got a few minutes. Everything you asked for is in the fridge, and I got the meat marinating at 10 o'clock."

"Cool, thanks." He nodded. We exited the car and got into the elevator. He always parked by the elevator in his building, it meant I could have a quick getaway if I needed it or a quick get to safety option. I appreciated it.

"So, Ms. Hamper says you might stay in Scotland for the summer." I chuckled slightly. I had been so pumped about that only a few minutes ago. Now I was just deflated.

"Hey," I looked at him, "It's okay to distract yourself from what happened. Not everyone gets even that."

"I just… it all feels like a betrayal now."

"Because your trying to move on without fulfilling your promise." I just nod, so he continues. "What would they want you to do?" I take a few seconds to think about that.

I sigh before answering, "They'd want me to be in my best shape- emotionally as well as physically- so that when he does resurface, I can take him down with no problem."

"Use that as your main focus. So long as he breaths you and your brother can never be reunited." He placed his hand on my shoulder, "Use that anger and very mediaeval temper of yours," I chuckled, which is what I knew he wanted, "To make his worthless, murdering, waste-of-breathable-air ass pay for everything that he has ever done." I nodded again, trying to hold back the tears.

The elevator dinged. We were at his apartment. The doors opened and we entered. My first instinct since I had moved in was to take a deep breath and check for any unusual smells. Nothing. It was always reassuring. I made my deep breath as well camouflaged as was possible, if anyone watched from the windows across the way, I didn't want them knowing what I was doing. Least of all him.

I wouldn't let everything my mom had taught me about survival go to waste. Nor what my dad taught me about self-defense and weapons. Bladed or otherwise.

Mr. Hydell looked at his grandfather clock. As a very successful divorce lawyer, he could afford one. 5:30, he had ten minutes to get ready for his date. He double checked his phone. The clock was right, it often was since I had cleaned it. It had had a bad habit of slowing down, so on a slow day when I was feeling very down, I grabbed my gun cleaning kit – my dad had given me one for my 15th birthday- and went to work. Mr. Hydell took care of his own guns so I wouldn't need to. He hadn't noticed at first but slowly he began to see a difference. Finally about a month ago he'd asked if I had done something and I said that I had cleaned it. I have an awesome memory, so none of the pieces had been misplaced. After that he'd made me the clocks official care taker - other clock places make you pay just to look at it. I loved that clock; I had a thing for vintage items. He often caught me staring at it, so last week he had amended his will so that I would get the clock when he died. As a shifter, obviously I aged slower than humans, so I'd still technically be young when he kicked the bucket. I didn't mind the wait.

"I keep forgetting that it works now." He shoved his phone in his pocket, "I've got to go get ready, you sure you're okay for tonight?" I nodded, he worried after me because my first night here I had awoken from a nightmare and went ballistic. I'd had no idea where I was and was very afraid about that prospect. I'd destroyed my room – thankfully, none of my stuff had been added yet and all of it was new, so easy to replace – it had taken him several hours to calm me down. Which wasn't easy in and of itself, I was in full dragon mode; size, and everything. I was still getting used to him and my new environment.

That was the first time he'd seen me for what I was. As a young shifter I'm not that big, but it still came as a surprise. He was a little angry that no one had told him that his new ward was a dragon shifter, but then again no one but me and Ms. Hamper had known. Two days after the murders, someone came out with info and proof of the existence of shifter. There was literally no way to stop him, he had incriminating evidence. Even against several governors who were actually good people. Needless to say those governors were fired and replaced. People fear what they don't understand, and humans more than anything. Though the only thing they should fear is their own species.

Ms. Hamper had known what I was the second she met me. Well I should say she knew I was a shifter; she hadn't narrowed it down to what kind yet. She'd been the one to calm Mr. Hydell down after I'd trashed my room. His silence meant my further safety. He'd chosen to defuse the situation wisely. He'd complemented me on my color. Magenta wasn't a shade commonly seen on a dragon. Mine especially. I was the more reddish shade of magenta, not overpowering but beautiful in its own right.

His chosen silence was helpful. It was bad enough what shifter kids were going through at their schools. I didn't need that too, not after everything I'd already been through. My brother didn't have that problem, other than revenge he had barely any kind of temper. Which is extremely odd for a dragon shifter, or any kind of shifter. All three of us had inherited it. I just had the worst temper.

"I'll be okay, I've got plenty to distract me." He been more worried about leaving me alone. He was afraid to come home and find I'd flown the coop, then maybe get myself badly hurt. All of that was understandable.

"All right. I'll see you later." He went into his room to change. I had a few minutes till I had to start dinner for myself, so I went into the bathroom to check my scars. My leg bothered me when I used it too much. Walking around at school and then walking to my appointment – only 'cause he was at work and couldn't drive me – plus I'd had gym today, rope climbing, so that really didn't help. I closed the door, undid my jeans, and slipped them off. The skin around the scar tissue was irritated, but that was my own fault, I hated wearing anything but jeans, cargo, or basketball shorts. Not much I could do about it, so I just rubbed soothing lotion on the scar, and took some pain meds. I never used aspirin, they also worked as blood thinners. I now had a small psychological fear of blood thinners.

I heard Mr. Hydell exit his room and leave the apartment. I now had the run of the place. Picking up my jeans I went into my room. It was painted a lovely shade of aquamarine and was covered in oceanography paraphernalia. I loved the sea. Most would say that was odd 'cause I did breath fire. I threw my coat, backpack, and jeans on the bed. Went over to my dresser – which had seashells painted on it – and changed into a pair of cargo shorts. I pulled my homework out of my bag. Not a lot for this week. I could do it as I made dinner.

I grabbed my mp3 player and went to the kitchen. Mr. Hydell had gotten me a mp3 speaker for Christmas. That way I could use that when my portable record player needed charging I could still listen to music. Music helped me stay in the here and now. I had a very wide range of genres to listen to, I wasn't too picky.

I took everything I needed for my dinner out of the fridge and cupboards, starting my music at the same time. 'Where Evil Grows' by The Poppy Family. I chuckled. I had completely forgotten that song was on there. Oh well, go with it. I didn't start dancing like Robotnik does in the movie that would come out a few years later, but I did sing along.

Tonight's dinner was one of my favorites, gyoza – or for those less inclined to culinary vocabulary, pot stickers. I loved pot stickers. This was a recipe my dad and I had come up with. Steak and Mushroom. I know people will say it's beef and mushroom, but no, you want plain ol' ground beef as your meat you go right ahead. I like steak, I am a Texas girl after all. My dad and I had both been big steak and mushroom people, we even came up with a very successful stew. The meat had been marinating for over six hours now – just like Mr. Hydell had said – so it was nice and tender. I'd chosen good steaks, so there wasn't a whole lot of gristle on them. My mushrooms of choice were portabella caps – really big ones – porcini, and, chanterelles. Although I didn't always use the chanterelles, sometimes I just wanted the portabellas and porcinis. The mushrooms had been pre chopped, I was surprised, I didn't take Mr. Hydell for a chef. He'd even rehydrated them. You can't get porcinis or chanterelles any other way here, they needed specific growing environments, unlike portabellas, they can grow just about anywhere.

I found the mushroom stock in the fridge by the meat. I'd add it to what was left of the marinade for the dipping sauce. I pulled out a cast iron skillet and sauce pan. Chopped the meat – after getting as much marinade off as I could – mixed that with the mushrooms and spices, plus mozzarella and parmesan cheese. He'd bought authentic Parmigiano-Reggiano. I held the chunk to my nose and smelled it, ah, heaven. I added them to a bowl and stirred, filling the wrappers was the arduous part. You had to get the perfect amount so that they wouldn't burst, not that I minded. Sometimes that was okay, it showed you never get it on the first try. I'd been doing it for a few years now and knew my portioning's well. Even when I made the wonton wrappers from scratch.

I got the marinade and stock cooking on a back burner while I filled the wrappers. A tail is quite convenient, when your hands are busy. I turned slightly to admire my tail. I'm not vain – which is another oddity among female dragons – but I did love the color. My eyes were the same shade. It was why my full name was Magenta. My siblings had laughed at me at first, because of my color. They were more common colors. Reggie was midnight blue, and Amanda had been Emerald green. My father had been as black as deepest night. When no stars or moon showed. My siblings ridicule was why I'd started going by Maggie. After so long I was just used to it.

The sauce didn't take long to heat through, so I did as Anne Burrell says to do, and brought it down to a simmer after it boiled for a few minutes. The pot stickers were all formed, with no filling or wrappers left – I hate it when that happens. I pulled the olive oil out. Most recipes said to use veggie oil, but I like the crisp that olive oil gives them, yeah I have to drain a little more oil, then again that's what paper towels are for.

I put six in the pan at a time, you should never crowd a pan. They only took five minutes to cook, and that was with the steaming. The kitchen filled with the scent quickly. My mouth began to water. I'd yielded over 30 pot stickers, that just meant leftovers. Yum.

Mr. Hydell liked my cooking, even if I still made enough for five people. My mom had been adamant about all three of us knowing how to cook. Most kids our age had no idea how to boil water without burning something. She said that was a damned disgrace. And one reason we both had watched Worst Cooks in American. It was fun seeing how some people reacted to the kitchen.

I made my plate from the first twelve. I ate slowly, so as not to get distracted, even if I was timing all three cooking intervals. Better safe than sorry. I sighed. Wrong choice of quote right now Magenta. I breathed deeply and slowly. Now was not the time to break down, not in the kitchen. The last thing we needed was a cooking fire. I steadied myself and began the next batch. The sauce was ready, so I poured that into a serving bowl to cool. The pot stickers were good without sauce but were even better with it. It took about 30 minutes to cook them all. I didn't mind. Some of the best things take the longest time to make.

Once I was done cooking the gyoza, I set them aside to drain and cool. Grabbing a barstool, I sat at the island to finish eating and go over some paper work my parents had left behind. I couldn't do either of their jobs, but I needed something to do. My dad had been a military combat trainer for several years, he'd retired to be closer to us after I was born. My sister and brother had been born in different states. He and mom had moved to Texas shortly before his final deployment, and that's where they had me. Dad had been ecstatic about a second daughter and had even insisted on my name.

When he had retired, he'd turned his skills elsewhere. He took up forging. I still had most of the blades that he'd made. One of the few swords that'd survived was a tanto that he had intended to give to me for my 18th birthday. Obviously now that would never happened. It wasn't finished, so I figured going through his old paperwork would give me some kind of clue. Mom had had some ideas too, so I included her high priestess notes for good measure. There! Near the end of her pile is a hand drawn picture. I immediately recognize the blade. Dad had made the Hamon line look like dragon scales, it wasn't easy, but he'd managed. Looking at the handle mom had designed, I couldn't **not** start to cry. It was the most beautiful thing I had ever seen.

The background color was pale aquamarine, the dragon silhouetted in it was a shade darker than me, and the waves that would be painted had a real sense of movement, there was even small but detailed fish swimming in the waves. The guard was the traditional circle but with a Chinese dragon cut into the inside, so that there was space between the two. Mom had even designed the sheath.

That was equally beautiful. The tail of the dragon was silhouetted there, and a leatherback sea turtle was painted at the very bottom, submerged beneath the waves. I'd finished eating, so I pushed my plate away. The tears were free flowing now. There was only one thing for it. I stood and walked to my room.

In my room I pulled out my violin. My grandpa had given me one when I was three, saying that he thought I should have an outlet for my emotions and the violin was a good one. He hadn't lied. I had progressed quickly – nowhere near as quickly as Lindsey Stirling – and I loved every second of it. I didn't have that violin anymore. A jealous classmate had smashed it in sixth grade. I'd been pretty mad at the time and had tried to smack her, but then grandpa came home with an adult one. I'd been so happy that I completely forgot about her, until the next school day that is. I'd outgrown my first one – my arm was now too long, so a new one had been in order anyway. The pieces of my old one had been collected and turned into a small sculpture. It wasn't the prettiest piece you'd ever see, but I adored it.

I pulled the bow from its spot in the case, rosined it, tuned my violin, took a deep breath, and started to play. The tune I played out was a mournful one, beautiful in its own way, not exactly uplifting, but comforting. The neighbor banged on my wall. I frowned at the wall. She wanted me to stop. Supposedly she hated the sound of the violin, viola, and cello. Our neighbor was a woman in her thirties **still** hoping to be discovered and become a pop star. Newsflash lady, if it hasn't happened yet, it probably won't. So instead of stopping, I played louder. She banged some more. Nope. Louder!

Sad to say but annoying her was helping, if she didn't like it, then tough shit! I need to let something out, I'd rather do it this way instead of crying. You'd think I would have run out of tears. It's amazing what things you can discover as time goes by. The next banging was on the door to the apartment. Still playing I went to the video com by the door. It was the building manager. Rolling my eyes I used my elbow to activate the shared video but not audio. I'd still hear him though.

"Mrs. Tomasino is complaining of a horrible noise." I glared at him through the screen.

"I don't want to tell you to stop – I can hear you through the door- I just want her to shut up."

"Then tell her to move out." Said Mr. Hydell coming up behind him. That was a quick date.

"Mr. Hydell, good to see you."

"Jim." They shook hands, "Ask yourself this, who are you more afraid of? A grieving teenage girl with a sever temper? Or a thirty-seven-year-old pop star wannabe who can't take a hint?" Jim looked at the screen, looked back at Mr. Hydell, and walked away. Smart choice.

I saw him knock on Mrs. Tomasino's door. I didn't hear what he said to her. I did hear her response though, I won't repeat it here, that woman is a terrible curser. And I don't mean that lightly. What she meant to say was 'tell that little bitch to stop before I call the cops.' Mr. Hydell grabbed his phone so hard his knuckles turned white. He stormed toward her door. That got me to stop. I'd never seen him that angry. Holy cow, he was Lord of the Underworld pissed. I guess that was understandable. This was the 17th time she'd complained about my playing.

He pushed past Jim and entered her apartment, I heard her start to shout, then gag. What?! Jim stood by her door; he was starting to look a little green. He even covered his mouth and gagged at one point. What the heck was going on? I went to my room and put my violin back in its case, I wanted to know what was up. He was closing the door when I got back. "What was that about?" I asked.

"I showed her some photos." He looked at his phone, like he wasn't entirely proud of what he'd done.

"Which ones?" He had several on his phone, including some of my leg, and the bodies of my family.

"One of your leg, one of each of your family, and of Tom and Marjorie."

"Ah." Tom and Marjorie were the two classmates I had put in the hospital because neither of them had known when it was time to shut their mouths. Marjorie had forgiven me a few days later, she'd been smart enough to realize that she had gone too far and deserved what I'd given her. Tom on the other hand… nothing yet. Then again he's been absent for this last week.

"Did the pics shut her up?" I asked

"That and Jim threatened to evict her from the building then send bad tenet warnings to all other residential buildings in L.A." I whistled. Way to go Jim.

"Which pic did she gag at?"

He chuckled, "I wanted to shut her up quickly, so I went straight for you mom's." I inhaled sharply. Yeah, Mom's pictures would do it. In his torturing of her, he'd mutilated her body in quite a few ways. It was later discovered that the only reason the cops hadn't arrived earlier, had been because Mr. Kepner had called in enough false reports that all the cops were deployed across the city. Most on the direct opposite side of town from our house.

"She got pretty green after that." He smiled deviously.

"I'll bet, is that what Jim caught a glimpse of?"

"No actually. The photos he saw over my shoulder were of your sister, grandma, and your leg."

"The stitches are what make those pics so bad." I said.

"Well they did have to do a rush stitch job just to make sure no fragments were lost."

"Wasn't the prettiest job, but it did the trick." I'd spent the hour after arrival and before surgery, mapping the stitches. Looking for some kind of pattern that, maybe, could tone down the whole situation. I'd had no luck of course.

"Did you say anything else?"

"Yes, I asserted myself and said that if playing woeful tunes – either on violin or mp3 – helps you cope with the pain, then she needs to fuck off. Your mental, physical, and emotional health is more important than her desires."

I was on the verge of tears again. "Thanks."

He gave a soft smile and came over to give me a hug. He was the only person I let hug me. Ms. Hamper was more because of the baby bump, hugs can get awkward. Plus I had a bad habit of knowing what the baby was going to be when I was in even the slightest amount of hand to skin contact. It wasn't so much the touch that mattered, it was the fact that I could sense the babies aura even before it was born. I can identify babies using just that. I'd even asked if she wanted to know. She said no, she wanted it to be a surprise. I was cool with that.

"You go ahead and go to bed, I'll clean up." He said, turning to the kitchen. I nodded and moved in the direction of my room. Oh, wait I was forgetting something.

"How'd your date go?" He turned as I asked, he smiled.

"It went well, the only reason it was so short is 'cause one of her clients had a panic moment and needed an emergency session." Right, his girlfriend was a therapist, though I didn't know which kind.

"So other plans were made?"

"Yep, we'll met up again tomorrow after work."

"Cool. Good Night."

"Good Night kiddo." He proceeded to the kitchen, depending on where they were in their meal when she got the call he might eat some himself.

In my room, I changed into my pjs, grabbed a book, and laid down in my bed. The book was one of the Alpha and Omega books by Patricia Briggs. And before you grill me on reading an adult book, I have different reasons for it. I'm nowhere near interested in the sex. What I need is details on the shifter mating bond. My dad and paternal grandparents were dead so I couldn't ask them. Reggie was in safety, and Amanda had never even thought about it. If Reggie had discussed it with dad I didn't know. For all I knew he had been too busy trying to become an astronomer to even think about a future mate.

The second reason is that books like these – shifter romances or reverse harem novels – were the only source of potential facts when it came to the mating bond. I know some of the authors actually were shifters themselves, I just didn't know which. Third, no one ever wrote about teenagers experiencing the bond, not even an early one. I had no other way of getting answers on something that honestly did worry me. If I ever did find my mate or mates – please be only one, two I could maybe deal with, but more than that – I had absolutely no idea how they would act towards me and my past. Would he or they say the same thing Tom did? Would he or they comfort me and become my rock or rocks? Good Gods, someone my age should not have to even contemplate these things.

There was some good news to the readings. In most cases the bond took place the second you made eye contact. So that's easy, just avoid any and all eye contact with the boys at my new school. The bad news was, if it didn't form immediately by eye contact, it could grow or fester into being just by being withing 1000 yards of each other. So that was just great. So, bottom line, no friends, whatsoever. No exceptions. I'd already seen what Mr. Kepner was willing to do to get to me, I would **not** put my mate or mates through that horror.

I fell asleep with the book in my hand. My lamp was still on. It was on a timer to turn off after about 20 minutes after I last touched it. It was a neat lamp. Nightmares were still a constant thing, but so long as I managed to wake myself when they got to gruesome, I'd be okay.

Chapter 2

"Kiddo, wake up, you'll be late for work!" Work? It was Saturday. Crap! It was Saturday! I jolted out of bed and turned to my clock. The clock read 6:45 a.m. I had 35 minutes to get ready and get there. I had over slept. I know most teens would say I'm crazy for waking up at 6:30 on a Saturday, well those teens didn't have a job. That was almost clear across town and by the coast to boot. Thankfully, I had a cheat for getting there **fast**.

The wind felt great as I flew. I didn't enjoy it as much anymore, for obvious reasons. I stayed high enough that no one who was out would see me. Of course the only person I was worried about wouldn't know if it was me or not. I was still cautious though. The last thing I needed – or wanted - to do would be to lead Kepner to my new home.

I saw my work place come into view. The smell of salt water strong in my nose. My fellow workers knew the drill and had the roof top tent all set. Folding my wings I made a careful landing. The first time I'd tried it, I miss timed it and got tangled in the tent, even whacking myself in the head with one of the poles. My co-workers still hadn't let me live it down. Stacy was there to meet me as I emerged.

"Bout time girl, we were starting to worry." I merely smiled and shrugged. Stacy wasn't my age, but I still couldn't talk to her. Ms. Hamper and Mr. Hydell were my limit right now. She and all our co-workers knew that. They didn't press, didn't hold it against me. They just took it at face value and gave me what support they could. It had been Mr. Hydell who had gotten me this job. The current manager had owed him a favor, and had been hiring at the time, so win-win.

I worked at the Aquarium of the Pacific, as a gift shop worker. I also did some volunteer work around the aquarium, some of it was pretty dirty, but I loved it. When I had told Mr. Hydell that I wanted to be a marine biologist, he'd jumped at the chance for me to work here. You can learn something new every day. My co-workers and I got along great, even with my not talking. I used the time to do more than just work, watching kids come in and look at the sea creatures in awe was full filling in and of itself. It helped me feel closer and closer to myself again. Which was something I definitely needed.

Stacy and I made our way inside, the tent would be taken down in about an hour, after everyone had been fed. The animals not the people. My job didn't last all day, the gift shop closes about mid-afternoon. So most people when they arrive later in the day go there first. Kids and all. The aquarium didn't open till 9, but there were 11,000 animals, with a diversity of 500 species living here, so everyone had to pitch in to help feed. It was 7 a.m., time can fly when your giving everyone breakfast.

8:30, okay that's it. Everybody's been fed. Now to finish getting ready to open. My co-worker Ben and I had the first shift at the shop, so we opened the security gates. The gift shop was just to the left as you entered the main building, the kids always want to go here first. We had all kinds of stuff, from sea creature anatomy books, to stuffed animals, to – of course – t-shirts, and jewelry. I had a few of the anatomy books at home, they had a lot of detail, plus the model that was part of the pages.

Everyone was ready when that final half-hour was up. People didn't pour in like they do at some places, but it was nice to know there were so many people who came. Either to learn or be amazed, depended on the person. My favorite part of the whole place was a tunnel where the seals and sea lions were. You go in and the critters could swim around and pass over you. Some kids loved 'playing' with them too. Moving fingers and hands up and down while the sea lion or seal followed. It had expanded greatly over the last few years though. Sometimes even I still got lost.

We were about an hour into our official day, when things took an interesting and somewhat unwelcome turn. I heard Ben inhale sharply. I turned, my look conveying my confusion, I thought he'd been hurt. Nope. Looking at me, he pointed out into the shop. Standing with a stuffed dolphin in his hands, was Tom. I sighed heavily through my teeth, clearly annoyed. I really did **not** want to see him. "Here he comes." Warned Ben.

I turned to look at him, he was still limping. Good. I'd broken his right femur and snapped his knee cap in two, in retaliation for his comment. So why was he here, in my one favorite place in the city? And why the hell was he holding the dolphin?! He went up to Ben first. Purchasing the dolphin. I put my smile back on to help the customer who had approached me. It wasn't hard, not once I saw the little girl with her. My family had learned early that I wanted to be a mother. And I mean early, I was eight. The little girl was jumping up and down in excitement, her mom was here to purchase the largest baby penguin plush we carried, and an adopt an animal subscription. I checked them out quickly, it's nice to see someone encouraging her child toward conservation. That was when Tom came over.

The first thing I noticed was a ribbon tied around the plush toys neck, with something hanging from the ribbon. Seriously. You do something like that for a girl your dating and trying to apologize to, not the girl who put you in the hospital. Crossing my arms I looked from him to the dolphin, and back. Raising an eyebrow at the end. He cleared his throat, as if nervous to be here in front of me for the first time in weeks. Serves him right.

"I wanted to apologize," uh, duh, "I uh… I had no right to say.. what I did… and I really am sorry." Arms still crossed, I just repeated what I had just done. He huffed. Like he wasn't surprised about my reaction but had hoped it would go differently. Nu uh.

He sighed, handing me the dolphin. I took it and finally got a good look at the card. Wait. It wasn't a card. What in the world? I looked back up at him. Confusion obvious on my face.

"This is a 4Ocean subscription." I said. Then went to pat Ben on the back as he had choked on his drink. Still coughing, he said,

"I'm fine." And went back to what he was doing, though he still looked at me in shock. Okay, so yes I talked. It's not like I couldn't at that moment, I was so shocked and confused. I paused. Oh great, the whole aquarium would know long before the day was done. Holding up the toy, I looked Tom in the eye.

"I know how much you love the ocean, I figured it was a good starting point."

"You figured giving me a 4Ocean subscription angry girlfriend style, was a good starting point?"

"Okay so maybe I didn't think the whole thing through. But I have been thinking a lot about what you said to me when you kicked my a- butt." The change in vocab was because a group of kids was next to him. No cursing in front of kids please. That day was somewhat of a blur still, I had blown for the first time. After I'd broken his leg, it had taken the whole football team to get me off him, many of them had come out with fractures as well – thankfully for them football was over for the year. Before that though, he'd said, 'gut it out girl, don't be a cry-baby about it. So a former teacher killed your family, doesn't mean you have to act like a killjoy all the time. Butch up! Grow a spine!' not sensing the danger, I'd hit him. Hard.

I'd been aiming for his groin, but he had moved to kick me in the ass, so his leg got the shot. As he fell, I went for his face. Pinning him to the ground, I'd reigned my strength in so I wouldn't kill him and started wailing on his face. Most girls thought I'd clawed his eyes out, there was so much blood and swelling to his handsome face. I'd hit him 12 times before the team pulled me off. Those 12 times weren't in a row, they were in spurts of threes 'cause of the team. When they finally got me off of him, the team using all their strength to just hold me, I looked at him with fire in my eyes and said, 'you wouldn't know humility if it bit you on the private parts, or reached into your chest, pulled out your heart, tore it to pieces, and then put it back in to heal on its own, so don't you dare tell me how to mourn.' I'd calmed down enough the team had loosened their grips, I wrenched myself loose, grabbed my backpack and left the school. It was only after lunch, so yes, I ditched. It was either that or go back and finish it.

When I got home Mr. Hydell had told me he'd been evacuated to the hospital and was in surgery. He'd tried to get his parents to sue. 'Not gonna happen.' They'd said. Several people had told them what he had said to me, they were sympathetic, both his parents had already lost one parent before he'd been born. So they knew loss.

"I've been absent this week 'cause my grandpa died."

"Oh." I said with surprise and sympathy. Everyone at school – even me – knew that he'd spent every summer at his grandpa's since he was a little kid. Both his parents worked, so he needed some kind of entertainment during the summer.

"I'm sorry."

"Don't be. I now know how you feel."

"You know some semblance of how I feel. I hope you never fully know my pain." He nodded in agreement at that. I picked the toy back up.

"Okay, this can be a good start." He sighed with relief. I wasn't fully forgiving him, but at least it was a start. We shook on it, giving each other a small smile. He left the store, then hesitated outside the shop doors. He looked around a little, then at me, then went to set up a visit time. Good on ya dude. Ben was still looking at me funny, "What?" I asked with another small smile.

"You talked." I gave him a look.

"I mean like.. obviously… it's just…. You talked."

"Could you be anymore dumbfounded?" I asked.

"Probably." He replied.

I had been half right. Yes by the time my first shift was over the whole aquarium knew that I'd broken my silence, but Ben had also shared a video of it with the whole staff. Darn you Ben. I ate lunch at the café there at the aquarium. It's more of a small food court but it works. Then when I was done, I worked my second shift at the shop. After my second shift at the shop was over I helped out with volunteer stuff. Today I was helping with a classroom tour.

I knew this tour. I'd taken it myself. Just before I'd started fifth grade my dad had been temporarily reinstated into the military to help train some amazingly inept recently recruited rookies – whoops, try saying that three times fast – and we'd moved to Vandenburg Air Force Base for that year. The elementary school there had a set of **awesome** field trips for the fifth graders. An overnight trip to L.A. was one. You even got to spend the night in the aquarium, sleeping by either the sharks or otters. Separated by boys and girls of course. Not including chaperoning parents.

The aquarium wasn't the only place they stopped; it was a two-day trip after all. The aquarium was just the last stop on the first day, and the first on the second day. I went with Sam; he and Tammy were acting as the official guides for the group. Several of the kids were amazed at how big the tanks were. Some even asked how the glass held all that water. Simple answer, it's not glass. It's plexiglass. Much stronger and lighter. It wasn't until we reached one of the tanks with sharks that everyone saw proof that I'd spoken.

One of the girls at the front of the group moved to the back. She seemed a little leery of the sharks, or so I thought. She was just collecting her dad. But as she waked by, I noticed she was wearing a Bones t-shirt. "Hey Maggie!" I looked up. Jameson, the scuba diver in the tank had said it.

"Hm?" I asked as a simple acknowledgment.

"Don't suppose you have any interesting facts for everyone here?" Jameson asked.

"Since we all know your reputation." Sam said, not entirely convincing in his subtlety. You guys want me to talk more. Fine.

"Actually I do." I turned to the kids, "How many of you have seen or heard of the show Bones?" Several of them raised their hands. The girl wearing the shirt lit up as well.

"Well for those of you who don't know, Bones is a show about a woman who's a Forensic Anthropologist. There actually is an episode of the show that features the aquarium. This tank especially."

"It does?" I turned to look at Jameson, I knew he watched the show. Apparently not enough.

"Yes Jameson, you didn't know that?"

"No, I must have missed it." The staff laughed; we didn't get many chances to tease Jameson.

"Well in that episode, Dr. Brennan – the anthropologist – and her partner agent Booth are touring the aquarium, and while visiting this tank, one of the fish coughs up a bone."

One of the boys raised his hand. Sam pointed at him, "How'd they see it then?"

"Well I never did say what fish it was did I?" They shook their heads. Whoops, my bad.

"Let me fix that," a grouper was swimming by just then. Perfect, "It was this big guy who up-chucked the skull, of the body." Several made sounds of disgust. The girl in the Bones shirt raised her hand.

"Yes?" I said.

"I always thought fish could digest bones." She stated.

"Well," I let it hang. "Maisie." Good, she was smart.

"Well Maisie, some fish can. Not groupers. Unlike some fish, crocodiles and alligators, groupers have to barf up what they can't eat, or it could clog their digestive systems."

A boy in the back said, "Like owls have to?"

"Exactly." Maisie raised her hand again. "Did Dr. Brennan get to go diving in the tank?"

"Yes, to get the rest of the skeleton. Hodgins went with."

"Cool." We all laughed, that had come from Jameson. After that, the kids asked more aquatic questions, but I could see that quite a few of them had enjoyed what I had shared.

Chapter 3

My day was over at 5p.m. I checked my phone on the way out. It was new, my old one had been destroyed in the explosion. Two texts. One from Mr. Hydell, '*Date is at 5:30. Text me when you get this.*' The other was from Ms. Hamper. '*Come to office after work. Details on scholarship.*' Oh. Better answer that right away. I dialed her office number. She picked up on the first ring.

"Hello, this is Ms. Hamper."

"It's Maggie."

"Oh good, you got my text. Is it convenient?"

"Yes, I'm on my way. I just have to let Mr. Hydell know first."

"Kay. See you soon." We hung up. Next, tell Mr. Hydell. I kept it to text, I do that walking much easier than I do talking. '*10-4 on your text. Headed to Ms. Hamper. New details about scholarship.*'

His answer took a few seconds. '*10-4 back at ya. Be careful. Get ride home if you can.*' I chuckled; he didn't do military lingo often. '*Will do.*' Ben usually gave me a ride after work. He would drop me off three blocks from my building. I would then take four right turns and four left turns before entering an alley and flying to the roof. As far as the other building inhabitants knew, I only left for school.

Ben dropped me at the office. His date had been cancelled so he volunteered to wait. He even agreed to wait on the street where there were more cameras and witnesses. Excuse me for being cautious and a good friend. I took the stairs up. I had excess energy from excitement. I was still in my work clothes, but somehow I doubted she'd care. My hair was neat at least. Lynda was at the desk when

I got there. She was a chain smoker, so I sneezed every time I came in while she was on duty. Today was no exception.

"Nice to see you too sweetie." She said in a snarky tone. She hated her job, hence the smoking.

"Is Ms. Hamper in?" I asked as politely as I could.

"They're both in there." Huh? Okay whatever. Wait! Possible panic!!

"What did the other look like?" She looked at me, realizing her mistake, quickly added.

"Sorry. The school super intendent. Very handsome. **Very** red hair. About 6'7. I'd say 350 – 360 pounds." I breathed a sigh of relief.

"Thanks Lynda."

"Yep."

That was about it with her. Mr. Kepner had had black hair, was nowhere near 350 lb., and he was only 5'9", damn. I'd never thought about how short he was. Eh, time for that later. I opened the door to her office. Holy fiery red head! Lynda wasn't kidding.

I was so surprised I stopped in the door. Looking at his head in disbelief. His hair was so red it actually hurt to look at it. Ms. Hamper cleared her throat while also suppressing a chuckle. I snapped out of it. I finished entering the room. And shook the large hand that he'd offered me. He stopped. He seemed stupefied. He was staring at my eyes. I cleared my throat. He snapped out of it.

"Miss Sharp, yes?" Wow, was his voice deep. Like the rumble of a ship's engine starting.

"Yes sir." I said, managing to keep my voice steady. This was a day for surprises.

"Very mannerful for a shifter. Most would just say 'yeah.'"

"I was born into a semi-military family, sir. Plus I'm from Texas."

"Ah, a southern girl. Well then let me just say it's a pleasure to meet you young lady."

"You as well Mr...."

"Mr. French." I didn't hide my surprise on that one. "Yes I know. Not a name one expects from someone like me."

"May I ask what exactly you are sir?" I asked sitting in the chair that he wasn't using.

"I thought it was rude to ask other shifters what they were." Said Ms. Hamper

"It can be. In some cases, but for this no. She most definitely is different." What did he mean by that? Yes, I knew my color – as a dragon that is – was very rare, and my mannerisms were not the norm, but how could one tell just by looking at my eyes. He gave his answer to my other question.

"I am a Cave Lion shifter." I gave a very surprised sound. He laughed.

"I get that reaction a lot." I don't doubt it. Cave lions were almost twice the size of today's lions.

"I assume by your silence sweetie, that's big?" asked Ms. Hamper.

"A modern lion would be considered only a little over half grown when compared to a cave lion. They were huge," I looked at him as I said the next part, "and you as a shifter must be positively immense."

"You're not wrong my dear." How could he say that so nonchalantly? He must've not been kidding when he said what he did a minute ago.

"Wow." I said, rubbing my forehead. Wait a minute. "And you run the school?"

"Indeed I do." He answered.

"I imagine most kids don't make trouble then?"

"You imagine correctly Miss Sharp. May I ask you a question?"

"You just did." I state. He gave a hard laugh.

"A young lady with a sense of humor. I like you." He was still laughing.

"Okay," Ms. Hamper interjected, "what happened today? That's the first joke you've cracked since the murders."

"Tom partially apologized." That shocked her. So I took the time to tell what happened at work.

"Smart lad." Said Mr. French. Okay I was gonna have a problem with that.

"Now for my other question, Ms. Hamper refused to tell me your real name. She insisted that I wait for you. So my question is, what is your real name?"

"Magenta, sir."

"Like the color?" I nodded.

"A beautiful name, is it just your eyes?"

"No sir, my scales are magenta as well."

"May I?" he wanted a demonstration. No prob. I gently shifted my left hand, the one closest to him. It was harder than expected. I'd forgotten that my hand had seized when the rescuers had been digging me out. I'd activated a pressure point in my arm to help support the tub, so it wouldn't finish crushing me. Sadly, the paramedics hadn't known that - my being unconscious didn't help - and had wrenched my arm loose. Sever nerve damage anyone. I had finished physical therapy two months ago.

I held it back though. Shifters can take signs of weakness differently. He looked at my arm. Watching it as I moved. I didn't go past the wrist. It still hurt when I shifted partially. Though I was fine when I fully shifted.

"Are you all right?" He asked. Reaching out to me as he leaned forward in his seat. Crap. Forgot, don't need to see it. Can smell it.

"I'm okay," I shifted back, clenching, and unclenching my hand, and breathing deeply, "I'm in the last stage of recovery for nerve damage." He growled. Yikes! I hadn't heard such a growl since my sister came home after curfew last summer. Mom and dad had been justly pissed. My brother and I had felt and heard the growl through the whole house.

Tentatively I said, "Sir…."

"I'm sorry, I didn't mean to do that." He paused, regaining his composure. "Ms. Hamper has informed me about the murders, I neglected to ask if you'd been injured. Or even there."

"We can give the full story if you'd like Mr. French." Said Ms. Hamper.

"No, that can wait. I need to fulfill why I'm here. I imagine you have questions, Miss Sharp." He made it a statement, not a question.

"Yes sir. Only three right now though." He gestured for me to continue. "One, where exactly is the school? Two, is it year-round or done like public schools? And three, would I still be able to work while attending?"

He looked at my shirt. "You work at the aquarium?"

"Yes sir, have you been?"

"I have. A most enjoyable experience." He thought. "To answer your first question. The location is kept secret, for protection purposes." Okay, to be expected. "To the second one, yes it is year-round. For the same reason." Understandable. "As for the third, that can be discussed." I nodded. Not exactly a straight answer, but I could live with it for now.

"The students do get summers, but we do insist that they give precise days to leave and return. Although, because you are or will be a new student it is mandated that you visit the school before the year begins. So as to choose from the available rooms and to familiarize yourself with the grounds."

"A day visit or over a few days?"

"A girl for details. Good. Two days. Usually. If more is needed we inform the parents. If they are non-shifters." I nodded.

"So, do you want the scholarship?" he asked.

I took a minute to think about it. It was an amazing opportunity. Finish high school and attend college. All on the same campus. Ms. Hamper and Mr. Hydell would be safe, because there would be literally no way to find me. Mr. Kepner would be screwed until graduation. And then screwed afterward for another reason. Plus the other students at school wouldn't have to worry about my possibly snapping again. A slow smile came to my face.

"I take it you accept?" He asked.

"Yes sir." He and Ms. Hamper both smiled. We all stood, he shook hands with us, and left to make whatever arrangements were necessary.

I left after that. Ms. Hamper had details to take care of and I needed to get home and eat. Ben was still waiting. He pulled out carefully. "That wasn't as long as I was expecting." He must've thought I'd had an appointment.

"Meeting about a scholarship. Not an appointment."

"Your leaving?!" He was shocked?

"Work, maybe. That's up for discussion. School. Yes." He sighed with relief. "You guys would actually miss me?"

"Yes. You may not talk often but you are fun to have around."

I smiled, "Thanks."

"Your welcome."

We performed our usual routine before we stopped, and I got out. He peeled out, maybe he was in a hurry. Or. Oh shit! I should have asked if anything odd or off had happened. I was getting lazy. Ok Magenta, slight change to routine. I pulled the hat I kept in my bag out along with the sunglasses. The hat helped hide my horns lightly growing out when I heightened more than one sense at once. The sunglasses were dark enough to hide the glow – and change, pupil wise - of my eyes. They were specially made and had been my dad's. Backpack on and I started walking. I kept my head up and my shoulders relaxed, so as not to give away that I was on edge. I knew the route well enough I could walk it blindfolded. Crap! Time to change that. So I did.

If anyone was following me they'd either notice the shift or had no idea. Ears sharp, nose open, and eyes never in the same spot for more than a second. My focus spread four ways. I pay attention and reading the Ranger's Apprentice series had taught me to use my peripheral vision more than direct line of sight. You're more likely to catch something that way. Like that! Someone ahead was looking behind me in a confused way. Like someone was deliberately driving slowly. My hearing said I was right.

The corners of my sunglasses had one-way mirrors on them. I turned left at the corner. A black car followed. I checked the driver's side of the windshield. Shit! The windows were tinted. This person was smart. Next turn. Still there. Third, and fourth. Yep he was following. I crossed the street. He didn't attempt anything. Time to identify my stalker. I pretended to look at the time on my phone, then sped up like I was in a hurry. He followed; he didn't pick up the pace to match me, but he was still there. I turned into the first alley. Sped up even more then transferred the momentum into a jump.

I flew seven stories up. The building was 20 stories. Hanging onto the fire escape I made another jump. Never making a sound. I was now at the 15th floor, one more and I'd be on the roof. Hup! Safe. I looked down at the alley, careful that only the top of my head showed. At the right angle you can watch people on the street and even if they look up they won't see you. So long as they are on the same side of the street as you are.

A car pulled in. I'd memorized the plate. So being halfway along the roof I could see the numbers. It was the car. It slowed but didn't stop. Less than halfway down it stopped. The driver's door opened. And Mr. Kepner got out.

Anger seized me. I so wanted to drop on him and rip him to pieces. But to do that I had to be a dragon. She began to fight for freedom. No!! The alleyway is too small, too narrow. I'd be the one at a disadvantage. Plus for all I knew he had more of whatever that smell was, that had incapacitated my dad. I wouldn't give in. Not now. I did, however, take out my phone. Carefully maneuvered it into position and using max zoom – which was super great – took his photo as he looked up. He'd shaved his head and grown a beard, but there was no hiding the scar on his cheek. The result of the explosion. He moved away from the car slightly. He was limping. No, he had a prosthetic leg! Way to go dad. A car door closed on the street. He must've assumed I was in it, 'cause he got back in and started down the alley, good, plate pic for the cops too. He finished backing out. I got up and moved to see which way he went. East.

I pulled out my burner phone and sent a message to the cops, the two pics and which way he was headed. The police officer I sent them to knew I had the burner and knew the number. He'd know what to do with the info.

I waited twenty minutes. I was still uneasy. I needed to get home before Mr. Hydell and eat. I was already hungry; I couldn't afford to be voracious. I took my storm crystals out of the hidden pocket in my bag. I chose fog. Fog can hide you easily, and this close to the coast it won't be seen as suspicious – especially not with a storm coming in. I said a small spell, activating the crystal. I then blew on it. Stimulating it until there was enough fog for me to start flying. Perfect! I put the crystals away and spread my wings. Yes just my wings.

I didn't trust my color in fog, I was too obvious. I flew carefully. I'd rather not hit a bird thank you. It was four blocks to home. I'd made enough fog for six.

Landing on the roof I rushed to the roof door, key already in hand. Our apartment was on the third from top floor. Running the whole way, I reached our door. It was already unlocked. My nose said just Mr. Hydell. Damn! I opened the door, he was standing by the window about to dial on his phone.

"Oh thank God!" he exclaimed. I closed the door and locked it, then turned on the video com's one-way camera. No one followed down the hall. I turned back to Mr. Hydell. His anger had dissipated.

"You saw him didn't you?" he asked, I just nodded.

Chapter 4

Two hours later, as the thunder storm escalated, we finally got word from the authorities. Mr. Hydell was more anticipatory than I was. I was still shaken, cowering in my room with my knees pulled up to my chest like a little girl. I know that was acceptable to most people given the recent circumstances, but with me, I hate feeling helpless. I always had. The night of the murders had only made that need for self-dependence and self-protection stronger.

I looked up when Mr. Hydell came in. I hadn't listened to the conversation. I didn't want to somehow jinx it if they found him or not. Mr. Hydell shook his head. Damn it! I put my head back down and screamed into my legs.

"They found the car, but he's gotten more careful. They found no DNA, no i.ds of any kind, and he bought the car under an assumed name. Even the address tied to the car was a fake."

"I should have just let my dragon out." I couldn't keep the tears out of my voice.

"That probably wouldn't have been a good idea kiddo." He said, putting his arm around my shoulders. Giving me much needed comfort.

"I know. She just wanted out so bad." I know better than to go into battle when my opponent has the upper hand.

The cops advised we stay somewhere else that night. So Mr. Hydell made arrangements at a hotel out of town, he even called the school and said I wouldn't be there on Monday. He was being cautious. We both packed a bag and using one of his other cars – one we knew Kepner wouldn't know – we left the building, then the city. As we'd left the elevator of the building I'd pulled my hair into my beanie hat and put a different pair of shades on. One that Hydell's girlfriend had given me. I didn't usually do designer brands, but for her I'd made an exception. I'd also pulled on a new hoodie and was zipping it up as we left the garage. He'd also called his office and girlfriend. His boss wasn't too happy about the sudden change, but he didn't make any complaints besides that. His girlfriend was more supportive. Turns out she was out of town visiting a friend and planned to meet us at the hotel. He gave her the name of the hotel in code. She was like me, she read spy and detective novels like it was a drug.

Mr. Hydell turned on the radio. Halestorm came out of the speakers. Not exactly an ideal choice when trying to listen for unusual noises outside, but then again I listened to Halestorm often and had even trained myself to filter out Lzzy Hale's scream singing – as Mr. Hydell called it – so that I could pick up other sounds without a problem.

While Mr. Hydell drove, I made myself look as much like a boy as I could. Not hard with a loose hoodie. I got one to two sizes bigger on purpose. I already preferred loose jeans, so no problem there. We both kept our eyes peeled, but thankfully no one tailed us.

He put his foot on the gas when we were finally on the high way. He wanted me as far from the city as fast as possible. He tapped my arm a few minutes later and indicated the glove box. Without any prompting I opened it. Inside was a revolver and a box of ammo. Using the hand not on the steering wheel he told me to load it. I carefully grabbed the gun and the ammo. A photo fell out as the box came. Whoops. Putting the gun and box in my lap I reached down and picked the photo up. It showed a three-year-old boy. He kinda looked like Mr. Hydell. *'I'll ask later'*, I said to myself. I returned the picture to the glove box and closed it. A minute later, the gun was loaded. I passed it to him, and he put it into a shoulder rig I hadn't seen him put on.

Twenty minutes later we pulled into a Holiday Inn. I wasn't surprised at the cheaper choice, Mr. Hydell didn't always like fancy hotels, and in this case he really didn't want fancy. He wanted inconspicuous. Most other lawyers wouldn't have cared for that.

We checked in, making sure to get a room with a view of the whole parking lot. I'd rubbed off. Gun in hand he stood by the window, the lights off, he watched the parking lot. We both knew what his girlfriend's car was. He kept his eyes open for hers and for any that might look out of place. I took a bath, I figured I might as well. My nerves were already on fire. Couldn't hurt to try and calm them down. When I came out, he was still at the window, gun well hidden by his leg. I decided to ask about the picture.

"Who was the little boy in the picture?"

He smiled before he said, "He's my nephew."

"He looks a lot like you."

"I know, that's why people think he's my son when my sister visits."

"How'd she react when she heard about me?" I asked.

"She was a little skeptical, but she understood my reasons." He froze. Then gestured to me. I came over to look over his shoulder. Sunglasses on, I looked into the 1997 Mercedes Benz that had just pulled in. The windshields weren't tinted, and Miss Jenkins was in the car alone. I sighed.

"Wait in the bathroom. I'll give you this knock when it's me and her." He tapped the knock out on my arm. Gotcha. I went in and listened to him leave. I stayed by the toilet, ready to grab the back's cover to use as a weapon if necessary.

Ten minutes later I heard two heartbeats enter the room. One I knew was Mr. Hydell's, the other I didn't know. I'd only ever seen Miss Jenkins from a distance. I hadn't been introduced to her properly yet. Knocks came at the door, three, two, then four. It was him for sure. I exited the bathroom. Miss Jenkins was the other heartbeat I'd heard; she was prettier up close. She was strawberry blond, about 5'3, and smelled like blueberries. Okay interesting choice of perfume.

She came forward to shake my hand, I noticed some flour on the edge of her blouse sleeve. So **that** was the blueberry smell.

"You've been baking." I said. She laughed.

"A very Sherlockian observation dear. Yes, my friend and I had been baking blueberry pies when Jack called me."

"I hope there's one in one of these boxes." Said Mr. Hydell, tapping one with a knuckle. It was only then that I noticed the Little Caesars boxes, and the smell of pizza.

"I thought you two had eaten on your date."

"We did dear, but that was more than two hours ago, **and**" she pointed at me, "if I remember correctly you haven't eaten since lunch."

"Oh good Gods." I said, covering my face and abdomen. In the stress of the last few hours I'd completely forgotten.

"That's what I figured dear." She gestured at the food, "Two of the pizzas are for you, Jack and I get the other one. The pie is for dessert."

"Thank you." I hadn't expected to be so quickly accepted by her. Today was most definitely a day for surprises.

Chapter 5

We spent the whole night at the hotel, she'd gotten a cheese, pepperoni, and meat lovers pizzas. I'd let them pick which one they wanted, though I did eat one slice of pepperoni. I ended up eating all but one slice of the meat lovers, and they had each eaten two slices of pep. So at the end we had five slices of pizza left over. The pie was really good. I didn't usually eat blueberry. I like pies that are an equal mix between sweet and tart. Unless it's pumpkin. She had somehow gotten the mix just right for me, so I really liked it.

By the time we were done eating, I was feeling tired. It was a two-bedroom room, so one for me and one for them. I changed into some pajamas that I'd packed. While in the bathroom, Molly – as was her first name, and how she wanted me to call her – knocked.

"Can I come in dear?"

"Yeah." I answered. She came in, I was wearing drawstring pants to hide my scars.

"I heard you hiss, are you okay?" Crap. For a human she had good hearing.

"I smacked my leg on part of the toiletries cabinet. I'm okay." I was favoring that leg actually, all that running and standing earlier had made it pretty tender.

"No you're not. Sit."

"You don't have to." I didn't want to bother; I was used to tending to it myself. Checking it usually required no leg wear. Kinda awkward when your guardian is a guy.

"Sit." She re-affirmed. So I did. "Can you get the pant leg up far enough? I'll be right back."

I pulled the pant leg up. It was pretty tight near mid-thigh, so nope. I'd have to remove them. I stood, groaning as weight was put on my leg again. I slipped the pants down and off, then wrapped myself in a towel. I could hear Molly talking to Mr. Hydell, she was wondering about why he'd never offered to help. The answer was simple. We hadn't known each other long enough the first time I'd had to tend to my leg at the apartment. Neither of us had felt comfortable. So he'd left it to me. I was fine with that. I had enough medical training to take care of it.

The door opened. She came in with… my poultice kit? She saw I was wrapped in the towel and my confused look at her choice of medicine.

"My great-grandmother had an apothecary. She taught my gran most of her medicinal poultices. My mother followed her father and became a devote Christian."

"Ah." Well somethings happen.

"She saw the poultices as witchcraft. Even my telling her doctors had used them for centuries before we had pills, wouldn't change her mind." I shook my head. She shrugged before continuing.

"My gran did teach me them though, and when I caught a glimpse of this in your bag, I figured it was the better option." She said.

I smiled; my family used poultices when pills were too expensive. And the blend for muscle pain was one I knew well. I'd been using it as often as possible these last six months. She pulled out the small bottle of dried calendula – or marigold – petals. Poured about half into one of the medium sized mortar and pestle I had and ground them up. Or tried to, this one was marble, so it weighed a bit more.

"I'll do the petals." I said. She looked up at me and smiled. I'm a big girl, she didn't have to do it all. She pulled out the smaller one and started grinding half my bottle of chia seeds. She was goin' for long term pain relief, rather than the usual twenty minutes.

Finally she left the bathroom and grabbed the warm water from Mr. Hydell. I set my marble mortar on the counter and she mixed the water with the finely ground seeds until it was a paste, then added the finely ground petals.

"Go ahead and take the towel off dear." She said without turning around.

"You sure? It's pretty bad." I said, making eye contact through the mirror.

"I saw some photos. I can take it." She said while turning to face me. Her resolve was good. But let's see. I partially removed the towel.

She swallowed a little, but she kept her composure. Nice. Most people couldn't. She kneeled down, gently touching the skin along one edge of the scar. My skin was hot from the pain and strain.

"How'd it get this bad?" she asked, meeting my eyes with concern. My gods the look reminded me so much of my mom. It was my turn to swallow. I really didn't want to cry in front of her. It was hard enough dealing with all the pain alone. I didn't want to unduly burden her with something that had happened so long ago and was very much a scar on my soul as much as it was my leg.

"When the bomb went off, I was thrown into the bathroom. Our house wasn't exactly new, so the old floor was," I shrugged, "basically turned to splinters held together with old glue."

"Jack said you'd had an old-style bathtub." She stated.

I nodded, "Cast iron."

"Geez." She covered her face. Almost fully realizing the whole picture.

"I went through the floor first. I bounced off my grandparents car and hit the garage floor. Then the bathtub came." I paused; I'd never had to actually describe how it fell. The paramedics had gotten a really nice view of it.

I continued, "The tub was one with a curved lip along the outside. When it hit..." I swallowed again. The memory of the pain still as intense as the night I got it, "the lip cut right into my jeans and leg." I looked up to meet her eyes.

"The tub met bone. Clean. The tub was perfectly parallel with the bone. My femur shattered into 73 separate pieces. It only takes 624 pounds of force to break a human femur. Not hard for a cast iron tub."

"Was there any infection?" she asked getting up to grab the mortar.

"A little, but it wasn't from the tub. The debris and dust were what the infection actually came from."

"Do you still have the plate?" With the number of pieces, a plate had been necessary.

"No. I got it removed last month. Even with me being a shifter, my body needed way more time to heal." I hadn't missed it. She knelt down.

"Here." She gave me the gauze. "I'll rub it on, then you hold the gauze down." I nodded.

She was very gentle as she applied the poultice. Never moving very fast so as not to aggravate the tender skin. When she was done I placed the two gauze pads end to end. She pulled the skin-safe medical tape from my bag. She taped the two pieces together then did along the borders. Leaving a little room at the knee so everything could breath.

"Thank you." I said when she was done.

"Your welcome." She said pushing a few strands of my hair back behind my ear. She got up and looking back at me, left the bathroom so I could change back into my pajama pants. Ms. Hamper was the closest thing I'd had to a mom since that night, the fact that Molly was willing to be one for me now when I most needed one, meant the world to me.

It also meant if Kepner found out about her she'd be in grave danger. For one day, why couldn't my life be safe and normal again?

I laughed without humor at myself. What was I even thinking? My life had become fucked up the second I'd chosen physics as my science class for sophomore year. I didn't even know what the hell it was about me that had caught his attention. My looks? My youth? My potential intelligence? I just didn't know, and that made it hurt only more. No matter how you looked at it, what happened to my family was my fault. You could tell me I was wrong for the rest of my life; it wouldn't change my opinion. You could say Kepner was at fault because of how messed up he was, that still wouldn't change anything. I'd been the one to choose physics. It would forever be a stain on my soul in my opinion.

Okay enough of the pity party. I stood, letting the towel fall away and picked up my pants. I had to readjust the pant leg a little but once I had them on, I again realized how tired I was. My leg was starting to feel better. I exited the bathroom and after moving the comforter, laid on the bed and was asleep the second my head hit the pillow.

Chapter 6

I awoke to the sound of music. Literally. I opened my eyes with a little difficulty, I was still feeling exhausted. Molly had the TV on and was watching the old movies channel. The Sound of Music was playing. I liked this movie, it really taught you something about moving on after the death of someone you loved. Too bad it didn't teach how to move on from losing everything. The movie Prom Night didn't either. The main character still had family to live with. I didn't. Reggie didn't count at this time because of the mutual danger. There was one book I knew about but couldn't read yet that might cover moving on after losing everything. That book was Dark Guardian by Christine Feehan. Over 18 years-of-age books, and in the case of her books I couldn't just skip any of the sex scenes. Patricia Briggs' books yes, they weren't explicitly detailed, but they were short.

I sat up, stretching my arms as I did. I could see from their bed that they'd took turns sleeping. The parking lot was lit so anyone showing up at night could still be observed. Right now it was just me and Molly in the room. Oh, no wait. The shower was running.

"Sleep well dear?" Molly asked, noticing I was up.

"I was pretty zonked. I guess that's a good thing."

She smiled and came over to brush my hair. Gods this woman would make a wonderful mother someday. Maybe soon, maybe not. It would depend on whether her relationship with Mr. Hydell lasted or not. She finished and then smoothed it out with her hand. My hair only went to my mid-back. I'd dyed it after Kepner did his evil deed. It originally was red. Nowhere near as red as Mr.

French's hair, but I missed my hair being red. Now that Kepner knew I'd dyed it I might have to change that too. First there was something I had to check.

"I'm going down to get breakfast. Do you want anything?" Molly asked after getting up from the bed.

I thought for a second, "A toasted bagel with cream cheese and a poppy seed muffin if they have any. Please."

"Drink?" she asked.

"Milk, please." She nodded, opened the door, and walked out. She didn't give a knock of any kind, but I knew her scent and heartbeat now – plus the door did have a peep hole – I should be okay.

Time for the other order of business. I grabbed the phone book, looked up the aquarium's number, found it, then dialed it into the hotel phone. I'd have to keep it short, so as not to draw possible suspicion. I didn't work today but I knew Ben did.

He picked up on the first ring. Reliable ol' Ben. "Aquarium of the Pacific." He said.

"Ben it's Maggie. Was everything okay after you dropped me off?"

"Yeah I was just in a hurry to get… oh crap! Did I scare you?"

"I'm glad you did." I heard him inhale.

"He showed, didn't he?"

"Yep. Time for routine change."

"Gotcha. See you later."

"Bye." Okay so that answers that. He'd only been in a hurry. I'd have to ask about what next time I was at the aquarium. The next time he worked was Tuesday. As was my next after school shift. Okay. I could work with that.

Mr. Hydell came out of the bathroom. He was drying his hair and was wearing what he'd been wearing when we left L.A. He looked around the room. "Where's Molly?" he asked throwing the towel around his neck.

"She went to get breakfast." He froze. Then turned.

"Did she give a knock for you to listen for?"

"No, I think she forgot."

"Okay. Wait here, I'll be right back. Don't open the door for anyone but us." I nodded. He went out the door. I kept my hearing high enough to keep track of him till he got in the elevator. So far so good. I got up and discreetly looked out the window at the parking lot. He'd probably check both cars for sabotage or little changes. He'd do it with gloves too. A neat person will notice the subtle changes to everything they had. Even the tiniest of things. This was a good quality to have. Especially when you're the only one in the area who touches your stuff. I didn't see any new cars, but there were a few that were already gone. I put the curtain back and thought. I kept my ears open though. If Kepner was still in the city, where would he go to find out where I was goin' for therapy? Every building that housed therapist offices, of course. It wasn't hard. If you watched a building long enough you'd see all the patients that went there. He'd had six months to watch and wait. That meant that he'd learned patience since we last encountered each other. Good for him. Bad for me.

Someone knocked at the door. My ears said the heartbeat was Molly's, she didn't sound anxious or uneasy. A little winded, but fine. I walked to the door. The carpet absorbing the sound. I looked through the peep hole. She was alone. I looked at her eyes. Subtle movements can indicate distress. Nope she was okay. I opened the door.

"I'm sorry dear. I should have given' some kind of knock to expect." She apologized. I took one of the plates from her so she could close the door.

"It's okay. Everything is fine."

"Where's Jack?"

"I thought he was going to check on you." Alarm bells. I went back to the window. Once again carefully moving the drapes. There he was. I'd been right. He was checking the cars. He'd do it again before we left.

"He's at your car." We both breathed a sigh of relief. I hate this part of my life. We sat at the small table to eat, finishing Sound of Music while we waited for Mr. Hydell to return.

He came back in 20 minutes later, with his own breakfast. Molly immediately got up, walked over to him, and smacked him on the shoulder. He'd put his plate down so his food wasn't in danger.

"Don't you ever scare me like that again!" She half shouted, so as not to alert the neighbors. She then threw her arms around his chest and hugged him. I suppressed a smile at Mr. Hydell's look. Not only would she be a wonderful mother, she'd be a formidable wife.

"I didn't mean to," he said as he returned her hug, "I saw you at the breakfast bar. I figured if I left slow enough you'd see me as well. I guess I was wrong. I'm sorry." He met my eyes; he was apologizing to both of us. I nodded. Apology accepted. She might take a little while.

Chapter 7

I showered about twenty minutes after Mr. Hydell returned to the room. The hot water felt good on my leg. The poultice washed off nicely. I'd need to visit the apothecary again on the way back into town. Not only did I need more marigold petals, but there were a few other things I needed to restock. I could barely hear what Mr. Hydell and Molly were discussing. That was fine with me. I didn't always like keeping my hearing at or near full power. Some things should stay private.

I never took too long in the shower, that would be a waste of water. I let myself air dry. I prefer that to toweling off. I feel it lets more moisture re-enter the skin that way. I had packed two sets of clothes when we bugged out. Today I was going to dress as low key as possible. I decided on my favorite brown long sleeve V-neck shirt with a piece of white fabric sewn infront, and a pair of jeans I'd had for a while.

I didn't know how we'd spend the next two days, but that was okay with me. Sometimes you need to get away. The hotel we were in was a few miles outside of Thousand Oaks California, so that meant Disneyland was out of the question. Once dressed I did my hair, wrapping it in the towel and carefully putting it on my head.

I left the bathroom. They stopped talking. That meant one of two things, or both. They'd been talking about me or had a plan for the next few days that they wanted to run by me. Well, time to find out.

"Did I interrupt?" I asked.

"Just about what to do for the next few days." Okay.

"Need me in on it?" I sat on my bed.

"Naw, you don't have to." I nodded, I didn't really. My nerves were still frazzled. Music time. I grabbed my mp3 and plugged in my earbuds. 'Halo' by Beyoncé. Soothing. Nice. I laid back on the pillow, I needed to try and think about anything but Kepner's presence. There was a really nice book store in Santa Barbara that I wanted to visit, plus the zoo and museum of natural history there, but I didn't know if they were open on Sunday. It was just after 8:00, so most people would be at church still. Well, might have to suggest them. I heard someone say my name. I pulled out an earbud and looked at them.

"Music up loud or too deep in thought?" asked Mr. Hydell.

"Deep in thought." I answered while sitting up.

"What was the name of that bookstore you wanted to visit? In Santa Barbara?" my eyes got bigger. He laughed. "Great minds think alike." Molly nodded. Apparently we had all been thinking Santa Barbra.

We used the hotel's Wi-Fi to check opening times on all three places I'd thought about. The zoo opened at ten, along with one of the museums I wanted to visit; the other museums and bookstore at eleven. Okay so we had a few hours. We decided to stop by Molly's country home just outside of Casitas Springs before headin' out. It was on the way to Santa Barbara, so it worked well. We paid and left the hotel. We made sure we had everything first. We did. Nothing we'd brought had gone far from our bags.

Mr. Hydell did indeed re-check the cars and those around them for tampering or bombs. Hey, don't ride the guy, his life was in as much danger as mine and Molly's were. He wasn't going to take any chances. He'd even brought the bug scanner. There were days I thought that was a little excessive, but then you watch things like crime shows and realize it's the best option for safety.

He gave the signal. No bugs and no bombs. We came forward, Molly going to hers while I joined Mr. Hydell. I checked the back seats, then threw my bag in the trunk. I saw Molly check her back seats as well. Take no chances.

She pulled out first, because she was closer to the exit. We pulled out of the spot carefully and followed her out. I did get to wondering though.

"What kind of therapist was Molly again?" I asked Mr. Hydell.

"She's a dual therapist actually. She's a couples therapist as well as a minor trauma therapist."

"The panic patient that ended your date early was one of her trauma patients?"

"Yep. Kinda like Evan in Freaky Friday." I laughed; Mr. Hydell had caught some of that movie a few months ago. I'd been watching it and had fallen asleep on the couch.

"So have you ever been to her country home?" I asked.

"Truthfully, I didn't even know she had one until she mentioned it." He admitted. Handy.

We made it to Casitas Springs not long after. It's a small place but has a really nice lake. We followed her through and then out of town, to a small – almost small enough to miss – private road that led to a large house on the lake. She clearly didn't use this property very much. Oh well.

The house was actually a Hobbit hole!? Cool! Mr. Hydell parked right behind her, I got out 'cause I wanted to ask about the part that actually shows above ground.

"Why is only part of it a Hobbit Hole?" I asked pointing at the door in front of us.

"It's not actually. Technically there are two houses on the premises. One is the one you see here, and the other is my cousin's. He's claustrophobic towards underground places, so I did mine as a Hobbit hole for just that reason. Although there is a tunnel that connects the two."

"You and your cousin don't get along very well?"

"Not really. Our grandfather left the land to both of us, so we just go back and forth. We are sometimes both here at the same time, but those times are rare."

"What does he do?"

"He's currently the assistant to the governor." She stated with a frown. Wow. "Anyway, I'll just be a minute." She walked up and opened the door to the Hobbit hole. I went back to the car. I got in the back seat this time. I placed my bag on the floor. Then she came back out but instead of locking the door, came over to the car and ask me to hand her my bag. I did. Then she locked the door, with my backpack safely inside as well. She then finally got in Mr. Hydell's car, and we began the rest of the trip to Santa Barbara.

Once we were back on the 101 I spent most of the time staring out to sea. You could barely see the Channel Island National Park. They were shadows at the horizon line. I'd lived in forests and mountains most of my life but even with how much I loved them, I was strongly drawn to the sea. Even my parents couldn't quite figure that one out. Sea dragon shifters had gone extinct almost a thousand years ago. Sure, my dad had had some sea dragon ancestors, but there was no way to guarantee that a descendant would have the gene. Let alone one so far into the future. The blood would be too diluted. I mean, that wasn't necessarily a guarantee that it wouldn't suddenly pop back up, but one never knows.

My grandma had once said that every now and then an ancestor would be so strongly drawn to the sea that they assumed they might have the gene, but every time they entered the water, nothing happened. She also said this was to be expected. Some things are out of our hands, and no matter how much we might wish it otherwise, some things just aren't meant to be.

At the time she had been talking about the sea dragon gene, but today that quote of hers applied to so much more. I hated how so much my family had said or done in the past was now so comparable to the murders. Even looking at the Pacific didn't help quell the sudden sadness and anger.

"Maggie, you okay?" asked Mr. Hydell.

"Huh?" Great. I was getting too habitual. This was the third time I'd been snapped out of something.

"You growled dear." Said Molly. Meeting my eyes through the rear-view mirror.

Oh. Whoops. "I was thinking about something my grandma said. That now is very comparable to the murders."

Molly reached back and patted my knee. "Try and think of other things hon. You had us thinking Kepner was following."

"Sorry." That explained why they both were checking the rear-view mirrors so much.

"It's okay kiddo." Mr. Hydell said. Despite the fact that I probably had put him further on edge.

"I was wondering if the two of you would like to stay at the Hobbit hole with me for the next two days."

"Yes." Me and Mr. Hydell said simultaneously. We all laughed.

"Well that's settled." She said with a big smile.

We still had about 15 minutes of driving left. Plenty of time to plan the day. Or at least the half before lunch.

Chapter 8

Because of when we had originally left, we arrived in Santa Barbara at 9:15. Only a 45-minute wait till the zoo opened. Might as well wait it out at one of the beaches. I didn't bring any sea worthy shoes, but then again that's why you don't wear shoes at the beach. And since it was still early the sand was still cool. Standing in the water with my jeans rolled up, I had some time to think. So little was known about sea dragon shifters. Other than they could spend days at sea with no problem. Where do you think some of the sea monster legends came from? Yeah some stories were actually monsters, but not all.

I stood at the tide line with my jeans rolled up, loving the feel of the water as it washed over my feet. I leaned my head back while taking a deep breath. Enjoying the sea's breeze in my hair. Oof. Something just hit me in the butt. I turned. A three-year-old girl stood behind me giggling. I chuckled. The ball at her feet had been what hit me. Her mother came up behind her.

"Maggie what did I tell you about that?!" she said. I laughed a little harder. Tears began flowing slowly.

"Mommy you made her cry." Dang it.

"I'm okay ma'am. Really." I said, trying to move the focus from my face.

"I am sorry about my daughter though." She said taking her daughter's hand.

"It's okay." I said while trying to stop the tears.

"Then why did you laugh?" she said accusingly.

"And why are you crying?" little Maggie asked before her mom could stop her.

"I laughed because me and her have the same name." I said to the mom.

"Oh, your…" she seemed slightly confused.

"Technically my nickname is Maggie."

"Oh." Even she couldn't quite hold back her small laugh. I kneeled down in front of her daughter.

"And to answer your question little Maggie," she squealed like a happy little girl, "I'm crying because when your mom yelled at you it reminded me of my mom."

"Where is she?" little Maggie asked looking around. Oh the sweet innocence of children.

"She's not here anymore." I said standing up straight. Her mother caught on to what I meant, but since little Maggie was still very young.

"Sweetie," she said, stopping little Maggie's next question, "what she means is her mom isn't coming back."

"Like granny?" she looked at the sky as if it held the answer.

"Yes. Like granny." She'd kneeled to speak to her daughter. So she rose back up now.

"And I really am sorry about her antics." She said as she picked up the ball.

"And I'm serious about it being okay. If you don't laugh at the little everyday things what can you enjoy." She nodded at my apparent wisdom. She then took little Maggie's hand and started to walk away.

"Bye, lady Maggie." She waved as she went.

"Bye, little Maggie." My gods she was so cute. No longer caring if my jeans got wet, I sat down. So many things can happen in a day, and so far, almost all had reminded me how gone my family was. Mr. Hydell was the closest thing so far. With Reggie safe, it was better for both of us not to think of the other as family.

Blood related dragon shifters could communicate at a great distance via feelings. If one was in trouble you just sent that emotion at them. If only Amanda had done that. Me or dad could have arrived in time. I know why she never went for the gun, but why not a call? Now I'll never know. I looked over to where Mr. Hydell and Molly were sitting. They looked so happy, and willing to give me something I no longer had. That was a blessing in and of itself. Molly and I had only known each other a day. Yet she acted so much like a mother that she treated me like her own daughter. I couldn't just give that up, even if they could be put in danger. Mr. Hydell already was because of his being my guardian. I knew he wasn't afraid of Kepner, but that might not necessarily save him should something come about. And I really didn't want either of them hurt. My heart was already such a torn, raggedy mess from the murders, who knew how long – or what - it would take to be truly whole again. I didn't want to think of them as family, but whether I liked it or not, they were my family.

I thought back to the night before. Molly hadn't hesitated to help me with my leg, even when she knew I was used to taking care of it myself. I'd have to ask at some point why. I knew how she felt for Mr. Hydell, but why have those feelings for such a broken girl you only just officially met? One of life's great mysteries I guess.

"Kiddo." Mr. Hydell called to me. The tears had stopped flowing, thanks gods. "Time to go."

I stood up, wiping the sand from my pants, before picking up my socks and shoes. I shook myself out of my revive. Enough sad for the day. Today **would** be a good and happy one. No questions or arguments. I was going to enjoy my two-day safe trip. No. Not safe trip. '*Call it what it was Maggie.*' A family trip. And I was going to enjoy it.

Chapter 9

The beach we were at wasn't very far from the zoo. Literally, it was right next door. So it was a very short drive from the waterfront. Mr. Hydell and Molly had both been here before, not at the same time though. Which was fine with me. We picked up a map at administration, before beginning our tour. I hadn't been here since I was two or three, I couldn't quite remember. Boy did I give my parents heart attacks. I had wandered off while me, my parents, and siblings were at the Wings of Asia exhibit. They had found me a few minutes later. I had walked myself back to the otter exhibit. They still freaked, but I should've expected that at the time.

Otters were one of my favorite animals. When I was two, I just couldn't keep myself away. Especially when they were so cute and funny. After that mom or dad had a hold of my hand at all times, never once letting go. Reggie had thought the whole thing was funny. Amanda hadn't understood why they were mad, she was only 5 at the time.

Now that I was 16, I didn't have to worry about wandering off. I knew better now. That still didn't stop me from staying at the otters exhibit for a while longer. The zoo had expanded within the last ten years, so we took our time to check out some of the new features as well. They now had a rock wall and a live show area. The live show area even had shows that featured guys dressed up as dinosaurs. Ha! That could be fun.

One of the things I liked about this zoo was that it wasn't level. Unlike most zoos, this one had hills and some of the animal viewing walk ways even looked out on a view of the surrounding land. So even the animals could look into the distance.

We spent about two hours at the zoo. I tried the rock wall with Molly. She didn't even make it half-way. I made it all the way. We all laughed at her for failing, she tried not to laugh at herself. We also stopped at one of the dining areas for lunch. The zoo served pretty good food. We then helped feed the giraffes and goats. That was fun. I'll never forget Mr. Hydell's face when the giraffe licked him on the nose. You couldn't not laugh. It was so funny.

It wasn't until about 12:30 that we stopped at one of the two gift shops. Me and Molly got a few pieces of jewelry and books. Mr. Hydell got a t-shirt and a pair of sunglasses. We stopped at the bigger one on the way out, I got a stuffed giraffe. Molly and Mr. Hydell got a few other things as well.

It was a 12-minute drive to the museum, we stopped at a gas-station to fill up and grab some snacks for later. Once at the museum, we took some pictures with the whale skeleton out front before going inside. My parents had taken my brother and sister here just before I was born. I'd never been before. We had a great time, although Mr. Hydell did get a little lost at one point. I really enjoyed the insect exhibit, while Molly and Mr. Hydell liked the mammal exhibits. We visited the gift shop last.

Mr. Hydell actually got a few maps, a printed mug, and an Albert Einstein cup. Molly and I both got a few pieces of jewelry. One I got was a pair of philodendron leaf blossom earrings. Plus we both got pairs of cherry blossom, trinity knots, and bonsai tree earrings. She also got a monarch butterfly necklace. I got two pairs of origami butterfly earrings, and we both got several bracelets.

After that we visited the museum's sea center. Molly said we probably should've gone there first since it was on the docks and was closer to the zoo. It only meant a 13-minute drive back to the waterfront. Can you say 'heaven' for the lover of the sea. Okay that came out wrong. Oh well. The sea center had a few things that the aquarium didn't have. Some of the touch pools had certain starfish and baby sharks. It wasn't very big though, so we were at both museums for about an hour and a half. It was fun though.

Once we were done there we headed to the bookstore. Mr. Hydell had to put the name into the G.P.S. but we got there. Turns out we had driven past it on our way to the Sea Center. How do you like that? We'd been a block away at one point. Again, oh well.

Paradise Found was great! Mr. Hydell decided to stay in the car to take an emergency call, so he gave me his wallet and said, "Go crazy." He smiled when he said it. Okay. I wouldn't go to crazy. Within reason. Molly and I went in and spent a good half-hour in there. Books were somewhat limited, but I did find a book on meditation and a copy of Practical Magic by Alice Hoffman. The book the movie was based on. We both also got some books on proper herb uses and I got a few crystals. I didn't need to replace my weather crystals, but sometimes have larger versions of them means the bigger you can go. Just in case. I even picked a few for healing crystals. Always be prepared.

The final things I got were several sticks of incense, – of course most in sea scents – some scented and unscented candles, and a few necklaces. Including a Hamsa charm, I was needing some extra protection. I did buy a matching bracelet set for Molly and Mr. Hydell. I didn't think he'd wear it, but you never know.

We both came back to the car with four bags. Good deals. We put everything in the trunk, making sure to put the bags on both sides so we wouldn't get them mixed up. We got back in the car.

"So where to now?" Mr. Hydell asked. Good question. It was only about 2:00, so we had a few hours before we'd have to go back to Casitas Springs. So where to? There were plenty more book stores we could visit. Plus the Santa Barbara Museum of Art Store was literally right across the street.

In the end we decided to indeed visit a few more book stores and the art store. We ended up headed back to Casitas Springs at shortly after three. I had tried to find Sherlock Holmes books but none of the stores we'd visited had any. I didn't mind though, Sherlock can be hard for some people to read because they're written in old English.

About half way back to Casitas Springs I remembered something, "So what was the call about?" I asked Mr. Hydell.

"I asked one of the officers who was looking into the sighting to call me if they got an update. They did."

"Really. What?" asked Molly.

"Kepner has rented several apartments in L.A. under several assumed names. Each building was discreetly visited and told to contact police if he shows."

"Wow." Good grief. I hadn't realized it was that bad.

"Not only that, they've gone back through security tapes for all buildings that house trauma therapists. He's watched and even visited several of them. Two or three have been broken into, and their records gone through. No finger prints though."

"But given how desperate he is. It most likely was him." I state.

"Yep." He says, somewhat nervously.

"So what do we do?" Molly asked.

"We continue with the plan. We lay low for a few days, then head back, but I think at this point it's time to change our living quarters." Mr. Hydell had three apartments in L.A., we could easily switch around.

"We can do that later this week. For now you both are staying with me at my Hobbit hole." Molly said.

Chapter 10

We arrived back at her home in Casitas Springs to the realization that her cousin was present as well.

"Great." She said, "I'll go let him know were here. You guys go ahead inside. I'll show you to rooms once I'm inside." She tossed her house keys to Mr. Hydell before exiting the vehicle and heading up to her cousin's door. We got out, unloaded the trunk, and went inside. It was very cozy. Traditional in its design too. With the wide circular arched doorways, hallways, and roofs. No stairs inside. We set the book bags in the living room, making sure not to mix them up.

The rest of the bags – which contained groceries – we took to the kitchen. It wasn't hard to find. It was a Big kitchen. Plenty of space, and a good-sized island. We placed all the bags on the island before putting everything inside in their proper places. Molly and I had chosen ingredients that we wanted to use for meals over the next few days. Mr. Hydell had also said that our time away may be extended if the cops advised it. My gut said they might. But one never knows.

I was looking around the hole when I heard raised voices. Whoops. My bad. My hearing was on high. I couldn't make out what was said, but from the tones, my guess was her cousin wasn't happy about total strangers – to him anyway – being in such close proximity to his house. Wah. Big baby.

I was actually standing next to the door that led to the tunnel that connected the two houses when she entered. I actually jumped. I had thought the door was a closet. She stepped through and locked the door. She was not happy. She started when she turned and saw me.

"Don't do that to me dear." She said with a soft laugh.

"Sorry, didn't mean to." And it was true. "Family dispute."

"Yes, but I don't want to talk about it right now. Come on. I'll show you your room." She turned back the way I had come and turned down a small hallway.

The room she gave me was awesome. It had a view of the lake, a computer, and a mini-fridge. I asked about the computer and fridge. She'd told me that a few clients had had to stay with her over the years, so she kept the place prepared. We spent a few minutes setting it up for me before she went back to discuss something with her cousin. Now that he'd calmed down.

I decided to use the computer to check up with Ben. I didn't know if I would be back for my Tuesday work shift and I was still curious about what he'd been in a hurry about. I used a dummy Facebook account, my friends and co-workers knew about it. So knew to check it if I was in hiding.

I logged on. I don't use Facebook often – mainly because of Kepner – but when I do I catch up with friends. Even the ones that were no longer speaking to me at school. They don't check it as often as my co-workers, but it's nice to talk to them sometimes. Good. Ben was on. I immediately started up chat.

"*How's it goin' Ben?*" I typed. He took a few minutes to answer.

"*Good, you?*" Can't complain but could be better.

"*Okay. So what was the rush the other day?*" he'd know what I meant but anyone snooping wouldn't know the specifics.

"*I'd forgotten that I had promised to pick up my grandparents from the airport.*" Whoops. Hope they weren't too mad

"*Ah. Any other problems?*" I really hate to get my friends in trouble.

"*Nah. They understood once I gave them details.*" By that he meant that he'd explained how he gave me rides to therapy.

"*Cool.*"

"*Yep. Hey, I gotta go, talk to you later.*" No prob. Not since he has guests.

"*Okay, Bye.*" He didn't say bye back. That's okay, when one is in a hurry you don't have to in my opinion. There was a knock at my door. I turned. Molly was there.

"If you're done, I'd like to finish the tour." She said with a smile.

"Yep, just let me log out." Once that was done I got up and followed her.

The hobbit hole was bigger than it looked. Not only was there the full-sized kitchen, but there was an underground garage, a pool, – plus hot tub – a gym, a large pantry, and a library. She did say that her cousin's house was a few rooms bigger – she had seven bedrooms, while he had 18 – but that she didn't mind the differences. She didn't like a lot of company, plus his house had a bad rep for being the party house where everyone left drunk. Not a good rep for a government worker. Hence why he wasn't here too often.

I really liked the library, it was spacious and had all kinds of books. Several fiction novels, and even some history books. But my absolute favorite section, was the old literature section. She had copies of Moby Dick, Dr. Jekyll and Mr. Hyde, Dracula, and… NO! Sherlock Holmes Galore! I rushed to that side of the aisle, every single story Sir. Arthur Conan Doyle ever wrote for Sherlock! Yes! Paradise!

"I thought you might like that. Pull down that first one there." She indicated the shelf above my head. There were two copies of A Study in Scarlett, the story that began it all. I pulled the one closest to her.

"Open it." She said. I did. Right to the copy-right page. Publishing year – 1887!! It was an original publication! Wait what's that? I turned a page. It was signed!! Sir. Arthur Conan Doyle's signature looked as fresh as over a hundred years ago.

I couldn't talk straight, "How… how did you get this? It must've cost a fortune."

"You know I never did ask my ex-husband that." I looked up from my admirations in shock.

"Yeah, I know," she continued, "I caught him cheating on me less than a month into our marriage." I cringed. Not smart dude.

"He gave that to me hoping to make amends. Didn't work. I kept it 'cause it was rare, but now since I know how much you also love Sherlock Holmes." She closed the book while still in my hands and placed my hands the rest of the way around it.

"It's yours dear." What? I was speechless.

"I couldn't possible accept this." I so wanted to but… it's an original.

"No arguments. This book had been on the shelf for two years. I want you to have it. You'll get more out of it than I will." Still holding the book, I hugged her. Best gift ever!

Still crying in excitement she left me in the library to read my new book. I chose the window seat looking out on the lake. A Study in Scarlett wasn't a long story, but it was a good one. To read how Holmes and Watson met, their first case together, and just how knowledgeable Holmes is. It's enjoyable, especially if you like to read old literature. Not everyone can. It can be a pain, but once you get used to it, it is very good reading. Though I will always come back to Sherlock. Not a lot of people wrote such intricate detective novels back then. It can really heighten ones learning capabilities, and intelligence.

I was there for about an hour before Molly came back to ask if I would help with dinner. Yes I would, I helped plan it. I put my new book in my room on the night stand. I'd do more reading before bed.

Chapter 11

For that night's dinner, we had decided on chicken alfredo. It was almost a quarter after five, so we had about an hour to make it. Molly and I had even decided to make the fettuccine noodles from scratch. She had the proper tools, so it wasn't too much trouble. She gave me the easy jobs, even though I protested slightly. My leg was tender after all the walking around. Oh great, I was even limping. I kept my prescribed pain pills in an inner zip up pocket in my jacket. I didn't take them often, I'm stronger than that. When I did it was with food. As recommended on the bottle.

"Do you have any sliced cheese?" I asked. She saw the bottle.

"Top fridge drawer." She indicated, "Need to take those with food?"

"Yep and thank you." I made a simple slice of bread and cheese, no need to make something big.

I ate it in about four bites while making the seasoning mix. I knew to use a bit more than you think you'll need. Any extra – that hasn't come in contact with raw meat – could be put back in the bottle. Either that or put them into the sauce. I took the pill after the sandwich was gone and I had taken a drink of water. I hate dry swallowing.

Molly started the dough while I started chopping the chicken breasts. The seasoning was waiting in a small bowl, while I put the chicken pieces in a medium sized one. There were only three chicken breasts, so I wouldn't be left with too much extra. Once I was done chopping the chicken and had washed my hands, I filled a pot with water and a pinch of salt and started it boiling. Once that was done I sat down on a bar stool for a minute. The pain pill hadn't taken affect yet.

"You okay dear?" she asked while kneading the dough.

"Yeah, still a little sore but I'm okay."

"I had meant to ask if you'd been in a wheelchair at all?"

"For the first few weeks," Nerve damage and all, "after about six weeks I was told I could switch to crutches or a foot cast. I chose a boot cast. It had to be specially made since it was my femur." I said.

"Why not crutches?" Oh right she didn't know about the nerve damage.

"I had nerve damage in my left arm." She coughed. I looked at her. She was again shocked.

"When the tub fell it wasn't exactly stable. I activated a pressure point in my arm to hold it up – using my dragon strength without actually shifting – and was still in that position when the paramedics showed up."

"Was it still activated when you got to the hospital?" she asked while attaching the rolling device to the mixer.

"Nope." She looked at me in surprise. "My hand had seized from the pressure point being stimulated for too long. I was out cold so I couldn't tell the EMTs about what I had done, and they wrenched my arm loose."

"Ouch!" she said giving a large cringe. "Did the pain wake you?"

"Oh yeah." I said nodding. "My scream was heard seven blocks away. Several of the people there had to cover their ears. I kinda then chewed them out."

"Well you had every right to!" Wow, she was mad. "Not knowing about pressure points. Did they even think to try and wake you first?" she asked while angrily rolling out the dough into ovals.

"One did have smelling salts, but he got overruled by majority." Should've used the salts. "That hospital ended up paying the treatment and therapy bills for my hand."

"Can you still shift it?"

"Yes but doing a partial shift with my left arm still hurts like hell. It doesn't hurt when I fully shift." Only because it technically goes from shoulder to fingers rather than the reverse.

"Do you still have the leg cast?" she paused in what she was doing.

"Yeah. There are some days I wake up and my leg won't hold my weight. So I use it." It was well designed to attach to my belt, wrap around my thigh & calf, plus with crisscross straps so I could bend my knee.

"Plus I was given a year-round elevator key just in case." I added.

"I would hope so." She'd started feeding more dough through the attachment.

I could stand again so I started mixing the herbs into the chicken and adding groups to the pan. I pulled out a second medium sized bowl to hold the cooked chicken. In a cast iron pot I got the sauce started. Alfredo sauce isn't that complicated, I actually had one memorized. It was my great-grandmother's, my mom had used it since I was little. My great-grandmother had remarried an Italian man and had kept his recipes. They had one child together, my grandpa had already been born to her previous husband. Great aunt Helga was still around, she just lived in Italy.

Molly got done with the noodles and added them to the water. I was just finishing the chicken. The cast iron pot was big enough that it would fit everything once they were done. We did have a bit of seasoning left and I had already added some to the sauce. Molly pulled out an old spice jar for the leftovers. I tasted the sauce. I thought it was almost there. I let Molly taste it. She agreed. A pinch more.

Once the sauce was perfect we put the rest in the jar. She drained the noodles while I added the chicken to the sauce. I added a scoop of pasta water to the pot to help thicken it a little more. Molly added the pasta just as Mr. Hydell came into the kitchen.

"I can smell that from the living room." He said, coming over and kissing Molly.

"Good." She said, "Good food **should** permeate the house."

"Before we eat, I was wondering what your cousin objected to." Mr. Hydell beat me to it. Saves me the trouble.

"He didn't like the idea of strangers being so close to his prize collection."

"Prize collection of what?" I asked setting out plates and silverware. The kitchen and dining room were next to each other.

"Antique pocket watches." She said.

"Okay, I guess I understand that." I said. Certain ones could be worth up to 12 million dollars.

"You may dear, but I've always believed a watch should be used, not on display."

"Maggie loves antique clock works." Mr. Hydell said, sitting down with a full plate.

"Really." Molly said while giving me a funny look.

"Oh yes. She even got my grandfather clock working properly again."

"All it needed was cleaning." I objected.

Molly and I sat down with our plates, "Besides, that love applies more to grandfather clocks. The pocket watch I have is modern. Well, had."

"What happen to it?" Molly asked while taking a bite of food.

"It was stolen." I was still mad about it. That watch had been a gift from my mom and dad for my twelfth birthday. A special gift commemorating my first shift.

"Oh honey I'm sorry." Molly said, patting my shoulder.

"Her parents never did find out who stole it. They left it at the store for cleaning and the store was robbed the day after they left it." Mr. Hydell told her.

"When was it stolen?" she asked while pulling out her phone. Okay.

"About a month before the murders. It was made with modern materials but was designed like original art nouveau, with a dragon instead of the usual plant." I was getting wistful, "My dad had even had the inside engraved."

"Something like this." She turned her phone for me to see. I nearly choked on my mouthful.

Still coughing I said, "That's the one!" I knew the design anywhere. I'd even drawn it out for the cops.

She chuckled, "Then I think we need to have a chat with my cousin."

"And he needs to have a chat with police." Said Mr. Hydell.

"What made you think it was mine?" I asked after taking a drink of milk.

"I was looking at his collection – thinking you might like to take a look, that set him off more than anything – and he mentioned that it had come to his usual guy about a week before the murders and had been there since." Made sense, anything depicting folklore after shifters were exposed was likely to go unsold.

"We can look as soon as he gets back."

"Where's he at?" I asked.

"Town, he'll be back soon."

"Did you look inside?"

"No," she said, "I only looked at it through the glass, I was taking the pic when he came in. He even checked the locks. Like I'm gonna open them, he keeps the key on him at all times."

It took him about twenty minutes to get back. I hadn't wanted to take my time eating – I was so anxious to get it back – but they made sure I did. I had just finished putting dinner away when I heard him pull up. I immediately closed the fridge door and called Molly. She met me at the connecting door. She unlocked it and we went up to his house. Technically it was a mansion, but right then I didn't care what the proper terminology was. We intercepted him at the top. I'd seen him on TV a few times, so I recognized him.

"Ugh," nice to see you to shithead, "what do you want Molly?" He gave me a disgusted look, like I was a piece of shit he'd found on his shoe. I growled, not just because of his look but because of how he'd spoken to Molly. He visibly blanched and backed away.

"Easy dear." Whoops, claws had appeared. "I need to see your silly collection."

"It's not silly," he stated, partially returning to his regular color, "those watches are worth fortunes."

"Bet you a thousand bucks more than half are cheap replicas." I said, crossing my arms.

"Oh and you'd know would you." He seemed offended that I might know more about antique clock works than him.

"Do you know how to open the back?" He gave me a look that said yes, "Then if they have a battery – which last I checked was perfected in the last century – it's a fake." I stated, keeping eye contact.

"Whatever. Now why do you need to see it?"

"Just take us there." She asserted. He rolled his eyes and shook his head, but he did shows us there.

He had about 150 watches. All on soft velvet pads. Most were definitely fakes. I could see that just from the artificial rust affect. Though a few were authentic. There are some designs even the best forgers can't mimic. The Victorian era ones were nice too. There it was. In the last shelf. One of eight.

"Take that one out." Molly said.

"Why?" he asked, fingering his pocket.

"Because it's four years old and belongs to me." I said, trying to hold myself back from forcing the door open. Two of the other watches in the cabinet were authentic and I didn't want to ruin them.

"HA!" he said, "and how do you know that."

"Open the cabinet and look inside the cover." Molly said, crossing her arms.

He walked forward, unlocked it, opened the door, and pulled my watch out.

"Is there an inscription?" Molly asked.

"Maybe." Liar. You can't fool a shifter.

"Does it read, 'To Magenta. Our beautiful, rare daughter who surprises everyone with her unknown beauty. Both of mind and spirit. To you on your twelfth birthday. Forever yours with our eternal love. Mother and Father.'" It did, I'd seen his shoulders tense as I spoke.

Plus Molly had walked up and read it over his shoulder. "That it does dear."

He was mad. I could smell it. I walked up and grabbed his wrist. I had sensed his muscles tensing, I really didn't want him crushing my watch. I pulled his arm down. He tried to fight.

"Dude." I said letting my eyes go dragon, he paled. "I'm a shifter." I started squeezing his wrist.

"Don't hurt him too much dear, he still needs to call the police and report his seller."

"Indeed." I said without letting go. He still held my watch. I squeezed a bit more. He fell to one knee.

"Take it, take it." He opened his hand and I snatched it out before he could change his mind. Only then letting him go. I opened my hand and the watch and examined it. It needed a battery, but it was the one. I closed it and held it to my chest.

"Why do I need to talk to the police?" he asked. Rubbing his wrist.

"Because you bought stolen property." Molly turned me back towards the tunnel and we left him with his pain and questions.

Chapter 12

I was in my room when Molly came in almost an hour after getting my watch. She had the biggest grin on her face. Whatever had happened with her cousin had been better than she'd hoped.

"Good news?" I asked with a smile.

"You bet dear." She said, sitting at the foot of the bed. "Not only did he go through his watches, but he discovered that you were right." She pulled a roll of money out of her pocket.

"I wasn't serious about a bet." I said.

"I know, but seeing his face was so worth it. So this is a reward from me." She passed it to me. It was indeed one thousand dollars.

"More than half – like 67% - of his collection was fake." Ouch. Sorry dude. NOT!

"How'd he take that?" I was trying not to smile.

She laughed so hard, "He was positively livid." She couldn't stop laughing. "He had the biggest temper tantrum I have ever seen." I joined her laughter.

"He did call the cops though." She said once she could breathe again. "Turns out his seller was wanted for selling stolen property and all kinds of embezzling."

"Ouch!" I started laughing again.

"Yep, so now my cousin has a partially worthless collection and has to find a new guy to go to." Not his year.

"Nice to know you can have leverage against him now."

"Oh," she giggled, "don't even get me started." She was very happy.

She left the room just after that. Oh today was a good day. I had more than I could ask for at the moment. More than I even wanted. I had been alone so long that I had begun to feel like I couldn't function with a family anymore. I could only imagine how Reggie felt. I decided to give in. I'm gonna check his Facebook account.

It took me a few minutes to find it. He'd been in the habit of changing his profile picture every few weeks. Some teachings don't go away. There! Rambo, seriously bro. I knew it was his page because of the name. He actually used his full name. Reginald Henry Victor Lockhorn Sharps. He added the extra 's' to his last name to play it safe. Although technically our last name was still only in half. Every shifter has a full name. It's what helps us track family history or blood. That one was Reggie's of course.

My dad's had been odd. Victor Jackson Susan Hemsworth Sharp. Don't even get me started, once my siblings and I had learned one of his middle names, we made fun of him. He took it on the chin though. That was dad. My sister's full name was easier and nowhere near as odd. Amanda Giada Martina Helen Sharp. Our last name was only fully given on formal occasions.

I didn't like to think about my full name. It brought back too many memories. Reggie as the oldest had been given our dad's name as a middle name. Amanda, our mother's – Helen. I had been given our grandma's name. Regina. Queen in Latin. I had never really understood why they chose it though. Even grandma had wanted them to pick something else. I didn't complain though. I like the name, it's pretty. The other reason I didn't think of my full name was 'cause of a warning my dad had given the three of us once we were all teens.

Long story short he'd told us never to say our full last name in front of other shifters or other fable folk. Particularly wizards with the name Parthenian. He'd never specified but had said that our two families had tried to destroy each other and that they had almost succeeded. If it hadn't been for two ancestors getting away, our family would be extinct. That being said, we'd never sought revenge. We had been feared and misunderstood. They called all dragon shifters monsters that should be destroyed. My family had never once caused harm to either humans, fable folk, or other shifters. The Parthenian clan hadn't cared. The only reason my family had tried to wipe the clan from the Earth was because they had tried to eliminate an ancestor's children in front of her. Not a smart move. After that was resolved no grudge of any kind was held. We were too smart for that. Hence why the surviving ancestors had changed their name and hidden.

I opened my brother's page. The usual astronomy stuff, eclipses, meteor showers, and…. He's dating?! Oh hold up now! Who is this girl? I clicked her profile. Her name is Matilda. She's a fellow student. Going for physics and biochemistry. Okay cool. Her birthday is next week and she's a year younger than him. Okay so far she's alright. Back to checking up on my brother. Oh geez.

He was in therapy for failing to be there for family. I wasn't even aware that was something you could be in therapy for. Man, Reggie was feeling worse than he had let on. You should have said something dumbass! Not much I could do to help, we were both better off alone for now. So long as he wasn't failing in school. Nope, straight A's. Good. Matilda was probably helping. Giving him something else to focus on as well as keeping him focused on school. There were some days where I wondered if he looked for my profile. Not that he'd get any results. My true account wasn't active, and I didn't think he knew about this one. Oh well. Nothin' I could do about that right now.

I logged out again and turned off the computer. Tomorrow I'd give myself a project. Something I could do with my hands. My violin was still in L.A. I hadn't brought it for obvious reasons. I looked at my new book and my watch. They were side-by-side on the end table. That's it! I'll make a box to hold them both. I was taking woodshop and needed an out of class project to turn in for my final grade. This could be it.

I ran to the room across from the master bedroom. The printer was kept there along with the main home computer. I went in and grabbed a few blank pieces of printer paper and a pencil. I semi-ran back. Damn leg. Once I was back I moved the computer slightly and sat down. I held the pencil loosely and began to draw. Any good artist experiments with designs until they find the perfect one. I went through three different potential designs before finding what I felt was the perfect one. Since both things I wanted to put in were either very old or looked old, I wanted something that paid homage to that.

Among the design I included aspects of Sherlock Holmes. A violin along one short side with music notes, a magnifying glass along the other, along the front I depicted a Victorian era woodwork, – like you see on some dressers or wardrobes – along the back I had Sherlock's pipe, and on the top I chose a cup of tea and a pocket watch. I'd made sure to add measurements to the drawing after measuring the length and width of the book and the distance I wanted between the two before making the final calculations. Most well-known engineering rule, 'measure twice, cut once.' I wouldn't be doing any cutting today, but it was always better to plan ahead.

I got up from the desk and placed the picture on the night stand, weighed down by my watch. I'd need to get a battery for it the next time I went to Walmart. I'd check the garage to see if Molly had all the necessary tools to get started, if not I could always talk to my woodshop teacher. Before I sat down I changed into my pajamas, it was late, and I needed sleep. I fell asleep while reading again.

Chapter 13

I actually over-slept. Wow. I hadn't done that in a while. I didn't count the other day for work. That was only by 15 minutes. Today I had gotten an extra hour-and-a-half. Either I had forgotten to set an alarm, or Mr. Hydell and Molly felt I needed a bit more sleep. I pulled my phone from my coat pocket – I'd hung it by the hood on the right headboard post. Dead battery. Whoops. I'd forgotten to pack my charger. Oh well. I'd leave it till later.

I maneuvered myself to get out of bed. My leg felt horrible. I hoped that didn't mean I couldn't use it. Only one way to find out. First I checked where Molly and Mr. Hydell were. The kitchen making breakfast. Ooh I smell bacon. I stood up, and promptly fell. Hard.

The scream I gave was heard in the kitchen, I'd heard them jump at the sound. They turned the stove off and came running. I gritted my teeth and tried to look as innocent as possible. I hated getting looks of sympathy. It only made the emotional and psychological pain feel worse.

Nope. No getting out of it. I was in too much pain. I could barely breath. Time seemed to slow down. Then the pain started to ebb. Wait. I know that feeling. *Damn it Reggie!! Stop it!!* I didn't want him to syphon anything. Least of all my physical pain. It was bad enough he couldn't be here. Him helping me in such a way only made my heart ache more.

"Stop fighting me sis. I want to help." Reggie said from a great distance. I started to cry. I hadn't heard his voice in so long.

"I don't want you to help." I didn't mean that in a bad way. I just didn't want him to share my pain.

He sensed that, "*I know, but I'm going to anyway.*" My gods he was stubborn. The pain started to lessen. I had actually fallen unconscious.

"*You're a jerk, you know that right.*" I laughed.

He laughed too, "*I know. I love you.*"

"*I love you too.*" Gods it felt so good to hear from him. I had come back to reality well enough that I could hear Molly and Mr. Hydell saying my name. I moved my hand in indication I'd heard them. I was lying on my left side. Ow.

I started to lean up. Ugh. Nope. Felt sick. Molly grabbed a pillow from the bed and placed it under my head as I laid down on the floor. I felt Reggie reconnect. Geez bro your insistent. Mr. Hydell placed a glass of water to my lips. I raised my head enough to drink.

"You okay?" Reggie and Mr. Hydell asked at the same time. I giggled.

"I'm okay, now." Reggie wasn't just syphoning pain anymore. He was helping my stomach settle.

"*Five weeks since the last collapse. You're getting better.*" I gasped, he was teasing me.

"*Eff off you over-protective dingleberry.*" I replied. He laughed. So did Mr. Hydell? Oops. I must've said it out loud too.

"What was that?" Molly asked, seeming a little consternated.

"I was talking to Reggie." I answered. Oh. Wait a minute! I held up a finger to fore stall any comments on my expression. "*You sneaky bastard! You've been checking up haven't you!*" I yelled.

"*Every few weeks. I've gotten good enough that you don't notice.*" He confirmed.

"*You know we agreed to not have any kind of contact.*"

"*You've been checking my Facebook account, I figured this was the best way for me to check on you.*" Well that confirmed my suspicions.

"*That's electronically. It doesn't count.*" I stated.

"*It does to me. I promise that I won't make this a habit, I just wanted to help. You tuned me out the other times. I miss you so much right now that my big brother instincts needed a reprieve.*" He said. I could hear the longing in his voice to see me. I felt myself start crying again.

"I miss you too bro. And I guess I needed a sibling reprieve too. Since I didn't fight this time." I could definitely give him that. Six months was a long time to miss someone. We'd gotten the funerals done in two weeks. So yeah. A long time. I sent him some of my love. I felt him start crying.

"Hurry up and kill that bastard." He meant it as a joke, and though I did laugh I could feel the rage that always came with those thought.

"Working on it. He's shown himself but he's not making finding him easy." I said.

"When?" He sounded scared. I knew why. Because he might not be able to get to me and help in time.

"Two days ago. He followed me from therapy and tried to follow me home." I could feel his growl in my bones. Something told me he'd had a growth spurt since we last saw each other.

"Don't worry. We left L.A. that same day. We've been away since." I reassured him.

"When do you go back?" he asked.

"Maybe later today or tomorrow. Depends on the cop's progress." I said.

"Okay. Be safe sis. I love you."

"Always am. I love you too bro." I opened my eyes. Molly and Mr. Hydell had moved me back to bed.

"You okay?" Molly asked.

"Yeah. But I'm clearly not going anywhere today." I said.

"I have a wheelchair in the garage. I'll go get it." She got up and walked out.

"I'll bring you some breakfast kiddo." He actually kissed my head. I couldn't help but smile.

He walked out of the room. Once he was out of hearing range I rolled to the left, put my face in the pillow, and just let it all out. I don't know how long I cried, but I did feel a little better afterwards. Not better enough to make a significant difference though. I heard Molly coming. No tissues close by. Oh well. I wiped my face as best I could. Then sat up without using my left leg. I groaned. Reggie had been right. I was getting better, and stronger. My leg could take movement more every time I managed not to collapse.

Molly came in, saw that I'd been crying, put the wheelchair out of the way, and retrieved some tissues. She then had me lean forward a bit more and brushed my hair. I went through three tissues before Mr. Hydell came back. He'd brought food and drink on one of the bed trays. He set in on the desk while Molly finished.

"You all right kiddo?" he asked for the third time. They weren't buying it then. Okay fine.

"I feel like someone has put lava inside my leg. Then covered it with liquid nitro. I'm sick and tired of Kepner. I'm missin' my brother bad enough I can't breathe. I don't know how much more I can take, and that makes me feel sick to my stomach and pissed off." I said without making eye contact. Molly hugged me from behind.

"So was that what the dingleberry bit was about?" He asked. I laughed.

"No, that was me chewing out my brother."

"Does that explain the look as well?" He also asked.

"Yeah. Turns out Reggie had been psychically checking up on me since after the funerals."

He was shocked, "But you guys agreed to no contact."

"We did, but since he's six years older than me he can do it without my noticing."

"Sneak." Molly said, she got up and fixed the pillows so I could lean on them.

I leaned back. "Thanks. And yes he is. He also syphoned some of my pain and nausea."

"You can do that?" Molly asked, she looked fascinated.

"If the ones involved are either blood-related, mate bonded, or pack bonded. Yes. Loners, no."

"Wow." She placed the tray on my lap.

"So much for my plans today." I started eating. Molly saw the paper under my watch.

"You could still do it dear."

"Not in a wheelchair. It would be too difficult." I said between bites.

"I have all you'd need, and the benches are adjustable, plus if there's a tool you need but can't reach, just call one of us."

"You wouldn't be opposed?" I asked.

"No dear. You need something to focus on. Plus looking at it, I think it would be a shame to cancel."

Mr. Hydell came over and looked at it. "It is beautiful. You plan on using it for your final grade too?"

"Yeah, but of course he'll need confirmation from you that I did it on my own."

"He'll get it. You don't like asking for unnecessary help." I smiled, he was right, I just knew when to accept it.

I had finished so they took the tray and left. Mr. Hydell closed the door as well so I could change. Easier said than done. I'd be working with tools, so no loose clothing. No prob, I didn't wear dresses or skirts often. I pulled on my jeans from yesterday, and my short-sleeved blue shirt that I'd packed. I managed to get in the chair without putting weight on my leg – don't say that's easy, try it sometime from a waist high bed. The chair was well made and very maneuverable. Good, I'd need it. I opened the door and wheeled myself out with the paper by my leg. I decided to stop by the computer room first though. I thought I'd seen an mp3 speaker. I like to work to music. Never too loud of course. I might need to hear this thing called an alarm.

I came up to the door. It was open. I went in. Yep. I was right, it was an mp3 speaker. I grabbed it and wheeled to the kitchen. Molly and Mr. Hydell were finishing breakfast.

"Molly," I said at the entrance, "can I borrow this?" I help up the speaker.

She nodded, "There's some bacon left if you want to finish it."

I decided to. I nodded and smiled. I put the bacon on a paper towel and headed to my room. Once there I grabbed my mp3 from my bag. I plugged it into the speaker so I wouldn't have to pocket it. Then off to the garage. Since there were no indoor stairs I was good the whole way. I opened the door. The cars were all parked outside so no obstacles. I put the paper, bacon, and speaker on a side shelf and began adjusting the work benches. That took a few minutes.

Okay, that was done. Time to work. I started by pulling down a 4x6. I double checked my measurements and began marking them out. The box would be nearly a foot long, about 5 1/2 inches wide and about four inches high. That's with the lid.

Once I had the dimensions marked, I put safety glasses on, pulled my mp3 from the speaker for safety reasons, and plugged in the speaker. Once that was done I put it back in and turned it on. 'I'm a Lady' by Meghan Trainor. There was another one I had forgotten was on there. Eh, not gonna argue. Like I'd said, I like music.

Time to work. I placed the 4x6 on the cutting saw, being careful, I cut off what I needed. I then put the leftover away and began cutting it at between the half and three-quarter marks I had made length wise. I had always done it that way. My teacher had never understood why. Once that was done I began cutting out the inner portions. I had decided that the inner support would stick up a bit passed the top of the bottom half and fit nicely into the lid.

Taking that out took about an hour. I can work fast when I'm focused. The music was still going so my focus was at the top. I started smoothing out the inside, then checked my measurements again. Perfect, right where I wanted them. I took a quick break. The next song started. 'The Girl You Think I Am' by Carrie Underwood. I loved this song, even if it made me cry now. I locked the breaks and leaned back a little. I'd enjoy the song before starting again. I even started singing along. I have an okay voice. There was a knock at the door when the song was finished. I started. It was Molly.

"Your pretty good dear." She said with a smile. I'd heard that before, but my nose said she wasn't lying.

"Thanks, but there would be some people who would disagree with you."

"Then those people don't know you very well." She said.

"One does. My brother always thought I sounded like dying cat." We both laughed.

"When was the last time he'd heard you?"

"About a year ago. Me and Amanda had been singing together." I said, he hadn't held back on his opinion.

"Was he right?" she asked.

"No. Not about me anyway. Amanda was the one who sounded terrible. It was just hard to tell who it was at the time." Mom had chewed him a good one for that.

"I came to see how you were doing."

I indicated what I had so far, "Pretty good."

"You want some lunch in about an hour?" she gestured at the clock. It was 5 after 10.

"Maybe in an hour and a half."

"Okay, leftover alfredo alright?"

"Yes." I said, I never get tired of chicken alfredo.

She patted my shoulder and left. Back to it. I stopped. 'Fight song' by Rachel Platten. I hadn't heard this one in a long time. This was one of my favorites. I decided to put it on loop. I started singing along with it too. Safety glasses still on I finished smoothing out the insides. Then using a small handheld tool, rounded the outside edges. Great, that was done. I moved on to the carving. I mapped them out with a pencil, then using the tools I'd located, started carving. I did the easy stuff first. Like the pipe, the magnifying glass, the tea cup, and the outline for the watch. Each took about twenty minutes.

By the time I had the watch finished Molly was coming back with a bowl of alfredo. I cleaned up before accepting it. She looked at the box, admiring it.

"You have so much talent dear." She said, gently touching the imprint of the tea cup.

"My dad was the one who suggested I take woodshop. I like taking something plain and making it beautiful in a simple way."

"He was right to send you in that direction." She said tucking a stray piece of hair.

"I just wish he'd be able to see this." I would not cry. Enough of that for today.

"I'm sure he'd love it."

"I'm not sure. He couldn't understand old English to save his life."

"That may be, but you'd made it, so I'm sure he'd love it." She insisted. I just nodded.

She left to take a call after that. I ate my lunch slowly. I really didn't want to throw up. Reggie's syphoning had helped, but of course such actions weren't permanent. I realized I needed a drink, I was still covered in stuff. I looked around. I couldn't text, my phone was dead. I noticed an intercom on the wall. I wheeled over. I tried the kitchen button first.

"Hello?" I waited.

"What's up kiddo?" answered Mr. Hydell.

"Could you bring me a drink please?"

"Sure. You still in the garage?"

"Yep." I answered.

"Gotcha, be right there." He let the button go.

Okay, that takes care of that. I went back over to the desk, I wiped off the wood chips into a dust pan I had grabbed. The trash bin was by the big door. Once I had that taken care of, I went back over to the desk. Mr. Hydell walked in with an insulated water bottle.

"Figured this was better than an open cup." He said handing it to me.

"Given what I'm doing, yep. Thanks."

"Welcome." His phone buzzed as he said. I caught a glimpse of the caller i.d. L.A.P.D.

Well, time to get the answer. He left the garage to take the call. I turned my music up a notch. I'd rather focus on what I'm doing than catch a word of what's being said. I wanted to finish my work. So I did.

Chapter 14

I took my time finishing the box. Once I had the simple designs done, I started on the harder ones. The violin side took about 45 minutes to get done right. The Victorian era side took me two hours, time well worth it. I then spent about twenty minutes adding holes in the front so I could attach a lock. The box looked amazing. I started sanding down the outside gently so as not to undo anything.

When I had that done, I cleaned up my mess. Tools and all. I even put the benches back to what they had been before I started. I ask Molly if she had any of the materials I would need for my planned finishing touches. I debated about staining the wood. I like the way wood can look as it is, but since I was putting something old in it, then I probably should treat the wood and try to fire proof it. I could use magic for that.

I wheeled out of the garage with everything I had brought. The chair had a bottle holder so that's where the bottle went. First I put my bowl back in the kitchen, then I put the speaker back. I put the box and my mp3 in my room, then went to find Molly and Mr. Hydell. My ears told me they were on the deck. I headed in that direction.

I heard their voices a long way off. They were discussing something important. I don't like to eavesdrop, so I knocked on the wall to get their attention. They jumped, but the end was what I desired. They knew I was present.

"I'm not interrupting am I?" I asked.

"No. I was just telling Molly the results of what the cops told me."

"What?" I asked. Please be good news.

"Kepner was spotted fleeing the city. It seems he's got someone giving him info and he knew he'd been spotted. He has officially left L.A., he was last seen headed inland."

"Did they follow?" Molly asked.

"They've got him under surveillance." He said rubbing his face.

"Go on." I prompted. I wanted as many details as possible.

"Their tracking his progress via traffic cams, but there's no guarantee that he'll be caught. All counties along his most likely route have been informed. Their hopes just aren't very high."

"So does that mean we go back?" I asked, I wasn't feeling very confident.

"So long as we go undercover of night, and use a less likely route. That's what they recommended." He said

"But do we?" Molly contemplated.

"My boss won't let me miss another day. This case I'm working on is pretty important and needs to be resolved."

"Neither will either of mine." Molly said, since she technically had two occupations.

"So we go back, just be extra cautious over the next few days." I said.

"That's the plan at this point." He confirmed.

"We can get started tonight," Molly said, "We'll grab dinner along the way. Or a second dinner." Nice hobbit thinking.

"We've got a little over five and a half hours before dark. Might as well find something to do." Mr. Hydell said. It was only after three.

"How's the box coming?" Molly asked looking at me.

"Almost done. I need to stain it and I want to get that done before I add the lock and interior stuff."

Molly thought for a second. "I don't have any, but I can check my cousins garage. Though I don't have high hopes."

He didn't have any either. Mr. Hydell decided to go into town to get some. He gave a honk order for us to listen for. He also said he'd text when he got there dand was on his way back.

"So, what do you want to do for the interior of the box?" Molly asked.

"I was thinking an elevated platform or a velvet inlay. If I do both I could also hide a small weapon in the bottom." I said, thinking out loud.

"Well. Let me see what I have." She got up and walked toward the master bedroom.

I followed. I figured might as well rather than make her walk all the way back. She pulled a medium sized bin out from under the bed. Inside were crafting supplies. She pulled out some of the velvet spreads. It wasn't fancy velvet, but it would work. She also pulled out some small wood pieces.

"I had done these a few years ago. I never could decide what to do with them." She handed to me. One was about the size of the book. The other was a small, shallow bowl.

"I'll be right back." I left the room with the pieces. I got back to my room, grabbed the book, and tested the fit. I little loose but a velvet inlay would fix that. The watch didn't quite fit either. The inlay would fix that too. I brought the pieces and the box back with me.

"They'll work." I said smiling. "Are you sure you might not need them?"

"Yes I'm sure." She had five separate colors of velvet. "Which one do you think?"

"Not sure." I placed the box on the bed. The black worked okay. The white was hurting my eyes against it. The yellow blended too well. The blue looked really nice, but so did the red.

"I'm torn between the blue and red." I said.

"Well let's wait and see what Jack brings back. He just texted me to say he'd arrived." She said.

"Okay." I thought of something. "You don't have any pocket watch batteries do you?"

She thought for a second, "I might. Wait here a minute." She walked across the hall.

She came back with a small bin filled with batteries. Of assorted sizes. She leafed through them. I looked back at the tub of craft supplies. A few of the things inside hadn't even been opened yet.

"Are these usually for some of your clients?" I asked.

"Yeah. Some of my couple clients ask me to watch their kids when I suggest a few days to themselves to try and resolve something without scaring the kids." Smart plan.

"Ah, will these work?" she handed me a pack of tiny batteries.

"I'll go and check. Thanks."

"Your welcome dear. I'll start putting this stuff away."

I went back to my room. I had packed my multi-tool. Using one of its attachments I opened the back. Good. No battery rot. I gently used the pliers to remove the plastic cover and the old battery. I opened the new pack then. I loosed one of the batteries and went to place it. I heard Molly shout something from down the hall.

"He's on his way back!"

"Thank you!" I yelled back.

There. The battery was in place. The watch started ticking. Yes! It works. I reset it to the proper time. I put the two covers back in place, then put my tool away. I didn't put the watch on though. Kinda hard while in a chair. So I put it back on the table. Molly came to me this time.

"Right ones?" she asked.

"Yep. Thanks."

"Your welcome. Go ahead and keep the other one." She said as I passed the pack back. Okay. I could store it in the bottom.

"Would a weapon fit in there?" she asked, looking at the box.

"A dagger would. So long as I put the handle under the watch."

"I've got some ribbon. Do you want to fit a hidden handle?"

"Ooh, good idea." I said. We went back to master bedroom.

She'd left the ribbon out. Clearly she'd had the idea before coming to check on me. She also had pulled out some small plywood pieces.

"I figured along with the handle we could glue some of these together to support the bowl." Another good idea.

We were working on that when Mr. Hydell got back. The stain he'd gotten would turn the pine wood a medium mahogany color. I decided to wait till it dried to make a final velvet choice. I took the box to the garage, where Mr. Hydell had taken the stain. He also set up a table by the big door so the fumes from the stain wouldn't stay in the garage. We both had stained something in the past, so we got the job going pretty quick. We decided to leave one edge unstained so that the wood wouldn't stick to the paper towels. One of us could came back and finish them later. He'd gotten the quick dry stuff. Cool.

Molly decided we could go for a swim after that. Mr. Hydell questioned it 'cause of my leg, but she told him how water exercises could be very beneficial for old wounds like mine. That won him over pretty quick. He did decide to supervise from the deck though. Fine by me. I didn't really mind. Plus better him than any unfriendly eyes.

I didn't actually have a bathing suit. I didn't swim much. The leg was only one reason. The other was my old one had been torn to shreds by Kepner. Like seriously dude. Why the swimsuit? The lake was huge, so us swimming off her small dock would be really private. When I mentioned I didn't have a swimsuit she immediately went to her room and came back with a nice black one with white flowers on it.

"I bought this last month. It was mislabeled, and I lost the receipt." She said. I took it from her and wheeled to my room. The suit fit great. It was a pain getting it on though. I then looked through the dresser drawers in my room. I found an old black shirt in the middle drawer. I put it on over the suit, then wheeled myself back outside.

"What's with the shirt dear?" Molly asked. She was wearing a light blue bikini that was one size too big.

"My mom made me, and my sister do it when we were little. She said it would be better than not wearing one."

"She ever say why?"

"No but we found out why one summer about two years ago." I said trying not to smile at the memory.

"What happened?"

I laughed, I'm sorry Amanda but that had been really funny, "Amanda went to a swim lesson at the public pool with me and had decided not to bring an extra shirt. Well after a few minutes, while she was wet - and thankfully only I saw – her chest fell out of her swimsuit."

Molly bent in half in an attempt to suppress her laughter, "That was why your mom had you wear the shirts?"

"Yep, turns out she'd had a similar incident when she was 15, so she wanted us to never suffer that."

"And the habit has stayed?" she asked. Still giggling.

I nodded, "Even Amanda kept it up. Since I was the only one who saw, she wasn't too embarrassed. But she still felt better wearing the shirt afterwards."

"I don't doubt it. Your mother must've never went swimming again."

"She avoided it for a long time. It wasn't until she met our dad that she felt comfortable enough to swim again." She'd told us that after Amanda's incident.

"How'd your brother and dad react?" she asked.

"Dad was relieved she hadn't been seen by anyone but me. Otherwise he'd have to beat off several boys with a stick. And those were his words." I smiled at the memory, "Reggie on the other hand said dad would have to hold him back first."

"Because he would have beat your father there?"

"Yep. Reggie always was the overprotective dingleberry I called him earlier." I paused. We were at the end of the dock, "Now I wonder how he'll be with me once we can be together again." I wasn't a kid anymore. Leg or no I could take care of myself. In more than one way.

She put her hand on mine and kneeled down by me, "It'll take time, but eventually he'll see how much you've grown. That big brother instinct won't ever go away, but he'll understand he doesn't always have to be there."

"I hope so." I didn't really have very high hopes. I love my brother, but dragon shifter's handle family differently than humans do. A friend of mine who was also a shifter had seven older brothers. Every single one of them was a helicopter brother. She was so very tired of them. She loved them but she couldn't wait to go to college. Her brothers went to college in the city, so they all still lived at home. She planned to go to college out of state. I didn't know if she planned to tell them where she wanted to go, but I understood if she wouldn't.

"You okay?" Molly asked.

"Yeah, just thinking about a friend of mine."

She patted my hand, "Come on. Let's get swimming." She dived into the lake.

I wheeled forward. There was a pair of wood blocks at the end. I parked between them, locked the chairs brakes, and – somewhat awkwardly – dove in myself. The water felt great! I could feel the pain in my leg ease. I was tempted to grow my tail, but I didn't want to outpace Molly. Mr. Hydell didn't want us to separate while in the water.

So we didn't. After about twenty minutes I looked up at the deck and noticed him coming back from the garage. He must've applied either the second coat or to the uncoated side. Either was fine. Oh great. Cousin incoming.

"Molly!" she looked at me. I pointed at her cousin.

"Ugh. What does he want?" she started swimming toward the dock. I stayed where I was, though I did put my ears on high.

"What?" she asked when she was close enough to talk without yelling.

"Were you in my garage?"

"Yes, I was looking for wood stain." She said.

"Why would I have wood stain?" he seemed peeved. Wah!

"I don't know. Maggie had a project she was working on and needed some." I waved as he looked at me.

"Why would you too even bother with that cripple?" What did you call me!!?

Uh-oh, he'd hit a button, and not just mine. "Don't you dare call her that!!" I started swimming back. I'll show you a cripple shithead. I made the ladder.

"Oh I'm so scared you little - Sweet Mother of God!" he spotted my scar as I got on the dock.

I was so pissed I could walk fine, "You asked for it." I shifted.

He screamed like a little girl. At full size I was only a little bigger than a female African bush elephant. My wingspan though was three times my length so I can look much bigger. I was surprised the dock took my weight. I didn't quite weigh as much as a full grown African bush elephant, but I was close. They can weigh six and a half tons, in dragon form I was a little over four tons of muscle.

He was as pale as a ghost as I stalked toward him. Molly on the other hand had a shit-eating grin on her face as she climbed out of the water.

Standing next to my head, she said, "A cripple wouldn't be able to shift." I lunged at him.

Still screaming like a little girl, he fell in the water. Oops. Say good-bye to your expensive suit dude. I leaned over the dock. When he rose to the surface the first thing he saw was my teeth. My **very** sharp teeth. He froze. Well. As best as one can while treading water.

"Please don't eat me." He was actually begging? Ugh, you really are pathetic.

Molly kneeled by my head at the end of the dock, "You ever call her a cripple again and next time I'll say she can drop you from 20,000 feet up into the lake." Ouch.

"You wouldn't." He didn't seem like he believed she was bluffing

"I would. Do you think I would dear?" she asked, looking at me. I tilted my head as if thinking about it. Then nodded once.

"I know she can reach 20,000 feet too." She said looking back at him. "So you better believe me when I say I will do it."

Still staring at me he said, "I believe you." He was telling the truth, even with how much cologne he was wearing I could smell it.

"Good. Come on dear. Let's head back inside." She said.

I shifted back. I left my eyes alone though. Then I picked up the wheelchair, folded it, and carried it over my shoulder. We were on the deck when he finally got out of the water at his own dock.

"What did he say?" asked Mr. Hydell when we got to the top. He sounded a little mad.

"He called Maggie a cripple." His eyes widened. He looked over at her cousin. Oh dear. He grabbed his phone and went inside.

"Where's he going?" Molly asked me.

"To make a call. Probably to your cousin's boss She seemed confused.

"Why?"

"Because he really doesn't like people insulting me." I wiped my face with the towel I'd left on the deck rail. "Our neighbor learned that one the hard way."

"The 'popstar wannabe' as you call her?"

"Yep. She was complaining about my playing sad songs on my violin and he showed her some pics of my leg and my family's bodies."

"Well, her own fault." Yep. No argument on that one.

Once we were back inside I unfolded the chair and sat back in it. I didn't want to take any chances of my leg giving out two times in one day. I went with Molly to the kitchen, we decided to make the pizza leftovers our snack. She asked Mr. Hydell if he wanted any, he said no. She gave me three slices while she ate two. A little while later, Mr. Hydell came back in from the front door.

"How'd the phone call go?" Molly asked as he sat down at the table.

"Not too well at first. His boss tried to blow me off. It wasn't until I mentioned him pissing off an emotionally traumatized dragon shifter that he started to listen." He said.

"How'd he take that?" I asked, I knew the governor was in favor of a new law that would allow shifter's to take office again.

"He was pissed. He asked how you handled it." He had a small smile.

"What did you tell him?" I asked. I could easily have screwed my species chances.

"I told him you had a bad temper, but that despite it, he was unharmed. I did also tell him that you made no threat and that any threat that did come, came from the humans in your life."

"And what did he say to that?" Molly asked. I was almost too afraid to know.

"He said that he would talk to him. He actually has family who are turned shifters, so he knows that there are good people amongst them. More than likely your cousin's going to get fired if he can't explain himself."

"He should have thought of that before he insulted her." Molly said, taking a drink of water.

"I know. Then again you did say he talks long before he thinks." He replied.

"What if he tried to lie?" I asked.

"I gave him the whole story. Then I advised him to have another shifter present when they talk. If I remember correctly you said most shifters can smell lies."

"I did, and we can. Even if you can perfectly lie there are still extremely minute traces of endorphins that are produced. Even one year old shifters can pick those up." I said.

"Good, so my cousin won't be able to get away with anything." Molly said. She sounded a little upset though.

"Are you okay hon?" Good. I wasn't the only one who picked up on it.

"Yeah. Me and him have never gotten along. Now that he's this close to possibly getting his comeuppance, I'm just not sure how I actually feel."

"Look at it this way. One way or another he gets a lesson that might actually stick." Mr. Hydell said.

She nodded, thinking about that. If he told the truth he'd keep his job but would be watched like a hawk for any misbehavior. Especially toward shifters. If he lied and had to be taught something that way, he'd be out of a job and possibly unemployable because of his attitude towards people in general. Gods knew what his boss would have in mind punishment wise. It was a possibility that he'd never go past where he was now in his occupation. Oh well. That would be his fault. Not everything or everyone could be treated like shit.

After that Molly went through some of her attic possessions to see if one had any spare locks and hinges. I realized I had forgotten hinges. Kinda makes a lock redundant without hinges. I went to check the box. It was dry, so time for the second coat. I applied it. Using the inside for purchase when necessary.

Once it was done fully drying about an hour later, it looked really great. I went back into the master bedroom with the now dry box. I checked the two colors I had. The blue didn't quite work. It was dark blue, so would work better with a much darker stain. Red it was.

The red looked amazing with the box. Molly had already glued the wood sticks together. They held the bowl well and made the fit in the box perfect. Tight enough to fit, but moveable. I used a glue gun to attach the velvet to the boxes while Molly had Mr. Hydell cut the ribbon. I had chosen a shade of red darker than the inlay. Not only would the ribbon act as restraints for the book and watch but would be the hidden handles to remove the inserts. Molly had found small Velcro tabs in the bottom of the bin and that was what we used to hold the ribbons closed over the book and watch.

We had the box finished by 4:30. The lock and hinges she had salvaged from a small old trunk that had practically disintegrated in her hands fit perfectly. The inside wasn't stained so making the holes for the hinges wasn't too big a problem. The lock even came with the key.

The box had probably been over 200 years old. That fact that it had survived so long was impressive. The key was pretty small but had a nice simple design to its end. The lock needed to be flushed with cleaner, but we got it working. The lock gave the box a much older look. I loved it.

I went back to my room to place the two items. Once there, I made sure my book mark wasn't showing, then placed it in the box. A Study in Scarlet fit perfectly, and the ribbons held it nicely. My watch fit too. It didn't fit as snugly as the book but then again it wasn't supposed to. The chain I laid out around the rim of the watch, holding it all down with the second ribbon set. I proceeded to test whether the Velcro would stay if I used them as handles.

Hey, what do ya know! They held. I could lift the inside out easily, and the dagger I planned to place inside would fit so long as it was from corner to corner. After the murders only two knives and one dagger had survived the bomb. Not including the ones my dad had made. They had been safe in the basement and were now some of the items in storage for me and Reggie. One was a kitchen knife. Useful but not ideal. The other was my pocket knife.

It had been on my person when I had been out. The paramedics had taken it off when they pulled me from the rubble. I had gotten it back the next day.

The dagger that had survived had been the one that my mom used to open the mail. That wasn't the daggers original purpose, but it was so small and sharp it handles letter opening well. It was well made and so was strong. I could use it for defense. Of course I still had my unfinished tanto. I might be able to finish that myself if I got to take woodshop or welding at the new school. I'd have to do research first, on what material was traditional for handles. I knew wood was popular, but micarta or acrylic could work to. Maybe even bone, antler, or horn. Hey wait a minute.

When my dad had fought Mr. Kepner one of his horns had been broken. I still had it. I grabbed a piece of paper, if I could remember the length of the horn in comparison to the tanto, I might just be able to use it. An average tanto was between 5.9-11.8 inches in length. My dad's horn was 12 inches long. Yes! It would work.

"What are you working on?"

"Holy Mother of the Gods!" I'd been so focused I hadn't heard Molly coming.

She started laughing. "I didn't think you could sneak up on shifters." She was still laughing.

I chuckled, "Usually you can't. Not unless one is extremely focused." My heart was still pumping.

Once she could breathe again I answered, "My dad left behind an unfinished tanto. He was planning on giving it to me for my 18th birthday before he died. It survived the bomb, and I have it with me." I paused, "My mom had designed the handle, and I found the picture of it a few days ago." I looked into her eyes, "I was planning on using my father's horn to make the handle."

"Where did you get a horn?"

"He'd lost it somehow in the fight with Kepner. It wasn't found until after two days, when the forensic team found evidence of bone chips that didn't match up with my mom or dad's skeletal systems. They looked in the bushes in front of the house and there it was. Me and Reggie hadn't even known he'd lost the horn until they asked us about it."

"Right because by that time shifters had been exposed." She stated.

"Yep. You can probably imagine our surprise when they found it." Dragon bones are hard to break.

"They didn't try to confiscate it as evidence?" she asked.

"No. All it proved was that dad somehow got his ass kicked. That scent still haunts my nightmares."

"You have no idea what it was?"

"No," I paused, "Reggie might, but describing scents is hard. And we're at too great a distance for me to share the memory of it with him."

"You could ask your new principal." Very true.

"I'll have to the next time I see him." I said.

"Which. When will that be?" Good question.

"I don't know. I didn't really think about it. I assume I'll see him again when I do the mandatory tour of the new school, and that will be done at the end of the school year I think."

"Ms. Hamper might be able to tell you."

I nodded, "Speaking of, I'll have to double check if the appointment and my shift will conflict." I should have covered that on Saturday, but I hadn't thought about it.

"Do you keep the schedule on your phone?" she asked.

"Yes, but my phone is dead. I forgot to pack my charger."

"You can borrow mine. I'll be right back." She turned and walked down the hall.

She came back with the charger. I plugged it into the wall by the headboard. Then plugged my phone in. I was about to turn it on when I hesitated. Kepner probably had been the one to break into the therapy offices. If he had done so in the last two days with my building, he'd have my number, and maybe could even track me. I dropped my phone on the side table. I couldn't give this location away. Not in the least. I didn't know if I was being paranoid or just cautious. I had already endangered them just by being in their lives, I couldn't give anything away.

I decided to do the smart thing. Check the internet. Building break ins would be trending about now. I booted up the computer. It didn't have a password, so I didn't have to worry about that. I opened Google and typed 'building break-ins in los angeles.' I didn't specify the type of building, I'd seen plenty of crime shows where they track people by 'key words' as they call them. Like if you're looking for a terrorist, key words would be things like bomb, a person's name, or a place that the investigators knew was the next target. I also knew that criminals with excellent computer skills could use the same method to track victims or targets that had gotten away. I was too smart to be specific in my searches. Who knows what Kepner had learned in the time between the murders and now?

The search went through. So long as there wasn't anything new, I could check my phone just fine. When I had gotten the phone I had cast a protection spell on it that specialized in keeping it from being tracked when it was off. Hence why my phone wasn't on a lot. I scrolled through the first page, any new break ins would be on the first page. I recognized the buildings that were listed, but none were my therapy building. The last therapy building break in was two weeks ago. Most likely one of the two or three that he'd gotten impatient with. Impatience was the only real possibility about him breaking into a few of the buildings.

Some people can recover from trauma quickly. Depending on the circumstances. Also depending on which buildings were broken into, would determine why he broke in. I checked which buildings they were. I knew them. They were some of the most expensive and high end offices in the city. They could get someone back on their life's course within a few weeks. He would've checked them first because he knew some semblance of my strength of character as a person. Once he found no trace of me, he would've moved on to the next building.

Eventually you get to the cheaper therapists. Those who are equally good at their jobs, they just focus on health rather than profit. Ms. Hamper had been chosen for me because of her impeccable record with teens who had suffered like I had. Loosing almost everything you had ever loved was sadly common.

Now that I knew my therapy building hadn't been broken into, I went and turned on my phone. I looked at my schedule. I got out early this Tuesday, right that was why the appointment wouldn't conflict with work. Tuesday was when Ms. Hamper had meetings with the father of her child, so I had to see her before 3:00 when I had appointments on Tuesdays.

I found her relationship with the father odd. They had dated for a while, then when she found out she was pregnant, she had wanted to continue as they were. He on the other hand had wanted to get married. She wasn't ready for that. Not because of her age but because her husband had left her for her 18 year old cousin. Or, he was 18 at the time of their eloping, now he was 23 and the two of them were happy, but he had badly scarred Ms. Hamper about marriage. The divorce hasn't been pretty either. She was still recovering from the sting. I'd said she should've sent her own therapy bills to him.

Since she was now 8 months pregnant, she had healed a great deal. She felt she was close to full recovery, but she wanted to take precautions about the baby's future before she fully committed to the father. As far as I knew, the deal was this. He either married her and stayed that way until the baby was 18 – or more if their feelings for each other were pure - or they stay a couple without actually marrying and provide for the baby fairly each way.

When I had first met Ms. Hamper she had only been two and a half months along. She hadn't even been aware she was pregnant. I hadn't been either. It wasn't until about a month later that I walked into her office for my appointment that I'd caught on. The look on her face when I realized where the third heartbeat in the room was coming from.

I turned my phone off and thought back to that day. I chuckled. Like I had said, she had known what I was the first time she saw me, so when I mentioned three heartbeats, she got suspicious. I hadn't mentioned it immediately. First I had looked around the room for a third person. None, obviously. She had thought the third heartbeat was a mouse, so I decided to focus my hearing, and there it was. The third heartbeat had been coming from her belly. I still laugh at the look she gave me when I said that she was pregnant. She hadn't believed me. Then three days later at my next appointment, she apologized for not believing me. She'd visited the doctor and he had confirmed it.

It was almost five at this point. I decided to head back to the library and read some more. I grabbed A Study in Scarlet and wheeled out. Old English is one you can take your time reading, even for those who could successfully grasp it. Sometimes it's good to slow down. Me reading old English novels helped with that. Once in the window seat again, I immersed myself in my book.

Chapter 15

It was 15 minutes past six when we decided to head back to L.A. Mr. Hydell, and Molly had looked at a map and decided to take a longer route back. They checked Google maps and found that the longer route was just over an hour and half drive. Might as well stop in Santa Clarita for dinner. We made sure to check the fridge for any leftovers. The only things in it were vacuum sealed, so no worries there, not once we finished the milk.

I had to be helped to the car. My little shift incident had **not** improved my legs state. My box was safe in my bag along with everything else we'd brought and bought over the last few days. Once the wheelchair was back in the garage and all doors and windows were checked and locked as necessary, we started back for L.A.

Molly took her car. She and Mr. Hydell had talked it out and agreed that she could split off when we came to her part of town, while we continued on to ours. Plus she only had the one car and would need it for work.

We made it to Santa Clarita at 7:35. Once there we stopped at a Subway for dinner, we all were needing a little protein, since it had been more than three hours since anyone's last meal. Mr. Hydell actually hadn't eaten since lunch, so he definitely needed food. Molly pulled in next to us. Mr. Hydell was in the handicap spot with the card hanging from the rearview mirror. He got out and asked if the restaurant had any wheel chairs. They did, and he and Molly helped me get inside. One woman gave us a dirty look. I had changed into shorts so all I had to do was pull my left pant leg up and say, "Crippling injury and we couldn't fit the crutches in the car." Don't accuse me of using the handicap spot when I don't need it. She had gone pretty green, but my scar had convinced her.

The sandwiches were really good. One little boy looked impressed when I managed to finish my whole sandwich in one sitting. We decided to stay until we were finished, that way we could take our time getting back. As we left someone else came in who needed the handicap spot. Mr. Hydell indicated for them to wait a sec while he got me in the car. Molly went over to apologize for any delay. I overheard them ask what was wrong with me, and Molly explain about my leg. The lady driving cringed but didn't complain. They just said take our time, they weren't in a hurry. I nodded my thanks at them. They nodded back. Not all disabilities can be seen, if someone has a tag don't always question it.

Once I was in, Molly took the chair back and Mr. Hydell pulled out. The other car moved in and waved at him. He waved back as Molly came back out and got in her car. Time to get under way again. I fell asleep on this part of the drive. Pain can do that. This bout wasn't over whelming like it had been earlier, but I didn't argue with sleep. Though in this case, I wish I hadn't slept.

My nightmare was really bad. I dreamt that Reggie had come home, that we were children again and all three of us were together again. We were playing in the backyard of our house in Texas, then everything got foggy. We lost sight of each other. Then I heard the screams. I'd heard Amanda scream in terror when we were kids, I still remember it. That scream of pure terror froze my blood. I started running toward it, there was a strangled cry. I tripped… and landed in a massive pool of blood. I stood quickly, then there they were, my brother and sister. Ripped to pieces, floating in the pool of blood. Their heads severed and floating closest to me. I could feel the pool getting deeper. I turned to get out of it, and ran into Kepner. He stood looking down at me, covered in the blood of my siblings and he smiled, "I've finished it, now we can be together." I screamed.

"Maggie! Maggie wake up!!" someone shouted, I felt cold water splash over me. I snapped out of it. I gasped as I came to. I looked around, we were on the side of the road. I tried to stand. Mr. Hydell grabbed my shoulders and held me down.

"You need to calm down first kiddo." He said. He was right, my heart was still beating at a frantic pace.

"Is she okay?" I heard Molly ask from up the small hill.

"What happened?" I asked. I was shaking so bad I was scared to hear what had gone down.

"You started growling like mad, then you lashed out." I smelled blood. I felt myself start to panic.

"It's not mine." He said, pushing me back down into the cool grass. My arms hurt. I lifted one. Shit! I'd fallen asleep with my hands on my elbows, now my arms were scratched all to hell. I think I even saw some bone.

"I'm coming down." Molly said. Whether to warn me or Mr. Hydell I didn't care to ask.

Mr. Hydell shined a flash light on my arms, "You slashed yourself pretty good kiddo." He wasn't kidding, it was worse than I'd thought.

"That must have been one horrifying nightmare." He said.

"Please. Don't remind me." I started to cry. It had been too real. I couldn't get the images out of my head.

My hoodie was a mess. It hadn't taken the damage at all. We weren't far from L.A. and there was a hospital nearby. They got me back in the car once I could breathe normally again. He called ahead and had them prep the emergency shifter unit. They were waiting when we got there. When they asked for details, Mr. Hydell gave them. There was no hiding that I'd inflicted my own injuries. They gave me a shot of antibiotics and some anesthesia. I would need stiches they said. They asked me if I wanted to be knocked out. I asked if you dream when knocked out. They answered no, so I said yes, but only if they fully knock me out. They reluctantly agreed.

I came to about two hours later. It was now almost 10 at night. My arms were sore and bandaged. My left arm was in a brace. Looks like I'd been right about bone. I was slightly nauseous. Molly and Mr. Hydell were outside, I heard them talking to the doctor.

"If the wounds are self-inflicted how long do they take to heal?" Molly asked, genuine concern in her voice.

"Depends. Since the wounds weren't a suicide attempt, they should be fully healed by next week. She can get the stiches out then." The doctor told her. His voice was deeper than Mr. French's.

"She'll be okay hon." Said Mr. Hydell.

"Did you have any warning sir? About what she was about to do?" the doctor asked.

"Nothing other than that growl. I've never heard her growl that bad before. It was like a… a… a get away from my child growl. Or a warning of impending death." He sounded slightly scared. "I wouldn't be surprised if the nightmare had been about her family."

"That's where I recognize her. Her families murder had been on the new last November." Said the doctor.

"Yep." Mr. Hydell replied. I could hear something in his voice. I couldn't tell what it was.

"When can she leave?" Molly asked.

"Normally we'd have her stay the night. To keep watch for any infection. But since she's a dragon shifter, she can leave as soon as she feels ready. Does she have any history of hurting herself?" he asked.

"No. The only reason she hurt herself was 'cause of how she fell asleep." Mr. Hydell answered.

"How'd she fall asleep?" the doctor asked.

"Like this." I guess Mr. Hydell demonstrated.

"Ah. Yeah. Her instincts wouldn't differentiate between herself or not in that pose."

"I kinda figured." Said Mr. Hydell.

"How'd you get her out without getting hurt yourself?" Molly asked.

"Once she started growling, I pulled over. I unhooked her seatbelt, got out of the car, went around to open the door, and that's when she started scratching herself. Once I got the door open I grabbed her by her hoodie's shoulders and threw her on the ground." Well that explained why my shoulders hurt.

"From there I removed her hands from her arms and held her down, then Molly dumped water on her." Thanks Molly.

"I assume in her nightmare she attacked her families murderer. Her arms just got the attack instead." The doctor said.

"More than likely. He resurfaced recently and she's been on edge since." Molly explained.

"Well, since she's not a danger to herself, and if she's able, we can release her shortly." The doctor told them.

I sat up as best I could, not easy, but not too hard either. Then I waited for them to come in. The doctor seemed surprised that I was coherent already. That was just me. I burn through knock out stuff quick. The Doctor was African-American, but his skin wasn't as dark as I expected. The voice didn't seem to fit.

"How are you feeling dear?" Molly asked. Sitting at the foot of the bed.

"Like a complete idiot." Why my instincts had not attacked the car, I don't know.

"Miss, if there is one thing you are not. It is an idiot." Doctor Iwahara said. I could see his name tag.

"Agree to disagree doc." I did feel like an idiot. "What all did I do to my arms?"

"Not nearly as much as you think." He said holding his arms behind his back. "Your lacerations were pretty severe, but the bone was not broken. Some of your arm was torn back and that is why bone was showing through. The bone itself was scored a bit but nothing permanent. Other than that the injuries are nowhere near as bad as they could've been."

"Any scar potential?" I asked. I really didn't want more.

"A few of them." He said. I dropped my head onto my knees.

"Ahhh." I didn't shout, I'm not petty.

"Which ones?" Mr. Hydell asked, since he had gotten a good look at them.

"Mainly the ones where the flesh was torn back. Where the bone showed." Okay that should've been obvious to me.

"How long should I keep the bandages on?" I asked after sitting back up.

"Until tomorrow at least. We've given your guardian some sleeping pills so you can get a full night's sleep, and we have requested that he call your school and absent you for another day."

"Thank you." I said.

He nodded and walked back out of the room. I needed to talk to Mr. Hydell. "Molly." She looked at me. "Can I have a moment with Mr. Hydell." She nodded. Her phone rang. Hey nice timing.

"What's up kiddo?" he asked. He looked concerned.

"Are you scared of me?" he looked at me like I had done something stupid.

"What on Earth would give you that impression?" he asked.

"You sounded scared when you described the growl." I wouldn't meet his eyes.

He sighed, I saw him run his hand through his hair out the corner of my eye. "I wasn't scared **of** you kiddo. I was scared **for** you." I looked up then. Now I was confused.

"I was afraid you'd hurt yourself more than you did. Or worse, you'd accidentally hurt me. I know that scares you more than anything. I was also afraid I'd have to use the sedative I always carry." Okay that was news to me.

"What sedative?" I asked. Getting angry myself.

"One that the judge mandated I carry as your guardian. Just in case I needed to put you out. He said it was for if you tried to kill a human. Mainly me."

"I wouldn't try to kill you." I said incredulously.

"I know. But the judge in charge of your case doesn't like shifters. He wanted to put you away forever. Not realizing it wouldn't solve anything."

"So he had you carry it because he deemed me dangerous." I stated. Arms crossed and leaning back.

"Not officially. Just in his mind." He said sitting on the side of the bed.

"How big a dose?" I asked. As a dragon shifter it would have to be either big or just a powerful sedative.

"15 milligrams." He didn't say of what. He didn't have to.

A week after shifters had been exposed, some foreign doctor had come up with a sedative that worked on shifters. It was called hydrochloral-fentinal. It was supposedly a combination of hydrochlorothiazide and carfentinal. A non-toxic combination. Yeah right. It was strong enough to put the largest shifter they could find to sleep for up to six days. The largest one they had found at the time to test it had been a bear shifter. Don't get me wrong, he was huge! The dose had only been five milligrams. He was out like a light. 15 milligrams for a female teenage dragon shifter – possibly on a rampage – would put me out for maybe a week.

"I made myself promise never to use it unless I felt you'd want me to."

"And since I didn't lash out until you were already out of the car, you felt I didn't need it." I met his eyes as I said it.

"Yes. I know you better than that judge does." He smiled and hugged me. "I won't let you down kiddo."

I didn't say anything, I just returned his hug. Hydro-fen was no laughing matter. Not with kids and teens. The drug already had bad publicity. A four year old shifter dying of overdose tends to do that. We stayed like that for several minutes. Molly came in a few minutes later and joined the hug. This was my family now. I couldn't destroy it by letting them down.

Chapter 16

Mr. Hydell had to carry me to the car. My leg wouldn't take my weight and I had decided to take the sleeping pills. I shouldn't wake up till about 8:00am. Mr. Hydell also decided to take the doctor's suggestion and excuse me from school for the day. I would still go to my appointment, and maybe to work. The attendance people did ask for a reason why of course. He merely said that there had been an incident that ended in injury for me. They knew that meant really bad nightmare that had resulted in my getting hurt. They know the drill.

I didn't react when we finally got home. Mr. Hydell had called ahead and had them prep the elevator so that he could carry me without a problem. After that it wasn't too much of a problem getting me into the apartment. Jim was waiting at the door, he helped Mr. Hydell get me the rest of the way in. Mr. Hydell told me later that Jim had asked if he wanted anyone looking for him to be told that Mr. Hydell wasn't here. He'd answered yes. So as far as anyone would know, the apartment was empty. That wouldn't necessarily stop Kepner, but it was a start. Mr. Hydell had also given Jim a copy of Kepner's photo. Old and new. That way no mistakes would be made.

I woke up at 8:30. First period wasn't even over. I'd have to check my computer for homework e-mails. There would of course be the usual stuff in preparation for finals next week. Prom was this Saturday. Gag. Why anyone saw that as a rite of passage, I'll never understand. Prom was stupid. Time to get up. I smell food.

I tested my leg. Nope. Still wouldn't take my weight. This time I had my boot cast. Mr. Hydell had even put it where I could reach it. I grabbed it after I had changed my clothes. First stop was the bathroom. The cast was well built like I had said. I could detach it from myself enough that I could use the toilet without a problem. Once that was done, I went into the kitchen. There was a note on the fridge.

'Text me when you're up. Breakfast in oven.' It said in Mr. Hydell's hand writing.

I took out my phone. *'I'm up. Thanks for breakfast.'* I texted him. He obviously had had to get to work lickety-split. That meant I needed to be careful today. Just to be safe. Not a problem

My phone buzzed. *'Thanks kiddo. Welcome. Security is on maximum.'* Fine by me. I texted *'Welcome'* back to him, and ate my breakfast. After that was done I did what little dishes there were, then went to the living room with my computer, my box, and the necessary spell components.

Time to fire proof my box. I had several red crystals and stones to use for the elemental focus. Come to think of it. I probably should also water proof it. So I went back to my room and got my water crystals and stones. You really shouldn't perform the two spells at once. It can confuse things. I'd do fire first. I place everything in proper sequence, lit some candles and incense, then began the spell.

"Here and now, elements hear my call

Of you I ask a favor small.

Protect this box from fire

Let it never be harmed by the pyre."

There was the tell-tale flash as my spell took effect. The crystals glowed and the candles got brighter. They stayed like that for a few seconds. Once they were done, I tested it. The book and watch were still in my room, so I held up the lighter I had grabbed from the kitchen after breakfast. I held it up to the box. The fire first acted like magnets do when you try to put the two positive or negative ends together. It moved away. Then it went out altogether. Good. Now for water.

I put my red crystals and stones away and switched them out for the blue ones. The candles and incense I didn't have to worry about. The incense was only half gone, and the candles could be reused. I also filled a bowl of water for testing later. I began the spell.

"Here and now, elements hear my call

Of you I ask another favor small.

Protect this box from water

So that all will remain in order."

The same result took place, everything flashed, then glowed brighter. Also once again, after they stopped, I tested it. I took the bowl and the box over to the sink. I held the box on my hand, then poured the water out of the bowl over it. The water moved off like the box was covered in silicone. Perfect. Now everything would be safe. Cast a spell on the outside, anything inside will be protected as well. Especially the stronger spells. Since the lock had been locked when I had performed the spells, when closed anything inside would indeed be as safe as the box.

I went back to my room. I put the book and watch back in their places, as well as putting my mom's small dagger in the bottom. I put the insert back in. Awesome. It fit perfectly. I placed the now completed box on my side table. I placed it next to the drawing of the finished tanto. I couldn't wait to start finishing that now.

Back in the living room, I checked my e-mail. I did have homework e-mails. I hooked up to the printer, and got copies of them. I'd do it again later today, so that I had all today's homework as well. I also had an e-mail from my woodshop teacher. A copy of the requirements for the final project. Including the part to be signed by Mr. Hydell that I had made the project myself. I plugged my mp3 into my speaker, then got to work.

It didn't take me long to finish my homework. Most of it was mainly study requirements anyway. But once I did have it done, there wasn't much for me to do. I didn't want to leave the apartment until later. Then I realized there was something I could do. Change my hair. Kepner had seen me with my new hair, so he knew what to look for. Time to change it up.

I got up and went into the bathroom. Mr. Hydell had a whole bin of hair-dye, just for me. I couldn't go back to red, could I? No. Better not to for now. It was already black. So brunette it was. I picked a medium chocolate color. I'd cut it too. Probably just down to my shoulders. I also pulled out some temporary tattoos. I could apply one to my neck. That would throw him off. Oh that reminds me.

I pulled my phone out. *'Could you grab me a new hoodie on your way home please?"* I put my phone down to wait for a response. I didn't expect one immediately, since he could be working right then. I got to work on my hair.

That took me about an hour. I had cut it first, only five inches. It would fit in my beanie hat that way. I had it done pretty quick after that. I looked good with brown hair. I still missed my red hair, but I would be fine with brown for now. My phone buzzed, *'Sure thing kiddo.'* The text said. Cool. I'd need to wait a few minutes to answer back. I had dye on my hands. I used my tail to turn the water on. I washed my hands thoroughly. Then I picked my phone up and sent, *'Thanks.'* He didn't answer back at all on that one. I didn't mind. He was a busy guy.

I went into my room when I was done. The remnants of my old hoodie were on my desk. You couldn't tell I had shredded it. Black clothes can do that. I picked it up. Geez. Just looking at my hoodie I could visualize how I had hurt my arms. My arms were still slightly numb so I couldn't quite feel where I had cut myself. The doc had written a few things down in case we forgot something. I went to the dining room where Mr. Hydell had left the papers. Okay, I should leave the bandages on for at least 12 hours. It was almost ten so I could remove them in a few hours to check the damage.

I put the paper down. I was bored. I didn't feel like reading so I sat on the couch and turned on the T.V. There wasn't much on that I liked. Eh. Bones was on. It was an episode I had already seen but I didn't mind, it was one of my favorites. The one where they visit the body farm at the college. And good I hadn't missed my favorite part of the episode. Exploding body!

Chapter 17

Bones was on most of the day, so I just sat and watched. My appointment was at 2:15. The clock read 1:45. Time to get ready. Mr. Hydell had texted me that he was on his way about five minutes ago. I decided I did want to go to work. I went in my room and changed into my long-sleeved aquarium shirt. I hadn't taken the bandages off yet, but it was best to avoid questions. I took my hat as well. I met Mr. Hydell in the parking garage. He was staying away from his Cadillac for now. He didn't want to take any chances that Kepner would recognize it.

"How you feelin' kiddo?" he asked as I got in.

"Better. What do you think?" I pulled my hat off.

He studied me. Then nodded, "It looks good. And I like the tattoo."

"Thanks." I had chosen an ivy chain to put around my neck, kinda like a choker.

"Your new hoodie is in the back seat." He said. Without taking his eyes off the road.

I reached back and grabbed it. It had angel wings on the back and Nordic runes down the arms.

"Cool. Thanks." I really liked it.

"Your welcome." He smiled.

It wasn't a long drive to the therapy office. He parked in the garage, but kept close to both the elevator and the entrance. We went up to Ms. Hamper's floor. Lynda wasn't on duty today. Bernie was though. I liked him, he got along with the kids who came in too. Bernie was about as skinny as Flint Lockwood, several of the adults called him 'beanpole.' I had once asked Bernie if he was a snake shifter. He had just smiled and said, 'I like to think so.' I guess that just meant he had shifter blood but couldn't change. I wouldn't press. He pointed us into Ms. Hamper's office. He seemed edgy. Never good when Bernie was edgy. It usually meant trouble. Either for the person causing the trouble or any adults who didn't agree with the new person. It would depend on who or what was involved today. The last time Bernie had been edgy, a seven year old autistic boy was told he was getting a new therapist. You can guess how that went down. Thankfully that incident had ended well. Today may not. Time to find out.

We entered Ms. Hamper's office. There was an unknown man inside with her. My shifter instincts kicked in. Ms. Hamper was also on edge and angry. I didn't like that. We both stopped just behind the chairs, neither of us sat down. I maneuvered a little closer to Ms. Hamper. Mr. Hydell extended his hand. The other man obliged.

"Mr. Hydell. To what do we owe the..." he hesitated, "circumstances?" Mr. Hydell did not consider this a pleasure.

"Mr. Mycini. I am here to re-assign Miss Sharp to a new therapist."

"Come again!?" uh- no! Not gonna happen unless it was for maternity leave. And based on Ms. Hamper's face, maternity leave was not the reason he was here.

"May I ask why?" Mr. Hydell asked. He wasn't happy either.

"Due to Miss Sharp's incident last night and with the recent reappearance of her stalker, we feel it is better for her to be re-assigned." So he was from the board.

"I'm quite happy with Ms. Hamper thank you." I said. Mr. Hydell and I both had our arms crossed.

"I'm afraid it's not your decision young lady." Was he being smug? I growled at him.

He took a step back, he seemed scared. The syringe of hydro-fen he pulled out of his pocket said that much.

I looked at Mr. Hydell in shock. HE had growled at him!

"You get that abominable thing away from her." Ooohhh quiet angry. Take cover.

Ms. Hamper looked impressed. "It may not be hers, but it is Mr. Hydell's." she said looking at me.

"Then you can tell the board that if they **ever,** suggest a change again I will sue every single one of them. Including you. Ms. Hamper is perfectly suited for Maggie and I greatly prefer that Maggie stay under her as a patient." He said while still speaking quietly and walking toward him to emphasize his point.

"The board does not feel the same." He said. He was scared of Mr. Hydell more than he was me.

"Why?" Mr. Hydell and Ms. Hamper asked at the same time.

He swallowed before answering. "Her condition…"

"Don't you play that bullshit!!" uh-oh. Now the pregnant lady was fully angry. "I am fully capable of being Maggie's therapist. Pregnant or not!" Back down dude. Be smart.

"Do I need to repeat myself?" Mr. Hydell asked. Looking him straight in the eyes.

He swallowed again and dropped his eyes. Good boy. "No. I will take the guardians consent for Ms. Hamper to continue as Miss Sharp's therapist to the board." He turned to leave.

Mr. Hydell grabbed his arm, "I don't believe you. I will accompany you, to make sure you do."

He looked like he was about to argue, but decided against it. He nodded and the two of them left the room. I barely held back my laughter. I had never heard Mr. Hydell growl before. You wouldn't know he was fully human, he growled so deep. I sat down.

"Well that was interesting." I said, meeting Ms. Hamper's eyes.

She giggled, "Indeed. I didn't think he could make such a noise." She laughed a little more. Then started. I jumped to my feet.

"I'm okay sweetie. The baby just moved. I think they find the whole thing funny too." She said with a smile.

I sat back down. "I'm glad to see that you're okay sweetie." She said.

I nodded, it wasn't hard to guess about what she meant. "How are you feeling?" I asked.

"Hey now missy, I'm the doctor I'm supposed to ask the questions." We both laughed.

"To answer your question, I'm fine. I was more worried about you. I was informed about Kepner's reappearance yesterday when I came in." I took my hoodie off without getting up, while she talked. I moved a sleeve up my arm a little to scratch an itch.

"I see they weren't kidding about the incident." She said, studying the part of my arm that showed.

"Yeah, well." I paused, "That's what I get for falling asleep when I'm not exhausted." I put my sleeve back down.

"Were they as bad as they told me?" she asked, rubbing her belly.

"One of them at least. I had clawed myself in one spot that showed bone. I haven't actually checked the others out yet." I said.

"Busy while at home?" she asked with a small smile.

"Homework, studying for finals, and a few other things."

"Do you feel you're ready for finals?"

"Yeah. I've been studying over the weekend when I can too." I said.

"Good. I have discussed a few things with Mr. French earlier today." She said.

"Like what?" she had my full attention.

"Well. Since the school is technically private, you will be given a councilor to talk to and they will e-mail me on any progression or regression."

"Even when you're on leave?" I asked.

"Yes. My partner and I both agree that it would be best." Okay fine by me.

"Anything else?"

"Yes," she sat up a bit more, "he would like to meet with you and Mr. Hydell. Later today if possible, to talk about your mandatory visit to the campus and the best moving time."

"Did he say how much stuff I would need to take with me?"

"No, he didn't specify, but he did say that – obviously – clothes and a few other things would be required." We both laughed again.

"I have his number here, so you or Mr. Hydell could call and talk to him- " I had sneezed. What the heck for? She gasped. There was the sound of water moving. Oh Gods!

"Bernie!" I shouted, getting up and moving her desk out of the way. Yep, her water had broken.

Bernie opened the door, "What's up?" He looked at Ms. Hamper.

"Her water's broken. Call an ambulance. Now!" He shook himself and went to the phone.

"I'm not due for three more weeks." She said, while still gasping, but she was smiling.

"You do know most of the time the baby picks when to come." I said, grabbing the wheelchair she kept in the corner.

"Very true, sweetie. Oh." She held her belly while I helped her into the chair.

Mr. Hydell came back in then, "Now that that's taken care of,- what's wrong?"

"Her water's broken. Bernie's called the ambulance." I wheeled her out into the lobby.

"Bernie, call Don, tell him I'm in labor." She said as we headed for the elevator.

"Yes ma'am. They had a unit in the area, should be here in two – four minutes." He said as I got her in the elevator.

"Thanks Bernie!" I said. Mr. Hydell grabbed my bag from her office before he joined us.

"Guess we'll have to reschedule." He said, we all laughed.

"The board have any objections?" she asked, begin to breathe la maz.

"Not a one." He said, "I'll give you the details later."

It was about a minutes ride to the main lobby. Once the door opened, people who were waiting got out of the way. Hey look. The ambulance was right outside. They'd made good time. Two other building workers held the door, while I wheeled her out. Once at the front steps, the medical workers met us and helped me get her down. Mr. Hydell took the chair back inside.

"Any contractions yet miss?" they asked her.

"I'm not entirely sure." She said, breathing heavily.

"She had one in the elevator about 0.53 seconds ago." I said without missing a beat.

One looked at me funny, the other asked, "You a shifter miss?" I nodded.

"Good, get in. We're shorthanded today." Ah, one was the driver.

"Yes sir." I turned to Mr. Hydell, "I heard. I'll follow behind." He ran for the garage, while I climbed in with Ms. Hamper.

The two guys separated and got in as well, "It will be about 20 minutes before we reach the hospital," he turned to me, "I need you to tell me everything." I nodded again. "Heart rate, breathing, the baby's heart beat if you can, and time the space between the contractions as well and how long each last."

"Gotcha." I put my fingers on her pulse. "Heart beat slightly elevated, but steady."

He nodded, "Baby's?"

I listened, "Steady."

"Good." He hooked her up to an i.v. Thank Gods it wasn't rush hour. There was virtually no traffic.

Chapter 18

Their calculations had been right. We reached the hospital in 18.9 minutes. Mr. Hydell met us there, a mere minute behind us. The doctors were waiting for us, the paramedic had remembered everything I had said, but he still had me give the final contraction times.

"When was the last contraction?" the doctor asked.

"13 seconds ago."

"How long till-" she screamed.

"The contractions are at every 14.5 seconds and getting closer." I said as we walked to the elevators.

"You and your father will have to wait here miss."

"No!" she grabbed my arm and squeezed. I winced slightly. Thankfully, it was my right arm. "She comes with me. Don's not here yet, so I want her with me till he arrives."

I met the doctor's eyes, "Yes ma'am." Mr. Hydell got in the elevator too. She screamed again, clenching at the same time.

"I'm sorry sweetie." She tried to smile but it came out as another contraction. "8.6 seconds." I said while looking at the doctor, "and I don't mind." I finished. Looking at her and smiling encouragement.

We left the elevator just after that. The maternity ward wasn't too busy. Only the father is allowed in the birthing room, so she reluctantly let go as they wheeled her into the room.

"I'll be right out here!" I shouted as they closed the door. I started rubbing my arms. I hadn't put my hoodie back on, but I had rolled up my sleeves, so the bandages were there for all to see. Mr. Hydell handed it to me. I put it on, then remembered something. I went over to the reception desk.

"Can I make a quick call please?" I asked the receptionist. She nodded and handed me the corded phone. I dialed the aquarium from memory. Then asked for the gift shop. Ben – as usual – answered on the first ring.

"Aquar-" I cut him off, "Ben it's Maggie. Listen I need to know if I can switch shifts."

"I was about to call and ask about that. Gracie said she needed to switch, and you were the only one available."

"Go ahead then. I'm with Ms. Hamper at the hospital."

I heard him choke, "She in labor." The loud scream was answer enough. "Okay then, I'll let Gracie know."

"Great. See ya later."

"Bye." He said, hanging up.

The elevator dinged and a tall Asian man walked out, "Don?" I asked. He nodded. I pointed at the door. He went right in.

Since she had progressed so quickly, the wait shouldn't be too long. A nurse did come over and ask if I wanted the bandages removed. I declined, I couldn't sit still. I was already pacing back and forth across the floor. Hugging my arms, not because I was cold, but because I was nervous. I had never been this involved in a birth before and I was worried for Ms. Hamper and the babies. Yes I said babies. I had known she was having twins the first time I sensed them. Her wanting it to be a surprise, well now she was most definitely getting one. Two in fact. The third heartbeat had been two perfectly in sync heartbeats. And on the ultrasounds the two had been perfectly lined up, so it had looked like one baby. I was also afraid she'd be mad at me for not saying there were two.

Mr. Hydell was sitting in a chair. Bouncing his leg. He had texted Molly, she should be here shortly. The elevator dinged. There she was. She came over and asked Mr. Hydell how it was going. I didn't quite register his answer. I was so nervous.

The door opened and the doctor came out. He looked exhausted. He was smiling though, so that must be a good thing. He looked at me and laughed. Dude. What was that for?

"You knew, didn't you?" he asked, still smiling. I just nodded. He laughed again. "The father just about fainted, he was so excited." He rubbed his face. That explained the laughter.

I smiled, "How'd she take it?"

He didn't lose his smile, "She was positively ecstatic. The first thing out of her mouth was, 'and she didn't tell me.'"

"She had said she wanted it to be a surprise." Now I couldn't stop smiling. Molly came over and gave me a hug.

"How are they doing?" Mr. Hydell asked. The biggest smirk on his face.

"All three are fine. She gave birth pretty quickly, there's only a three second difference between the twins."

I chuckled, "One girl and one boy right?" I asked.

He looked at me in surprise, "Yes. You could tell that too?"

I nodded, "It's just something I do." There was no way to explain it.

"Scuse me, but uh…" Don stood at the door, looking befuddled, but happy, "she wants to see Maggie." We all looked at the doctor.

He nodded, "Go on." He said to me.

I didn't wait. As I walked passed Don I said, "Congratulation." He chuckled. "Thank you."

I finished entering the room. Someone had used a pencil to hold up her hair in a makeshift bun. Whatever works. She held both babies in her arms. She was glowing with happiness, and there was a new ring on her left hand. Well. Looks like that will be official. She didn't look up as I got closer, she was too busy admiring her new babies. One wore a pink hat, while the other wore a blue one. They were both wrapped in homemade blankets with their names sewn into them. I couldn't read what they were, but I could ask.

"So who's the oldest?" she looked up at me while I asked. I was beginning to cry.

"This one." She looked at her daughter. I walked a little closer. "You knew the whole time. Didn't you?" she asked.

"Yeah. I was afraid you'd be mad at me for not saying."

"No, never. You just made it all the better." She said, trying to hold her own tears back.

"What are their names?" I asked, I could see the girl's began with an M and the boy's with a G.

"His name is Gregory William Hamper-Lawson. Don insisted on Gregory."

"It's nice." I said.

"I think so too," She looked up at me, "we'd made a deal that if it was one or the other we would pick a name that way, but we both had planned one out just in case."

"And hers?" I asked. She turned to look at her daughter.

She smiled, took a breath, and said, "Magenta Guinevere Hamper-Lawson."

I covered my mouth, now I was crying. She had named her daughter after me. I didn't know how to respond to that. Don, Mr. Hydell, and Molly came in then. I guessed they had heard, 'cause Don patted me on the shoulder, while Molly and Mr. Hydell gave me a hug. I grabbed a tissue after they let me go and blew my nose. I tried to catch my breath. I looked at her and the babies. I really didn't know what to say.

We left shortly after that. She needed rest and the babies needed to feed. Don told us he would call later to give an update. Once in the car, I still couldn't speak, though I did text Ben to say that she and the babies were okay.

I grabbed my bag when we got back to the apartment, I had planned on showing her my handmade box. As part of my recovery program. Obviously, that would have to wait now. I didn't mind. I was more happy for her and Don then I was for myself. Not only were they now parents, but they would be getting married.

It was only then that I remembered the card she had given me. I had moved into my room to put my bag away, I put it on my bed and went back out to the living room. I pulled the card out of my coat pocket and handed it to Mr. Hydell. He took one look at it, and instead of asking me for specifics, immediately started punching in Mr. French's number.

It was officially 3:00. Time for a snack. Wait. Had I even had lunch. Crap! I had been so preoccupied with my homework, studying, and protection spells I had completely spaced on lunch.

No worries, we still had leftovers. I pulled out some of my gyoza leftovers, Mr. Hydell had eaten some of them, but not a lot. I'd still have about twenty left.

"Hey, how much of those are left?" Mr. Hydell asked.

"Including the ones in my hand…" I counted, "27." I said turning to him.

"Okay. Do you think you're willing to make more for tomorrow?"

Okay, I shrugged. I like making gyoza, "Sure."

"Cool." he turned back to his phone call.

I placed the seven I had on a plate. I might eat more if I was hungry enough. I also pulled out the sauce and heated them up together in the microwave. Making sure to put a paper towel over the bowl of sauce, so it wouldn't cover the inside. Mr. Hydell hung up and came over to heat some up himself. Or so I thought.

"What's up?" I asked as I pulled my snack/lunch out.

"Molly's coming over. I told her about these," he held up a bag of gyoza, "and she wants to try them."

"So a stay home dinner date then?" I said, smiling.

"Pretty much. That and I think she's feeling," he paused as looking for the right word, "motherly."

After what had happened over the last few days, I wasn't too surprised. "So how did the call with Mr. French go?"

"He said due to an emergency he couldn't make it tonight. So we planned that he could come here tomorrow night and we three could discuss things over dinner." He said.

"Three as in you, me, and he. Or you, Molly, and him?"

He chuckled, "You, me, and him. Molly will be working at the time that we agreed upon."

"We'll need to stop by the store first, but I don't mind making more." I said while grabbing some chop sticks.

It would be a little while before Molly showed up, so we went to the store after I was finished eating. I grabbed some skirt steaks, mushrooms, barbeque sauce, some spices we were low on that would need to go in the recipe, wonton wrappers, and two different cheeses. Everything else we got was grocery related. Although I also grabbed a new shirt to replace the one I had covered in blood. Not that it would make much of a difference at school. I almost never take my hoodie off while at school. Not even on really hot days. Some people have asked if I was cold-blooded because of my hoodie wearing. I always laugh at that, and just say that I'm used to it.

I put everything away when we got back. Mr. Hydell had gotten an emergency call and had gone into his office first thing after coming in the door. I pulled out some of the necessary equipment for making gyoza. I wouldn't start the next batch till tomorrow, but having it out before dark helps against taking extra time. I did decide to re-heat the gyoza in the over, to re-crisp the bottoms. The sauce I could do in a sauce pan.

Chapter 19

Molly came up about fifteen minutes past six. She had had a busy day. The only reason she had shown up at the hospital was because it had been her lunch break. After she had returned everything had become chaotic. Three of her patients had been late, two had missed their appointments entirely, and one had had a very serious relapse. So other than the births, not a good day. I was in the bathroom getting ready to remove the bandages when she arrived. The gyoza were in the oven on low, they'd only take about 5-10 minutes to re-heat 'cause of their size. The sauce was in the pan on the stove. Mr. Hydell was watching that. I heard the two start talking as she sat down on one of the barstools.

"Day was that bad huh?" he asked, pulling the gyoza out of the oven.

"Yeah. I might stay over tonight. I need to relax."

"Fine with me, though Maggie might need a little help with those bandages." He said as I came out.

She turned to look at me. "You okay?" she asked.

I smiled, "I'm still overwhelmed about Ms. Hamper's name choice," in a good way of course, "but other than that I'm okay."

"Trouble with the bandages?" Mr. Hydell asked.

"No, I just wasn't sure I wanted to see the carnage yet." I said, sitting down.

"That's to be expected. They were pretty bad." He said.

Molly placed a hand on my arm, right where Ms. Hamper had squeezed. I unintentionally jumped. She withdrew her hand.

"Oh I'm sorry dear." She got up. Worried she had hurt me.

"I'm okay. I swear. I just must be a bit more tender than anticipated." I said, rubbing my arm.

"Well Ms. Hamper did squeeze your arm pretty hard. Twice." Mr. Hydell said.

I got up and grabbed a bag of frozen peas, "I'll be fine." I said to Molly.

"I'd prefer to get those bandages off now dear." She said as Mr. Hydell set down a plate in front of her.

"Eat first. I need to check my e-mail anyway." I said heading to the living room with my plate.

I probably had homework e-mails and maybe something from the aquarium. Ben or Stacy would have sent something about the shift change. More than likely when Gracie had been supposed to work. I sat at the couch, my plate on the coffee table next to my computer. I opened my e-mail account. I had started a new one after the murders, and had made sure to route it through several servers so that I couldn't be located when I accessed it. I knew it was probably an over-precaution, but better safe than sorry. I had three new e-mails since earlier today. One was the rest of my homework for the day, another was a spread sheet for finals studying, the third chilled my blood.

It didn't say who it was from, but it didn't take a genius to figure it out. I didn't outwardly react, I didn't want to alert Mr. Hydell. Yet. I'd let him know later. The e-mail only had three words on it. *'I'll find you.'* The e-mail was from Kepner. I immediately printed out my homework and finals e-mails, then forwarded the Kepner e-mail to Officer Steele. Plus an attachment about who it was from and that I would be cancelling my e-mail. I knew the Kepner e-mail was several hours old, but it might still be useful. I heard Mr. Hydell react to the printer start up. My stomach was churning. I put a gyoza in my mouth and started chewing. That helped a little. I went to the main page and cancelled my e-mail address. I had already cleared it out earlier. I wouldn't be making a new one.

Mr. Hydell came over with my homework. He noticed that I was edgy, but he didn't make a comment. I took my papers from him, my hand was shaking slightly. He raised his eyebrows questioningly. I just shook my head. He didn't need details. Officer Steele would let him know them. Officer Steele was only one of the men in charge of my case. He wasn't the head guy, but he was the tech guy. He was the one who got emergency e-mails from me. The only reason he hadn't gotten the pics three days ago was because he didn't handle surveillance. Just the online stuff.

I finished eating my dinner. I was glad I still tasted it. The fact that Kepner had somehow figured out my e-mail was still freaking me out. I'd check my Facebook once I was a bit more settled. That didn't take long though. I opened Facebook. Thank Gods. My user name was so far from my own that nothing out of the ordinary was present, not even a new friend request. I'd still be careful over the next few months. The last thing I wanted was for Kepner to learn my habits and schedule. I leaned back and thought about his e-mail. What exactly had he been conveying when he wrote it? Promise? Anger? I couldn't tell and quite honestly I didn't want to know. If he meant it in an angry way, that might mean that when he did find me, he would kill me. I wasn't too apprehensive about that. If he meant it as a promise – good or bad – that meant he would kill Mr. Hydell and Molly if he could get to her. Either would die to protect me. **That**, I was apprehensive about.

I got up and walked to the bathroom. I needed to focus on something else. Might as well remove my bandages. I'll take that carnage right now please. Before entering though I decided to go to my room and change into a tank top. No sleeves would make it easier to check. Molly met me at the bathroom.

"You don't have to if you don't want to." I said to her.

She gave me a look and pointing into the bathroom said, "In." I chuckled.

She left the door open, I guess Mr. Hydell would be helping too. Okay. Not gonna argue. I looked at my arms in the mirror. I could see some of the stitches through the bandages. I had removed the brace yesterday, so that wasn't in the way. Mr. Hydell came in with a bowl of warm water. He placed it on the counter by the sink. I sat down on the toilet. Molly and Mr. Hydell both grabbed stools and sat opposite each other. Parallel with my arms.

"We'll be as careful as possible kiddo." Mr. Hydell said, grabbing a pair of medical scissors.

I just nodded. My arms were starting to tingle, the stitches were itching. I hate that.

Molly found where the tape holding the ones on my right arm were and undid it. She started gently unwrapping it. The brace had been on the back of my right arm. Close to the elbow. Ms. Hamper had grabbed me closer to the wrist. I didn't look at my arm as she unwound it. I did watch Mr. Hydell cut the left ones though. I didn't know what to expect but I did know that the doctor could have been wrong about scar potential. I already had my leg, I really didn't want more.

"Good grief." Molly said. I looked at my arm. It was pretty bad, but not as bad as I was expecting.

"Well," I said turning my arm a little, "at least most won't scar." I could see where I had exposed bone. Yeah, that one was gonna scar. You could see where my fingers had gone as I had attacked myself. Thankfully my thumbs had been up against my hands, so they wouldn't have done any damage. When I had moved my thumb claws had gone into my hands. Those had been small enough they had healed before Mr. Hydell had even removed me from the car.

"Those won't. I don't think he got a good look at these before they were bandaged." Mr. Hydell said.

I looked over at him, then my arm, "Shit!" I said.

He was right, I'm right handed so my left arm got more damage. The four marks would most definitely scar. My thumb had caught a little, but that one was so small it was the only one that would fully heal. My index finger on the other hand had come really close to my artery. If he hadn't woken me when he did, I would have cut right across it. Maybe even with three of four fingers. I felt like an even bigger idiot.

"That's just great." I said, lowering my arms to my lap.

"Can you even twist your arm?" he asked. I tried. It hurt. A lot!

"Great. As if nerve damage wasn't bad enough." Now I was just angry with myself.

"Can you heal yourself?" Molly asked.

"Not at will. That would require skills I don't have yet. As a wiccan anyway." She seemed confused.

"Very few shifters can actually heal themselves at will. Healing usually is done the same way as humans, just much faster."

"Ah, but you could use a healing spell."

"For the scratches, yes. The nerve damage no. I'm not high enough in spell work to do healing spells that advanced. Poultices not included."

"I see." She said. I turned my right arm. There was a bruise where Ms. Hamper had grabbed me. It covered a few of the scratches.

Mr. Hydell chuckled, "You took it better than most husbands do."

I chuckled, "Most husbands know better than to take a birthing mother's hand." I looked back at my arm, "Honestly the only reason it's showing is 'cause she was having contractions. Any other time it wouldn't show at all." Not on a shifter anyway.

"It's still a good thing it was your right arm. I can only imagine how bad she would feel if she had grabbed your other arm." Molly said. I nodded. I honestly would be surprised if I could successfully shift after this.

"Did the doctor say how long I should wait before shifting?" I asked.

"He said you should wait till the stitches come out." That made sense. He did say I could maybe get them out next week. Best to be safe.

"When can I get the stitches out?"

"He said to visit your usual doctor this weekend, and to have her give the final prognosis." I nodded, that also made sense.

"At least they were clean cuts. Not ragged." I said.

He nodded, "Do you want to re-bandage them?" he asked.

"Yeah. I'd rather not have any of the stitches get caught on something and pulled." That had happened to friend once. Not pretty.

Mr. Hydell and Molly did the bandaging. It was faster and I didn't need to move my arms too much. Then a thought occurred to me. I looked at Molly as we left the bathroom.

"So how did you like the gyoza?" I asked with a small smile.

"Ohh, dear those were delicious!" She said with a smile. "I ate like ten of them."

"Including some off my plate." Mr. Hydell said. I laughed.

"Now I hate to kill your mood, but what was the rection earlier?" he asked.

I took a deep breath, "I had an e-mail from Kepner." Both of them stiffened. "I already forwarded it to Steele, and I cancelled my account."

"Good girl. But, how did he get your e-mail address?" he asked.

"I have no idea." And I didn't.

They both got phone calls that instant. I went over to the coffee table and started my homework. Most of it was done quickly, then I got to English. Crap. I hadn't been reading Hamlet. I might have to pull an all-nighter. Why couldn't they teach Sherlock in English class? I'd ace that easy, but romance. Ick. I hate romance novels. I know technically Hamlet is more tragedy than romance but still, it can get messed up. I had read Taming of the Shrew willingly. That was the only Shakespearian novel I actually liked. It wasn't long past seven, if I got started now, I might get everything done before ten. I went to my room and grabbed Hamlet. I decided to lie on my bed and read, my homework could stay where it was for now.

I had been about halfway through when I'd stopped. By 9:30 I had finished. I was mentally chewing out the king for being so stupid. Come on dude, if your gonna poison someone make sure you do it in such a way that your wife isn't going to drink from the same cup. I mean duh. Second, if you don't trust the fencing sword to work, kill him in his sleep. Then again if the queen had been smart she wouldn't have married her husband's brother after his death in the first place. Oh well. If you want everyone to die in the end, that's what you write.

I finished my homework pretty quickly after that. I was in bed by 10:15, after eating a snack. I left a note for Mr. Hydell to start the meat marinating at eight. He left for work at 8:30, and since we had bought enough for me to double the recipe – it's a cave lion shifter, play it safe – the meat marinating an extra hour or two would help.

I also left the spices out. He knew how much would be necessary. Either that or Molly would beat him to it. She didn't have to be at work till nine tomorrow.

I decided to play it safe and take a sleeping pill with my milk. I really did not want to have nightmares tonight. I also plugged my mp3 speaker into the wall, turned it on, and laid down. Not long after I was glad I'd decided on the music. I started hearing things coming from Mr. Hydell's room. Turn up the volume just a tad. Good, no other noises. I fell asleep quickly after that.

Chapter 20

I woke up at six. My head felt a little fuzzy. Probably from the pill. First things first. Bathroom. No, actually test my leg. I got partially out of bed, making sure to keep my arms on the bed frame. Nope. My leg wouldn't take my weight. Great, that meant a shower would be difficult but not un doable. I put the brace on and walked to the bathroom, from there I did my usual morning routine. Toilet, shower, inventory on scar and arms, then it was back to my room to change into school appropriate clothes.

Mr. Hydell and Molly were still asleep. That usually was the case. I made some coffee, enough for all three really. I needed it because of how fuzzy I was still feeling. I don't usually take sleeping pills. I don't like to chance a possible addiction to them, not with my injuries. And before you say shifter's have hard times getting addicted to things, think again. A shifter can get as addicted to something just as quickly or as strongly as humans. All it depends on is the substance.

Breakfast was a bagel with sausage, egg, and cheese. I like to get a high protein breakfast on school days. Especially since I had gym first thing. I gathered all my homework and finals papers into my backpack, I then checked my phone. I had one text from Ben.

'Saw that your e-mail was cancelled. Gracie was supposed to work at 3:30 today.' Okay, so it was long-sleeved work shirt again today. I sent a reply, even though he wouldn't get it till about 8 a.m.

'No prob. See you at work.' I kept it short. That way he wouldn't have to focus too much when he got it.

Once my breakfast was gone I rechecked the bandages, nothing was loose, and no stitches were poking out of them. Good. I stuffed my work shirt in the front most pocket of my backpack. I'd change at work. I put my coat and backpack on, and walked out the door. I normally took the city bus to school, but today I was feeling apprehensive. So instead I'd fly. The morning was already pretty foggy so it wouldn't be too big of a problem getting there. Landing on the correct building was. I had once accidently landed on the building across the street. Since it had happened before the murders, all I'd had to do was jump to the ground and walk across. I couldn't do that anymore. If I even would be able to do it again was heavily debatable. So the school had given me special permission to either land on the roof – they kept a roof door key hidden up there for me – or land in the teachers parking lot. Whichever was easier for me. Since I was wearing the boot, I would land in the parking lot. It was also right next to the gym.

I stayed relatively low as the school came into sight. The teacher's parking lot was mostly full. I decided to land next to one closest to the door. I made sure to be careful. One of the teachers pulled in at that moment. I rolled my shoulders as I put my wings back. It was my gym teacher. He got out and took one look at the boot.

"Another incident?" he asked.

"Pretty much. Too much walking and not enough sitting." I said.

He nodded, "So long as you can do the simple exercises for finals, it's all good." He smiled.

He held the door for me as we walked in. Since I couldn't participate in class, I walked over to the bleachers and sat down. I'd do some more studying while everyone else worked up a sweat. I made sure to sit so my leg was stretched out and my left arm wasn't in danger of getting hit. I heard music start playing over the speakers. Mr. Kray – the gym teacher – liked to play classical music in class. Some of the kids hated it and worked harder so that they could get out of there faster. Me and some of the others like it though. I'm a fan of Beethoven. Mr. Kray didn't play him often.

Other kids started coming in, heading straight for the locker rooms. I pulled out my phone and sent Mr. Hydell a text that I was at school without an incident. He'd be up by now. I wasn't sure about Molly. He responded back pretty quickly. *'Gotcha. Thanks. Meat in marinade.'* Cool. I texted back thanks and that my phone would be off till later. I always turn it off for school.

I had just replaced my phone in my pocket when the bell rang. Mr. Kray came over. He had some printed papers in his hands.

"Do you think you'll be able to do these exercises?" he handed me the papers. Sit ups, push-ups, chin ups, and a few other exercises.

"What day next week is the gym final?"

"Wednesday. Odd periods on Monday, evens on Tuesday. Gym and swimming on Wednesday. And of course Thursday is the last day." He said.

I nodded. Looked back at the sheet and said, "I'll have to go easy on the chin and pull ups, but I shouldn't have too much of a problem."

"Okay. Keep those, just in case." He said. Then walked over to begin class.

I spent most of the time studying, a couple times people asked me to throw the ball back. Some were even all the way on the side of the gym. Easy when you're a shifter. Two or three others got the idea of studying and passing the ball. They had me ask a question and the person who had the ball when it stopped moving would have to answer. Eventually the whole class was in on it. Mr. Kray even started keepin' score. When it hit five minutes till end of class, I left. My next class was on the second floor. I needed to get to my locker and the elevator before the hoards were released.

I finally reached the elevator just as the bell rang. Once in I breathed a sigh of relief. It's murder trying to get through such a crowd with a bum leg. Obviously it's a short ride to the second floor. I almost ran into Mary on her way down. She was one of five kids at school who had Down syndrome. I held the door for her and even pushed the button. She smiled at me. We got along very well.

Once at my locker I was ambushed by two of the prom committee. Yay. Not. Emily and Amber were heads of the committee. They were adamant that everyone should go to the prom. Even me.

"Can we please not do this today guys? I've had a really hectic weekend." I said. I was already feeling tired. It was only second period.

"We just wanted your opinion on some things." Emily said, passing me a spread sheet. It showed some final pieces for decoration and some hair designs. Amber handed me some for dresses and coats.

"For you two?" It wasn't a secret that the two were dating, they liked to keep their outfits matching.

They nodded, "All right. Any colors in particular?" they both pointed at one and we all three went on our ways. I'd see them at lunch, so I could give them their answers then.

It wasn't a secret at school that I had an eye for color coordination. Quite a few of the popular girls willingly came to me for fashion advice. Even some of the guys they were dating came to me some times. They weren't necessarily because they wanted to be fashionable, just not 'screw up' their girlfriends whole outfit. There had been a few times that girls had gone home to change so that they matched what their boyfriend was wearing. That was when they started coming to me. Their parents giving them an ultimatum helped too. No more coming home to change, or no more car. No guess as to which they chose. It was basically a no brainer. Marjorie had already told them about my abilities with colors.

I sat down in math class. I handed my homework to the teacher as he came by. Easier to pass it to him then dig it out standing by his desk. I leaned a little more on my right hip. That's the only small disadvantage to sitting how I was in gym. Half my butt hurt.

Once the bell rang everyone got busy studying. The teacher would quiz us by surprise to test us. It was a good system. It weeded out the liars. I could already see two or three people on their phones instead of studying. The teacher looked at me. Since everyone had their heads down, I signed at him who wasn't studying. His children were deaf, so he knew sign language. In three separate languages. He also was in charge of sign language club, which I attend. And don't rag on me for tattling. I was raised to tell the truth. Even if it meant selling out people not doing school work.

I knew he wouldn't call on them immediately. He'd make it as random as possible, best way to make it seem he'd found them by chance. He also wouldn't pick me. I never asked why, but I think it's because he knows I already know it all. There's no reason to test me.

He picked the three kids before class was over, they'd all gotten their phones confiscated, and their parents were e-mailed. Shame, shame. Oh well. Their own faults. I finished studying about ten minutes before class was over. So I took out the papers that Emily and Amber had given me. Emily had picked a purple color. Okay, not a lot of options on that one. I thought about a few things. She was a cheerleader, like me she got straight A's, she was on the debate team. Those aspects I could work with. I decided on a deep lavender colored dress. Now for her hair. I looked through those. She had picked quite a few. I eventually decided on a partial bun style hairdo.

I left at five till again. My next class was woodshop. I wouldn't have time to look over the papers there. Too much goin' on. I took the elevator down to the first floor and walked across the courtyard to the shops. Wood, metal, and auto shops were all in their own building. I was one of two girls in my class. Priscilla and I didn't talk much. We didn't get along, she was only taking woodshop to fill space in her schedule. She sucked anyway, she never got higher than a C on her grade. I took it because I wanted to take it.

I entered class just as Mr. Graham was coming back from the metal shop. He actually taught both, so the two periods were never available at the same time. I had wanted to take metal shop at the beginning of the year, but it had been full, so I went with my second – but just as much wanted – choice. I almost immediately sat down once I got to a table. I was sweating slightly. I usually did when I made that walk with my cast. Mr. Graham placed a water bottle on the desk. He kept a mini-fridge in both rooms. I wasn't his only student with some kind of disability. One of his other students actually had type one diabetes and needed daily insulin injections. He took both shops so both fridges had emergency packs in them.

Speaking of him, he walked in. Ian often stopped at his locker between the two classes. He liked to sit next to me. He was actually one of my friends. We had grown up together. He and our other friends still didn't actually talk to me, but it was nice to still see them.

Once the whole class was seated, Mr. Graham got down to business. We'd be practicing with some of the machinery as well as being quizzed on safety. Three student needed to finish their end of term projects – the in class ones anyway. All they had left was the sanding. Two others had to stain or varnish. Ian needed to assemble the pieces of his, and I needed to lay in the final details to mine.

Everyone got to work. Safety goggles in place, I grabbed my project and a small grinding tool. I needed it to smooth out the edges. My in class project was a plaque, embossed with a Japanese cherry blossom branch. I had spent last week carving in my pattern. Not easy, but I didn't want to do a rose. Most people did roses. I like roses fine, but I think the Japanese cherry blossom is prettier. Plus being able to do a more intricate design was part of who I am.

I gently placed my plaque in one of the vices. This one was specially positioned so that I could use it without standing up. I put a face mask on and started grinding. I spent about twenty minutes smoothing the edges. I would have it finished by the end of class. There were a few smaller details I wanted to add once the smoothing was done.

I smelled something suddenly. I couldn't pin point it though. I pulled my mask off and took a deep breath. Fruit? In wood shop? Wait. Ian! I turned toward him just as he collapsed. He needed four injections a day because of how sever his diabetes was. He would only collapse if he skipped one.

"Mr. Graham!" I shouted over the machines. He looked, and needed no further prompting. He opened the fridge and tossed me one of the insulin syringes. I was qualified to give them in an emergency situation.

I didn't have time to stand. I caught the syringe and threw myself out of my chair, pulling the safety cap off at the same time. I landed on my right side, just close enough to get the shot into his leg. Once the syringe was empty I pulled myself into a partial sitting position and stopped at his head. Mr. Graham had gone around telling everyone to kill the machinery. I started patting Ian's cheek, trying to wake him up. Just as I had done since middle school when he fainted. Finally he started coming around and I breathed a sigh of relief. Ian was like a brother to me, I knew what could happen in an unprepared emergency.

Mr. Graham came over and took over getting Ian on his feet enough to get him in a chair. I on the other hand picked myself up and sat back in my chair. I'd made that jump a few times in the last few years, so my hip didn't hurt too much. It was my leg I was more concerned about. That last jump had been about two months before the murders, so I hadn't done it with my leg the way it was till now.

On one note, it didn't hurt, but it was somewhat stiff. I began flexing my leg, trying to ease it back to normal. I had used both legs to get me close enough to him. Ian was finally able to sit up. Mr. Graham and one other boy picked him up and helped him sit in a chair.

"You skipped an injection didn't you?" Mr. Graham asked him. Meeting his eyes.

"Yeah," Ian said while nodding, "I forgot to grab something from first period and had to run all the way back. I didn't think about the injection until just before I fell." Which explains why he'd grabbed the table first.

"Stay put. I'll call your mother." Mr. Graham said as he walked away.

Ian winced. His mother hated it when he missed injections. He'd be lucky if she didn't excuse him from school for the rest of the day. He'd had a near death episode only last month in one of his other classes. His mother had been on pins and needles ever since. I heard Priscilla giggle.

"Stupid idiot. Maybe he should ask his mom for a new body." She said under her breath with a very mocking tone.

I growled, the others wouldn't have heard her, but I had, "Shove it Priscilla! You wouldn't know a sever medical condition if it bit you on your abnormally tiny ass!"

Everyone was looking at me, this was the first time I had spoken in class in months. Most of them had looks of shock, Ian was suppressing a laugh, and Priscilla was staring at me as if I'd offended her. Suck it up girl, you heard me.

Mr. Graham finished his call, "Mag, did Priscilla say something?"

Before she could respond I said, "She called Ian a stupid idiot and that maybe he should ask his mom for a new body." I looked at Priscilla. Now she looked confused and freaked.

"Oh, really." Ian said. He wasn't happy.

"Miss Zanof, will you please come with me to the office." Mr. Graham made it a statement instead of a question.

She wouldn't take her eye off me, "Oh. Didn't you know that I'm a shifter." I said in a slightly sarcastic tone.

Now she only looked disgusted, I just chuckled. I was used to such looks. Mr. Graham came forward. She switched her gaze to him as he pulled a well-hidden recording device from beneath the desk. It was an expensive one too. It would most definitely have picked up what she'd said. Keeping his eyes on her, he played it back at full volume. The whole class heard her words come out. This would make the third strike against her, and I wasn't even responsible for the first two.

"Everyone please take a seat and wait for my return. Miss Zanof, principal's office. Now." Mr. Graham made sure she stayed in front of him.

"Freak." She said to me as she passed.

"Thank you." I said. You want to throw off a bully, take the insults as compliments.

It definitely threw her off, she looked back at me as if I'd offended her again. Not this time. I will gladly be called a freak and take it as a compliment. I'm weird by nature.

Ian sat down next to me as they walked out, "Thanks for the quick save Mag." He and all our friends called me that.

"Anytime. Dork." We both laughed. I missed my friends. I was going to be hard to tell him I wouldn't be at school next year. I decided not to wait.

"Ian," he looked up at me, "I won't be here next year." He looked confused.

"What? Why?!" He was like family, so this was going to hurt.

"I've been given a scholarship to a shifter school. With Kepner still loose, it's safer for everyone if I disappear for a while."

"But… but, we made a promise that we'd graduate together. All of us." He was getting angry.

"I know that," I kept my voice even, "but unlike this school, shifter schools can't be located. I don't want you or any of our other friends hurt or killed. He's already taken so much from me." I was angry enough that I was beginning to cry. I hate that sometimes.

He heard the break in my voice, he rubbed his neck, then said, "What are you guys looking at!?" The other boys immediately found something else to do.

I turned too, "Please don't spread this around school."

They each put both hands up and said, "Promise." I nodded thanks. They went back to what they were discussing. I knew they'd keep their words, I could smell it. It was no secret what Kepner had done, so they had no problem keeping it on the down low.

"Do you really have to?" Ian asked. Not meeting my eyes.

I nodded, "Yes."

He looked at me, sighed, and said, "Okay." He put a hand on my shoulder, "Will we be able to communicate again?" he asked.

"Maybe. It depends on if he's caught or not." Neither of us liked the situation, but it was a necessary evil. We had to take it on the chin, no matter that it hurt almost as much as zero contact with my brother.

"I'll tell the others. Don't be surprised about any reactions." He said.

"I'll be expecting several." And I would be. Most of my friends wouldn't be happy, but they would understand.

Mr. Graham was coming back just as I was getting ready to leave. Obviously Priscilla was in more trouble than just this classes three strikes. Ian decided to escort me to my next class. With permission of course. We left the shops building and headed to the main one. I started having trouble at the stairs. I was sweating again. He pushed the doors button once I made it. He was wise to escort me. I made the elevator. He accompanied me the whole way to English.

He made me wait by the door while he got my English book. We knew each other's locker combo's for obvious reasons. He came back with it just as the bell rang to switch classes. He headed off for his next period while I waited for the door to clear. We waved at each other before he turned the corner. It would be some months before we would be able to speak again.

Chapter 21

English passed without incident. Thankfully. I even spent the last few minutes of it choosing Amber's dress and hairdo. I took my time going to the cafeteria, I really didn't need to collapse. I was allowed to get extra if I needed it. I kinda hoped I wouldn't. Today's lunch was something good, the school made awesome cheese burgers. I took only one, but the lunch ladies knew to keep one in reserve just in case. If I didn't need it, it would go back into circulation. I did however grab two chocolate milks. I wanted something sweet right then.

I chose a table and sat down. I usually ate alone but since Emily and Amber needed fashion advice I knew they be joining me once they got food. I pulled their papers out of my backpack. I'd had a little trouble with Amber's dress. Amber was in orchestra with me, also got straight A's, and was on the volleyball team. Don't make that girl angry on the court, you will regret it. She wanted red and their weren't a lot of reds that complimented deep lavender while also being complimented by it. Magenta was out 'cause the two just hurt your eyes when seen together. Any pale versions were out too, they looked horrible with deep lavender. Fuschia was too bright – and hurt my eyes. I had finally decided on a cherry red color. The two blended well without being overpowering. For her hair I picked a really pretty braid that she'd printed out.

The two sat down across from me. I handed them their final results, leaving the rest on the table. They were ecstatic. They kept saying 'thank you' for the rest of lunch. I was getting ready to leave after finishing my food when Emily said, "You're sure you can't come?" she looked at me as if disappointed that I wasn't.

"Even if I wanted to I couldn't." I patted my leg.

"Not even if I showed you the dress I designed for you?" she held up a small notebook. That got my attention.

I stayed where I was as she opened it to one of the very back pages. I gasped, I normally didn't do dresses at all but the one she'd designed was gorgeous. And something I'd definitely wear. It was the same shade as my eyes, had full length bell sleeves, a high collar neckline, and a one layer ball gown skirt. The embroidery details on the skirt were of a Chinese dragon, while the bodice had a more elaborate design. I couldn't quite tell what it was though. I was speechless.

"I even designed it so that the skirt was detachable. You could wear a pair of leggings or shorts under it with no problem." She said.

"It's gorgeous." I admitted it. I loved it.

"I know you still probably won't go but I really wanted to do something as a thank you." She said, beaming at my praise.

"You wouldn't have to make a whole dress." I said, looking at her.

"I know. But I have already started it, and I intend to finish it." She took on her stubborn smile.

"I'll be doing the embroidery." Amber said.

I huffed, "I don't have any say in the matter do I."

"Nope." They said together.

"Well in that case, I don't know how to say thank you." I said.

"You don't have to. This is our way of thanking you, we haven't been able to solve our color coordination for months. This is how we repay you."

"I still have to say thank you." And I did. The dress was stunning, and no one had ever done something like this for me.

"Your welcome. Should I just send it to your home address when it's done?"

I got out a sticky note and wrote it down for her. She placed it on the page with the design and we all got up to leave. I'd have to hoof it to next period, but I didn't mind. I was feeling better after her surprise. It wasn't until I was seated in chemistry class that I realized I'd forgotten to ask Amber what the embroidery on the bodice was. Eh, I'll ask when I see her in final period.

Chemistry also passed without incident. Physics had been discontinued for the year because the school had been unable to find a replacement teacher after Kepner's crimes. I didn't mind too much, chemistry was cool. Mrs. Banks was a nice teacher, she even made studying fun. She split the class into two teams and did the game Jeopardy style. Telling one student a clue to get the right answer. History class was okay, our teacher could be dull sometimes, but Mr. Hanley didn't always mean to be. Next and last was orchestra. I had started using a school violin so I could play at home when I needed to. Due to the circumstances I didn't have to pay rent for instrument. For those of you who have never played an instrument, don't assume the final is playing. Nope. The final for orchestra and most other classes involving music is symbol identification. And it's not as easy as you think, some symbols look alike in a small way and can get mixed up. Understandable but not necessarily fun.

Amber played viola, so once studying was done I moved over and asked her my question. She thought for a moment and decided to pull out her notebook and draw the pattern instead. She took her time. Finally when she was done she showed it to me. While the bottom pattern was a Chinese dragon, the bodices design was of Japanese cherry blossom branches, she'd even found a way to make the branches go part way down the sleeves. The pattern would stop just short of the elbow, where the bell sleeves began.

"Why the cherry blossom?" I asked.

"Samson said they were your favorite flower." She said, putting her notebook back in her bag.

That made sense. Samson was another one of my friends, he was also one of Ian's cousins. The two had been raised together because Samson's mom had died in childbirth and his dad – whoever the hell that was – had ditched the second he'd found out Samson's mom was pregnant. He didn't plan on finding his dad. He figured the ditching had partially caused his mom's death. Which was a possibility, according to his aunt, his mom had been deeply in love with the father. Talk about a sword to the heart at that one.

I stopped in the school bathroom after I left class. I changed into my work shirt, and after heading outside, took the bus to the aquarium. While on the bus I turned on my phone. I had two messages. One from Mr. Hydell and one from Molly. Plus one voice mail. I read the text messages first. *'Text when you get this and when work is done. I'll pick you up.'* I sent a reply back, *'Only have to work half an hour. Starting at 3:30.'* I'd get done at four, plenty of time to make the gyoza before Mr. French arrived. Molly's message said, *'Save me some of those gyoza.'* Plus an emoji of a potsticker. I had her hooked. The voice mail was from Ms. Hamper. 'Hey sweetie, just called to let you know me and the babies were released at noon, and are now home. I'd like some color advise to redo their room. Call me when you can to reschedule appointment.' Sensible, since our last one was cut short. My next appointment was supposed to be on Saturday, but I would need to throw in an extra one now. I'd check my schedule on the way home.

Chapter 22

Work actually went by pretty quickly. Not that unexpected since it was a week day. Ben walked me out, he was a little jumpy now that Kepner had vanished. Mr. Hydell was waiting in his Cadillac. Ben was heading back in as I got in the car.

"How was work, kiddo?" he asked.

"Good. I'm guessing by your face the school called." I had noticed the slightly hidden look of pride.

"They did." He was smiling now. "Priscilla, was that her name," I nodded, "thought so. She's been expelled from the school."

I was shocked, "Why?" I had meant to get justice for her comment, not get her expelled.

"You and Ian weren't the only ones she'd picked on. Apparently she'd been bullying all the special needs students and her comment in woodshop was the last straw."

"Wow." She was worse than I had thought. I wasn't shocked anymore.

"Yep. The school had been waiting for an excuse to kick her out. Her remark about Ian was it." He chuckled slightly, "Her parents were livid about her treatment of others."

"And how do you know that?" I asked.

"I could hear her parents chewing her out in the back ground." He answered.

Oh well. Too bad for Priscilla. She'd finally gotten her comeuppance. She had tried to pick on me at the beginning of the year. I'd proven unflappable to her bullying. She'd hated it. Though I hadn't known just how far her bullying had gone. If I had I would have kicked her ass, and taken whatever consequences. Not that I would have gotten any. My mom was a very formidable woman when it came to trying to punish those who did the right thing. You can't always go to a teacher when bullying is occurring, by the time you get back both parties are gone. You might not necessarily have to resort to violence, but interfere somehow. Otherwise the trouble could escalate very quickly and may have a disastrous outcome.

I took my phone out of my pocket and opened my schedule. I didn't have to work again until Saturday, and both Thursday and Friday were open after school. I'd probably do the replacement appointment tomorrow, even things out a bit. I dialed her work number, it would forward to her cell since she wasn't in the office. I had to leave a message, though I did state that a video chat might be the best option.

I had just finished the call when we pulled into the garage. The security guard checked us and let the thing up. Mr. Hydell parked in his usual spot. We got out and got in the elevator.

"You feeling up to making dinner?" he asked. It was 4:08.

"I'll eat a snack and take a pain pill. That should give me enough time to rest. I'll get started once I'm done eating."

"All right. He should be here at six." That gave me a little over an hour and a half to make the gyoza.

I went into my room after grabbing an apple from the kitchen, tossed my backpack on my desk, and fell backward onto my bed. My leg was pretty sore, it really had not liked my jump. I took my time eating, thinking about how the meeting might go. Mr. French didn't know about my leg cast. I don't even know why I still called it that. It technically wasn't a cast anymore, just a brace. Oh well. I was more worried about how he'd react, given his reaction to my nerve damage. Then there was my arms. I had spent some of school thinking about the scratches. I had come to the conclusion that all of them scarring was definitely a possibility, I'd just have to wait and see. I know for a fact that the two that had exposed my left ulna most definitely would scar.

I sat on my bed till 4:30, the pain had started to recede, but to play it safe I took a pill. I really didn't want to collapse again. First

I changed into more comfy clothes. I switched my jeans for shorts and my work shirt for a short sleeved one. I debated about taking the bandages off, then decided against it. I didn't want olive oil jumping into one. It hurts enough on unwounded skin. I put the cast back on and walked out my door.

Mr. Hydell was in a heated discussion on the phone. I quietly walked to the kitchen and got started on dinner. Repeating all the same steps from a few days ago, I had over sixty gyoza ready to cook by 5:50. Mr. Hydell finally finished his phone call about a minute later.

"Good or bad?" I asked.

"Pretty bad. The father is demanding more time with the kids. Even though he's the abusive one. The mother is debating whether or not to send the kids to her parents in the Rocky's and try to end all this without any emotional fallout." He said.

"If he's that bad someone should just shoot him." His client's husband had beaten her for years and was about to move on to his children.

Mr. Hydell chuckled, "A typical Texan answer. I wish it was that simple." He'd figure it out. He always did. One reason why he was the best divorce lawyer in L.A.

"Since Mr. French is going to be here soon, I think it wise to warn him about my arms before he sees me." I indicated my arms while closing the last three gyoza. 67 total. New record for me.

He cringed, "Good idea." I cocked my head as I heard the elevator ding down the hall. Even from here I could smell lion. I didn't know the difference between normal lion and cave lion. Mr. French was the first cat shifter I'd met. Well, as far as I knew anyway.

"He's comin' down the hall." I said.

Mr. Hydell went to answer the door while I put a small amount of olive oil in the cast iron skillet. I had been apprehensive about using anything made of cast iron for a few weeks after the murders, but now that it had been a few months I was over it. I didn't pay attention to what the two said, my focus needed to be on the food. Because of how thin the meat was it could over cook easily, even if it was marinated. I got out the little kitchen timer and set it for the first three minutes, I also filled a one cup measure to the first quarter mark. I then grabbed a pan lid from the cupboard and set it by the timer.

I turned as the door open and the two walked back in. Mr. Hydell looked a little nervous, and Mr. French looked… well I couldn't really tell what his look was. I had seen such a look only once. When my sister had told our parents that she and her boyfriend had had sex and that she might be pregnant – that ended up being a false positive thankfully – but the possible meaning had been unclear.

I decided to let him tell me, I really didn't want to try and guess the look. My parents had been pissed that she had done something so irresponsible – the unprotected sex part anyway – but they had been willing to help take care of her and any possible child that came about. My sister had been relieved when the second test had come back negative. Even then she'd known she wasn't ready to be a mom. Though after that she and her boyfriend had been more careful. She'd had to get on everyone's good sides after that too. Mom and dad had gotten over it faster, they had liked her boyfriend well enough, but me and Reggie. Neither of us had spoken to her for weeks after the near baby incident. We weren't mad about the prospect of being an aunt and uncle. We just really didn't like her boyfriend. He'd tried to pull her away from her religion at first. She'd been adamant about staying the way she was in a relationship, he hadn't gotten the picture at first. Reggie and I had found him going through our mother's high priestess supplies and trying to either destroy or 'purify' them as he'd put it. We had almost gone dragon on him. I had actually dragged him from the room and tossed him down the stairs.

Amanda had tried to intervene on his behalf, until we told her what we'd found him doing. She had lost it. She didn't transform though, that was good. He finally got the point that she wasn't going to change religions when she'd said, 'If I can't be myself with you, then we are done.' Being herself meant keeping her religion. No if, ands, or buts about it. After that me and Reggie wanted nothing to do with him. So anytime he came over, we left. Either together or separately. It wasn't until almost three months after the baby incident that we'd started talking to her again. And that had been last year.

I turned my attention back to reality when the timer went off. I added the water and covered the pan, then reset the timer for one minute. I set up the cookie sheet to take the done gyoza and checked the sauce. It was done. I carefully poured it into a bowl, then added a small ladle to serve it into smaller bowls.

"How are you doing Miss Sharp?" Mr. French asked as I took the lid off the pan and reset for another minute.

I turned and leaned on the counter, "Sore, but can't really complain."

He was sitting at the bar with Mr. Hydell, "I'm glad." No he wasn't, he was tense. I raised an eyebrow.

"Alright, I'm glad you're not injured further than you had been, but I'd like to find this Kepner, myself and show him shifter justice." Now that, he was truthful on.

"You and me both." I said, turning to take the first batch from the pan. I always cook six at a time.

I put the next six in the skillet, "May I see your arms?" I set the timer for three minutes and came around the island. It was only then that he saw my cast. Brace, damn it! His growl shook the floor. I stopped in my tracks, my claws even extended. His eyes briefly changed before he got himself back under control.

"I'm sorry." There was a wistfulness in his eyes, he knew pain. Like I knew it.

I calmed down myself and finished coming forward. I undid the bandages quickly. I didn't want to take too long for gyoza sake. He barely suppressed a second growl, looking over my arms with the air of a father. He paid more attention to my left arm, though he did look questioningly at the bruise on my right arm.

"The bruise is from Ms. Hamper. Contraction." I explained.

"Ah." His tone said he knew that one. "Which one exposed bone?" I pointed to it, wincing slightly at turning my arm. At least I could turn it some now. He turned his attention to the brace. Ha! Got it!

"I never did ask for the details of your families murder." He said. Not taking his eyes off it.

"Well. I've got about 60 more gyoza to cook. I'll tell it to you." I moved to add the water. "You want the full story or the condensed version?"

"Full story please." He said. I put the drained gyoza on a plate, "and you eat first. It's only right."

I took a deep breath, trying to keep myself centered. He would be the first person I'd told the whole story to in a long time. I decided I wouldn't sit down. I'd use the process of cooking to keep my head where it needed to be.

It didn't take as long to tell it as it had the first time. By the time I had the gyoza done, I'd finished the story. Mr. Hydell knew it well enough, but Mr. French looked about ready to charge out the door and track Kepner down. Fine by me. The Punisher had said it best. Sometimes the law is inadequate.

"You are just a child," his tone had changed, he must be really old for it to do that, "you never should have had to endure such pain." I set a plate with gyoza down in front of him. He set to. He calmed down a bit.

"We must accept the hand that the universe has dealt us." I said, giving Mr. Hydell his plate.

He looked at me, confused, "That's a mature way to look at it. Who said that?"

"I doubt you'd be familiar. It's from the Ninja Turtles." I said, finally sitting down with my own plate.

"As in the Teenage Mutant Ninja Turtles." He said, looking at me with a small smile.

I laughed, "Yeah, them. It's from the most recent animated series, season three, episode one. Mikey technically is quoting Master Splinter."

"I see. May I have more?" the gyoza were completely gone.

I chucked, "Why do you think I made so many sir."

"They are very good. Better than most I've eaten from my personal chef."

"You say that like he's oriental." I said, putting ten more on his plate.

"He is. He wanted to work for Chef Morimoto, but he didn't have the skill."

I looked at him in disbelief, "Wow, ambitious. Are you a fan of potstickers?"

"I am. Ever since I visited Japan about a decade ago." He said, eating another.

I refilled Mr. Hydell's plate before he posed his next question, "If it's not too invasive, may I see the scar?"

"I'm almost used to actually showing people, in fact I had to show it to a woman the other night who thought we were using the handicapped spot without a tag." I sat on the stool to his left, facing away from the island. My leg was starting to feel tingly. I pulled the leg up to almost my hip. They were loose shorts, so it wasn't too hard.

"Mother of the Gods." He said as he got a full look. He didn't touch my leg, but carefully examined it. You could still partially see how the tub had landed.

"Has it always looked this bad?" he asked, keeping his composure, even though he was fighting his lion.

"No. It looked much worse after the first set of stitches." I said, putting my shorts leg back down.

"First set!?" he was starting to lose that fight.

"I have pictures." Mr. Hydell said, pulling his phone out.

I went back around the island to my seat. I sat back down, and started eating more. Mr. Hydell showed him the pics of my leg after the stitches that the paramedics had applied had been replaced. Of course those were several hours later, after the surgeons had finished the puzzle that was my femur. Even the rig to hold the bone together had left scars. Small ones, but they were there. They would eventually no longer be visible, but the obvious one would be with me for the rest of my life.

"Can you shift with your leg like that?" he sounded concerned now.

"Yes. The scar doesn't even show when I do."

That surprised him, "Have you shifted since the other night?" he asked, indicating my arms.

"Not yet, I was instructed to talk to my regular doctor for a final heal estimate before shifting."

"A wise option." He said.

"Speaking of that, your appointment with her is on Saturday. About an hour before Ms. Hamper." Mr. Hydell said, double checking his phone. I nodded.

"Also speaking of appointments, I have drifted from my original purpose here." Mr. French said.

After that all talk turned to my transferring. He wanted to see my room to determine how much stuff I could bring. Mr. Hydell showed it to him, I was having trouble standing. He came back with my dad's tanto and my new box. One thing I had wanted to ask about was my weapons.

"Is this your work?" he asked, admiring the blade.

"No," I sniffed and wiped my eyes, "It's my dad's work. He never got to finish it." No crying Maggie.

"His skill is impressive. It seems he passed it to you." He meant the box.

"I can weld okay, but I've never tried my hand at forging."

"We have such facilities at the school." Yes! Thank you!

"Any rules about weapons?" I asked.

"Only that they are allowed. We do after all require our students to be proficient in combat."

"Yes!" I said, putting my arms in the air.

He chuckled, "How many do you have?"

"Not a lot. I have a few of my dad's unfinished ones, most of the finished ones, and a pocket knife he and mom got me for Christmas a few years ago. I know how to use guns, but those are all in storage."

"Well we can remedy that." He smiled.

He and Mr. Hydell discussed a few more things after that. I put what was left of the gyoza and the sauce away, making sure to put the separate baggie for Molly elsewhere. I took the time to rewrap my arms, since the bandages were sans blood, I just reused the ones from earlier. Mr. French also took some leftovers, I guess I now had him hooked. I double checked my homework, I hadn't missed anything. I'd done some at work, the rest I could do here in a sec. Not that it was much. Just before Mr. French left he turned to me and asked if I had any martial arts training.

"Yes, but I haven't been able to practice since this happened." I indicated my leg.

"We should be able to help with that as well." He said, with a thoughtful expression.

"I'd really like that."

"What forms?"

"Wing chun, karate, ninjutsu, and dragon style kung fu."

"Really?" he looked impressed. I just nodded.

"I also know Tai Chi, my dad insisted on it so that we could regain control of our natural tempers faster."

"A wise precaution." Again I just nodded.

"I'll have the staff make sure that the grounds are up to date then. You aren't going to be the only one with such skills at the school." He said.

He left shortly afterwards. It was officially 7:30, I had a few hours before bed to do the rest of my homework. Just before I got started Mr. Hydell called me to the living room. It seems that Mr. French had given him some floor plans of the rooms at my new school.

"All the rooms are the same, you'll just be able to change it up to how you want it when you choose one." He said.

"Cool." I leaned over the couch arm to get a better look. The rooms had two doors?

"Okay sorry check that. Most of the rooms are the same. All third floor rooms have launchpads. That's what the second set of doors are." He stated after reading another set of papers.

"Cool. So any and all flyers are on the top floor."

"So it seems. And speaking of new rooms." He leaned forward, like a father about to give his children the news that they were moving. I speak from experience on that one.

"Let me guess. You want me to fully disappear by taking all my stuff to the school." I had suspected that from the amount of time they had spent talking in my room.

He chuckled, "Can't hide much from a shifter." He tapped his fingers together, "That is it in a nut shell. Now that Kepner has popped back up, it's safer for all parties involved if nothing of yours stays here. It would give him no way to track you anywhere."

"I agree. It's the most logical thing to do." I'm not a petty little girl to cry or complain.

It really was the safest option for everyone. Kepner had already proven how dangerous he was in his pursuit of me. He'd killed his own daughter for crying out loud. Who knows what he'd do to Mr. Hydell or Molly. I didn't even want to think about him coming after Ms. Hamper.

"I don't want to do it Maggie, but…"

I grabbed his arm, "Like I said, I agree. And I do understand. His popping up and disappearing is of great worry. It is indeed safer for everyone if I vanish too."

He gave a sad smile and placed his hand over mine, there were even tears in his eyes. I moved closer and hugged him as I had done my dad a few days before he'd died. We stayed like that for several minutes. Neither of us wanted to move. I'd be spending the next three months in Scotland, I didn't know if he and Molly had any plans, but knowing him. I decided to broach the question.

"Are you and Molly gonna do anything while I'm in Scotland?"

"Yes. We both need time off, so we've decided that while you're in Scotland, we're going to go to Australia, Japan, and maybe Nepal."

"Cool. Bring me souvenirs from each." I said.

"Same to you kiddo."

The phone rang then, making us both jump. We both got up, he went to answer the phone while I went to my room to finish my homework. I put my mp3 player on. 'Blown away' by Carrie Underwood. It's a good song, one I really like. I didn't want to eavesdrop on Mr. Hydell's conversation. I could tell from how he'd answered that it was his boss. Something must be going down at the office. But since lawyers have the whole client confidentiality thing, I didn't listen in. Though I found out a few minutes later my zoning the conversation out was unnecessary. He came into my room a few minutes later, he looked heavily relieved.

"You remember what I'd told you before dinner." He asked, rubbing his face tiredly.

I nodded, "The one I said to just shoot."

"Well he wasn't shot," Come again? "He's been run over by a drunk driver. The doctors called it twenty minutes ago." Karma dude!

"Is the widow relieved?" I asked.

"Yes. Though she's gonna break it to the kids as easily as possible."

"That's understandable." I couldn't really believe her luck. I was happy for her though.

"I'll let you get back to your homework."

I did turn back to it as the next song started, 'Wasting all these tears' by Cassadee Pope. Another that I'd forgotten was on there, but one of my all-time favorites. I'd played it once for my sister, she'd enjoyed it. Up until she realized why I was playing it. The boyfriend before the one who'd almost gotten her pregnant and was there when she died, had been cheating on her. He'd even been shallow enough to put the moves on **me**. Needless to say, I had been supremely disgusted with it and had told him if he ever came near me again, I'd rip his private parts off.

The next week he'd fondled my ass. So I elbowed him in the throat. Reggie had seen him do it and had then thrown him out the door. I had played the song for Amanda like....thirty minutes later. When she was wondering where he was. Reggie and I then proceeded to tell her what he'd done. She had believed it somewhat. It wasn't until she went over to his apartment and found him fucking another girl that she'd been hit with the cold hard truth.

That was the first time she'd been cheated on. She had grabbed all the pictures of him and went with dad to the gun range. She unloaded seven separate mags into his pictures. She then sent him a pic of the carnage and told him that if he ever showed his face to her again, the pictures wouldn't be the ones getting shot. He would.

Listening to Cassadee reminded me exactly why me and Reggie hadn't liked her last boyfriend either. She was an adult, she had been so convinced that he was the one. We were shifters for Gods sakes! It wasn't as simple as it was with humans. You could think someone was the one, but be surprised later when your body betrayed you and bonded with someone else entirely. It wasn't something you could fight. Not as a full grown adult anyway. That was another reason I was desperate for whatever info I could find about the mating bond. I'd have bet my life that were Amanda alive today, she'd have gotten lucky and bonded with someone more deserving of her. Not that jackass she'd been seeing when she died.

I mean, there was a possibility that her fated mate would have been human, but one never knows until it happens. That's half of what scares me about the mating bond. Is that you don't see it coming. I don't always like the unknown. If I can plan something sure, I'm fine with it, but you can't do that with mates. Not even true psychics could tell you who your eventual mate was. That was all my dad had been able to tell me about the bonding process. I had wanted to cheat a few years ago, he'd told me it wasn't that easy. Sure humans could go to a psychic and be told when they would meet their other half, but oh no not shifters.

I missed my dad so much right now. There were so many questions he had yet to answer for me. I had no doubt that Reggie and Amanda had asked the same questions. I just didn't get the chance. Kepner had stolen that and so much more from me. I certainly wouldn't go around asking other shifters what I needed to know. That would be too awkward.

The music changing to Halestorm snapped me out of my thinking. Enough with the heavy thoughts, I need to focus on finishing my sophomore year. I turned back to my homework.

I finished just before nine. I decided to get a bedtime snack and take a sleeping pill. Nightmares were the last thing I needed right now. I ate about two handfuls of pistachios, drank a glass of milk, and took the pill. I said good-night to Mr. Hydell, then went to my room and changed into my pajamas. Sleep took me within twenty minutes of lying down.

Chapter 23

School on Thursday passed without incident, even with most of the school knowing about the incident in the woodshop. I was glad for it though, I really didn't want any attention. I was making my way to the city bus by the school when I got a text from Molly, '*Jack working late. I can pick you up.*' I texted back asking where she was. '*Two minutes away.*' I sent back that I'd wait for her. Ms. Hamper had returned my message this morning on the way to school. She had agreed with me about a video conference instead. The carpets in her office were being replaced. For obvious reasons. She'd set the appointment for when I got home.

I sat down at one of the benches outside the school and waited. That's when I felt it. Someone was watching me. Without taking my phone out of my pocket I sent Molly a text to wait and call the officer in charge of my case. I put my sunglasses and beanie on. I took a second to focus my thoughts and expanded my senses. I tuned out the students walking and talking past. I tuned out the vehicles, animals, and phone rings. The only other noise was the wind. When that stopped, I picked it up. My eyes were closed behind the sunglasses, but the person with the camera taking my pictures wouldn't know that. Especially not since I was turning my head like I was looking around.

I sent Molly a text with the photo taker's coordinates. I maneuvered my arm just enough to see the reply, two units in area. Approaching suspect on foot. It didn't take long. I heard rather than saw the officers take the man by surprise. I got up as Molly pulled up a block away. She was playing it smart. I looked two blocks west. I could barely see the officers shoving the man into the squad car. His camera in one piece in another officer's hands.

I hopped in Molly's car and she peeled out, barely waiting for me to buckle up. Good. I didn't want to stick around. Completely vanishing to a new school was sounding better and better. I wanted to ask Molly how she felt about it, but I chose not to distract her.

She pulled up to my building and went inside with me. I hadn't said a word the whole way, everything felt like it was unraveling too quickly. Why couldn't he just roll over and die!!? I'm too broken to lose anything else in my life. I realized I was jumping to conclusions, for all anyone knew the photographer was working for the local paper and wanted a story. I doubted that theory highly though. Kepner wasn't stupid. He'd probably hired the guy to keep tabs on me and report back to him.

Running my hands through my hair as we entered the apartment I went to the bathroom and almost emptied my stomach. I barely managed to run water over my face to calm down. I was trying to finish the school year, I did **not** need this now.

I came back out to find Molly on the phone with Ms. Hamper. So much for that appointment. I started pacing, I was so anxious for answers on who that damned photographer was. I grabbed my backpack from where I had dropped it on the way in and threw it as hard as I could into my room. I was losing my mind, I would have given anything at that time to be normal again. Molly came over with the phone still in hand, and stopped my moving by hugging me tight enough that I couldn't move at all. I couldn't quite return the hug. I still felt sick.

I heard Ms. Hamper say over the phone, "Put the phone in her hand." Molly complied as I fell to the floor. Both legs having turned to jelly.

"Maggie, can you hear me sweetie?" she asked.

I pulled myself together enough to answer, "Yeah." I swallowed pretty hard.

"Focus on my voice, okay." She started saying other things, I just focused on her voice, not bothering to pay attention to the words. Suddenly there was a cry in the back ground.

"Oh crap, hang on." One of the babies was awake.

I began to regain my breath, listening to her put Gregory back to sleep. I chuckled a little, he was only a few days old and already being stubborn. I moved so that I was up against the wall. I needed something a bit more solid right then. Gregory took a good fifteen minutes to go back to sleep, by the time she came back over to the phone I could breathe normally again.

"Already stubborn huh." I said as she picked up the phone.

She laughed quietly, "Yes. Just like me as his father puts it." I took a deep breath. "How you feeling now sweetie?" I guess we're doin' the appointment after all.

"Sick to my stomach. I still can't really breathe, and I just want to disappear." I answered.

"Mr. Hydell already told me about what he and Mr. French discussed. I think it's best too."

That made me feel a little better, "I'd feel better if the four of you did too." I admitted.

"Sweetie, then I wouldn't be able to give you therapy." She sounded more worried than angry.

"You have other priorities now. Once Kepners dead you can be my therapist again. He's already killed one baby. I don't think my heart could survive two more." My voice had broken by the time I finished the sentence, and Molly had come over.

I heard her sigh, "Okay, if you think it's for the best."

"I do." I didn't want to lose her as my therapist, but the needs of the many outweigh the needs of the one.

"Alright. Don and I will make the arrangements. I'll miss seeing you sweetie." I could hear the held back tears.

"Me too." I said.

We hung up. It would be a long time before we would speak to each other again. That didn't worry me then. I just wanted her and the babies to be safe. I could use whatever therapist they had at my new school.

Molly sat down next to me and pulled me into a hug. She didn't say anything, she didn't have to. We stayed there for I don't know how long, just waiting for Mr. Hydell to get home and give us whatever news the cops came up with.

Chapter 24

I didn't eat dinner that night, I couldn't. My stomach rebelled at water. Molly hadn't left my side the whole evening. Eventually I had fallen into a fitful sleep against her shoulder. I didn't lash out in any way thankfully, but she still never let go of me. Mr. Hydell had arrived after ten o'clock. He'd gently woken me and moved me to my room. I didn't even bother thinking about my homework. I could try and do it on the fly in the morning.

That ended up coming sooner than I would have liked. The nightmare that had ended in my new scratches tried to repeat itself. I woke myself just in time. I decided not to go back to sleep. I grabbed my mp3, put my earbuds in, and blaring the loudest music I have on it, I stayed up all night doing my homework.

At 6:30 the next morning I got off my bed and went to make enough coffee for the whole day. I wasn't drowsy, but also wasn't going to take any chances. I barely registered Mr. Hydell come out of his room, I was more focused on the mug of coffee in my hand. I was disheveled from little sleep, but I just didn't care. He did apparently.

I heard him huff in consternation, "You didn't sleep at all did you?"

His tone reminded me of my dad, choking on my words I said, "I slept a little. I decided not to after my last nightmare tried to repeat itself." Now I wasn't so sure I wanted to go to school.

He became sympathetic and came over to hug me, "I'm sorry kiddo."

I leaned into his shoulder, after a few seconds I asked, "What was with the photographer?"

"Kepner paid him $100,000 to check on you and send him pics." He said, moving to the toaster.

"Where the hell did he get the money? All his accounts were frozen." Great.

"No one's quite sure, but needless to say the guy has no idea where the money came from or where Kepner even is."

Mr. Hydell jumped as the mug in my hand shattered, spilling semi-hot coffee over my right hand, "Great, just another thing for him to fuck up!" I ran medium cold water over my hand. It was slightly red but since I'm a dragon, it wouldn't burn. Just be irritated for a little bit.

Mr. Hydell passed me a towel and started wiping up the spilled coffee, "Do you want to stay home today?"

"Not really. I don't want to go to school either, but I need something to distract me. Schools the best way to do it."

Work wasn't until tomorrow, but after everything that had occurred over the last two weeks, I was forming a plan. If I was gonna disappear, that would mean quitting my job. No matter how much I didn't want to. Or at least ask for leave of absence until Kepner was dead.

I flew to school that day too. I wanted the cold spring air of June 2nd on my face, I didn't care if I was seen. Not that it mattered, the fog was so thick you couldn't see an inch in front of you. I kept my eyes dragon so that I could see just fine. I also decided to land on the school roof. My leg took it okay, I could finally walk without the brace. Although knowing me I'd be limping by lunch.

My morning periods passed without incident, in fact they'd been kinda boring. I don't get bored easily, so that was sayin something. I was at my locker dropping off my book when I heard someone wheeling down the hall in my direction. I knew who it was by her expensive but well moderated perfume. I turned to see what Marjorie wanted.

I thought back to when I'd hit her. Her crime had been worse than Tom's, so her still being in a wheelchair after two months wasn't a surprise. I had been in exactly the same spot I was now when she had tried to get herself killed. She'd walked up behind me with her posse of friends and groupies, and had started saying really stupid shit.

"Hey everyone look. It's Kepner's little whore." Her friends had laughed, but I'd ignored her.

That didn't stop her, I don't remember the other attempted insults to bully me had been, but when she saw that I was unaffected and her groupies were starting to laugh at her instead of me, she moved to more dangerous territory.

She'd leaned against the locker to the left of mine, tried to look me in the eye, and said, "Maybe you should ask your parents for a school transfer." I heard her friends and groupies gasp, "Oh, wait." Then she'd laughed, not sensing the danger. The others had though and stood there behind me trying to make themselves as small as possible.

She turned to look back at me, and watched as the coat hook I'd been holding after getting my jacket, was suddenly pulled forward and down, taking the wall of the locker with it. The sound of shearing metal had traveled down the hall, making several people cover their ears. I turned my head to look her in the eyes, only then did she see how much danger she was in. My eyes were full dragon, glowing and menacing. She'd turned to run. I swung around in a circle, hitting her in the back with my fist.

I'd missed her spine, but she still flew almost half way down the hall. Her friends didn't move, afraid I'd move on to them. The groupies scattered, just trying to get to safety. I stalked down the hall to where she lay. She was groaning in pain at my blow. I stopped next to her, and not holding back on my strength, punched the floor next to her head. The dent was still there.

I then crouched next to her, the abject terror on her face not affecting me at all, and whispered, "You ever talk about my parents like that again, and next time the floor won't be the target." I paused, "Do you understand me?"

In tears, she had nodded vigorously. I then stood, closed my locker, and for only the second time in my high school career, ditched school. I had nearly killed her, I needed to get away. I didn't go back to school for three days after that. I had spent both times after the incidents outside of the city. When I had come back, Mr. Hydell told me that her parents had tried to sue, but she had actually told them not to. Apparently my actions had shown her the wrong she had done, and she was taking it for what it was.

We hadn't spoken since, I generally avoided her. Even though we went to therapy in the same building. I closed my locker and leaned against it. It had been repaired while I'd cooled down. I waited for her to get closer.

"I heard Ms. Hamper is going into hiding." She said by way of greeting. I just nodded.

"I am sorry, for what I said. I had no right to say that." She paused, "I know you'll probably never forgive me, but I truly am sorry."

"I just hope you never know my pain." I didn't know if I could forgive her. "Don't tell anyone else, but I won't be here next year. I've accepted a scholarship to a shifter school." I looked at her expectantly.

She placed both hands on her lap in full view, "I promise I won't tell."

I nodded, "Thank you."

She gave a small smile, "Will you still see Ms. Hamper?"

"When Kepners dead. Yes. For now. No. But I will contemplate your apology."

"That's all I really expected. Thanks for being honest." She meant it, I could smell it.

My act had humbled her. I hadn't expected that, but then again life says to expect the unexpected. I watched her as she wheeled her way down the hall. I decided to stop at the bathroom before heading down to lunch. While I washed my hands, Priscilla's friends tried to jump me.

Looking up into the mirror I said, "Don't say I didn't give you fair warning."

I turned, "You three really want to do this?" my phone was hidden on one of the doors, pointed at the four of us. I had placed it there before leaving the stall.

They drew in closer, I shrugged. I hadn't dried my hands, so as one tried to punch me – man her form was terrible – I slapped her with one still wet hand. Another came and got the same thing. The third stopped short and tried to kick me in the leg, bad move. I ducked under it and growing my tail, I tail-whipped her in the ass. Then did the same for the others. A teacher came running at their cries.

An hour later the three were leaving with their parents, suspended for the last few days. They – like Priscilla - would miss finals. My phones video had been incriminating, there was no getting away with it when I was involved. Mr. Hydell had been called and informed of the situation, and I was released to finish the day. I went to a vending machine to get a snack to make up for no lunch. I ended up getting three things from the machine, I wanted to play it safe. I also grabbed a V-8 v fusion from another machine. By the time I made it to orchestra, my stomach wasn't growling, but I would need to eat again before I got home.

Mr. Hydell picked me up after school. He brought me a burger from McDonalds. I ate the meal on the drive home. He didn't say anything about the bathroom incident, but I could tell from his shoulders that he was exasperated. By me and my behavior or theirs I didn't know. It wasn't until we got home that he actually broached the subject.

"Did you actually slap them?" he seemed confused.

"Yes. With wet hands." I confirmed.

"You don't slap. Usually you go straight for punch." He's smiling now.

I shrugged, "Punching with a wet hand doesn't hurt as much, and I wanted my point of 'leave me alone' to get across very quickly. And technically I only slapped two of them."

"The tail-whip was what I liked. Did any of them see it coming?"

"Nope, and two of them need to really work on their aim. The second one missed my face by a good five inches, and the third one would have hit my waist instead of my leg."

"No critics for the first one?" he asked while getting a soda.

"Ugh, don't even get me started on her form." I'm a martial artist, of course I notice these things.

He's fully laughing now, "So you were exasperated with their behavior, not mine." I stated.

"Yes." He paused, "I'm tired of people seeing you as the criminal when they got what they deserved."

I nodded, "Marjorie apologized today." I took a sip of water that I'd just gotten from the tap.

He looked surprised, "You didn't accept did you?" he knew the story.

"I told her I'd contemplate it."

"Was that all she expected?" I just nodded. "Good."

I sat at the island peeling a banana for my snack. I did Fridays homework right there, I didn't feel like going to my room. I had found a dent in my wall where the backpack had made contact. I felt seeing it would bring me right back to yesterday. Better to not think about it for now.

Homework was done before dinner. Mr. Hydell ordered pizza instead of having me cook. The Domino's delivery guy almost went to the wrong floor, he realized his mistake as the doors opened. He brought up our three pizzas and got a good tip for his trouble. Mr. Hydell and I ate in the living room while watching more episodes of Bones. I had some memorized so I could warn him if any got to gross. His stomach wasn't quite as strong as mine was.

He called Molly before he went to bed, I gave myself a little reward for finishing the last homework of the year before going to bed myself. I gave in and took a sleeping pill. I had three weeks' worth, but since I didn't take one every night I could make them last longer. I'd probably sleep in again. I didn't have to be at work till noon.

Chapter 25

I did in fact sleep in, a good two hours. When I awoke I could hear Molly in the living room. My brain was still a little fuzzy, but I did remember that Mr. Hydell had work today. He must have asked Molly to stay over with me. It made sense. My appointment was at one.

I got up slowly, taking my time. Not just because of my leg but because I could feel some of the effects of the pills still in my system. I'd rather not fall on my face thank you. When I did get up, I went over to the window to look outside. I got ready to move the curtains when I noticed something buzzing. At first I thought it might be a drone outside my window but then I realized where the buzzing was coming from. My bed. It was my phone. I quickly went back over and picked it up.

It stopped buzzing as I grabbed it. I had one missed call. Whomever it was hadn't left a message. I didn't recognize the number. It started buzzing in my hand. The same number, I was about to hit decline but decided against it. Maybe they'd leave a message this time. They did.

"I'll find you." Click. I knew that voice anywhere, and now I knew how he'd meant the e-mail. That he'd go through whomever he had to, in order to get to me.

With a roar I threw my phone at the wall, shattering it into a million pieces. I then went over and – eyes going dragon – scanned the buildings faster than was humanly possible. There! He was IN the building directly across from us. One floor lower. He was just hanging up his phone. I heard Molly enter. I growled to stop her.

I yanked the curtains closed, took a deep breath, and took control of myself.

"Kepner's in the building across the street." I said. She was already on the phone.

Fifteen minutes later the cops had news. Once AGAIN Kepner had gotten away!! Two weeks in a row! I couldn't stand it. I was pacing in my room. Molly had called a friend of hers and we were waiting for him. She also called my doctor to reschedule my appointment. It was now on Monday after school. Molly was going to take me to her apartment as discreetly as possible. Before we planned to leave I wanted to place a lock spell on my room, my gut was telling me it would be a good idea. I've never not listened to my gut. I made sure to plant some spy cameras around the apartment as well. If he showed up – like I felt he would – the cameras would pick him up. They were so well hidden only the one who had placed them could find them.

I borrowed some of Molly's business clothes and using some more hair dye, turned myself blond, and using a very complicated spell, regrew my hair until it passed my waist. I then put it in a hairdo that was very tricky. Something you could never do with a wig. I had taken a movie make-up class for fun a few years ago, I applied those learned skills now. I made my face look as French as possible. My face isn't exactly conducive for it, my being a mix of Polynesian and Scottish. My skin tone wasn't that dark, but it wasn't pale either. My magenta eyes needed to be covered as well. I don't have contact lenses, but I did know a very simple glamour spell that would work.

I mumbled it under my breath, and when I opened my eyes, they were green. Perfect. He'd never recognize me now. I stood up to perform the lock spell. Wait. I lived here year round, he could use anything in the apartment to track me. Either with technology or magic. I grabbed my stuff and went out to the very center of the apartment. Placing candles at the four compass points, drawing a pentagram with salt, and placing a small group of crystals and stones at my feet as offering, I began the spell.

"North to South, East to West

Strength from the best

And the worst of me

Take this offering I give freely

And from now until then

Grant me this protection for when

My enemy should arrive

Nothing within shall leave this homely hive."

There was a hurricane like wind that blew around the apartment. Touching every object within the walls. I opened my eyes when it stopped and saw that the candles were half what they'd been when I'd started, the salt circle was gone, and – oddly- the crystals and stones were still at my feet. Why? There was a knock at the door. I would have to get the answer to my question later. I checked who was at the door. Molly. I went and opened the door. She was alone. I ushered her in. She looked around, and turned back to me.

"Wow," she said with a start, "if I didn't know it was you I would have asked who you were."

"Kinda the point." I moved the remains of the candles back to my room. "Did you get them?" I asked when I came back.

"Yep." She help up a long coat, stiletto heels, and a fancy briefcase. She had gotten them for me so I could keep my cover.

I locked the door as we left, making sure to use some gloves I had as well. The heels were killing me, but I had to look as little like myself as possible. Which meant no limping. I had a pair of Molly's sunglasses on as well. We made our way to the roof to board her friends helicopter. As we were taking the stairs my ears picked up a recorder of some kind. I scanned and found an out of place air conditioning unit. My eyes and ears told me there was a two way receiver inside.

I put on a really thick French accent and asked, "So where did you send her?" wow. That was convincing.

"She's using the subway. She can be very sneaky when she needs to be." Molly said.

Kneeling down under the rotor blades, I said, "But where will she go?"

"That's up to her, she insisted on my not knowing."

We got in the chopper and put the headphones on as requested. Molly sent an emergency text to the cops about the unit and where it was on the building. She had gotten a new phone from her bag to send it, now she sent one to Mr. Hydell. Whether or not he'd respond was debatable.

The chopper ride passed quickly, I didn't notice though. I spent the whole ride wondering how the hell Kepner had found where I lived. It's not exactly rocket science I know, but still. It was disconcerting. The only sanctuary I had now was the aquarium, and that was one I'd have to sever as well.

Chapter 26

Molly's apartment was spacious. It didn't have the white painted walls of ours, but it was relaxing in its simplicity. I sat on the couch and took the heels off. My leg was screaming in pain. I'd almost been forced to leave the brace behind, but thankfully it had fit just fine in the briefcase. I could finally breath normally again. I had been rattling the question of how'd he'd found my home the whole way here. One option was the internet, – obviously – but both Mr. Hydell and the officer in charge of my case had pulled some heavy strings to keep my address hidden.

He probably could have pulled the same shit Victoria pulled in Twilight, hacking into the schools database. My report cards had to go somewhere. He also could have broken into my therapy building, or bribed someone at one place or the other. Whatever he'd done, our apartment was no longer safe. We could either move or go ahead with our travel plans. That would throw him off the scent for at least a few months.

I sat back up as Mr. Hydell came into the apartment. He visibly jumped when he saw me. I couldn't hold back my laugh.

"Holy Shit kiddo, you could go to Hollywood and make a killing." He said with an amused smile.

"Glad I fooled you so well. Maybe Kepner will fall for it." I said.

"There's news on that, one of the cops found a bribe at the school."

"What?!" that came from Molly, who'd only just reentered the room.

"One of the attendance workers was an old friend of his. She didn't believe the murders were done by him – despite the damning evidence – and gave him our address. As well as my name."

Now I was pissed, "So what's the plan now?"

"I pulled some strings and am having your school monitored from Monday to Thursday. Your finals will still be held there, but you should be okay to attend."

"Fine by me. And for the weekend?" I asked.

"For that, I've decided that we'll go to a hotel up in Sacramento, or San Francisco. We'll spend the weekend laying low."

"Which in this case means a super fancy and expensive hotel." Yay. Not!

"One with lots of security too." He added.

Lots of security was fine with me. The more security there was the less likely Kepner would be to show up. There wasn't a guarantee though, but it was better than nothing. I reacquired my heels, got a new phone from Mr. Hydell – a flip phone this time, - and we made our way to the roof. We were going to take the helicopter again. It had been refueled, checked, and was ready to go. We all three hopped in and as the sun began to set, made our way north.

It would be a three hour flight to San Francisco, I thankfully had brought a book, so I'd be preoccupied. I willingly kept the heels on for the whole flight. I heard over the roar of the engine that Mr. Hydell had our building on high alert in case Kepner paid a visit. There weren't enough headsets for everyone, so I went without. Didn't matter much, not with my being able to filter out noises for what I want to hear. I kept my attention split the whole way, I wanted some kind of warning in case the pilot needed to land suddenly.

I went through a mental check list, I had my brace, my sleeping and pain pills, and a book. I'd be covered for tomorrow. I could hardly believe that Saturday was almost over. I did **not** like the feeling of losing a whole day to panic. I had called Ben shortly after Kepner had resurfaced, making sure to use a neighbor's phone. I had asked for an appointment with the boss. Now that Ms. Hamper was going into hiding, any therapy appointments were postponed until further notice.

I made sure to pay attention to our surroundings outside as well. Even with the helicopter going I could hear about seven miles in every direction. So far, there weren't any other flyers in our immediate area. Kepner couldn't fly anything, but that wouldn't stop him from hiring. A picture of him would only prompt bribe or appearance change. He may have shaved his head bald, but he could add some pretty convincing tattoos or even piercings if he was desperate to stay unfound.

The helicopter gave a shudder as we finally reached San Francisco, we landed at the airport and were going to take a limousine to our chosen hotel. We would keep up appearances though, I the friend from France visiting Molly and meeting her boyfriend. I spoke French well enough to make it look convincing, but just don't put me into a conversation with someone who spoke French fluently. I almost collapsed on my way off the chopper, I had just enough warning from my leg to compensate with some of my dragon strength and keep myself standing. I looked around like a tourist, making sure to keep the accent thick. I could tell Mr. Hydell was impressed with my acting skills. Good. I'm glad I could be so convincing.

I removed the heels once we were in the limo, I grabbed an apple from the bowl of fruit available inside, I ate it very quickly. I hadn't realized until then that I hadn't eaten anything at all today. Were my parents here I'd be grounded for a month for that. Once the apple was gone I grabbed a bottle of water and took a pain pill. It would be a seventeen minute drive to the hotel, it should be enough time for the pill to kick in.

I don't know how but I had managed to keep myself from sweating from pain. I lay on one of the limos seats, stretching out my leg. I had a headache coming on now. Great! Just what I needed. I took the time thinking how I would explain to my boss about needing to quit or get leave of absence. Either would be acceptable. I just hoped that once Kepner was dead – by either my hand or the police – I could start working again.

Speaking of the aquarium, I needed to start doing research on schools that offered marine biology. I also needed to think on where I wanted to go to school. Not an easy task, I couldn't even remember what states had schools offering marine biology. I knew I could easily take college classes online, but I didn't want to. I wanted as much field experience as possible. To help strengthen my leg. Obviously states along the coasts would offer it, I just had to specify which ones. I was kinda hoping UCLA offered marine biology. I decided to hit the computer once we arrived and settled in.

I groaned when Mr. Hydell told me we had arrived. I really didn't want to put the heels back on, but I had to. I needed the cover to work for as long as possible. The limo stopped at the front of the hotel.

"Holy shit! Are you kidding!?" I asked when I saw the hotels sign.

"Nope. I got a two bedroom on the top floor." Molly said.

We were in front of the Hotel Via. My sister had talked about this place only a few years ago, she had wanted to do a siblings day here. Me, her, and Reggie. A dream that now could never be. Me and Reggie could do it in her honor one day, but certainly not soon.

Molly checked us in. I didn't have to fake my amazement this time. The hotel was beautiful, and very fancy. I could barely keep my eyes from wandering. I had never been in such a fancy hotel. I heard Molly ask for the Wi-Fi password, I guess she might have brought a laptop. We made our way to the elevators and went up to the top floor. The room she got had a view of South Beach harbor and Mission Bay. Not out to sea but I was happy about it. The room did have two beds, so we all would be comfortable. Mr. Hydell closed the curtains while I sat on one of the beds. My leg was extremely close to collapse. I did not know how I would handle the next day. Molly sat down next to me. She gently patted my knee, and winced. She could feel the heat from my legs pain through my skin tight pants. Well, they were skin tight on the thighs anyway. My thighs are wider than hers, not by much but enough.

"If you can sit up dear, I have something for you." She said.

With a bit of effort, I sat up. She had brought her work bag with her. Before we'd left though she had used one of Mr. Hydell's bug detectors to check both it and her clothes. I also had seen her check them again at her apartment. From inside the bag she pulled out a brand new computer.

"Jack told me you didn't have a computer. So I got you one."

It was an HP Pavilion, in steel grey. A gaming laptop! This one alone could be over $800. I was flabbergasted. The most expensive thing anyone had ever given me was my phone. No scratch that. The sunglasses she had given me, and those had been almost $200.

"Are you trying to spoil me?" I asked with a tearful laugh.

She laughed too, "No. I just have more money than I know what to do with sometimes." She hugged me around my shoulders. "Do you like it?"

"Yes! I love it!" and I did.

"Jack told me you'd had your eyes on this one for a while. I figured you could use one."

"And it will give us a way to stay in touch while travelling." Mr. Hydell said. "I also took the privilege of making sure your phone couldn't be tracked unless you dial 911."

"Cool. I'll have to get some pretty good virus protection on this."

"No need dear. I had the guy at the shop put Norton on it, and it is registered as mine. So you should be able to use it without a problem." Molly said.

"Thank you." I said. To both of them.

Chapter 27

Mr. Hydell got up to order room service. Molly helped me get to the bathroom for a shower. The movie make-up I used was dissolvable and eco-friendly. I could wash it off while also relaxing my leg with the hot water. I gaped at the bathroom. Marble counter and shower walls. I had never used such a beautiful bathroom. Molly had me sit on the toilet and undid my hair.

"How did you get your hair so long so quickly?" she was awed. She must've thought it was a wig.

"Magic is a wonderful thing. It's was a growth spell my mom taught me. Normally I use it for plant growth, but it works on almost anything. Except people and animals of course."

"I would have thought wig, but I know this hairdo wouldn't work with a wig." She said, running her fingers through a tangle.

"Which is why I chose it." I said.

"I'll let you get in. If you need anything, let me know." She exited the bathroom.

I looked down at my leg, I decided to try something. I could partially shift my arms and have my wings out in human form, why not try shifting my legs. I peeled off Molly's pants, and focused my energy on something I hadn't done before. I felt my legs lengthen and contort. When I opened my eyes, my legs were long and scaley. The scar wasn't visible, and my leg took my weight. Awesome! My claws were dull enough that they wouldn't damage the floor in any way, and because of how much time I spent outside in dragon form as a kid, my feet were tough and slip resistant. I wouldn't be falling tonight.

The shower roof was tall enough that the extra inches wouldn't be a hinderance. I finished undressing, wrapped a towel around myself, and got the hot water going. I would make sure to slowly unshift my upper legs so that the hot water could sooth my leg, but I wouldn't go past my knees. Once the water was where I wanted it, I got in. It felt really good. My leg started relaxing and some of the tension started easing from the rest of my body. I could barely feel anything, I hadn't realized how tense I had been. It took about five minutes for everything to finally relax enough that I could move without being stiff. I grabbed the hotel soaps and started to wash.

I got out less than fifteen minutes later. I was feeling much better. I had returned my legs to human for a few minutes. A small test to see if I could stay that way. Nope. My leg started trembling. I quickly shifted my legs back to dragon. That's better and will have to do for now.

Now that my hair was longer I put it up in a towel again, and toweled off this time. I could smell food and I was starving. Molly had put a pair of pajamas on the counter while I'd been washing. I wasn't familiar with them. Must be something she bought. I carefully pulled the drawstring pants on. I managed not to get any claws stuck. The pants were a few inches short of course. I didn't mind, it's not like anyone but them would be seeing me. I pulled the shirt on. I didn't bother putting my bra back on.

I walked out of the bathroom to find that Mr. Hydell had ordered quite a bit of food. I won't go into detail, but it would produce quite a room service bill. Most of it was for me of course. Since I hadn't eaten in almost twenty-four hours. A young dragon shifter going that long without food is **never** a good thing.

It took me almost an hour to eat all the food that Mr. Hydell had ordered for me, but Man was it good! I usually did any cooking so eating pro chef food was out of the norm. It was delicious! I even managed one of the three desserts he'd ordered. Chocolate French Macarons. Ha, ha very funny. I ate like six of them.

They were surprised to see me exit with my legs the way they were, but they didn't comment. I ate at the small table in the room, my leg elevated on a chair. Once I was done though I got into the bed. I let my legs return to normal as I fell into an exhausted sleep.

I didn't dream that night. Thank Gods! I needed some reprieve from pills and tension. I didn't wake up till about 8:30 again. I had fallen asleep at ten. A good ten hours of sleep. I felt much better. I turned to see if they were still in the room. They weren't but there was a note on the night stand. 'Listen for 2, 4, 1.' Knock sequence. Gotcha.

I sat up and touched my leg through the pants. It wasn't warm anymore. Thank Gods. I saw another note on the bathroom door. I didn't get up. I wanted my leg to rest as much as possible. I zoomed in with dragon eyes. 'Change into the robe on the bathroom door and I'll get you some fresh clothes.' Molly's hand writing. I got up carefully. Once I was sure my leg would take my weight, I grabbed both notes and flushed them down the toilet. I also grabbed the robe after I actually used the bathroom. All that food meant a very full bladder. Now all I had to wonder was what was for breakfast. At such a fancy hotel, one never knows.

I was waiting on the bed in the robe when the sequence came. I double checked with my dragon senses. It was them. With breakfast. I opened the door. The room service guy left the food on the table and left. Molly gave me a bag of clothes and picked up the discarded dirty clothes, despite my protests. I could've done it easily.

We spent the rest of the morning just sitting in our room, them watching t.v. and me doing college research on my new laptop. I found plenty of colleges within the U.S. that offered marine biology. I might have to spend the next few years deciding in which state I wanted to attend. There was one school that was out and that was in Chicago. If I want to study sea animals, going to school in Illinois seems redundant to me. It would defeat the purpose.

I was closing an ad for a clothing website when it hit me. I sat up quickly. I had written my address down for Emily and Amber. If they had thrown the sticky note away or lost it, anyone could acquire it. Anyone who knew me well enough would know my hand writing anywhere, especially Kepner. I suddenly felt sick. I could very well have screwed the three of us over.

"You all right kiddo, you look a little green?" Mr. Hydell asked.

I moved my laptop, in case I did need to vomit, "Did the cops ever say who was bribed." I knew one of the attendance administrators was Amber's aunt.

"Someone named Jennifer." I collapsed back on to my pillow with relief. Amber's aunt was named Zelda.

"I gave another student my address. She needed it so she could send me something."

"Does she still have it?" he asked.

"I honestly don't know. I never thought to ask them to destroy it in anyway."

"Who'd you give it too and why?" Molly asked.

I bit my lips in embarrassment, "Emily and Amber designed me a dress as a thank you for solving a dress color coordination issue they were having for prom."

He was dumbfounded, "You don't do dresses. The only time I've ever seen you willingly wear one was for school concerts."

"I know, but what they've designed is something that I would want to wear."

He actually laughed and covered his eyes, "Who are you and what have you done with Maggie?"

That got all three of us laughing, "That must be some dress." Molly commented, still laughing.

I'd show it to them when it arrived. I was still apprehensive about whether or not they still had my address or if out of habit had thrown it away. I'd just have to ask Amber tomorrow in orchestra or lunch. Whichever one I saw her in first. I picked my computer back up and continued my research.

At noon the three of us went out to lunch. Molly had gotten me more comfortable heels so I could keep my French cover a little easier. The skirt she got me would allow me to wear the brace without anyone seeing it. I did my hair back up in the complicated style I'd used yesterday. This would be the first fancy restaurant I had ever visited. I hoped they offered sparkling water, I looked in my twenties with this disguise, and I know that the French really appreciate wine.

Thankfully we didn't go somewhere super fancy. We stopped at Café Okawari, a place not far from the hotel. Japanese food with a California twist. Sounds good. We sat at a table and ordered our drinks, Molly and I got tea while Mr. Hydell got an espresso. I like Matcha tea. Once we were ready for food, I found me and Molly getting the same thing. Their Chicken Katsu plate, while Mr. Hydell chose their Veggie Curry. He must really like spice.

While eating we discussed how we'd travel back down to L.A. Right now the option was rent a car and drive back. I needed to finish school and they both needed to be at work tomorrow. It was either drive or chopper back. One was faster obviously but they left it up to me. To be honest, I was apprehensive about driving back after what happened last week. I had decided though that I didn't like someone else doing the flying. I'm a dragon, I can do my own flying.

Molly and Mr. Hydell left a very good tip when we left. The food had been excellent. I now understood Mr. French's love for it. We took our time going back to the hotel. Mr. Hydell was on his new phone – having smashed his while at the office as he told Molly this morning – looking up car rental places in San Francisco. He found an Enterprise rent-a-car a few blocks inland from the hotel. It was a five and a half hour drive back.

We ended up deciding to stay a few more hours in San Francisco before heading south. Me and Molly gathered our stuff from the hotel while Mr. Hydell took a taxi to pick up a car. Imagine our surprise when he pulled up in a minivan. Hey good cover.

In order for us to spend more time in San Francisco, we went to the movies. Mr. Hydell wanted to see Guardians of the Galaxy Vol. 2, I wanted to see Alien: Covenant. Both had only just come out this month. I like Marvel, but I'd been on pins and needles since Prometheus. Molly ended up being the tie breaker. Both! Okay then, both of them would be about two and a half hours, we'd leave for L.A. by five or five thirty, and get home about ten. Perfect. Purchasing tickets for both, we went inside to find seats. Guardians of the Galaxy was playing first. Time to go watch Gamora kick ass!

Chapter 28

The movies were great! I really enjoyed both, but Alien: Covenant gets my vote. Once again Ridley Scott delivers. Super cool movie. Mr. Hydell couldn't stop laughing about Drax getting dragged behind their ship. And seriously if you haven't seen it shame on you or sorry about the spoiler, but seriously it was hilarious.

We hopped back in the minivan at 5:45, and started south. Molly checked a map and saw that we could stop in Bakersfield for dinner. That would mean dinner at nine, but truthfully I don't think anyone cared.

Once we were out of the city limits Mr. Hydell hit the gas. He was doing that a lot lately. Though his reason this time was different. I had seen him checking restaurants in Bakersfield and I guess one he wanted to visit closed before nine. I was busy checking my new phone for messages when I heard him tell Molly about a place called the Black Bear Diner. I remembered him mentioning it last month, when he'd been about to take over a case from Bakersfield. When his firm had given the job to someone else, he'd been upset. We couldn't exactly travel for fun much.

With his pedal to the metal driving, we made Bakersfield by seven, plenty of time to eat and make L.A. by dark. He found the diner pretty quickly. I got some odd looks, but I didn't care. I was hungry. We all ordered soda when we got our seats. The brace wasn't visible thankfully. I really didn't want to get asked questions. When we got our drinks we were ready to order. I picked one of their steak dinners while both Molly and Mr. Hydell got sandwiches.

Oh my Gods the food was fantastic! My steak was juicy and tender, and Molly's sandwich was so filling she couldn't finish it. I ended up doing that for her. We didn't want to risk leftovers since we still had almost two hours of driving left.

Both of them left 50 dollar tips for the waitress when we left. I would have left one too if I'd had my wallet. I was actually full. We had been tempted to get dessert, but we realized that since tomorrow was Monday, we all needed to get up early and should get home and get to bed before it gets too far past nine.

We left the restaurant at 7:50, if he drove fast we could be home by 9:20. Though knowing Mr. Hydell, he'd either put pedal to the metal again or take his time. He chose pedal to the metal.

We got home at just after nine. Molly decided to stay the night with us again. Mr. Hydell went to interrogate the building manager before we went up. Smart choice. Jim was happy to tell him that as far as he knew, no one had even approached our apartment while we were gone, but he did accompany us up. I smelled him the second I set foot on our floor. My growl was warning enough.

The three adults stopped while I took a deep breath. The scent was almost a day old. That sent a shiver down my spine. He had been in the building while we were at the hotel. I followed the smell. Kepner had been in our apartment. I noticed a small smell. I held up my hand to Mr. Hydell before he placed the key in the lock. I knelt down in front of the door. There was a tiny bit of wax on the keyhole. I grabbed a tissue from my pocket and wiped it off. I'd give that to the cops.

Were I not such a Sherlock Holmes fan, I wouldn't have seen it. I then expanded my other senses, to see if there was a bomb on the other side or a trap of some kind. I can't see through walls, but dragon senses come close. Other than Kepners foul odor, nothing was out of the ordinary.

Mr. Hydell unlocked the door. I immediately went over to one of my hidden cameras. I took out my laptop as Mr. Hydell and Molly told Jim to contact the police officer in charge of my case. I really needed to ask who that was so I could stop just saying officer in charge.

While my computer booted up the video, I turned and asked, "What's the name of the officer in charge of my case?"

"Detective Hopkins, did you set up cameras?" he asked.

"Yep, just before we left. I also performed a lock spell on the apartment."

"A lock spell?" he asked.

"To make sure nothing left the apartment, he could easily use an item from here to track me. Either with tech or magic."

The cameras had been a good idea. Every one showed footage of him in our home. Looking around, touching something, or even trying to destroy something. Damn, my lock spell must have worked really well. The camera in my room showed him sitting on my bed and smelling my pillow. Eww. That bedding was either going to be washed or burned. In Mr. Hydell's room, he'd tried to destroy a picture of me and Mr. Hydell from February, when he'd taken me to the Daytona 500 in Florida. Best weekend ever! Needless to say he had been literally unable to even pick the photo up off the dresser, and had resorted to punching the picture. Childish much.

The rest of the footage showed him trying to remove various objects from the apartment. To no avail. When I cast a spell I mean business. Every single thing he touched had stayed put.

An officer finally arrived to collect the footage. He had three other cops with him, to make sure the evidence made it without trouble. He was impressed by what I'd gathered. He was skeptical about the wax until I told him where I found it. He left after only a few minutes. Mr. Hydell put the security system on high, Jim did the same with the whole building, and we all went to bed.

I changed into really comfy pajamas after checking that all my homework was where I'd left it. It was, thank gods. I rubbed some poultice on my leg, wrapped it in gauze, and laid down. I also checked my arms. I hadn't unwrapped them since Friday. I was getting more movement back in my left arm finally. I decided to put one of my long sleeve shirts on. I had to change out of what I had picked but I really did not want the stitches to snag on anything. When all that was done I pretty much fell on my bed. I had taken the time to change the sheets. I could smell him on the other ones. I'd wash them first and if his scent was still there I'd burn them. I was truly exhausted now. I pulled the blanket up to my chin. Once again putting my music on to drown out the two adults in their room.

Chapter 29

I woke up before my alarm even went off. I hadn't dreamt at all last night, which was a relief. Until I realized why. My last thought before waking was of another nightmare, one I hadn't had in months. One that I did **not** care to see again. I sat up. Great. My leg was stiff. The brace wouldn't do it today. It was going to have to be a wheelchair day. I hate wheelchair days. So many people give my sympathetic looks I get mad.

I grabbed a pair of crutches out from under my bed. I got up slowly, I now had yet another reason to despise heels. Concerts didn't count because the heels I wore for those was only half an inch. Manageable with a bum leg. I made my way to the bathroom, this was not a favorite thing of mine to do with a stiff leg.

Molly was up as well. She was making pancakes. Cinnamon and chocolate chip pancakes. Yum! I went back to my room to get dressed. I put on my jeans carefully. I was wincing by the time I was done. I had trouble getting my breath back. I'd need a pain pill after breakfast, I hate doing that so soon in the day. At least my shirt and hoodie weren't such a pain. Double entendre intended.

I sat at the bar at first, but changed my mind with how much it hurt my leg. I went into the living room after that. I rarely ever eat on the couch. Given the circumstances though. Molly placed three pancakes on a plate for me. I managed to add the butter and syrup myself. I sat back into the couch to eat. Mr. Hydell came out at a quarter to seven. The first thing he noticed was the crutches. He gave a heavy sigh.

"I'll call the school to have a chair ready." He said.

"Thanks." I said. At least it was finals week. I had two days of recovering before gym finals. That was going to be interesting.

Molly gave me a ride to school. We all three left at the same time. Mr. Hydell also reminded me about my doctor's appointment at three. I'd be done with orchestra finals so no worries. Molly drove carefully but with enough speed that she made good time. I had time to think about my finals on the drive. I honestly wouldn't be surprised if the school pulled some scheduling strings for my benefit. They'd done it before. I should have asked Mr. Hydell before we'd left. Oh well.

My hunch had been right. Mr. Kray was waiting with the wheelchair when Molly pulled up. What was the school's plan. I got out slowly. Molly had me leave the crutches in the car. She'd pick me up later. I grabbed my bag and put it in my lap. She pulled out and headed to work. I turned myself around to ask Mr. Kray my question.

"I take it the schedule's been changed?"

"Yep. An e-mail was sent to all parents and guardians that the finals schedule was changing. All odd periods are being done today. So gym first." Crap.

He opened the door and let me through, "I've modified the rig so you don't have to pull yourself up very far for the arm exercises. You can do the full amount if you want but you don't have to."

He wasn't kidding, "What about the leg exercises?" I asked.

"Your exempt, I didn't want to try anything." Fair enough, though I didn't think many students were going to be happy. "I know how high you can jump and how fast you can run anyway."

"True." He and everyone in class had seen me play basketball and soccer.

"Also 'cause of the chair you'll be allowed to leave a little sooner than normal."

"So only today and Wednesday have changed?" I asked.

"Yep. All even periods are still tomorrow, and Wednesday is now the last day." He confirmed.

I positioned myself beneath the modified rig. I could do this distance easily. It only made sense to have me go first for chin and pull ups. The sit and push-ups counted as leg exercises so none of those for me.

Once class started Mr. Kray found a job for me when I'd finished the arm exercises. Helping him time the other students. He made the test a competition. To try and fully gauge their abilities. The last test was the long dash. It was Mark vs. Kim. Our two most competitive class mates.

"GO!" Mr. Kray shouted. They shot past. I had the stop watch for Mark.

I hit the stop button, when I saw what it said, exclaimed, "Holy Shit Mark!" that surprised everyone.

"What was my time?" He asked from a sitting position.

"3.6 seconds." I said.

"For the thirty meter dash!?" He asked. He couldn't believe it.

I nodded, "You should try out for the track team next year."

Mr. Kray checked the stopwatch, "Damn. She's right. On both."

The average male covers a thirty meter sprint in almost five second. He could do the Olympics someday if he wanted to. I checked the time and saw that it was time for me to head out. I told Mr. Kray and he saw me out. He stayed near the door while I made my way to woodshop. I had my box in my bag. It was empty of its precious contents. Though the velvet covered insert was still there. I also had the papers that Mr. Hydell had signed.

I wheeled into shop. Ian was already there. He was admiring my in class project. I had managed to finish it on Thursday. His project was on the table in front of him. It was a beautifully done piece. He'd get a good grade. I didn't see his at home project though. Must be in his backpack.

I sat myself at the table behind him. I pulled my project out. I had it wrapped in a kitchen towel to protect it from abrasion with other things in my backpack. I could feel the tension coming from Ian. I wanted to turn and say something, but what does one say when things are the way they are at this time? Finally I heard him turn to say something….then the bell rang, and Mr. Graham came in with the written part of the final. Whatever Ian needed to say would have to wait.

The final covered the basics. Identification of parts and procedures, safety precautions, and of course, types of wood. I was done by the hour mark. That left half an hour of free time. I leaned back in my chair, before handing my final to Mr. Graham.

"At home papers please." He said.

I handed those to him, "Should I wait to show it?" he nodded.

Ian placed his test on Mr. Graham's desk next. Now it was the waiting game. I was grabbing my book when Ian tapped me on the shoulder. He indicated the other side of the classroom. By the equipment, where we could talk and not disturb the rest of the testers. I wheeled over while he grabbed a chair.

"Why are we talking now?" I asked when we were both seated again.

"I asked Mr. Graham. He said we could so long as it was over here."

"I'm guessing this is about my leaving?"

His shoulders tensed, "Yeah." He wouldn't meet my eyes.

"What did the others have to say?" I asked, somewhat dreading the answer.

"They all think it's a good idea. Good enough in fact that…" he stopped.

"That they feel it's best for all of us to vanish." I finished for him.

He hung his head, he was crying, "Yeah."

"Because you all heard about his double appearance?" I asked. He just nodded.

"So what are your parents planning?"

"Homeschooling. From Washington. And then moving back down here once it's safe."

What? "Is that what the others are doing too?" I could **not** believe it.

"Yeah. All the parents think it's best. I think It's terrible."

"Ian, it's not safe for any of you." I whispered somewhat harshly.

"I know that," he whispered equally harshly, "but I love you like family and I worry about what might happen to you."

He hung his head again, "That bastard has already taken so much from you, it's unfair that he should by extension take us too."

"It's better than being dead. I can handle move, not death." There were tears in my eyes now.

"That doesn't make it any more right."

"I know that, but I need to know you are all safe. Ms. Hamper and her family already are. If vanishing is the best solution then so be it."

He was going to argue, time to pull out the big guns, "The needs of the many, outweigh the needs of the one."

He chuckled sadly, "Leave it to you to quote Spock and show how right you are." He leaned back and after a few minutes finally came to a decision.

"Alright. I'll go along with the plan willingly. On one condition." He said.

"Okay, what?" He got up and went back to the tables. The others were finished, and Mr. Graham started us on showing our out of school projects. Ian asked to go last. Mr. Graham was fine with that. The other boys had some really good stuff. Not all of them were as detailed as others but that was fine. Finally Mr. Graham called on me. I unwrapped my box. There was a chorus of whoa's from the class room.

Mr. Graham came over to inspect it. He was looking for a purchase tag. *You're not gonna find one.* I thought to myself. He opened it and was struck dumb. He hadn't expected me to do a box insert. He lifted out the piece and examined the inside. We all could see that he was impressed.

"This is damn good Mag. A+." Yes! "Alright Ian let's see yours."

Ian went over to his backpack, he pulled out a shoebox, "I don't regret what it implies sir."

That raised a few eyebrows, Mr. Graham opened the shoebox, "I see. Morbid, but the detail is exquisite." He pulled a statuette out of the box. My heart warmed in a sisterly way.

The statuette depicted Kepner with a Scottish claymore through his heart, and coming out his back. Mr. Graham did the same with his project, examining it bit by bit. He even nailed the scar Kepner had received from the explosion. I started to get teary eyed. My friends were more like family, the fact that they all wanted a piece of Kepner for his crimes was heartwarming.

Mr. Graham chuckled, "I'll have to take off a few points for what it depicts but A+ as well."

He handed it back, "Thanks."

"One can dream." I said looking at the statuette.

"Yeah," he held it out, "the one condition is that you accept this as a gift."

I took it, "I accept." I held the statuette, thinking that the Scottish claymore through the heart was a lovely thought, but not what I had in mind for Kepner.

Everyone returned to their seats for the rest of class. I had about five minutes before I had to leave. I rewrapped my box, and after getting the shoebox from Ian, put the statuette in my bag as well. I'd keep them both with me for the rest of the day. I didn't trust my locker at this time.

At five till I headed to the cafeteria. I wasn't feeling hungry, but I knew I had to eat. I was more anxious about whether or not I could talk to either Emily or Amber about my address. Since I was in a chair, I got let through the easy door. I grabbed my food and parked at a table. Neither Emily or Amber showed, must be having a meeting or something. Prom had passed, so probably one of their other extracurricular activities. Someone had left a school paper on my table. I saw my name on the front page. Wearily I picked it up. Someone had nominated me as prom queen? Eww. No thank you. That was a waste of someone's time. Most kids at school already knew how I felt about school dances, why bother nominating me.

Once I was done eating I went to history. That passed without incident. Finally I had to get some help getting to orchestra. There was a small staircase that led to the room after going down the hall from the elevator. One of the bass players ended up carrying the chair down while I hobbled down holding the hand rail. Going up the stairs was gonna be fun. Amber was already seated in her section. I decided to get the question off my mind before class began.

"Hey Amber, the piece of paper with my address on it, do you still have it?"

"No, I kept it in my bra until I got home, then once I had it memorized I burned it." She said.

I visibly sighed with relief, "Thank you." I said.

"I heard about Kepner popping back up, I didn't want to take chances. Especially not since my aunt told me about her co-worker spilling the beans to him."

"You have no idea how much I appreciate that." I said with a grateful smile.

"Your welcome." She said with a bigger smile.

Orchestra passed quickly after that. The final was straight forward enough. Our teacher even let us watch a movie for the rest of class. She had the same bass player help me out of the classroom when it was time for me to leave for my appointment. Amber caught up with me at the front doors. Before going outside she turned to say something.

"I have a dentist appointment, but I wanted to explain why you were nominated for prom queen."

"Okay." The could be interesting.

"One of the guys on the committee nominated you because he felt that it might be a good way to apologize for how some people have treated you since the murders."

"I'm guessing that didn't get far."

"Not really. Most of us felt that the only apology that you'd accept would be from the two of them. If at all."

"One more than the other." I said.

She nodded, "I said no because I knew you weren't even gonna be there and I felt making you prom queen would just create more potential victims."

I nodded at her thinking, "Safe thought."

"Yeah. He's already proven what he's willing to do. Making you prom queen would have just given him more targets. Not make you feel somewhat better."

"I do appreciate the thought, but you were right to say 'no.'"

"I hope your new school is less of a shit show."

I laughed, "How many people actually know about that?"

She caught my concern, "Only your friends. I accidently overheard them talking about it."

"Can I ask it of you not to spread that around?"

"No problem on that one. The secret is safe." She said.

"Thank you." I saw Molly pull up.

"Your welcome."

Her parent hadn't shown yet so she stayed inside. I wheeled out to the car and – after some difficulty – got in. Time to go see my regular doctor. Thinking on it, I wondered if the new school had an onsite doctor or if students went to the mainland for it. I only said mainland as a thought. Most shifter schools that I'd heard of were on islands. Remote and naturally well protected. It only made sense that my new school would be on an island.

Mr. Hydell was waiting at the office for us. Molly had to get back to work so she left after I disembarked. Mr. Hydell and I went up and checked in. I liked my doctor. She was a shifter as well, thought I never did ask what kind. A nurse called us back. With some help I got weighted. I had lost ten pounds. She wouldn't be happy about that. I had been steadily losing weight. It was attributed to grief and survivors guilt, but something I still needed to turn around.

Dr. Jones finally came in. I was right, she wasn't happy about the weight loss. She was even less happy about my most recent collapse. We left with me being given a strict diet chart and a new exercise plan. Plus a date to shift again. Two more weeks at least. Great. I hate waiting.

I was quite on our drive home. I really hadn't wanted such a long no-shifting sentence. It was bad enough being unable to shift until only a month ago. When my leg was healed enough to take it. My shifting the first night with Mr. Hydell didn't count. I envied my brother now. He could shift fine, but me no. No shifting of any kind until June was half over. I turned the radio on. Trying to undo my frustration a bit by listening to more of Halestorm. I always listen to rock or metal music when I'm mad. It just seems to fit for me. I made sure the volume wasn't too loud. I really didn't want to distract Mr. Hydell from his driving by acting like a spoiled rotten brat.

Once back at home. I retreated to my room. I wanted privacy for a few minutes. My previous sheets were folded on the bed. I picked them up and took a deep breath. Not a single whiff of Kepner. Thank Gods. The last thing I wanted was to wake up smelling him.

Dr. Jones had refilled my pain pills. Even though I had said I didn't need it done. She had insisted. Saying it might come in handy with my arms. The good news was that I could sleep without covering them now. The ends had been trimmed so that they were less likely to get caught on anything. I turned my mp3 speaker on and started up Halestorm again. I tried to relax as much as was possible.

I stayed in my room until Mr. Hydell called for dinner. Molly had brought home KFC. Fine by me. I like fried chicken as much as most Texan girls. We told her the results of my appointment. She did say that the time limit was a little excessive, but probably better than what some would get. It didn't really make me feel better though. I had hoped it might, but I had already spent so much healing time trapped in my own body, the thought of more healing time just made me mad.

She treated me to dessert, trying to help me cheer up. Mr. Hydell didn't like cheesecake, he thought it was too sweet. I made one a few months ago that was toned down, he liked that one. Molly bought blueberry cheesecake. She paired it with hot fudge sauce, to tone down some of the inherent sweetness. It tasted pretty good.

I went to bed with trepidation. I really didn't want to take a sleeping pill. I decided I'd keep a pill and glass of water near my bed. If I needed to wake and take it, so be it. I changed into my pjs and turned my music on. Maybe that will help.

Chapter 30

I slept well. Thankfully. The pill had been unnecessary. I was really happy about that. I tested my leg on the way to the bathroom. I was limping a little. No wheelchair, but the brace would be a smart idea. I decided to wear a short sleeved shirt, the hoodie still wouldn't come off, but I saw from my clock that it was gonna be warm today. Another day of people wondering how I can handle a hoodie on such a day.

My shirt depicted the Ninja Turtles. It was one of my favorites, and one of the few of my t-shirts that had survived the explosion. I found that kinda ironic in a funny way. I put the brace on after checking it over for wear and tear. Looked good. It was kinda stiff though. I'd have to get it checked for rust.

Molly made French toast for breakfast. Yum! I ate a whole three pieces. After a glass of milk and orange juice I was ready to go. Mr. Hydell had the day off, so he gave me a ride to school. Second day of finals, time to finish the even classes. I thought on how tomorrow would have been gym final. My school did it so that all kids with gym or swim class would be in that part of the building all day. Except for lunch that is. I didn't fully get it though. This is L.A., why do it that way if only two grades have physical related classes. A small town high school I could understand. Oh well. Not something for me to bother with. I was just glad the year was almost over.

I got out slowly. My leg was already complaining. I took a deep breath and walked inside. I would make the end of the day on my feet. I got in the elevator and went up to math. Once again holding the door for Mary. She looked a little flustered but brightened as I did her a kindness. I would miss her when I started my new school.

My math teacher had a funny lookin' box at the door. It didn't take me long to figure out what it was. A cell phone box. So no cheating or slacking.

I went to put my phone in, "No. You have a medical problem. You keep yours. Plus I know you won't touch it." He said.

I nodded and went to my seat. After the bell rang some kids tried to get away with sneaking their phones in, but Mr. Anderson out smarted them. He had e-mailed every student's parents and asked if they had left home with their phone. He'd gotten a lot of affirmative responses. So the same three kids and two others had to give up their phones. Mr. Anderson pulled another one on them. All phones were sent to the office. And I mean all.

Every single cell phone but mine and a few others were sent to the office, and there they would stay until the end of the day.

English went well. For me anyway. Two kids were caught cheating and were automatically failed in their English final. Both sets of parents were e-mailed as well. Lunch went by without incident, then it was up to chemistry. I froze at the door. Something wasn't right here.

"Everything alright Miss Sharp?" Mrs. Banks asked coming up behind me.

"No. Something is off in here."

She knew I meant it, "I'll get security." She moved off to do so. Telling other children coming to chemistry to stay out of the room.

A few tried to laugh her off until they saw me standing stock still like a dog on alert. I stayed right there until she returned with the campus security guards. I moved back to let them in. They went in cautiously. Not taking any chances of danger. The other students jumped when the bell rang. I was too busy to notice, my focus was on trying to figure out why this room felt wrong.

It wasn't until I turned my focus to my sense of smell and sneezed, that we all realized the smell of rotten something. Covering my nose I pointed at Mrs. Banks' office. The security guys walked slowly in that direction. Upon opening the door, the smell became over powering and several kids began to gag and cough. Two threw up right there. The security guys decided to call an evacuation.

Mr. Hydell arrived about ten minutes after the evac had been called. The latest details said that someone had left a dead and mutilated cat in Mrs. Banks' office. School was called shortly after. Any and all last even period finals would be finished tomorrow. I couldn't get the smell of long dead cat out of my nose. The most disturbing fact was that no one knew who had left it.

I had my suspicions of course, but they weren't all that convincing. Something like this was beneath Kepner, and nowhere near the point of him trying to get to me. It's not like Mrs. Banks and I are friends, she's just my chemistry teacher. So why would he do something like that? The answer was simple, he wouldn't. It had nothing to do with me and those close to me. Priscilla and her friends could be likely suspects, but this didn't feel like them.

Two of her friends were really squeamish when it came to things that were dead. Plus all three of them had cats. Priscilla was the only one who didn't, and she had been nagging her parents about it. So that put the four of them out. They wouldn't stoop so low as to murder a cat and mutilate it's body just to make a point. I couldn't really think of anyone else at school who would be capable of such an atrocity. Or if not someone at school, who?

Mr. Hydell was extra cautious when we got home. It felt weird to be home so soon. And I mean that, I hadn't had a sick day in years. I started pacing, trying to Sherlock Holmes the incident. If it wasn't anyone at school, then what purpose would the cat serve. Getting everyone out of the school was one thing, but there were other ways to do that. No, someone wanted the school to be evacuated. I started racking my brain for a likely scenario. The phones? No, too much trouble. A student? Maybe, but too many variables. A prank? Again maybe, but why? To scare people, prove a point, mess with everyone? Okay so maybe not a prank.

I thought about an episode of Bones. One where a woman had been murdered merely because the bad guy needed her apartment for a sniper shot. That didn't fit either, so I eliminated it. I still didn't believe it was for one particular student, the evac would make it impossible to follow or grab that student, especially with the teachers doing head counts. What then!?

Then I had a thought, these were all the obvious choices to get people out. What about a less likely option. Like trying to test the schools response time to an incident. I immediately thought of Benghazi, the kids using the bottle rockets to test the soldier's response time. But again, why? Maybe to get something from the school. Then it hit me, several of Kepner's things had been left at the school after the murders and never confiscated by the authorities. Rumors said that some of the things he left behind were possibly dangerous.

I immediately told Mr. Hydell about my suspicions. He then called the cops that had showed up at school. The chemistry room had been sealed off, but the physics room was connected to it by a closet that met in the teacher's offices. It would also be several minutes before any news came back.

"What made you think about his belongings?" Mr. Hydell asked a short while later.

"'When you have eliminated the impossible, whatever remains, however improbable must be the truth.'" I said, using one of Sherlock's most memorable quotes. Well memorable for me anyway.

"Evacuating the school would mean absolutely no one would be inside." He said with realization.

"Leaving the building perfectly empty. A perfect opportunity to get in and retrieve them."

"He wouldn't be able to do it himself, he'd have to get someone else to do it."

"Yes he would." I said.

I sat down on the couch. Kepner obviously had an accomplice. But who and why would anyone help him? The whole city knew who he was and what he was wanted for. No one would willingly help him. I leaned back. Maybe someone who owed him a favor, someone who thought him innocent of his crimes. I hope not on that one. It just didn't make any sense.

I decided not to dwell on it. As far as I knew the schools security cameras had still been operating. Whomever had got in would be on tape. A few minutes later we both got an answer. Kepner's things were indeed gone, and the perp was caught on camera. Whether or not they were responsible for the cat was yet to be determined.

Any further information would have to wait. Now it was just a waiting game on finishing school. Mr. Hydell got an e-mail just before dinner about a small adjustment to tomorrow's schedule. Sixth period would be extended so that all finals could be finished without a problem. So seventh period would only last half an hour or so. None of the students or staff complained. It was better than some results. None of the students even bothered to complain about their phones still being at school.

The day passed by a lot quicker than usual after that. Mr. Hydell and I just ate leftovers for dinner and watched a little t.v. before going to bed. This time I did take a pill. I'd rather not have nightmares involving mutilation. I didn't play any music that night. I wanted nothing impeding my hearing. Just in case something unexpected happened.

Chapter 31

Nothing unexpected occurred that night. What happened that morning was a little bit of a surprise though. Mr. Hydell was making breakfast. He didn't usually do that. Most mornings he either just had coffee or coffee and toast. This was the first time I'd ever seen him do bacon and eggs.

My leg was feeling better, but for safety reasons I was gonna wear the brace again. I sat at the bar with a glass of milk while Mr. Hydell finished the bacon. He put a plate in front of me and we both dug in with gusto. He did bacon and eggs well it turned out. It also turned out that there was news from the school.

"The police found that guys finger prints all over the office and his DNA on the cat's body." Mr. Hydell informed me.

"Well that guy was sloppy."

"Yep," he said, "not enough though. Kepner's things weren't found on him or at his apartment."

Damn, "Why'd he do it though, was he that stupid?"

He shrugged, "Don't know yet. Maybe they'll have that answer by the end of the day."

I hoped so.

He gave me a ride again. He wasn't comfortable letting me out of his sight just yet. He only left after I was actually inside the school. I was a little nervous today. And maybe a little apprehensive. This would be the last time I would walk through these hallways. I would miss this school. This was where both of my siblings had graduated, and where I was always supposed to graduate from. It felt a little like betrayal to my siblings and friends that I wouldn't finish here. Maybe if Kepner died before my senior year, I could start up here again and finish how I'd wanted. With my friends, following in my siblings footsteps. I shook my head. That likelihood of that happening was remote at best. Kepner had only just recently proved how wily and sneaky he was. I mean, he'd out run the authorities twice in the last two weeks. Not a good ratio to try and top. Especially when you add how easily he got away from the authorities after he killed my family.

I put thoughts of Kepner out of my mind, I needed to focus on my last day of school. I wasn't exactly looking forward to chemistry. I might still smell the cat over whatever cleaner they would've used. Trust me, the smell of something dead mixed with Lysol is **not** pleasant.

I was saved thankfully. Mrs. Banks had the door closed and had taped plastic around the door. There would be no smell getting through that. I nodded at her with thanks. She returned it.

The chemistry final went by without a hitch. Everyone was finished before the modified bell. Other than the final test, the other classes had been enjoyable. Even gym. Orchestra finishing short was weird though. None of us minded, but the feeling of unfinished was there for everyone.

I decided to fly home. I had returned the keys to the office and made my way to the roof for the final time. Another thunder storm was coming in. I breathed in the smell of rain mixed with sea water. Oh boy. That meant the storm was coming in from sea. Not always good. I saw several kids start running. They smelled it too. This one was gonna be bad. I didn't take the chance of full change. I'm lighter and more maneuverable as a human.

Jumping as best I could, I started flying home. The wind felt nice. I kept as low as possible. The last thing I wanted was to get struck by lightning. I could smell ozone. There would definitely be lightning later. My trepidation grew as I got closer to our building. The clouds were much darker and very thick. My sister would have loved this. She would have grabbed her camera and started snapping pics like no tomorrow. Any aspiring meteorologist would definitely love this.

As I landed and made my way inside, taking the stairs down, I realized that that was the most I had thought about my sister's future career choice in a while. I chuckled a little. Our parents had been surprised that all three of us had chosen scientific futures. The astronomer, the meteorologist, and the marine biologist. Two focused on the sky and one on the sea. It was a little ironic. It only showed just how much of an oddball I was compared to other dragon shifters.

I felt tears threatening. I pulled myself together. I needed all senses open once I got to my floor. I opened the door to the floor above mine, and walked to the elevator. I pressed my floor and rode down. I only did this because my leg was starting to throb. Although the sudden change wouldn't be anticipated, so that was good.

I discreetly took a breath as the doors opened. Nothing out of the ordinary. So far so good. Our apartment door was ajar. I stopped. I didn't like that. I turned my hearing up. Mr. Hydell was inside, and he was laughing. Okay, that's a good sign. I listened a little more though. His laugh sounded natural, not like it was from a recording.

I knocked on the door. There was a second scent, one I recognized. I peeked through just as Mr. French exited Mr. Hydell's room behind Molly. So that was the other scent. Okay, so panic unneeded. I indicated the door.

"Sorry about that dear, that's my fault." Molly said, coming over to close it, "I was in a slight hurry when I heard Mr. French was in here. I wanted to meet him, and I guess I didn't get the door closed all the way."

"It's okay. A little practice for me for later." I said jokingly.

She chuckled, "I still apologize."

"As do I," said Mr. French, "I should have called first, but I was in the neighborhood and decided to stop by to check on you."

"Well you probably should either make plans to stay the night or make a run for it." I said.

"Why?" Mr. Hydell asked, just as a room shaking blast of thunder rocked the building.

"That's why." I said.

Everyone looked out the window. The rain was so thick you couldn't see the building across the street. The power went out a few seconds later. I immediately put my dragon eyes on. Mr. French put his lion eyes on as well. We could see in the dark. Molly and Mr. Hydell not so much.

"Wait here, I'll get some candles." I had spare, unmagic related ones in my room. As well as some lanterns and flashlights.

Mr. French followed me in and back with the candles. We set them up around the bar and from there lit them and then set about distributing more around the apartment with flashlights. A few minutes later, the place was better lit. We could all see just fine now. Mr. French came over to me when I took a seat on the couch.

"How'd you know the storm was going to be so bad?" He asked with a small smile.

"My sister wanted to be a meteorologist. She would go on and on for hours about the weather." I dropped my head, "She would have loved this storm." I wiped a tear away.

Mr. French grabbed my hand, stopping me, "It's okay to cry. You obviously miss them very much."

"I hate showing weakness." I said, not bothering to reclaim my hand.

"It's only natural."

"Showing weakness or hating it?" I said with a wistful smile.

He chuckled, "Both I suppose." He sat down next to me. "I encourage my students to put aside normal shifter reactions to weakness. It can only cause trouble."

"Which no one causes, I'm guessing."

"Sometimes. There are a few times when students lose control and revert to the normal reactions. It's to be expected. You can't just get rid of thousands of years of instinct overnight." He said.

I nodded, "Speaking of overnight, I think for safety sake, it would be better for you to use the guest room. If the powers out it could be dangerous driving. Even for a cave lion shifter."

He chuckled again, "I think your right." There was a flash of lightning. Anyone not prepared would be temporarily blinded.

"I'll go discuss it with your guardian." He got up and walked back to the kitchen.

I heard the two of them discussing it. I didn't listen in though. I was trying not to cry my eyes out. Every single blast of thunder and flash of lightning was reminding me of my sister. I remembered back to one incident when I was four and Amanda was seven. Reggie had celebrated his eleventh birthday during a thunderstorm much like this one. Not even one third of the way through the storm, Amanda had grabbed her raincoat, boots, a waterproof camera, snuck to the garage and biked to the edge of town. This was before we moved out of Texas.

Mom and dad had noticed pretty quickly that she was gone. Me and Reggie had just laugh about how long it took though. Amanda arrived back about twenty minutes after mom and dad had noticed. She was so excited about her pictures and data that she hadn't even noticed mom and dad trying to yell at her for going out in such a storm. A tornado had even been produced a few miles away. All she could focus on was showing her siblings her pics, and explaining the data she'd gathered. Several of her photos had survived the explosion. She'd hung them in her room. Reggie hadn't even minded that she'd kinda took over his birthday party after that. We both thought it was really cool that she'd done something like that.

Her fearlessness and tenacity were part of how she got a full scholarship to M.I.T. for meteorology. I remembered back to two days before her high school graduation. The absolute astonishment and overwhelming joy on her face, when the acceptance papers had shown up in the mail. She had practically fainted in nervousness before she'd even opened the packet. Our parents had been thrilled, they never expected M.I.T. to accept her. We had celebrated her success that night. And she even got a mention at her graduation. I saw several kids look surprised, they were the ones who thought of her as a screwup. Not my sister. If she wants to go to one of the best colleges in the world, then she'll do it.

With another flash of lightning, I couldn't take it anymore. I got up and ran to my room, slamming the door shut in my wake. I turned my music up loud and launching myself on my bed, balled my eyes out onto my pillow. Amanda had been so ready to take on the world to accomplish her dream. Now she never would, the world was a lesser place without her in my opinion. Yeah she'd made mistakes, we all do that, but she would have made an excellent scientist.

I stayed in my room for I don't know how long. I finally stopped crying, but still didn't feel like I had cried my last. My nose felt puffy from crying. I grabbed a tissue from my backpack and blew my nose. I only then realized that I had never removed the two wood items from it. I got up and taking by backpack over to my desk, extracted my box, and the shoebox.

I replaced my book, watch, and dagger in the box, then opening the shoebox, extracted the statuette from it. The thing had shifted slightly and was wedged inside. I just tore the box a little to get it out. At some point I would find another box to transport it in. I placed the statuette on my desk. I turned it a few times like anyone would, to see which angle it looked best at. Finally I just turned it, so it was parallel with the wall. A nice view of the sword going through him.

I went back to lie on my bed. I didn't want any company right then. Showing weakness around my parents and siblings was one thing. My running to my room was the most either Mr. Hydell or Molly had seen from me. I had trouble controlling it around Ms. Hamper, but then again she was my therapist. I'm supposed to show weakness. That didn't make it any more comforting for me.

I ended up falling asleep shortly afterwards. I don't know how long I slept, but at one point I woke to go to the bathroom, and realized that the brace was still on. With clumsy fingers I removed it, then made my way to the bathroom. Once finished washing my hands, my stomach growled. Great.

I opened the door and went to the kitchen. Mr. French was there, sitting at the bar. That was a surprise. I know he and Mr. Hydell had agreed that him staying the night was the safer option, but I hadn't expected him to be up.

"Couldn't sleep?" he asked as I made my way into the kitchen.

"No. I just woke up." I said, grabbing gyoza leftovers. "You?"

"No. I've been up for the last hour."

I only then noticed the time, "2 a.m. Mr. Hydell won't be happy with me."

"I've wanted to ask why you still call him Mr. Hydell?"

"Because he never said to call him anything else." I said with a smile.

He laughed, "Maybe you should remedy that."

"Maybe. It's up to him really."

"Are you feeling better?" he asked, giving me a fatherly look.

I sighed, "No. I feel like someone has torn open my chest and undone some of the healing I've only just managed to gain." I said, putting the gyoza and sauce in the microwave.

"Have you told this to anyone? Ms. Hamper?"

"No. I'm too used to talking to my siblings about such feelings and Ms. Hamper has gone into hiding, so can't talk to her."

"Why just your siblings?" he asked.

I shrugged, "They wouldn't try to fix it. They would just hug me and tell me that I'm stronger than either of them and that if anyone could come back from rock bottom ready to conquer a kingdom, it would be me."

He chuckled, "Interesting terminology."

"Yeah," I sat down with my plate, "all three of us were like that. We were closer than most siblings our various ages."

"How much distance?"

"Three years apiece. Reggie is 22, and Amanda was 19."

"I see why you say closer than most. Some six year old siblings won't react well to someone new." He said.

"Yep. Reggie was the exception. He was super excited to have another sister." I popped a gyoza in my mouth.

"I had a sister. She was seven years older than me." he paused, and laughed, "My parents told me that the day they brought me home, she threw a temper tantrum 'cause she thought our mother was just getting fat." I laughed with him, "It took her several years to finally accept that I wasn't going anywhere except maybe where she was going. I annoyed her to no end on those occasions."

"Is she still around?" I asked tentatively.

"No. She died a few centuries ago. Protecting her daughter."

"I'm sorry." I said.

"Thank you." He looked at me, "You remind me of her a great deal."

"How so?"

"She was stubborn about showing weakness to others too." I chuckled. "But she also had a strength about her, one that you wouldn't find in anyone who hadn't suffered extreme loss."

I pushed my now empty plate away, "I don't know if I'd call it strength."

"It might not seem like it at first, but eventually, it will."

"I just feel so lost right now. It's one reason why Ms. Hamper mentioned me going to Scotland this summer."

"Is Scotland important to you?"

"Yes," I paused, "most of my ancestry comes from there, and I've been in love with it for as long as I can remember.

"Most of your ancestry?"

"My paternal grandmother was Hawaiian. One of the last members of the pacific islanders dragon clans, or the mo'o as they are called. Her mate was from Scotland. They both died when my dad was in high school. Back in the eighties. Over 700 years old."

"And your maternal grandmother?" he asked.

"Both her and grandpa were from Scotland. He was a metal worker, and she was a healer."

"Which is where your mother got her wiccan abilities."

"Yep, and where me and my siblings got it too."

He seemed amazed, "You inherited magic? Other than what comes with being a shifter?"

I nodded, "I've actually performed several successful spells since I was small. I even did two on my box."

He still looked amazed, "May I see?"

I got up and went to retrieve my Sherlock box. I came back out with it and my Kepner statuette. I wanted to perform a protection spell on that too. Knowing Kepner, if he ever saw it he would try to destroy it. I was not gonna let that happen. Ian had worked hard on it. I got out some matches and two bowls. Filling one with water, I came back over to the island. I set everything down and began my demonstration. I held the box and lit a match.

"Amazing." He said as I moved the match down the side. I blew it out, my spell had worked so well that the smoke never touched it either.

"Watch this." I poured the water out over the box into the other bowl.

"You truly are amazing." Once again the water reacted as if silicon was involved.

"Thank you." I put the box down.

"What is this?" he asked picking up the statuette.

"A classmate made that as his final project. He gave it to me as an end of the year present."

"Now I know what that bastard looks like. The detail is wonderful."

"I thought so too." Smiling affectionally at it.

"What are you going to do with it?" he asked, placing it back on the counter.

I pulled out my crystals, "I'm gonna place a protection spell on it."

He seemed fascinated, "Do you oppose to an audience?"

I chucked, "Normally I don't give a damn, but in this case I actually need a second pair of hands for the spell I have in mind."

I placed the statuette in the middle of my circle of crystals. I had one to represent each element, and a dozen others around it. I took out a small hammer, and grabbed a stick lighter from the cupboard. I also grabbed a small cup for the water. Handing the hammer to Mr. French I explained to him what I needed him to do.

"When I finish the line, 'protect what is mine' I need you to swing the little hammer at the statue as hard as you can. That will emphasize to the spell how much force to protect it from."

"And you want me to do it because since he's human, he can't match a shifter's strength." He noted.

"Yep."

I took up the lighter and cup, then began the spell.

"Earth to wind, fire to water

So that what I love won't be torn asunder

Keep safe this object from harm

Both physical and of charm

Here and now in this day and time

Protect what is mine."

Mr. French swung the hammer while I poured out the water and held the lighter close. The telltale wind blew through the room as the spell took effect. The hammer bounced off without leaving a scratch, the water and fire never touched it. The spell had worked perfectly.

Mr. French sat back down on the barstool with a look of astonishment on his face. I grabbed my crystals and started putting everything away. When I got back I grabbed a towel and started to wipe up the spilled water. It wasn't until I put my empty plate and bowl in the sink that Mr. French finally said something.

"I've never seen such a powerful spell."

"My mom taught us well. She theorized that maybe because of our strong Scottish ancestry was why our spells work so well. Either that or the dragon blood. But I've also seen Hawaiian magic, and it's pretty powerful too."

He chuckled, "It's a possibility." He seemed to have a thought, "Is Sharp your full last name?"

"No. I know what it is, but my dad made all three of us swear to never say it to other shifters, fair folk, or magically inclined peoples of any kind."

"Why?"

"Something about an ancient family feud that nearly wiped out our family."

Now I had his attention, "With whom?"

I hesitated, "The Parthenian clan."

He was visibly shocked, "The wizard clan."

I nodded, "Only two of our ancestors got away."

"That's not possible, they claimed to have searched the house top to bottom, killing all they found inside."

"Yeah well, they lied." Wait a minute, "How do you know which family they attacked?"

"Did your father never tell you the story?"

"No, he planned to tell us when we were all adults. Obviously he never got that chance."

"What **is** your full last name?"

I clamped up, a promise was a promise, no matter if the one was dead or not, I shook my head.

He became placating, "I promise I won't tell anyone what you tell me. I swear on the blood of my ancestors."

Okay, that was acceptable, "Do you want my full name or just my last name?"

"Just the last name."

I sighed, "Sharpwingclaw."

He fainted, "Jeez Louise." I said in surprise. I had **not** been expecting that.

I went around the bar to check on him. He was out cold. Wow. I didn't think my last name would have such an effect on anyone. I took a risk and shifted to dragon. It would be easier to get him to the guest room that way. Using teeth and tail I lifted him onto my back and walked down the hall to said guest room. The door was already open.

It was a tight squeeze, but I managed. Tipping him off my back onto the bed, I sniffed his head, checking for blood. None, good. I shifted back to human and left the room. Closing the door behind me. My arms felt funny.

I went into the bathroom and turned on the light. I only then realized that I was still wearing my hoodie. I took it off and got a huge surprise. My arms were HEALED! How the hell had that happened!? The stitches were even coming out on their own. That creeped me out a little. But I had been right, all but three on my arms healed. The ones my left ring and pinky fingers had left were fully gone, and as I had correctly predicted, the right thumb mark was gone too. I had a thought. I removed my jeans in a flash. My thighs skin was a normal color again. The scars were still there of course, but the wound looked several years older now. It felt six months old, but how the hell did it look so old now? I'd have to ask Mr. French about it at some point, if he could even talk to me again.

I was still reeling from Mr. French's reaction when I finally settled down to sleep again. Why was my last name such a surprise? I know my family was still technically in hiding from the Parthenian clan, but I didn't think it was that significant. I decided to take a risk. I would contact Reggie tomorrow, and see if he'd gotten more about our family history from dad before he'd died or not. He was the only one who might know something.

I finally changed into my pjs and got into bed properly. As the storm finished its final hurrah, I drifted off to sleep to the rain on my window. I had a dreamless sleep.

Chapter 32

I stretched like a cat the next morning. It didn't even hurt. I looked at my arms and legs. Nope, that hadn't been a dream. I used the sunlight to reexamine my leg. The scars from the restraining piece to hold the bone together were almost completely gone. I could only see them when I turned my leg in a certain direction. That was technically a really good result. I still felt a little weirded out though. I looked at my arms. The marks where the stitches had been were completely gone. There wasn't a single trace of them.

I got out of bed and changed into shorts and a tank top. I couldn't hear anything from the kitchen or living room. Everyone was still asleep. Well, two were still asleep, one was still unconscious. I chuckled a little. I could still hardly believe that Mr. French had fainted.

I put my hair up in a ponytail, and made my way out to the kitchen. I decided to make breakfast burritos for everyone. It would give me something to focus on while I thought about how to ask Reggie what I needed to ask. I also fantasized how everyone would react when they finally saw my arms. I knew there wouldn't be any happy reactions, especially not when I mention shifting way ahead of what my doctor said.

I got the chopped potatoes in one skillet, and started scrambling most of the eggs. Mr. Hydell had two 18 count packs in the fridge at all times. I used all of one for today's breakfast. Two shifters were eating, better safe than sorry. I got the applewood smoked bacon out and set it aside for the moment. I flipped the cutting board over and started cutting the bacon in half. I put that in a pan of its own and stirred the potatoes. I stood on tiptoes to get the tortillas from a cupboard. Whoa, I could stretch my left leg. Wow! What the hell had happened last night?!

I heard movement from both rooms. It would be a few seconds before either room was emptied, so I gathered my thoughts and nerves. I was really apprehensive about how Mr. Hydell and Molly would react. I took a deep breath and flipped the bacon. I started pacing through the kitchen. I decided to try and think about how to contact Reggie. I hadn't started a telepathic communication with him from such a distance before. The farthest I had ever gone was with Amanda, and that had been my limit at the time. Ten miles was one thing, more than a thousand was a stretch. I knew he wasn't in New York anymore. Well, I guess if he can do it, maybe I can. He had six more years of experience on me.

Mr. French was the first to exit his room. He didn't come any closer yet though. That had me a little concerned. I don't know why but it did. I was saved by Molly and Mr. Hydell coming into the kitchen, they both looked a little bleary eyed.

"Did you sleep well Mr. French?" Molly asked.

"Please, call me Bram." He said, coming to sit on one of the barstools.

"Alright, did you sleep well, Bram?"

"Yes. Although I must confess I was awake at 2 a.m., I don't usually sleep through thunderstorms."

"Did you ever get back to sleep?" Mr. Hydell asked, retrieving his cup of coffee.

"Yes. Although I don't know how I made it back to my room." I bit my lips. Here it comes.

"To tired to comprehend maybe." Mr. Hydell said, sitting back down.

"More likely I think Maggie was involved." I turned. He was looking at me.

"Let me get these eggs in the pan first." I removed the seasoned potatoes, and replaced them with the eggs. "I hope no one minds if everything is cooked the way I like it."

There was a chorus of 'no's. I then went over to extract the tortillas from their package. That's when Molly noticed, "What happen to your arms?!"

I turned, holding up one of them. She grabbed my wrist and turned it. It was my left arm, so I winced a little. She apologized and continued examining it. I couldn't quite tell what she was thinking from the look on her face. I smelled burning. Some of the bacon was getting too crispy.

I gently pulled my arm loose and went to remove them from the pan, "Maggie," Mr. Hydell said, "let me see your arms." I stirred the eggs a little first.

"Not much to see." I turned to him and showed him.

"How the hell?" He held my arms and looked completely stupefied. He looked up at me.

"I have no freaking idea. It happened after I…" I hesitated.

"After you what?" he took on a fatherly tone.

"After I shifted to get Mr. French back to his room, after he fainted from shock after hearing my full last name." I said, somewhat quickly.

"You shifted!" He stated.

"I didn't have much choice." He crossed his arms. Okay fine, you wanna go there. I crossed my arms and said, "It was either that or try to drag over 300 pounds of dead weight," I pointed at Mr. French, "to his room with my bad leg and an arm still recovering from nerve damage." As if to emphasize my point my fingers started twitching. They hadn't twitched in weeks. Yet more proof of nerve damage.

Mr. Hydell had a resigned look now, "Fair point." He said with a heavy sigh.

Mr. French chuckled, "So you **were** responsible."

"Yes. I may be able to use my strength in human form, but it was wiser to go dragon. Despite what my doctor said." I said the last bit as I went over to stir the eggs some more.

"What did she say?" Mr. French asked.

"No shifting for two weeks." Molly answered, with an equally resigned look on her face, I guess she was expecting to reprimand me as well.

"Hold on a minute," Mr. Hydell said in a thoughtful tone, "you told me that you weren't allowed to tell anyone your full last name."

I put the last of the cooked bacon on the paper towels, "Yes, I wasn't and technically still am."

"But I made a promise that I would never tell anyone what she told me." Mr. French said.

"I see." Mr. Hydell said.

"Why **did** you faint? I expected some kind of reaction but not **that**." I stated, moving the eggs to a bowl.

He gave a sigh, "Because yours is a name I haven't heard in centuries."

"Is that significant?" Molly asked.

"Has she told either of you?"

"Molly no, me, yes. I have no magic of any kind. Her father never forbade her from telling humans."

"True." I said. I had never actually told him it. He'd caught it over my shoulder one day last month.

"To answer your question Molly, every shifter has a full name, whether it's only two to three words, or sometimes up to seven. In Maggie's case, our world believes her family long extinct." Mr. French said.

"What!?" Molly didn't like the sound of that.

"My fainting last night was due to surprise," he paused, "and I awoke this morning feeling incredibly happy." Huh?

I assembled the first burrito, "Why would knowing my name make you happy?" I placed the folded burrito in the skillet to crisp up the outside.

"Because it helps explain why you are different from other shifters." He answered.

"Different how? You mentioned it at the meeting with Ms. Hamper." I flipped the burrito.

"In many ways. One of which you demonstrated last night."

"Speaking of which why were you up at 2 a.m.?" Mr. Hydell asked accusingly.

"I woke up and realized I was hungry. I didn't check the time till just before I put my dinner in the microwave." I said.

"And what exactly did you demonstrate?" He asked.

"A protection spell. Ian gave me a gift for the end of the year, and I wanted it protected from harm."

"Like the one you preformed on the apartment?" Molly asked.

"Similar but not as vast."

"What is your full name dear?" She asked.

"Sharpwingclaw." I felt a lump in my throat.

"I meant-"

"I know what you meant." I interrupted. I was trying to reign in my tears. I couldn't breathe right then.

She looked upset, "Too soon." I just nodded and turned to start the next burrito.

"Sharing a full name with someone can be difficult for traumatized shifters," Mr. French explained, "it can make us feel alone, or worse, in some cases."

"Even when it's someone who's like family?" She asked with a confused tone.

"Especially then. It can make the shifter feel, undeserving of family." He said.

"This full name business feels unnecessary if you ask me." she said.

"It can seem that way sometimes, but it has its purposes. Honoring family, identification in case of people with similar names, and of course, telling what kind of shifter you are." Mr. French explained.

"How does full name length tell what kind of shifter you are?" Mr. Hydell asked.

"Anything more than five words means dragon shifter." I answered. "Dragon shifters being the strongest and most ancient of all shifters, means that we get the most respect from other shifters. Usually."

"And with that respect comes a sense of title. Which is why dragon shifters have the longest names. It can feel like a royal saying their title to others." Mr. French added.

"But you don't ack like a royal dear." Molly stated.

"It's the implication that matters. Dragon shifters have an inherited wisdom, which is why we don't flaunt ourselves before other shifters." I said.

"Her kind are old enough to have been humbled as a species, partially thanks to humans."

I placed a burrito in front of Mr. French, "Thank you." He said.

I put the next one in front of Molly, "Thank you dear. If it's not to invasive, why does the shifter world think your family is gone?"

"A wizard clan tried to wipe it out centuries ago." I said, giving Mr. Hydell his.

"Why?" Mr. Hydell asked.

"I don't know." I said while putting mine in the pan.

"The clan was jealous of her families power, and the love they received from the neighboring villages."

"Huh?!" this was news to me.

"Your family was cherished by the villages, for their healing abilities, the protection they provided, and everything else they did for the communities. Human and shifter children grew up together, playing in the fields, helping with chores. Your family was the first to ever show that humans and shifters could co-exist in perfect harmony."

I removed my burrito from the pan, set it on my plate, set the plate on the counter, and promptly slid down the island to sit on the floor. My family had nearly been wiped out because of jealousy! Then I had a thought, I jumped back up before anyone could come around from the other side to check on me.

"What about an incident when the clan tried to kill an ancestor's children in front of her?" I asked.

Molly and Mr. Hydell's eyes widened at that, "That was the clan trying to vilify your family to the villagers. It had the opposite effect." Mr. French told me.

"Rather than making my family look like monsters, it showed how well a mother dragon protects children. Her own or otherwise." I said.

"Indeed."

"So why did they attack my family's house?" I sat on a barstool.

"They waited until the night after the village was attacked by raiders. Everyone was exhausted so an attack would have been unstoppable."

"But the villagers would have run them out later." I said, starting to get angry.

"The clan took the armor from fallen raiders and used hidden wands to perform their attack. Your family only had two children at the time – since shifters live so long – the clan had no trouble dispatching all the adults."

"That still doesn't make sense, even when weakened by battle dragon shifters can fight." I knew my stamina.

"The clan had access to illegal plants. Particularly dragon's bane."

"Dragon's what?" I asked.

"A plant that stops dragons from shifting, leaving them in their weaker form. A dragon shifter can't even use their strength when affected by dragon's bane."

I thought back to the night of the murders, the funny smell, "Is this plant still around?"

"Yes, but it is heavily guarded and only a few herbalists are trusted with it." He paused, "Why do you ask?"

"I'll explain later, continue please."

"The clan figured if they could make it seem that the remaining raiders had killed your entire family, they could swoop in like saviors and take over."

"So they tried to kill everyone in their sleep." I said.

"Yes. Or, they said they did. Since your standing here and told me about the two children escaping, I don't know how they convinced the village of your families eradication."

"I never said it was the children."

"Easy guess."

"But how would children survive? Shifter or not?" Mr. Hydell asked.

"Only one way to find out." I said before popping the last of my burrito in my mouth.

I got up and almost ran to my room. I went to my desk and opened the drawer where I kept all my crystals and stones. I pulled out my brother's birthstone. A pearl about the size of a golf ball. His birthday was at the end of the month. The lump returned to my throat. Clutching the pearl, I swallowed down the lump and sat on my bed. Holding the pearl in both hands in front of my chest, breathing deeply, and closing my eyes, I reached for my brother.

It didn't take long, *"What's up? I can sense your anxiety."* He said.

"I need to know if dad ever told you anymore about the feud."

"No, but I did overhear him as he told mom."

"Sneak. What did he say?"

"That after the clan killed everyone inside the house, they searched it. They knew about the two kids but couldn't find them. They then decided that even if the children escaped them, they'd never survive the night."

"But obviously they did." I said.

"Obviously. The next day when the raiders attacked again, the villagers were able to repel them on their own. The clan tried to stop the raiders themselves but were thrown out of the villages when all the raiders were dead. They couldn't understand why they weren't welcomed as heroes until one woman started calling them murderers. They never did find out how the villagers knew they had killed our family."

"Because a certain set of children came to the only other safe place they knew and spilled the beans."

"That's what dad said. The clan still assumed our family was wiped out 'cause they never found evidence of the children making it back to the village. Their tracks ended at a river." He stated.

"The dumbasses assumed they drowned while trying to cross."

"Dad said the two did that on purpose. Part of the whole going into hiding piece."

"Was sensible. The villagers would protect them as their own anyway."

"Yep. While it was nice to chat with you sis, I gotta go. I'm supposed to be studying." He said.

"Nice talking to you too bro, sorry for the interrupt. Love and Miss you."

"Love and Miss you too sis." I felt his reluctance as we broke contact.

I leaned back on my bed, laughing to myself. It was nice to know that our family was damn good at outsmarting people. I thought about how the two kids would have arrived at the village. Maybe covered in the blood of their parents, scared shitless, angry. There was a multitude of possibilities. Anyone would have given them the protection they needed.

I got up and after putting the pearl back, went back out to the kitchen. All three adults were still there, and I could see that Mr. French had made himself another burrito. When they all saw me they asked what I had been doing. I sat at my chair with a smile, and told them all that Reggie had told me.

Mr. French was laughing by the end of it, "No wonder the clan told a different story."

"Serves them right." Molly said.

"They still should be punished for what they did." Mr. Hydell said.

"Oh they have been." Mr. French said.

"Please explain." Mr. Hydell stated.

"A few years – almost a century – after the murders, the eldest remaining member of the killers was visited by a witch. She was from one of the villages she told him and was a good friend of the two children that had died."

"I'm guessing she was actually one of those children." I said, taking a sip of milk.

"Her name was Romillda Vienna Adaira Grace Sharp."

I laughed, "They didn't put two and two together."

He shook his head, "They didn't know about shifter full names then, they just assumed she took sharp as a last name in honor of your family."

"Idiots." I said.

"She cast a spell on them. Saying that their family would be cursed to die young until one of your family forgave them."

I was actually shocked about that, "And here I thought my family didn't do revenge."

"Normally no, but since the clan wiped out everything the two girls knew – much the same as Kepner has done to you and your brother – they made an exception."

"I didn't know both kids were girls." I said.

"The witch mentioned later that she and her sister were living peacefully with husbands and children of their own."

"I see, and I'm guessing since the clan thought them all dead, that they assumed they would be trapped forever."

"Yes." Mr. French confirmed.

"And since Reggie and I are now the last, it would be up to us to forgive them or not." He nodded.

I shrugged, "Well if I ever meet one, I'll see if he or she is repentant." I took another drink of milk.

"There's one at my school." I nearly choked on said drink.

Coughing I said, "You couldn't have waited to say that till after I swallowed."

We all laughed, "I apologize for that."

I nodded, "You know it's almost poetic." Everyone looked confused, "My family is systematically slaughter twice, centuries apart, and both times, only two children survive."

"And each set seeking revenge." Mr. Hydell said.

"Yeah, well. In my case Kepner won't get cursed, he'll get dead. And he will know mine and my brother's pain."

"A fitting death." Mr. French said.

"This student whose a Parthenian, what's he like?" I asked.

"He's repentant in my opinion. He recently learned from his mother about the slaughter and I've known him for years, he despises killing anything. He's one of my few vegan students. He's always going on about how if anyone from your family survived, he'd be the one to apologize. He's the last of his family, much like how you and Reggie are the last of yours. His mother has been diagnosed with terminal breast cancer that has spread. He's your age, and she's only 36."

"Still technically young." I said.

"Yes, but I will let you be the judge on whether or not he and his family deserve forgiveness."

"I'll get time to judge once school starts." I said.

It was now approaching 9 a.m., Mr. Hydell had to get to work and Mr. French had to head home. It would be just me and Molly for the whole afternoon. I had a lot to think about now. Knowing that my family's killers from so long ago were so dwindled came as a surprise, but then again so did finally having the full story. It made me wonder what Amanda would have to say to all this. Also what Reggie would think about there being only two Parthenians left. Just like us, and whether he would be willing to forgive. If this one boy was willing to repent for his ancestors crime, then he at least deserved a trial period. To test whether he was telling the truth or not.

I could always contact Reggie again later and tell him what I had found out. About the curse, and the clan. Did dad even know about the curse? I'd never get that answer. Or if he had known, did he ever talk to mom about removing it. Spells could be undone, curses couldn't. A curse must run its course. If you tried to stop it before it was finished the curse would rebound and kill you, especially if you had cast it in the first place. What my ancestor had cast was technically a spell that acted like a curse. That was one that could be undone, so long as one had the original spell. My mom had several ancestral spell books, I didn't know about my dad. I could always look through our stuff in storage at some point.

Aw Crap! I only now remembered that I never asked Mr. French about why my saying my name would do what it did to my scars. I had been so caught up in learning my family's history that the thought had completely slipped my mind. I also never explained why I'd asked about the dragon's bane. I'd just have to take care of both issues the next time we got a chance to talk.

Molly called me to the living room. I took a breath and went to see her. I decided any other questions could wait. Molly had the day off and she wanted to spend it with me. I might have to change my shirt if we went out, but I intended to enjoy myself.

Chapter 33

Close to noon the mail arrived. It was late for a Thursday. I didn't mind though, 'cause in it I found info that Ms. Hamper had sent me about staying in Scotland. I brought it back up to the apartment to look it over. I was glad that her uncle was still willing to let me stay the summer. Now that I had the necessary information, I was excited to get summer started.

The packet contained plans of the grounds as well as maps of the house itself. It also gave the location so I could find it on Google Maps. I pulled out my computer and typed in the coordinates. I could not believe where the estate was located. The estate was on the south west side of the Isle of Skye. I was super excited now. The only habitation within miles was a small town called a hamlet. The town itself was called Eynort, it was at the very end of Loch Eynort. I looked up the elevation of the estate. High enough to see the ocean. Awesome! Google maps didn't show the lake that Ms. Hamper had mentioned, but then again she had said it was small.

The Isle of Skye was over 200 miles north of Glasgow, Scotland. That just meant a long drive or a small plane. I could see that there was a length of the road to the estate that was straight enough to act as a small plane runway too. The trees were even far enough apart. You'd still have to be a damn good pilot to land there. I looked through the rest of the papers, they gave me a list of rules. There weren't as many as I was expecting.

Rule one was of course no leaving the estate without informing someone about where I was going and when I intended to be back. Fair enough. Number two was expected; stay out of the main bedroom. Three, clean up any messes I make. No duh. Four, I don't have to help with anything, but I can if I want to. Five, that if I wish to practice my martial arts, I have to do it outside – except when it rains, then I can practice in one of the spare rooms. Also fair. Six, any and all magic related occurrences must be performed while in the forest or if they must be done indoors, that I should inform the head of the house, i.e. Ms. Hamper's uncle. Fair as well. And finally rule seven, everyone at the estate would be informed about my status as a dragon shifter, but any shifting must occur outside at all times. No problem there. I prefer to be outside when I shift anyway, the only times when a shift takes place indoors is for one of two reasons. Like relocating a fainted lion.

The plans and maps of the castle and grounds were pretty straight forward. The castle itself was four stories, each with ten to twenty rooms depending on size. The master bedroom and mine were marked. There was a library, a dining room, a sitting room, a media or gaming room, the kitchen, and lots of guest rooms. The basement held the pantry of course, and a door to the underground garage. The roof had a viewing platform. I couldn't wait to go stargazing in Scotland.

The back of the estate had a beautiful garden, with what looked like a fountain, but I couldn't quite tell. There also was the staff housing, multiple family homes on the premises. The garden of course was more like what a Scottish person would have rather than an English garden. Full of native Scottish flowers and trees. Somewhere I could sit and read a book for hours, or practice my martial arts with a peaceful air. This trip was sounding better and better by the minute.

Near the end of the papers I found a note, *'cover story already in place. Items necessary to arrive later. Have fun sweetie.'* Ms. Hamper had taken the liberty to make sure I was safe. I'd most definitely thank her the next time I saw her.

Depending on when she sent this packet, the items for my disguise should arrive either later today or tomorrow. The ticket provided in this packet said my flight left on Saturday at eleven a.m. I had to be ready for a thirteen hour flight. Joy. From Glasgow airport, a personal pilot friend of her uncle would pick me up and fly me to the estate. After that I could do all my own flying. Speaking of flying though, I needed to do research on Scotland's shifter laws. I reopened the google tab on my computer.

The results were good. Scotland was a shifter friendly country and even allowed shifters to roam freely. Wolves were given special access to national parks on full moon nights, and dragon shifters were free to fly from city to city. Even landing at the airports if they needed to. There were a few stipulations of course. No attacking people without provocation, No eating anyone, – gross - and all kills made while on a moon run must be registered. Plus dragon shifters – if they wanted to land at an airport – had to call ahead and say they were coming. Understandable. I've seen on t.v. what can happen when a dragon shifter and a plane collide. Not pretty.

Everything was in place. Now all I had to do was wait, and plan out everything I'd need to take with me. I got up to go to my room while Molly took an emergency call. It didn't sound good. I grabbed a notepad and pencil from my desk. Necessities went first. Clothes, obviously. Toiletries, not necessarily needed but a possibility to consider. Books, maybe, would depend on how much reading material was at the estate. One book was at least necessary for the flight over. Computer, definitely, one to communicate with Mr. Hydell and Molly, plus I could install the kindle app and use it if I needed to. Also there would be movies on it. Phone, yes. Phone charger, no duh. Passport, duh. I'd have to do further research about customs and age travel requirements.

Carryon bag would consist of computer and a book. My phone would be on me at all times. Maybe a water bottle if it was allowed, and some snacks. No weapons of course, but then again I myself am a weapon. I probably wouldn't take any jewelry. I also should e-mail Emily and Amber about the dress. I'd hate for it to arrive here and no one be there to receive it.

I heard Molly make a noise in the living room. I walked back out with the list still in hand. She didn't look too happy. Something must be up.

"Everything okay?" I asked.

She sighed, "No. One of my patients has had a nervous breakdown and needs an emergency session."

"So you have to head in?"

"Yes," she looked at me, "but I'll be taking you with me. Our office playroom manager is out sick, and I know how good you are with kids. She'll be bringing her daughter and son, so they'll need to be entertained."

"I'll go change then." I turned and walked back to my room. I put on a pair of jeans and a long sleeve shirt. The last thing she needed was the kids needing therapy too.

She called and left a message for Mr. Hydell, I checked to make sure the lock spell was still going, then we got into her car and drove to her office. It wasn't a long drive since her office is a few blocks from where I got therapy. Once inside her assistant explained that her patients son was a really badly behaved boy and needed someone with a strong will to watch him. Molly pointed at me and said I'd be watching him. Her assistant was pretty skeptical.

We were brought up to her office and while she went in to where her desk was, I went into where the kids were. Ducking as a ball was thrown out, and catching the sippy cup that followed. I looked at the sippy cup like it was something I was mad about, then looked at the two kids in front of me. The little girl looked contrite while the boy looked angry that I caught it.

"Hey Molly," I called, "quick question, does the mom want any spanking done if necessary?" I didn't take my eyes off the kids. Little girl looked shocked that I would even suggest it, the boy got this look that said he'd hit me if I did. News flash little dude, I hit back.

I heard her talk with the mom, "Only if necessary, and please. She says maybe you could knock some sense into the son."

She said it so low that only I could hear her. Challenge accepted. I walked into the room, putting on a smile. I heard her assistant close the door behind me. The two were twins from what I could tell, and about four years old.

"So, what are your names?" I asked while crossing my arms.

"Addy and Billy." The little girl answered. The boy just looked at me like I was something gross.

"Well Addy and Billy, while your mommy talks with my friend, I'm gonna keep the two of you entertained."

"You're not our mom!" Billy shouted.

I didn't even flinch, "No I'm not, but until your mom comes back in, I'm in charge."

Billy looked confused by my not recoiling at his shout. You don't scare me little dude. He then proceeded to pick up one of the little chairs – as best he could anyway – and tried to throw it at me. I simply swiveled my hips and it never even touched me. Addy looked impressed, but Billy looked pissed.

"Since your so adamant about throwing things, why don't you try to throw those balls in the hoop." I said. He looked down at them and decided to make it look like it was his idea. Fine by me.

I took Addy's hand and walked over with her to the blocks, we spent the next ten minutes building a tower. By the half hour mark, Billy was content with the basketball hoop and Addy was playing with a puzzle. She kept smiling at me every time she got a piece without help. There was a knock at the door, Molly's assistant was bringing in snacks. I got up to answer the door. I took the tray from her as there was a cry of pain from behind me. I turned.

Billy had hit his sister. Hard. A bruise was already forming. The smile on his face vanished when he turned and saw me. I had my angry mom look on. I knew the look well, thanks to my mom. I turned back to Molly's assistant.

"When the door is closed, is it soundproof?" I asked. She nodded.

Good. I set the tray down, closed the door, and turned back to Billy. He turned and tried to run to the other side of the room. Like lightning I reached forward and grabbed him by his pants, picking him up off his feet. Addy looked impressed, but her brother was trying to hit me. Keeping him at arm's length I walked over to the adult chairs and sitting on the end chair, put him over my knee, held him down, - despite his screaming - and started spanking him. His sister was shocked at it, but it was necessary. I hate people who tell you spanking is child abuse. IT'S NOT! It's discipline, me and my siblings could speak from experience. Amanda was the least spanked of us, hence the sad number of mistakes she'd made. And those were her words, spoken a few weeks before she died.

After about ten hits, I let him up. He grabbed his butt and had tears in his eyes. He tried to stare me down. It didn't take long for him to realize I was the dominant one in the room. He lowered his eyes, smart move.

"No wonder your mom had a nervous breakdown." I said. Getting up to check the tray. Why was there a raw egg on it? Oh wait, Molly had an idea.

Still crying Billy asked, "What do you mean… a nervis breakdown?"

I turned back to him, "It means this." I picked up the egg and sat down, placing a plastic cup under the egg.

"Do you guys know what's in here?" I pointed at my head.

They both nodded, "The brain." Addy said.

"Good, now pretend that this egg is your mommy's brain. A nervous breakdown is when people start going crazy," I met both of their eyes, "and your" I pointed at Billy, "really, really bad behavior, is causing your mom's mind to do this." I crushed the egg.

Their eyes widened. And don't grill me for doing it. There are somethings you cannot explain to children with words. You need examples.

The example worked, Billy hung his head in shame, and started crying. Addy looked troubled, like she wanted to comfort her brother but understood that he needed to be punished. I got up from the chair and went over to Billy. I kneeled down and I pulled his head up to look me in the eye.

"Do you understand now Billy?" I asked.

He nodded, "I'm sorry."

"It's not me you have to apologize to. Your mother is there to take care of you, or someday when you need her, she won't be there. You need to love and appreciate her. Okay?"

He nodded again, and I pulled him into a hug. I rubbed his back to show him it was okay. Addy came over and joined the hug. I heard another knock at the door. We all looked, Molly's assistant was standing there and looking at her hand. She must have moved her hand in her jaw dropping moment. I got up and grabbed the tray of snacks. I bought it over to the table and, having a thought, went back to the door.

Opening it I asked, "Any chocolate?"

She nodded and passed me some from the cupboard that was by the door. Hershey's, perfect. I closed the door and sat at the table with them. There were graham crackers on the plate, pretzels, gold fish, and mini marshmallow. I held up the chocolate.

"I will give you guys a few pieces if you promise to behave better for your mom. That means no more throwing things, no more hitting each other, no more screaming at her, no more complaining about what she gives you for food."

"Even if we don't like it?" Addy asked.

"Yes, even if you don't like it, and I learned as a kid, if you eat the stuff you don't like, you have a better chance of getting either dessert, or something you've wanted for a while. Both hands where I can see them please."

They both raised their hands and said, "We promise." I smiled.

I spent the rest of their mom's session, showing them fun combos with the snack material. Including s'mores. By the time she was done, Billy had stopped crying. The assistant knocked at the door again and gestured for us to come out. I got up with them and exited the room, switching off the light and tossing the cup with the egg in the trash as we left.

Their mom came out of Molly's office looking a little better, and once Billy saw her, he rushed over and threw his arms around her. With a teary voice he apologized profusely to her. I chuckled slightly at the look on her face, she was utterly shocked. She started crying and kneeled down to hug her son. Molly looked at me over her head, 'well done' she mouthed. I winked.

As the three left, Molly's assistant couldn't stop staring at me like I was a mythical creature. Technically I was, but she didn't know that. Eventually she got up the courage to ask me how I had tamed such an unruly little boy.

"I just applied the same techniques my parents used on me." I said.

"It's mainly the father's fault, he spoiled the two of them." She told me.

"Where's he?" I asked.

"He died in a building fire a few months ago." Molly answered.

"Ah." That explained why the kids took my lesson at full seriousness. They were already down one parent.

"Well, I think her life is gonna be much easier now." The assistant said.

"Life maybe, motherhood, definitely." Molly said.

Molly called the security officer on our way down, checking if anyone had approached her car. She got a negative report. There was one officer in the garage on every level at all times. Once outside the building she decided to go for lunch. We stopped at a Dairy Queen drive through, got our orders, and went back to Mr. Hydell's apartment. She also called Jim and had him check the security cameras as well.

He also gave her a negative report and we went back up in the elevator. I did my usual deep breath and smelled Mr. Hydell. Home early, on a week day? I sent him a quick text, *'you home early?'* his response was pretty quick, *'yep. Waiting for you guys.'*

I was still a little skeptical. So we approached the door with caution. Mr. Hydell actually opened it. I breathed a sigh of relief. We walked in and joined him for lunch. Molly laid out what happened at the office. Mr. Hydell was laughing by the end of it.

"Did you really crush an egg?" he asked.

"Yep, and a good idea on that one Molly."

"Thank you dear." She said, taking a fry from Mr. Hydell.

"You must be some kind of miracle worker." Mr. Hydell said with admiration.

"Maybe for some others. Too bad I can't do that with my own problems." I said a little wistfully. I shrugged, "Such is the life of an empath."

"Maybe that's why you're so different from other shifters." Molly said.

"Maybe." I replied.

"So, why were you off early?" Molly asked Mr. Hydell.

"Well since my current case is resolved – by outside means – I officially am on vacation. All we have to do now is make the plans." There was smiles all around.

Chapter 34

The rest of the week went by fast, by the time Saturday arrived, all three of us were ready for travel. The package with my cover story in it had arrived the day after the plans like I predicted. Inside I'd found a makeup plan for my face, and a full outfit. My passport was changed to the new cover as well. The FBI – as it turns out – was closely monitering my case, and had great interest in my safe travel. The airport officials were informed of the situation even. The new passport said I was 18, and native American. Works for me.

Mr. Hydell, Molly, and I separated at the terminal, my flight was getting ready to leave and they still had an hour long wait. We all hugged and said our goodbyes. I would miss them greatly. They made me go through my checklist again as well. I waved at them as I was walked into the boarding platform.

Once seated, I double checked my phone. I had received a text from Emily saying that my dress was delayed due to lack of embroidering materials. I responded saying it was okay, and that they should take all the time they needed to finish it. When that was done, I turned my phone off, and asked when I could use my computer. The flight attendant told me once we made cruising altitude. Reading first then.

I pulled out my copy of Eragon, buckled myself in, and waited for the flight to begin. I never did get another chance to talk to Mr. French about my scars healing or the dragon's bane. I didn't mind though, I could ask about them when it was time for me to visit the school.

I ended up getting the whole row to myself. There was a newlywed couple in front of me, and a school field trip behind me. Hey, wait a minute! I turned around, and looked at the row behind me. I recognized two boys from my history class. Their eyes widened when they saw me, - recognizing me threw the make-up - then they just started to laugh. Jimmy had taken my spot after the murders, and here he was sitting behind me.

Mr. Hanley came forward to see what they were laughing about. I just waved at him. He then joined them in merriment.

"And here I thought you'd be spending summer at home." He said.

"Not this year. Thanks to my therapist." I said with a big grin.

"How'd your therapist score you a trip to Scotland?" Jimmy asked.

"Her uncle owns an estate on the Isle of Skye." Their jaws dropped.

"Lucky." Kevin said, with a pretend sulky look.

I laughed, "It's to help me try and heal you dork."

"Still. You get to stay in a fancy estate. We get to go hoteling." Kevin replied with a dorky smile.

"I don't think hoteling is a word Kevin." Mr. Hanley said.

"It is, just not in the sense that Kevin is using." Jimmy said. We laughed at the face Kevin made.

The announcement came over the p.a. to take seats and fasten seatbelts. I turned back to front facing, and held my book. This would be my first plane flight, I was a little nervous.

The taxi wasn't so bad, but I gripped the arm rests pretty hard as we lifted off. I heard the metal groan under the pressure. Okay, no doubt about it, I prefer my flying to planes. It took a few minutes to reach cruising altitude, but once we did, I got out my computer. I sent Mr. Hydell an e-mail that we'd reached it. Also saying that I'd send him one when we were an hour or so from landing. His reply would be a little bit, but I knew he'd respond.

They had decided to go to Australia first, which meant they had a fifteen hour flight ahead of them. Two more than me. So I probably wouldn't get an answer until late. After I did that, I reread the e-mail that my boss at the aquarium had sent me. I had been granted leave of absence until further notice. I was really glad about that. It meant I could return to work after Kepner was dead. I really hoped that didn't take more than a year.

I put my computer away and picked my book back up. I was strangely feeling a little tired. Maybe I was one of those who slept through flights. Only one way to find out. Within a few minutes, I was asleep. I was only woken later when a flight attendant asked if I wanted dinner. I nodded, and she passed me a menu. I heard snoring behind me. I turned my head a little, Kevin was fast asleep. Jimmy looked like he wanted to hit him over the head. I chucked a little. I reached in my pocket and pulled out a small pack of M&M's. I passed them to Jimmy.

Everyone at school knew about Kevin's 'addiction' to M&M's. We even knew he could be woken up just by passing some under his nose. Jimmy did so now. Kevin woke with a start and accepted the bag from Jimmy.

"You sound like a horse when you snore, you know that." Jimmy said. Kevin just nodded.

The stewardess came back, and I told her what I wanted. I wasn't too hungry, so I went with a chicken salad, and some orange juice. Plus a chocolate chip cookie for dessert. I heard the boys get menus as well. I picked my book up from where it had fallen from my hands. I checked it. No damage sustained. Good.

She came back again with my meal only a few minutes later, she even gave me a couple packets of ranch dressing. I gladly used them. The salad was really good. Crisp and fresh, the chicken was more moist than I was expecting. Really tasty. I drank my orange juice slowly, the citrus gave a little more freshness to the salad. I was done soon, and moved on to the cookie. That was really good too.

Once everything was cleared away, I opened my computer back up. I had two responses from Mr. Hydell. The first said thanks, and the second said they were boarding. They were now in the air too. I checked the clock in the corner. 8:30. I had been asleep a little over eight hours, that meant another five hours of flight time. I realized I needed to use the bathroom. I put my computer away and asked Jimmy to keep an eye on my bag. He nodded, and I got up to go.

I came back less than a minute later to find a baby in the seat next to mine. It was sound asleep. I looked at the boys.

"You were already in there so the mom went up to use the first class bathroom. She asked us to watch him." Kevin said. I nodded.

Making sure not to bump the seat, I got back in mine. I couldn't help looking at the little cutie. He was snoring slightly in his sleep. He reminded me of Gregory. It made me wonder where Ms. Hamper and her family had gone. They were safe, so I wasn't too longing in my query. The mother came back a few minutes later, she looked a little flustered.

"I'm sorry, I didn't mean to inconvenience." She said.

"No inconvenience ma'am. I didn't mind." I said.

She smiled and picked him back up. She went a few rows forward and sat down next to her husband. Who only just woke up as she sat down. We could hear him apologize for dozing off on her. Dude, you're a new dad, it's to be expected.

The boys and I settled back into our seats, and relaxed. I felt myself dozing off again. This time I didn't notice I'd fallen asleep until Jimmy was shaking me awake saying we were half an hour from landing. I thanked him and quickly sent an e-mail to Mr. Hydell. They had another two and a half hours at most till they landed.

It was close to ten in the morning in Scotland. The eight hour time difference was a little confusing, but once I had it figured out, it was no trouble. I shut my computer off, put it in my bag, and started reading again. I could barely focus though, at this point we were between Ireland and Scotland. I was super excited. I had a thought. Maybe at some point I could ask Ms. Hamper's uncle if the school trip could stop by. The Isle of Skye was on the tour list, it wasn't a bad idea.

About twenty minutes away the stewardess served breakfast. There was a slight weather delay, so we wouldn't land for an extra five to ten minutes. I ordered a bagel and cream cheese, and some milk or apple juice. I got the apple juice.

When I was finished I put my book back in my bag with my computer, double checking that it was still off. I kept my bag between my feet as we got the fasten seat belt sign. I did so and watched out the window as we started our descent. From what I could see a quick rain shower had passed over before we had reached Glasgow air space.

We actually bounced slightly as we landed. I really didn't like that. I honestly thought I was gonna puke. Thankfully I didn't. The disembarking took a half hour. When I finally got off the plane, I made my way to the front. The baggage collection spot was only slightly crowded. My suitcase was one of the first ones to come out. I waved at Mr. Hanley and the history class as I made my way over to the waiting area.

Ms. Hamper had included a small picture of her uncle's friend. I knew what to look for and didn't have long to wait. The picture hadn't said what his name was though. I saw him walking my way after only ten minutes. I stood and shook his hand.

"Your Maggie?" he asked.

"Yes."

"Names Mack, I'll be flying you up to the estate."

"Ready when you are." I said.

He led me outside, passed the main tarmac, and over to one of the smaller runways. His plane was a single engine Cessna. He put my bags in the back and secured them. Then he had me climb in and strap myself in. He also had me wear the headset, even thought I'd be able to hear him just fine without it. He radioed into the tower and got the go ahead.

His takeoff wasn't as bad as the 747, but I was still a little uncomfortable. My stomach felt a little queasy from the multiple altitude shifts. He noticed and passed me a pack of vitamin c gummies. I chewed slowly, and after a few minutes I felt better.

Even with clear skies it was gonna be an almost two hour flight to the estate. I found myself unable to sleep on this one. I was enjoying the scenery immensely. Glasgow was out the right hand window. I remembered that my history class would spend the first week there before moving on to explore the rest of the country.

"Ever been to Scotland before Miss Maggie?" Mack asked over the headset.

"No, but I've always wanted to. And you can just call me Maggie." I answered.

"Then I hope you don't mind if I act like a tour guide while flying."

I shook my head, "It'll help me remember landmarks." I said with a smile. He then spent the whole flight pointing out mountains, and other landmarks. Telling me what the locals called some places and what their names were in Gaelic.

Finally the Isle of Skye came into view. I was getting a little angsty to fly, but I was extremely excited to finally be here. We couldn't see the estate yet, thought the surrounding country was breath taking.

"Say how far can you walk with that bum leg of yours?" Mack asked.

"Not very far, maybe one mile." I answered.

"That bad huh." I nodded, "What kind of shifter are you again?"

"Dragon."

"Right," he chuckled, "I'm so used to working with wolf and bear shifters. I've never gotten the chance to even talk to a dragon before."

"Well now you have. Why do you ask on the walking?"

"There's a tourist spot called the Fairy Pools in the mountains. It's technically almost six miles from Eynort, walking. So a two and a half hour walk." He explained.

"But since I'm a dragon.."

"Yep. You could fly and save yourself the pain."

"Sounds like fun." I said.

"Take a day to settle and get to know the place. I'll point it out on a map when I come back tomorrow."

"Gotcha."

"Alright, prepare yourself kid. We're coming in for landing." He said.

He wasn't kidding, right in front of us was the straight stretch of the estates road. I swallowed my nerves and watched him land the plane. He got it down without bouncing. I appreciated that. When he came to a stop, I was smiling. That was actually fun. I saw a car back up toward us.

"That'll be your ride the rest of the way. It was a pleasure to meet you."

"Same here, and thank you." We shook hands and I got out. I grabbed my bags from the back and made my way to the car.

The driver was dressed in a suit and said he was the valet. He took my bags – despite my protests – and put them in the trunk. I waved to Mack as he turned the plane around and took off again. I hopped in the back of the car when the driver opened the door. Apparently I was gonna be treated like a lady for the summer. Honestly, I'm not sure how I felt about that.

The drive was short. Like literally two minutes, and I got my first view of the castle. The pictures hadn't done it justice. It's beautiful, and the grounds add to its splendor. The hedges are well trimmed and have several gardeners currently tending them. I see the window to the room I'll be using, the curtains are being moved by a maid.

The driver stopped at the steps to the door and a small group of people come out. I could see from her dress that one of the woman is the head of staff. She had another maid open the door before I could even unbuckle myself.

"Miss Sharp?" she asks in a thick Scottish accent. I nod. "Excellent, I'm Mrs. Granger, head of staff. I'll be looking after your needs while you stay with us."

The driver came around the side with my bags, "I can take them." I said.

"Oh nonsense young lady." Mrs. Granger says, "Our employer has made it abundantly clear that we are to do any heavy lifting. He'd rather you didn't do any undo harm to your leg." So they had been informed about that. One less problem to worry about I guess.

Deciding not to argue, I allow one of the staff to grab the bags. Even though one only had like three things in it. I followed Mrs. Granger up the front steps indoors. The foyer was tidy and very spacious, with a beautiful crystal chandelier hanging from the ceiling. A small table took up the middle of the floor and had a vase of roses on it. There were several paintings on the walls, several depicting long ancient battles. Some of it, Scottish scenery. One or two had people in them.

Mrs. Granger led me upstairs while a butler took my bags from the boy who'd brought them in. He looked at my smaller bag like he expected it to weigh more. I was led to the fourth floor and shown my room. The master bedroom was down the hall and had double doors. That wouldn't be hard to miss.

My room was lovely. The stone walls were visible, and the view of the sea was wonderful. The window even had a seat with several pillows. An excellent spot to sit and read. The four poster bed even had the wrap around drapes, in a deep green color. I could see patterns woven into them. I took a second to admire them while Mrs. Granger began talking again.

"Lunch is in half an hour, and please, feel free to explore the grounds. We look forward to your time here." She said, before leaving the room with the butler.

I sat on the bed, it gave slightly under my weight. I couldn't believe I was finally here. In the land of most of my ancestors. I chose to stay put for a little while. I didn't want the staff to see me cry. I laid down on the bed and stared out the window. The tears started flowing freely. There was no holding them back. What would my family think of all this? My parents probably wouldn't believe it, Amanda probably would've been a little jealous, and Reggie I know would be happy for me, and proud of me for taking the opportunity. He'd had his distraction in school, and his new girlfriend. School hadn't worked for me of course, but now I had my distraction, and I intended to use it.

I got up and started unpacking. I separated my clothes into different dresser drawers, and put my computer on the head table between the bed and window. Eragon was placed next to it. When I was done, I sat down again. Trying to reign in my emotions. This was my chance to recover, and I was going to use it.

Chapter 35

I got off the bed, but before heading downstairs I traded the jacket I'd been wearing since before the airport, for my hoodie and headed down to the dining room. I had memorized the house plans on Friday after the second package had arrived. I took my time getting there. I was looking at everything and still having a hard time accepting that this whole place was basically at my beck and call all summer. Such treatment would most definitely take some getting used to. Ladylike wasn't me.

When I got to the dining room, Mrs. Granger was waiting with one of the other maids. She directed me to a seat at one end of the table. I was at least able to pull my seat in myself. She spoke to the maid so fast I didn't catch anything but haggis. Cool, I've always wanted to try haggis! I know it can gross people out, but I've heard from plenty of people who've actually tired it that it is very good. Even Guy Fieri from Food Network said so. Look it up.

"Lunch today will be haggis, with mashed turnips dear." Mrs. Granger confirmed for me.

"Thank you." I said, giving her a genuine smile.

She seemed impressed, "Most Americans balk at the mere mention of haggis."

"Most Americans don't do their culinary research." I stated. She seemed pleased with that.

The maid – who looked about my age – came back from the kitchen with the meal on a plate and took a sec to tell me that her name was Gretchen. She had removed the innards from the stomach and served it next to the mashed turnips. I actually had never had turnips either and was eager to try both. Before either left, I asked what I should do with the dishes once I was done eating. I was told to go ahead and leave them where they were. Gretchen also brought me glass of milk, saying just in case it was too spicy.

The haggis was awesome. Really earthy and meaty. I did get some spice but nothing overpowering. It also was a really moist dish, there were some bites I mixed with the turnips, which were also really good. When I was finished, I stood and took the dishes to the kitchen. I was feeling a little uncomfortable being waited on, so I washed them myself. I'd let Mrs. Granger or Gretchen know at some point.

I didn't have to wait long though. While I was setting the fork in the drying rack, Gretchen walked in. She looked rather surprised that I'd take the time to do it myself.

"I could have done that." She said, her strong accent coming out, indicating the now washed dishes.

I shrugged, "I'm nowhere near used to this kind of treatment. I was raised to be independent as well as polite." I leaned against the counter.

"I kinda figured miss," she said, "our employer mentioned you would be different from the other shifters we sometimes take care of."

So I wasn't the first to be given this opportunity, "Does he do this often? And please, just call me Maggie." I asked.

She smiled, "Not as often as Mrs. Granger would like. She enjoys having young shifters in need of healing around. She says that being pamper can heal anything."

"I disagree. Some people don't like to be pampered." I stated.

"True," she agreed, "but that won't stop her. Especially with what our employer has told her about you." She looked confused.

"What has he told her?" I was curious now.

"That you've suffered more than most of the young ones he sends, and that we shouldn't force you to accept anything. He never really gave her all the details. He said that was for you to do."

"Ah." I felt a little confined now.

"If it's not too pressing," she started, "may I ask why you're in need of healing and what kind?"

She wanted specifics, good, "I'm suffering from depression and survivors guilt. I need physical therapy as well as standard therapy," I paused, trying to hold back tears, "and I'm on two different meds for pain and sleep."

She didn't react like I expected. She dropped the towel she'd been holding, walked up to me and gave me a hug. I returned it somewhat shocked. Most people just look at me like I should be put into a mental institution. Even if they did it wouldn't last long.

"Needing outside help isn't something to be ashamed of, and whatever has caused such pain, we will help in whatever way we can." She said, still hugging me.

When she did finally pull away, I started wiping the tears away. She didn't press or admonish me in anyway, just handed me a tissue and went into the dining room. I stood there, rooted to the spot. Whomever Ms. Hamper's uncle was, he seemed to be a very generous person. I remembered back to the first time she'd told me about him, that he had suffered much the same way I had. It would explain why he took on shifter kids in pain. The isolated estate would be a perfect environment for coping or healing processes.

Tossing the used tissue in the trash I decided to take a walk in the garden. The kitchen had a door that led outside as well. Once outside, I started looking around a bit. The flowers were at peak of bloom. Scottish bluebells had always been one of my favorite flowers. It was much like the Japanese cherry blossom in its simplistic beauty.

I couldn't name all the flowers in the garden, but I didn't mind. Looking up I saw that what I thought was a fountain was actually a statue. A perfect rendering of Boudica, Queen of the Iceni. She stood in full scottish dress, and holding a scottish claymore specifically made for her.

I was a little surprised at this, but then I thought about it. Boudica was a queen who had been tortured in so many ways; the theft of her property by the Romans after her husband's death, the rape of her innocent daughters, the attempt at subduing her, the imprisoning of her people. The Romans had taken so much from her and yet she rose up to kick their asses up between their ears. A phoenix among falcons as my mom had called her. A perfect example of coming back fighting, and a good inspiration for people who've suffered some kind of adversity.

No one knew how she'd died, or what happened to her daughters afterward. You could ask thousands of different people and get hundreds of different opinions. If people even knew who she was. Even shifters had theories. Some of my kind said her daughters had gone on to live happy lives after their mother's death. Others weren't so sure. Back then rape was used as a different power play. It made a woman less likely to get married, effectively ending a bloodline. Her daughters had been abused and violated by so many men, I honestly was one of the few who believed they took their own lives alongside their mother. I wouldn't have blamed them, not after everything the Romans had done to them.

After admiring the statue, I continued around the garden. Several of the gardeners waved at me as I walked by. I waved back, and enjoyed the scenery until the clouds started looking ominous. Another rain was coming in. Time to head back inside.

It started down pouring half way there, I made a run for it. I regretted it once I got inside though. My leg started to throb. I sat on one of the chairs that was placed along the wall by the door. I started breathing deeply, trying to control the pain. I stretched my leg out and yelled as the pain suddenly intensified. A door down the hall opened and I heard someone coming in my direction. I barely comprehended Gretchen as she knelt next to me.

"Maggie, are you all right?!" she looked really concerned.

Threw shaky breaths I said, "My room, there's a metal rig-" I clenched my teeth, "it's a brace for my leg, I need it. Along-" damn this hurts, "with the taller of the two bottles on the head table."

She immediately stood and ran for the stairs. She was fast. I continued my labored breathing as the pain went back and forth from dissipating to growing. Clearly my saying my full last name hadn't been as beneficial as I had hoped.

Less than a minute later, Gretchen came back down the stairs with the brace and my pill bottle. She gave me the brace, set the bottle down, and ran to the kitchen. I undid the braces buckles and started putting it in place. I tried to do my calf, but the pain was too much. It was only then that I heard shouting from the kitchen.

Gretchen finally came back with a glass of water, she looked annoyed. I saw why a second later as Mrs. Granger followed. She stopped in her tracks when she saw me though. I opened the bottle and taking the glass from Gretchen, took two pills. Which was only recommended in extreme cases. This was one of them.

Without asking Gretchen, she started doing the buckles on my calf. Which I greatly appreciated. I finished the water, and went back to trying to catch my breathe. I was clenching the chair pretty hard. I ended up leaving indentations in the wood.

When I could finally breath again, I looked up at Mrs. Granger, she was looking a little pale. Gretchen was looking worried. She didn't say a word, but her eyes said enough.

"I'll be fine. Eventually." I said, still taking deep breaths.

"I'm going to make a call." Mrs. Granger said, going back through the door she'd come out of.

Gretchen shook her head, "Can I help you get anywhere?"

I nodded, "My room if it's not too much trouble. I need to lie down."

She nodded, and put her arm around my waist while I put mine over her shoulders. It was a long walk, but we managed it in five minutes. It helped that there were hand rails on both sides of all the stairs. We had to turn sideways to get into my room, once we did though, she helped me get over to the bed and lie down. I wasn't breathing heavily anymore, and my leg wasn't throbbing as much. Both were good things but not necessarily how I would end my day. I could still end up completely crippled for the week if not careful.

"Maybe we should move you to one of the ground floor rooms." Gretchen commented as she sat on the foot of the bed.

I shook my head, "I'll be alright. Plus it would go against doctor's orders, I have to take the stairs to help strengthen my leg."

She nodded, "Okay."

"I hope I didn't get you into any trouble." I said.

She chuckled, "No, she gave me a chore and only argued because she thought the water was for me. She believed me when she saw you of course."

"Yeah, I can have that effect on people."

"Shocking them into silence." She said with a smile.

I nodded, "I never wear anything shorter than my knees, so people don't see why I have a limp."

She seemed surprised, "It's on the surface?"

"The evidence of the wound, yes. The wound itself, no." I shifted position slightly, "I have a scar that goes from here," I traced it with my finger, "to here."

Her eyes widened as she followed my finger from knee to just below the hip joint, "What could cause such an injury?"

"An old fashioned cast iron tub with a lip around the outside edge." I answered.

Her eyes got so large I thought they would pop out of her head, "How does one come into conflict with a tub?"

I laughed, "I've never heard it worded like that." I couldn't stop laughing.

"I still wonder." She was giggling to herself. I guess she hadn't realized how'd she'd phrased it.

"To answer your question, one comes into conflict with a tub, when a bomb planted by a deranged lunatic to kill your parents misfires and destroys the floor. Sending you and the tub into the garage, where you lie prone and unable to stop the tub from falling through the ruined floor to land on your leg." I look up to see her reaction.

She's staring at me in horror, "Who could do such a thing?"

"Did you ever see the American movie Prom Night, from 2008? Or read Dark Guardian by Christine Feehan?" I asked.

"I've read the Feehan book." Her expression changes when she realizes what I'm talking about. "A man killed your family because he wanted you to himself!"

I swallowed the lump in my throat as I nod, "Almost my whole family."

She looks angry as well as horrified, "How did it happen?"

"Kinda similar to how it does in the movie I mentioned. I went to a movie by myself to try and calm my nerves, and when I got home…" I paused, "everything was wrong. My maternal grandparents were already dead." I paused again as my emotions took over and I started crying as I talked, "My older sister, died in my arms."

She covered her mouth in shock, "When I went to try and kill him, since he was still in the house, I noticed the bomb too late. When it went off I was thrown into the bathroom and from there received this permanent injury," I indicated my leg, "I lost consciousness when the tub landed." I paused to clear my throat, "When I came to, he was outside. Torturing my mother, I was forced to watch her die at his hands. He then somehow defeated my father, shooting his leg off before shooting him in the chest with a shotgun at point blank rang."

There were tears running down both our faces now, "My father lived long enough to tear the attackers leg to shreds. He only then was able to notice that I'd seen the whole thing. He died, in front of me. Just as the ambulance arrived."

She was pale as a ghost now. Unbidden, she got up, walked closer and sat down next to me. Pulling me into a friendly and comforting embrace. I returned it gratefully. I heard a quiet gasp from outside the door. Gretchen hadn't closed it when we'd come in.

There were actually several heartbeats outside the doorway. We had passed a few other workers on our way here. I hadn't realized they'd followed. I realized one of them was Mrs. Granger. She was crying into a piece of cloth, a handkerchief I think. If the short and ugly version wasn't good enough to convince people of my desperate need for time to heal, I didn't know what was.

"You said almost your whole family was killed. Was someone not there?" Gretchen asked quietly.

I took a breath, "Yes. My older brother was away at college when the murders happened."

"How did he react?" I knew what she meant.

"He was appalled that he hadn't been there. Like me he suffers from survivors guilt. He wishes beyond belief that he'd been there that night. Maybe we both could have done something."

She relaxed with relief, "I'm sorry I doubted."

"You don't have to be. I've always known that he could've reacted one of two ways."

"Where is he now?" she seemed surprised that he wasn't here with me.

"Safe. I have no idea where he is. We mutually agreed to end all contact until Kepner – the man who killed our family – was dead."

She shook her head, "You are very strong then."

I chuckled, "Sometimes."

We sat in companionable silence for the next several minutes. Everyone outside the door had dispersed by then. When she did leave to take care of other chores I took out my computer and logged in. I had to readjust a few things for the new time zone and country. Plus of course get the Wi-Fi password from a passing staff member.

Once that was done, I sent Mr. Hydell a message about my arrival. I realize it was a few hours late, but I didn't think he'd mind too much. Let's see. It was 1:08 here, so in Sydney it would be just after ten in the evening. He wouldn't have any trouble getting the e-mail then. I logged into Facebook next. I could still check on my friends at least.

It was as expected. All my friends had deleted their accounts. Good. Even if Kepner found this account, he wouldn't be able to find my friends. I didn't have high hopes about this account staying hidden though. He'd already found my e-mail and phone number. He may find this eventually. The only good thing was that he'd be unable to find me with it. Molly hadn't been kidding about the security she'd had put on this thing.

I put my computer away once I got a response from Mr. Hydell. He griped a little about not telling him immediately, but he didn't argue with it. I decided to test my leg. I moved to get up off the bed. Even with the brace, my leg gave. Okay so no more walking for today. I sat back down and rolled to the other side of my bed. I sat up, grabbed my book, and hopped on one leg to the window seat.

I opened the window a little before laying my leg out straight and settling back to read. I loved this book. The whole series really. I would sometimes wonder if maybe the author was a shifter – like I commented earlier on some authors being shifters. It wasn't something to ask though. Some shifters are more comfortable blending with humans. Fine by me, just don't lie about it.

Mrs. Granger came up a few hours later to ask if I wanted dinner brought up to me. I tested my leg first. I could walk, so I followed her back downstairs. I took my time of course. She waited patiently at the bottom of the staircase for me.

The dining room was empty again. I kinda had thought the staff would be eating here too. I guess not, since looking out the windows I saw the staff houses had lights on. So obviously they'd eat with family.

I sat at the end of the table again, this time getting help with the chair. I was however surprised that I hadn't been told to dress up. Since I'm being treated like a lady in her castle.

"I hope you're hungry young lady." Mrs. Granger said. I nodded.

"Good. Given the events of today I felt a supper of Cullen skink was appropriate."

Ooh. Sounds good. For those of you not brushed up on your Scottish culinary knowledge, Cullen skink is a fish chowder. Made with potatoes and haddock. My mom made it once for my birthday. It was really good.

I could smell it before the chef even left the kitchen. He brought the whole soup into the dining room. It smelled amazing. He placed the tureen on a wood platform and started ladling into the bowl in front of me. My mouth was beginning to water. He set a small bowl of parsley flakes down and also put a loaf of bread near me.

He bowed to me, seeing my smile he got a big grin on his face as he left. Mrs. Granger also left me to my meal. She wasn't away long though, she came back in with a laptop.

"I have a few more things to take care of so I won't be joining you. I've set up a movie on the laptop to play for you while you eat dear. Please enjoy."

I nodded, "Thank you." I said sincerely.

She smiled. Then bowed herself and went back into the kitchen. Leaving me alone with the soup. It was divine. Creamy and thick, the fish gave it a mild salty flavor and the fresh parsley was nice. The bread was excellent and reminded me of my grandma. Warm and fluffy inside, crispy, and crackly on the outside. I did watch the movie that Mrs. Granger had set up. Brave. Ha! Very appropriate.

Chapter 36

I ate about half of the soup in the tureen, and a good quarter of the bread loaf. I was stuffed for the first time in a long while. The chef came back out before the movie was done and was surprised at how much I'd eaten.

"A girl with an appetite. Always a good thing." He said with a wide smile.

"It was delicious. Thank you."

"You are most welcome miss. And I see you enjoyed the bread as well." He chuckled as he carried the tureen back to the kitchen.

I leaned back in my chair. Relishing the feel of a full stomach. Both he and Mrs. Granger came back in about five minutes later. I paused the movie to hear what they had to say or ask.

Chef went first, "First, you may call me Malcolm. And I hope you have some room for dessert later."

I smiled, "I think I will Malcolm. What would it be?"

"A little something called cranachan. Are you familiar with it?"

I nodded, "I've done plenty of research on traditional Scottish foods." I knew cranachan was kinda like a trifle or parfait. Made with fresh Scottish raspberries, oats, cream, honey, and whiskey traditionally.

"Excellent. I'll exclude the whiskey if you wish." He said.

"I'll try the authentic version first I think."

He smiled, "I'll get everything started then." He went back towards the kitchen.

I turned my attention to Mrs. Granger, "Since tomorrow is Monday, I have to inform you that this is the staff's day off. Do you have any objections to this?"

"No ma'am." No one should work seven days a week.

"Alright, I also wish to know if you are allergic to anything or have any food preferences or dislikes."

I took a minute to think, "I have an allergy to pickling liquids, and of course anything made with them." I paused, "Preference wise, not much except I'm not over fond of oatmeal – or porridge – but I'm not unwilling to try a few things mixed with it. Dislikes are few. I really hate American potato or egg salad, also I'm not fond of hard boiled eggs. I prefer scrambled. Other than that I don't have a lot of dislikes."

"I'll inform Malcolm then." She smiled at me.

Just before she entered the kitchen I had a thought, "oh um…" she turned, "I am put off by things made with blood for personal reasons," she nodded knowingly, since she'd heard the minute details of the murder, "but I'm not opposed to trying the black pudding at least once."

She nodded, "No opposition to suet or organ meats?" I shook my head.

She nodded again and finished entering the kitchen. I pulled the laptop closer and started the movie up again.

Malcolm came back about thirty minutes later with a small mason jar of cranachan. He handed it to me with a smile, which I returned. He then said good night and left through the kitchen doors. The dessert was delicious. Creamy and fresh. The raspberries bursting with flavor. The whiskey gave it a slight tang which was balancing for the sweetness. Really good dessert. I finished it at the same time the movie finished.

I left the laptop there on the table and took the jar to the kitchen. I rinsed it out, and set it beside the other dishes. I cleaned the spoon as well. Going back into the dining room I saw that the laptop had been collected, so no trouble for me on that one.

Saying good night to Mrs. Granger as I passed by her room, I went up to bed. I stopped at the bathroom across from mine first. My chest clenched slightly as I saw the cast iron bathtub. It wasn't exactly the same as the one that we'd had, but it was close.

I got my nerves back together and looked in the mirror. I'd decided earlier that I'd put my hair back to normal. I looked okay as a blond, but I wanted my red hair back. I didn't technically have a hair changing spell, but everyone makes their own at some point. I went into my room and took out some of the crystals and stones I had brought with me. Before I got started though I remember rule number six. Any and all magic to be performed outdoors or to inform the head of house if needed to be done indoors. It was raining pretty heavily, and I didn't want to go outside in the dark. Not after the murders. I wasn't comfortable with that.

I went back down the hall to Mrs. Granger's room. The door was open, and she was still awake, she was on the phone though, so she held up a finger and I waited patiently for her to finish.

Once she hung up she said, "Yes dear."

"I'm going to perform a spell in the bathroom across from my room, is that okay?"

"Yes, go right ahead."

"Thank you." I said.

"Your welcome."

I walked back to the bathroom with my stones and crystals, working out how to word the spell as I walked. I stood in front of the mirror, and separated the red stones from the rest. I took a second to remember which way was north and set the crystals up. Keeping my voice low so as not to disturb Mrs. Granger, with my hand held over the stones, I began my spell.

"Earth to sun, Night to day

Listen to all I say

Here in lands of old

Please let my magic unfold

Earth, Air, Fire, and Water

Please return my hair to its natural color."

The wind was subtle this time. I guess taking que from my voice level and staying quiet. Once it stopped, I looked up. I smiled at myself in the mirror. My hair was red again. The mild ruby red color I had been born with. To explain its shade better, think a few shades darker than Ariel's from the Little Mermaid, but not as dark as Fiona's from Shrek. I also took the time to redo the growth spell and make my hair even longer. Now my hair reached my knees, and was beautifully thick. I put my stones and crystals away and ran a brush through my hair. I was feeling much better than I had this morning. It was a little hard to believe that I woke up in California this morning and will be falling asleep in Scotland.

I decided to check my e-mail before changing into my pajamas. Molly had sent me pictures. I'd take a look at them tomorrow. Mr. Hydell had also sent an e-mail saying that he was suffering from jetlag and probably wouldn't be ready to explore tomorrow. I chuckled a little. If Molly had her way, he'd be up and out by seven a.m. and ready to go just fine.

I changed into my pjs after closing my door. I chose to leave the window curtains open, though I did close the window. I moved the bed drapes around a little so that the morning light wouldn't hurt my eyes when the sun rose. My room faced west so I wouldn't get the sunrise.

I went to the bathroom to take my sleeping pill. Once again taking a chance to admire my hair. I put the small cup back down and swallowed. That done, I could sleep peacefully tonight.

Back in my room, I shut the door, pulled the foot drapes closed, and climbed in bed. I wasn't feeling tired, so I grabbed Eragon and started reading. I just managed to place my bookmark inside when I felt myself nod off.

Chapter 37

I awoke slowly the next morning. The pill had worked better than usual last night. Probably because of the stress and a full stomach, who could say. I looked out my window, it was a clear day outside. A good day for a fly.

I sat up and cringed. My leg was really sore. That wasn't a good sign. I really wanted to go flying, I guess I could remain in dragon form the whole time. But there were pro's and con's about that. I laid back down for a few minutes, trying to think of something. I couldn't shift with the brace on, and it was clear that I would need it today. I'd just have to see where the day took me I guess.

I got up, put my brace on, and went to the bathroom. I had trouble obviously, since the brace didn't do well without belt loops. I should get that modified. Once I was finally done, I went back to my room to see that yesterday's clothes were gone, and something new was out. I usually pick my own clothes, but I guess someone decided to save me the trouble. My hoodie was still there though.

Amazingly enough the brace works fine with cargo shorts, although it looks weird against a bare calf. Oh well. It's nice out, might as well dress accordingly. I still wore my hoodie out of compulsion.

I didn't have to take as much time getting down to the dining room this time thankfully. Mrs. Granger was already there, surprisingly. She had breakfast out, I was actually expecting to have to make my own breakfast. The look on her face when she saw that my hair was different was priceless.

I actually laughed, before asking, "What's all this?"

"I figured with your leg it was easier if someone else did breakfast today." She explained.

"Thank you ma'am." I said, nodding as well.

"So polite for a shifter." She said with awe.

"I was raised well." I sat at the same end of the table as the two previous meals.

Breakfast today was a dish called kedgeree. A spiced rice dish with smoked haddock, peas – sometimes, and parsley. Usually it's done with hard-boiled eggs, but since I'd told her I prefer scrambled, she did the eggs to my preference. There was a wedge of lemon on the side as well. It looked and smelled really good.

"I have to head to town for some things, so I'll be back later. The staff are on hand if you need anything, but I do encourage sometime in the woods. Might help with your leg." She said with a reassuring smile.

"Thank you. I plan on some flying if that's doable." I said.

She thought for a second, "Given your legs sensitivity I would recommend launching from the roof. It should make it a little easier." I nodded.

She grabbed her purse and after giving me a final wave, left the dining room. I heard the front doors close as well. Only then did I dig in with gusto.

I normally wouldn't have thought to do fish or rice for breakfast, but the kedgeree was actually really good. The lemon added a nice citrusy note, and the cup of milk I had grabbed kept the heat in check. It wasn't as spicy as some people have said, but it did have a kick.

Keeping my weight off my left leg as much as possible, I washed the dishes after I was done eating. I left them on the rack to dry, then chose to head outside and sit in the garden for a little while. The day was nice, so it was an excellent opportunity. And at least this time I won't have to rush inside.

Sitting on a bench next to the Boudica statue, I admired the view of the garden, and the small edge of the ocean that I could see from here. One of these days I'll have to go for a swim.

In the distance I heard a plane engine start up. I'd already heard one of the staff say in passing that Eynort's store hadn't had what Mrs. Granger needed so now she needed to head down to Glasgow. My guess was Mack had either been called in earlier or had been staying somewhere not far away. The Isle of Skye was bigger than some people think, plenty of open space. You'd be surprised where some choose to live.

I watched the little plane gain altitude for about twenty miles, then even out and head south. I thought about the Fairy Pools that Mack had told me about. I'd have to get a map out so he could show me where they were later. For now though, I felt like exploring. I got up from the bench and walked back inside. At the edge of the kitchen I left a note along with my brace. I can walk as a dragon just fine. I hopped back outside, and steadying myself leaning against the wall, I started to shift.

It felt good to go dragon again. Now that I didn't have to worry about my doctors two weeks diagnosis. My legs went first of course. Once I was done changing, I let my eyes adjust to the changes as well. Everything was more detailed in my dragon eyes. Colors sharper, distance wasn't a challenge, and I could filter the sun better. If necessary of course.

I started walking, my leg feeling surprisingly stiff. Great. Not so immune in dragon form anymore. I performed some stretches to try and loosen the muscles. That seemed to help, so I started walking again. It felt good to be able to move freely. I followed a path into the woods, keeping my wings close so as not to get caught on anything.

Not that far in I found a large boulder in one of the staff's backyard. I – for some reason – decided to lie on it and sun myself. I don't usually do that. Amanda yes, me, no. I had no inclination for it, but some instinct told me to sun myself.

I jumped up on the boulder, got comfortable, and laid down. Almost instantly I stated feeling sleepy. What was going on? After less than two seconds, I nodded off.

I don't remember what happened in my dream, but I do recall what woke me up. Something was moving my tail. I opened an eye and chuckled. Or well, chuckled as well as a dragon can. There was a one year old child playing with the end of my tail. It must have slid off the rock while I was asleep.

Keeping my eye partly open, I twitched my tail tip a little as the child reached for it. The child squealed and erupted into giggles. This also drew the attention of the family member just inside the house door. The person inside looked around frantically so I twitched my tail again. The same result occurred. The family member looked outside, and I realized it was Gretchen.

She came outside, "Keelan, don't you scare me like that." She admonished him.

"Dan-dan." He pointed his little fingers at me. It was only then that she fully noticed me.

I turned my head to look at her, her eyes were pretty wide, "Maggie?" she asked.

I nodded, feeling little Keelan grab hold of my tail. Gretchen voiced my thought as well by saying, 'aww.' It truly was cute. I gently lifted my tail, he got this huge grin on his face, and started laughing. Gretchen followed less than a second later.

"Mr. McHaddish told us you were good with children." She said between giggles. I tilted my head to the side. She got it.

"Our employer. The man who owns the property. He also said you were a dragon shifter, he neglected to tell us your color."

"Dan-dan." Keelan said again.

"Yes little brother I see the dragon." She laughed again.

I'd never spoken in dragon form, so I went for telepathy, *"Can I ask you something?"*

She looked surprised and amazed at what I had just done, "You can speak telepathically?"

I nodded, *"Comes in handy when one's vocal cords aren't old enough for it."*

"I see." I wouldn't be able to speak in dragon form for years. "What was your question?"

"This boulder I'm sitting on, does it have any magic related abilities?"

She thought for a second, "I don't think so, but then again this is the Isle of Skye."

"Very true." I said.

"What exactly is your color? I can see it's not quite red." She asked.

"*Magenta. Which technically counts as a reddish-purple, or a purplish-red. Depending on which side of the color scale your coming from.*"

"Ah. It's beautiful. Is that why your full name is 'Magenta'?" I nodded.

I put her brother back down and tried to take my tail back, his grip tightened, "Dan-dan." My gods he was cute.

Gretchen giggled again, "It's time for your nap anyway little brother."

She grabbed him, but he just refused to let go. He had a strong grip for a one year old. When Gretchen finally did get him loose he threw a fit. He wouldn't sit still. I gently hopped off the rock and laid down in the yard. I used a blanket of his that was on the porch and made a little nest in my now curled up tail.

Gretchen looked at me gratefully and set her brother in the proverbial nest. He moved around a little, getting comfy. Once he was, he fell asleep almost instantly. We both chuckled quietly. Gretchen went back inside and came back with a camera. Her parents were never going to believe this. He started snoring softly. Which only made the scene all the cuter. Gretchen started taking pictures like a fiend. I didn't mind, her brother looked absolutely adorable where he was.

I heard a car pull into the drive way. Me raising my head told Gretchen all she needed to know. She put the camera on the porch and went inside, her sneakers squeaking on the kitchen floor. I looked up at the sky, noticing the tree coverage in her yard. I was still confused about why I'd had such an urge to lie on the boulder. I mean yes, the Isle of Skye had some of the most Scottish legends attached to it, but that only partly explained what had just happened.

I looked back down at Keelan as I felt him move. I adjusted my tail just enough to keep it from falling asleep, but not to disturb him. I looked at him adoringly. He also reminded me of Gregory, and that made me a little sad. I couldn't not think about Ms. Hamper and the babies. I so wanted to know where they had gone to be safe.

I wasn't stupid enough to inquire though, that could only lead to them getting killed.

I turned my attention back to the kitchen door, Gretchen was leading her parents back quietly, I could see she had her finger to her lips. She smiled when she saw he was still asleep. I caught a glimpse of her dad first. I recognized him as the staff member who'd given me the Wi-Fi password yesterday. He looked surprised to see me.

I hadn't seen her mother yet at the estate, but she had a prosthetic leg. That caught me a little off guard. When the two finally saw their son, her mother started gushing she thought it was so cute. Her father started giggling a little. I saw the look on his face change and he suddenly made a run back into the house. He came back a few minutes later with a tape measure?

"Scuse me darling." He said to his wife, who was crouched by my tail.

"What on earth are you doing darling?" She laughed.

He measured the nest I had made, "If he sleeps like this, we can finally sleep."

"*Ah,*" I said, "*they're at the sleep strike stage huh.*"

"Aye, I've even been woken by him a few times." Gretchen answered.

"Who are you talking to dear?" her mother asked. She pointed at me. Her father had an idea.

"Is your tail fully touching the ground?" he asked me.

I moved my tail a little, "*No, only the outer edge is, and from there it gets higher. He's asleep enough if you want me to lift him and see for yourself what I mean.*"

Her mother took the initiative and picked him up, blanket and all, very gently. He father saw that my tail was flexible enough to almost perfectly resemble a spiral. It also had a slight bowl shape, which I knew helped babies sleep much better. He grabbed the camera from where Gretchen had left it and took a couple picture from different angles. Once he was satisfied, he stood and went back inside. His wife followed, taking little Keelan with. Gretchen looked at me and smiled. She seemed more relaxed now that her brother would sleep better.

"I can't thank you enough for your help Maggie."

"Not a problem Gretchen." I said.

"I'll ask my mum about the rock if you like."

"I would please, and I was also wondering where this lake my therapist mentioned is located."

She thought for a second, then turned toward the path, "Follow the path for just under a mile, you'll find a small deer path that turns off. That deer path leads straight to the lake."

"Thanks Gretchen."

"Your welcome. See you later." She waved as I got up to go and she went back inside with her family.

I got walking. The path was very easy to follow, so finding the deer path wasn't too much of a challenge. With my dragon senses I found it almost immediately. It really was a **small** path. I didn't walk down it though, I didn't want to scare any deer from using the path again. So walking about five feet to the side of the deer path, I followed it until I smelled water.

There it was, the small lake that Ms. Hamper had spoken about. It was beautifully clear. No fish but the bottom was perfectly visible. It was about thirty feet in circumference and from the look of it, twenty feet deep. So not as small as I had envisioned.

I gently dipped my snout in only a half inch and took a drink. It was crisp and clean. Very refreshing. I walked around the lake for several minutes, I'd have to come back here with my swimsuit and go for a swim. I took a sniff and smelled raspberries. I turned around and moved a little ways from the lake. Only about eight feet downhill from the southern shore, was a small grove of berry bushes. They smelled so good. I decided to eat a few for a snack.

Scottish raspberries are at peak season in June, so they tasted fantastic. I was full before I even got through one half of the bush. I'd have to see if this was where Malcolm got his berries for the cranachan.

I walked back to the lake and at the last second got a running leap and used the open spot over the lake to clear the trees and head back to the house. I brushed the tops of the trees with my wings as I went. It felt good to do my own flying. The wind carried so many scents past my nose it was a surprise that I could tell where anything was coming from. I could smell sheep and cows to the north, the fishing villages to the south, and oh so many woodsy smells from the forest all around me. The best scent of course was of the sea. I turned my head just enough to see a few miles out to sea. I spotted a pod of whales breaching off the coast. Humpbacks.

The castle came into view. I circled the grounds before picking a spot close to the kitchen door. I was small enough to make the path to the outdoor kitchen pavilion work. I saw Mrs. Granger standing by the door holding my brace and waving to me. I indicated where I was going to land and just saw her nod of affirmation.

As I got lower a sudden sharp pain seized me. I cringed and roared in pain. I barely managed to land without crashing. It wasn't until I was on the ground and breathing through the pain that I realized where the pain had come from. My wings. Not my leg.

I was staring at my wings in confusion when Mrs. Granger finally reached me. My wing muscles were still partly spasming from the sudden pain that I had trouble getting on my feet. I tried shifting back but the pain was too intense. I saw a fresh log by a wheelbarrow and grabbed it with my teeth just before the pain became so intense that I'm surprised I stayed awake. I kept my roar as quiet as possible so as not to deafen Mrs. Granger when she knelt by my head.

"What is it dear?" she asked with motherly concern.

With tears streaming down my face I said, "*My wings. They hurt.*" I bit down a little more as the pain spiked again.

She saw that there was nothing wrong with them, "Stay here if you can, I'll be right back." She left my brace on the ground and ran back to the house.

I kept my breathing as steady as I could, it wasn't easy since the pain was doing what it had done with my leg yesterday. Ebbing then intensifying. My jaw was starting to hurt too, but since that was because of me biting the log, I could use it as a focus. When the pain finally started decreasing and not escalating, I let go of the log. I kept it close though, just in case.

Only my leg had ever hurt that much, what was up with that then? Why and what would cause my wings to feel like someone was pulling them apart with a hot iron bar? I didn't remember either of my siblings going through something like this. But I did remember that shortly after they'd each turned sixteen, our dad had taken them on a trip out of town for the weekend. They had been fine when they left and had seemed okay when they'd come home, so what the heck were the trips for? Something more to ask Reggie. When I could get my thoughts straight again anyway.

I was finally able to focus enough to notice Mrs. Granger coming back with something in her hand. She crouched down in front of me and held the glass up. It was a one cup measuring cup with tea inside. How long was I trapped in the throughs of pain.

"Drink this dear. Mr. McHaddish said it would help." She told me. I drank it without complaint. It tasted horrible.

"There, you'll feel better shortly. He also said that if you can, you should stretch out your wings to their full length and let them absorb some sun. Do you think you can do that?"

I tried to move one wing, I couldn't. it just hurt too much, "Okay, stay put, I'll gather some of the staff and we'll move them. How much room do you need?"

I took a second to think about that. Tip of tail to tip of nose I was 32 feet long, that meant I needed 96 feet of space for my wings.

"My wingspan is 96 feet." I answered.

She looked dumbfounded. In an impressed way. She nodded, stood up, and ran toward the staff housing. I looked around me, there were only a few things that would need to be moved. I laid my head down after shifting my body a bit so I was comfortable. I laid on my belly as best I could, like I had in Gretchen's backyard.

I felt everyone coming before I saw them. Your head touching the ground will do that. I saw Gretchen coming too. She knelt down by my head and placed a hand on my nose. She smelled like ginger. Odd.

I barely comprehended the staff members moving the various items out of the way. I re-grabbed the log before they touched my wings. Very carefully and slowly, the thirteen people Mrs. Granger had brought back, started moving and unfolding my wings. I bit down on the log, it hurt more than I wanted to admit. They took their time and had the task down in about six minutes.

Once they were done, I was on the verge of blacking out. I was glad I'd readjusted before they actually got here. My wings hurt so much that I now was surprised that Reggie hadn't made contact. He'd been so quick to do it when I collapsed a few weeks ago, what was different about this time? I'd think about it later, right then I just wanted to let oblivion take me and rest right there in the sun.

Chapter 38

I didn't register the time when I finally came to. All that I could tell, was that by the suns positioned, about three hours had passed. It was now close to two. I felt sore from head to tail. I lifted my head a little, feeling the headache as I got more than four inches off the ground. Great.

Gretchen was there with a bowl of water. She tilted it into my mouth, the dryness started going away. The tea had helped with the pain, now I just needed to try and get up. I decided against it when my legs started shaking. I figured I might have the energy to change back to human. So taking a breath, I started to shift.

Thankfully I was successful. Once I was human again I rolled onto my back and laid there. My back muscles were on fire. My leg wasn't though. Fine by me honestly. I heard my stomach rumble. I hadn't eaten since breakfast. I felt a little queasy from all the pain from earlier.

Gretchen knelt down by me, "How are you feeling?"

"My back is on fire, and I'm starving." I said. There was sweat on my forehead.

"I forget that dragon's wing muscles come from their backs and shoulders. Can you stand?"

"Maybe with a little help and my brace. I don't trust my leg."

She got up and ran toward the house. She came back a few minutes later with Mrs. Granger and my brace. With her help I was able to get the brace secure. Then with both of them helping, I was able to get up.

The three of us walked back to the house, only separating when Mrs. Granger walked inside first in order to open the door to the dining room. She had pulled a chair from the table as well. The table was set with lunch and tea.

"Thank you." I said to both as I sat down.

"You gave me quite a scare when you fell dear. I was worried you'd crash." Mrs. Granger told me.

"I'm sorry. It just happened so suddenly."

"What was it?" she asked.

"I honestly have no idea. I'd have to communicate with my brother to find out." I said, wiping the sweat from my forehead with a napkin that she handed me.

"But you said your brother was hidden." Gretchen said.

"He is. Dragon shifter siblings can communicate telepathically, even at great distances."

"Well you must eat first. You can speak with your brother when you're finished." Mrs. Granger told me.

I didn't argue. I was so hungry I could eat a whole buffet by myself. They both left me to my meal once I'd poured myself some tea. She'd gone for simple and hearty today. Meat and cheese sandwich with tomatoes and lettuce, and homemade chips. I could tell from the smell that the chips had been baked instead of fried, so they were healthier. The tea was good too.

She'd made five sandwiches. I ended up eating all of them when I saw the small note saying they all were for me. The note also said that a large meal was recommended by her employer. Due to how much calories would have been burned by the pain.

The food was really good. I managed to eat and drink everything by the time Mrs. Granger came back to clean up. I tried to help but she wouldn't let me. She said I was to head up to my room and rest for a little while. I decided she was right, all that food was making me sleepy, and after what had happened a nap was definitely advisable.

Without any argument, I made my way upstairs to my room. I was having trouble keeping my eyes open when I reached the final landing. I didn't bother taking the brace off when I reached my bed. I just kinda collapsed down on it. I had just enough thought left to remember that I had brought the pearl with me. The same one I had used to contact Reggie earlier last week. I'd have to try and talk to him either later today or tomorrow. It would depend on how much energy I had when I woke up.

I was semi awake when Mrs. Granger came in to place another glass of the nasty tasting tea on the night stand. Gretchen must have told her about my being sore. I'd thank her for that later. I nodded off again right after she left my room.

When I finally woke up enough to stay that way, it was after three. I went into the bathroom and grabbed a drink of water before I swallowed the tea. I went back in my room and swallowed the tea quickly. It wasn't as bad the second time around, but not something I would want to drink every day.

I sat back down on the bed and contemplated my next move. Obviously, I needed to ask my brother if he knew what had just happened to me and what the hell it was about. Thinking on it, I was reminded of a Star Trek: The Next Generation episode. In that episode, Counselor Troi thought she'd lost her empathic abilities for good when the ship accidentally got caught inside a two dimensional being that was made up of thousands of minds.

She later learned that she still had her abilities, she'd just been overloaded by the quantity of emotions so badly that her abilities were inactive. It wasn't until the Enterprise had finally separated from the being that she could feel the emotions of others again. It was possible that because of how much pain I had experienced, my brain had been overloaded and Reggie made unable to sense my pain.

It was the only working theory I had. Might as well put it to the test. I grabbed my bag with the stones and crystals and opened the hidden pocket in the back. I kept the pearl in there, along with my sister's birthstone. I just couldn't bring myself to get rid of it. I pulled the pearl out and made my way to the roof. The stairs for it weren't hard to find. I passed Mrs. Granger on the way, so she knew where to find me.

On the roof I found the viewing platform and a sitting area. I chose one of the chairs and moved it to the western most point of the roof. My back muscles protesting slightly from the weight moving. There was now at least an ocean between me and my brother. This was going to be the hardest communication either of us had performed.

Taking the pearl from my pocket and placing it between my palms, I said his name. I continued to focus on that for several minutes. I don't know how long it took but when I finally felt him make contact, the first thing I noticed was his relief.

"Maggie! Thank the Gods, I was worried you'd been seriously hurt." He said.

I gave a small smile, *"I'm in pain but not hurt. I promise."*

"Where are you? I'm having to focus really hard to talk with you."

"I'm in Scotland. On the Isle of Skye."

I could sense that he was impressed, *"What in the world are you doing there?!"*

I chuckled, *"My therapist's uncle is letting me stay at his estate for the summer. To try and heal."*

"Lucky." Were he here he'd stick his tongue out at me.

"I hope your summer has started okay." I said.

"Can't complain. Costa Rica's beautiful."

What! *"Please take plenty of pics."*

He laughed, *"Same to you sis. Of the night sky too please, and I want a rock."*

"Sea shells and a rock in your case bro." I giggled.

"You got it." He paused, *"As much as talking to you feels so good right now, I'm guessing that's not why you called."*

I sighed, *"I wish it was, but you are correct."* I took a sec to gather my thoughts, *"I need to know why dad took you and Amanda on those trips shortly after your 16th birthdays."*

I felt him cringe, *"Oh man those were some of the most painful days of my life."* Huh!??

"What do you mean?" I asked, apprehensively.

"The reason our full last name is the way it is, is because of the extra claw we have on our wings."

I was confused, "*The claw at the joint?*" Not the joint where the wing met shoulder, but the joint that was at the halfway point on a wings length. The thumb claw if you will.

"*No, that claw comes standard with all dragons.*" He started, "*In our case, we have a second claw that grows from the very tip of our wings.*"

"*I see.*"

"*What you experienced earlier — I think — was the first stage of final growth for that second claw.*"

"*Great.*" I said sarcastically.

"*Trust me, I know what's in store for you over the next few days. 'Cause you do remember that dad excused Amanda from school so that she could be gone for a few extra days.*"

"*I remember. I also remember how both of you came home.*" They'd looked like they'd been kidnapped and beaten several times. Dad hadn't looked much better. "*Why had dad looked so terrible too?*"

"*Because he'd had to restrain the both of us when we reached the final finishing stage. The pain made us both lash out so bad that anyone who got too close was in grave danger of being killed in some way.*"

"*Oh my Gods.*"

"*Yeah,*" he paused, "*dad came out with broken bones both times.*"

I started hyperventilating, what was going to happen when I reached the final finishing!? My dad was dead, he wouldn't be able to restrain me. No one would! I could seriously hurt or kill someone. My thoughts went straight to Keelan. If I hurt him…. I couldn't even finish the thought.

"*Is there any way to delay or stop it?!*" I asked in desperation.

I felt his hesitation, "*No.*"

I couldn't breathe, "*So what do I do!?*" I was scared. I didn't get scared often.

I could feel him thinking, trying to find a way for his baby sister to get through something that our dad should be here to help with.

Finally, he said, "*I don't know. You always were stronger than me and Amanda combined. Dad would've been the only one who could restrain you. Maybe if you know a potion that could knock you flat out when the final finishing comes, it might help.*" He was grasping at straws, but at least it was something.

"I'll see what I can find, but I don't have high hopes for it." I really didn't.

"Maybe we should consider temporarily ending the no contact agreement. You're going to need me."

I thought about it, *"Give me 24 hours. If I can't find a doable spell or potion I'll contact you again."*

"Contact me whether you find something usable or not." He paused, *"I **will** need to know that you're going to be okay."*

I sighed again, *"Okay."*

I felt his relief, *"Thank you. I love you sis."*

"I love you too bro."

We broke contact at the same time. I wrapped my arms around myself. I felt queasy again. This was officially serious. Both of those trips had lasted almost a week apiece. That meant that since I'd experienced the first part of the final growth, I had less than five or six days to come up with some kind of plan.

My thoughts went to Mr. French. A cave lion shifter wouldn't be able to restrain me once the final finishing took hold, but maybe he'd know someone who could. I should talk to Mrs. Granger, see if she or her employer could help me contact him in any kind of way.

I put the pearl in my pocket before standing and putting the chair back where I found it. I nearly ran back down the stairs. I looked down the hall way, no sign of her. I stood still and opened my senses. I found her heartbeat on the second floor. In the library. She was talking on the phone with someone.

I walked to and down the stairs to the second floor landing, she was just exiting the library when she saw me coming. I walked up to her.

She held up her hand so she could talk first, "Mr. McHaddish has decided to come here. He wants to make sure you're alright himself."

I nodded, I could talk to him then, "When does he get here?"

She sensed my nervousness, "He's already on the plane. He should be here by tomorrow afternoon."

I sighed with relief, "Thank you."

She came closer and rubbed my shoulders, "Go back up to your bathroom and take a hot bath. It will help with your soreness and nerves."

I nodded and turned to go, running my fingers through my hair at all the stress. A bath would be good.

I climbed the stairs slowly. I closed the bathroom door and started the water. I added some scented soap as well. I removed my brace and clothes and climbed in once I'd turned the water off. It did indeed help. For now. Come tomorrow, all that stress of the final finishing would return, and I could only hope that whomever this Mr. McHaddish was, that he'd be able to help me get through this.

Chapter 39

After my bath and putting my clothes back on, I went down to the library. I walked through the shelves to see what was available. All kinds of old novels, both from the United Kingdoms and America. I saw Hawthorne, Melville, Dickens, Jane Austen, Shakespeare, and even Jules Verne. The only French author in here. And yes I did the research, Jules Verne wasn't English, he was French. I'd been really surprised by that.

I grabbed Moby Dick and found a chair to sit in. I hadn't read it in a while. Seeing it again reminded me about the first time I'd read it. Amanda had come home, seen it, and done a double take. She'd then told me that I wouldn't make it half way through. She'd been wrong. Me and Reggie were the ones who could read old world or era novels without trouble. Amanda, not so much.

Reading did help me keep calm. Unfortunately my back muscles spasmed a few times. I probably should've taken a pain pill. I really didn't want to go back upstairs, but I also didn't want to bug anybody on their day off.

So, gritting my teeth, I put Moby Dick on the coffee table located between all the chairs, and walked back upstairs to take a pill. I swallowed it quickly, I wanted to get back to reading. I was sweating again. I decided to take a risk and left my hoodie on the hook behind the door. I relaxed when I finally got back to the library. I sat still for a few minutes before picking Moby Dick back up. I shifted positions slightly so I was lying on my back with my shoeless feet hanging over an arm of the chair and my head resting on the other with a pillow behind my neck.

That done, I got reading again. Every now and then I'd kick my feet, feeling comfortable for the first time that afternoon.

I was reading for more than an hour when one of the younger staff guys came in. He was just walking through from what I could tell, so I went back to my reading. I heard him pull a book from the shelf and walk in my direction. I kept reading. It wasn't until he yelped and jumped that I actually put the book down and looked at him. okay, what was that about? I looked up. In front of me stood a tall boy of about 17 in jeans and a t-shirt, with brown hair, blue eyes, broad shoulders, and a decent amount of muscle. I guess you could say he had the same amount as Zac Efron does in High School Musical.

He stooped to pick up his book, "I'm sorry, I didn't see you in here." His accent wasn't as thick as Gretchen's. He was reading Jules Verne.

"That's alright, I should have probably said something." I replied.

He sat in the chair opposite me, he seemed nervous. I didn't know why. I could feel him repeatedly glance at me as we sat there. It wasn't until I turned a page and looked at my arm that I realized what he must be looking at. I closed the book and gave an exasperated sigh. I should have kept the hoodie.

"It's my scars. Isn't it?" I asked. I met his eyes.

He dropped his, and put his book on his lap, he still seemed nervous, "I don't mean to. I was just, surprised."

"It's my own fault, I should've kept my hoodie on."

"I.. I didn't mean that." He paused, running his hand through his hair, "I've never seen a girl with scars before."

"But you've seen guys with scars." I smiled, meaning it as a joke.

He did as I'd hoped, he chuckled, "Well, I am sorry. I really don't mean to stare."

"I appreciate your apology, and I really don't mind. You're not the first to stare at me for one reason or another" I opened my book back up.

"If it's not too um.. pressing, how did you get the scars?" he met my eyes as he asked.

I closed my book again, "I don't know what you've been told about why I'm here,-" I paused.

He adjusted his position a little, "My dad told me that you're in therapy for survivors guilt and are in hiding from your family's killer."

I nodded, at least his dad was honest with him, "I still suffer from nightmares about my family's killer. A few weeks ago, I had a bad enough nightmare that I reacted in my sleep. The scars are the end result."

"You scratched yourself?!" he looked stupefied.

"Not intentionally. I fell asleep with my hands on my elbows, and in my dream, I went to attack him," I paused, thinking on how to explain it, "I guess my instincts just, went for it, and I scarred myself as a result."

"Did a doctor say anything?" he seemed concerned now. Good grief boy, pick an expression already. I thought with humor.

"The doctor at the E.R. said to speak with my regular doctor for a final diagnosis, and he told me to take sleeping pills if necessary to avoid any more incidents."

"E.R.?"

"Emergency room. It's the part of the hospital where people go after accidents or other medical needs that can't wait."

"Handy." He said.

"I guess living way out here any medical emergencies can be taken care of onsite." I said with a small smile.

He nodded, "I broke my arm a few years back. We splinted it and called a doctor in to look at it. He said just keep it splinted or go down to Glasgow if I wasn't okay with the splint. My mum ended up overruling me and took me down to get it put in a cast."

"Jameson! Where are you son?" a woman shouted from the hall.

"In here mum!" now he looked really annoyed.

I turned as a woman in her thirties came in. She looked a little disheveled. She glanced at me, and did a double take at my arms. I gave an apologetic smile and picked my book back up to start reading again. She cleared her throat and started talking to her son.

"Sweetheart, I've told you several times to ask before coming in here." Oh great, a helicopter mom. I could tell by her tone.

"And I've reminded you mum, that Mr. McHaddish said I could use the library anytime I wanted." He sounded annoyed. I now understood why he'd been overruled.

"I don't care what he said, you are my son, not his." I rolled my eyes. Her back was to me so she couldn't see.

He sighed in frustration, "What do you need mum?"

"Your friend Bill just dropped off a downed tree. It needs to be cut." She sounded like she was gonna throw up just by asking him.

He huffed, "Alright. I'm coming." He stood and placed the book on the coffee table between us.

I returned my attention to my book as they walked out, "She really should cover her arms."

"Mum!!" he sounded horrified.

That was it, I stood, "Thank you very much." I placed the book on the table as gently as I could under temper. Walking past I said, "Thank you very much for reminding me just how self-conscious I am about myself now that I have these permanent marks marring my skin!" I'd stopped in front of her at 'much'. I held up both arms, "Curtesy of the man who murdered my whole family in front of me!"

She looked horrified, but also ashamed of herself. Good. I didn't look at Jameson, I couldn't tell how he felt, but I think he was at a loss. I stormed out of the library, and ripping the brace from my leg, ran down the rest of the stairs, and out the front door.

I shifted as my feet touched the gravel, and still running, took flight just before touching the gate. I gained altitude and pointed myself toward the coast. I needed somewhere far from people right now.

I landed at the beach after a five minute flight. I started pacing back and forth. I really did not need criticism right now. I'm supposed to be healing Damn it! Her saying that only made me mad. Who was she to say what I should do?! I have my own rights to not wear coverings for my arms if I want to.

My frustration hit a peak and I whacked a rock out to sea. It flew pretty far, and even skipped over the water. I laid down in the sand. Keeping my head up and looking out on the horizon. I missed my family now more than ever. Why did people have to make stupid comments that sent me ballistic? I know some people would say I was the problem on that one. That I took some things too seriously. Well someone once said 'never judge anyone until you've been in their shoes'.

I didn't know what her situation was, but that didn't mean she had to make me feel bad about myself. Her comment had hurt. It was bad enough how some people at school had treated me.

I was breathing hard now. I chose to let it out. I roared as loud as I could, out to sea. I only stopped when I ran out of breath. Panting, I let the tears go. Again. Why did my life have to be so fucking miserable? I don't complain often, but when I do, I prefer to be alone.

Chapter 40

I stayed on the beach until after midnight. I just didn't want to go back right then. Finally it was my stomach that had me flying back. I didn't want to try fishing. I hate getting water up my nose.

The lights of the observation deck were on. I circled a bit, before choosing to land. I aimed the down draft from my wings toward the ground when I landed on the edge of the roof. Jameson was standing by the deck seats and had a table set up. I tilted my head a little in confusion while walking further onto the roof. He smelled faintly of sweat and… bear?

I shifted back and looked at him questioningly. He shrugged and seemed nervous about saying anything. It was only then that I noticed that the table was covered with food. There was even some sodas in a cooler by the foot of the table. I smiled while raising an eyebrow.

Finally he said, "I wanted to apologize for my mum's rude comment. I figured we could have dinner and do some stargazing."

I bit my lips, "So is this a date?" I smirked.

"Oh God no." then, "Not that you're not uh…"

I chuckled, "I'm joking Jameson."

He chuckled too, "I'm sorry. I've never actually done something like this."

I smiled, "I get it. And I accept your apology. This is really nice." I meant it. It was a nice way to apologize.

His smile got bigger, he led me to the table, acting like a gentleman and pulling my chair out for me, "I hope you don't mind, I did all the cooking myself." He said while pushing the chair back in.

"I don't mind." I kept the smile.

He sat down opposite me and with a flourish, removed the cloth he'd been using as a cover for the main course. I laughed.

"You made hamburgers." I couldn't believe it.

He smiled shyly, "I've always wanted to give more American food a try. I figured this was an okay place to start."

They smelled really good, "What meat did you use?"

"Beef. I had to grind it myself, but the recipe I looked up said that beef was the most common meat used." He said.

I nodded, "It is, and they smell fantastic."

He smiled proudly, "Well I hope they taste just as good."

We started assembling our burgers. They were still warm, so the piece of cheese I placed on mine started to melt slightly. He'd even made the ketchup. Wow! It wasn't too sweet and actually tasted like tomatoes. I applied some, place a slice of tomato and a piece of lettuce on the bottom bun, put the burger in its place along with the top bun, and started eating. Man those burgers were delicious.

"Mhh. What seasonings did you use?" I covered my mouth to ask the question.

He swallowed, "Garlic, thyme, oregano, and a little paprika."

I nodded, "They're really good." I took another bite. He smiled happily.

The burgers were juicy and definitely had lots of flavor. The paprika hit in the back of the mouth but it wasn't over powering. He leaned down and pulled out two sodas. I saw they were Scottish when he handed me mine. Irn Bru? Okay, interesting name for a soda, but then again this was Scotland. I opened the can and gave it a taste. I liked it. It was really good.

We talked about all kinds of stuff while we ate. Turns out we had a lot in common. Taste in books, music, and movies. We even had a similar background, minus the murders of course. He'd moved around a lot as a kid, his dad being former military as well, but his dad had been army. So he'd lived in quite a few places and knew how to make all kinds of foods. America was the only place he'd never lived, and he'd been a little disappointed about that when his dad retired. His dad promised to make it up to him though. Neither was sure exactly how, but his dad would let him know when he finally settled on a plan.

He'd made twenty burgers in all, must have had a lot of meat. We both ate five, fixins and all. The guy could cook.

"I don't think I could eat another bite." He said with a chuckle.

"Me either." I joined his chuckle.

We sat in companionable silence for several minutes. Just watching the night sky and listening to nocturnal animals. Plenty of stars were out, more than I had ever seen in L.A. When I spotted ursa major, a thought hit me.

"Can I ask you something?"

"You mean other than that." He said jokingly.

I laughed, "Yes other than that." I said, still laughing.

"I'm gonna guess it's about my mum." His smile dropped a little.

"No actually. I was gonna ask why I smelled bear when I landed."

He seemed relieved, "I'm actually a bear shifter." He said with the same shy smile.

Wow. "Really?"

"Have you never met a bear before?" A quizzical smile replaced the shy one.

I shook my head, "Not that I know of. I have a friend who's a wolf shifter, she and all seven of her brothers as a matter of fact."

"Good grief. I feel sorry for her. That must get annoying."

"She loves them, but you are correct. It gets very annoying."

"But other than her and family, no other shifters that you know of?" he asked.

"I know my regular doctor is a shifter, I've just never asked her what kind. And I do know one lion shifter. We met only recently though."

He nodded, "I'm a little surprised about that."

I shrugged, "My mom and dad didn't like us interacting with many of our own species. They were highly distrustful of them for several reasons, but my siblings and I never really argued. We just took it on the chin and made friends with people we had things in common with."

"I know how that feels." I focused on his face, he'd sounded upset on that one.

"Can I ask?" I asked.

He nodded, "My mum is the way she is, because of my birth father." My eyes widened in shock.

"My birth dad was a very abusive man," he paused, "he would beat my mum until she was black and blue. When she found out she was pregnant with me, she ran away"

"I'm sorry for yelling at her."

"Don't be." He said, meeting my eyes. "She needed to be told off for that one."

"How'd she meet your dad?"

"He was the doctor that delivered me. She went into labor so quickly that the closest hospital was the military one."

"Where were you born?"

"You first." His smile came back.

I chuckled, "Texas."

"Cool." I could tell from his tone that he meant it. "I was born here in Scotland. My gran was really surprised when my mum remarried a military doctor."

"Did she disapprove?" I asked.

"No, she was thrilled about it. Said it was a good choice. Especially with my birth dad out there hunting her down."

"Oh my Gods."

He nodded, "My birth dad had learned that she was pregnant and went after her 'cause he wanted me. I get my shifting from him, and knowing how protective shifters can be toward family, I at first thought that was why he was looking."

"But later found out that wasn't the reason." I guessed.

"Yep." He paused, "I was four, when he finally caught up to us. We were living in Geneva at the time, and he ambushed us at the store." He was getting angry, "He grabbed me and made a run for it. The front door was blocked by people, so he went back in and found the stairs to the roof." He paused again.

I reached across the table and placed a hand on his arm. This was a pain I knew as well. Having been hunted by Kepner. He looked into my eyes and saw the empathy there. He shed a few tears in what I believe was appreciation. He took a deep breath and continued.

"My parents caught up with him on the roof. My dad pointed a gun and told him to let me go. My mum was in hysterics, begging him not to hurt me. He walked to the edge of the building and realized he had nowhere to go. It was a tall building and even with his shifter strength he didn't want to risk the jump to the ground." He took a drink of his soda, "Finally he started yelling at my mum for taking me from him. Saying that she had no right to do that. He jumped down from the edge, and started cursing her out for what she'd done." He looked away for a moment, "He called her a weak bitch who deserved to die at his hand." He clenched his hand, "That was the final straw for me. While he was distracted saying that shifters were superior and that he was gonna raise me so that I could follow in his footsteps instead of my dad's, I shifted."

He smiled at the one piece of good in that memory, "That was my first shift. Mum had told my dad what my birth father was. He hadn't really believed her until he saw me do it."

"Why didn't your dad shoot him?" I asked.

He thought for a second, and realized something, "Because I was being held out over the precipice." My eyes widened again.

"He knew that it was a guarantee that he wouldn't be shot if I was in danger of dying, since he hadn't brought a weapon with him."

"I see."

He nodded again, "He never realized what I was doing until he paid attention to my dad's face. When he turned to look at me, I took the opportunity. I used his momentum and my own to slash him across the face. I tore his cheek bone out and nearly separated his nose from his face."

I nodded with an impressed smile, "Nice."

His smile returned again, "He managed to spin all the way around, bringing me back to the safety of the roof and that's when my dad took the shot. Put two bullets through his head."

"Shifter or not that kills all. Usually."

He chuckled, "Yeah, excepting a lucky few." He rubbed his face, "Thankfully not his. As soon as he let go I ran to my mum. I didn't shift back until we heard the police coming up the stairs."

"I'm sorry you guys had to go through all that." I said sincerely.

"Thanks. But it can't be worse than what you went through."

I lowered my eyes, "Honestly no, it's not. You at least got to keep your parents."

We both turned as we heard someone coming up the stairs. I felt his muscles tense a little. There are some scars that take longer to heal. The psychological ones are among the hardest to get over. I kept my hand on his arm as Mrs. Granger showed herself. We both gave sighs of relief.

She smiled as she got closer, "I'm sorry to interrupt Jameson, but your mother is throwing the biggest fit of the year downstairs."

"I'll take care of it." He gave her a half smile.

She turned and walked back inside. I stood and started helping put everything in their containers. He'd been smart to bring some up for leftovers.

When we had that done, I turned to him and said, "I really enjoyed this Jameson."

He smiled broadly, "I'm really happy you did."

We carried the leftovers to the kitchen and placed them in the fridge. Saying good-night to each other, he headed out the kitchen door to meet his mother. I went back out the dining room, and made my way upstairs to my room.

Someone had brought my brace back up and placed it on my bed. I'd have to thank someone for that, but right then I was tired. I checked the clock. 2A.M. I changed into pajamas and was asleep not long after my head hit the pillow.

Chapter 41

I was running, I couldn't breathe. Was I too late, were they all dead? I kept running, my feet like feathers, never fully touching the ground for longer than a second. My leg was on fire. I didn't care, I used it as a focus. I had to reach them, I had to stop him. I finally made the house. It was dark. I ran inside, breaking down the door as I went. The blood was everywhere. Soaking the walls and carpet. My family lay in pieces on the floor. Kepner stood unharmed in the middle of it all. I began to growl, he turned, and something went boom.

I jolted awake. I was breathing very heavily. My eyes couldn't focus. I closed them and started taking shallow breaths. When I opened my eyes, Jameson was kneeling over me, holding my arms down. Another boom sounded. I jumped, beginning to panic.

"Maggie!" I met Jameson's eyes, "It's just the storm."

I turned my head just enough to look out my window. Rain was coming down in buckets, a flash of lightning in the distance the only prelude to the next boom of thunder. I closed my eyes and started taking deep breaths. Finally my heart started beating slower. I opened my eyes back up. Jameson was still holding me down. He looked extremely worried.

"I'm okay now. You can let me up." I said.

"Are you sure?" He was worried for me.

"Yes. Why do you ask?"

He answered by looking at the sheets around me. I turned and lifted my head, and was met with carnage. My bed sheets were torn to shreds. Claw marks as long as my arm crisscrossed every one of the sheets. I groaned and dropped my head back down. I'd been so tired last night I hadn't even thought about taking a sleeping pill. Mentally I checked my body over. Not a scratch. I took a deep breath and looked Jameson in the eye.

"Yes, I am sure and I'm fine. The sheets got all the rage."

"Okay." He let go of my wrists. He got off his knee and stood by the bed.

I leaned up and looked the bed over again. The duvet was fine, as were the pillows, only the sheets were the worse for wear. The clock read 9:30. Geez, I hadn't slept that late in a long time. Fully sitting up, I turned my attention to my wrists. They were bruised! I was actually amazed, I didn't bruise easily. I heard Jameson make a noise. I looked up at him, he looked sickened with himself.

"You must be stronger than you look to succeed in holding me down." I said with a small smile. Hoping to alleviate his concern.

"You're no slouch yourself. I had to use every ounce of mine just to hold you down." He wouldn't meet my eyes for long.

I stood up, walked toward him, and using my fingers to lift his head said, "Thank you."

His eyes showed his relief, "You're not mad."

I shook my head, "I'm grateful that you happened to show up."

His shy smile showed, "Technically I wasn't just passing by." I'd noticed the butler uniform he was wearing.

"I'm still grateful. I've only had two other nightmares get that bad, both didn't end well. So I'm glad that someone was there to stop it before it got worse."

"Jameson, are you up here?" We jumped apart as Mrs. Granger came toward my room.

"In here Mrs. Granger." He said. Was he blushing?

She came in. She was about to say something when she caught sight of my bed. I lowered my eyes instinctively. Like a child when they know they've been caught doing something bad. She came forward and started looking me over.

"I'm fine. The sheets took the hit." Jameson chuckled. Trying to hold back his smile.

"And these?" She asked angrily, she held up my wrist. Sadly it was the left one. The sudden movement wasn't good. I shouted in pain and sat down on my bed. Clutching my arm to my chest. My reaction surprised Mrs. Granger, but Jameson's reaction surprised both of us.

The second after I sat down, he was between us. The growl he gave shook the floor, making Mrs. Granger back away from me. His growl was aimed at her. I gasped through the pain and using my right hand, reached over and grabbed his arm. He was trembling, from what I couldn't tell. He turned and looked at me. His eyes had gone bear. Time to defuse the situation.

Putting as much authority into my voice as possible I said, "I'm fine." I met his eyes. I would make this a dominance challenge if I needed to.

He closed his eyes, swallowed, and said, "I'm sorry Mrs. Granger. I really don't know what came over me." When he opened his eyes, they were back to normal.

Mrs. Granger swallowed and said, "It's fine dear, but will someone please explain the bruises."

My hand started twitching, Jameson saw and sat down next to me, "The bruises are from me holding her down."

"I was having a nightmare again and he kept me from hurting myself." The twitching was hurting a little. I grit my teeth and breathed through it.

"I'm guessing from your sheets dear, it was a pretty bad one."

I nodded, "But not as bad as the one that gave me these." I indicated my arm scars.

"And the twitching?" she asked.

"Nerve damage. Caused the night my family was murdered." Jameson's eyes started to turn. "The damage was my own fault. I pressed a pressure point and fell unconscious before the medical team arrived. They wrenched it loose not knowing about the pressure point being active."

They both cringed, "Are you still in therapy?" Jameson asked.

"For this no. I'm in the final stage of recovery so therapy isn't required. Although it does get examined every time I go to the doctor."

"Why would you even need to activate it?!" He asked.

"An answer you'll have to get later dear. She needs to eat and you need to get back to work. You can talk again on your lunch break." Mrs. Granger reminded both of us.

He nodded and rose to leave, but not before taking one more look at me before walking out the door. Mrs. Granger followed after telling me that she was going to check that my breakfast was on the table, and that she'd come back up to remove the sheets.

Once she was out the door I laid down, staring at the ceiling. Why had Jameson reacted that way? There was no need for it. I decided not to dwell on it. Sitting back up I started to get dressed. I pulled another pair of my jeans on, put a long sleeved shirt on, and finally my brace. My leg was feeling tingly from my dream. I started removing the sheets myself. I'd destroyed them, I might as well do as the rules had said and clean up my own mess.

With the sheets off I saw that I'd hit the mattress a couple times. None of the marks were too deep thankfully, so they'd be easy to fix.

I had the sheets rolled into a ball when Mrs. Granger came back to my room. She gave me a mildly amused look.

"I could've easily done that dear."

I shrugged, "One of the rules was I clean up my own messes. This one counted as my own."

She gave a resigned sigh, "Well, just give them here and head down. I'll take care of these."

I did as she said and handed the bundle to her, then went down to breakfast. Malcolm had made oatmeal and cranberry juice. There were a few additions to it, though. Fresh apple slices, raspberries, and some mini chocolate chips. I sat down. Mrs. Granger had been true to her word of making me comfortable food wise. There was even some cinnamon in the oatmeal. I broke some apple slices into smaller pieces and added them. Also some of the raspberries and chips.

The crunch from the apple pieces and chocolate chips helped me ignore the oatmeal's texture, but all together breakfast was really good. The oatmeal wasn't too without flavor thanks to the cinnamon, and not as slimy. I ate every bite, and drank the glass of juice.

Once I was done I took everything to the kitchen. Malcolm wasn't there so I washed the dishes, ate the rest of the apple slices, and put the bowl of raspberries by the other fruits. The chocolate chips I was confused about. Then I spotted a ceramic jar with 'chocolate chips' written on it. I took the lid off and saw the same mini chips. I then emptied the bowl of its contents and placed it in the sink. I washed that too.

I went back into the dining room just as Mrs. Granger entered it. She was on the phone with someone. She indicated for me to wait. I stopped next to her and waited for her to finish.

"I understand sir. Thank you." And she hung up, "Well, that was Mr. McHaddish, he's on Mack's plane and they should be here within two hours."

I looked outside at the still going storm, "I'd be surprised if they were, those winds look pretty bad."

She nodded, "I'll be surprised as well. Where shall I find you after he arrives?"

"The library ma'am. I want to read more of what I was reading yesterday."

"Before Mrs. Billings became involved." I nodded, "Then I shall see you later dear. Enjoy your book."

"Thank you ma'am."

I left the dining room and walked up to the library. Both of our books had been returned to their shelves. I reacquired Moby Dick, and sitting down in the same chair as yesterday, began reading again.

I was about halfway through it when Mrs. Granger came into the library. At first I thought she was coming to collect me, but she wasn't. Instead she placed a cup of tea on the coffee table, smiled at my thank you, and left again. I leaned forward and took a sip. It was warm, lemon tea. One of my favorites. And just the right amount of sugar added too. I leaned back in my chair and continued reading.

It was close to noon when Mrs. Granger finally came up to tell me that Mr. McHaddish had arrived and would be ready to see me in ten minutes. I thanked her and finished my tea. I placed my book back on the shelf after memorizing the page I was on. I then did a little pacing. I honestly was nervous about meeting Mr. McHaddish.

I was also curious. You don't drop everything you're doing just to come and check on your temporary ward. What was it about me that had him doing so? I mean, yes, what had happened yesterday was odd, but not necessarily something you'd have to get personally involved in. Some would call that overkill.

I was on my second round of pacing when Mrs. Granger came back down. She indicated for me to follow and I did. She informed me that he would be seeing me in his third floor office. We walked up to said third floor. His office was about halfway down the north hallway. Once again the double doors made an appearance. She stood in front of them and knocked. A barely audible voice from inside said 'come in'.

She opened the doors, led me in, and I stopped in my tracks. The man standing in front of me most definitely was not who I was expecting.

"You!!" I said in shock.

Chapter 42

Mr. French stood in the middle of the room. Looking amused at my shock and surprise. He was wearing the same suit he'd worn the first time we'd met. His hair was as red as ever. Mrs. Granger looked confused at my outburst, but she didn't say anything.

Mr. French chuckled and said, "Thank you Jenny. I'd like to speak with Maggie alone."

She bobbed her head and walked out. Closing the doors as she went. I turned my attention back to him and shook my head. Somewhat laughing at myself for not seeing it. I covered my face with one hand, piecing it all together in my mind.

"Your Ms. Hamper's uncle." That explains why she wasn't intimidated by him when we'd been introduced.

"Correct." He had this smug smile on his face.

"Does she know?" I asked, meeting his eyes.

He chuckled and moved toward his desk, "Yes, she does." He leaned against his desk, "How are you feeling?"

I wrapped my arms around me, "Depends on which way you mean."

"Every way."

I sighed, rubbing my neck I said, "Tired, emotionally and psychologically. Physically, I'm okay but could be better. Drained and confused."

He nodded, "Jenny informed me about what happened in the library yesterday and about what happened this morning."

I bit my lips, "She's not in trouble is she?"

He knew who I meant, "No, but I have informed her not to do it again. You need support, not criticism."

I nodded, he continued, "What I want to know is if you accepted her son's apology."

Again I nodded, "He told me about his birth father last night, so I understand why she's a little judgey and jumpy."

He laughed, "Judgey and jumpy. I won't tell her you said that." He rubbed his jaw, "Although I am surprised that he told you."

I shrugged, "I guess he felt I deserved an explanation. I did appreciate the clarification."

He nodded this time, "And this morning?"

"I appreciate that too. I was just too tired to think about the sleeping pill."

"May I?" he held out his hand.

I rolled up my sleeves and stepped forward to let him examine my wrists. He was gentle with my left arm, and he didn't seem too surprised that my arms had scarred. He looked at the bruises with a father's eye. Judging why they were there.

"They don't hurt?" I shook my head, he let go of my hands and I pulled the sleeves back down. "When did you return last night?"

I took a deep breath, "After midnight." His eyebrows raised. "I was mad. I wanted as much time to cool down as possible. It wasn't until I got hungry that I came back. I honestly didn't expect Jameson to still be awake."

"I forget that moon rise happens earlier in June. I usually don't come here till September. To make sure everything is still functioning before school starts."

I nodded, just before a sudden burst of pain in my back took hold. I shouted in pain and dropped to my knees. I managed to stay on my hands and knees while the pain fluctuated like it did yesterday. When I could finally breath again, I opened my eyes and kept taking deep breaths. Mr. French was kneeling next to me. I played for lightening the mood.

"Do I still have to call you Mr. French?" I asked.

He laughed, "Nice to see your sense of humor survives, and no. You can call me Mr. McHaddish if you find that easier."

"I honestly do." I laid down on my back. Groaning as the pain spiked a little.

There was a knock at the door. Mrs. Granger opened one of them and came in with a cup of tea. He must have called down to her when I was trapped in my pain. She passed it to him and walked back out, saying as she went that lunch was ready. He thanked her and then helped me up enough to drink the nasty concoction.

I made a face as I swallowed it. That done, I laid back down. There was a sheen of sweat on my forehead again. I wiped it off with my shirt sleeve. This was going to get troublesome. I needed to get ready for the final finishing before the week was over, and it was only Tuesday. If my calculations were right, I'd be incapacitated by the pain by Saturday.

Thinking on it, I'd have to discuss this with Mr. McHaddish over lunch. Him being a cave lion shifter, he might be able to restrain me when the final finishing took place. Either that or he could combine his strength with Jameson's.

Leaning down, Mr. McHaddish helped me stand up. I groaned the whole way up. I also was pretty stiff walking down the stairs. If this and yesterday were just the beginning of it, what would the end be like.

It took me fifteen minutes to reach the dining room, Mr. McHaddish staying with me the entire time. Even though he didn't have to. Both Jameson and Gretchen were waiting with lunch. I at first thought it was Cullen skink again, but instead it was my mom's version of potato soup. How in the world did anyone but me and Reggie know that recipe? There also was a whole platter of homemade bread rolls, and a plate of seasoned butter.

"I thought something a bit more familiar would be welcome." Mr. McHaddish told me.

"How'd Malcolm even know this recipe?" I asked while sitting down in the chair just to the left of the end seat.

"He and your mother met in college. She shared it with him there." He answered.

I was surprised about that. My mom hadn't shared a lot of her recipes with anyone but family. She and Malcolm must have been good friends for her to give him a copy. My mom's version was done with both solid chunks of potato and pureed potato, and ham. With bacon and cheese as a topping. Sometimes chives were included, but not always.

I sat staring at the soup a little apprehensively. I hadn't had my mom's potato soup since my birthday last year before the murders. I finally got up the courage to ladle some into my bowl and add some of the bacon and cheese. I grabbed a bread roll as well. I started ripping it to shreds and dipping it in the soup. It tasted just like my mom always made it. I felt my chest tighten. I breathed past it though, I was hungry and needed to make up the calorie burn of intense pain.

When the clock read 12:30, Gretchen and Jameson joined us at the table. Both digging in with gusto. I chuckled quietly under my breath. It was nice to see my new friends enjoying something I'd been eating since I was little.

I finally leaned back into my chair when I was full. I hadn't eaten as much as I used to. Then again I hadn't had anything made by my mom in so long. Or, something that was originally made by her and replicated by a friend. When both Jameson and Gretchen were done, she got up and took all the bowls to the kitchen. When Jameson made a move to follow her, Mr. McHaddish lifted his hand and indicated for him to remain seated.

Once Gretchen was gone Mr. McHaddish said, "I believe there was a question Jameson wanted an answer to earlier."

Jameson nodded and said, "Yes sir, and quite frankly it's been driving me crazy all day."

I took a deep breath, Gretchen had come back in as he'd spoke. She knew what I was going to say, and stayed anyway.

I met Jameson's eyes and said, "I had to activate the pressure point because of the cast iron tub that had fallen through the ceiling." He looked at me in shock. That was to be expected.

From there I took the time to explain to him everything that had led up to the murders, and everything that had happened afterwards. Only ending my narrative when I reached the part about arriving at the airport for the flight here. He'd gone pretty gray about half-way through. I was impressed by that, most people react very differently.

"Did those two kids ever apologize?" he asked finally.

"Marjorie did, and Tom partially did. Both of them have learned their lessons. I was only a contributing factor."

"What do you mean by 'partially'?"

"He wanted to work up to a full apology, 'cause he didn't see that what he'd said to me was all that bad until his grandfather died."

"I see." Jameson seemed okay with that answer.

"Speaking of them. I know that some part of your family's maturing stage is happening, and I've done a careful calculation of your strength." Mr. McHaddish said.

"My brother called it the final finishing. He wants me to contact him later today to let him know if I've got a plan for getting through it without killing anyone."

"Maturing stage?" Gretchen said with a questioning face.

I got up and grabbed a piece of paper and a pencil from the middle of the table – that I had only noticed yesterday, - I sat down again and started to draw a dragon wing.

"Do you know how shifter names work Gretchen?" I asked.

She nodded, "The number of words in it tells what sort of shifter you are. Also that because of the length of some last names, they are shortened sometimes."

"Well my last name is one of the shortened ones, and its full meaning has to do with this." I pointed at the picture I had drawn. Both she and Jameson looked at it.

"But that's not there, not on your wings anyway." Gretchen stated.

"Correct, that's because it doesn't grow out until children in my family reach the age of sixteen. My brother and sister already went through it. Now it's my turn."

"But why is that claw even there? Such a claw isn't seen on other dragon shifters." She asked.

"We think it might be an evolutionary mutation. Something that only her family does because of an extra gene in their DNA." Mr. McHaddish said.

"That still doesn't fully explain it. Why would a Scottish family of dragon shifters need an extra claw on each wing." Then it hit me, "Unless of course it's because of how rugged the mountains in Scotland are in the first place."

He nodded, "Dragons in general prefer to live in the mountains. Since most of your heritage comes from here, its why the gene is still going."

"So, what **is** the plan?" Jameson asked.

"I have an idea, but I'll need your full cooperation Maggie." Mr. McHaddish said.

"I'm guessing it's not what I had in mind." I said somewhat quietly.

He shook his head, "Like I said, I managed to have your strength levels calculated."

"How?" I asked.

"The hole in the floor."

"Ah." The hole in the floor was what students at school called the dent that I'd made when I attacked Marjorie.

Both Jameson and Gretchen looked confused, "It's the dent I made in the floor at my old school." I explained.

They nodded, "Indeed. From the information gathered, it's understandable why your father separated your siblings from civilization when it came time." Mr. McHaddish continued.

"And restrained my siblings on his own. Our inherited strength is no joke."

"So couldn't you and I hold her down when the final finishing occurs?" Jameson asked.

Mr. McHaddish shook his head, "No, even combined the two of us would never keep her down. Not even bringing her brother in would work."

I huffed, "So I'm stronger than the three of you combined? How is that even possible?"

"Even I can't answer that, though I have been looking into it." He placed his elbows on the table and twined his fingers, "My plan at this point is to do similar to what your father did. Isolate you in the mountains until the pain subsides, and the claw finally grows out."

"My brother suggested a potion that could knock me flat out. I don't have many high hopes for that."

"Your right not to. Based on what happened yesterday, the pain would override the potion and you'd wake up almost immediately." I dropped my head onto the table.

"But your brother's idea gives me one." I picked my head back up to see the thoughtful expression on his face. "It's a long shot, but I know a potion that will extend the time of pain. Basically take a one hour pain and make it last all day."

"Making it easier to deal with." I finished.

"Correct. It could take the pain of five or six days and make it take five to six weeks. If I brew it right." He thought some more, "We'd still have to keep you active though. Just in case the potion doesn't affect the final finishing as I'm hoping."

"Why not a hike through the mountains?" Jameson suggested.

"That could work." I added.

Mr. McHaddish nodded, "I like your idea Jameson. It gets her active and keeps her far from humans as a last resort."

"It'll be good for my leg too."

He nodded again, "That's settled then. I'll have everything prepared, and we'll leave for the mountains tomorrow. But before we do that. I know this will sound cruel…"

"You want me to go dragon outside and see if there will be any more of what happened earlier in your office." I finished for him.

He smiled sadly, "Yes."

"I'll do it. If there's more than I want it over with." And I did. What had occurred in his office was barely anything compared to yesterday.

"Alright. I'll get to work on the potion after some final calculations." He left it there.

I got up to go outside when I remembered something, "Why would saying my full last name that first time, have the effect it did on my scar and wounds?"

He hung his head and thought for a second, "That's a complex question with an equally complex answer. One that I will give you when the final finishing is complete."

I gave a resigned sigh and walked out the kitchen door after removing my brace. The storm had ebbed quite a bit, so the rain wasn't as bad, and the thunder and lightning had stopped. Very slowly, I shifted. I stretched out to full length before doing the same with my wings. I even flapped them a little to see if they were stiff from yesterday. I carefully looked them over as well. There weren't any outward signs of damage or any growth, but that really only meant little.

As I was giving them one more flap, the pain started again. It was worse than yesterday by a long shot. There was no stopping the roar I gave off. Like earlier, I collapsed to the ground. Breathing heavily, trying to control the pain. Then I felt the connection.

"Maggie!" it was Reggie.

"Don't interfere bro. I need to do this one myself." I was panting now, but at least I was getting a sense of where the pain was emanating.

"Even though I want to I can't. Literally. I can feel the pain as an ache, but I can't syphon. At all."

He sounded annoyed, *"Your in dragon form, aren't you."* I stated. That was the only reason we could communicate across an ocean without amplifiers. His pearl acted as mine.

"Yes. I'm in the mountains hiking. I felt you collapse and thought it was your leg." He explained.

"Not this time. But a plan is in place for my final finishing." I told him.

"What is it?" he asked, and I spent the next few minutes explaining it to him. It only took that long because of me pausing at bouts of pain.

When I was done, I could feel his relief, *"I'm glad he's willing to help."*

"Ms. Hamper said that he knows our pain, so him helping isn't that big a surprise to me."

I could feel his chuckle, *"I've got to go. Humans are coming. Love you sis. Be careful, and good luck."*

"Love you too. I will be and thanks."

We broke contact just as Mrs. Granger approached me with an umbrella, and another glass of tea. Thankfully shifting back was easier this time around. I took my time standing up of course, but once I did, I drank the tea, and limped back to the house. Mrs. Granger gave me my brace, and I managed to get it on with only a little bit of discomfort. She then handed me a couple of chocolate chip cookies and a cup of milk.

I thanked her and went to sit in the dining room. She stopped me and said I could take my snack to the library and read some more if I wished. I did, so I walked up. I found Jameson there, in the same seat he'd sat in previously. I grabbed my book from the shelf and went to sit down. I couldn't see the title of Jameson's book, but I knew it was the same one from yesterday for him as well.

"Which one?" I asked, indicating his book.

He smiled, "20,000 Leagues under the Sea."

I laughed at the irony. We were both reading books that primarily took place at sea. He realized it too when I showed him mine's title. He leaned over with laughter.

"Have a thing for the sea do you?" he asked, still smiling.

I nodded, "I've wanted to be a marine biologist since I was seven."

"Really? Cool."

"You?"

He chuckled a little, "Navy."

My eyes widened, "Really? Cool." I said, mirroring him.

He laughed some more, "I've wanted to join since the incident. I figured they'd accept me if they didn't know about shifters. Now I'm not so sure."

"Did you try looking it up?" the U.S. military took shifters, why not the Scottish military.

He tilted his head, thinking, "I guess I never really thought about it. Plus mum doesn't have a computer, and the one here is in Mr. McHaddish's office."

I finished my second cookie and the milk, then said, "Come with me."

We left our books on the table, along with the glass, and went up to my room. I went around the bed – which I could see had been repaired – and fired up my laptop.

"Hey, are you on break or?" I let the sentence hang.

"No, I'm actually done for the day. I prefer to hide in the library. My mum doesn't know I only work half the day."

"For obvious reasons?" I asked.

"For obvious reasons." He confirmed.

My computer was awake and I opened google. Patting the spot next to me, I typed 'Scottish military acceptance requirements' into the search bar. He sat down next to me as google took a few seconds to open results. The storm may have been mostly over, but it still was causing interference.

Finally the results popped up. I clicked the first link, which connected directly to the Scottish military's website. I clicked the 'Navy' option and waited. When the requirements finally showed up, we both looked through them. At the bottom was written, 'All shifters welcome to enlist.'

Jameson gave a sigh of relief and flopped down onto the bed beside me. I chuckled at him. It only made sense that most countries would allow shifters into the military. They could do things humans couldn't and could be valuable assets to a team. Of course all the same things that keep certain humans out could also keep a shifter out. But since Jameson was in peak shape, he wouldn't have too much of a problem.

I exited out of google and put my computer back. Jameson was still lying down, his hands over his face. Thinking I bet, about his next move. His dad would be thrilled, his mom on the other hand, was another matter altogether. There was one of two ways she could react. Either the same as her husband, or say 'no'. Not that she'd have any say. It would be his choice. The only thing she could really do would be to try and talk him out of it.

Suddenly a thought hit me, "Why the Navy?"

He moved a hand, "Why do you ask?"

"Well, kinda for the same reason someone would ask a cat shifter, not all bears react well to being surrounded by water. Or being underneath it."

He sat up, a knowing look on his face, "I see what you mean, and really I just never thought about it." He paused, "The navy just, felt right I guess. Anytime I imagined myself enlisting into another, it just, didn't feel right."

I know that feeling, "What about you, why marine biologist?"

I smiled, "I've been in love with the ocean since before I could walk." I paused, remembering. "When I was only a few months old, my parents took us down to Galveston island," he looked confused, "it's a small island right along the coast of Texas."

I was caught in fond memory, "They stopped at the beach to let us play in the sand. Amanda and Reggie started building a sand castle, I just, wandered off. I walked straight up to the water and started splashing and laughing. I even picked up a sea shell and kept it. I still have it." I paused again, "I've always felt at home near the ocean. Like it's calling to me."

"Kinda like 'Moana'." He said.

I laughed, "Yes, almost exactly like that."

"Odd though, given you're a fire breathing dragon." He stated.

"Normally I'd agree, but then again not many dragon shifters know if they have sea dragon shifter ancestry."

He looked at me in surprise, "You have sea dragon shifter blood?"

"Heavily diluted as far as anyone can tell. The only way to know is if something happens when I swim in dragon form."

"But then again any and all manuscripts about sea dragon shifters were destroyed centuries ago." He finished for me.

"Yep." I thought about my grandma, "My maternal grandma was trying to piece some things together. She'd been a genealogist before retiring, and when my dad asked, she looked into it."

"So she was trying to find out what happened to them?" he asked.

I nodded, "She'd told my dad that maybe someday someone would happen upon the gene, and finally resurrect the species, but so far any of my other ancestors who've had the gene – as far as they knew – didn't shift at all in the water."

"Maybe they did it wrong."

"Maybe. I plan to find out at some point."

We sat there for a few more minutes until Mrs. Granger kicked us out so that one of the other maids could put the new sheets on my bed. We went back down to the library and went back to reading. I drank the last drops of milk in the glass and took it to the kitchen. I thanked Malcolm for the soup before heading back. I finally sat down opposite Jameson again and immersed myself in Moby Dick.

When I was almost done, I saw Jameson pull something from a drawer in the coffee table. I leaned my head a little to see what it was. He held up a remote and was aiming it at a spot on the wall above us. Suddenly music started to play. I knew this music.

"You like Lindsey Stirling?" I asked.

He nodded, "I played viola in middle school, as you call it."

"But you don't anymore?"

He shook his head, "Never really took to it. I like listening to stringed instruments plenty, just never really had a knack for it." I nodded, "You?"

"Violin since I was three." I said with a big grin.

"Do you still play?"

I nodded, "I'm nowhere near as good as Lindsey, but I have a talent for it."

"There's a music room on the third floor. Maybe you could play some time."

"I just might." With that we both returned to our books.

Chapter 43

Once I was done with Moby Dick, I put it back and went down the hall to the bathroom. I used it and took a pain pill. I'd decided while we were sitting on my bed after checking google, to carry some in a plastic baggie at all times in my pocket. That way I wouldn't have to go all the way back up and down all the time.

Back in the library, I started searching the shelves again. I hadn't even gone through the whole place yesterday. I looked into the shelved books passed the sitting area. There I found even more English authors, including Sir Arthur Conan Doyle. I actually shouted 'yes' and went back to my chair, carrying The Hound of the Baskervilles in my hand.

I practically jumped into my chair, "Excited are we?" Jameson asked with a huge smile.

I held up my book, "One of my favorites."

"Sherlock or that story?"

"Both." He chuckled and once again, we both went back to our reading.

I hadn't read Hound of the Baskervilles in three years. My mom had forbidden me from reading it until I was older than fifteen. She'd read part of it and found it too scary for a thirteen year old. We'd disagreed of course, but I'd been overruled. Unbeknownst to them, I had snuck the copy from them and finished it at night. Unfortunately I'd fallen asleep after finishing it and been caught when dad had come to wake me up the next morning. I'd been grounded for a month and the copy hidden somewhere. Now that everything was in storage, I could look through it and claim it. Or fight Reggie for it.

When he'd seen me reading it, he had laughed under his breath. He had known how mom and dad would react and not even warned me. Needless to say I'd been upset with him about that. He had then spent the next month trying to make it up to me. It wasn't until he admitted to me that he'd been jealous of my reading it when he wasn't allowed to that had us both rethinking things. I had had to explain to him that I'd started reading it without mom and dad's knowledge. I hadn't had permission. Why he thought so was odd. He then explained that our parents hadn't let him read it because of how easily he got nightmares from scary movies. They'd figured Hound of the Baskervilles would yield the same result.

Eventually mom had caved and let him read it. Obviously it was shown that they'd been overreacting. Amanda had teased them endlessly after that, and had called them silly for not letting me read it.

I felt the tears come to my eyes thinking of her. I put my book down for a few seconds to wipe them away. As I went to read, a thought occurred to me. I had dreamt about her last night, before the nightmare started. She'd told me to revisit the boulder in Gretchen's backyard. Saying that it was important and that someone hadn't been able to set up a good connection. What had she meant by that? Now I really needed to talk to Gretchen.

"You okay?" I jumped at Jameson's question. Making us both laugh.

"Yeah uh," I bit my lips, "just thinking of my sister."

"Seemed like some pretty deep thoughts."

I nodded, "Some possibly important ones too."

"How so?" He asked, genuinely curious.

"Well," I took a sec to gather my thoughts, "last night, before the nightmare started, I had a dream about her. In it, she told me to revisit a boulder in Gretchen's backyard."

"The one with the Celtic runes on it?"

"You know which one I mean?"

He nodded, "Gretchen and I used to play on it when we were preteens. I noticed the runes the day before my mum forbid me from jumping off it."

"I didn't see any runes."

"They're hard to spot, but I could show them to you." He offered.

I gestured for him to lead the way and leaving our books on the coffee table, walked to the dining room, where I removed the brace.

"Can you run?" he asked, with concern.

"Given my adrenaline right now. Yes."

We jogged out the kitchen door, and upon reaching the statue, broke into a run. It quickly became a race. I was lighter on my feet, but he'd been training himself for military basic training. We were a match made in heaven. Each overtaking the other, only to be passed again and again. It was over too soon. We reached the boulder, barely even breathing hard. My leg didn't even hurt.

He jumped down off the trail and into her yard. I followed, noticing Gretchen at the window. She came out to join us as I gently came down. He knelt in the wet grass and started clearing away mud from a spot low down on the boulder.

"Is he showing you the runes?" Gretchen asked.

I nodded, "Did you talk with your mom?"

"Yes. She told me that when my ancestors lived here, they would correspond with the fae. This boulder was often used as a meet sight."

"Here!" Jameson partially shouted from the mud.

Gretchen and I both knelt down to see. The runes were painted onto the boulder. I knew this method, having done a report about it as extra credit in my freshman year.

"I don't know what it says, but it always felt important when we were preteens." Jameson said.

"I do. My dad made Celtic runes a requirement when the three of us were little."

"So what does it say?" Gretchen asked with peaked interest.

I got a little closer, to make sure I was reading it right, "Here where all elements meet, a portal to faery I do create. Let me speak to them, and they to me."

I laughed quietly. I had thought such portals didn't exist anymore. To find one so well protected was amazing.

"A portal to Faery? As in the home of the fae?" Gretchen asked in fascination. I nodded.

"Is that a good idea?" Jameson was looking at it from a warriors point of view.

"Portal didn't always mean one you could walk through. In this case, it meant a communications portal. A way for people on good terms with the fae, to talk with them, or pass information back and forth in times of war." I explained.

"Okay that's actually pretty cool." he admitted. "Do you sense anything now?"

I shook my head, "Some portals need all four elements to work, and in this case it says, 'where all elements meet' I'd need to come here when the sun was out."

"Like yesterday, when you were here before the pain started." Gretchen stated. "Why?" she then asked as she stood.

"When I was asleep last night I had a dream where my sister said to revisit this because someone supposedly couldn't get a good connection." I explained.

"Someone wanted to talk with you. That explains why you were napping on it." She said.

I nodded, "There was a slight breeze, but when I arrived the sun wasn't fully shining on the boulder."

Gretchen knelt back down beside us, her hand under her chin as she thought, "You know, the boulder is drenched in sunlight at about five o'clock in the evening. It even hits the inscription itself."

"So maybe you could stop by tomorrow before you leave." Jameson suggested.

Gretchen shook her head, "The rain forecast is for the rest of the week, it'll have to wait till she gets back."

"Fine by me. It'll give me time to try and figure out why someone amongst the fae wants to talk to me." I said.

"You don't know any fae do you?" Jameson had a contemplative look on his face.

"Me, no. Someone in my family, maybe."

"Maybe that's why. This person might have a message from them for you." Gretchen said.

I shrugged, "For whatever reason, it'll have to wait." We all stood up, "I do appreciate the help you guys."

They both smiled, "We're glad we could be of help." Jameson said. Just before it started downpouring.

Gretchen and I squealed and we all made a run for her back door. We all started laughing once we got inside. Her mom was in the kitchen getting dinner set up. Keelan held on her hip while she blended spices. She set him down and handed us each a towel to dry our faces and arms. Keelan seized his chance when their mom went over to the stove. He came forward and wrapped his arms around my legs.

"Dan-dan." He said.

I looked down at him in surprise. Gretchen started trying to hold in her laughter. Jameson not so much. He openly laughed. Drawing Gretchen's mom's attention. She peeked at my lower legs and saw him there. I shrugged when she met my eyes. She chuckled and went back to what she was doing.

"How can he even tell it's me?" I asked with a smile.

"I honestly have no idea. Your eyes maybe." Gretchen couldn't stop giggling.

I looked down at him, "Dan-dan." He lifted his arms. I knew what that meant. I knelt down and picked him up. He got the biggest grin on his face.

"How about some tea to warm you all up?" Gretchen's mom asked.

"Yes please." I said.

"Thanks Mrs. Lochlan." I mouthed 'thank you' at Jameson. He mouthed 'you're welcome' back. Gretchen didn't notice, she'd gone forward to get some cups for the tea.

Jameson and I walked up to the island in front of us and sat on two of the stools that were available. Keelan wrapped his arms around my neck once I was seated. The Lochlan's kitchen was really nice. Lots of space and had a rustic finish to it. Keelan raised his hand, pointed his finger at my eyes, and moved his hand forward a little. I went cross-eyed as his finger got closer. He started laughing. Mrs. Lochlan turned to see. She got a confused look no her face.

"He doesn't usually laugh at that."

"Well he does like her mum. Maybe it's because she's following his finger."

Mr. Lochlan walked in, saw me and said, "I really must thank you for your help yesterday Miss Maggie. That bed I made from the measurements was a life saver."

I smiled, "Glad to be of help."

Jameson looked confused, so I explained what had happened yesterday after I had napped on the boulder. He chuckled at how cute Keelan had acted. Even at the little nest I had made to get him to sleep.

Mrs. Lochlan passed each of us a cup of tea. We both thanked her and took a sip. It was really good. I felt myself warming back up from it too. She tried to take Keelan, but he just refused to let go. I chuckled, the little guy really liked me for some odd reason. Eventually she gave up. Looking at him like he was the most stubborn baby on the planet, and at that moment he was. I was tempted to grow my tail and give him something to play with, but with Mrs. Lochlan still moving around the kitchen, I thought better of it.

Finally Keelan allowed himself to be taken, and put in his playpen. The rain was still going, but it was no longer a down pour. Mrs. Lochlan offer her umbrella to us for the walk back. The winds were still pretty bad, so we politely declined. Neither of us wanted to lose it.

"So how will you two get back without catching cold?" she asked in her mothering tone.

"We shift." Jameson told her.

She didn't argue with that. In fact she seemed to see the sense in it. Part of the porch was covered, we could use that as the starting point and go from there. Jameson was the technically smaller one so he went first. He stepped out the door and stood just below the eaves. Aiming it so he would go down the stairs as he shifted, he started to change.

"Don't be a stranger dear. And good luck on your hike." Mrs. Lochlan said before I walked outside.

"Thank you ma'am." I said.

"Oh, please, call me Mrs. Lochlan."

I nodded, and went out to take my turn. I did as Jameson had done, also noticing that he'd vacated the backyard. He must be pretty big if he'd give me this much room. I put a little more oomph into my shift, making sure to clear the steps with my front legs. I'd rather not send my tail or wings through a window.

I planned it well. The tip of my tail was the only thing to touch the house as I finished shifting. I gave a last bob of my head in good-bye to Gretchen and her mom as I walked across the yard to the trail. That's where I found Jameson, a ways back into the trees. I stopped in my tracks as I caught sight of him.

He was positively huge! He hadn't mentioned he was a grizzly. He was a little bigger than me when you didn't include my wings. The size of one and a half full grown African bush elephant bulls. I was amazed at his size. Most grizzly bears are inherently big, but he could put the whole shifter group to shame.

I only realized I was staring when he chuffed at me. I immediately closed my mouth and lowered my eyes. Were I human, I'd have blushed. That being said, I clearly was acting shy. I don't usually do that. Jameson walked closer and seemed to be studying me. He hadn't seen me in dragon form yet. The shift earlier had been done while he was heading to the library to hide from his mom. I came a little onto the trail, and he started circling me. Okay, what was up with that? It wasn't until he nudged my wing with his nose that I understood. He wanted to see my full size. Well, not a problem, except that the trail was pretty narrow.

I lined myself up so that my body was perpendicular with the trail. I then unfolded my wings so that they went down the path easily. My tail tip the only thing even reaching Gretchen's backyard. Even with his bear eyes, I could see the awe in his gaze. A 96 foot wingspan might not seem like much when the wings were folded, but it was impressive when fully stretched out.

Once he was done admiring my wings, he switched his attention to my leg. He sniffed it, and looked at me. It was the correct leg, but he hadn't seen the scar. I decided to try and make contact telepathically.

"The scar doesn't show when I'm in dragon form." I said.

I could tell he'd heard me by his reaction, *"Your telepathic?!"*

I nodded, *"And telekinetic. Although I can't move big objects yet."*

"What counts as big?" he asked. I could sense his smile.

"Anything bigger than a grapefruit. At this point."

We both looked at the sky as a rolling boom of thunder sounded. Folding my wings back up, we pointed ourselves toward the main house. My legs were longer than his by a small amount, so he walked in front. He'd only insisted 'cause my leg started tingling. Must have been all the running. Oh well. I need to strengthen it.

Some of the gardeners did a double take when we reached the gardens. It's not every day you see a grizzly and dragon shifter leave the forest together. Jameson traversed the hedges and flowerbeds carefully. He was wider than me. I chuckled slightly to myself. I only laughed a little harder when he stopped to look back at me. With barely — I snickered — contained laughter, we continued walking to the house.

Mr. McHaddish was waiting at the door with a small awning set up. He also had my brace in hand. That explained the chair that was present as well. Jameson went first, after shaking off most of the water. The look he gave me when he finished made me laugh again and turn my head in the classic 'I didn't do anything' move. That only made him laugh. Looking back at me several times, he walked into the house so that I could shift.

I could hardly fit underneath, but then again I only needed enough room to fit my human form under. I made sure to grab the chair before I was finished. I sat down and accepted the brace. Strapping it on, I followed Jameson inside. Mr. McHaddish insisted on taking the chair himself. There was a small cauldron going in the fireplace. I tilted my head at the sight of it. My mom had had one, but she'd only used it in summer, when we could cook outside. I caught a whiff of the contents. It wasn't food.

I sneezed and looked at Mr. McHaddish, "The potion I mentioned."

"Ah." Was all I could manage, my nose really didn't like it's smell.

"It'll be ready by about 3a.m., so we can leave after ten."

"Okay."

I couldn't take the smell anymore and followed Jameson to the dining room. It was after five, so dinner wasn't for another hour and a half. I could get some more reading done.

I left the dining room, ducking into a small alcove as I saw Jameson and his mom moving toward the front door. She didn't sound happy, and he looked mad. I stayed hidden until they were out the door. Jameson had looked back before it closed and met my eyes at the last second. I gave him a sympathetic smile, which he returned. I still understood why she was the way she was, but if she didn't open her eyes soon, she'd possibly lose Jameson.

Chapter 44

I waited a few seconds before leaving the alcove. I really did feel sorry for Jameson. I had seen how helicopter parenting could end sometimes. One of two ways most often. Don't even get me started on helicopter siblings. Walking up to the library I thought about my friend Gene. Some of the times I'd been over to her house, her brothers had looked at me like I was a bad influence. Other times, like I was a bomb about to blow. She laid into them on every occasion about treating me that way.

Then there was Ian's mom. We had grown up with her being the helicopter. Things finally hit a peak when Ian turned 13. Me and Samson had wanted to take him to the fair for his birthday. His mom had taken one look at the rides and said no. Eventually we mostly pulled a sneak out. He and Samson snuck out – they lied to me and said permission was given – while I did have permission to go.

We actually had fun at the fair. We even met up with the rest of our friends and did some games. It wasn't until his mom had gone out to get some groceries that they'd been caught. Traffic had been stalled due to a crash and she'd taken an alternate route, right past the fair grounds. Somehow she caught a glimpse of Ian. Not believing her eyes, she'd called his phone. Him answering it was her confirmation. The guys at the ticket gate had let her in without a fight. She was that mad.

I had spotted her first. The look on my face when I turned to the two of them not only confirmed to me that they had lied, but told them that she was coming. In response, Ian had looked up, met her eyes, grabbed the two of us, and made a run for the Moby Dick ride.

That was a fun ride. I honestly had never seen his mom go so green. We rode the thing three times. Just before the third ride started loading, he'd passed the insulin injection to me and indicated where to stick it. His mom practically fainted as I stabbed the needle into his leg. Samson had been impressed that he'd trusted me with it. Then the third ride had begun. I'm still surprised that his mom hadn't collapsed. Finally at the end of our third ride, she'd shouted at him at the top of her lungs for him to get off the ride and come to her that instant. His response had been to merely say 'make me'. The ride operator looked like he was gonna side with Ian's mom, until Samson said it as well.

From there the situation caught the attention of the whole fair. Ian trying to make his stand and his mom putting her foot down. It wasn't until my mom showed up that Ian finally got his say. My mom had been there to pick me up, and had heard a great deal of the argument. Boy had my mom laid into her! It had even made the news. But my mom had gotten her point across. Trust her son to know his own limits and give him his freedom, or he could and would run from her. In one way or another.

Ian's life had gotten much better after that. Yeah his mom would have a moment every now and then, but she managed not to smother him.

Based on what I had already seen from Jameson's mom, an incident was fast approaching. Were my mom here – or even Ian's – either could talk sense into her. At this point though I think either Jameson or his dad would be the only one to get into her thick skull. Mr. McHaddish probably wouldn't be enough. She clearly respected him, but felt when it came to her son, that she was the superior one.

Once back in the library, I was able to relax again. I was a little upset that Jameson couldn't join me to finish our books, but whatever reason his mom had collected him for was possibly something important. I'd just have to ask later. I sat down and picked Baskervilles back up to read.

Mrs. Granger brought dinner to me rather than have me come to the dining room. When I asked, she told me that the smell of the potion had permeated the dining room, which meant just about everything smelled unappetizing. Hence why dinner was pizza, made in her own oven. For me she had made two medium pizzas. One cheese, one pepperoni. When I asked what everyone else was eating, she told me that because of the potion, everyone – including her – were eating dinner in their own homes, or going out.

She brought napkins and another of the Scottish sodas that Jameson brought last night. I made a small spot on the coffee table for my plate and used a napkin as a coaster. The pizza was already sliced, and really good. The bottom was crispy enough to hold itself up, and the cheese was nice and melty.

I had most of the pizza eaten when Jameson came storming in. He looked livid enough to shift. I cleared my throat to get his attention. He saw me and almost immediately started to calm down. He started pacing, taking deep breaths as he went. Finally he was calmed down enough to sit down. He ran his fingers through his hair and gave an exasperated sigh.

"Have you eaten?" I asked.

He tilted his head a little, one hand still in his hair, "No." he answered, shaking his head.

I gestured to the pizza, "I'm full. I know it's not a lot."

He shook his head again, "It's plenty, given my mood." He took a slice and ate about half in one bite.

He finished the pizza, and my soda. He did that one by accident, he was so mad at his mom. I didn't say anything though, he needed some time to himself. Hence why he was here.

"Should I ask?" I asked, placing my book on my knees.

He thought about it for a sec, then said, "She wasn't happy about my going for a run in the woods with you."

"Was she mad about the run in the woods or the fact that it was with me?"

"The run itself. I guess you moved fast enough she never even noticed you." He smiled on that one.

"Either that or your white shirt was the only thing she saw at all."

He laughed, "Yeah, I've been trying to study camouflage, but anytime I try my mum freaks."

"Hence the white shirt all the time."

He nodded, "She can see me very well that way." He dropped his head, his eyes were starting to change.

"I could teach you." I said. He raised his head and seemed amazed that I would offer.

"You really could?"

I chuckled, "You honestly think a magenta colored dragon doesn't know how to blend in." he chuckled as well. "I don't exactly mesh well color wise in most environments." I lowered my eyes as I thought of my dad.

"My color is so rare that my dad made it a requirement for me to learn all forms of camouflage. Anytime he had the three of us compete in war games, I won, every time."

That definitely got his attention, "War games?!"

I nodded, "Yeah, he'd set up all kinds of obstacles, all of them based on military basic training obstacles. Rope climbs, mud crawls, 30 yard sprint, plus of course the standard exercises. When we did stealth exercises, he would always set one of us up as the sniper. He modified an old m-1 Garand to fire paint balls, I could sneak up on both of my siblings when they played the sniper, and tag them when I was sniper."

He looked fascinated, "Could you seriously coach me?"

"Yes," I giggled, "I remember everything my dad put us through. I could definitely help you get ready for the military."

He leaned back, put his hands in the air, and said, "Yes!" then he had a thought, "What about navy exercises?"

I nodded, remembering those exhausting summers, "He did navy ones too. Including the mile swim, scuba practice, hypothermia awareness and avoidance – and of course treatment, hand-to-hand combat under water. He covered a lot of stuff."

"I wish I could've met him."

I laughed quietly, "He'd have liked you." I had a thought, "I might be able to talk with someone from his old squadron, they could give any info I've missed."

"Was he a military trainer?"

"Technically only once after I was born. Before, he'd been deployed a few times. When I was in fifth grade, he was reinstated so that he could whip some hopeless recruits into shape. It was him training us that got him noticed, and of course why he was effective as a trainer. While he was doing that, he got a few of his old buddies in on it."

"Are you still in contact with them?" he asked.

"Technically no, but I could send an encoded message to either one of them or my brother."

"Works for me." he said with a smile.

"Does your dad know?"

"He knows I want to join, he's just not fully sure what all to have me cover. Since I'd be joining a different branch."

"Some stuff is the same. Not all but a good portion." I said.

We were interrupted by Mrs. Granger coming to collect the remains of what she'd brought me. It was only then that Jameson realized that he'd drunk the rest of my soda. His ears got so red. I chuckled and said that if I'd wanted to complain, it would've been as he drank it. I giggled at his expression. Mrs. Granger did too.

After she left, Jameson got up to retrieve his book and sat down. He took a while before opening it though. I guessed from his expression that he was thinking about his mom, and how she might react about his future career choice.

"Did you or one of your siblings ever consider the military?"

I nodded, "Yeah, we all did at one point."

"What changed?" he asked.

"Well, Reggie, ended up having a severe allergic reaction on one training day. After that, he figured that the odds of him being deployed somewhere where his allergy wouldn't be aggravated were remote at best, is when he changed his mind."

"What was he allergic to?"

"A combination of the standard military camo makeup, sweat, and pollen. Literally any kind of pollen that came in contact with the stuff could activate it. Even arctic areas have pollen, so he decided against it."

"Shame."

"He wasn't too upset about it. It actually was after that that he discovered his passion for astronomy."

"What about you and your sister?"

"Amanda was different. She was considering the military as her second option, in case she didn't get into the college of her choice."

"Did she?"

I nodded, tears springing to my eyes, "She got accepted to M.I.T. the summer before she was killed."

"And you?"

"Secondary option as well. Or it was. Now that I have this," I indicated my leg, "even if I learn to live with it, there's no way I'll be able to join. Shifter or not, it will always affect me, and that's what has always disappointed me. It's a guarantee that I can't join." I felt a tear run down my left cheek.

He nodded. Then we turned our heads as we heard Mrs. Granger in the hallway, it sounded like she was having an argument with Jameson's mom. I indicated for him to hide behind my seat. He grabbed his book and jumped for it. Literally. I wiped the tear away, leaned back into my chair, and looked as inconspicuous as possible. The two entered and his mom looked around. Finally she looked at me. Arms crossed.

I shrugged, "He left like two minutes ago." I lied.

"Did he say where he was going?" his mom asked. Her accent thicker with her high emotions.

"Just that he was heading home." She seemed to sag with relief. Not bothering to thank me, she turned and walked out. Her feet stomping the whole way.

I shook my head. One of these days she's gonna get yelled at for stomping around like a child. Mrs. Granger than looked at me. Her arms were now crossed.

Meeting my eyes she asked, "He's still here isn't he?" Jameson's laughter was answer enough.

He stood, and looking at me over the back of the chair, said, "Thanks."

"You're welcome." I said. Chuckling to myself.

Mrs. Granger shook her head, trying to hide her smile, "Well if you want to beat her home you'd better get moving."

He nodded, and rose from behind my chair, "Thanks again Maggie." He put the book on the coffee table and booked it out the door.

Mrs. Granger gave a conspiratorial grin, "His mum finds out about this and she's going to explode."

I shrugged, "I hate to say it but she needs to loosen that leash. The tighter you hold the more they fight."

"You speak from experience."

I nodded, "A friend of mine from back home had a helicopter mom. She learned the hard way on that one."

"I see. Well, maybe Mr. McHaddish can do something." She moved to leave.

"On this one," she stopped, "it's better if it's her husband or Jameson. That's the only way for the lesson to hit home."

She lowered her head in thought, then nodded, "Perhaps your right." She paused, "There's dessert down stairs if you'd like some. The smell has gone, so the dining room is safe again."

We both chuckled. I put Baskervilles back, put 20,000 Leagues away, and followed her to the dining room. Ice cream with fixins. Simple and enjoyable. I used some homemade chocolate sauce, some sprinkles, and a maraschino cherry.

Once dessert was consumed, I made my way up to my room. I needed to let Mr. Hydell know that I'd be out of contact for the next few weeks. I fired up my laptop and had the e-mail worded in my head before it was fully awake. I typed it out and sent it within three minutes. Now to wait for his response. I'd explained the final finishing, as well as the plan to get me through it. I didn't know what to expect from him, let alone Molly. The chance of the two of them agreeing to the plan was a heavy chance, but one I was willing to take. There were too many people here at the estate for me to risk trying to get through the final finishing here. The stakes of hurting someone were higher here than in the mountains.

Finally my computer pinged that an e-mail had been received. I opened it to see that they were worried for me, but if Mr. French felt it was a good idea, then they wished me luck. They also said to contact them the minute I got back. No matter what time it was in either time zone.

I replied that I would, and put my computer to the side. I went into the bathroom to use it and change there. I showered, and put my hair up to dry. Back in my room, I read the responding e-mail. Thanking me for agreeing to their terms. I then shut it down, and sat in the window seat. The storm had abated, and the skies were semi clear. The clouds were numerous, but at the right pass you could see the stars.

Once my hair was mostly dry, I took the towel off, and laid down. Then immediately sat back up and took a sleeping pill from the bottle. Quickly revisiting the bathroom, I took the pill, then went back to lying down. The sheets smelled fresh, and clean. I turned to face the window, and fell asleep watching the clouds roll by.

Chapter 45

I dreamed of Amanda again, despite the pill. She told me the same thing, to revisit the stone. I managed to reply that the weather wasn't conducive to receiving whatever message, and that I was leaving tomorrow for the hike.

The conversation felt so real. The sympathy in her eyes when I mentioned why I was going on the hike. She'd even thrown her arms around me and wished me luck.

I awoke with a start. The phantom feeling of her hug still there. It made my gut clench and tears started flowing. Why was it so important that I go back to the boulder to speak with someone. That much was obvious now. Someone wanted to talk to me. Someone who was fae. But why? Why would the fae want to talk to me, and what about? It's not like I had info they needed. Unless they had info I needed. About Kepner maybe.

I decided to let it sit. I would have to just deal with it when Mr. McHaddish and I got back from the hike. Which I needed to get ready for. I had packed my hiking boots, planning to hike in the first place. Along with appropriate clothing.

I pulled on one of my long sleeved shirts, and some loose fitting jeans. The brace was debatable. I'll just have to talk with Mr. McHaddish. I also pulled out my emergency medical kit. I placed my two pill bottles inside. Planning out how many I would have left, and if I'd need to get them refilled. Could I even do that here? Another thing to ask Mr. McHaddish.

I took my bag down to breakfast with me. The brace was on my leg. I also brought my rain breaker jacket. This is Scotland. Better to have something that keeps you dry. My boots were waterproof as well. I made a list in my head as I walked down. Other things I needed were extra socks, some eco-friendly soaps maybe, and my camera. If Mr. McHaddish was okay with it.

He and Mrs. Granger were waiting for me in the dining room. Breakfast was granola with fresh berries. I poured my milk over it and the berries, then started eating.

"I called and spoke with your physical therapist about the hike."

I swallowed, "What did he say?"

"That he wants you to wear the brace every day for the first two weeks. Sleep with it on as well. Taking one night off every two days."

I nodded, "And after that?"

"On and off over the next few weeks. We're not fully sure how long we'll be out there. It depends on when the claws fully grow out."

"So the claws fully growing out is the deadline?"

He nodded, "Working your leg is the second project."

"Okay."

After breakfast, we gather the rest of the necessities. Just before 9:30, he had me drink the potion he mentioned. He'd done calculations based on metabolism, strength, and my calorie burns from the pain. I took a deep breath and tossed my head back, to get the potion in my system without tasting it too much. It was nasty, but we'd see how effective it was shortly.

The staff came by to wish us luck on our hike. I was able to separate Gretchen and Jameson from the crowd. I'd had a thought this morning while going over my list. I looked to make sure Jameson's mom wasn't within hearing range and quickly told him my thought.

"If you get a chance, find and watch the movie 'The Abyss.'" I told him.

"American?" I nodded, "Why?" he asked with mild curiosity.

"Most of the movie takes place underwater obviously. There's info about deep sea training in it, specifically how someone can pass a test, but not pass the real thing."

"That can happen?!" He asked, dumbfounded.

I nodded, "The tests are there to weed people out, but they don't always work. Some people react differently to tests than they do the real thing."

"That's why their called tests." Gretchen said. "I have a copy of it. You can borrow it this weekend."

He nodded, "When my mum heads down to Glasgow for school shopping. Any other movies with such examples?"

I thought for a second, nodded, and said, "A movie called 'The Last Days on Mars', it has the actor Liev Schreiber in it. His character suffers something similar."

"Liev Schreiber, as in the actor who does sabretooth in one of the X-Men movies?" he asked.

"Yeah, the same one that also stars Ryan Reynolds." I confirmed.

"Maggie. It's time to get going." Mr. McHaddish said.

I turned and said, "Coming." I turned back to say, "Good luck. I'll see you guys when I get back."

"Good luck to you as well." Gretchen said.

Both gave me a hug before I went back over to Mr. McHaddish. Waving good-bye to everyone, we made our way down the same path I had traveled yesterday and the day before. Everything was muddy today, from all the rain of the storm. Some of the flowers were in bloom, and were all over the place. I let my senses expand as we walked. I've always loved the smell of rain in the forest. It was so much better with my dragon senses too.

"You seem so at peace already." Mr. McHaddish commented as we walked past the boulder in Gretchen's yard.

I gave a sad smile, "I've always loved this weather. It's one reason why I want to live in either Washington state or Maine. Whichever one has this weather the most."

"You could move here to Scotland." He stated, looking back at me with a fatherly smile.

I chuckled, "I've thought about that too."

"Where did your siblings want to settle?"

I chuckled a second time, "Amanda couldn't decide. She was the wandering soul of the three of us. Wherever a weather phenomenon occurs, she'd have wanted to go." I sighed, thinking of her world map that hadn't survived the bomb. I had never seen so many push-pins in one map before.

"And your brother?"

I actually laughed on that one, "Temperamental as the weather that one. He could never stick with one decision for long. The only constant was that he'd settle somewhere on the coast. Along the sea like me."

"Maybe you both inherited some sea dragon shifter traits." He gave a contemplative shrug. I shrugged as well.

Truth be told, neither of us had really thought about it. Plenty of people could feel a pull to the sea, for one reason or another. I had always felt it, my brother on the other hand had grown into it. It wasn't until I'd shown him some pictures taken by a friend's uncle that he'd realized how much the sea had to offer to someone with a love of astronomy. Rock or sand deserts aren't the only places to enjoy the night sky. A watery or icy desert works too.

My brother had been mesmerized by those photos. He had actually paid fifty bucks to keep the ones I'd shown him. I'd called him 'crazy' for it until he gave one to me. Not only did the picture feature the galaxy, but the person taking the pics had caught a humpback whale breaching at the same time. Sadly that photo had been destroyed in the small fire that occurred after the bomb went off. I didn't know if my brother or my friend's uncle had any back-ups. I'd have to find out after Kepner was dead.

We kept walking. The forest got thicker about two miles from the house. I kept hearing the wildlife moving about around us, and wondering if I could identify them by smell alone. My siblings and I had each specialized in a different form of tracking. Reggie by smell, Amanda by sound, and me by tracks. I had already spotted several small animal paths as we walked, I decided to try my sibling's methods.

Keeping my head on a swivel, I brought my senses of smell and hearing to highest power. I mainly got the wet forest, but once I filtered that out, I could pick up some other smells. Deer and bear were easy, some of the smaller wildlife, they proved a bit more elusive to name. How Amanda managed to decipher which animals made a certain sound – when so many sound exactly the same – was impressive.

I actually kept the practice up until we reached the edge of the woods. It was so much of a surprise that I stopped in my tracks. I turned and looked around. I then just shrugged it off and laughed at myself. I hadn't realized how absorbed I was in my task.

I put a bit more speed into my walk. Catching up with Mr. McHaddish at the top of the small hill. I stepped over a rock and felt my leg twinge. I groaned as quietly as I could. I turned and looked in the direction of the estate. I could just barely see the roof from here, but nothing else. Seeing the roof reminded me about getting pictures for my brother. All the constellations would be the same, but there would be more to see. Certain the fact that the Isle of Skye has one of the lowest population counts in Scotland.

I stood by the rock I'd stepped over and pulled my camera out of my coat pocket. Turning it on, I pointed it out toward the estate. The view was beautiful, even with the sea so far away. I slowly turned in a circle, doing a panorama. When I was fully turned toward Mr. McHaddish, he stood for one picture, then ducked behind a nearby rock as I continued. I chuckled quietly. His consideration reminded me of my dad. I wished he was alive, he'd have like Mr. McHaddish as well. Unless the two had already met. I'd have to add that to my growing list of things to ask him.

I put my camera away when I was done with my rotation. The wind blew in from the sea as I did. I took a deep breath, just as the first of the pain came. The potion was working well, it hurt, but it was bearable. Not quite a dull ache, but intense enough to be a small nuisance.

I turned back to Mr. McHaddish, breathing through my teeth as I did, and started walking up to where he stood. I took another deep breath at the top. The pain was ebbing a little, but by now I knew better than to think it was over. If the pain was only this bad at the start, then maybe I could take the final phase without too much trouble.

Chapter 46

Over the next several weeks, Mr. McHaddish kept me busy. By the end of the third week, not only were the claws finally visible – though not fully grown out – but I could walk six miles without the brace. I could even finally run more than three without it too. It felt so good to be as close to normal as I used to be.

He'd also started teaching me Gaelic. I picked it up with surprising ease. He'd been impressed when I could converse with him in Gaelic before the second week was out. I'll never forget his face, he'd nearly choked on his coffee. On the 26th, he'd gotten a hold of Mack and had him fly us down from the village of Culnacnoc to Portree for the Skye food and drink Festival.

That was the most fun I had that summer. We weren't able to stay long but what we get to do was lots of fun. I even got to try the black pudding. I know it's made with pigs blood, but it was actually really good. The mix of spices meant you couldn't taste any blood, and it had a slightly prominent onion flavor.

We even checked into a hotel for a day and showered. We spent the night in two rooms, and spent the rest of the next day attending the festival and he took me on a tour of the place. We stopped at a few shops as well. The Or gift shop was cool, but the most shopping we did was at the outdoor clothing and equipment shop across the block from it. We restocked on our food supplies and replaced a portable stove that had fallen from one of our packs and been cracked.

Our final two shop stops were at a jewelry store, and a book store. Both had some really nice stuff. I only bought three necklaces, and two bracelets. At the book store I got some books in Gaelic so I could try my hand at reading in the language as well. Plus I bought a few children's books for Gretchen's brother that Mr. McHaddish mentioned they didn't have.

After that he took me to one of the most popular tourist spots in Portree. It was called the Lump. Don't ask why but I think it had something to do with the shape of the hill. We even took a ferry ride after I took several pictures from the top of the hill. Our luck on the ferry ride was awesome. We not only saw a pod of whales, but several of them breached as well. Oh so many pictures for me. One of the other tourists actually asked Mr. McHaddish if his daughter had never seen whales before. We'd both laughed. Mr. McHaddish then explained that I wasn't his daughter but was a friend's child who was staying here for the summer, and that yes I had seen whales before, just not so close.

Once our small trip in Portree was done, we met Mack at the same road on the outskirts of town so he could take us back up to Culnacnoc. Both flights he made good time on. By the time we reached the same road we'd taken off from the day before, both of us had replaced our boots and had resorted our packs.

We landed and Mack took off again, taking our bags from the festival and the tour back to the estate. It wasn't long after two, so we could cover quite a few miles before dark. We only took about ten minutes to get everything ready. We camped that night on a mountain slope. We woke the next day to overcast skies and a quick breakfast. The third week ending with bitter coffee.

It was now the beginning of the fourth week, and we finished breakfast in record time, getting ready to make up some lost time. I was washing the portable coffee pot in a small stream when I remembered what the next day was. June 30th, Reggie's 23rd birthday. I'd have to get him something really special for him.

I felt the tears prick my eyes as I walked back to camp. The sky was clear today, with a slight breeze from the main island. I looked to the south west, where I knew my brother was still enjoying his summer vacation in Costa Rica. I had left the pearl at the estate. I was too afraid of losing it to bring it with me. Pearls of that size are not easy to find.

I sat down on the rock I'd used as a chair and looked at the sky. Inspiration struck. I could give Reggie a panoramic photo of the night sky on his birthday. I had plenty of space left on my camera for it. I smiled to myself, he would be blown away by it. I'd have to wait of course, to give it to him, but it would be worth it when I finally could.

"How are we feeling today, Mag?" Mr. McHaddish asked as he sat down as well.

I shrugged a little, "Okay. Thinking about my brother."

"That's right. You said his birthday was tomorrow." I nodded.

"Do you plan to contact him?"

"No. I left the pearl at the estate, and we can't communicate at this distance without both being dragons. I'll contact him afterwards." I said.

He nodded, "I'm sure he'd be proud of how well you've done over these last few weeks." He had this look of nostalgia on his face. I decided to ask the question that had been bugging me for the last few days.

"I remember you said your sister died protecting her daughter, can I ask how, Mr. McHaddish?" I asked. He didn't react as I expected. I had figured he would shut me down, not actually answer me.

He sighed, and said, "She died protecting her daughter from a rival shifter for our family's land. I was away on other business when it happened. My niece was seven when my sister died." He paused, "When I did finally return, I learned that over those several months of absence, the rival shifters had slowly killed the rest of our family, including my thirty year old son. Thinking they had won the land, they bragged to the nearby village about their deeds. Not knowing that I was back, I heard every word they said." I recognized the look in his eyes as he spoke the next sentence.

"I lost control. I killed their entire clan, including the only child they'd succeeded in having. He at least died quickly, but no seventeen year old should be so stupid as to attack a seven year old girl, the way he did my niece." He paused again. The look in his eyes showing just how far away He was.

"After that my niece and I disappeared. I took her to the main land and we lived out our lives as best we could in the Carpathian mountains. She also swore to never marry a shifter. That's why Ms. Hamper has almost no shifter DNA."

"So how many greats are on her?" I asked.

"Only seven. Because of how old my niece was when she finally married." He said with a smile.

"Can I ask just how old you are Mr. McHaddish?"

He chuckled, "I will celebrate my 4000th birthday in seven years." My eyes widened. He was that old. That was honestly amazing to me. My dad had only been within his first century and my grandparents within their first Millenia.

He laughed at my face, "Yes. I get that reaction too."

"Sorry." I couldn't quite contain my own mirth.

"You don't have to apologize. Your ancestor had almost the exact same reaction when I told her my age."

"Which ancestor?" I took a bite of my bread roll.

"Boudica." He told me.

I nearly choked on my bread roll. "Boudica!? As in queen of the Iceni celts? That Boudica!?" he must be joking.

He patted me on the back several times before answering, "Yes," he was laughing as well, "the very same."

Once I had my breath back, I said, "That's impossible, no one knows what happened to her daughters."

"No humans do. It, however, is knowledge only certain shifters have." He said.

I still couldn't believe it. Boudica's daughters had disappeared from history after her death for a reason. The Romans had already destroyed their lives enough, who knows what would have happened to them if the romans had gotten their paws on them again.

Mr. McHaddish interpreted my expression correctly, "Your one of the people who believed the three of them committed suicide?"

I nodded, he continued, "I don't blame you. Most people do believe that."

"But, why would only shifters know their fates?" I asked.

"Would you like me to explain the full story?" I nodded vigorously.

He chuckled before starting, "Most of the story is of course, well known. The rapes and flogging, the ensuing chaos, the death of Boudica, but what is only known to shifters, is how and when she died." He paused, gathering his thoughts, "The final battle between the Romans and Boudica's army did indeed end badly for Boudica, but contrary to popular belief, Boudica did not die from suicide. She was killed on the battlefield by one of the Roman soldiers."

He paused, once again gathering his thoughts, "Sadly her body and those of her army were not properly buried, but her daughters were able to mourn her. They did in fact disappear from history afterwards, but willingly. They had no other family except for some of the surviving villagers. They of course, took them in and for their safety changed their names and spread the rumor that the three had committed suicide."

"What were their names changed to?" I asked. Their birth names were lost to history as well.

"Elizabeth and Guinevere. They lived out their lives under those names. Never once speaking their birth names afterwards."

"Did they ever marry?"

He nodded, "Although of course they swore off men after the rapes."

"It's understandable. Other than family and fellow villagers, what man would they let within ten feet of themselves." I stated.

"Indeed. But that all changed when Elizabeth – the older of the two – was thirty. She was out gathering berries, when she was attacked by a wayward Roman soldier. She held her own very well, until the Roman landed a blow to the back of her head. Neither of them had known that a dragon shifter was nearby watching her. He didn't step in until the Roman stood over her and was removing his belt." I growled, then gave an apologetic look for the interruption. He shook his head and said, "No need to apologize, most other shifters react the same."

He'd started the fire and some food cooking while he'd been talking. The bacon was done now, so he split it between us. Breakfast for the last few weeks was always bacon and bread rolls. Sometimes he included sausage or eggs, but since those don't handle long treks that well, they weren't on the menu often.

While we ate, he continued, "Elizabeth witnessed his transformation just before she fell unconscious. When she awoke, she remembered that the shifter had saved her and thanked him. The Roman soldier's body was never found. He politely escorted her back to her village and made sure she arrived home to her sister safe. After that, Elizabeth couldn't stop thinking about him. Though the two had sworn off men, they hadn't until then met shifter men."

After swallowing my bite of bacon, I asked, "How'd her sister take it?"

"Guinevere was skeptical at first, but she enjoyed seeing her sister so happy. The same shifter came back frequently, and eventually, the two were married. That shifters name, was Marcus Sharp."

My eyes widened in disbelief, "As in Marcus Anatolis Anton Grievious Sharp. The one and only member of my family to be kidnapped by the Romans and raised as one. And my great, great grandfather"

It was common knowledge in my family what had happened to him. His father had been killed in combat with a Roman soldier, after that soldier had tried to marry his daughter without parental permission. His sister had killed herself to save herself from the same soldier. His mother – who was human – was subsequently raped and beaten to death, and he was taken to Rome itself. He was raised there until he was in his mid-teens. To save himself from being drafted into the Roman army, he'd run away. Back to his home country, faking his death along the way. All family records said that he'd met his wife while he was in his late thirties, and that he'd been completely dumbfounded when he found out that his mate was human.

"The same. He even found and killed the surviving Roman soldiers who'd raped her and her sister." Mr. McHaddish interrupted my thoughts.

"He treated her like she deserved."

He nodded, "Your family accepted the two of them into their arms without question. Even Guinevere married a Sharp a few years later, though sadly they never had children."

"But Elizabeth and Marcus did." I stated.

"Seven children. Only the two who inherited the shifter gene lived more than a hundred years."

I laughed quietly to myself. It all seemed too impossible to be real. Me. A descendent of Boudica. One of the only living descendants of her. It was all so surreal. I wondered if Reggie knew about this. I doubted it though, since I hadn't. Unless of course it was one of the many things dad would have eventually told me. It just, boggled my mind.

I was still thinking about it when the next bout of pain began. They were starting earlier and lasting longer now that the claws were showing. Before they'd showed, the pain had lasted about seventeen minutes, but had been easily manageable with continued movement. The potion was doing its job well. What had at first lasted seventeen minutes, instead took seventeen hours. Now of course the pain lasted almost nineteen hours and required at least one stop during the hike. Hence the light breakfasts and all the more moving around.

After about twenty minutes, when the pain was ebbed a bit, we packed up and started moving again. We were heading south along the eastern edge, following the small stretch of sea that separated the isle from the main island. There were a few days when we camped near the shore. I loved those nights, I could observe some of the night crawling sea creatures.

The pain intensified greatly about a quarter to one. It got bad enough that we had to stop walking. I became confused, by this time only four days of the final finishing was done, I had at least two more days. Why was the pain this intense?

Finally the pain ebbed enough that I could focus again. There was sweat on my forehead. Not a good sign for me.

"Are you alright?" Mr. McHaddish asked, kneeling down next to where I had sat.

Taking a deep breath, I answered, "No. I think the pain might be overriding the potion."

"Hold still." He felt my pulse and timed it on his watch, "Damn! You might be right. Something about your metabolism must be affecting it."

"That can happen?" I asked.

He nodded, "Your leg getting back up to snuff must have kick started your metabolism. Your almost back to full health." He looked worried.

Shit! He should be. Me getting back to full health was the one thing both of us had forgotten to factor in. It had never even crossed my mind, not since both Reggie and Amanda had been at peak health during theirs. It hadn't occurred to me that my health could be a factor.

"What do we do?" I asked between breaths.

"We head inland. The mountains aren't far from here. We can hike through them until the potion runs out and the claws finish growing."

I nodded, "I'll be ready to move in a minute."

He nodded and stood up. Looking inland, he mapped out a route for us to take. The mountains only inhabitants would be wildlife. We were near the coast directly opposite the Loch Snizort Beag. And yes, that is an actual name. The mountains were almost perfectly between the two masses of water.

Once I had my breath back, we made our way inland. He set a slow and steady pace. Even though I wanted to get there as fast as possible. The pain worked its way down my back to my leg. I hissed in pain as my leg complained for the first time in days. I looked ahead to where Mr. McHaddish was standing. He got this determined look on his face and removed his pack.

Looking me in the eyes, he said, "Get on." I was confused for a moment. Until he started shifting.

Holy mother of the Gods! I had been right. he was positively huge! He was easily the same size as Jameson. It would be a job and a half just to climb on his back. He was magnificent though. His fur was a pale shade of grey, and thick enough to withstand a Russian winter. His mane was the size of two armchairs. It was a wonder in and of itself.

He gave me a pointed look and indicated a rock next to his pack. Limping over to it, he knelt down, and I was able – barely – to throw my left leg over his back and straddle his spine. Thankfully since he was all muscle, I couldn't feel his spine. Picking up his pack with his teeth, he started walking in the direction of the mountains. At the pace he set as a lion, we'd reach them by seven in the evening at least. I kept still as he walked, only really turning my head to look around as he moved. It felt weird to ride a lion. I'd ridden a horse before. This was nothing like that.

I kept quiet as well. My only indication to him about the pains rise or fall was me clenching his fur slightly every time the pain got worse. I at one point had him stop and poured out some water into a bowl. I knew enough about big cats to know the signs of thirst. While he drank from the bowl, I took a drink from my water bottle. It was almost empty. I'd need to refill both at the next stream.

That came rather quickly after I returned to my position on his back. I took my time refilling all the water bottles and canteens we had brought. We were just about to enter a tree line, and I indicated that I could walk just fine now.

He shifted back, though I could tell it was reluctantly. He had already been walking with me as a passenger for almost three hours and had missed lunch because of it. I didn't want to be that much of a burden on him.

I spotted movement at the tree line. My hunting instincts activated when I identified the buck grazing in the grass. It was about sixty feet to our right. I carefully and gently placed my water bottle and pack down on the ground. Mr. McHaddish was too busy checking his pack over to notice the deer.

Moving quietly, I shifted. I stalked the buck for about twenty feet. Stopping only when it's head was raised. Thankfully the wind had shifted to downwind, so he couldn't smell me. Once I had covered half the distance between us, I paused. Then, like lightning, I lunged at the deer.

I snapped it neck clean. It never even registered what had attacked it. I took the deer in my teeth back over to Mr. McHaddish. He was laughing to himself. He'd been so concerned for me, he hadn't noticed his stomach growling a few minutes ago. I stepped over the stream and laid the dear at his feet. It was a good sized buck, enough to feed him for lunch. I wouldn't be able to eat. The pain was only helping my nausea.

Shifting back, I sat down by the stream and started eating some crackers. Mr. McHaddish smiled at me, picked up the carcass, and walked into the woods. I took the liberty of turning back toward the east. Lying back, I watched the clouds go by, even dozed for a little while.

At five o'clock, Mr. McHaddish emerged from the woods, having eaten the whole buck down to the bone. He had the antlers in his hand, and after passing one to me, tied them to our packs. From there we started walking inland again. We followed a deer path through the small group of trees that had hidden him and his lunch. Taking our time once more, to save me any unnecessary effort.

I wouldn't have minded had it not been for the knowledge that the potion was more than likely going to run out in a few days. Or maybe tomorrow. I got butterflies in my stomach at the thought of the final stage. Once more I wished my dad were here to help me through it like he had my siblings. And of course the more I hated Kepner for ruining my life and forcing me to go through this thing effectively on my own. I was thankful for Mr. Hydell, Molly, and Mr. McHaddish, but their support wasn't something I could ever repay.

Chapter 47

It was in fact just after eight in the evening when we finally reached the foot of the higher mountains. We both almost collapsed from exhaustion. Thankfully we had just enough energy to make camp and start a fire.

Mr. McHaddish had caught two rabbits less than an hour ago, and had them on a spit roasting over the fire almost as soon as I had it going. I got the pot and filled it with some water from a canteen. I then took out some potatoes I'd collected and chopped them using my claws. I put them into the pot before placing the pot into the fire, between where the two rabbits were hanging.

The sun was yet to set, but low enough to create twilight. I looked out to the east as Mr. McHaddish walked a distance away to relieve himself. I opened my bag and took out my pain pills. I hadn't taken one in more than a week, and I had taken only one of my sleeping pills throughout the entire trip.

I was turning the rabbits when Mr. McHaddish came back over. He was putting his phone away. I had left mine at the estate since it wasn't compatible with his portable solar charger. He seemed a little at ease, but not by much.

He knelt down and said, "I just spoke with Mrs. Granger. There's some news about Kepner that they've received," I took a sharp breath, "and I've asked her to store it in my office until we return."

I nodded, "Good or bad?"

"Not sure. She didn't actually read the message, but she thinks it might be serious." I nodded. "On a different note," he pulled a small bottle from his pack, "I had been hoping you wouldn't need this."

He handed me the bottle. I unscrewed the cap and took a whiff of the contents. It was more of the potion to prolong the pain. Like before, I took a deep breath and threw my head back, swallowing it quickly. It was just as bad the second time as the first. I sat still while I waited for the potion to get into my system.

After only three minutes, I didn't feel queasy anymore. I took a drink of water to wash down the last dregs of the potion.

"I've also run a few more calculations. Factoring in your being almost back to full health, that second helping **should** extend the potions effects for another two weeks." Mr. McHaddish told me, while stirring the potatoes.

"You're sure?" I asked hesitantly. Several things could happen in two weeks.

He nodded, "You weren't fully through the first dose, so adding on should work just fine."

I nodded. I trusted him. You don't get to be 4000 years old without perfecting your potion making skills. I looked at him as he carefully scooped out the taters once they were done. Him being as old as he was, made me wonder a few other things.

"If it's not too invasive, is your niece still alive?" I asked tentatively.

He nodded, "She is. She currently lives at the school as one of the teachers."

"Cool. What does she teach?"

"She's the weapons teacher. Quite a few of my students are intimidated by her because of her vast knowledge on bladed weapons."

"I can't wait to meet her." I really couldn't. She sounded really cool.

He chuckled, "She'll like you, you both have a lot in common."

"That we do." I agreed.

He paused to remove the rabbits, "I'm guessing you have one more question."

I nodded, "Did you ever have any other children?"

He shook his head, "After my son was murdered I became afraid to have more. For obvious reasons. Also I was now raising my niece like my own. It was close enough."

He gave me one of the rabbits just as another thought occurred to me, "How'd you know about Boudica being my ancestor?"

He smiled, thought about something, then answered, "I met your father when he was a very young boy. He introduced me to your grandparents and they filled me in on some unanswered questions."

"What questions?" I asked with interest.

"At that time, obviously no one knew that your family was still alive but I was doing research for a friend about families from Scotland that had either vanished or abandoned their homeland. He was looking for someone in particular. I eventually found him, but the information your grandparents gave me got me curious about things. That was how I actually met with them again to ask about Boudica."

"And they knew?" now I was intrigued.

He nodded, "It's a secret that has been passed down your family line for two thousand years. Sadly your grandparent died before they could tell your father though. That was knowledge that usually wasn't shared until someone's one hundredth birthday."

"Which my father never reached." I clutched my bowl until my knuckles turned white.

Mr. McHaddish placed a hand over mine, "But now you know. And you can share that with your brother." He smiled, and I returned a small one.

With tears in my eyes I asked my next question, "What were they like? My paternal grandparents?"

His gaze became sympathetic, clearly this was a question he'd answered before for someone else. More than likely his niece.

"Your grandmother was as fierce as could be. No one stood in her way. Her tenacity knew no bounds, especially when it came to family." He paused, "But with her children, she was always gentle. I remember the last time I saw her, it was just before your father finished high school, she told me that your father had met a nice young woman and that she was more than likely his mate. She was ecstatic to be so near becoming a grandmother for the first time."

I choked back my tears. Hearing that, reminded me of my dad. It was no wonder he missed grandma so much. He was every bit her son. He and mom had been a force to be reckoned with together. Not even any of our teachers had argued with them.

"Your grandfather was another matter." He chuckled, "Always had his nose in a book, he never could get enough of learning. He passed that to your father, and clearly to the three of you." He paused, "Your grandmother was breathtaking as a dragon. Her scales the palest of blues, yet in a certain light, her scales shimmered as if made of water."

My tears were free flowing now. My dad had never told us about his parents as dragons, only ever as humans. Hearing this made me think of my brother. His shade of midnight blue had been picturesque.

"Your grandfather was interesting color wise." He said.

That got my attention, "How so?"

He smiled, "His color – like yours – was not one commonly seen amongst dragons." He stopped and openly laughed.

Okay, what? "What color was he?"

Trying to contain his laughter, he said, "Bright neon green."

I practically died of laughter. I'm sorry grandpa, but it's no wonder why dad would dodge the question whenever one of us had asked him. I'm also sorry 'cause that is just plain funny. I could only imagine how my siblings would react if they knew that.

I paused in my laughing, then frowned in confusion. Why had I worded that sentence as if Amanda was still alive?

"Are you alright?" he'd stopped laughing too.

I shook my head, "I'm… just wondering why I've been thinking like Amanda was still alive."

"How do you mean?" he looked confused.

"Well," I gathered my thoughts, "both the night before we left and the night before that, I dreamt about her. In both, she said to revisit a boulder, but in the second one, for some reason… I reacted and told her about the hike and the final finishing." I paused, thinking on how best to explain the rest.

Finally I chose to just say it, "When I was finished telling her, she gave me a hug, and said she wished that she was there to help me. Then I woke up, the feeling of her hug still there. As if she really had just hugged me."

He seemed intrigued and troubled at the same time, "These were the only times you've had this dream?"

"Yes."

"What boulder did she mean?"

"The one in Gretchen's backyard." I said.

"The fae speaking stone?!"

"If that's what it's called, then yes." I answered nervously.

Now he looked really worried, "Did anyone in your family know any fae?"

I shook my head, "Not to my knowledge."

"What else did your sister say?"

"That I needed to revisit the boulder because someone hadn't been able to get a good connection. I had napped on the boulder the first day of the finishing and apparently because of when I was there, only three of four elements touched it, so the connection wasn't strong enough."

"That doesn't mean you should go back." His look was fatherly again.

"I know, but every time I've thought about it, some instinct says that even if I don't do it there, then someone will still try to contact me. For whatever reason this someone wants to speak with me, I need to do it." I paused, "The thought of ignoring it… makes my stomach hurt."

He sighed, "You truly feel this needs to be done?"

I simply nodded, he sighed again and said, "Alright. But I will accompany you to the stone. There are reasons I had that stone declared off limits."

"I'm not gonna argue with that." I said with a small smile.

We finished our meal in silence after that. I could tell he was nervous about the prospect of my eventual chat with a member of the fae. Despite some children's tales, not all fae can be trusted. A good portion were – and/or still are - indeed dangerous, but the fae can and will return favors without causing trouble. So long as the deed was done in kindness. But it still left a burning question. Why would the fae want to speak with me? As far as I knew no one in my family history had ever done anything worthy of a fae favor. Unless one of my siblings had done something for a fae and not realized it.

Wait a second. Two years ago my sister had found an injured rabbit and nursed it back to health herself. The fae could sometimes disguise themselves as animals to move around without hinderance. Maybe that rabbit had been a fae. Come to think of it, she'd never explained the bracelet she'd worn afterwards. Nor had she ever taken it off. Was the bracelet somehow tied to the fae?

Good questions both. But the answers would have to wait. Right now I had to focus on getting through the final finishing without hurting anyone. Including myself and Mr. McHaddish.

Chapter 48

The next two weeks went by quickly. Every day was pretty much the same routine. The only add on was that Mr. McHaddish got me started on my martial arts training again. Now that my leg could take the vigorous movement better. He would have us stop at random times during the hike and have me perform a different one each time. He'd brushed up on his martial arts training after I had mentioned which ones I practiced, so he made a good sensei.

On the second to last day of our hike, I took my camera out to look at the panorama I had gotten on June 30th. I'd had to wait until a little after midnight before I could begin. I hadn't wanted the light of the moon to drown out the stars. Although I did get some awesome zoom shots of the moon with my camera. Not to mention how often I had pulled the thing out during the hike. I now had more than 200 pictures, plus plenty of room to spare.

I put my camera in my pack, I felt a sense of anticipation mixed with apprehension creeping up on me. I stood and looked around, Mr. McHaddish was nowhere to be seen. Our camp was directly between the small settlement of Sligachan and the mountain Glamaig, so he'd chosen to go into the settlement to get some medical supplies. On both of the last two days, the tips of my wings had bled bad enough to require them. The claws hadn't grown any further though and that had me worried. I of course couldn't contact Reggie to find out if his or Amanda's had done the same, so for now I just assumed that they had.

We were now almost perfectly opposite the estate. That wasn't necessarily a good thing, but it did mean that if the claws finished growing soon, we could cut across the island to get to the estate and I could take some much needed rest.

At this point the plan was simple. If the pain overruled the potion – and I was betting it would – I was to make a break for either Glamaig or one of the further away mountains. I'd recently memorized a map of the isle, so knew where the nearest ones were. My choice wasn't Glamaig, it was too close to a human population for my liking, so my choice was a mountain called Sgu'rr nan Gillean. It was a very rocky mountain and extremely isolated, a perfect choice for someone about to potentially go ballistic with pain from claws growing out of the ends of her wings. Not to mention if I could successfully fly there, I wouldn't have to worry about not hurting Mr. McHaddish.

I started pacing, it was approaching noon. My nervousness was rising by the minute, not only for the finishing but for Mr. McHaddish's return. I had already worded and written a note for him, explaining where I was going and that the potion had indeed run out. It was currently in my coat pocket, only to be pulled out should I actually need to get moving before he got back. Which if my calculations were correct, would be soon. Whether he returned first or not.

For once, I got a warning. My leg started to pulse with pain, as did my arms. I'm smart enough to get the picture. The final stage was about to begin and I needed to get moving before the pain blinded me. I pulled the note out, folded it, and placed it under a rock by Mr. McHaddish's pack. Pointing myself in the right direction, I got a running start, shifted, and took off.

I wouldn't need to fly for long, a 96 foot wingspan moves a lot of air. Within seconds of starting, the pain started to intensify. It wasn't debilitating yet, but I knew better than to hope otherwise. I flew at full speed, well over 300 hundred miles an hour. I reached Sgu'rr nan Gillean within five seconds, just before the pain caused me to fall from the sky.

That was the first time I actually crashed. I hit the ground head first and rolled. End over end. For a good 70 feet. When I finally came to a stop, I had carved a nice set of grooves into the ground. Panting, I lifted my head enough to look around. Nothing, absolutely nothing in my surroundings but rocks, trees, and grass. Good.

I stood shakily. The pain had abated somewhat, enough for me to move closer to the base of the mountain a bit more. I had landed in one of the valleys between the northern two sets of peaks that come off Sgu'rr nan Gillean. Even better. That meant that any roars I gave off would be contained by the mountains and trees. My legs weren't that steady though, so I wouldn't be moving at all once the claws were fully grown out. I took a few second to look at the ends of my wings. The claws had started as stubs less than an inch in length. Now they were about two inches. I had never seen my sibling's claws, but I had caught a glimpse of my dad's, and his had been about eight inches long. Each.

I didn't have much time to think after that, the pain lanced through me so bad that my vision instantly turned red. The roar I let out would've been heard on the mainland had I not crashed where I did. And like any creature caught in the throughs of pain, I lashed out. Swiping at trees with claws and tail, at one point I managed to shatter a microwave sized rock. A granite rock doesn't always crack easily, let alone shatter. The force required for it is well into the 10,000 pounds range. Egyptian pink granite goes at over 65,000 pounds of force.

I don't know how long I was in pain, all I did know was that when the pain finally faded to an intense ache, the claws were fully grown, and about six inches long. Dragons don't sweat, but it certainly felt like I was. It wasn't until my vision cleared some more that I realized I wasn't wet from sweat, but from rain.

I lifted my head in appreciation. The cooling rain felt wonderful against my heated scales. The pain was now gone, but the after ache was agonizing. It felt as if someone was pinching all of the nerve endings in both wings individually. I opened my mouth enough to get a drink. Man I was so thirsty. I started panting again, the slight movement of my neck from swallowing had sent an aftershock down both shoulders, which then moved to my wings. I lost my footing, and then consciousness.

I barely came to sometime later. The only thing that registered was the movement of the trees from the wind. Then the sound of chuffing. At first I thought it was Mr. McHaddish, but my brain just wouldn't work. I slipped back into oblivion.

My wing was moving. Why?! I could barely move, but I could at least open my eyes. My head wasn't positioned to see what was moving my wing, so, with what little strength I had left, I moved my head just enough to view my right wing.

A grizzly bear? My vision focused a bit more. Jameson?! How'd he even know where I was? And what was he doing here? Besides gently cleaning the blood from my new claws.

I made to move my wing away from him, but he just as gently caught the membrane and pulled it back to him. I groaned a little. No matter how gently you clean them, it still hurts. With jelly legs, I managed to shift my body a little to a more comfortable position. For once, I noticed just how chilled I was. Most of my body heat was in my wings. So the rest of me was cold from the rain.

Seeing me shiver, Jameson rose from his position and moved toward me. Being careful of my legs, he laid down beside me, providing me with some much appreciated warmth. I spotted a puddle a few inches from my nose, I was thirsty, but didn't have the stamina to move toward it. Jameson took the initiative though. He rose once again, and very carefully lifted my head with his snout, and moved me toward the puddle. Once I was close enough to it, he put my head back down on the ground. I was close enough to drink, but not to drown should the rain fill the naturally occurring divot in the ground any more than it already had.

I drank my fill. Then moved my head just enough to look Jameson in the eyes. I made sure that he could see the thanks in mine. He placed his head on the ground, his nose only a few inches from mine. I could see his welcoming look as I lost consciousness once again.

I don't know how long I was out that time either. The first thing I noticed was the sound of a raised voice. Only just managing to open one eye, I saw Mr. McHaddish on the phone with someone. Whomever he was talking to either was the unhappy one, or he was. I didn't care at that point. The only thing I really did care about was the fact that Jameson was still lying next to me, never once moving away as I shifted position in discomfort.

I tried to move my wings to a different position, but only managed to send pain shooting down them both. Mr. McHaddish noticed. I didn't register what he told Jameson, but I did feel my wings carefully move. I quickly lost consciousness once more when they stopped moving.

The sun was setting. That meant I had been out for over nine hours. It felt like much longer. I slowly raised my head, being careful not to send any movement down to my shoulders. Jameson was snoozing beside me, while Mr. McHaddish was sitting nearby. He'd set up camp, and seemed annoyed. Most likely at me. Since I did something so reckless as go off on my own like I had.

I used my tongue to grab a stick and tossed it at him. I hit him square in the shoulder. He turned and looked at me. Yep, I was the one he was annoyed with. He stood and started pacing like the angry father he'd once been. I shook my head a little. Not at him, but at the dizziness that was creeping up on me. I really did not want to fall back into unconsciousness. I was hungry and wanted something to eat. Finally Mr. McHaddish stopped pacing and looked at me.

"Do you have any idea how angry I am at you?" he said. Trying not to give it away. I did the dragon equivalent of raising my eyebrow. No duh I knew how angry he was.

He shook his head, "Do you realize how serious you could've gotten yourself hurt?!"

Okay, that one had to be answered, "*I couldn't care less about myself. I'd rather go through every second of that again, then even think about what I could've done to you or anyone else.*"

He tried to argue, but couldn't.

"*You said it yourself. I'm too strong for you, Jameson, and my brother combined.*" I finally caught a glimpse of my surroundings, "*Nature can recover from this kind of destruction. The lives of humans and shifters cannot.*" When I need to make my point, I will.

I could see he wanted to argue, but all he said was, "Damn it young lady."

He ran his hand through his hair as he started pacing again. He grabbed a deer carcass from behind the rock he'd been sitting on, and dragged it over to me. It wasn't as big as the one I had killed two weeks ago, but it would feed me for at least a few hours.

I ate slowly, not wanting to throw up what little I had eaten today. It was the bones I needed the most. The calcium in them would help my system recover from the intense pain of growth faster. Also it would make sure the new claws were strong and not brittle. I ate the heart, liver, and lungs as well. I'll never forget Mr. McHaddish's face as he saw me eat the eyes also. Sadly the laughter hurt.

I finished the deer shortly after eleven. I then laid my head down with the intent to sleep, but a nagging at the back of my mind had me staying awake. The nagging was Reggie, attempting to make contact.

"*I'm here sis.*" He said.

I gave a content sigh, "*I know.*"

"*I could barely control myself when I felt it begin for you. I'm glad you decided to isolate yourself.*"

"*At least you are. Mr. McHaddish isn't entirely happy about it.*" I said with a small smile.

"Yeah well, it was your choice." I awoke some more as Jameson moved. That got my brothers attention. *"Who's your pal?"* uh-oh, big brother instincts coming up.

"He's a friend. His name is Jameson." I said.

"Is he your boyfriend?" he asked with barely contained brotherly hostility.

"NO! We only met a few days before the hike began." I told him.

"He seems a little more familiar than a friend."

"Like your Matilda?!" you want to go there, I'll go there.

I felt him cringe, *"Touché."* I then felt his slightly aggrieved sigh, *"Okay, you say he's just a friend, I'll believe you."*

"Damn right you will. You know I'm nowhere near emotionally ready for that." The after aches were making me testy.

He seemed contrite, *"Fair enough. I'm sorry."*

I gave a grateful sigh, *"Thank you, and apology accepted."*

"Now get some sleep sis. Your gonna need it."

With that, he broke contact. Leaving me with my thoughts. Good grief, and I thought my reaction to his girlfriend was bad. He hadn't reacted this way with any of Amanda's old boyfriends. So why react that way with a friend of mine? I had told the truth. I wasn't anywhere near ready for a relationship beyond friendship. I mean, I could understand if he reacted that way because of everything we've been through in the last few months but sheesh bro. Overkill much.

I didn't have much time to think about it though. By the time that Jameson woke up I was close to full sleep. His movement only served to remind me that he was there. I also noticed that Mr. McHaddish was on the phone again. I only just caught him say Billings. Jameson's mom! That can't be good. Unless she somehow has no idea that he's even left the estate, but how that could be, I didn't know. I'd just have to find out in the morning after I woke up.

Chapter 49

I awoke to find Jameson gone, and Mr. McHaddish at the fire cooking breakfast. I moved a little, and started to shift. It took several minutes, but eventually, I was human again.

Once I could stand, I walked over to the camp and sat down on a folding chair that Mr. McHaddish had set up for me. I gladly took the breakfast that he passed me. Bacon, eggs, and sausage hash. I ate slowly, not wanting to overwhelm my stomach. The hash was really good.

Mr. McHaddish remained quiet for the entire time I ate. He even passed me a cup of warm coffee. The only reason it was warm was because of the chill in the air. I still drank it gladly though. When I was done with everything, I placed the dishes down on the rock between us, and looked up at the sky. Some clouds drifted by, but it was mostly clear. A good day for a fly, if I could manage it. I looked at Mr. McHaddish as he rose from his position.

"I know what you're thinking, and I want you to wait at least a full day before attempting to fly." He told me.

I nodded, I kinda figured that I would need more time to get used to the new claws. I rolled my shoulders. I could also feel new, stronger, muscles in my back and shoulders. It made sense when I factored them in with the claws. My ancestors had used the claws for purchase on rocks, it was only logical to have stronger muscles too.

I leaned back in my chair. I was still exhausted from yesterday. It made me wonder how or when we would start heading back to the estate. I didn't have long to wait.

"If you're up to it, we can start walking back soon." That would be a long walk.

"How far from here is it?" I asked.

"A little over seven miles. I'll do most of the walking since you need to rest as much as possible." He answered.

"How long did it take Jameson to cover that?"

"In bear form at top speed, only about ten minutes." A normal grizzly could reach 40 miles an hour. So Jameson could run at more than double that speed.

I nodded, "Not bad."

"Indeed. So, what do you say? We can even stop at the fairy pools for a rest."

I thought about it, then said, "Okay." We both rose from our positions and started packing camp. Once done, he shifted, and with no argument, I climbed on his back.

He covered ground quickly. We moved about three miles inside of an hour. If the estate was within seven miles, then the last four should take him just over another hour and a half at most. Though we did stop at the fairy pools. They were beautiful, pristine even. I don't know how many pictures I took. Of both the pools, and the surrounding lands. It felt wonderful to be so close to my normal self once again.

We ate a quick snack before moving again. Mr. McHaddish let me walk for a little while from there. He'd shifted back to human form about a mile before we actually reached the pools. He hadn't wanted to scare any tourists that might be around, and there were about twenty of them when we arrived.

It wasn't long into our walk that I needed to rest. I had known I wouldn't be able to reach the estate walking, but it still felt good to walk for at least a little ways. He shifted back to lion form, and we continued our journey back to the estate.

I hadn't actually asked what time it was when I had woken up, so I assumed it was close to ten in the morning when we reached the lands of his estate. He took the same path in that we had taken out. He didn't shift back until we were right next to the kitchen door. Mrs. Granger was waiting for us. She had a chair next to her as well, more than likely for me.

Mr. McHaddish laid down so I could disembark. I did end up sitting down from sudden pain in my leg, so good thinking on her part. Neither of us smelled very good, but it wasn't atrocious. Kinda hard to take a shower when out on a hike.

Mrs. Granger made us eat before she'd let us go inside to shower. She brought us each two meat and cheese sandwiches, and a glass of milk. I ate mine pretty quickly, I was starving at that point. I finished mine first and was allowed to head up to the bathroom across from my room. I went into my room to grab some fresh clothes first though. There was a box on the bed, I walked over to it. It had my name on it, as well as a card. I could tell from its size that it was a dress box. The address said it was California. This couldn't be the dress that Emily and Amber had been working on. I had given them my home address, why send it here?

I decided to leave it for now, I hadn't showered since the festival and needed one for multiple reasons. I walked across the hall and closed the door. I did lock the door, not wanting to be walked in on. I remembered one time last summer Reggie had done so. He'd been so embarrassed about that.

I took my usual twenty minute shower, feeling much more relaxed afterwards. I changed into my clean clothes and made sure to leave yesterdays in the hamper by the door. I unlocked the door and found lunch in my room. More haggis. Yes!!

I sat down to eat, letting the box wait. Mrs. Granger came up to retrieve the tray about fifteen minutes later. Before she left, I asked about the box.

"That arrived a few days ago. Your guardian called to tell us it was a gift from them. They're currently in Japan." She left after that.

Oh right. I'd forgotten that the two of them were in Japan for the month. I wondered what was in the box now. I had asked for some souvenirs from each country, maybe this was one.

I sat down on the bed and pulled the box into my lap. But before opening it, I put it back down and grabbed my computer, choosing to check my e-mail before anything else. I plugged it in to charge as it woke up. I had over 200 unread e-mails. Geez.

Most were spam or ads, so I just deleted those. That narrowed it down to sixty. None from Kepner. Thank the Gods. Most of them now were from Mr. Hydell and Molly, details, and pics from their trip. I opened them and started saving the pics to my computer. They'd gone to Australia Zoo! Lucky. My siblings and I had grown up on Crocodile Hunter episodes. We all three had been huge fans of the Irwin's, and had been devastated when Steve had died.

The rest were from friends sending me their new usernames. One was from Reggie. Pics of his trip so far. Cool! Most of them were of the native flora. Costa Rica had some very beautiful flowers. I sent him a reply e-mail thanking him for the pics and sending him some from my camera. I also told him about the birthday present surprise I had for him. The next e-mail was from Emily, telling me that the dress was done and that they were going to send it to me once I got back. No argument there. The final e-mail was from Molly, telling me about my box and that she knew it was something that I would like. On that note, I put my computer aside and opened the box.

Chapter 50

Holy Crap! I was gonna hug Molly the next time I saw her. She'd sent me a Japanese kimono, anime cosplay Lolita dress. Black with white, pink, and purple flowers on it. It was beautiful! I was in love with it the second I unfolded it. I couldn't believe she'd gotten me one of these. I checked the tag. Made in Japan. I put it down and closed my door. I removed my shirt and tried it on.

It fit perfectly. I looked in the mirror. I actually looked really good in this. The jeans didn't quite work with it, but I had a pair of leggings at home that would work great. I turned back to the box and picked up the card. It said, 'To Maggie with love from Mr. Hydell and Molly'. I smiled.

I placed the card in the box and started to remove my new kimono. I had it off my shoulders when the door suddenly opened.

"Why is this-"

"Jameson!" I shouted, pulling the kimono hurriedly back onto my shoulders.

"Shit!" he cursed as he quickly closed the door.

I redid the kimono and while blushing, went over to the door. I opened it and look out into the hallway. Jameson was standing in the middle of the hall, facing the opposite wall, with his head turned down. I could see that he was blushing as well, his ears were bright red.

I cleared my throat, "It's safe." I tried to hide my smile.

He turned slightly, "Are you sure?"

I chuckled, "Yes I'm sure. If I wanted to flash you I'd have done it when you opened the door."

He fully turned, his face wasn't as red as his ears, "I'm sorry about that, I didn't think you were back already."

"You haven't seen Mr. McHaddish yet?" I asked.

"No." he answered, shaking his head. He then got a confused look on his face, "and what the hell does 'flash me' mean?"

I chuckled again, "It's from the sixties era. It's when a woman lifts her shirt to show off her chest, and in most cases the woman wasn't wearing a bra."

His eyes widened, "I'd heard that phrase before, but when I asked my mum what it meant she said I didn't need to know."

"Did you ask your dad?" I asked.

He shook his head, "Didn't think about it."

I nodded, "And I accept your apology." I smiled at him. He returned it gratefully.

"Although if I may ask, why were you opening my door?"

He started blushing again, "I got so used to the door being open while you were gone that it just seemed odd for it to be closed, and since I hadn't known you were back…"

"It was instinctive." I finished. He nodded.

"What's with the shirt?" he asked, gesturing at me.

I looked down at it as I answered, "It's a gift from my guardian's girlfriend. I don't usually wear something like this but I've like kimono's since my sister and I discovered anime."

"It suits you." He said. I smiled.

We heard Mr. Granger call his name. He smiled and waved as he went back down the hall. I waved back and stepped fully into my room. This time I locked the door before I changed back into my shirt. I gently refolded the kimono and placed it back into its box.

I looked at my clock. 1:45. I could go outside for a little bit, or read. I also remembered what Gretchen had told me about the boulder. Depending on the cloud cover at five, I might just be able to finally find out who needed to talk to me and why. I could admit to myself that I was extremely curious about why, and about actually talking to a fae for the first time. My gut was telling me that the rabbit and bracelet I had mentioned earlier were involved somehow.

Before heading outside though, I went down to the library. I hadn't looked through all the Sherlock books before we'd left and I wanted to confirm which ones I had seen. I walked back to the shelves and counted. Sir Arthur had written four novels and 56 short stories about Sherlock and Watson. And Mr. McHaddish had nine books in total, obviously the 56 stories composed into their five groups. Yes! I could easily read through the entire works in one summer. Molly's library had had all sixty as well, but since we'd only stayed the one night. I mentally went over the list of ones that I had read, and it wasn't very long.

I had read all but one full novel and only about five of the stories. My high school library had at one time had some of the stories, but since most kids either can't read old English or aren't interested in Sherlock at all, so they'd donated them to a book store in Seattle. I'd been disappointed about that, and they had apologized to me.

I grabbed one I hadn't read before and went over to the seating area. The Case of the Five Orange Pips was one that Reggie had told me about. I had been impatient to read it since I'd seen it in my high school library before they'd been donated. I sat down and started reading.

It didn't take me long to finish it. I felt sorry for their client, but that's the thing with secret societies, they take redemption to overkill sometimes. Oh well. The story itself was good though, definitely not something you'd read every day, but might just for kicks. It was just after three, so I got up and grabbed The Sign of the Four. I'd read it twice and liked it, not quite as much as Hound of Baskervilles, but it was good.

At ten to five, I put my book on the shelf – after memorizing the page – and started outside. I knew that Mr. McHaddish wanted to come with me so I went up to his office first, to see if he was there. I ended up almost running into him on his way downstairs. From there we both headed out the kitchen door, saying hi to Malcolm on the way. I even asked what he was making. Scottish beef stew. Sounds good to me.

We walked back down the path to Gretchen's backyard. She was waiting for us. Mr. McHaddish jumped down from the bank to give me room to shift. Keelan came running out just as I started. Gretchen turned just in time to grab him before he got too far. It's not a good idea for one year old's to see someone shift, it can be bad for them psychologically.

I finished just before her brother finally wiggled free of her grip. He made to start climbing the bank, but Mr. McHaddish grabbed him and held him out of my way. I stepped down and he was allowed to come forward at last. I chuckled, although it sounded like chuffing. With him sitting on my right front foot, I walked forward a bit more. I lifted my leg a little, gently bobbed it up and down, as if trying to shake him off. It had the desired effect, he started giggling up a storm. Gretchen tried to hide her smile but Mr. McHaddish openly laughed. He hadn't seen me around kids yet, so I could see that he was surprised by it, in a good way though.

I placed my foot back down so Gretchen could extract him as the sun began to illuminate the boulder. He didn't fight as much this time. I was getting nervous about this, I really wanted to know who wanted to talk to me but the apprehension was almost overwhelming. Finally I took a deep breath as the feeling to lie on the stone came upon me again, and jumped up on the boulder. I made sure to position myself in the exact same way I had the first time. It didn't take long for the need for sleep to overtake again. Just as the sun fully lit up the stone, a slight breeze started up as well, and I was out.

That was one of the strangest experiences of my life. First it felt like I was floating, then like I was very heavy. Kinda like when someone is under the effects of hypnotism. When I could finally focus, I saw nothing but golden light around me. I turned in a circle, only then noticing that I was in human form. I was about to call out when a black blur appeared. That blur eventually manifested into a humanoid shape, which then took the form of a fae male.

He was about 6′7″, had short brown hair, and piercing blue eyes. He was wearing a black suit in full display. I looked at him suspiciously. He was clearly glamoured. I could just make out a fuzziness at the edge of his features. The only thing he didn't hide were his ears. Fully pointed.

He smiled, and said, "It's a pleasure to finally meet you Miss Sharp."

"And to whom do I have the interest of meeting?" I asked, still eyeing him suspiciously.

He bobbed his head in acknowledgment, "I'm glad to hear your sister kept her promise of secrecy."

My chest tightened at the mention of her, "So this **is** about Amanda." I said.

He nodded, "I've waited a long time to contact either you or your brother. Unfortunately there aren't a lot of ways for one of my age to speak with the mortal realm easily. Also their aren't very many communication stones left intact in your world."

"I understand, so what exactly is it that you have to tell me?" I asked.

"I'm here to tell you about your sister's agreement with me."

"So you were that rabbit that she nursed back to health two years ago." I stated.

He nodded, still smiling, "I was indeed, and I owe your sister a debt for that. A month after she released me back into the forest, I returned to her in a dream."

"Like with my dreams last month?"

He nodded again, "I told her that I was extremely grateful for her help and her kindness. And of course as a fae, I am obliged to repay such deeds. I told her that I wanted to give her a gift. One that hadn't been issued to a human in centuries."

"The bracelet." I said as comprehension started to dawn.

"Correct. I told her never to remove it, so long as she kept it on, I could one day return the favor."

"So what exactly was the bracelet?"

"What did you notice about it?" he asked.

I thought about the bracelet for a second, "I noticed that every time I was near it, I could feel a magical aura. Also the tree emblem on it that was next to the S shaped divide between the two ends. The biggest thing that I noticed was that it was made of elm wood, and never once took any kind of damage no matter what accidently happened to it."

He chuckled, "Your sister wasn't kidding about your perceptiveness. I assume that comes from reading Sherlock Holmes."

"Part of it does."

"What do you now of resurrection tokens?" he asked.

"I know their name is literal." Wait. "Are you saying that her bracelet – from you – is a resurrection token?" My voice had risen slightly as my emotions started growing. Tears were flowing as well. This couldn't be true.

"Her bracelet is, indeed, such a token."

Holy Mother of the Gods!

Chapter 51

I started hyperventilating. He wasn't kidding, such tokens were almost never given to humans centuries ago. The fact that Amanda had been given one. I still couldn't believe it.

"This can't be happening. This… this is impossible." I stated, pacing, running my hands through my hair in slight agitation.

He came forward and grabbed my shoulders. I got a feeling of his immense power, "It is not impossible. Not in this case. I knew your sister was destined for a disaster to happen, I just didn't know what kind."

"So you gave her the bracelet not only as a thank you, but to give her a second chance, like she did you." I pieced the facts together.

He nodded, "I would have died if not for your sister's compassion. She deserved a second chance as well."

I took a deep breath, "So that's why when I had those dreams about her, it felt so real. Because she was really talking to me." I shuddered, as tears flowed even more, "And actually did give me a hug."

He nodded again, "She's been in limbo since she died in your arms. Her spirit is still active, and moving through the netherworld. Keeping an eye on the two of you. When she heard about you beginning the final finishing, she was more agitated than I have ever seen."

"I'm not surprised on that one."

He chuckled, "I wasn't either until she explained the process further."

"So," I took a deep breath, "how does the token work?"

He returned his arms to his side, "It was activated when she covered the emblem on the bracelet in her blood. That informed me that her life was in danger. The spell immediately sent her soul to limbo once she died."

I nodded, "Okay. So what has to be done to get her back? We cremated her body." I was worried now.

"No you didn't." I raised a questioning eyebrow. He started to specify, "We replaced her body with a cadaver while you were trapped under the rubble, but before the medical workers arrived. An exact replica of her body, to be autopsied and buried. Her true body is hidden, so that when the final resurrection steps are taken, she can be reanimated. Her bodily wounds have fully healed, we just need the final steps to be fulfilled by you and your brother."

Eagerly, I asked, "What steps?"

"One, Kepner must die."

"No problem on that one." I felt my anger boil.

"I didn't think so, but for this one, both you and brother have to kill him. As the last of your family it is only right that it only work if both of you finish him."

I tilted my head slightly in thought, "Not too big a problem. We both have plans for him."

He smiled, "Two, both of you must be present when we rejoin her soul with her body. We will need a blood sample from both of you to reactivate her bodies functions."

"Also not a problem."

"And three, we will need proof of Kepner's demise. The spell can only be undone when death of one's enemy is confirmed."

"That, can and will be accomplished. My brother and I will not be merciful in his death. Nor quick."

"I wouldn't expect you to be."

"Is anything specific preferred as proof?" I asked.

He shook his head, "Other than pictures, a piece of him is the best form of proof."

I pictured what I'd be bringing, "Kept fresh or not?"

He laughed, "Fresh enough to tell that it's from him please."

"Easily done then. But how do I contact you when the deed is done?"

In answer, he opened his hand, he held a necklace with a tree pendant, "This is similar to your sister's bracelet. The emblem is mine, so I will know when it is done immediately." He placed the necklace in my hand. Closing my finger over it with his own. I felt the magic of the pendant emanate through my hand. It gave off warmth of its own.

"Just hold it in your hand and whisper 'it is done', and I will send you coordinates to come to. From there, everything can be finished."

I held the necklace to my chest. I so wanted to say thank you, but I knew how the fae can take 'thank you's.

"You can say thank you on this one. I am repaying a debt, and I won't take it how my people usually do." As in he wouldn't see it as me owing him a favor. "The only thing I ask is that you don't tell anyone outside of trusted family and friends about the tokens. Either yours or your sister's."

"Thank you, and I promise." I said.

He smiled, and without another word, began ending the communication. I was a little dizzy when I woke up. Obviously I was still lying on the boulder, but no time seemed to have passed. I shook my head as I lifted it. I looked at Mr. McHaddish and Gretchen. Both seemed confused as well. I felt something in my hand. I opened it and found the necklace he'd given me.

I looked for Keelan. He was inside the house. I quickly shifted back and placed the necklace over my head. I tightened the strings and hopped off the stone. I wobbled a little, the dizziness wasn't fully gone.

"Are you alright?" Mr. McHaddish asked as he help me steady myself.

"I'm fine."

"You were barely even out. What happened?" he asked.

"I'll tell you on the walk back."

Gretchen joined us on the way back to the main house. As we walked, I told both of them what the fae had told me. I trusted them both very well. I knew neither would reveal any of the things I told them. Gretchen was amazed by it all. Mr. McHaddish was blown away. Once Gretchen left to take care of her chores, he told me that he'd known someone centuries ago who'd had such a token. He'd used it to resurrect his son, who'd been murdered by a rival man. His son had then lived to old age, and had a very good life. It was reassuring to know that Amanda could go back to her life once she was resurrected.

Chapter 52

While Mr. McHaddish went back up to his office, I sat in the garden for a while. It was still so overwhelming. Amanda was going to get a second chance. I couldn't say just how much I missed her, remembering that night still hurt way too much. Her dying in my arms had only made it hurt even more.

I looked at the necklace in my hand, it was beautifully done, enough that you'd never know it was a fae token. I felt my heart constrict some as I thought about it not working at all. That fear of everything coming to naught hurt more than anything. I'd have to find a way to contact Reggie and tell him everything. Also see what he thinks of it all. He'd probably say he wanted some kind of proof that the whole thing was true. Maybe if Amanda got involved, he'd believe it better. One way to find out.

I may have left the pearl up in my room but I could still talk with him if I concentrated hard enough as a dragon. I moved away from the seat that I'd occupied for the last several minutes, and shifted. I took a few seconds to examine my wings for the first time in full detail. I'd have to test the claws out at some point.

I closed my eyes and took a deep breath. I focused on Reggie and waited. He took his sweet time getting the message. Eventually, I felt him begin to respond.

"Your insistent this afternoon sis." Hmm, he was annoyed. Too bad!

"Well excuse me if what I have to tell you is more important than your date." I replied, annoyed with him now.

He seemed embarrassed, good, *"What's up?"*

I laid out what I had been told, *"What do you think?"* I asked.

He reacted as expected, *"I'm not convinced. I'd like some more proof that this is possible. I mean, if Amanda could say so herself, then I would most definitely be inclined to believe this whole story of yours."*

"I expected nothing less from you."

"I guess that means I'm getting predictable." He seemed worried now.

"And you remember what dad said about being predictable."

"Those who are predictable, are the most likely to end up dead. Unless doing so to confuse or trick one's opponent."

"Yep." Our dad didn't sugar coat.

"Okay, then I'm willing to give the situation the benefit of the doubt. But would still like some kind of affirmation of it all."

"Thank you, and I do apologize for interrupting your date."

"Thank you. I'll talk with you later."

With that we both broke contact. I felt better knowing that he was aware of the situation, and was willing to be openminded about it. I looked up toward the sky as a plane flew overhead. It only served to remind me that I had to wait a full day before I could fly. I huffed, and began the shift.

Once human again I walked back inside. Malcolm wasn't in the kitchen, but the stew was cooking on the stove. It smelled really good. My mouth started to water. I checked the time. It would be done in about an hour. May as well head back to the library and get some more reading done. Maybe even enjoy some quiet time with Jameson. So long as his mom didn't show up.

Jameson wasn't in the library when I got there, so I went back and grabbed my book and sat down anyway. I didn't realized I'd sat in his seat until I decided to put some music on. I laughed at myself and reached over to the coffee table. The drawer with the remote also included the music channel list. I read the list over and picked the strings section. I was in the mood for either Lindsey or something classical.

I pushed the button for strings and Beethoven's fifth symphony started playing. One of my favorites. I leaned back in my chair and continued reading.

At half past six, I got up and put Sign of the Four back in its place on the shelf. I had finished it at about the same time I finished the sixth Beethoven piece I'd been listening to. Having replaced it, I walked back to sitting area and turned the music off. I then started walking down to the dining room for dinner. I had barely eaten most of today, so I was really hungry. I wouldn't be surprised if I ended up eating most of the stew myself.

Mr. McHaddish was in the dining room when I arrived, the soup tureen already in its place on the table. A large loaf of fresh bread, bread rolls, and a plate of soft butter, were present as well. I sat down next to Mr. McHaddish as he started serving himself.

He finished and handed the ladle to me. I took three scoops then grabbed a bread roll, I also took a slice of the bread loaf and spread some butter on it. I dipped the roll in the soup and took a bite. The stew was delicious. You could taste notes of the red wine and Worcestershire sauce, plus that slight sweetness from the currant jam. The meat, potatoes, and carrots were all tender and juicy. I'd have to ask Malcolm for a copy of this recipe. It is that good.

Mr. McHaddish and I both ended up eating three bowls, plus most of the loaf and rolls. We didn't talk much at the beginning, we were both really hungry. When I was finally full, I got up and put my bowl and spoon in the kitchen sink, which was full halfway with soapy water. I came back out and was about to exit the dining room all together when Mr. McHaddish gestured for me to sit. I did, and he folded his hands, as if about to deliver bad news.

I was right, "There's been news of Kepner, you remember?"

I nodded, "You'd said it had to wait till we got back."

"I did," he took a deep breath, "the news isn't good. Not only has he disappeared completely, but the police were finally able to find the list of items he'd left at the school, and they have a theory what he's obtained."

"What?" I asked.

"A talisman. One he stole from a witch who lived in Sao Paulo. It allows him to locate that which he feels belongs to him."

"I.e. me."

He nodded, "So far though, from what they can tell, there's something causing interference. He's been unable to locate you."

Wait, "How do they know that?" I asked.

"The witch he stole it from still has a connection with it."

"And she's told them about the interference." Okay, that made sense.

"Yes. She's not sure who or how, but she's glad that it is so effective." He paused, letting me put the pieces together.

"You think Amanda might be the responsible party."

"Either her or the fae you spoke to earlier." he said.

"Was there anything else?"

"Yes," he paused again, "the authorities are worried Mr. Hydell and Molly are being followed."

"By someone working for Kepner?" He nodded. "Understandable. If he can't find me with that talisman, he'd assume I was with them."

He nodded again, "That's why the two of them have been notified and put under surveillance until further notice."

"For their safety."

"Yes." He confirmed. "I spoke with them earlier and they've requested that you avoid contacting them for a few days, they've deleted the other e-mails you've sent so there's no way to track you that way. But they would like you to play it safe." I nodded, "I also want to ask you that if Amanda does contact you, to ask her if she can somehow get Kepner's location. She can then tell you and I can inform the authorities."

I nodded, "Okay."

He placed a hand over mine in thanks, "Now on up to bed. We both need our rest. And don't forget to take a sleeping pill."

"I won't. Good night."

"Good night." He said as I stood up from the table.

I slowly walked back up the stairs. I didn't know how I felt about the police not knowing where Kepner was. I wasn't angry. It wasn't the first time he'd alluded them. Maybe upset about it. I just didn't know. Everything I'd learned over the last few months had scrambled my emotions pretty good.

I reached my room and put the box with my new kimono on the dresser where all my other clothes were kept. From there, I took the time to open a secret pocket in my rock bag. Inside I pulled out the only surviving picture of me and my siblings. It was taken last summer while we were hiking in the Rocky's. Reggie had inherited our dad's blond hair, and of course his blue eyes stood out behind his glasses. He'd tanned the least that summer, so his skin was still semi-pale. At that time he's stood 5'7", who knows how much he'd grown since.

Between the two of us was Amanda. Her long brown hair shone a darker shade in the summer sun. Her green eyes shining when she'd noticed the storm clouds moving in behind our parents. She'd stood 5'3"before she'd died. The only thing about her that had surprised me was that she'd been jealous about my chest growing faster than hers. But then again she'd been the skinniest of the three of us. I'd been the oddball. With my magenta eyes and red hair. With a heavy sigh I put the picture back into its pocket and closed the bag.

I grabbed my pajamas and went into the bathroom. I changed and took a glass of water into my room with me. I wanted to get my bed ready before I took the pill. I pulled the covers back just enough for me to sit down, then moved the curtains how I wanted them. I pulled my pills from my bag. I'd have to call these in for refill soon. I took a drink, then the pill, and put the rest of the water on the side table, just in case I needed a drink later.

I sat down after closing the door, and after grabbing the corner of the covers, laid down to sleep. I hadn't taken one in several weeks, having fallen asleep mainly from exhaustion in that time. Finally, the pill took effect and I fell into one of the deepest sleeps I'd had in months.

Despite how deep the sleep was, I felt that same feeling I'd had when Amanda had contacted me before the hike began.

She must have been serious this time. The contact took hold so quickly, I was actually dizzy from it. I mentally shook my head and focused on my surroundings. The same golden light was around me, but this time the blur didn't manifest into a fae. It took the shape of my sister.

I began to cry. Without really thinking, I rushed forward and grabbed her in a dragon hug. Think getting a hug from four bears at the exact same time. I cried into her shoulder as she returned my hug with just as much ferocity. Suddenly there was a third set of arms. It was Reggie.

He squeezed the both of us so hard, it got a little hard to breathe. Finally we all separated and looked each other over. Reggie most definitely had grown since we'd last been together. He now reached 5'11" easy, and looked to weight a good 250 pounds. Of pure muscle none the less.

"What have you been doing dude?!" I asked.

He chuckled, "Nothing new. This just kinda happened a few months ago." He gestured at his abdomen. His shirt – we could see – was loose for a reason.

Amanda laughed. You'll never know how good it felt to hear it again, "I told you there would probably be some more growth to come. You know the male body doesn't stop growing until twenty-five." She said.

"I only just turned 23 two weeks ago." He retorted.

"Doesn't matter." Back and forth. That felt good to hear again as well.

She sighed and turned to me, "You're looking much better little sis." There were tears forming in her eyes.

"Even more knowing we can get you back." I said, trying to keep my own tears contained.

"So all of that is true?" Reggie asked.

Amanda nodded, "Rowen – the name he gave me – said that the spell is ancient. I'm the first human to be given a resurrection token in 500 years." She paused, "Of course, the only way I'm coming back requires you two to accomplish a few things."

Reggie nodded, "Mag told me. None of those things will be a problem. Although I express myself curious what Mag plans to bring as proof." He looked at me pointedly.

I shook my head, "Nope. I'm saving that for a surprise."

"I'd be surprised if you didn't sis. What I want to know is how you two plan to kill him." Amanda told us.

I won't tell what we had planned. Yet. But Reggie and I took a few minutes to lay it all out for her, and I will tell you, that his death most definitely would **not** be quick. A devilish smile spread over Amanda's face as we told her the gory details.

Finally when we were done, I asked the question, "Amanda. Why didn't you grab the gun?"

Reggie took a sharp breath, but she answered, "Truthfully, I thought I could convince him otherwise. I was so stupid! I went to get the gun as a backup plan, but that's how he got me. I spent so much time just standing there like an idiot, contemplating on whether I really wanted to grab the gun."

I had always figured that her pacifism would come into conflict with her training. It came as no surprise to be proved right.

"It's not your fault sis. The fault belongs to Jake." Reggie said. Naming the boyfriend who'd talked too much. And had turned her against everything our dad had ever taught us.

"True. So lets just say that all of this, has been a slap upside the head. I'll never disrespect our dad by turning away from it again." She seemed uneasy. Time to pull out the big guns.

"It is better to be violent, if there is violence in our hearts, than to put on the cloak of nonviolence to cover impotence." I said.

Reggie chuckled, "The A-Team. Seriously."

"Don't forget who said that." I threw back.

"I didn't see the A-Team." Amanda said. Right. I'd forgotten about that.

"It's a Gandhi quote. He may have been a man of peace, but even he knew – and accepted – that violence was sometimes necessary to accomplish one's goal."

Amanda chuckled, "Leave it to you to hold on to such things."

"Wisdom can be a terrible price, especially when people don't listen." I shrugged as I said it.

"What you said to Mr. French a few months ago was good too."

I chuckled, "You heard that huh?"

"It's not every day you quote Splinter." She said.

"Technically I was quoting Mikey as he quoted Splinter."

"Huh?" Reggie asked. I told him, "Right, now I remember that episode. But is this visit purely business or did you want to say something else?" Reggie asked.

She sighed, "For now it was just to show you that Maggie was serious. I did however want to talk some more. I can't keep an eye on both of you at the same time so I'm under informed on a few things."

"So we make an appointment." Reggie said. We all laughed.

"That's the idea." She said. I then remembered what Mr. McHaddish had asked me earlier.

"Hey, uh, Mr. McHaddish – that's his other name – wants to know if you're the one causing interference for Kepner." I said.

She smiled wickedly, "You bet your ass I am."

"I kinda figured. He also asked if you might have an idea where he is. The police have no clues at this point."

She shrugged, "He's been moving about as often as a busy bee. Last time I saw him he was approaching New York. From what I've seen, he's got some old college friends that he's lied to about the whole situation. They think you're being held hostage from him."

Reggie growled, "Maybe we could change that." His brows were raised in thought.

He and Amanda laid out their plan. Amanda might not be able to influence people's minds, but she could influence paper and pencils. She could tell the police somewhere about Kepner's friends and help get him caught. Meanwhile Reggie could spread some rumors on social media using a false account, and I could pass info from Amanda to Mr. McHaddish. Then of course the police get that info as well. This plan had a high chance of success. So long as Kepner didn't get wise before the cops found and arrested him.

"I'll get started on my part as soon as we're done here. That should give us a good start." Amanda said.

"I'll tell Mr. McHaddish what you told me."

"And I'll come up with something for Facebook and Twitter. Maybe I'll get lucky." Reggie finished.

We said our good-byes, and Amanda broke contact with us. I woke up with a small start. It was still dark out. I checked my clock, it read 3:30. What had woken me? I knew it wasn't the pill wearing off, I could feel the drowsiness trying to put me back to sleep, so the pill was still working. I pulled back the covers and stood up to look around.

My room had an eerie feeling to it. I let my eyes go dragon and looked again. In the western most corner, I could just make out a distortion. A magical distortion. Something about it gave me a really bad feeling. Quietly, I shifted. I made sure to stay small as I did. This house was old, so I didn't want to damage the floor by going full size. I carefully moved closer to the distortion. My mom had taught us to identify spells via scent. Each spell – no matter the caster – gives off a particular smell. My nose told me this was a visual tracking spell. Hard to cast unless someone had a talisman of some kind. Kepner.

I growled. Either Amanda's interference wasn't working, or he'd found an amplifier. Either was an option, but I didn't take the time to guess which it was. I knew a really good counter spell. I carefully leaned up to the top of the poster bed roof. Someone hadn't dusted this thing in quite a while. Good. I turned and using my tail, beat the roof until the dust was nearly cascading off the top. I made sure to aim my strikes so that the dust went straight for the distortion. The dust was only a temporary block, but it would serve long enough for me to get the spell going.

Shifting back, I grabbed my bag of stones and yanked it open hard enough that I almost tore it. I pulled out my crystals, and about half my stones. I also pulled my ceremonial dagger from the protected pocket. It was a small dagger, as was the pocket it was hidden in. My mom had placed the spell that made it undetectable when under an x-ray device. Including airport scanners. And Thank the Gods for it too.

I quickly and quietly placed the crystals and stones in proper formation and realized I needed salt. I quietly left the room, then sprinted down to the kitchen and grabbed the container of salt. Thank goodness the girl in the yellow dress label is so easy to spot. I sprinted back up and quietly reentered my room. With steady hands, I made a circle, then drew the pentagram in the middle with my stick of chalk, repositioning the crystals accordingly. I grabbed the small bag of candles I'd brought with me and lit one at each compass point. Once everything was properly set, I stood in the middle of the pentagram, and took the dagger in my left hand. I began the spell.

"Here and now, in lands of old

Let my will and strength unfold

He who is my enemy wishes to find me

Make it so he will never see

Take of my blood, not bone

And protect me from magic not his own."

As the wind began, I dragged the dagger across my right palm. Never making a sound as the blade bit into my skin. I let the blood drip at all points on the star, and compass points. I then turned in a circle, following the salt. The air felt heavy, and began to smell of magic. I finally stopped my movement and faced the distortion. It started to pulse, then it started to fade all together. At the last second, it seemed to fight it. Then finally, with a loud bang, it disappeared entirely. I breathed a sigh of relief. Now that talisman was useless to him. He'd forever be in the dark as to my location. I opened my hand and looked at the cut. It wasn't deep, but it was still bleeding pretty good.

I jumped and turned as the door moved a little. Mr. McHaddish stood in the doorway. He seemed flustered, as well as amazed. My guess would be that he'd watched me perform the spell. He saw my hand and came the rest of the way in. He took a handkerchief out of his pocket and pressed it into my hand using his own. I hissed a little at the sting. He gestured toward the bathroom.

Carefully stepping over my things on the floor, I complied. Once inside, he removed the hanky, and examined my hand. It was already healing. Since the wound was self-inflicted for magical purposes, it would heal slowly, but not human slowly. I'd still have to wrap it though.

"That was incredible." The admiration was clear in his voice. "But may I ask why it was necessary?"

I nodded, and answered. Explaining it all out as he bandaged my hand, "My mom always said, to emphasize your seriousness in a blood sacrifice, you should take blood from your dominate hand."

"How'd you even get the dagger past the airport?" he asked as he threw the alcohol wipes away.

"A specially crafted spell my mom cast on the hidden pocket in my crystals bag. For just such occasions." I said. My head started to fall. I shook awake.

He chuckled, "Now that this is taken care of, you need to get back to bed."

"I need to clean up my stuff first." I stated.

He shook his head, "I'll do that. Do you have a preferred place for the crystals, stones, and candles?"

"The candles go into the smaller bag, but let them cool first, so that the wax doesn't stick to anything it shouldn't. The crystals and stones just go straight into the big bag, but put the candle bag in first or it won't fit right." I managed to explain as he led me back to my bed.

"Okay. Now get some sleep. I'll take care of the salt and chalk as well."

I was so sleepy that I didn't register him actually moving my legs into a better position so that he could pull the blankets back over me. I slept all through him replacing my candles and crystals. Then him actually grabbing a scrub brush and kneeling down to clean the chalk and bloody salt. I was just glad that he wasn't mad at me for performing a spell without telling him. I'd have to ask why he'd been up in the first place and when he'd seen me. Finally I entered such a deep sleep that all thoughts vanished completely.

Chapter 53

I woke up with a long stretch. I felt refreshed for the first time in a while. Which wasn't too big a surprise given the long hike we'd just gotten back from. I sat up to find that Mr. McHaddish had been true to his word. The chalk and salt were cleaned up, and my bag was on the shelf. The surprise was the breakfast sandwich and glass of milk on the side table.

I moved the covers and sat on the edge of the bed. The sandwich consisted of bagel, breakfast sausage, bacon, and a scrambled egg shaped into a circle. The bagel was even toasted. I picked it up and started eating. It was really good and very filling. I drank the milk while I stood to look in my crystals bag. I opened it to find the candles bag in the bottom like I had said. I'd have to thank Mr. McHaddish when I saw him later.

I finished the milk as I got changed. I checked outside first though. The sky was clear. A perfect day to go flying and test my wings. I closed the curtains until I was done changing. I reopened them to see that a small wind was blowing. So long as it didn't get too strong, I could fly in it easy.

I grabbed the dishes and walked down stairs. I left the dishes in the kitchen sink and went outside. I almost walked straight into Jameson. I stopped just in time. I looked up into his face. He seemed agitated, not a good way to start a day.

"Are you okay?" I asked.

He took a deep breath before answering, "No. My mum found my navy recruitment pamphlet and she completely wigged out. Said

I was forbidden to join any military branch and to look elsewhere for a future occupation."

I shook my head, "It's your choice. Not hers. She can be unhappy about it all she wants. In the end if you feel it's the right choice for you than you do it. Any repercussions from her can be handled later."

He met my eyes as I spoke, then chuckled, "I do feel the military is right for me."

"Then she either needs to give you the familial support you need or get over it."

He laughed, "Don't say that to her face. She won't take it kindly."

"Neither did a friend's mom when my mom gave her an earful about such things." I stated.

"I just want her to support me, and not treat me like I'm a small child anymore."

"Then tell her you want to talk, and when you sit down to talk, tell her you want her to promise to not say anything until you are done speaking. Ask her to listen to everything you have to say. Tell her why you feel the military is the right choice and tell her that you'd prefer her support. Because either she gives it or she could lose you forever. That nearly happened with a friend of mine back home. It wasn't until he put his foot down – and my mom got involved – that she finally listened."

"I tried to tell her why I thought it was right." he said with a resigned sigh.

"There's a difference between hearing and listening. Hearing means they aren't paying attention to what you are saying. Listening means they are." I told him.

He looked in the direction of his house, "I think I'd better let her cool off first."

My dragon hearing told me she and her husband were in a heated argument, "Probably a good idea."

He nodded, "I was on the way to ask Mr. McHaddish if I could go down to Glasgow for the day. Mack's in the area, so it wouldn't be too much trouble."

"I actually needed to tell him something, so I'll join you."

He smiled at that, and we made our way up to the office. We found him having a heated conversation with someone over the phone. We indicated that we'd wait till he was done and sat in two of the available chairs.

"I don't care what her father says, it's not happening." And with that, he slammed the receiver down. "Sorry. Now what can I help you two with?"

"I'll let Maggie go first. My gut tells me there is quite a lot." Jameson said with a smile.

I smiled back, "One, Amanda did in fact contact me last night." He leaned forward in his chair. I told him everything that transpired during our talk. "After that you know what happened."

He nodded, "You awoke to Kepner trying to use the talisman."

I nodded, "And thank you for cleaning everything up." Jameson's eyes widened.

Mr. McHaddish chuckled, "Your welcome. But there was no way you were going to do it, not with how tired you were."

I nodded, "If it's possible, I'd like to go flying today."

He thought for a moment, then nodded, "It's been almost 24 hours, I think a field test is safe at this time."

I smiled as Jameson said, "I was actually going to ask if Mack could take me down to Glasgow for the day sir." That got his attention. Jameson then explained what had happened with his mom.

Mr. McHaddish gave a single nod and said, "I think a day away from your mother is a promising idea, but I'm afraid Mack left about fifteen minutes ago."

Jameson hung his head. I got an idea, "I could do it." Both of them gave me odd looks, I chuckled, "I've given other people rides before. All anyone has to do is modify a horse saddle a little and give him a parachute for safety reasons."

Mr. McHaddish laughed, "Your serious?"

I nodded, "How do you think my friends found out about me in the first place. My parents kinda forgot to explain to us that shifting in front of friends was a bad idea."

"If she's willing to do it I'm willing to try." Jameson said.

Once again Mr. McHaddish thought about it. Finally he said, "If both of you are sure, then I don't see why not."

From there Jameson and I made our plans. We'd use one of the old horse saddles that Mr. McHaddish kept in the garage, and modify it enough to fit onto my back. The garage was surprisingly empty, but large enough that I could be full size.

I shifted as Jameson lifted the saddle. I laid down so that he wouldn't have too much trouble placing it. He adjusted it a little and asked where it should be adjusted. I told him and he marked the spots. The saddle we were using was designed for a Clydesdale, so there weren't that many spots to adjust. Jameson grabbed a small blow torch to reheat the marked areas. He expertly reworked the leather until it fit without an issue.

Once he had the saddle finished, he went to the very back of the garage where Mack kept the spare parachutes. He grabbed one and tried to properly put it on. It didn't take him long to figure it out. The straps really aren't that complicated, they just seem like it. He double checked the instructions about which was the primary pin, then grabbed a helmet, gloves, goggles, a bandana for his face, and strapped the saddle onto my back, being careful of my wings. It felt weird wearing a saddle after so long. I stood and moved around a little to get used to the feel.

Finally we were ready to leave. Mr. McHaddish came down and told us that he'd called the Glasgow airport and told them to await the arrival of a dragon shifter and one passenger. They had told him to tell me to fly at 2000 feet. That level would be kept clear until I arrived. I nodded and agreed. He opened the garage door and I was able to walk outside. He also told us that he was going to inform Mrs. Billings of our departure after we'd left. So that she couldn't try and stop us.

Jameson climbed into the saddle using my leg as a boost. He settled himself before tightening the leather straps he'd added with industrial staples and buckles. He'd be perfectly secure once they all were done. Mr. McHaddish shook the saddle to make sure it was tight enough not to move, but not to kill me from suffocation. That done, I looked back at Jameson and told him to hold on with his knees as much as his hands, and to lean forward until I told him it was safe to sit up again. He tried to swallow his nervousness as he nodded. He leaned forward, I felt his knees tighten. Good.

I turned to Mr. McHaddish and told him we would call when we arrived, and when we were heading back. He nodded and told me thanks. I looked forward, took a breath, and started to run. Just before the wall, I jumped and started flapping. I felt Jameson clench as I left the ground.

I reached 2000 feet quickly. It may not be the highest I've ever flown, but the view is beautiful none the less. With great care, I turned myself in the direction of Glasgow. I tilted my head just enough to look back at the estate. I caught Mrs. Billings running toward Mr. McHaddish as he waved at us. This was not going to end well. For one or the other.

I turned my attention to Jameson. I could see through the goggles that his eyes were closed. I knew he'd flown before, I just hadn't thought to ask him if he'd had his eyes open at all or not.

Finally I said, "*You can open your eyes. The view is amazing.*"

Wisely, he answered telepathically, "*I'm not used to flying anymore. So just give me a minute.*" He didn't sound annoyed, so that was a plus.

"*I'm sorry if my take off was a little rough.*" It had felt fine to me.

"*It wasn't you. It's just been close to eight years since I've flown.*" He told me.

"*I see. Take your time then.*" No need to push. I did ease my flying a little though. The last thing I wanted was to unnerve him from flying permanently.

A plane travels from Skye to Glasgow in just over two hours. At my top speed, I could cover it inside of an hour. Inside half an hour really, but then again I can nearly reach supersonic speed thanks to my wingspan. I wasn't going to fly anywhere near that fast today. I didn't want to over exert myself or make Jameson sick. It's not exactly pleasant to try and barf with something over your mouth.

It felt great to fly again. I looked at each wing as we went. Turns out the claws helped with my aerodynamics as well. I'd have to try them out climb wise at some point this following week. Today was Saturday the 15th of July. I'd have to see if there was any way to attend the Lomond folk festival at the end of the month. I felt Jameson move a little. I involuntarily shivered. It had tickled. He stiffened back up.

"*Don't tickle.*" I said with mock annoyance.

I felt him laugh, "*My moving tickled.*"

"*Yes.*" He moved deliberately, "*Stop it!*" I squirmed beneath the saddle. That tickled way too much.

He stopped only because he was laughing too hard. Two can play that game. I gave a small belch. One I knew he would smell no matter the altitude, or facial protection. Dragon breath smells no matter how often you brush your teeth. I felt him recoil as the wind brought the smell to him. I started laughing at his reaction. He joined in.

"*I guess I deserved that.*" He said, still laughing.

"*Yep.*" I agreed.

I then felt him relax as he finally opened his eyes. We were just passing over the village of Glenfinnan. The view of the surrounding terrain and Loch Shiel was beautiful. I'd have to remember to visit Loch Ness at some point this summer. Within a few minutes we'd pass over Loch Linnhe, and from there, would make Glasgow within thirty minutes.

Jameson was getting more relaxed as we went. He looked around more and more as the miles went by. He even started pointing out landmarks to me just like Mack had. I didn't mind, it help to cement them in my memory for future reference.

Half an hour later, Glasgow airport came into view. I angled myself to come in directly from the west onto the shorter of the runways. I could see the man standing with the light wands awaiting my arrival. I gave Jameson a heads up and began my descent. I came in slowly, to give the man with the wands enough of a warning. He saw me coming and started waving. I knew enough about his movements to understand that he wanted me to slow down a bit more. I did so, and his pattern changed. He signed that I had a fifty foot stop stretch. More than enough. He must have thought I was bigger than what I actually was.

I reached a hundred feet off the ground. I began moving my wings in landing formation. I slowly brought us down. I used my tail to steady myself as I touched down. I jolted a little with the stop, but it wasn't too bad.

I made sure not to move as Jameson dismounted from the saddle. He wobbled a little as he stepped down. Once he'd regained his balance, he undid the saddle. I shifted back and stretched out. The great thing about scales is that chaffing doesn't happen unless worn for very long periods of time. We turned as Mack called our names. He came forward and led us to his plane. He had us store the saddle and everything that Jameson had brought with him for the flight.

He then informed us that Mr. McHaddish wanted us back before nightfall and he wished us a good time in town. This could be fun. We hopped in the shuttle that came by and were taken toward the main building. One of the men who worked in the radar room came down to tell us that we needed to give them an hours heads up before departure. Not a problem.

We left the airport by the main entrance and took a taxi into the city. That wasn't a long drive, but Jameson did have the driver stop at a tourist spot. It wasn't until I saw the advertised map for the Devil's Pulpit that I saw what he was up to. We exited the cab after he paid and we walking into the small building. He exchanged a few words with the guy at the counter, and after a few minutes, we were ready to go.

"So, the Devil's Pulpit. Have you been there before?" I asked as we grabbed our now rented bikes.

"Yeah. I thought you'd like to see it. It is truly a wonderful place to see."

"I would definitely like to see it. One doesn't come to Scotland and not see it."

He smiled, "Your leg up for the ride?"

I tested my leg a little, "I think so. I might need to rest at the half way point, but since I've gotten it strengthened, I should be okay."

He nodded and we headed off. On bikes, it would be about an hour and a half of riding to reach it. And that was without any possible stop we'd have to make for my leg. About a third of the ride would be through the city. He pointed out quite a few spots for both tourists and locals as we went. I mentioned lunch – which would be soon – and he mentioned there were several places to eat along Drymen road. Part of our city route, so not that hard to find. We kept a good pace together. Like that day before the hike, we made it a race. As shifters we both had untold amounts of stamina when in human form.

We rode along A81 until we reached the roundabout at A739. That took about thirty-five minutes. From there, we connected to Drymen road. It was mostly residential, but the further we went, it began to diversify a little. I noticed a Pizza Hut just past Station road, but he seemed either to not see it, or had his mind set on something a little further on.

Finally we reached Thorn road and he stopped. At first I thought he was looking at the café just down the street. But when I reached him and asked, he said no.

"I know there's a Domino's around here somewhere. I'm just trying to remember where."

Finally he pulled out his phone, hit ignore on his mom, and pulled up a map. He scrolled through it for a few minutes.

"Okay there it is. We're a few blocks short. We need to go up to Kirk road."

I chuckled, and he looked at me funny, "Sorry. I can't hear kirk and not think of Star Trek."

He gave me an interesting look then, "You watch Star Trek?"

"All series and movies." I smiled.

His smile got even bigger, "Thank you. A woman with a taste for science fiction."

I laughed. Most people didn't react that way when I mentioned Star Trek. They either called me a nerd – which of course led to me explaining the difference between nerd and geek – or they shook their heads like they thought I was uncultured. I can like what I want, thank you very much.

We rode down to Kirk road after crossing the street, and then turned down it toward the Domino's. We hitched our bikes to the poles across the road, plus our helmets, and walked over. As we entered I asked him why he'd wanted to come here.

In answer he said, "My mum never took me here when I was a kid. She said it was where she met my biological dad and that it only ever brought back bad memories."

"So you wanted to come here while you were alone, so that she wouldn't be able to stop you."

He nodded, "That and I've always wanted to try it. Gretchen has had their pizza and has told me its good. Although she likes Pizza Hut better. What about you?"

I shrugged, "I'll eat just about any kind of pizza. Well, unless it's got something pickled on it."

"Why?"

"I'm allergic to pickling brines. Doesn't matter what the pickle is, it's the brine that affects me. I break out in an itchy rash, and start to have trouble breathing."

He quickly checked the menu, "So we avoid anything with pickles of any kind."

I nodded, "Thankfully there aren't a lot of pizzas that include pickled items."

He was still careful to read over every single ingredient mentioned for every pizza. When it was our turn, we ordered a medium meat lovers, and a medium cheese. That amount would get us a good portion of the way there and back. We could always stop by again if needs be, or go to one of the other restaurants or cafes in the area.

We took a seat and waited for our pizza to get ready. While we sat, his mom called again. This time he answered. He made sure to keep his voice low though, so as not to disturb anyone around us. He of course couldn't hide the conversation from me. But he didn't seem to mind that fact.

"*Where are you!?*"

"Glasgow. We're getting lunch."

"'*We*'?" She asked.

"Me and Maggie. Who did you think I was riding out of the estate?"

"*I want you home. Now!*"

"That's kinda hard to accomplish mum. We've already ordered and I wanted to show her the Devil's Pulpit. We'll be back before sunset. I promise." He told her.

"*That's not good enough!! You are my son, and I want you home, NOW!!*"

Uh-oh, he had a rebellious look now, "I am your son, yes. But I am also Richard's son and he gave me permission for a day trip to Glasgow. I am a big boy and can take care of myself. I've also got excellent back up if I need her." With that he shut his phone.

I kept silent for a moment before saying, "It's Ian and his mom all over again."

He looked confused, so I told him the full story of the event. When I was done he said, "So I'm at the near final stage of possibly getting it through my mum's skull."

"Possibly. She can either react one way or the other. It just depends on if our earlier discussed plan works or not."

He lowered his head in thought, "I really hope that works. I love my mum, but treating me like a newborn puppy or China doll got annoying years ago."

"The tighter you pull the leash, the more they fight."

"Who said that?"

"I did. It's my interpretation on the original quote. I sometimes forget the full one."

"What's the full one?" he asked.

"The tighter you try and hold on to something you're afraid of losing, the more you are pushing it away." I could only remember it now because of the situation.

"Rhonda Byrne. I learned a few of her quotes in school."

I nodded, "I saw one of her books in Mr. McHaddish's library. Maybe you should give it to her."

"Seems like a good idea."

Our pizza arrived. We made room for the platforms and pulled a piece off. The waiters looked at us like they doubted we could finish both. Oh we can finish them no problem. You just wait and see.

While we ate we talked about Star Trek. We compared our favorite episodes and movies. We also talked about somethings we'd done growing up. He asked a few questions about the U.S. as well. I told him about L.A., and other parts of the U.S. that I'd visited with family before last year. He seemed really interested about Montana.

"Any particular interest?" I asked.

"My dad was born in Montana, and since he officially adopted me, I have dual citizenship in America."

"Cool," I swallowed the bite of pizza, "Montana's beautiful. Lots of wide open spaces. Texas too, but Montana has mountains and forest along the western edge. It also actually has nine national parks. Two of them are known country wide, the rest aren't as far as I know."

"I know about Yellowstone, but what's the other one?"

"Glacier. It's in the north of the state, containing part of the Rockies and Canada."

He pulled out his phone, "One sec."

I at first didn't know whether he was looking up Glacier or just pictures. When my family had visited, we'd been astounded by its natural beauty. Then the amount of lakes contained within. More than 700 in total, but only 131 actually had names. My siblings and I had made a bet that we could eventually see all the lakes – named or otherwise – by the end of summer. Our parents had won that bet. We only saw about a hundred. On the way back to L.A. we'd decided that we'd go back every year at some point and see them all, no matter how many years it took. Last month I would have said all three of us going would be impossible. I fingered the necklace at my throat. Now I knew we could.

"Whoa!" Jameson exclaimed.

"What?" I asked, taking another bite of pizza.

"This." He turned his phone to me. I smiled.

"Lake McDonald. The largest lake in all of Glacier National Park."

"Is it always that clear?"

"From what I've seen, yes. My family and I camped around it a few summers ago."

He looked at the picture, "Maybe I can talk my dad into taking me next summer."

We finished our pizza shortly after that. Not a single slice left. I left a tip, despite Jameson saying it wasn't necessary. It was polite in my mind, and I explained how expected it is in America. It can become habit too.

Outside, we put our helmets back on, he ignored another call from his mom, and we got back to our ride. We followed Drymen road until it met Stockiemuir road – I know, that one's a mouthful – and followed that out of the city. We passed another residential area, then it was mostly open country from there.

We biked for about fifteen minutes and reached what we considered the three-quarters of the way there mark. The Carbeth Inn. We had spent a little over fifteen minutes at the Domino's, so we were almost to our destination. About another twenty minutes of riding – or less – and we would arrive at the gorge that housed the Devil's Pulpit. We did however stop at the inn to use the bathroom. To play it safe on the journey. We also refilled our water bottles, then we were off again.

The rest of the bike ride passed without incident. Until we reached a paintballing spot just short of Craighat. We tried to pass it by, but apparently there were some boys from Jameson's school who saw us coming and decided to set up an ambush. I asked him about them and he told me that they'd bullied him in elementary school, and were unbearable now that they were all in high school. Of course he used the U.K.s terms for the schools, but it's easier to do it our way.

Eventually I suggested that we pedal like mad passed. As shifters we'd be passed them before they even had time to register that we'd mounted our bikes. He took a breath, and nodded. We stood ready, and very suddenly, we started pedaling.

We shot passed the waiting boys. They never even saw us go by. We turned to look back at them just after we reached the tree line. We burst out laughing. The boys looked annoyed and confused, like they couldn't figure out where we'd gone. We saw one boy gesture that we must have turned around. Nope!

We turned and continued toward our goal. On the way I asked if they knew he was a shifter, he shook his head and said his mom had forbidden him from telling anyone at school.

Finally, we rounded the second to last curve and spotted where we could stow the bikes. We went a little ways into the trees, and tied them to a tree. I tied mine in such a way as the tires were as secure as the body. Jameson copied me after a moment, then we made our way through the trees.

"What do you know about the stairs?" he asked as we walked.

"I know they look like they belong in a long abandoned place instead of here. They're dangerous if one isn't careful enough, and not recommended unless someone **really** wants to go down, but I don't know where they are." I said.

"They are slippery as hell. We could always just jump down the seventy feet."

I chuckled, "I'm not sure my leg is ready for that." It was started to throb a little.

He chuckled as well, "Okay. You take the stairs and I'll wait for you at the bottom."

We reached Finnich Glen as it was called. We located the stairs. Jameson was true to his word, he jumped down from above the bottom step, and I made the precarious walk down. It was a dry day, so the stairs weren't as wet as usual. The climb was okay, but the stairs seriously either needed to be replaced or repaired in some way. They looked like they could be featured on Mysteries of the Abandoned. If they were actually abandoned.

Jameson was waiting patiently at the bottom when I reached it. Just this part of the gorge was great to see. We made our way down the glen, hopping over to the other side in some places. Since it was summer the water level was lower than normal, and not as red as some pictures. At high flow, the river is called Blood river. The red sandstone that the place is made of is what gives it it's color. That would be awesome to see.

We walked the whole glen. Even stopping at the famous stone itself to rest temporarily. On the log nearby that is, it wasn't against the rules to actually touch the stone, but neither of us felt the inclination to do so. Something about it gave both of us a strong otherworldly feeling. Which was understandable if you know a good deal of the ancient folk lore behind the stone and the area itself.

I recognized the rock from a few episodes of Outlander. My mom had loved the show and books. The Devil's Pulpit was one of the things that had helped amp up my interest in Scotland. I was wishing that I'd brought my camera. Then I realized that Jameson had been taking pics on his phone for most of the journey. He promised to e-mail copies of them all to my laptop later. I thanked him, and we spent the rest of our time there exploring.

Chapter 54

We stayed at the glen for over an hour. It was now close to three. Eventually we started back toward where we'd left our bikes. It had drizzled, so the stairs were wet enough to be a problem. We both decided to remove our shoes and climb via our clawed feet.

It felt funny having jeans over scaly legs. But our claws made the climb all the easier and safer. We replaced our shoes at the top before hiking back toward the road. We found the tree that we'd secured the bikes to. The bikes were still there, along with the helmets, but there was also the smell of other people. Jameson groaned. Looks like his bullies had followed us.

I expanded my senses and found the whole group of six across the road. Waiting to ambush us once we left the tree line. This gave me an idea though. There was only one way those boys were gonna leave Jameson alone.

I told him my idea. The large grin he acquired was answer enough. Splitting up, I walked out of the trees and crossed the road. The trees weren't as thick on this side as the other, but they would be enough for me to shift and sneak up on them. Holding back my laughter was the hard part. I knew how my parents would react about this, but it had to be done. Otherwise Jameson might hurt them at school, like I had Tom and Marjorie.

I shifted as quietly as possible. It wasn't too hard, not after so much practice. The shade was thick enough that I looked red instead of magenta. I followed their scents until I was right behind them. Each was holding a thick branch. Not a good idea boys. I started stalking them. Creeping forward until I could just about lick one of their boots.

Finally I lifted my head just enough to create a small breeze on one's neck. He shook his head, but didn't turn. Then I blew a full breath at him. I sensed him stiffen, and saw him begin to turn. His eyes widened a fraction of a second before he shouted and swung his stick. I dodged easily, but one other boy thought it was a clever idea to throw his at me. It hit me square in the nose. That just pissed me off. He looked smug until he saw me bare my teeth and snarl at him. I let the smoke creep out of my teeth as I prepped a fiery shot. All of their eyes widened in realization.

They fled toward the road, only to see Jameson shift in front of them on the road. They collapsed to the ground as he roared in their faces. All but one peed his pants. When Jameson was done, we both shifted back. I walked out of the woods rubbing my nose.

While walking I said, "Well, I think that's incentive enough. Don't you agree Jameson?" my nose was a little bloody.

"Are you okay?" Jameson asked with the concern of a friend.

I pointed at one of the boys, "He thought it was a good idea to throw his branch at me." I pulled a tissue from my pocket and wiped the blood away.

The boy raised his hands in defeat at Jameson's deep growl, "It was instinctual."

"I trust this means you'll leave me alone now." His eyes were still bear.

"You will, won't you boys?" I said, with my eyes dragon.

They all nodded vigorously. Good. That problem is solved. We turned and grabbed the bikes. Which Jameson had brought to the road just before he'd shifted. We buckled our helmets, and giving a wave to his former bullies, started the long ride back to Glasgow.

We did end up stopping at one of the café's near the Domino's we'd stopped at for lunch. Café Crème it was called. We both ordered tea and a muffin. The tea was good, nice and warm. The muffins were really good too. Fresh out of the oven. We didn't talk much while there. Just enjoyed each other's company. He did ask at one point if my nose was okay. I told him it was. I'd been healed before even leaving the tree line.

We stayed there for only about twenty minutes before paying and starting up again. We reached the tourist spot we'd started from, only thirty minutes after leaving the café. We returned the bikes and helmets and received word from the manager that his mom had shown up about thirty minutes or so ago. That meant she was on her way to the Devil's Pulpit, and we'd passed her on our way here. Jameson asked if she'd been alone and if he'd told her our mode of transportation. He'd responded that yes, she'd been alone, and no, he had not told her our mode of transport, just where we were going. He then asked what his mom had taken. His answer had been the bus, and that he'd seen her sit down on the opposite side of the driver. Remember that the drivers column is on the right side of vehicles here. So she was sitting in the left hand side of the bus. The opposite side of where we'd been riding.

We had seen a bus go past just as we were leaving the café. She would never have seen us. We left the building shortly after. The look on Jameson's face was impossible for me to interpret, so a few minutes away, I touched his arm and asked what he was feeling.

"Honestly, I have no idea. I'm angry that my mum would follow me here like that. If the boys from school see her, shifter or no they'll start up again. On the other side, I'm antsy, I guess."

"We can walk around Glasgow for a bit. Sunset's not till 6:30, so we've got time." I said.

We stopped and he looked around, then nodded, "There are plenty of places I wanted to show you here anyway." He smiled.

Like a gentleman, he held out his arm. I chuckled and wrapped my arm through his, placing both hands on his forearm.

The first place he took me was the Glasgow Necropolis. Only a mile from the concert hall we'd stopped outside of after leaving the tourist building. I know most girls wouldn't consider that a romantic place to start, but I liked it. It was interesting to see so many grave stones near the Glasgow cathedral. So many of them looked really old. Not to mention the view was nice too.

We even went on the cathedral tour. It was the oldest cathedral in all of Scotland and the oldest building in Glasgow. It was built in 1197. That put it at over 800 years old. I was so amazed by it. This gothic style church was only thirty-four years younger than Notre Dame.

The inside was beautiful. I'd never been inside such a big place of godly worship before. I'd visited a few churches back home, but nothing like this. And yes, there actually is a difference between a church and a cathedral, I looked it up.

After the tour ended, we walked further into Glasgow. We stopped at several shops as well along the way, despite my minor objections. We did buy a few things, mostly souvenirs for me. We even at one point spotted my history class at one of the hotels along North street. I tried to wave at them, but they were all facing the other direction. Jameson actually decided to head over and meet some of them. I was hesitant at first. My classmates knew I was distancing from my friends for their safety, but he insisted. Saying maybe they could get a tour of the estate sometime. Or at least more of the Isle of Skye.

Eventually I agreed and we walked over. They were all really surprised to see me. Jimmy, Kevin, and Mr. Hanley especially. I introduced Jameson, and we all just started talking. They were about halfway through the country tour and were expecting to attend the Lomond folk festival at the end of the month. Jameson mentioned if they'd be going up to see the Isle of Skye, and Mr. Hanley answered.

"Maybe sometime in August, but it depends on how much we can successfully squeeze in."

"You should if you can. I just spent most of June hiking around it. Some really great spots for tourism." I said. Not going into detail on why the hike took place.

Mr. Hanley pulled out his schedule book and did some calculations. He nodded and smiled after a few minutes. I guess he found enough room to squeeze it in.

The group had to get moving after we talked, so Jameson and I headed north west. I asked him where we were going and he told me it was a surprise. A few blocks on, he stopped by a parked taxi to ask if he was in service. I looked toward the sky, smelling rain. I couldn't see any clouds, but that didn't necessarily mean anything. I heard Jameson open the door. I turned back and with a gentlemanly flourish, he gestured for me to enter the car. I chuckled and did so.

Apparently he'd told the cabbie where he wanted to go before he'd gestured for me to enter, 'cause a little over six minutes later we arrived at our destination. I barely got a look at the small sign on the fence. My eyes widened in realization.

"The gardens?!" I said.

He nodded, "I figured it was a good place to end the day. And maybe lose my mum for the rest of the day."

"Works for me."

He paid and we exited. We walked inside the small brick building and paid for our entry. He also took a few seconds to speak with the desk clerk about something. The young man hesitated for a moment, then seemed to remember something, and gave Jameson the go ahead on whatever it was that they'd been discussing. We walked out a second later.

I turned to him and asked, "What was the discussion about?"

"The son of the man who owns the place owes me a favor, so I had the guy call him and let him know that I'm here and need to talk to him."

"What about?" I asked with a small smile.

He placed an arm around my shoulders, "I remembered you saying at lunch earlier that you have a thing for historical or abandoned places, so I wanted to show you the ruins of the railway station that are here."

"Wha- really?!" I exclaimed.

He nodded, this huge grin on his face, "I know the gardens themselves are old and very beautiful, but the ruins seemed more your style."

I hugged him around the ribs, "You are amazing." He returned my hug and we continued inside.

Chapter 55

We walked around the gardens for almost an hour before a boy about our age came over. He told Jameson that we had forty-five minutes to explore the ruins. Plenty of time for two shifters. Jameson also asked him to text him if his mom showed up. We both doubted she would, but it was best to play it safe.

We were next to the rose gardens, Jameson thanked him and we turned toward the Kirklee residential area directly to the northwest of the gardens. I looked at him in confusion, but he just held up his hand to forestall any questions.

We carefully walked down a small incline and from there he pointed at the tunnel that led to the abandoned station. I smiled at the rare opportunity we'd been given, not even safety workers came here often as far as I knew. We walked around the spray painted barricade and walked down the tunnel.

It's too bad the ruins are too dangerous to be explored for humans. Shifters obviously have an advantage when it comes to such things, since we can move faster than a building collapse by a long shot. We tread carefully though, just because we were fast didn't mean we should throw caution to the wind. Only stupid people do that. Shifter and human alike.

The over grown moss actually added a really nice look to the old concrete pillars and platforms. And amazingly enough, the graffiti – in the right light – brought a beautiful splash of color to the whole place.

I even commented on that fact, which led Jameson to say, "I've heard that some people still actually use the tunnels as a short cut when walking places."

"Faster than going around the gardens." I stated. He nodded, and we kept moving.

We came out the other end just in time to finish our forty-five minute time limit. My skin tingled slightly from the sudden rush of warm air, compared with the chill from the tunnels. We walked back toward the building called Kibble Palace. Yes, that is its name. Half-way there, we both got this sense of foreboding. Expanding senses, we found out why. Jameson's mother was just ahead, standing just outside the glasshouses western most door. Hidden from our view by the trees and bushes.

We stopped in our tracks. We could tell from her breathing that she hadn't seen us yet. Jameson checked his watch. It was five o'clock. We turned and ran toward the small brick building that we'd entered from. Jameson flagged a cab, and we began a quick journey to the airport. Up until he asked how long the drive would take. Twelve to fifteen minutes. Not enough time for the airport to prepare a safe flight path for us. They'd said to call an hour before we would plan to leave.

I came up with a plan. Obviously since his mom had found us, she must be tracking him in some way. So all we had to do was lead her on a wild goose chase for at least a half an hour, then head to the airport for the trip back to the estate.

Jameson whole heartedly agreed, and had the cabbie change course. On the way, he called the airport to tell them we'd arrive at either five-fifty five or six exactly. They thanked him for the heads up, and we exited the cab at the Riverside Museum.

The museum was a lot of fun. Despite our somewhat hurried tour, thanks to his mom. We spent most of our last hour there. We left at ten to six. Jameson told the cabbie to get us there inside of those ten for a fifty dollar tip.

That cabbie knew the meaning of pedal to the metal. He got us there within seven minutes. We still had all our purchased items from earlier, and made suitable time getting inside to report to air traffic control. They had everything ready. All of Jameson's equipment, and the saddle were waiting for us. The man came over to tell us that we were cleared for 5000 feet and to ask how much clear air we would need. I consulted with Jameson, and he stated that he wanted to get back as fast as possible. So full speed was fine with him.

I did some quick calculations and told the controller that we would need only about twenty seconds of clear air. He looked at me like I was silly. So I told him to make the calculations himself. A wingspan of 96 feet can move how much air in one flap? He did the math, and the look on his face of realization at how fast I could fly, was worth the extra seconds we were taking.

He called up to the tower and told them our necessary time space. He even had to pass it along to them to do the math. I vaguely caught someone ask how muscular I was, he was able to pass the info on right after I shifted. Given that my wings muscles were now fully matured, I was extremely muscular. I rotated my wing joints as Jameson got the saddle in place. He made quick time in getting it situated, and then getting himself situated. The main launch control man led us to the same small runway we'd come in on. I got the fastest running start in my life that day. I'm pretty sure I'd left claw marks in the asphalt.

I gained altitude quickly, making sure not to jostle Jameson and the saddle too much. I reached 5000 feet in altitude, and brought my wings to full length. I quickly told Jameson to fold himself forward as far as possible, to avoid any injury. He did so, and I gave a flap.

I hadn't moved so fast in a long time. The fast moving air felt invigorating against my scales. I pushed with all my strength. Within seconds, I reached my full speed. I almost didn't feel the sonic boom that occurred. I turned my head to make sure Jameson was alright. I could feel through my back that his heartbeat was steady, and his breathing was normal. I must have been producing some kind of air pocket as I flew.

The estate came into view only seconds later. I deliberately flew in circles over the entire place as I descended, so as to lose as much momentum as possible before landing. I spotted Mr. McHaddish coming out the front doors as I made my final circle. I came down slowly, and giving one last flap, brought the two of us safely down.

I cringed a little as my back legs met ground. My left leg wasn't happy with all the hurried walking only a few minutes ago. Mr. McHaddish came forward as Jameson came down from the saddle.

"I'm so sorry you two. I tried to stop her." He said.

"How'd she even get to Glasgow so fast?" Jameson asked as I shifted.

"Mack came back early. That's how."

"I don't suppose you know anything about her putting a tracker on me?"

Mr. McHaddish looked thoughtfully confused, "I don't think so Jameson. But I wouldn't put it past her."

Jameson groaned and rubbed his eyes, "Great."

I placed my hand on his shoulder, "Lets head inside and get some dinner. We can worry about your mom when she gets here."

"I agree." Mr. McHaddish said.

Jameson nodded, and after putting the flying equipment back in the garage, we made our way to the kitchen for dinner.

Mrs. Granger was waiting in the dining room with a large tureen of Cullen skink and more fresh bread. I hadn't eaten this since the first few days I'd been here. The smell was very enticing, along with the bread.

Mr. McHaddish sat at the head of the table, while Jameson and I sat to his right. He sat to his immediate right while I sat to his other side. This way, should his mother show up – and we knew she would - there would be at least someone between him and her. We hadn't seen Mack at the airport, but that hadn't meant much.

Not when his mother was already proving to be very annoying in her helicopter habits.

Jameson and I ate pretty heartily, while Mr. McHaddish ate slower. Constantly turning his eyes toward the doorway. It wouldn't make much difference, not when we all would hear her coming the second she entered the building.

Jameson's father eventually came in, we could just barely see the phone in his hands. We could easily hear the conversation between him and his wife. Obviously, she was rather livid.

"He's here at the estate. He's fine. He looks a little peeved at you but he is perfectly fine." We heard his father say.

"*How could you let him off the estate like that!! He could have been hurt!!*" She shouted.

"He's not a child anymore Mildred. He is a grown man!" Well this might not end well.

"*He's seventeen!*"

"He's old enough then, to know who and what he is and wants to be!"

"*I will not have my son moving about like his birth father! It's bad enough that that floozy of a girl took him to Glasgow!*"

Excuse me! "She's not a floozy dear! She is an emotionally traumatized young woman who came here to heal! If Jameson chooses to help her, than you should be encouraging him, not hurting him!"

"*How could you say that to me?*"

"Because I've been doing a lot of reading, and how you treat him… it's not healthy."

"*For whom? I'm trying to protect him.*"

"For him. The tighter you hold on to something for fear of losing it, the more you push it away. Look at how he reacted when he found you following him in Glasgow." He paused, "He did everything he could to get away from you."

"*I don't believe that was him. Ever since that girl showed up, he's been acting different. The entire time she was gone he wasn't himself.*" I looked at Jameson, he wouldn't meet my eyes.

Finally Jameson couldn't take it anymore, he stood and walked to where his dad was talking, we heard him take the phone from his father, "I was the one who had us running all over Glasgow from you. Maggie had nothing to do with it, and I would appreciate it if when you get back, you be willing to sit down with me and talk. If not, then I have nothing more to say to you."

With that he hung up the phone. Handed it back to his dad, apologized, and instead of coming back to finish his food, went outside. Most likely to blow off steam, as far as I guessed. I didn't blame him. His mom was very close to losing her son forever. He obviously loved her, but too much apparent 'love' can drive anyone crazy.

I finished my soup, and went up to my room. I figured Jameson needed some alone time. Ironically, that's where I found him. I tilted my head in confusion. Why my room? Maybe in his anger he hadn't realized where he was going. I cleared my throat. He about jump out of his skin, then looked around in confusion himself.

"Sorry, I don't know why I came in here." He said, not meeting my eyes.

"It's okay." I came over and sat down on the window seat. Directly opposite him.

"I'm sorry about what my mum called you."

I shrugged, "I've been called worse. Trust me."

He chuckled softly, "I honestly find that hard to believe. You're such a nice person."

"Believe what you want. Your mom isn't the first to call me something." I hesitated, "Was that true, what she said, about when I was on the hike with Mr. McHaddish?"

He twisted his hands together, "I'd rather not talk about that at this moment."

I nodded, "Okay."

He sighed, "I've been meaning to ask what kind of hobbies you have?"

I chuckled, "Curious?"

"Well, that and, Gretchen's mum suggested it."

I laughed, then paused, "Honestly, I haven't practiced – let alone thought about – my hobbies since before the murders."

"Didn't feel right anymore?" He hit that right on the nose.

I nodded, "Nothing did. Most things still don't."

He stood and came to sit by me, he put an arm around my shoulders and pulled me into him, "You can talk to me." he said in a whisper.

I felt the tears begin to flow. So many people had told me that, and yet, here with him, it felt the most right. I took a deep breath. He knew the details of the murders, just not all the emotional baggage that had come with the afterward shit.

I was about to start talking when we heard the front gates bang open. I'd forgotten that my room faced not only the sea, but the front lawn. We watched his mom walk up the path toward the house, but she didn't see us – I hoped. We weren't at the right angle for her to see us from where she was standing any way. And she was standing now. As well as talking with someone. I leaned back and opened the window just enough so that the two of us could hear her at full volume.

"Where is my son Mr. McHaddish?" she sounded peeved.

"I know he's still on the estate, but not his exact location. He left in a hurry after hanging up."

"I want that girl gone. She's interfering with him."

We saw him shake his head, "Maggie isn't going anywhere until the end of summer. And the only one interfering with Jameson, is you."

"Why do you care so much about her? She's just some girl from America." I scoffed. Oh, yeah you know me so well lady.

"I care because I've been in her shoes. Being unable to prevent the murder of one's family is not something you get over quickly."

"I don't believe that her family was murdered. She seems perfectly fine to me."

Okay, that's it! I got up, grabbed my laptop, and sat on my bed. I had pics of my family's bodies in a file. Mr. Hydell had sent them to me after Molly had given me the laptop. Just for such occasions. To steel myself, I opened the first picture. It was of Amanda. Even though I now knew she was okay, it still hurt to look at the photos. Although, looking at this one, I could see how it was the cadaver instead of Amanda's actually body. The three freckles on her right cheek were off by about two centimeters. As her sister, I'd notice something so small and insignificant.

I heard Jameson swallow. I'd been so busy studying the photo that I hadn't heard him come over. I quickly backed out of the picture and showed him how many there were. He took the hint. He gently took my computer from my hands, and went out the door.

I got up and moved back to the window seat. He'd closed the window before coming over, but his mom and Mr. McHaddish were still at the front steps. I saw Mr. McHaddish turn as Jameson opened the door and came out. His mother breathed a sigh of relief and went to hug him. He held up his hand and even from here I could see the look of extreme anger on his face at her disbelief. He turned my computer and touched the mouse pad.

His mother's reaction was one I hadn't seen in a long time. She immediately paled, and backed away. I didn't reopen the window. I didn't want to hear what they said. I saw Jameson start to scroll through the pictures. I had them all memorized. I was wondering how she'd react to my mom's pictures. Three to go. Two. One. There.

She took one look and vomited into the grass. Jameson looked confused, until Mr. McHaddish said to pass him the laptop and take a look himself. His mother tried to stop him verbally, but to no avail. Jameson looked about ready to puke himself when he saw the first picture. Now I did open the window.

"That is all that remained of her mother. It wasn't quick."

"He tortured her?!" Jameson asked. His mother looked up from her vomit pile.

Mr. McHaddish nodded, "Not knowing that Maggie was trapped beneath debris only twenty feet away. She saw everything that he did to her mother. Forced to watch because her mother was protecting her."

Jameson shook and sat down on the steps. I was both surprised and impressed that he didn't puke. Mr. McHaddish then knelt by his mom and continued scrolling through the pictures. She tried to look away, but found herself glued to them. She about puked again when he got to the picture that showed my dad's chest. Yeah, that hadn't been pretty. But then again, close range shotgun wounds never are. I reclosed the window and hugged my knees to my chest. His mom really was not making my healing process easy. I mean, yes I understand why she's afraid for her son, but children need to be allowed to make their own decisions at some point or they never learn. If her son wanted to be friends with an emotionally traumatized young woman, then that was his choice.

I put my thoughts of her away as they turned toward my own mother. I would definitely need to take a pill tonight. Even just sitting here, I couldn't get the memories of her being tortured out of my head. I felt my chest clench as I was taken back to those moments. My breathing became ragged and shallow. I started crying, but I managed to keep myself from rocking back and forth.

I didn't register my door opening, or my name being called. It took several moments before I even registered that Jameson was now next to me and gently shaking my shoulder. I didn't know why then, but him suddenly being there made me feel better. With shuddering breaths I started coming out of my memory relapse. I lifted my head enough to see that Jameson had tossed my laptop on my bed before coming over to me.

I started taking deep breaths. Trying to get control of myself again. I felt my leg twinge. I winced as I stretched it out again. Then took a sharp breath through my teeth as the pain intensified. I started rubbing my leg as Jameson went for my bag. He successfully pulled out the medicine bag and brought it over. He opened it and not knowing which container to pass me, handed me both.

I opened the correct one and he went for a glass of water. My stomach was still full from dinner, so I'd be okay taking the pain pill. He passed me the water when he got back to me. I thanked him and took a mouthful. Then popped the pill in my mouth and swallowed. It would still be a few minutes before I was better.

"I'm sorry my mum needed the extreme measures." He looked sadly down at me.

"She's not the first one to need them." I said, leaning back against a pillow.

"That, I believe." He sat down on my bed and put my computer to sleep. Then said, "I mentioned your suggestion to my mum. About talking."

"What did she say?"

"She'll do it. She mentioned we could talk after dinner. But I still plan on making her promise not to say anything until I'm done speaking."

"Always good." I winced as my leg throbbed.

Jameson looked worried, "I thought the hike was supposed to help heal it."

I shook my head, "Just strengthen it. So I can handle day to day stuff again."

"Is there no way to fully heal it?" He asked.

I shook my head again, "Even as a shifter I'll have this for the rest of my life. Don't believe a shifter who tells you that you can heal from wounds caused by your own stupidity and anger."

He seemed confused, "How does it have to do with stupidity and anger?!"

"Because when Amanda 'died', I was so angry, that my anger blinded me to the danger of the bomb. The stupidity comes from not letting my father's training take over instead of my dragon instincts."

"So in a way, you are responsible for the injury." He surmised.

"Partially. If I had stayed put even for just a few seconds, the bomb wouldn't have sent me flying, and the tub would've landed in the garage just fine. Also I would've been able to kill Kepner right then and there."

"Why did he even have the bombs?" he asked.

"He knew that we weren't human. Well most of us weren't. He left the bomb for my parents, but he did something wrong with the first one and it went off too soon."

He looked angry, "Was he at least hurt?"

"Oh yes!" I paused, "He received a scar from the explosion, and then after my dad got home, he left with his leg hanging on by a thread. He now has a prosthetic leg."

"Which one?" there was a slight growl to his voice.

Okay, "Left. It takes up most of his leg."

He looked confused again, "How do you know that?"

"He showed himself before school was done. He followed me after a meeting with my therapist where I met Mr. McHaddish and we made the first plans for this." I ended my sentence with a gesture around the room.

"Did he see you?"

"Nope. I was twenty-one stories up when he got out of the car."

Jameson shook his head, "Why you?"

"If I knew I would tell you, but I don't. All anyone else has are guesses. I mean, Amanda might know, but it's easier said than done talking to her."

"I hope he dies a slow death." He said with vehemence.

"Oh, I plan on it."

He looked at me like I was crazy, "You plan to let him catch you?!"

"No. Good Gods no." I paused, gathering my thoughts, "I plan to kidnap him after the police find him, then kill him."

"If they find him."

"If my sister is able to get him caught, they will."

"How hard could that be?"

"It depends on how fast she can find him. From what I can guess about limbo lore, you could turn just the slightest and end up going the wrong way."

"So not very reassuring." He surmised again.

I nodded, "But with my sister's tenacity and stubbornness, I'd call it even money."

We ended our conversation shortly after that. I needed to take a shower or hot bath so my leg would stop hurting, and he had some chores to take care of. I ended up taking a bath because I couldn't stand for very long, even with dragon legs. I also made sure to let

Mrs. Granger know I would be in the bathroom in case someone tried to enter by accident.

About an hour later I emerged from the bathroom feeling much better. I took a brush through my hair when I got to my room, and checked the time. 8:00. Just enough time for me to check my e-mails before bed.

There wasn't much, just some pics sent by Mr. Hydell and Molly from their trip in Japan. They'd gone hiking on Mt. Fuji. Cool. They also planned on visiting a few ancient temples and forging shops. Mr. Hydell even asked which kind of sword I wanted. Tough choice. The tanto and wakizashi were both short swords and good for concealment, but I already had a tanto in the works. So really my choice was between a wakizashi, katana, or the Zanbato. The Zhan ma Dao was the Chinese cousin of the Zanbato. The key difference was the Zanbato was longer by a few inches.

I took some time to think it over, and decided that I wanted a Katana. I could try my hand on the wakizashi later if I get the chance to learn forging.

Chapter 56

The next few days went by pretty quietly. I didn't see much of Jameson or his mom. Gretchen and I got to spend some time together though. I showed her how to identify poisonous plants, and how to tell the difference between poison ivy and it's identical – but harmless – look alikes.

The first look alike was easy. There was a sample of box elder on the property. This was one of three plants often mistaken for poison ivy, and for good reason. Poison ivy grows in groups of three leaves, but so does box elder. Eventually I told her an old nursery rhyme I'd been told by my mom about poison ivy.

"Leaves of three, let it be."

"Because of the groupings?"

"Yep. It applies to poison oak as well."

"Why the rhyme though?"

"It's a useful learning tactic. Another is 'black on yellow, friendly fellow. Red on yellow, deadly fellow'." I said.

"I know that one. That one has to do with two snakes that have the same three colors on them, but in different order."

I nodded, "Another good tip is to carry a small handbook with you at all times. Either bought or made by you that includes pictures of the plants and anything that looks a lot like it."

"Does poison oak have any look alikes?" she asked.

"Only if you get it confused with box elder. Which isn't as doable as with poison ivy."

"How come?"

"Because box elder has only one point to its leaves, whereas poison ivy and oak have multiple. Maybe even three or more, but no more than five."

"So definitely get my hands on a guide book." She said, I nodded.

I also showed her poisonous mushrooms. Including the red one with white spots that appears in children stories for some reason. She had asked me about this stuff because of Keelan. She wanted to make sure the surrounding forest was safe for him to explore as he got older. Knowing what was poisonous and what wasn't would be useful.

It was a good thing she did too. We found a patch of destroying angels not far from her house. I recognized them immediately. Their snow white color and tea plate sized caps were well embedded in my memory. There was even some young ones just beginning to sprout. I had Gretchen stay put while I ran back to the estate to tell Mr. McHaddish.

He followed me back with a group of gardeners. Each gardener was prepared to pull them up by their roots. They came with thick gloves and axes for wood chopping, so that once all the mushrooms were pulled, they could be burned.

He had me and Gretchen head back to her house before the gardeners got started. They'd handled them before and were therefore prepared, we on the other hand were not.

On the walk back she asked how I knew so many poisonous plants and fungi. The answer was simple. My mom. She'd kept all kinds of botanical books at home before the murders. Most had been destroyed in the blast. My siblings and I had memorized every picture in those books. For good reason. Such knowledge is never useless, especially out in the woods.

Her collection of plant books had been extensive. Large enough to cover every plant on every continent. There wasn't a single plant we couldn't identify. Or so I had thought at the time. I still needed to ask Mr. McHaddish if he had any kind of reference to this dragon's bane plant. I could easily find wolf's bane, but dragon's bane was something new to me. Plus once I knew what it looked like, I could share it with my siblings.

Gretchen and I made it back to her house just in time to see Jameson storm down the trail toward the main house. I was tempted to call to him, but decided against it. He looked like he could use some space. So Gretchen and I proceeded to her house for some lunch.

Her mother made us some meat sandwiches on wheat bread. She also had some homemade chips ready. We told her about the mushrooms we'd found, and she admitted that she was glad they'd been identified and were being properly dealt with. She looked toward the living room where Keelan was sleeping. Just a small piece could kill a perfectly healthy adult. It was scary to think what it could do to a baby. I even drew her a picture of the destroying angel compared to the button mushroom. The two can and have been mistaken for each other. The best way to tell the difference is the destroying angels 'egg' stage as it's called. In the 'egg' stage, the entire mushroom is encased within a sac that protects it from insect predation. Button mushrooms don't have this sack, and I've noticed that with button mushrooms, the stem is smaller than the destroying angel's, but you should still be very careful when mushroom hunting.

After a few minutes, Gretchen's mom left the room to deal with Keelan, and I finally posed the question I'd been wanting to pose to Gretchen. The one that I'd been reminded of when we'd seen Jameson.

"Did he really act differently when I was gone?"

She knew whom I meant, and nodded, "It was like he was someone else. He couldn't sleep, he barely ate. He was angsty as hell. Kept pacing around like he wanted to go bear and go chasing after you to make sure you were safe." She paused to take a drink, "After the first two weeks, I called Mr. McHaddish and told him. He then called Jameson every night for the rest of the hike to tell him you were okay."

I shook my head in disbelief, "Why in the world would he act like that?"

"Normally, I'd call that a male's reaction to his mate being away from him. But neither of you are old enough for a mating bond to form. Aren't you?"

I nodded, "Shifters have to be physically mature for the bond to form. Don't ask me about shifters younger than 18, that's one place where I'm still in the dark."

"Couldn't you ask Mr. McHaddish?" she asked.

I shook my head, "One, I'm not ready for those answers, because of the emotional trauma from the murders. Two, it's not something a teen shifter asks of anyone but a parent or sibling."

"Why not ask your siblings?"

"One, I have no idea if my brother has even bonded, and two, I know Amanda never did. And they both are physically mature."

"So in other words, any and all mate bond questions will have to wait till after Kepner is dead."

I nodded and we finished our lunch in silence. Her mother came back in looking a little disheveled. I guess Keelan had been stubborn about going back to sleep.

I made my way back to the main house not long after we finished eating. Gretchen had some school lists to look over, and I wanted some alone time to think. Mainly about Jameson's behavior over the course of the hike. I just couldn't wrap my head around it. Why act like an over protective male, when we hadn't even known each other for very long at the time?

I was still turning the thing over in my head when I reached the Boudica statue. I almost tripped over Jameson's legs. I managed to catch myself, but tweaked my leg. Not good. Groaning and hopping, I made my way to the bench.

I was about to chew him out when I got a good look at his head. There was a little blood at his hairline. Forgetting my leg, I knelt down beside him. He was out cold, with a cut and small bump where he'd either hit his head or been hit by something else. I looked around us, there wasn't anything to trip on. Then I noticed his shoes. One set of laces had come untied, and the evidence of him stepping on the lace was obvious. I then checked the bench I'd been sitting on. There was a little bit of blood. I wiped a small drop from the bench and sniffed it. Yep, it was Jameson's blood.

I looked up and around for someone. I noticed movement in the kitchen window. Grabbing a nearby stone, I chucked it at the window. Even from here I heard the thunk of it hitting the window. The person inside looked out and I waved both arms to get their attention. They saw me and came running. It was Malcolm.

He took one look at Jameson and asked me to shift, so that we could get him to the kitchen. I did, and with a little effort, got Jameson on my back. I stayed small so that I could fit though the door. It was a tight squeeze, but I made it. We laid him down on one of the benches in the kitchen, and Malcolm made a quick call for Jameson's dad. I only then realized that his dad must also be the estates onsite doctor.

His dad wasted no time getting there. Once he was inside he knelt by his son and asked what had happened. I explained how I'd found him and what I saw had happened. He asked how long ago I'd found him. I also did some quick math and deduced that he'd tripped about ten to fifteen minutes ago.

Without warning, Jameson woke with a start and grabbed his dad's wrist. I heard the bones start to break and grabbed Jameson's arm. He immediately met my eyes.

"Let go Jameson." I put some authority into my voice as I said it.

He turned to look, and quickly let go, "Sorry dad."

His dad shook feeling back into his hand, "It's alright son. A natural reaction. How do you feel?"

"Dizzy, I have a headache, and my ears are ringing." He answered.

His dad held a small light and shined it in Jameson's eyes. He immediately turned away. His dad and I looked at each other and said, "Mild concussion."

"Huh?" Jameson sounded concerned.

"You tripped and hit your head son." His father explained.

Jameson felt his head, "Ow. Yeah, now I remember. I feel like a numpty."

"Your anything but son. The fact that you remember what happened is good."

"So what do I do?" he asked.

"No sports, t.v., or video games for a few days, and some headache meds. Also not a lot of socializing. So basically, relax quietly as much as possible for the next few days."

"Got it." His eyes widened, "Oh God, mums gonna freak." He covered his face with both hands.

"I'll talk with her. Make sure she has all the details first." His dad said, rising to head back. First, he turned to me and said, "If it's not too much trouble, take him up to the library and read to him for a little. It might help."

I nodded, and as he left, I tapped Jameson on the chest. He moved his fingers enough to look at me, and I gestured for him to get up. He had to lean on me for the whole walk to the library, but once there, I sat him down in one of the chairs and asked what he'd been reading lately. The Hunt for Red October by Tom Clancy. A good book and movie.

It didn't take long to find it. I grabbed it from the shelf and came back over. I sat in the chair next to him, groaning as I went, and opened it to his bookmarked page.

"Before you start reading," he said, "how'd you know it was a concussion?" I couldn't quite interpret his look that day.

"My sister and brother both ended up with one. My sister when she was six and my brother when he was eleven."

"Do you remember your sister's?"

I nodded, "I remember being scared. She bled quite a bit. More than a head wound usually does anyway."

"How'd they get them?"

"My brother fell from his bike and glanced off a rock, and my sister was kicked by a colt."

"A baby horse?!" he asked.

I nodded again, "Smaller doesn't mean anything when one gets startled very badly. He kicked her pretty hard."

"And she made a full recovery?"

"Only thanks to her shifter blood and the fact that my dad saw it happen and got her to the hospital very quickly."

"That's good." he looked down at his hands like he was still embarrassed.

"Do you mind if I ask why you were so angry before you fell?"

He gave me a curious look, "I thought you were here at the main house."

I shook my head, "Gretchen and I were out walking through the woods. I was showing her poisonous plants and how to identify them. We actually found a patch of poisonous mushrooms. It was after we informed Mr. McHaddish and were told to go back to her house that we saw you go down the trail."

"Ah," he ran his hand through his hair, "I asked my mum if I could transfer to Mr. McHaddish's school."

I recoiled in surprise, "Why?" I asked.

"Because of the boys who used to be my bullies." He paused, "My mum received phone calls from their mums, and apparently they're less than happy about my defending myself. Plus they don't believe their sons that I'm a shifter."

Okay, what! "What did your mom say?"

"She was bealin," he saw my look and chuckled, "angry, that I revealed my ability to them. More so because I used it to scare them into leaving me alone."

"It was either that or attack them out of anger at the school. Believe me I know what it's like to attack a fellow student out of anger, and it is not something that you want to happen. Especially not if they deserve it." I saw his look too late. I turned and saw his mom standing behind me. This was exactly why I never sit with my back to a door.

Thankfully for me, she seemed upset at herself, "Is that true?" she asked.

"Is what true mum?"

She cleared her throat, "That you attacked other students out of anger." She wouldn't look me in the eyes.

"Unfortunately, yes. They both said things about my family's murder that they shouldn't have, so I reacted."

"Were you punished?" she sounded only slightly accusatory.

I looked at her with fire in my eyes, "No." I placed the book on the table and stood, "I was not punished because **I** was in the right." I stood in front of her as I finished, "Tom told me to 'get over it' instead of mourn. Marjorie said, and I quote 'you should ask your parents for a school transfer,' then said, 'oh wait,' and laughed. Like my family's murder was a joke. You want the details of their injuries, call my guardian."

Without looking back, I stormed out of the library. But I did sense her shudder as I walked away. I didn't care, I just wanted to get away from her. I didn't want to go for a walk, with how I was feeling, it wouldn't help.

Eventually I found myself outside the media room. I really shouldn't break anything so first-person shooter video games were the best outlet. I opened the door and found several game consoles set up below a large wide-screen TV. I opened the cabinet door that held the games and pulled out Halo 4. I walked over and knelt down in front of the Xbox 360 slot.

Once the disk was inserted, I grabbed a controller and sat on the couch directly opposite the TV. I activated the controller, created an account, and started playing.

Chapter 57

I was in the media room for about four hours. Playing it safe so that I wouldn't explode when I saw Jameson's mom again. Finally I paused the game and rubbed my eyes. It was only eight days till the first day of the Lomond Folk Festival, but I felt I needed a day away **now**. Maybe both Jameson and I would get lucky and his mom would go on a business trip or something. That would give us both some peace from her.

I looked up just as both Jameson and Mr. McHaddish entered after knocking on the still open door. Jameson did a double take when he saw which game I was playing. He chuckled and looked at me.

"You play Halo?"

"Yep, since it first came out."

"Video games aside," said Mr. McHaddish, "I've come to tell you both something."

That got our attention, "What?"

"One, for some reason Mrs. Billings has invited several of your former bullies mothers here. Two, your father has convinced your mother to give my school a try, Jameson."

Whoa! Nice work Richard, "Wow. I never thought my mum would agree." Jameson said with a very happy smile.

"She has some stipulations of course." Mr. McHaddish told him. "She wants to see the school, campus, and dorms before you actually go. So, I've convinced her to take a holiday with her husband to Los Angeles. But with the condition that they make absolutely no mention of you" he pointed at me, "in any way, shape, or form."

"No offense to Mrs. Billings, but I have my doubts she'll succeed. I also don't mean you any offense Jameson."

"None taken and I can ask her as a favor to me." Jameson said.

"It's worth a try, son." Mr. McHaddish said.

"When do they head out?" I asked.

"Next week. After they get everything packed. Your father has a plan set for their trip portion of the travel." He said the last bit to Jameson.

"I don't doubt it." Jameson said.

"Speaking of going places. One, when do we," I gestured at the two of us teens, "start school? Two, is it okay if I attend the Lomond Folk Festival next Friday?"

Mr. McHaddish chuckled, "Still a girl for details." I shrugged and smiled, "Well to answer the first one, school for humans in L.A. start on August 15th, while for shifters, it starts on September 5th."

I nodded, "For discretion purposes."

"Correct. For question two, yes. Plus I was planning on having the staff spend time off, I think it would be good for everyone to get in some actual vacation time before any school starts. I can easily take you and anyone else who wishes to go. It's only a short drive from Glasgow to Balloch."

I nodded, "Sounds good to me."

Mr. McHaddish had a thought, "We could even visit the local aquarium. Yes it's not the largest aquarium in the country, but, an enjoyable visit none the less."

I leaned forward, of course I'd go to an aquarium. No matter the size, "Should I pack a bag?"

He laughed, "I think it best. But not yet," he was trying to stop laughing, "wait a few days first. Plus it will give me time to get a schedule ready." He left the room trying not to chuckle to himself.

Meanwhile, Jameson came over and sat down beside me, "I'm sorry for what my mum said, she didn't have to say that."

"Thanks, but truthfully I'm more concerned about what went down after I left."

"Went down?" He looked at me funny.

I laughed, "Do I have to explain?"

"No, I've just never heard that in person. I told her that both incidents happened after shifters were brought out, and that it could happen with me, which is why we did what we did."

"And what did she say?"

"That she understands now, and wants to cement that fact to the other mums."

"Cool. So that will finally be fully out of the picture."

He nodded, "So, you up for a few rounds of player vs player?"

"Hold up buddy boy, your dad said no video games for a few days." I said, knowing that a video game induced headache with a concussion was bad.

"That was before he remembered I was a shifter. He said so long as I play with adequate lighting, I should be okay."

"You're sure then?" I questioned.

"Worried I'll beat you?" oh, are you challenging me?

I saved my game and said, "Bring it."

Needless to say I kicked his butt. He took each defeat as learning experience though, and became more evasive as time went by. Eventually though we had to quit and head down to dinner. The score was still twenty seven to zero. He did ask for a rematch later.

As we sat down to pizza, I asked, "So, how did the talk with your mom go?"

"Pretty good actually. She kept her promise and let me talk until I was done. I even mentioned the incident with your friend and that got her thinking that maybe she really should ease off."

"Good. I'm glad it went well."

"I also told her that she needed to ease off with you or one of these days you might just snap."

"What are the chances she'll listen?"

He paused with the next slice in midair, "If she actually does contact your guardian, pretty high."

I nodded, "I hope so. 'Cause I really don't want to lash out at her. I could've killed both of them with one blow."

"Just ask the floor at your old school." I chuckled, "You know you started talking with a Scottish accent as you yelled at her."

I nearly choked on my drink in laughter, "Seriously?"

He was laughing as well, "Yes. I swear I was trying not to laugh at the fact that you didn't realize it."

We finished eating in silence. For a few minutes anyway. Mrs. Granger came in just as we were cleaning up and taking everything to the kitchen. She said that his mom wanted to see the both of us out on the front lawn. We both assumed the mothers of his former bullies had finally arrived and were about to get their proof that Jameson was a shifter.

Mrs. Granger had us head out while she cleaned up the dishes. We didn't say much as we walked, but I was honestly surprised when we saw the entourage that awaited outside. The mothers hadn't come alone. Their sons and husbands had come too. Well this could get interesting.

The boys immediately hid behind their parents when we both came out. Several said, 'that's them'. I was the one they were surprised to see. They must have assumed I was staying down in Glasgow. We both turned as Mr. McHaddish followed us out.

"May I ask what this is about?" he said to Mrs. Billings.

"These numpties don't believe my son is a shifter."

I just managed to keep my expression normal, I really didn't want to laugh, "She called them here to prove it."

Mr. McHaddish scrutinized Mrs. Billings with a newfound respect, "Very well, but only so long as Maggie is on standby as backup."

"Hence why I asked for both of them. Maggie, if it's not too much trouble."

"Not too much trouble for what, dance a jig?" one of the fathers commented with a laugh. Several of the other parents joined him, but the boys all backed away.

I shook my head, "Your sense of humor is dull and lacking in its wit by…seven centuries."

Jameson burst out laughing, "Finally, someone said it."

The father that made the comment was about to say something when his wife raised her hand. The look in her eyes said she was gonna try and pull the mom card. Not gonna happen lady. I walked a few steps forward and shifted. This time I was full size. I hadn't been this big when we'd scared the boys in the woods, so even they were moving farther back. Several of the offending adults moved back hastily, two even fell on their asses. Serves them right.

I waited as Mr. McHaddish came around to stand on the gravel path. I moved off of it and laid down. Claws and teeth in full display, as I opened my mouth to discourage laughter. I saw one father attempt to hold it back. His wife, seeing the smoke emanate from my mouth elbowed him in the ribs.

"Her name is Magenta for a reason, Mr. Hanes." Said Jameson.

"She's pink." The father said, and openly laughed.

"Darling, she's a bloody dragon! I don't think laughing at her is wise." His wife said.

He attempted to stop, but his stupidity was on high today. Not bothering to get up, I extended my wing and stabbed my end claw into the ground in front of him. My wing only a few centimeters from him. I heard him swallow as reality set in. Especially once I pulled my wing back out. His eyes widened when he saw the six inch claw at the end, and it had him gulping in fear.

"Magentas a reddish purple, not pink, Mr. Hanes." Mr. McHaddish said.

"Well, we'll believe that she's a dragon, but I still don't believe your son is a shifter." Said one of the mothers.

"No? Darling." Mrs. Billings looked toward Jameson.

He walked forward with his hands in his pockets. He stopped at fifteen feet from them. The boys stayed as close to the gate as they could get, as Jameson shifted. Every single parent shouted, and moved backwards. The wives clutched their husbands, and the husbands tried to look brave, but failed miserably.

Bears had been extinct in the U.K. for centuries, so seeing one of his size was very impressive. So long as one wasn't on the receiving end of his teeth, or claws. A good look at his paws showed they were the size of car tires, and his claws the length of two human hands. Several of the parents nearly peed themselves. They would if it was me they were disbelieving of. Jameson let out a large chuff that sent them recoiling. All predator shifters have bad breath in animal form. At least in this case, it meant the parents understood they weren't hallucinating.

Jameson's mother came forward, "Were my son going to secondary school with your sons again, I'd say to leave him alone, as he has already asserted. But, thanks to my employer here," she gestured to Mr. McHaddish, "he will no longer be anywhere near your sons. But should I ever hear of them doing anything adversely to my son, I will not hesitate to show you just how angry I can get." She walked forward as she talked, emphasizing every word as she went.

Mr. McHaddish came forward as well, "Now that the message has been rammed home, please leave my property." He growled at the end of his sentence.

The boys had already opened the gate and were getting into their respective vehicles. The parents followed, not wanting to find out what Mr. McHaddish was. I stood and stretched out my wings. Quite a few of the parents looked back to see them. Even marveling at my wingspan. They didn't need much prompting to get in their cars and leave though.

Jameson and I shifted back, "That felt good." Jameson said.

"It did." His mother agreed with him.

Jameson and his mom headed home not long after we lost sight of the long line of cars. I had a little excess energy after the angry rush earlier. I told Mr. McHaddish where I was heading and made my way back to the media room to play a few more levels of Halo 4. One at the most, depending on how I was feeling.

I stopped by the kitchen to grab a glass of water before going up. I made sure to place the glass on the table by the couch arm, so that if it fell in anyway, the consoles would be safe.

Mrs. Granger stopped by to tell me that I had an hour left before I really should get to bed. I thanked her and returned to my game after she left. I was beginning to think that I should spend the next day meditating, that way I could stay calm during at least one day this week.

With about twenty minutes left, I saved my game and turned everything off. I made a quick stop at the kitchen to drop off my glass and grab a small snack. I grabbed a handful of almonds and made my way up to bed. When I passed the library I remembered Jameson's book and went to see if it needed to be put back. It did.

Once I'd replaced it I finished walking up to bed. I brushed my teeth and changed into my pajamas. Back in my room, I brushed my hair and opened the curtains. It was a beautifully clear sky. The crescent moon wasn't too high just yet, but the light was high enough that I could set out my crystals and stones for purification. I'd have to do it again when the full moon was out, but what I could get for now would work.

I took out my phone and checked when the next full moon occurred. August 7th. I could make that work. I set my phone down as it shut off and turned on my alarm clock. As I sat down I got another sense of foreboding. Standing up again, I cast a quick protection charm on my window. Making sure it was one that would make me invisible to anyone looking through with either technological or magical means.

That done, I was finally able to lie down and go to sleep. It was only after a few minutes that I remembered that I needed to take a sleeping pill. I quickly roused myself and grabbed a glass of water from the bathroom. I took my pill and finished my water. I was exhausted enough that the pill took affect within ten minutes.

Chapter 58

The days before the Lomond festival were actually pretty quiet. Thankfully I didn't end up needed to meditate much. Gretchen's parents even asked me to baby-sit Keelan for a few hours while they went down to Glasgow to start school shopping. They told me that Gretchen had actually started college – or university as they say – courses at school and needed a few extra materials.

The Thursday before the festival started, Mr. McHaddish got a call from the school and had to make arrangements to head back to the U.S. on Sunday. That meant we'd only really have one day to attend the festival. Jameson and his mom were heading down tomorrow to finish school shopping as well, so we'd be doing the festival on Saturday the 29th.

Neither Jameson or I were too bummed about it, there were future festivals that we could attend. Either together as friends or individually. We both spent that Thursday planning out what we would need after I got done babysitting. We consulted Mr. McHaddish on additional classes and made our list from there. Other than the usual classes, there was also weapons training, hand-to-hand combat, survival training, advanced botany – for multiple purposes, and herbology.

The herbology was a mix of herb therapy – poultices and things like that – and what you hear about in Harry Potter. Identifying plants and how to use or avoid them. This was the class I was most looking forward to. None of my mom's books had included magical plants. This would also be my opportunity to learn what dragon's bane looked like, and maybe, how to make myself less susceptible to it. If that was even possible. I was really hoping it was, then I wouldn't be affected by it when Kepner finally found me. After everything that had happened since just before school ended, I'd accepted that it was only a matter of time till he did find me. The right amount of determination mixed with stubbornness can accomplish a lot more than some people realize. I wasn't dwelling on it though. So long as I made sure I was prepared for him in as many ways as possible, I'd make it out alive, and he wouldn't.

That night before bed I made sure to take a sleeping pill. My sense of foreboding had been getting stronger and stronger as July came to a close. It had gotten so bad that I'd taken to checking up on Mr. Hydell and Molly every night. I'd even tried contacting Amanda to try and see what Kepner was up to. So far I hadn't been successful. I didn't want to take the risk of not taking a pill before bed, the last thing I needed right now was a really bad nightmare.

I made sure to renew my protection spells that night as well. With that stolen amulet now useless to him, he'd be on the hunt for a new way to track or find me. I already knew that there were hundreds of magical ways to find someone, it all depended on what he could get his hands on quickly. Some would be more reliable than others, but it was all a matter of ingredients.

Thankfully I slept like a rock that night. My paranoia definitely was causing some repercussions in my health. Knowing Mr. McHaddish, he'd inform Mr. Hydell, and from there my doctor would be told. That was an earful I wouldn't be looking forward to. I looked at my clock. 8:30. The festival started at eleven, plenty of time.

I went down to breakfast to find Mack at the table with Mr. McHaddish. He seemed excited. I sat down without interrupting their conversation, and set to my toasted bagel and cream cheese.

I was still a bit groggy from the effects of my pill that I didn't catch any of their conversation. Eventually I caught my name and turned toward them.

"Are you up to riding in the plane or flying?" Mr. McHaddish asked.

I gave it a moment's thought, "I'm okay with riding in the plane."

Mr. McHaddish nodded and returned to his conversation with Mack. Apparently his plane was due for repairs, and would be serviced while we went to the festival. It would be ready by ten that evening if all went well.

We'd be taking his plane down to Glasgow, and then driving up to Balloch for the festival. It was a twenty-three minute drive without heavy traffic. So should the repairs go well, we'd leave for back here at half past ten at best. That made me a bit nervous. Sunset would be half past nine, and night flying was tricky, even more so with a small plane. They're harder to find should they crash.

I hadn't flown at night much since an incident when I was seven. I wasn't counting plane flights, that's not me doing the flying. My siblings had both crashed into a barn during a training flight. I'd seen it at the last second and been able to pull up. Thankfully it was on family property, but you can imagine the earful my siblings got from our grandparents for reckless flying. The two of them had been egging each other on before they'd crashed. They always got so competitive during such exercises. Dad had paid most of the damage, but he'd made the two of them do the work of repairing the roof and rafters.

After that none of us flew at night. Dad didn't trust the two of them to not get into it. He'd done any other night exercises on the ground. Not all that easy when you're supposed to do some of them in flight.

Plane wise, it was obvious. My flight here from the U.S. had been partially at night, so I was a little comfortable there, but not enough to choose it over my own flying. I made a note to myself to try and bring a book with me. To try and keep myself as distracted as possible if necessary during the flight.

I made quick work of my breakfast and went upstairs to grab my hoodie and boots before we left. I nearly ran into Jameson on his way down. We apologized and went our own ways. At my floor I paused. Had he been nervous? I thought the moment back over in my mind. It felt like we both had been nervous. Why? We were just friends, there would be no reason for it.

I shrugged it off and continued to my room. I stopped at the door. Something felt off. I expanded my senses and looked through the wall. And no, it doesn't technically count as x-ray vision. What this is counts as bending light to make things invisible. Similar, but not the same.

The distortion was back. It was stronger this time. I growled deep in my throat. There wouldn't be time for a block spell. Maybe a quick glamour spell? No, I didn't have a small rock with me. I didn't want to wait for the distortion to go away. He might just watch my room until I walked in. My next option was to ask someone else to go in and get them. I hated the idea of giving him someone else to possibly track down just so he could find me. That would put that person in danger.

The decision was made for me. Mrs. Granger came up at that moment and saw me standing there staring at the wall. She came forward and without another word, walking into my room. My hoodie and boots were both by the door, within easy sight of the distortion. I was about to go in and pull her out when she came out with both items.

"I made sure to keep my face in the wrong direction dear." She handed me my boots and hoodie.

I swallowed the breath I'd been holding, "He could still have seen enough to identify you."

She met my eyes with motherly concern, "I'll be fine. I promise." She rubbed my cheek and left.

I watched her move back toward the stairs and reran the memory. She had indeed kept her face pointed down and in the opposite direction of the distortion. There would be no way for him to find her based on nothing but her back and hair. And I'd done the research, the estate was on the historical landmark list, but the staff list was not included.

I sat down on one of the hall chairs and put my boots on over the socks I'd been wearing. I took a deep breath to steady my nerves before standing. I checked my room. The distortion was still there. I guess whatever he'd gotten hold of just showed him the space I was currently occupying. At least, that's what I hoped.

I slipped my hoodie on and made my way downstairs. I met Mr. McHaddish at the bottom. He placed a hand on my shoulder encouragingly. I could tell by his expression that Mrs. Granger had told him what had happened.

I wasn't as reassured as he'd hoped. He gave me a wait here look and went upstairs. I sat down on the bottom stair and placed my head in my hands. I was starting to feel trapped. Not just here at the estate, but inside my own head. I was gonna need to talk to someone soon. I really wanted to talk to Ms. Hamper, but since she and her new family were in hiding that wasn't going to happen. Not unless Mr. McHaddish actually knew how to contact her.

I almost didn't register Jameson coming down the hall. He stopped when he saw me. Without a word, he sat down beside me, and placed an arm over my shoulders. I stayed the way I was though. He started rubbing his thumb across my shoulder. I removed my hands and after folding them against my chest, finally leaned into his shoulder.

I was starting to feel sick to my stomach. My bagel wasn't sitting well at this point. I definitely needed to get out of the house soon or I was gonna go nuts.

Mr. McHaddish came back down, kneeling in front of me he said, "I've made a few arrangements with the staff. One of them knows a protection spell that should work."

Mutely, I nodded. He smiled, and stood back up. He told Jameson that Mack would be ready for takeoff in about fifteen minutes. The main car and driver were waiting outside to take us the short drive to the long stretch of road that also served as runway.

Jameson stayed there with me until it was five minutes till takeoff. He stood and offered his hand. I met his eyes as he gave me a small smile. I took his offered hand and stood. We walked out to the driver and got in the car. Mr. McHaddish and Gretchen quickly joined us. The two minute drive was subdued at best. I was starting to feel like a downer.

We exited the car when he stopped by Mack's plane. The engine was already going and Mack was already in the pilot's seat. Gretchen and I got into the very back while Jameson and Mr. McHaddish climbed into the forward seats. Mr. McHaddish made sure we were all secure before he climbed into the co-pilot's seat.

Since there were only two sets of headphones, Mr. McHaddish put them on, and we got started on our way down to Glasgow. The distortions appearance in my room had made me forget about grabbing a book, so I was stuck with trying to contain my nerves for the flight. I was saved by Gretchen pulling out a deck of cards.

We spent most of the flight playing war. I had to show them both how to do it, but they enjoyed it thoroughly. Although they both made objections when I said my siblings and I considered the ace card as the highest card, beating even the king.

By the time we landed, both of them wanted rematches. One against me, the other against Jameson. We had to wait outside Mack's plane for a few minutes before a shuttle showed up to take us to the main building. Once it did, the four of us got on and from the main lobby, grabbed a rental car and drove up to Balloch. It was only a twenty-four minute drive from the airport, during which Jameson and Gretchen both told me about which bands would be performing that year. The ones they liked best were Smokey Valley, The Dead Flowers, and the Trongate Rum Riots. I honestly laughed at the last one.

As I said they both liked all the aforementioned bands, but disputed greatly on which songs were their bests. I told them I'd like to hear whatever they performed and then maybe buy some c.d.'s of theirs and make my own opinions.

I didn't have very long to wait though. When we finally wheeled into north Balloch, we saw that we'd arrived a little early. Mr. McHaddish decided that we'd make the aquarium our first stop. It was just after ten-thirty, so it was open.

Chapter 59

Mr. McHaddish hadn't been kidding when he'd said the Balloch aquarium was small. It was only a half hour visit. I still enjoyed it greatly. It felt… well, it made me feel myself again. Which was getting harder and harder for me. I just hadn't realized it until I was back inside someplace that always gave me peace.

Mr. McHaddish noticed the change in me as well. I don't know what he planned when he pulled his cell phone out, but I was hoping it was along the lines of me working again when not at school. We grabbed a snack at one of the restaurants surrounding the aquarium before finally heading to the festival grounds. They weren't that far from the aquarium, so we could easily walk. Mr. McHaddish, however, chose to drive so as to give my leg a chance to rest before all the walking the festival would give us.

The festival was Great! Jameson and Gretchen couldn't stop showing me around all the vendors stalls, of course including all the food stalls. I really enjoyed the trinket stalls. I stopped counting all the bracelets and necklaces I bought. I even bought some hand crafted jewelry boxes to hold them all when I got home.

Gretchen practically dragged me to the first performance by Trongate Rum Riots. I was glad she did though. I liked them enough to buy a c.d. of theirs. Jameson then followed by taking me to Smokey Valley and Dead Flowers performances. With likewise results. I bought two more c.d.'s to take home.

It was approaching late afternoon when the day took an unexpected turn. Jameson and I were waiting for Gretchen at one of the food and drink stalls when I noticed a teenaged girl looking at me with daggers in her eyes. I shrugged her off at first, then decided against it when I sensed her moving closer to us. I especially noticed her sharply inhaled breath as Jameson put his arm around my shoulders. Okay, that deserved some looking into. I heightened my hearing. Being careful to filter out the sounds of other people. Her heartbeat was rapid, but steady. I knew what that meant.

"Do you know the girl over my left shoulder with shoulder length blond hair?" I asked Jameson.

He looked up and in the direction I'd indicated, and groaned, "Yes I do."

I looked up at him, I saw he was trying to hide his expression from her, "Who is she?"

"Her name is Elizabeth. She's a lass from my school."

"I'd say from her expression, that she has a crush on you and doesn't like the idea of me being here with you."

"Well she can deal with it. I was never interested in her. She's a rich spoiled brat who thinks she can get what she wants." He said with slight vehemence.

Jameson heard a call from a friend from school and went over to talk with him for a few minutes. Leaving me on my own at the stall. I made light conversation with the vendor while waiting. It was then that Elizabeth decided to make her shallow move.

"Stay away from Jameson, ya hear meh?" she said trying to sneak up on me.

I pretended to not hear her, looking around like I'd heard a funny noise instead, before looking her in the eyes, "Oh I'm sorry was that you? I thought it was a cow mooing."

Her eyes widened at my words. "Do you know who I am?" she placed her hands on both hips like a three year old.

"Don't know don't care. All I do know is that Jameson is his own person and you have no right to dictate who he interacts with."

I'll give her this, she's got great reflexes. I never saw the slap coming. My head never moved, and she shook her hand afterwards as if in great pain. That's what happens when you slap a shifter.

My eyes were dragon as I looked up at her. She recoiled in fear, "Do you want to know what happened to the last person who slapped me?"

There was a growl in my throat, but the most notable thing was my southern accent. That only came out when I was about to fully lose my temper. I felt a hand on my shoulder. My nose said Jameson. I calmed a little. And I mean only a little.

"That was a very stupid thing to do Elizabeth." He said, not taking his eyes off her.

She tried and failed to regain her composure, "I was just talking with her, there was no need for her to insult me."

"You can't lie to a shifter Miss Davenforth." Mr. McHaddish said, coming up behind her.

"I would like to know what happened to the last numpty to slap you Maggie." This was from Gretchen as she walked up to us.

My eyes never left Elizabeth, "The last idiot to slap me, ended up with their arm in a cast. I broke every bone in her right arm with a flick of my fingers."

I caught Jameson's look over my shoulder, he was impressed, "How old were you?" he asked.

"Twelve. The girl wasn't getting the hint that my brother wasn't interested in dating her, so I said it in plain words for him."

Gretchen got a fake thinking look on her face, "Hmm, history shows its unwise to piss off a dragon shifter. Who'd have thought?" the last bit was with a sarcastic tone.

"D-d-dragon shifter?" Elizabeth stuttered.

I let the smoke billow from my nose. I know that looks odd as a human, but it got the point across. Elizabeth backed up until she came up against Mr. McHaddish. She started, then moved around him, thinking that hiding behind him would work.

"You'll find out eventually Elizabeth, but I'm leavin' school." Jameson said.

"What!?" she came out from behind Mr. McHaddish, "No! You can't! I forbid it!" she stamped her foot like a three year old now.

"It's not your choice!" Jameson said, "I was never interested in you in the first place. You might as well know it. Plus now that I can attend a shifter school, I'm going to."

"You're not a shifter. The whole school would've known." Her accent was getting thicker, she was almost hard to understand.

Jameson let his eyes go bear without blinking, "I **am** a shifter. My mum pulled some strings to make sure the school kept it quiet."

"And before there is any further incident, I need to get my three teenagers back to the airport for the flight back to the estate." Mr. McHaddish said, coming up to pull all three of us away from the stall and toward the parking lot.

"Good-bye Elizabeth." Jameson said as we were lead away.

Once in the car, Mr. McHaddish called Mack to check on the planes maintenance. The news wasn't very good. One of the pistons was cracked and needed to be fully replaced. That repair however was almost finished, and once it was, the rest could be done. That would be another two and a half hours of work. So we wouldn't be heading back till full dark. Close to midnight.

Neither of them was comfortable with that option, so the decision was made for the four of us to stay at a hotel in Glasgow, while Mack stayed at one near the airport. Mr. McHaddish could make do without luggage for his flight, he said. He planned to drop us off with Mack the next morning after breakfast, then wait until it was time for his plane to leave while we went back to the estate.

We reached the airport and were about to head further into Glasgow, when Mr. McHaddish just decided to pull into the Holiday Inn across the street from the main parking lot. He got us checked in, with two rooms. Him and Jameson in one and us girls in the other. He made sure we had robes as well so that we could get our clothes washed for the next day, and told us we could order whatever we wanted from room service.

We didn't go crazy, we each ordered a sandwich, plus what we wanted from the dinner menu, then of course dessert. While eating, we watched a little t.v., and talked about the festival. Gretchen commented that she'd noticed Elizabeth just as she was heading to the restroom after we'd arrived at the stall where the slapping took place. She hadn't thought much of it though.

Jameson wasn't upset, apparently it wasn't the first time that Elizabeth had made a scene because of her jealousy toward other girls who got Jameson's attention. He talked about one of the many she'd committed at his school. He'd been talking to a cousin of his named Rochelle that lived in Glasgow, and she'd 'accidentally' spilled her coffee on his cousin. It hadn't been very hot but his cousin had still needed to go to the nurses office. She'd sustained first degree burns because of the amount that had been poured.

Elizabeth had been let off with a warning because none of the school cameras had caught the incident, but after that Jameson had been careful to keep his eyes open when talking to girls. Rochelle had slapped Elizabeth when they encountered each other after school, and explained that she was Jameson's cousin. Thankfully for Elizabeth's sake, she believed her.

"Is your cousin a shifter too?" I asked as we ate our ice cream sundaes.

He shook his head, "Our mums are related. Rochelle's dad died in a car accident when she was three. He was fully human as well."

"Do ya think she'll try anything now that you won't be there?" Gretchen asked him.

He shrugged, "I don't know. If we went to the same school, I'd ask you to let me know."

"You guys don't go to the same school?" I asked.

Gretchen shook her head, "I go to a private school on a full scholarship. He was attending the public school."

"Speaking of the transfer, do you know where the school is located?" Jameson asked me, just as I put a spoonful in my mouth.

I chuckled at his bad timing and Gretchen openly laughed, Jameson just looked amused. Once I swallowed, I answered, "No. Mr. McHaddish hasn't told me. But that's for protection purposes. All shifter schools are hidden via location and glamour spells. Though I think the school is somewhere in California."

"Will the spells protect you from Kepner?" Gretchen asked.

I nodded, "The spells are ancient and renewed yearly according to the original ritual. Kepner would need a specific talisman to get anywhere near the location."

"And I know from you that certain talismans are hard to get." Jameson said.

"When did I tell you that?" I asked.

"You didn't, but I heard Mr. McHaddish mention it as he was walking down one of the halls at the estate."

"Ah. Well, in the case of anti-glamour talismans, those are not only hard to find, they are hard to make and stupid expensive."

"Really?" Gretchen seemed interested about that.

I nodded, "The spells and materials to make them are themselves hard to get ahold of. And any that already exist cost all four limbs in cash to rent."

"So in other words, he's screwed." Jameson surmised.

"No. He's screwed to the deepest depths of Tartarus." I stated.

Our conversations after that turned to movies. A Trailer for Ferdinand had started playing just after I'd finished my sentence, and I had deliberately watched it. I was really happy to see Ferdinand get a movie. I went on to explain that it had been my absolute favorite children's book growing up. I still had our original copy on my book shelf back home. The trailer got all three of us laughing.

The laughter got the attention of Mr. McHaddish. He came over to say that since it was getting late we needed to head to bed. Jameson got up and walked out while me and Gretchen wished them goodnight.

While showering, I realized that I hadn't planned to stay here for the night, and was without a sleeping pill. I almost started to panic, when I remembered that I'd seen chamomile tea on the room service menu. I breathed a sigh of relief. I was heavily susceptible to chamomile. My mom had used it to help me sleep after nightmares when I was small. One glass – or as my mom had called it, a cup and a half using liquid measurements – had worked perfectly when I was little. I'd sleep like the dead with a few cups now.

I exited the bathroom in my robe. Gretchen had volunteered to get our laundry done the next morning. I picked up the phone and ordered four glasses of chamomile tea. I would need maybe three to put me out. The fourth was a backup just in case. The room service man brought them up a few minutes later. I explained them to Gretchen as I downed the first two in one swallow each. I then advised her on what she should do should I have a nightmare despite my precautions. She wasn't fully happy about going to get Mr. McHaddish, but since she was human, there was significant risk of injury or death to her. She accepted the plan after that.

I decided to play it safe though. I drank the other two and laid down. Gretchen turned out the lights and we both nodded off.

Chapter 60

My precautions weren't necessary. Thankfully. The four glasses of chamomile worked their magic perfectly. I did indeed sleep like the dead. I didn't wake up till Gretchen came back into our room with our now clean clothes.

The amount of tea had the same effects as the pill, I was pretty groggy. Gretchen fixed it by also bringing up two large cups of coffee. I added milk and sugar to mine after we were dressed and went down to get breakfast. I got odd looks about adding milk until I explained I was American. We both went back up with cream cheesed bagels, and muffins. We nearly ran into Jameson as he went to knock on our door. Seeing that we were now up, he went in to grab his breakfast and join us again. He informed us that we'd need to leave within the next fifteen minutes. Mr. McHaddish's plane would take off at seven-thirty. Just twenty minutes from now. He'd called the boarding office to say that he'd be there within the time and would be without luggage.

The three of us finished our breakfast as quickly as we could, still being a bit tired all around. When we were done, we tidied up our rooms, and gathered everything we'd bought the day before, then after leaving the rooms, went down to meet Mr. McHaddish at the front door. We took the rental car the short distance to the main terminal and watched as Mr. McHaddish got on his plane without a problem.

Meanwhile the three of us met up with Mack and loaded our stuff onto the plane. He told us that the maintenance was finished and was ready to head back up to the estate. We had to wait our turn to taxi out, but once we were airborne, the three of us just zonked out. The last indication of what had happened was Mack's chuckle.

The three of us didn't wake up until the plane touched down along the road. We all rubbed our eyes and stretched out while Mack got the plane slowed down. He was chuckling as we disembarked to hop into the car awaiting us. Mack took the liberty of unloading all our stuff, despite our protests. The driver asked if he would be joining us. He answered no, that he needed to head back down to take care of some final paperwork. He re-taxied along the road while we were driven back to the main building. I sat up straighter as we passed through the gates. We all could feel the slight pressure differential as we passed through. I looked back as the driver pulled up to the front steps. I could just make out the distortion of an extremely strong protection spell. The one that Mr. McHaddish had mentioned yesterday. I was glad that it was in place.

We walked up the stairs to meet Mrs. Granger at the door. She surprised us with news that we each had mail waiting. I wasn't too surprised that Gretchen and Jameson did, but why did I have mail? I didn't live here year round like they did.

Gretchen's was school related, Jameson's was a postcard from his parents. They seemed to be enjoying their vacation really well. I held up my envelope, flipping it over and over by the corners. I'd seen this type of envelope only once before. I grew a claw and opened it, carefully sniffing the opening to check for anything that might be harmful.

Jameson looked at me funny, "There's a show called NCIS back home, in one episode, one of the agents opens an envelope and blows on the opening. He ends up releasing a deadly virus into the office. I was being safe."

The two nodded in understanding. That one episode I mentioned wasn't the first time I'd ever heard of that had involved sending viruses or other deadly materials through the mail. It was an unfortunately effective method. I turned my attention back to the letter. It was indeed a wedding invitation. I opened it and nearly screamed with delight when I saw whom it was for.

"What is it dear?" Mrs. Granger asked.

"My guardian has asked his girlfriend to marry him." I said, trying to hold back the tears of joy. I covered my mouth and chuckled happily.

Both Jameson and Gretchen hugged me and congratulated Mr. Hydell and Molly. I pulled the letter back from my face and read the date. They planned to wed on Christmas Eve. I was to be the maid of honor. There was a small note written in the corner that asked me to be ready for a video chat on the thirty-first at eight a.m., which if I remembered correctly, meant that it would be five in the evening for them. I double checked my phone. Japan was nine hours ahead of Scotland, so my calculations were correct.

I made my way upstairs a few minutes later. Feeling elated that the two of them were going to be getting married. I was even more glad that they were going to involve me in such an important role. I would have expected to be a brides maid but never the maid of honor. I was only a little nervous about actually being involved in a Christian ceremony. I think. I pulled the invitation back out of the envelope. It didn't specify which ceremony would be used, just the church in which it would take place. Okay, I could live with that. It wasn't the first time I'd been to a wedding. The first had been for a friend of my mom's. My mom had been one of the bride's maids and had received enough passes for her whole family.

I didn't remember much of the ceremony though, I'd only been five. I had spent most of my time trying to stay awake. I did later apologize to the bride and groom for it, but they'd gladly brushed it off, saying they were surprised I'd succeeded in staying awake. They even gave me an extra-large piece of cake at the reception.

I sat down on my bed and decided to check my laptop to see if either of them had sent me anything. I found only one e-mail from them. It was from Molly specifically, asking me for color coordination advise. She'd sent me a few of her ideas. I pulled up google images and compared her choices.

I immediately discarded the pale blue and cream mix. The blue over rode the cream easily. The deep sea blue and emerald green combo was nice, but in the end I chose the peach and turquoise combination. The two blended nice and were very appealing to the eyes. I sent a reply e-mail with my answer. I wasn't sure exactly when she'd get it, but I knew she would like my results. I really liked that they were trying to get their favorite shades into the ceremony in some way. I didn't know what the colors would be used on, and at that moment, I didn't mind or care.

Thinking about the upcoming wedding between the two of them took me back to the other one. My siblings and I hadn't been too psyched about it, but we hadn't complained.

I decided to check up on my brother. I pulled up a new tab and went to Facebook. He hadn't changed anything yet, but I knew he probably would at some point once he got back from his vacation. I pulled up some of his vacation pics. He'd tanned since we'd last seen each other. A few photos even showed his new girlfriend.

She was pretty, I'll give her that. She looked Hispanic, but I couldn't quite tell. The first pic of her wasn't under very good light. I clicked to the next one. Better. She was definitely Hispanic, with some Chinese ancestry it would seem, based on her slightly more almond shaped eyes. Cool.

Seeing how happy my brother was with her, it made me decide that I liked her and wanted to meet her. I scrolled to the next pic and sat up. He'd caught her by surprise I think, because she had jaguar eyes in it. I exited out of my brothers pics and went to her page for a minute. Yep, it said shifter, cat shifter to be specific. That could definitely be interesting. As far as I knew, we'd never even encountered any cat shifters. Well, that is up until Mr. McHaddish.

There was another question I would have to pose to either of my older siblings. Our parents hadn't told me why we didn't interact with other shifters – aside from my friend Gene and her family - whether or not my siblings had been told was unknown to me.

I exited out of Matilda's page and went back to my brother's. It was a good thing I did too. There was a message being typed as I got back. My gut wrenched. Instinctively, I grabbed my stones bag and pulled out the pearl. My intuition was right. The message being typed was from Kepner. I read it quickly, then moved my computer off my lap and focused on my brother. I sent a quick and simple message.

"Cancel your Facebook account! NOW!!!!" I shouted at him. Sending all my sense of urgency along with it.

He didn't respond. He didn't need to. I refreshed the page once I came back to myself, and found the page no longer existed. It was then that he contacted me.

"Destroyed my phone too. Send you the new number at later date." He said, trying to send calming vibes at me. It didn't work.

I began to panic. My breathing increased and my vision began to blur. Kepner's message to my brother still circling around in my brain. I knew my brother hadn't seen it. I didn't want him to, but it made no sense. There was no way in Hell that Kepner could've found out my brother's account username. A thought suddenly occurred to me. I quickly went back to my dummy account. There was a message there too.

I didn't read it. I was already too far into a panic. I immediately canceled my dummy account. I checked the clock. All of this had amazingly transpired inside of one minute. Not long enough to track me. I shut down my computer and started trying to regain control of my nerves.

His message to my brother wouldn't leave me alone. It started swimming in my brain so fast that I wanted to scream. Everything felt too loud. I covered my ears even though there was no noise. I didn't comprehend my rocking back and forth. I began to hyperventilate. I could hear my own heartbeat in my ears as I finally did scream. The message to Reggie was the last thing I saw in my head as I lost consciousness.

"She belongs to me!"

Chapter 61

At first, all I heard was voices. Panicked voices. I couldn't identify them. Each of them just sounded too far away to bother trying to understand. Then everything went quiet again.

The next thing I knew, there was the strong scent of bear around me. That jostled something. Jameson? But what was he doing in my room? I tried to wake up, but something kept me from coming to. I tried to shake it off, to no avail. The panic began to set in again and the smell of bear got stronger. Why couldn't I wake up?! The panic only got stronger as my instincts took over.

Something clicked. With a roar, my heartbeat immediately steadied and I woke up. The panic was so strong that I went from human to dragon in one second. Roaring, I wheeled around and started attacking the first thing that came toward me. Or I tried to. The only thing in the room was me. I felt confined and that didn't help my sense of panic one bit. I heard the window shatter as I moved around, the stones in the wall groaned as well, trying their best to hold up against my panic.

"MAGENTA!" someone shouted. The panic was too strong. I needed to get out.

"JAMESON, NO!" a woman's voice. But why was she yelling?

Something was in the room with me, but it didn't feel threatening. Over shouts from the door, I stopped moving and began to focus on the presence next to me. I closed my eyes and started slowing my breathing. I concentrated on the other creature in the room. It wasn't human. It was a shifter. I felt a wet nose touch my own and I leaned into it. I caught the groan of concern that came from the other shifter.

My panic finally began to abate. I took one deep breath after another. My legs gently gave out from underneath me and I was able to lie down. I took one more breath before opening my eyes, and met Jameson's as I did. He was matching me breath for breath. His forehead was against mine as I finally got my panic under control. I swallowed and pulled my head away to look at my surroundings. We were in my room, but all the furniture had been removed. It was just the two of us in the room and there was hardly enough space for both of us, while standing in the doorway, Mr. McHaddish held Mrs. Billings back. Wait, how long had I been out? Mr. McHaddish had only just left for California and she should still be in L.A. with her husband.

Seeing that I was calmed down, Mr. McHaddish loosened his grip, but not enough that she could come running into the room. I looked further about the room. The walls, roof, and floor were all still intact, but the window was a hopeless tangle of a mess. The only other weak point in the room was the door to the hall way, and it was untouched.

I hung my head in exhaustion. I was now breathing steadily, but heavily. Jameson came over and nudged my head. I barely comprehended his mother's reaction, 'cause right then, there was only one thought occupying my mind. That was the moment it clicked.

We were mates. That was the only explanation for him being able to center me in times of pure danger and terror. It was the only thing that made sense and explained everything that had happened since we'd met. Our being perfectly comfortable around each other, his behavior during the hike, everything. The emotional connection was there, but since neither of us was over eighteen, the full mate bond wasn't in effect yet.

Jameson nudged my head again, this time turning it into him rubbing his shoulder along mine as my head moved along his back. As he turned I returned his nudge. He then laid down beside me and placed his head atop mine as I laid mine on the floor. He leaned into my stubbed horns as his mother finally got loose from Mr. McHaddish.

She got about two steps into the room before Jameson gave the deepest growl I'd ever heard from him. His mom stopped in her tracks and looked genuinely scared. Then she shook herself and looked Jameson in the eyes.

"Jameson, you get up and out of this room this instant. Now." Her Scottish lilt got thicker with each word. She was definitely angry.

Jameson just chuffed at her and stayed put. He didn't even bother raising his head. I paid more attention to Mr. McHaddish as he came into the room. He placed a hand on Mrs. Billings' shoulder and leaned down to say something.

"This wouldn't have happened if you had just let him come in here sooner." He said. Again, how long had I been out?

She smacked his hand off and said, "That girl is dangerous, and he is my son. I won't put him in danger so long as she is so volatile."

"The only thing that is dangerous now is you trying to take Jameson away from here." He grabbed her arm and forcibly removed her from my room.

Needless to say she protested the whole way. When Mr. McHaddish finally had her out, he closed the door behind him and locked it. I chuckled as best I could, the lock wouldn't keep us in any more than it would keep her out, but it was a nice gesture.

It was only once the two of us were alone that I allowed myself to purr. Yes, dragons can do that too. I felt Jameson relax as he felt the vibrations. If he'd been able to, he probably would've smiled. That being said, I'm pretty sure he actually did.

We stayed like that for several minutes, before Mr. McHaddish came back. He unlocked the door and walked in with… Ms. Hamper!

I grunted in surprise and lifted my head. Jameson didn't quite move quick enough and got knocked on the chin. He grunted with the impact and I immediately regretted my sudden movement. He shook his head and gave me a look that said he was okay. I turned back to Ms. Hamper as she came closer, not in the least bit afraid of me.

"I'd been hoping I'd one day get to see you as a dragon." She placed a hand on my nose, and I pushed into it. I had missed her. But what was she doing here?

"You'll need to change back now Maggie." Mr. McHaddish said from the doorway. Most likely keeping his eye out for Mrs. Billings.

I removed my nose from Ms. Hamper's hand and closed my eyes. Taking my time shifting back. I was shaking as I finished the change. Jameson knelt down next to me. Placing his hands on my shoulders to try and help me up. I gestured that I wanted to stay on the floor and he sat down next to me. Ms. Hamper came and knelt down in front of us both. She lifted my chin and looked me in the eyes.

"You've lost weight dear." She said.

No kidding, I felt like I hadn't eaten in weeks. I didn't smell very good either. Okay, now it was time for me to find out how long I'd been unconscious. I looked up at Mr. McHaddish.

"How long was I out?"

He took a deep breath before answering, "Three weeks."

"What!!?" No fucking way!

"It's true," Jameson said, "we've been trying to wake you since we found you passed out on your bed."

"Jameson was the first indication that something was wrong. Mrs. Granger said he came barreling into the house and nearly changed on the way up here."

I leaned back into Jameson and rubbed my face, "So she then called you."

He nodded, "She said that while he charged up the stairs, the whole house heard this piercing scream come from your room. It took her half an hour to calm Jameson down enough for her to be able to do anything."

"Then after she called him, he called me." Ms. Hamper said. "He told me you were going to need me after you woke up."

I groaned, "Three weeks."

Ms. Hamper gave me a sad smile, "Why don't you shower first and we can talk after you eat as well."

I nodded, and only then let Jameson help me up. I was so weak from my coma – might as well call it that since I couldn't be revived – that Jameson had to help me all the way to the bathroom. He sat me in the chair by the shower stall and left the bathroom.

I groaned as I pulled my clothes off and dropped them on the floor. I didn't have the energy to put them in the hamper. I climbed into the stall and turned the water on. I let it get hot and left it there. I'd worry about temp later. I ended up having to sit down 'cause my leg wouldn't take my weight. I heard the door open and registered Gretchen coming in to collect my clothes and leave fresh stuff.

"I'm glad you're finally awake." Was all she said as she left the room and locked the door behind her.

I took my time. Making sure every part of me was clean before I could finally leave the stall knowing I no longer smelled like a wildebeest. I toweled off and put my hair up. I pulled on my fresh clothes and sat down. My leg hurt really bad. I was gonna need to put my brace on.

I limped back to my room, expecting it to still be empty. Surprisingly enough, everything was back, and the window was covered. I pulled my brace out of my suitcase and put it on. I made my way to the stairs and was about to walk down, when Jameson suddenly scooped me up. Where the heck had he come from?

I didn't bother protesting as he carried me down the stairs. I was way too drained for it. The smell of food hit me before we even made the second landing. My stomach growled so bad it actually hurt. I gagged slightly at the thought of just how empty my stomach actually was.

Jameson carried me all the way to the dining room. He placed me in the chair that Mr. McHaddish pulled out, then hearing his mother, went off to deal with her. Malcolm came out of the kitchen carrying a dinner platter of haggis. Already removed from the stomachs. There was enough for ten or twelve haggis on that platter.

I managed to keep from shoveling it into my mouth. Mostly. Only between drinks of milk and juice did I actually slow down. Malcolm also brought out two loaves of bread, and a roasted vegetable medley that smelled divine.

Mr. McHaddish once again stood in the doorway. I guess he really didn't want Jameson's mother coming anywhere near me. Fine by me. She was the last thing I wanted to deal with. It was only then though that I realized, I never got to do my video chat with Molly and Mr. Hydell.

I swallowed my mouthful and turned to Mr. McHaddish, "Does Mr. Hydell know?"

He'd turned as I'd spoke, then answered, "Yes, I had Mrs. Granger call and tell them. I also called them myself while you were in the shower to tell them you'd woken up."

I nodded, and said, "Thank you."

"They want you to call them later. So that they can get the full story."

I nodded again and turned back to my food. I polished off the haggis and vegetables, leaving half a loaf of bread when I was finally full. I leaned back in my chair, feeling much better than I did an hour ago. I reached forward and finished my glass of milk off – the juice was already gone – before turning back to look at Mr. McHaddish as we both heard Mrs. Billings' voice come up the hall. Thankfully she didn't get any closer and I chose to ignore her by clearing my throat to get Mr. McHaddish's attention.

When he looked at me I asked, "When did you get back?"

He chuckled slightly, "The next night after I left. Mrs. Granger's call reached me in the air, so for emergency purposes, the plane was rerouted to Montreal, and from there I boarded a different plane and came straight back."

"You were that worried about me that you postponed school business." I couldn't quite believe it.

He nodded, "Me and my staff managed to work it out over the phone."

"And Mrs. Billings?" I asked as her voice became louder. I guess she was shouting now.

"She received a call about Jameson a few days after you lost consciousness. I wanted her to finish their vacation, so I waited." I nodded, "How much do you remember?"

My throat tightened and my stomach clenched, "Everything."

He came forward and knelt down beside me, "Take your time and explain it slowly."

I nodded again as Ms. Hamper came in to join us. She suggested we move to the library and talk there. Just in case Mrs. Billings came looking. I doubted she would though, not unless Jameson joined us. I wanted him to, but I knew he needed to settle this with his mother before any other problems came up between them.

Mr. McHaddish carried me to the library. Once again I didn't bother protesting, my leg was no longer in the shape the hike had put it in. He sat me down in one of the big arm chairs when we made the library, then went over and shut the double doors, making sure the latch caught so we'd have warning should someone decide to come in.

While he did that, I turned to Ms. Hamper and asked, "How're the little ones?"

She smiled brightly and said, "Wonderful. They're actually here at the estate with Don."

"Where did you guys go?"

"Virginia. A friend of mine owed me a favor. We were there up until Uncle Bram called me." she answered. Gesturing to Mr. McHaddish as she did.

Nice to know that was indeed Mr. McHaddish's first name. I thought it suited him. He came over and sat down next to her, bringing a glass of water and one of my pill bottles with him. Where did he get those? He handed both to me and I saw it was my pain pills. I took one gratefully. My leg was starting to feel stiff. I moved just enough that my leg was draped over the chair arm. That felt much better.

"I'm wondering. Is there a particular reason I couldn't wake up on my own?"

Mr. McHaddish nodded, "Your panic attack was so far gone that Mrs. Granger injected you with an herbal mixture to stop your body from going into shock. The mixture she used was one that we commonly use to knock someone unconscious." He paused, "After that we worried that waking you up might cause some kind of problem, so we decided to let Jameson stay put and calm you down in hopes that you'd wake on your own. It wasn't until Gretchen explained how susceptible you were to chamomile that we discovered that one dose was probably going to put you out for a few weeks. I decided against trying to wake you using another mixture."

"Is there even an elixir that counter acts the first one?" I asked.

He nodded, "There is, but I still felt it best to let you wake up on your own. We also suspect that some outside influence might have been keeping you asleep."

I shook my head, "There wasn't any. My mom taught us how to recognize that kind of thing, and I can honestly tell you that wasn't the case."

"That's good. I feel much better knowing that." He said.

We all turned as the doors latch unhooked and was redone after someone entered the room. All three actions were done quietly, but not for our benefit. We all turned as Jameson came over and sat down in the chair next to me.

Ms. Hamper didn't seem to mind, since she gestured for me to go ahead and talk about what happened to cause the panic attack. It felt relieving to talk about it with her. Both Jameson and Mr. McHaddish had to be given moments to calm down. Neither of them was happy about what had happened and the events that caused it. I felt a lot better after I was able to talk about it. Then Mr. McHaddish asked the question that I'd been dreading.

"Does he know where your brother is?"

"I have no idea. He probably did three weeks ago when the message popped up. My brother mentioned on his account that he was on vacation, just not where."

"It unfortunately wouldn't be impossible for him to figure out." Jameson stated.

"No it wouldn't," I agreed, "but Reggie has the same survival training I do. Once he knew he was in danger he would've gotten out of there in whatever way possible. And he'd be sure to take his girlfriend with him."

"So what are you thinking he'll do?" Ms. Hamper asked.

I shrugged, "I don't know. Whatever he's got planned, he won't share it with me unless he needed to."

We were interrupted from further conversation by a commotion at the door. Mr. McHaddish got up to see what was going on, while I suddenly got a tingling sensation at the back of my head. I shook my head, trying to get rid of it. Then it hit me. I knew that tingling anywhere. I got up and despite my leg's protests, listened at the shelf to what Mrs. Granger told Mr. McHaddish.

"There's a young man and a young woman at the door. They're demanding to see Maggie."

The adrenaline kicked in then. Ignoring my leg, Jameson, and Ms. Hamper, I shot passed Mr. McHaddish as he left the library and practically charged down the stairs. The three of them calling my name as Mrs. Granger just looked after me in surprise.

There was a commotion at the front door as they were forced open. The roar of a jaguar obvious as someone tried to stop the one person I'd wanted to see in so long. I didn't bother stopping until I stood on the last few steps that led into the main foyer. Standing just below the crystal chandelier was a beautiful jaguar, and next to her, stood Reggie.

Chapter 62

I barreled down the rest of the steps and tackled Reggie as he came toward me. I can't describe how good it felt to finally hug him in real life again. The tears I'd been holding back began to flow freely. And judging from my own shoulder, he was crying too.

Seeing me embrace my brother seemed to calm everyone down. I barely noticed Jameson, and the others coming down the steps after me. I was just so happy to have Reggie near me that he was all I cared about in that moment. It wasn't until he actually looked up and realized our audience that he even made an attempt to pull me back and look at me. We placed our foreheads together, drinking each other in. He smelled slightly different. I couldn't tell why though.

"Maggie?" I turned to look at Mr. McHaddish, "Are you going to introduce them?"

I cleared my throat and wiped my face, "Everyone, this is my older brother, Reggie. And his…"

"Mate." Matilda answered, having changed back.

My eyes widened, so that was the difference in his smell, "Mate, Matilda."

She smiled at me, a genuine one too, "It's a pleasure to finally meet you Maggie."

I returned her smile, "You too." I turned partially as Mr. McHaddish came forward, me and Reggie hadn't let go of each other, "Bro, this is Mr. McHaddish."

"Ah, the cave lion shifter who runs the school you'll be going to." He extended his hand as he talked.

Mr. McHaddish accepted and shook the offered hand, "Indeed. I'm glad we got to meet. Although I wish it was under better circumstances."

"I do too sir."

"I take it you're here because of your sister's panic attack?" Mr. McHaddish asked.

Reggie nodded, "Yes sir. I wanted to make sure she was okay in person."

"Hmm." Matilda groaned. Reggie dropped his head as if trying not to laugh, "You ever make me fly like that again mi amor, and you'll never hear the end of it."

I gave my brother an odd look, "I flew here myself." He answered.

"Si, and it was very cold. I'm a cat, mi amor, I don't take well to my feet being off the ground against my will for extended periods of time."

I chuckled, "I'm sorry. I don't mean to laugh."

She shook her head, "It is okay." Her smile showed she was just venting.

"Shall I make up one of the other guest rooms sir?" Mrs. Granger asked.

"Yes. Reggie, Matilda, this is Mrs. Granger, my head of household."

"Ma'am." Reggie shook her hand before she left to attend to the room.

Jameson had been standing back the whole time. Reluctant and nervous to get anywhere near my brother should Reggie react adversely to his presence. It was only then that I let go of my brother and went over to Jameson. Sadly that was when my leg decided to fully give out.

Jameson caught me just before I fully hit the floor. I heard Reggie growl at him and – surprisingly – my growl toward Reggie. That got his attention. Jameson quickly picked me up and carried me over to one of the rooms off the foyer. I groaned as he sat me down on the couch that was available. I gave Reggie an 'knock it off' look as he came over and nearly growled at Jameson again.

He graciously swallowed it back and sat down beside me, on the opposite side of me from Jameson. Matilda grabbed one of the foot rests and brought it over. She then gave Reggie the same look I just had. He looked at her with a 'seriously' look on his face. Which she just gave him what we would later call the wife look, and he dropped his head. I chuckled, he was gonna be in for it over the next few years.

"So.." he paused, "I guess your Jameson."

"Aye, and it honestly is nice to meet you." Jameson answered as he placed a pillow behind my back.

Reggie nodded, then looked at me, "I thought you said you weren't ready for a relationship?"

"I'm not. But that doesn't mean I have to – or even can – argue with a mate bond."

Jameson nodded, "We can still just be friends until she decides otherwise."

That surprised Reggie, "You're okay with that?" he asked.

Jameson just nodded as Mrs. Granger came in with a platter of sandwiches. Gretchen not far behind with a platter of tea cups. Surprisingly, Ms. Hamper followed with the tea kettle.

"Reggie, Matilda, this is my friend Gretchen and my therapist Ms. Hamper." I indicated both as I spoke.

Reggie shook Ms. Hamper's hand, "Pleasure ma'am. And you as well miss." He shook Gretchen's hand as well.

Ms. Hamper sat down on the couch opposite us, "The pleasure is mine. I'm glad we actually got to meet Reggie."

"Ah thought the two of you were still in Costa Rica." Gretchen stated.

"We were. Until three weeks ago when he sensed his sister was in danger." Matilda replied.

"Aha," Gretchen looked at Reggie, "I'll never get that scream out of my head."

"I'm sorry." I said.

"The fault isn't yours Maggie. The fault belongs to Kepner." Mr. McHaddish said.

"I figured he was the reason you told me to cancel my account." He reached forward and grabbed a sandwich. He looked at me first.

I shook my head, "I've still got twelve servings of haggis in my stomach, plus one and a half loaves of bread and roasted veggies to digest."

Reggie looked mildly impressed, "Twelve servings of haggis."

I shrugged, "I needed to catch up on protein."

Mr. McHaddish went on to explain to him and Matilda what had transpired over the three weeks that I'd been unconscious. Mrs. Granger took the time to pour out the tea and then left the room, taking Gretchen with her. Reggie and Matilda ended up polishing off most of the sandwiches. They explained that they hadn't eaten yet that day, and it was just after noon.

After that, the two of them went on to tell how they had gotten here from Costa Rica without getting in trouble for crossing borders illegally. Simple really. They'd crossed the Atlantic itself, taking rest stops on certain islands as Reggie flew. Even if he had to fly part of the way through the night. Then resting for a few days on each island they stopped at so that Reggie wouldn't overly exhaust himself. Obviously he'd been super anxious during those rest stops, but he'd known better than to try and continue when he was tired. I wondered what dad would've said. Then a thought struck me.

"Have you been in contact with Amanda?" I asked.

He shook his head, "Not since the first week. She was freaking out because Kepner had found a new way to try and find you, and she can't interfere as much as she wants to."

"What way?" I asked, sitting up straighter.

"A blood talisman. Which he needs a relative's blood to get working. A close relative." He said.

"I.e. you." I stated.

"Yep. Thankfully my school has allowed us to extend our time away indefinitely until we can return safely."

"So what do you two plan to do?" Ms. Hamper asked.

Reggie shook his head again, "As much as I would like to share ma'am, I can't. Technically me and Maggie are still in danger so our original agreement is still in effect."

I nodded, "No contact what so ever."

"Yep." He agreed.

"The two of you must at least stay a few days to recuperate." Mr. McHaddish said.

"That was part of the plan sir, although it originally was going to be down in Glasgow." Reggie confirmed.

"Well the two of you are more than welcome to stay here. It's not like I don't have the room." Mr. McHaddish mentioned as Mrs. Granger came back in to tell him the room was ready.

Jameson and I stayed in the living room while Reggie and Matilda followed Mrs. Granger up to see their room. Mr. McHaddish went outside to talk to some of the men that worked on the estate about fixing my demolished window. Ms. Hamper went up to check on her twins, which left me and Jameson alone. I could tell that Jameson had something on his mind, and that he wasn't sure how to actually broach it. So I did it for him.

"What's on your mind?"

He chuckled, then said, "I was wondering if you wanted to come down to Edinburgh tomorrow. Well, maybe you, your brother and his girlfriend."

"Were you in need of something?" I asked.

"Besides time away from my mum. Again. I wanted you to see some more of Scotland before you left. There's an aquarium down in Edinburgh and I know how much you love them, plus it's right on the ocean, I figured we could spend the day there and help you feel better."

He was up to something, but when I thought about it, "Sounds like a plan."

He smiled brightly. I didn't know what else he had planned, but I like surprises sometimes. Whatever he had in mind would have to be either important or just something he wanted to do together. I wasn't sure which. Then something came to mind.

"Were you serious, about what you said earlier?" I asked.

"About being okay with just being friends until you decide otherwise?" I nodded. "Yes I was. You've been through hell one too many times already, finding your life mate at our age just seems like a little too much too early." He paused, "Even if it takes until we're in our twenties, I won't push you."

I chuckled, "I probably won't have to wait that long to be ready, but I do appreciate the thought."

Reggie and Matilda came back down shortly afterwards. The four of us spent the time afterwards talking about everything that had gone down between each of us up till that moment. Reggie even told me how the two of them had met. Without revealing where he was now going to school that is.

They'd met in a very unconventional way. She'd been working as a janitor at the local hospital and been on her shift when Reggie went in for an annual appointment. He'd been so distracted that he'd run right into her cart and knocked it over. She'd laid into him about him making her job a little harder and possibly getting her in trouble. She'd shut up though once they'd made eye contact. Thankfully she hadn't gotten in trouble, since her supervisor had seen my brother crash.

He of course then asked how we'd met. Once that was explained, he wanted to see my new scars. I'd been wearing a long sleeved shirt, so I had to pull them up to show him. He immediately came over to get a better look at them when I did.

"And you did these in your sleep?" he was pretty horrified by them.

I nodded, "They healed a lot quicker a few days later."

"They did?! How?"

"I said our full last name."

"You did what?!" he asked.

"Don't give me the big brother shit right now Reggie." I was not in the mood for that, "I only said it because Mr. McHaddish promised he wouldn't tell anyone else."

He sighed, "And what did he say after that?"

"He fainted dead away."

"Huh?!" that confused him.

"He explained it the next day. He thought our entire family was wiped out, so me telling him our last name caught him by surprise."

"But why would saying it cause your scratches to heal almost instantly?"

"I'm not sure it was just my saying it. I had to shift in order to move him afterwards, I think that might have contributed."

He thought about that for a few seconds, "You might be right. Does he have any theories?"

I shrugged, "He had either that or a full idea. But he said that was an answer that would have to wait till another time."

He stood, "Well I for one don't want to wait."

He pulled me to my feet, and with both Jameson and Matilda following us, carried me most of the way up to Mr. McHaddish's office. We caught him on the phone with – from the sounds of it – Mr. Hydell. We all paused at the doorway as he looked up. He then beckoned me over and had me reassure both Mr. Hydell and Molly that I was awake and okay. If still a bit shaken.

They hung up reassured that I was indeed fine. They even encouraged me to spend some time with Reggie if at all possible. When that was done, Reggie got right down to business. He didn't waste any time laying it all out for Mr. McHaddish about wanting to know if I was right about what we'd discussed down stairs.

He sighed before saying, "Maggie's guess is correct in a way."

We all sat down, "Please explain." Reggie said.

"By saying her name out loud, it basically means that she accepts who she is because of it. Her shifting afterwards only cemented the fact, and allowed her to access the ancient healing powers your family was always famous for."

"I'm not sure I fully understand." I stated.

"When your ancestor cast the spell that cursed the Parthenian clan, she basically cast one on her own family."

It clicked, "Because our family focused on healing and harmony, her cursing the clan was basically the opposite of what we stood for."

"Correct." He folded his fingers, "You saying your name basically claimed it back, and your helping me after I was incapacitated, signified that you were ready to take back the powers your family had been blessed with for thousands of years."

"I'd always thought that all dragon shifters healed quicker than the rest." Reggie said.

"Dragon shifters do, but your family is unique in the fact that under normal circumstances, you heal almost instantly."

Reggie and I looked at each other, and without the slightest bit of hesitation, I grew a claw and sliced my left palm open. The blood flowed for not even a second, before the wounds closed back up again.

"Holy shit." Reggie whispered.

"She can do it because she's already reclaimed her name. You will only heal that quickly once you do the same." Mr. McHaddish said to Reggie.

Reggie got the same look on his face that I had when faced with actually saying our name out loud in front of other supernatural beings. I didn't blame him, a promise was a promise. He took a deep breath and swallowed. He looked like he was about to be sick.

"I promise I won't tell anyone mi amor." Matilda said, reaching over and placing her hand on his arm. "I've been wanting to ask what it was anyway."

He smiled, and without looking at her, said, "Sharpwingclaw."

She withdrew her hand so quickly that she actually cut her arm on the chair she was sitting in. Reggie reacted instantly. He moved and knelt in front of her, grabbed her arm and applied a small poultice I hadn't known he was carrying. She looked at him like he was from another planet.

"It can't be possible. That line was wiped out." She said in some awe.

He chuckled a little, "Maggie and I aren't the first in our family to be good at hiding."

Reggie and I weren't able to do much after that. Mr. McHaddish noticed that we both got a little angsty after he bandaged her arm, that he practically banished us outside. Saying now that both of us had reclaimed our name that we needed to spend some alone time together. As dragons, not humans. I was up for it. Maybe it could help my leg.

Jameson and Matilda accompanied us outside. We barely made it out the back door, we were so excited to finally spend some flight time together that we couldn't contain ourselves. I only just managed to get my brace off before changing.

Once we were in dragon form, Reggie took the time to examine my wings, now that I had the family telltale claw. Standing next to each other, you could see that he had a good foot and a half on me in height. That didn't stop him from leaning down and rubbing his head with mine. Jameson exclaimed to get going. His mom was approaching.

Reggie and I got running starts and took off just before hitting the garden shed. Once airborne we turned in a circle to see our respective mates wave as we gained altitude. We reached a thousand feet before Reggie made mental contact.

"Where to? You've seen most of this beautiful isle."

I thought for a second, and an idea formed. Neither of us had ever been given the opportunity to use our end claws for their original intended purpose, so why not put them to the test.

"To Kilt Rock. Follow me." I turned north by northeast and we were off.

Chapter 63

It wasn't a very long flight. Even with Reggie admiring the isle's beauty, we made good time. Kilt Rock and Mealt falls were only a little over two miles north of Culnacnoc. Along the eastern side of the isle.

Reggie expected me to land near where the tourists were standing. Nope. We gave the tourists an interesting view though, before flying a little ways north of the viewing areas and down to the stones at the bottom, there was no beach. Reggie took one look at the cliffs above us and gave me a 'race you' look. Gladly big brother.

Kilt Rock was 90 meters high. That translated to 295 feet of cliff to climb. With our dragon strength, that wouldn't be a problem. Before starting though, I took a moment to enjoy the ocean breeze. While standing there, my tail got itchy for some reason. I lifted it and shook it. It had fallen into the sea while I'd been standing still. I looked over at Reggie and we both moved closer to the cliff and got a grip.

We started off just using our arms and legs, wanting to get to a more preferable height before actually trying to use our wings. I was smaller and could move faster, but Reggie had six years more climbing experience than I did, and therefore, his muscles were better prepared for it.

That didn't stop me from trying to overtake him. My back right leg grabbed a not so stable stone and it fell into the sea. I missed a hold with my front leg, but thankfully caught one with my right wing. Two of them actually. Both claws hooked on two separate off shoots. I could feel the muscles in my back working as I pulled myself back up using them.

I was glad that I'd spent time on the hike working my back to strengthen the muscles just for this purpose. I looked over at Reggie as I climbed higher. His claws looked to be about seven inches long each. I wondered if that was the length they had started at or if they'd grown to it after time.

"Were your claws seven inches when they first grew?" I asked.

He grunted as he got a better grip before answering, *"No. They were at six and a half. The next half inch grew in when I hit eighteen."*

"What about Amanda?"

"Uh," he paused in climbing, *"let me think."* He started moving again as he did, *"If I remember correctly, hers started at six inches, and grew a full inch when she hit eighteen."*

"And dads were eight inches."

"Yeah. I don't think dad ever said how long grandpa's were."

"Not to my knowledge either." I caught up with him. *"What do you think about any future growth?"*

"I think it might be possible. You remember that ten inch horn we had on display in the living room?"

"The one that was shattered into several pieces by the first bomb." I answered.

He nodded, *"Dad never said where it came from, but I think it used to be one of gramps' claws."*

I thought about it, *"He did spend an awful lot of time staring at it. As if he missed someone."*

"If it is a claw, we should get it DNA tested when we're safe again."

"Agreed." I got just above him, *"But speaking of gramps, did dad or mom ever share why we didn't interact with other shifters besides Gene and her family?"*

He stopped, as if only just realizing something, *"You know, I don't think they did. It never really occurred to me to ask."*

"You never found it odd?"

"Oh no I did, I just assumed it was for a good reason. Maybe we could ask your temporary guardian about that."

"Well, he did mention that he'd known our grandparents before they died."

He nearly lost his hold, *"He did?!"*

"Yeah. He met them and dad not long after dad met mom." He looked at me until a rock hit him in the head.

"Okay, lets finish this discussion at the top."

"Then pick up the pace turtle boy." I moved faster.

"Oh! You get back here!" he scrambled up after me.

I beat him to the top by a good fifteen feet. I made sure to stick my head over the top before planting my wings for the final pull. I'd rather not accidentally skewer a human. I was panting as I walked a few feet back from the edge. I shook myself down as I waited for Reggie. It was a beautiful day and the view was spectacular. I laid down to get the weight off my leg, just as Reggie came over the top.

"I win." I said as I laughed at the look on his face.

He stuck is tongue out at me before coming and laying down beside me. Admiring the view as well. A rabbit scurried away as we sat there. It went in the direction of the tourists, which were only a hundred feet away. Several raised their phones or cameras, asking for pictures. I didn't mind but I looked up at Reggie first, since he was between me and the tourists. He simply shrugged and nodded in the humans direction and several people started taking pictures.

I jumped slightly as I felt something move next to my tail. I stood and looked down at the culprit. A European viper. Joy. It must have been stalking the rabbit as me and Reggie had come up. I wasn't too worried, snake fangs can't penetrate dragon scales. Not even highly venomous ones like this one.

The viper didn't seem to know that. It reared up and had the nerve to hiss at me. Several people shouted in surprise when they saw it rear up in their cameras. Then it decided to try and strike at me. Not a wise idea. It backed off when I hissed back at it. It got a good look at my teeth and slithered away.

Reggie chuckled at me. Or, as well as a dragon can chuckle. I laid back down next to him and we just enjoyed each other's company. It was only when the humans started to disperse that we changed back to human in record time. We walked over to one of the viewing benches and sat down. Well, he walked, I limped. I sat down next to him and rubbed my leg.

"I thought the hike fixed that." he said.

"It did. But being comatose for three weeks didn't help it at all."

"Oh. So, go back to the part about Mr. McHaddish knowing our grandparents."

Over the next hour I told him all that Mr. McHaddish had told me. Including how we were descendants of Boudica. He nearly choked on that one. I told him I hadn't quite believed it either, not until Mr. McHaddish had laid it all out. After I was done, he took some time to think it over. I did some thinking of my own, mostly about how Kepner could have found Reggie. Then it hit me like a runaway train.

"Our plan!" I nearly shouted. I placed my hands on my head 'cause I felt like an idiot.

Reggie jumped when I said it, and came out of his thoughtful revive, "What are you talking about?"

"The plan we set up with Amanda to find Kepner. That must be how he found you. It's not difficult to back trace an account that suddenly shows interest in someone."

"Shit." He smacked himself in the face, "He must have back traced my dummy account and it would have led him right to my real one."

"Were the two linked?"

"No. I made sure to use a completely different name for my dummy account. I didn't leave any kind of clue."

"It still must be how he found your account."

"Then I'm off the grid. Me and Matilda will disappear." He said without hesitation.

"There is something I want to set up first."

"What?"

"You remember those instant transport spells mom taught us?"

His look said yes. Without another word, we stood and got a running start toward the cliff. We jumped and fell for about twenty feet before changing and using the momentum to skim the water, and gain altitude. Once high enough, we turned and started back for the estate. Despite my brothers wingspan being thirty feet shorter than mine, he kept up easily.

We didn't bother landing in the garden. We went straight for the roof patio. From there, we ran down the steps to my room. The staff were in the process of fixing the window, so I was able to grab my stones bag, as well as my ceremonial dagger, and leave without causing any trouble.

Reggie went outside to choose two stones, while I went to inform Mr. McHaddish of my plan to perform magic. I grabbed a spare knife and a permanent marker from the kitchen, then met Reggie at the Boudica statue. We moved to the edge of the forest.

This spell was the most complicated that our mom had ever taught us. It required both of us to speak the incantation at the same time, in perfect synchronization too. This would be the first time either of us would perform the spell for real world purposes rather than training. But rather than do it in English, we chose to do it in Gaelic. My rocks and crystals were all set up in the circle.

"Are you ready?" I asked as we knelt down on the grass, the two rocks between us, with the necessary symbols written on them.

"Damn straight." We held the knives I had grabbed and began. For translation purposes, I'll write it in English.

"North to South, East to West

Here and now at our behest

Fire to Water, Earth to Air

Take me from here to there

As trouble brews for loved ones dear

Take me there without fear

Blood to blood, and unshed tears

In two seconds, take me there!"

We dragged the blades across our palms as the wind began to stir. We squeezed our hands to get the blood to drip before the wounds closed. The blood dripped onto the two rocks at our knees. They began to glow as the spell took hold of each. We only looked away when the glow reached a peak. Once it stopped, we checked our hands. The wounds were closed. We looked down at the rocks, the glow was still there, but it was steady. We each picked one up and held it. I could feel the power thrumming from it. The rocks were small enough that we could carry them with us everywhere in a pocket, and when they were needed, all we'd have to do was crush them, and the magic would be released to perform it's intended purpose.

Mr. McHaddish approached us as we were putting my rocks and crystals back in their bag. He seemed amazed once again. Obviously he'd been watching from the house. Behind him were Jameson and Matilda.

"That was pure dead brilliant!" Jameson exclaimed, I laughed.

"What kind of spell was that mi amor?" Matilda asked with this amazed smile on her face.

"It's an instant transport spell." He held up his rock before slipping it in his pocket.

"Like in Harry Potter with the apparating?" Jameson asked.

I nodded, "Just without the danger of splinching." I placed mine in my pocket.

"And you put the spell into the rocks?" Mr. McHaddish asked in fascination.

"Yep. Makes it easier to take with us and or activate." Reggie answered.

"Not to mention, we'd be able to keep them should we be searched." I added.

"Very true." Reggie agreed.

We all walked back inside to find Mrs. Billings waiting in the dining room with her arms crossed. Jameson instantly and openly groaned as we walked past her. Reggie gave me a questioning look as we four left the dining room while Jameson went over to see what his mom was on about.

"Helicopter mom." I answered.

Reggie made a sympathetic face as he caught the first half of her sentence, "What the bloody hell is wrong with you!!?"

Mr. McHaddish paused in his stride, "I think it best we take a moment to listen." He said to the three of us, while he turned around to face us. We were stopped by the bottom of the stairs and could hear every word.

"Mum, there is no reason to be bealin." Jameson said, trying to remain calm.

"No reason. No reason! You walked into a room with a psychotic dragon!"

"How would you react if you found out the man who killed your family might be this close to taking the last surviving member away from you!?" he countered.

We heard her attempt to answer, but fail, then, "I don't know. But I cannae stand the idea of you being hurt because some girl can't control herself."

"She would never hurt me. Not on purpose anyway. Any other injury would be me own fault."

"You don't know that. You barely know her, and this little crush you have on her will only last so long."

We heard a slap, "Haven't you been paying attention to what Mr. McHaddish has taught me."

"Three years here is not enough time to learn all you need to know about being a shifter."

"It is too. It's not a 'little crush' as you call it." Jameson was clearly close to losing it.

I walked closer to the doorway of the dining room, "It is so. I've seen it enough times in other teenagers."

I stopped and stayed out of sight, "How many of those 'other teens' were shifters, mum?"

She stammered, "I don't know."

"Then you have no idea about what shifters go through." I heard him start to walk away, in my direction.

"Jameson! Get back here! I'm not finished!" she shouted.

"Well I am. Until you talk to Mr. McHaddish and hear how we shifters find love."

I started moving as he came out the doorway. He automatically took my hand as we walked toward my brother. I looked up the stairs to see Matilda and Mr. McHaddish already moving up. We moved into line as his mother came out. Jameson without hesitation, picked me up and carried me the rest of the way up the first flight of stairs. Once at the top he put me down and walked up to Mr. McHaddish.

"I hate to ask it…" he didn't even have to finish.

"I'll talk to her." He gave Jameson a sympathetic smile.

With that, he walked back down the stairs to head her off, and turned her back toward the dining room. Jameson breathed a sigh of relief at the thought of his mother possibly, finally understanding that shifters work differently than humans do.

I grabbed his arm and rubbed my other hand up and down it to try and help him regain some of his composure. It seemed to help. He placed his opposite hand over mine as I stopped moving it. He then stood straighter and turned to look Reggie in the eyes.

"I was wondering if you and Matilda would like to join us," he gestured at me, "for a trip down to Edinburgh tomorrow?"

Reggie looked surprised, but Matilda looked excited, "Of course." she said without hesitation. Reggie looked at her with even more surprise, then just smiled and nodded.

Jameson smiled back and said, "I'll go and see if Mack is available."

He pulled his arm from mine and went back down stairs and out the front door. I went upstairs with Reggie and Matilda while explaining who Mack was. I also had to explain why Jameson's mom needed to be educated about shifters. They were both surprised when I explained how his mom was ignorant about most aspects of shifter life, and of course horrified about Jameson's biological father's treatment of her. I did mention that he was long dead.

I spent the rest of the day with Reggie. We both felt great amounts of relief at being able to spend time together after so many months apart. These would be memories that would fuel us for the rest of time that Kepner was alive.

It wasn't until after dinner that we separated. He and Matilda greatly enjoyed the round of haggis that Malcolm prepared. Reggie did comment on me possibly being tired of it after the amount I had eaten earlier. I'd just shaken my head and kept eating. Malcolm was extremely pleased that Matilda enjoyed it. She told him she was originally born in New Mexico, but her ancestry was predominantly from Panama. Her great-grandfather was from China.

We all dispersed after dinner for different reasons. I wanted to spend some time alone. Today had been one of the craziest that I'd had in a long time. I ended up taking a bath to try and ease my leg. From there, I took a pill and drank a glass of chamomile tea. I really didn't want to take any chances that night.

Chapter 64

My precautions were for naught. The nightmare I had that night was the most real I'd had in several months. It started out differently too. Now that I had found my mate, it began with Jameson's death. Run through with a sword in front of me.

I was instantly awoke though. I was immensely grateful for that. I sat in bed panting as Reggie came in. I wasn't too surprised to see him, when I was little he'd always been the one to come if mom wasn't able to. Now that she was gone, obviously, Reggie would be the only one. He sat down next to me and let me lean on him, wrapping his arm around my shoulder. It was close to dawn, so neither of us went back to sleep. It would be pointless at this point.

Our bodies had other plans. The first indication either of us had that we'd fallen asleep, was the sound of a camera. We both startled awake to find Matilda standing at the side of my bed, her camera held up to capture the two of us. Her wide smile making Reggie laugh with slight embarrassment, and me smile and rub my face.

Reggie and Matilda left my room shortly after. I laid there trying to fully wake up. My leg was feeling stiffer than usual. That was never a good sign, so I started rubbing it with the ball of my thumb, hoping to ease the tension.

It worked for a little bit. I decided to put my brace on before I stood up. I tested my leg to see if I could go the day without a hot bath. My leg would've collapsed on me had I not been wearing the brace, so that answered that question. I grabbed my chosen clothes and walked to the bathroom. I made sure the water was as hot as it would go, and got in.

Thankfully it didn't take long for my leg muscles to relax enough that I'd be able to walk several miles. To be on the safe side though, I chose to wear my brace. I limped most of the way down stairs, but I was used to it by now. I wondered if Mr. Hydell had told my physical therapist about my comatose time. More than likely he had, but whether or not Mr. McHaddish had been contacted was the question. I'd just have to ask him when I finally made it down to the dining room for whatever breakfast was left.

Half way to the kitchen I stopped. I knew that smell anywhere. I hurried as best I could, my stomach suddenly grumbled. I nearly bumped into Jameson standing in the doorway.

"That is what you made for breakfast Malcolm?" he asked with amusement.

"Outta my way handsome." I said, moving around him.

He and Reggie laughed as I moved to the chair I usually used and sat down. Biscuits and gravy was one of my absolute favorite breakfasts. I grabbed four biscuits and poured the still hot sausage gravy over top. Malcolm even brought over a plate of bacon. Applewood smoked from the smell of it. I grabbed a handful and crumbled it over the gravy.

"I cannae remember ever making somethin' like this for breakfast before." Malcolm said to Mr. McHaddish as he entered the room.

He chuckled, "How many of my temporary wards are from Texas?"

"Fair point. I might just have to make a few more southern American recipes before yeh head home." He said to me before he went back into the kitchen seeming pretty excited about trying something new from my home.

I looked up at Mr. McHaddish as he sat down, "I suggested it. I thought you might like something from home today."

I nodded in response, I had a mouthful already in and didn't want to be rude, "Maggie always appreciates biscuits and gravy." Reggie said as he sat down.

I swallowed, "Ya damn straight." I said.

Jameson sat down opposite me, "This is a Texan breakfast?"

"Technically it's a southern American breakfast. Found from Texas to Florida to Kentucky." I corrected.

Jameson just chuckled and loaded his plate, copying me in amount and style. I'll never forget the look on his face as he took his first bite. He devoured his food after that. I might just have to introduce him to Texan barbecue at some point. Traditional Texan barbecue. I'd have to check and see if Malcolm had all the spices I would need, plus of course get ahold of either brisket or ribs of some kind. Either pig, goat, or cow would do.

About an hour after breakfast, we heard from Mack, he was stranded down in Glasgow trying to solve some mix up with one of his ordered parts, and wouldn't be able to fly us down. It was Reggie that suggested that we do the flying. Jameson was all for it, but Matilda was a bit skeptical. She was a cat shifter after all. But once Jameson showed her the saddle that he'd modified, she was up for it.

Jameson took the time to modify a second saddle for Reggie. At the shoulders and chest, Reggie was seven to ten inches wider than me. Don't even get me started on his wing joints, Jameson had to re-fit it three separate ways before it would finally fit around him.

By the time we were ready to leave, each of us was eager to get going. Mr. McHaddish found an extra helmet and goggles for Matilda, plus a scarf. Just as we were leaving, Mr. McHaddish caught us and informed us that the Edinburgh airport was too busy to accommodate us. We discussed it quickly, and decided to land at Glasgow and get transportation from there.

We ended up having to leave in a flash to avoid Mrs. Billings again, but I honestly didn't mind. I was just glad to be able to shift with my leg acting the way it was. Jameson had my brace tied to the saddle as a precaution should we need it. I had a feeling I would and was happy with the thought of taking it with.

Reggie and I kept our pace steady, and not too fast. We flew the same path that Jameson and I had used earlier in July. At the pace we set, we arrived in Glasgow in just under an hour. We'd already called into the airport before leaving, so once again, one of the tarmac workers was waiting for us. Reggie had me land first, since

I was the smaller of the two. I made room quick enough though, the last thing I wanted was for Reggie to land on me by accident.

He was a bit rusty, from the looks of it. It must have been a lot longer since he'd flown to an airport than I'd guessed. He nearly knocked his nose into the tarmac. I tried not to wince. Once the saddles were removed and we'd shifted back, I turned to Reggie.

"When was the last time you landed on something other than ground?" I asked.

He thought for a sec, then, "It's been more than a year. I've never liked landing on rock, of any kind."

I didn't blame him, rock can be rough on feet, even ours as dragons. I didn't mind it as much, I'd always liked walking barefoot outside as a kid, so my feet were better prepared for it. Amanda had once again been the odd one there, but for landing on rock she had a really good excuse for hating it. The first time she'd landed on rock, she'd ended up with a three inch gash on her foot from a discarded piece of glass. So justifiable in her case.

As we left the airport, we learned that Jameson had called and made plans for a river boat tour along the Union Canal. We'd reach Edinburgh by the Falkirk Wheel, which connected the Union Canal to the Forth and Clyde Canal. Me and Reggie were pretty excited about that, it was one of the few things that all three of us had on each of our bucket lists.

We took a cab to the boat tour dock. I hadn't paid much attention to the route we'd taken there, because I'd been too busy pointing out different landmarks to Reggie that I had seen here last month with Jameson. He mentioned possibly going to see the Devil's Pulpit with Matilda at a later date. Both me and Jameson definitely recommended it. The cab pulled up outside the main building for the river tours and we disembarked.

Matilda was a little nervous about getting on a boat, but was more than willing once she saw it had a small café on board. We all greatly enjoyed the scenery along the way. All total it would be a 43 to 50 minute trip to Edinburgh, depending on traffic. And yes there could possibly be river traffic.

At one point during the trip, Reggie and I got some alone time. He wanted to make sure my leg was doing okay. It was, since we'd been smart enough to bring the brace. I mentioned to him that we'd never actually talked to Mr. McHaddish about why our parents didn't interact with other shifters. He commented that it could wait till later, when we got back from our little day trip. We also – of course – talked about Amanda.

"Is that the token?" he asked, pointing to my necklace.

I nodded, "Yep." I touched the little charm. Feeling the magic hum through my fingers.

Reggie gave a small smile, "I honestly can't wait to see what you plan to bring as proof."

I chuckled, "You know me. A little old fashioned when I need to be."

It was then that we came to the Falkirk Wheel. All four of us were rather impressed by it. 115 feet tall, and the only boat lift that worked by rotation. The passengers on our boat waved to the other boat – who did wave back – as we took the five minute ride down to the lower canal entrance. I checked my watch. We had covered a little over twenty minutes of our journey to Edinburgh, we had twenty-one minutes or so of travel to go. Plenty of time for a hot chocolate.

I met up with Matilda at the café and decided to ask her a question, "So how does the Chinese ancestry come in?"

She smiled, "My Panamanian family is nearly religiously traditional in its practice of only mating with other shifters found in Panama. My great-grandmother chose not to."

"Just like that, huh."

She nodded, "Her parents had matched her with a neighboring jaguar male, but when they met, there was no chemistry and the bond didn't take hold. As it turned out she'd made a deal with her parents. If the bond didn't work, they'd give her enough money to travel, then she would try again."

"And it was during this traveling that she found her mate." I stated.

Again, she nodded, "While hiking along the Great Wall. Sadly, when her parents found out that she'd been bonded to a snow leopard, they were less than accepting."

"How much is less?"

"She was forever banished from the tribe. And Panama. Along with any and all descendants."

I gave a horrified look, "No offence but your tribe is fucked up."

She laughed heartily, "No offence taken, estoy de acuerdo." 'I agree' for those who don't speak Spanish.

I was glad she agreed with me, "So what happened afterwards?" I asked.

"She and her mate moved to America and started their family. Mi abuela was the only one who became a jaguar, while her siblings all became snow leopards. She eventually visited Guatemala and that was where she met her mate. Who as it turned out, was from a neighboring tribe to my great-grandma's."

"Happy coincidence maybe?"

"She thought so at the time, but then heard that breeding in her mama's tribe was getting too inbred, and that even they were starting to outsource."

"So what your great-grandma did, actually inspired some of the younger generations, because they could see what the older ones could not."

She nodded with this huge grin on her face, "The tribe elders ended up pardoning her, and her extended family. She still never went back, but her children and grandchildren did. Reggie and I had plans to visit before you called, but we can always do it later."

"I am sorry about that." I said, leaning against the counter.

She placed a hand on my shoulder, "You don't have to apologize. I just hope that you two get the chance to make that monster pay."

I nodded, "Thanks."

"Your welcome. Plus I'm glad Reggie could get the chance to see you before you started school."

We rejoined the boys shortly after that. During the rest of our boat trip, Jameson told us that the wheel had replaced a succession of eleven locks that used to ferry boats between the two canals. Reggie's jaw practically hit the floor when he heard the number. I'll admit mine almost did too, it was a staggering amount to think about, not to mention the time consumption of it. No wonder the wheel was checked daily.

The boat made its way through Falkirk until it came to two beautiful sculptures called the Kelpies. My brother and I took a bunch of pics as we passed out of the canal and onto the river that joined it. Then from the River Carron, we passed into the bay, under three separate bridges, and after some distance of coast, into the Newhaven Harbour just north of Edinburgh. It was marked as a historical landmark, so we took the time to look around and at the lighthouse just across the waterfront. Once we had disembarked from the boat, we grabbed yet another cab, and rode down to Edinburgh.

Chapter 65

We had a great time in Edinburgh. The four of us went to several different tourists shops, Jameson took us to several tours in historical buildings, and we did indeed visit the aquarium that Jameson told me about. Deep Sea World as it was called, wasn't technically in Edinburgh, it was in North Queensferry, just across the water. I'd never seen so many different sharks in one aquarium. We came away with good memories and some other great souvenirs.

Our final stop of the day was to the Edinburgh Castle. I can't tell you how much we all enjoyed that. Reggie and I the most. This fortress had stood most likely since the iron age. Reggie and I knew that this place was tied to our ancestry, but we couldn't quite remember how. We almost didn't want to leave. We took some pics and grabbed a pretty late lunch there before we did though. I most definitely recommend visiting.

We were back on the boat for the return trip at five o'clock. We spent the whole trip back to Glasgow talking about our day. By the time we reached the airport, Jameson had received a call about something taking place later that week. After hanging up he seemed really excited, then refused to tell any of us what he was excited about. I was tempted to mess with him until he spilled the beans on the flight back, but decided against it. I needed to concentrate on flying safely and quickly or I'd never hear the end of it from Reggie.

We touched down in time for dinner at the estate. Mr. McHaddish had us all take our newly acquired stuff to our rooms before letting us come to the dining room. Malcolm had tried his hand at Brunswick stew. It smelled awesome. And upon sitting down, we discovered that he'd omitted the okra. Merely because he couldn't get ahold of any. Neither me or Reggie minded, we only liked okra fried. Any other way we didn't like it. We all four dug in with gusto. Malcolm had done an awesome job. The stew had great flavor, and the meat was nicely done. I couldn't help but laugh at Matilda's face when Malcolm told us he'd done it with rabbit meat instead of cow.

After we had finished eating, I asked Malcolm if I could do something for either lunch or dinner the next day. Turns out he had the next day off anyway, so he gave me free range of the kitchen. Cool!

I spent some time in the kitchen getting everything I would need for me to do barbecue. Reggie came in and asked if I could do my steak and mushroom gyoza as well. I said 'yes' since I hadn't made it in a while. Plus he hadn't eaten it since before the murders, and had been craving it. I made a list of things I would need, and went about the kitchen to see if everything was there.

Almost, I would need either brisket or rib meat for the barbecue I had planned, and neither was available. Malcolm had everything else, including the spices and herbs I needed. The wonton wrappers I could make myself, and dehydrated mushrooms were perfectly fine.

I went up to my room feeling happy that I could do some cooking the next day. I might even throw in some baking, but that was up for debate. We'd just have to wait and see.

I took extra precautions that night. Two cups of tea and a sleeping pill. I was nearly falling over before I even hit the bed. Thankfully it worked. I ended up having the first dreamless sleep in a long time.

Then of course, I slept through breakfast. Obviously no one minded. I woke up to find – once again – a breakfast sandwich waiting with a glass of milk on my nightstand.

Breakfast eaten, I dressed, brushed my hair, and went down stairs to find that someone had bought two racks of ribs, plus a brisket, and some steaks had been brought out and prepped for me. I smiled. I wasn't going to argue with it. Whomever had done it must have either heard me talking to Malcolm or he'd done it himself. Either way I was happy.

I immediately got to work on the brisket and ribs. They would need at least ten to twelve hours of smoke time. I mixed my rub, and patted it onto the meat. I chose my woods, and got the outdoor smokehouse – which Malcolm had pointed out to me earlier – going. Once it was warm, I got the meat in.

I invited Gretchen and Matilda to help me with lunch. Both of them were interested in trying the gyoza, having heard about it from Mr. McHaddish and Reggie. Matilda turned out to be a wizard when it came to dough, so I let her handle the wonton wrappers. Gretchen and I handled the rest. The meat had apparently marinated overnight, and was super tender.

Reggie's mouth was watering so bad when he came to check on lunch progress that he had to be banished from the kitchen. Jameson wasn't much better. He kept trying to sneak into the kitchen after once again avoiding his mom. I guess his stunt with me had undone some progress. I might have to fix that.

When lunch was finally fully put together, neither of the boys could sit down fast enough. Reggie of course didn't waste any time getting at least a dozen on his plate the second the platter hit the table. Good thing I'd planned out for about a dozen shifters to be eating. We had close to one hundred gyoza when finished.

Mr. McHaddish came down to eat while I took my plate back into the kitchen to get the rest of the accompaniments to my barbecue started. I needed to make mac and cheese, cornbread, and maybe cobbler. No peaches, so apple pie it was.

I took my time with everything. Not just because of my leg, but because I wanted to enjoy myself. It had been a while since I'd been allowed to actually cook more than one thing for a meal. I am a southern girl after all. By the time three o'clock rolled around, I had a new energy about me. Everyone noticed too. Even Ms. Hamper when she came down to make some formula for the twins. I felt a bit more like myself again.

I went out to check the meat at a quarter to four. The meat thermometer said 175. Not quite where I wanted it, so I closed the door and left it alone for another two hours. I fully removed them from the oven twenty minutes before they would be served. It was ten to six, so I wouldn't be cutting into either until 6:10. Just enough time to finish the cornbread.

Mrs. Billings came by to see what I was doing. She practically laughed at me when I had it all explained to her. I guess she thought I was trying to win Jameson over or something. I just shook my head and ignored her, especially after Jameson came in and nearly shooed her away.

I had covered the meat to retain the heat, and removed it now. It smelled amazing. I grabbed a knife and cut off a piece off the end of both. I popped them in my mouth individually and immediately shut my eyes both times. They were perfect. The crust gave it a crunch and they was super juicy. I called in Jameson to help me, and we got everything to the table for dinner.

Jameson couldn't get enough of the brisket, or the ribs. Had he been left to his own devices, he'd have eaten the whole things himself. I was amazed he even had enough room left for dessert. That any of us did, Mr. McHaddish included.

"It's been a long time since I had classic southern food." He explained when asked.

"I'm just glad you got to actually make something from home sis." Reggie said past a mouthful of pie.

"Don't talk with yer mouth full." I said, deliberately using my accent.

He'd finished chewing and just about died of laughter, "Yes ma'am." I threw my napkin at him.

"No throwing things please." Mr. McHaddish said, "Some of us are still eating." He added before taking another bite of his pie.

"I could get used to this kind of food, Maggie." Jameson said.

I chuckled, "Good, 'cause as a southern girl I love feeding people." I took a drink.

"Then I'll probably get fat." He said jokingly. Which made us all laugh.

There wasn't any pie left when everyone was done. Everything else had leftovers, but then again I had only made the one pie. I might just have to make some more later.

I decided after dinner to show Reggie the panorama that I had made for his birthday. I had wanted to show him the night sky, but even with the new moon, it was cloudy out. So showing him the perfect night sky of the isle would have to wait a few days. I pulled my computer out and got it started, then I went down to Reggie's room and told him to come up to mine when he had a chance.

While I waited, I finished the final touches needed to make it work as a panorama. Should we ever get the opportunity, we could do this as a ceiling in the room of a house. Wherever he and Matilda decided to live when it was safe for us again.

He knocked on my door about five minutes after I finished. I waved him over and turned my computer in his direction. His face lit up when he saw the vast sky.

"This is from my birthday?"

I nodded, "I took it while we were on the hike. I figured you would love it."

He kissed me on my forehead, "I do. Your awesome sis."

He gave me a hug, and left. I was supremely glad he liked it. I shut down my laptop and put it aside. I was glad to see that my laptop hadn't been damaged in anyway when I had the panic attack. Some people can react really bad when gripped by fear. I looked out my now fixed window. The sea that I could see was a little choppy. I wouldn't be surprised if a storm was brewing out to sea. Either that or it was just me. Feeling exhausted, I changed into p.j.'s and crashed into – thankfully – another dreamless sleep.

Chapter 66

The next few days were interesting. Jameson actually went camping in the woods without his mom knowing. Needless to say, she came into the dining room while Mr. McHaddish was eating and practically went off on him. He wasn't happy about it.

I eventually heard that she'd been given the whole spiel about how we shifters 'find love' as Jameson had called it. She wasn't happy about the prospect that it just happened. That two souls could connect in ways that human ones never could. What bothered her the most was the fact of it not being voluntary. That wasn't something bad in shifter eyes. The concept of soul mates is taken much more seriously by us. Yes, it left almost no room for dating other people, but it also simplified the whole process in a way.

In the end she wouldn't shut up until Jameson was found. So, without anyone but Reggie knowing what I was doing, I walked into the woods to find him.

Turns out, that was all part of his plan. He was waiting for me near the berry crop with two hiking bags. Okay, that was a surprise. Then he told me his idea. There were technically five castles on the Isle of Skye, three in ruins, two not. We currently lived in the only one that had been restored from a previous state of disrepair. He was taking me to all the rest of them. He'd already informed Mr. McHaddish, Reggie, and Ms. Hamper of his plans.

His look asked what I was waiting for. I looked back over my shoulder, trying to see if anyone was coming, then rushed forward and grabbed the other bag from him, and we were off.

Turns out, he didn't intend to do a lot of walking. At top speed, he could cover three miles inside of two minutes, faster depending on flat land versus rocky. But since it wasn't even ten in the morning of August 25th, we had basically all day to explore the castles of Skye. The first two were at the north of the isle. Mr. McHaddish and I had seen them while on the hike. The other two were in the south, on the Sleat peninsula, so much further away, but worth it. The whole isle was only fifty miles across, so not that large when compared to other islands. It was still going to be a workout for Jameson to cover in one day. When I mentioned it to him, he just shrugged and said it was his turn to be the ride, since I'd done four trips.

As he went, I did some quick math in my head. Breaking down miles into feet and hours into minutes, I was able to calculate that Jameson could move three point seven times faster than a standard grizzly bear. They can run a maximum of 35 miles an hour, and that's not counted as a sprint, so Jameson was running at 129 - 130 miles an hour. That's as fast as NASCAR racecars. I took a moment to imagine that scenario, a grizzly shifter running next to a NASCAR driver, and laughed. I could only imagine the look on which ever drivers face.

Jameson heard my laugh as we reached the first castle. Dunvegan Castle, the western most castle on the Isle of Skye, and the oldest continuously inhabited castle in Scotland. We had stopped near the public parking lot just across the way from the castle itself. I hopped off Jameson – to the interest of several other tourists – and hobbled over to one of the closer vehicles. The car's owner graciously gestured for me to sit on the hood to rest my leg. I thanked him as Jameson went behind a large bush to shift.

He came over with a smile on his face, "What was the laughing I heard?"

I chuckled slightly, "I did some calculations about your speed, and upon reaching my conclusion, imagined a scenario with you running alongside a NASCAR racecar, and the possible look on the drivers face."

Jameson thought about it for a second, then laughed himself, "That would be hilarious to see."

We stood and joined the owner of the car as he walked across the road and into the trees surrounding the castle. We stopped at the ticket stand and Jameson purchased two. They tried to give him the disability discount because of me, but when I stated I would be fine so long as the brace was on, they relented and allowed him to pay full as he wanted. The gate was opened and our group was allowed to start the long walk to the actual castle. The first full view of Dunvegan we got was very impressive. It wasn't as far back from the trees as I had expected, and the low wall was a surprise, but not all that unexpected.

Jameson and I greatly enjoyed the tour. It was a little like walking through a more modern castle instead of one that was over 700 years old. Most of the rooms were very nice, though I preferred the rooms that still had their stone walls exposed. I spent a good ten minutes admiring a mantle – at least I'm sure it was a mantle – or a mirrored desk that was very beautifully carved. I tweaked my leg looking, but the owners were very gracious about letting me use one of the available chairs to sit before moving on.

Before leaving the castle, we stopped at the gift shop. Despite my protests, Jameson bought me a pocket watch, a letter opener, a journal, a notebook, and a necklace and earring set, all three of which were Celtic knots. We then after leaving the castle, enjoyed a walk through the gardens and down to the shoreline – or what little walkable shoreline there was.

Once that was done, we walked back to the parking lot for lunch at the onsite restaurant. He insisted on paying here as well instead of me. It was after noon, so we both ordered the tomato soup, plus some sausage rolls, and I convinced him to try the gluten free brownies for dessert. He also chose coffee for both of us before we sat down. When our food finally came, we took our time eating. Everything was delicious, including the brownies, which really surprised Jameson. Apparently his mom had tried to make some at one point and they hadn't turned out well. I didn't usually drink coffee made by another person, but the coffee that Jameson ordered for me was really good, I even ordered a second cup before we left for the next castle.

As we left the restaurant, Jameson's phone told him that there would be rain over at Portree, several miles east of us. Jameson wasn't worried, the rain wasn't scheduled to last long, and we wouldn't be approaching Portree for at least two hours. Any weather advisory for the Trotternish peninsula was what he would focus on if it popped up.

Just north of the parking lot, Jameson shifted and we began our trip to the northern most castle on the island. Duntulm castle. This wouldn't be a straight line trip though. We would have to backtrack a little ways in order to get around Loch Snizort Beag, which was the only lake to separate the two castles. In a car, this trip would take almost an hour, and those roads were twisty, almost never straight, despite the nearly flat ground. Jameson at his run could cover the trip inside of an hour.

As with most ruined castles, there wasn't much to any of the last three castles, but of them Duntulm had the most left to it, we spent most of the time enjoying the view from the top of the hill. The moisture from the waves at the bottom of the cliffs gave it all a nice atmosphere too. It was nearly one o'clock before we started down to Dunscaith castle. The second most southern castle. In a car it took one hour and 45 minutes, Jameson covered it in just that forty-five. He took his time at my insistence. No need to make the trip as fast as possible. Not with his mother possibly once again trying to bring him back to the estate like a troublesome kid.

I enjoyed Dunscaith the most of the ruined castles. The view was almost equally great, but Dunscaith had a rocky coastline that I could hike along as a dragon. That alone allowed me to get my leg some of the exercise I needed to get it back up to where it had been last month. Plus of course the human tourists had a blast photographing me among the ruins.

As we were making our five minute trip down to Knock Castle – this one wasn't included on most tourist brochures or maps because of how small it was – Jameson's phone sent him an alert. We had just passed Loch na Doireanach – I know, that's a mouthful – when he finally stopped to see what it was about. I was sitting on a rock when he gave an exclamation of surprise.

"What's up?" I asked, rubbing my knee.

"There's another castle just a few miles southwest of here." He said, his finger going mad over his phone as he found info on said sixth castle.

Okay, that was a surprise, "How did you not know that?"

He shrugged and gave me a genuinely confused look, "I don't know. I could've sworn that I specified all castles in Scotland."

"Does it mean anything for your plans?" I asked with a conspiratorial smile.

He returned it and said, "It just means we're away from my mum for longer. Also we'll need to make up some time as we move to mainland Scotland."

"Wait what?" I asked. Where was he going with this?

"Nope, that one stays a surprise." He said as he helped me up before shifting.

We didn't get to stay at Knock Castle for long. Jameson's mom somehow learned of his plans, and tried to intercept us as we arrived. We were only at the ruins of Knock Castle for twenty minutes when he spotted her coming. We ended up losing her by walking down the narrow shoreline to the nearby beach.

Once that was accomplished, we made our way to a taxi service in town and took the seven to eight minute car ride down to Armadale and it's ruined castle.

We ended up spending most of the rest of the day at Armadale. This ruined castle included a museum, a library and archives, wildlife walks, a shop, and a restaurant. It turned out that the head librarian was an old friend of his grandma, and allowed us to trace our family histories in the archives without an appointment. We found a lot of interesting stuff. Including just how much my family tree diminished after the Parthenian clan attack.

Us hiding there was part of the reason Jameson's mom wasn't able to find us. Most of our time though was spent on the trails, I especially enjoyed watching some of the ocean life from the hills. We even spotted a pod of humpback whales feeding. The museum was excellent, as were the two shops, and the food was fantastic. We chose to eat an early dinner there before heading back into town to get some supplies for later tonight. Apparently he planned on camping out on Carn Eige for the night before continuing to our final destination. Which he still wouldn't disclose to me.

Once again successfully dodging his mother, we began the trip to mainland Scotland. It was nearly eight, so we had just over half an hour to get to the Skye bridge and cross it. By bike it would take almost two hours, but since Jameson was in a hurry to avoid his mom, he left the towns limits at a run.

We reached the Skye bridge with a good ten minutes to spare. There were a lot of people who reacted with shock at the sight of a bear nearly stomping into town before the bridge. He didn't want to risk shifting in front of people, so we stopped outside a building within walking distance of the bridge. He emerged a minute or so later, and we began the little over twenty minute walk across the pedestrian's bridge. Fun fact, the Skye bridge is **not** a toll bridge. We did spot a troll under it at one point near the halfway mark. I couldn't quite make it out until I used my dragon eyes.

"A fragglewump." I exclaimed.

"No!" Jameson sounded fascinated.

I pointed it out to him just before it fully retreated to its lair. Those of you who have seen Hellboy 2: the Golden Army will know what kind of troll I speak of. It truly is very ugly.

Once across, Jameson wasted no time in finding a place to shift. It didn't take him long to circumnavigate the town and head out into the country side. Even with the waxing crescent moon, bears have excellent night vision, so Jameson had no trouble navigating the country side until we reached the base of Carn Eige. He may have taken his time, but he still made the journey in almost two hours.

We stopped and made camp about a quarter of the way up the mountain. At 1,183 meters above sea level, it wasn't technically that high, Carn Eige is only the twelfth tallest mountain in the British isles, but the tallest in northern Scotland. We found some flat ground and made our tents. I'd done it before so I was finished first. I got a fire going while he finished his, and started a hash in the 16 inch cast iron pan he'd packed, with some of the ingredients we'd bought in Armadale.

The hash eaten, we sat and watched the semi clear sky. He held me in his arms until about midnight, then a light rain started. Laughing, we retreated to our tents to sleep.

Chapter 67

It wasn't until I smelled more hash being cooked the next morning that I realized we'd left without either of my pills. I shrugged it off though, I'd been thoroughly exhausted last night. I stretched, changed my clothes, then emerged from my tent, stretching even more. I sat down next to Jameson, and accepted the plate he offered me. That was when I realized something; his caloric intake might not be where it was supposed to be for this trip. As a dragon I maximize my caloric use, hence why I needed high in protein meals, but no more than the usual number of meals each day like a human.

After one mouthful I posed my question, "Don't you need more calories than this?"

He swallowed before asking, "How do you mean?"

"A standard grizzly male needs 100,000 calories a day, you being a huge grizzly shifter would need," I paused and did the calculations, "holy shit, 500 to 600,000 calories a day. At least. And your still growing!" I finished.

He laughed, "I guess it's a good thing that I don't need to hibernate than." I just gave him a confused look, so he explained, "I don't need to use my fat reserves for hibernation. I learned a long time ago that it was more efficient for me to use them in a different way."

It clicked, "You learned to maximize your caloric intake."

"Yep. My dad said that because of some long term operations in the military, even soldiers are trained as such, I just got started on mine earlier than most people."

"Well good, 'cause you had me worried." I replied, and we finished our meal shortly after.

We got moving about an hour later, after we'd washed the pan and packed the tents. He still insisted on doing all the walking and running, saying that his stamina needed the training. I chuckled at his excuse to stay the 'work animal' as he put it, but I didn't argue.

He didn't actually run, it was more of a jog, but we reached our final destination in just over an hour and a half. My eyes widened and I just lit up when I saw where we were heading. I knew Loch Ness anywhere. I'd seen enough pictures and videos. Giggling like a mad fool, I slid off Jameson's back and hugged him around the neck. I felt his pulse quicken as I did so. When I pulled back, he had the biggest smile on his face. I quickly hopped back up and he made his way down the hill toward Drumnadrochit.

A friend of his met us at the Loch Ness Centre and Exhibition. From there he gave Jameson a set of tickets – after Jameson shifted of course – and loading our bags into the trunk of his car, had us get into the back and we all drove down to Blairbeg Park. I noticed just how crowded it was when we arrived, then it hit me.

"Are these the Highland Games?!" I'd always wanted to see the Highland Games!

Jameson nodded, "The Glenurquhart Highland Games. Held here every year."

Once again, I grabbed Jameson and hugged him. It wasn't until we were actually outside the car that I gave him my full appreciation. I grabbed his shirt collar and pulled him down, kissing him full on the mouth. I'll never forget the look on his face when I pulled away after a few seconds. It wasn't until his friend chuckled at his expression that the blush appeared and he tuned back into reality. Just as he'd done in Glasgow after we'd returned from the Devil's Pulpit, he offered his arm, and I took it. We walked down to the stands to find our seats.

I can't tell you how much fun it was watching the games. His friend had gotten us some awesome seats near the front of the viewing stands. We spent the entire day watching the games. We came away with some cool souvenirs too. Two t-shirs apiece, plus Jameson bought himself a water bottle, and me a Scottish tartan with a standard plaid pattern.

Wrapped in said tartan, we took a boat tour on the Loch after the games were over. Jameson had already made plans to spend the night at a nearby hotel, so we were covered there. I was minding my own business with Jameson at my side, when the boat started rocking violently. Jameson managed to grab hold of the rail, but the sudden momentum didn't agree with my leg, and I went over. I felt Jameson grab my tartan and it came off just before I hit the water.

The freezing cold water stunned me really badly. I nearly lost the breath I was holding. Thankfully my dad's cold water training kicked in, and I was able to save my breath. And don't shout at my dad about the cold water training, we all three of us asked for it before he'd even thought about adding it to our regime.

I shook my head and looked around before starting back to the surface. I stopped looking when I saw the giant pair of eyes attached to the creature that had been rocking the boat. Nessie, in all her glory.

I couldn't believe my eyes. I closed them and shook my head again to make sure I wasn't seeing things. She was still there when I opened them. I reached out a hand to touch her snout, and she pushed forward into my hand. I laughed in awe the best I could.

"You are never alone little sister." She said telepathically, before turning and swimming away.

As she swam, I could see that she wasn't a plesiosaur, but a plesiosaur-like sea dragon. A long nearly serpentine body, with long slender flippers down her belly. I watched her swim away until she was out of sight, then swam to the surface.

Sputtering, I accepted the rope someone had tossed over broad for me to grab. Once back aboard, I was wrapped in blanket after blanket to try and warm me up. They needn't have worried, as a dragon, I technically couldn't catch hypothermia or pneumonia. But I didn't tell them that. Jameson came over with my tartan in hand and placed it as the last item around my shoulders.

The boat quickly made port. They asked if we wanted an ambulance, but since I knew everything I needed about keeping hypothermia at bay, they called a cab instead. From the boatyard, we were taken to the small but comfortable Aslaich Hotel on the River Coiltie. Because of the games, it was almost fully booked, so the only room left was a couple's suite. That meant only one bed. Honestly, it was fine by me, just because I couldn't catch hypothermia didn't mean I like being excessively cold. Sharing a bed would be good for me health wise.

Once in our room, Jameson started a hot shower. I moved around to keep my blood flowing as he did. When it was ready, he left the bathroom and I was left to bathe. I felt much better not long after.

I came out of the bathroom to find Jameson had ordered room service and had a plan for the bed. I would sleep under both sheet and blanket, he'd sleep under just the blanket. It was a beautiful comforter and thick enough to cover both of us without a problem.

We talked as we ate. He was amazed that I had not only seen the Loch Ness monster, but had been spoken to by her. If I hadn't seen and felt it all myself, I might not have believed it.

I had lain down for bed when someone came by to collect the dishes from our dinner. Jameson waited until I got comfortable before he laid down himself. He made sure I was fully covered before he placed his arm over my waist, and his head behind mine. I smiled, his warmth was reassuring as I drifted off to full sleep.

It was only then that I realized something; how in the world had Nessie known I was in that boat? It's not like I advertised my presence. So how had she known?

The question would have to wait, I needed to get some sleep. I once again began to drift off. For the first time in months, I had a really good dream. One that I remember to this day.

Chapter 68

After breakfast the next morning, I found out Jameson wasn't done with our trip to Drumnadrochit. We hadn't gotten to see the ruins of Urquhart yesterday and we both wanted to visit. We made sure we had everything collected when we packed up. I made up the bed, and straightened things around before we actually checked out. The weather was cloudy and cool, so I wrapped my tartan around me like a shawl, and we went off into main Drumnadrochit.

We both greatly enjoyed walking around the Urquhart ruins. There was one family there that we'd encountered at Dunscaith who recognized us. Their son asked if I would go dragon here like I had on the shore back at Dunscaith, I told him I was unsure if it would be okay with the people who looked after the ruins.

He was pretty disappointed until the very caretakers came over and said they didn't mind. They actually thought it would help raise their tourist money if a shifter was seen there. Turns out they'd been down on money the last few months and needed the extra help. So Jameson and I both decided to help out. The little boys eyes lit up. We asked the family to keep an eye on our bags while we obliged the caretakers.

We ended up spending over two hours at the ruins. Neither of us minded, we were both having a good time. The little boy couldn't leave me alone, he was so happy to see a real live dragon.

When we were finally able to leave, Jameson and I took a cab back up to the center we'd met his friend at. We took that tour, as well as one available at Nessieland – only half a block away – and stopped there for lunch before visiting the available gift shops. We also took cover from the light rain.

Once again despite my protests, he bought me a slew of jewelry at one said shop. My Gods don't even get me started on the price of some of the things he bought. I know the difference between dollars and pounds when it comes to actual money. Here's one example, one of the necklaces he bought me cost 147 pounds, that translates to 170 American dollars. Eventually I asked if he was trying to spoil me. His answer honestly surprised me.

"No." he paused, with a wistful smile on his face, "My grandmother on my mum's side left me a proverbial fortune when she died. She also gave me a piece of advice. That when I met my mate, I would take care of her in every way possible. Like you, she suffered from severe depression when her brother committed suicide in front of her when she was younger. My grandfather helped her get back to normal."

"How?" I asked.

"He did the same thing I've been doing. Not to spoil her but to give her plenty of keepsakes that she could fondly look back on and remember good times."

I chuckled, "Did it work?"

He nodded, still smiling, "She eventually was able to move on and pull through. She was buried with her favorite pieces and left the rest to my mother."

I smiled sadly, "Least you got to say good-bye to yours." I tried to swallow back the lump in my throat, but it wouldn't go. I also did my best to keep my emotions in check as I felt tears threaten. I would **not** cry here in public.

He came forward and wrapped his arms around me in a sympathetic hug. I quietly chuckled to myself. Here he was buying me jewelry for one of the most unexpected reasons ever, and I had been worried he'd run out of money he might need for other things.

It also made me wonder how his mother felt about him inheriting the money rather than her.

I decided to leave that conversation till later. From Nessieland, we went down to one of the waterfalls that was within driving distance. The Falls of Divach. A one hundred foot tall waterfall that feeds into the River Coiltie, then down to Urquhart Bay. Despite it's spelling, it's actually pronounced 'jeevach'. I spent the time watching the water flow, and admiring the brooch pin that Jameson had bought me at the Center gift shop. I was using it to hold my tartan closed so I wouldn't have to.

The next falls were across the lake, so we took one of the other available boat tours, neither of us really wanted to take the nearly hour long drive around the lake. And that was going either north or south. Jameson kept a strong hold of me the whole way. He really didn't want me to take another dip like I had last night. I spent the whole boat ride wondering how Nessie had known I was in the boat last night. Thinking on it, most dragons could sense each other once within a certain distance. But that wasn't a guaranteed method when applied to Nessie. Even the shifter community wasn't 100% sure if she counted as a dragon or not. Most said sea serpent, but the two were almost perfectly identical, so any differences – no matter how small – barely counted. Now that I had seen her for myself, I was convinced that she was indeed some kind of sea dragon. Maybe not one of my ancestors who could take human form, but a dragon none the less.

The boat landed at the adjacent dock only about twenty minutes after we'd left the first one. We stopped at the Loch Ness Shores Camping and Caravanning Club site and rented some bikes that he'd called ahead about the day before. The club didn't usually rent out bikes but they made an exception for Jameson. I finally asked how so many people were able to owe him favors. He responded by saying he'd tutored several of the various family teens and they had promised him whatever favor he would call in. I guess high ranking high schools have their advantages.

The day was still cloudy, but it had warmed a little now that it was just after two o'clock. We passed quite a few other tourists on the fourteen minute ride to the Falls of Foyers.

Unfortunately we didn't get to enjoy our time there. A certain jealous ex-classmate was on site with her rather small number of groupies. I smelled Elizabeth's excessively strong perfume before Jameson did. We made it to the parking lot before we actually saw them though. Obviously Jameson was less then pleased.

We dismounted out bikes as she started walking up to us. Her friends tried to hold her back, she did look pretty hysterical. Jameson left our bikes and me by the ramp leading up to the attached café. I leaned against the rail of said ramp while he went over to buy the trail map. I didn't take my eyes off of Elizabeth. Her friends had succeeded in holding her back, but she was staring at me with such malice that I was more worried for the safety of her friends than hers.

We moved off down the appropriate trail when Jameson came back with the map. We tried to enjoy the walk but Elizabeth was at the forefront of our minds the whole way. We did finally relax a little when we arrived at the falls upper viewing area, and were able to put Elizabeth out of our minds entirely by the time we made the lower viewing area. We really shouldn't have.

Jameson once again had his arm over my shoulders when we heard the surrounding wildlife flee. We both heard Elizabeth running toward us, but only I recognized the smell of metal in her hand as a gun. I pulled out my phone and carefully placed it on a rock, making sure to place loose plant life around it to keep her from seeing it, but not keep the camera from recording the next few moments for future purposes. I was really glad I did.

Jameson stood between me and her, with my phone being given a perfect view. Elizabeth stood panting before us, her hair now wild from her run through the woods after us, her arms and lower legs scratched up from shrubbery, and the Sig Sauer p238 in her hand shaking as she held it in a death grip. A modern version of a six shooter as my dad called it. Where she had gotten the gun I didn't know, but I knew enough about the possible situation to keep on my toes.

"I won't let you leave Jameson. If I can't have you. No one can." Was all she said before raising her hand.

Jameson beat me to the punch. He pushed me down as the bullet took him in the left shoulder. Time seemed to freeze as I watched Jameson fall backward from the sudden force of the blow. Then instinct took over. Pulling my tartan over my head, I dropped it over Jameson and turned back to Elizabeth. She still held the gun, but now she only had five shots left in the mag. I shifted just before she pulled the trigger again.

I placed Jameson beneath me and folded my wings over my front legs while keeping my head over them. She aimed the last four shots at my head when she realized that my wings had deflected the last bullet. She kept pulling the trigger after she was empty. In her further hysteria, she threw down the gun and pulled a knife from the back of her shorts. Smoke billowing from my mouth and nostrils, I let her run at me. What she didn't see was my tail waiting just behind my wings.

Quick as lightning, I lashed my tail forward and gripped her around the throat, not bad enough to kill or wound her, but enough for her to drop the knife as I lifted her off the ground. I could easily have killed her for hurting Jameson, but I knew he wouldn't want that. Seeing her friends coming up the trail with two police officers also kept me from strangling her.

Her friends stopped about thirty feet away from me. The officers however kept coming, neither carried a gun, but they did carry batons. Elizabeth was too afraid of me to start talking, but Jameson was more than capable.

"Back here officers." Was about all he could manage. They made to move around me, but stopped when I growled at them.

"Are you all right son?" the older one asked. His brow covered in sweat from his long run.

"I've been shot. This dragon is my mate." He explained. The two officers seemed confused.

One of Elizabeth's friends spoke up, "Jameson is a bear shifter sirs."

The officers nodded, "I see." One said, "Well could you ask your mate to stand down."

Without Jameson doing so, I gently moved off so that they could examine him. I growled every time he winced as they checked his shoulder. They managed to keep their heads though. It was then that Elizabeth decided to try and move the situation in her favor.

"This bitch is the one who shot him! He's delirious! Don't believe a word!" she shouted while trying to pry my tail off. I simply tightened it a little. Finally one of the officers looked up.

"It's just a graze, it bounced off his collarbone." The older one informed me.

"I'm afraid son, we might have to take the young lady's word for it." The younger one said as he helped Jameson up.

"No you won't." Jameson walked over and removed my phone from its hiding spot, his right hand over the open wound the whole way, "My mate recorded the whole thing."

I watched Elizabeth out of the corner of my eye and saw her sag in defeat as she realized that the jig was up.

The ride back to Drumnadrochit was not in any way pleasant. Not only had his mother been called, but so had Mr. McHaddish and Mr. Hydell – once a signal could be acquired anyway. No need to explain how his mother took the news. I cannot however say how the other two reacted. I was more worried about Jameson. The officers had been right, because of how Jameson had moved, the bullet had only grazed his collar bone. It didn't stop him from being in pain though.

Thankfully when we arrived at the police station, it was Mr. McHaddish waiting for us instead of his mother. He took one look at both of us and ushered us in himself. The gun and knife were in my backpack inside of two plastic bags. They were pulled out as the officers reviewed the footage on my phone again. Their station chief commended me on my quick thinking, both with the phone and protecting Jameson. He also asked why Jameson wasn't healed yet. Simple answer; there was dirt in the wound, it needed to be cleaned first.

The first parent to arrive was Elizabeth's father. He refused to believe a single word of the story until the chief showed him the video. I dare not even describe the rage on his face as he turned to look at his daughter. He didn't strike her, but his features left no doubt of future punishment for her stupid and dangerous actions. And of course as a rather highly respected family, her actions were shameful and she'd be paying for those as well.

I didn't give a damn about the respect implications one bit. Mr. McHaddish finally had Mr. Hydell on the phone and I needed to explain the situation to him and Molly. One of the other officers came out with a med kit so that Jameson could clean the graze. Once it was cleaned, the wound finished closing, leaving a very light scar behind.

Mrs. Billings arrived with her husband while I was on the phone. Thank goodness for me on that one. It meant she would have to wait to try and grill me. Jameson tried to beat her to it though. He wrapped his uninjured arm around me and kissed my head. I smiled up at him before he moved off to try and waylay his mother.

Needless to say that ended our trip to Drumnadrochit. We met up with Mack at the Inverness airport a little over half an hour away, and were flown back to the estate. Jameson's mom was glaring daggers at me the whole forty five minute flight back. I didn't care. We had both done what we were supposed to do by ancient law. Protect our mate. Yes, Jameson had been hurt, but it's not like it was a permanent injury like mine was. Just before landing, Jameson placed his hand over mine and gave me a reassuring smile.

Thankfully his mother's verbal repercussions against me were once again waylaid by Reggie and Matilda waiting for me at the front steps. Reggie's arms were crossed in front of him as I exited the car and Matilda came over to ask if I was okay. I gave them the quick and ugly version. Reggie's mouth got a pinched look as I explained the incident. The unexpected bit was what really got Mrs. Billings going.

Reggie came down the steps, placed his hand at my back to lead me back inside, turned to Jameson and said, "Thank you."

Jameson simply nodded, but from the smile on his face, I could tell that Reggie's 'thank you' meant a lot to him that day. His mother on the other hand, got this look on her face like she couldn't believe that someone had actually been glad that her son was hurt. The three of us however, kept walking inside so that Jameson could explain to her what my brother actually meant.

I made it back up to my room with my bag before Reggie and Matilda left me alone and went back to theirs. I closed and locked the door. I really wanted to know if Jameson and his mom would be able to work it out, but I resisted the impulse to walk over to the window and open it. This wasn't a conversation I needed to overhear. So instead, I began unpacking my bag. I sorted my new jewelry and placed it all inside my suitcase. I then held up the plans that Ms. Hamper had given me three months ago. I double checked when I would be heading home. My return ticket said the 30th. Today was the 27th. I had two more days in Scotland.

So that gave me two weeks before school started to reacclimate myself back to California. I put the packet away and pulled out my laptop. There were two emails from Mr. Hydell that he'd sent yesterday. One was a thank you for the color choices, the other was about getting the apartment to myself that first day back. Apparently, there was some problem with their tickets home, and they were going to have to wait a day. I sent back a reply letting them know I understood.

I then realized that I hadn't gotten either of them a souvenir like I had promised. I face-palmed and got thinking. I'd noticed Jameson had bought me a necklace that I had already bought at another place, I could easily give Molly the one I had bought and keep Jameson's. Mr. Hydell was another matter. Then I remembered the water bottle I'd bought at the outdoors store we'd stopped at in Glasgow back in June. So there, they were both covered. I knew that neither would mind how I had chosen the gifts.

That done, I looked at my phone to check time. I know I should've done it before I'd shut my computer off, but it hadn't occurred to me until it was already off. Noon. I put my laptop aside and left my room to get some lunch.

Chapter 69

I made a quick sandwich and grabbed a couple handfuls of various nuts from the kitchen and took everything up to the library. I settled into my usual chair after grabbing a Sherlock Holmes novel and ate my lunch quietly.

I finished my food before my book, but I wasn't able to finish the book at all. Jameson's mom ended up having a shouting match with Mrs. Granger right outside the library. I only started listening when I heard my name. Not even trying, I snuck over to the door and listened.

"What do you have against Maggie in the first place Mildred?" said Mrs. Granger, trying to defuse the situation.

"What I have against her is the fact that she is driving a wedge between me and my son." Oh, yeah, right. That's your doing lady, not mine.

"No she is not. You are. You can't hold onto your son like this forever."

"What do you know Jennifer? You don't have any children." Mrs. Billings asked.

I heard Mrs. Granger's sharp intake of breath, "I do in fact have a daughter. And a sister who has two sons. I know from watching her that you are having an extremely negative affect on your son."

"I'm sorry, I truly didn't know."

"Clearly." Said Mrs. Granger. Ouch. Burn.

I heard Mrs. Billings swallow back her first response, "When does Maggie leave?"

"Why do you want to know?"

"I'm curious." You don't lie very well Mrs. Billings.

Mrs. Granger sensed it too, "She leaves sometime this week, after Ms. Hamper's evaluation."

"Evaluation for what?" oh good grief.

"Her mental and emotional state," Mrs. Granger stated, "or did you forget why she was here in the first place."

Mrs. Billings had the decency to feel guilty, based on her tone, "I honestly did forget."

"Well could you at least put aside your animosities toward her about your son long enough for her to receive a positive evaluation."

"Yes. I can." Mrs. Billings stated.

Somehow I doubted it. But I was willing to give her a chance since she was Jameson's mom. I stayed by the door until I heard Mrs. Granger walk away. I was about to head back to my chair when I caught Mrs. Billings saying something to herself.

"My son is going nowhere near that girl again. I'll cancel the transfer and get him back into his school here."

Oh I don't think so miss lady. I waited and listened as she moved back downstairs. Then sent out a psychic wave to locate Mr. McHaddish. Once I found him, I gathered my dishes and went down to the kitchen. I found him discussing dinner plans with Malcolm. I pulled him away long enough to inform him of Mrs. Billings' plans.

He immediately went off to talk with her. From his demeanor, it would not be a polite conversation. That done, I was about to make my way back up to the library when Jameson called my name. I turned to meet him at the bottom of the stairs.

"What's up?" he asked.

"I just told Mr. McHaddish about your mom planning to undo your school transfer." I stated.

He got this look on his face, like he was about to be sick, while also being extremely angry. He clenched his hands into fists, then without much warning, he grabbed my hand and led me upstairs. We continued up until we reached the roof.

He stopped just short of the patio furniture and turned to look me in the eyes. He seemed to hesitate, then he did something I had never expected. He pulled a small box from his pocket. I was about to protest when he held up his hand.

"I'm not proposing." He chuckled at the relief on my face, "But I am giving you a ring."

I raised my eyebrows, "I don't understand."

"My mum doesn't know it, but I met my grandparents on my biological father's side. They are nothing like their son used to be, thank goodness."

"And?"

"And my grandpa gave me this ring. He said that it was a tradition in his family that the male give their mate a ring before the actual engagement as a sign of love."

"A promise ring basically." I stated. Blushing slightly at the prospect. He smiled, "Yeah."

Without another word, he opened the box and pulled out the most beautiful ring I had ever seen. A gold band in the form of two dragons holding a small black fire opal in their conjoined hands, their tails intertwined on the opposite side of the gem. Both the dragons' eyes were sapphire chips that shone as much as the gold. Engraved within, was the saying 'Simply meant to be.'

He grabbed my right hand and placed the ring on my ring finger. Obviously it was enchanted, because it shrunk down to perfectly fit my finger. I nearly started crying as I admired it. Jameson put the box back in his pocket and took my hand in his. Using his other hand, he lifted my face to meet his eyes.

"Tha Gaol Agam Ort." He whispered. 'I love you' in Scottish Gaelic.

"I love you too." I whispered back. We began leaning in to kiss.

"JINGS, CRIVENS, HELP MA BOAB!!!!"

We both started at the sudden shout from the doorway. We turned to see his mother standing there. Her face a very livid shade of red. She stormed forward and pulled back her hand. We both knew what was coming. Jameson stepped out and grabbed her wrist before she could fully bring it toward my face.

"Don't touch my mate mother." Anyone with sense would've backed down. Clearly she didn't.

"I would speak with you my son. Now."

"About what, you deciding to cancel my school transfer without speaking to either me or dad."

Her face said it all. Then she turned to me, I just shrugged. It was not wise to keep such information from ones mate, not when it could affect both of them.

"I would speak with my son alone." she reiterated.

I looked up at Jameson and he nodded. So, quietly, I moved away and started walking toward the door. I was almost there when I heard his mother whisper 'thieving bitch'. Without really thinking, I turned and went back toward her. Thankfully Jameson caught my arm before it reached her. Now she looked worried if not afraid. Serves you right bitch.

"Maggie." Was all Jameson said.

I looked up to meet his eyes. He wasn't happy with her or me. So taking a steadying breath, I yanked my arm from his grip and finished my journey back inside. But now I was seething. I could feel the smoke coming out of my nose. I stopped at the bottom of the roof stairs. My hands began twitching. I needed to do something to work off the anger, so I analyzed my feelings. Video games wouldn't do it, I'd be liable to destroy either the controller or other pieces of the room. I didn't feel like going flying, and my brother was preoccupied, so no sparring.

Finally I caught the scent of wood oils. I then remembered that the music room was one story down, and Jameson had mentioned there was a violin inside.

Making up my mind, I went to the stairs and made my way down a landing. I had to look around a little to find the room, but when I did, I felt myself calm down a little. I walked around, admiring the assortment of instruments available. I finally found the violin and picked it up. I took a minute to tune it, then started playing.

It felt good to play again after a few months. I played until my fingers were sore. But it allowed me to vent my frustrations without hurting anyone. At one point, I looked up at the clock on the wall and saw that I'd been playing for almost two hours. I lowered the violin to rest, then noticed the small audience at the door. I suddenly felt very shy.

I saw that both Mrs. Granger and Gretchen had tears in their eyes. I only realized then that I'd lapsed into mournful music a few songs ago. Amazingly enough, I felt liberated about that. Like I had finally let something go. Then I heard sniffling, and recognized Reggie's breathing.

Moving past everyone else, he pushed his way into the room and came toward me. I set the violin down and returned his hug, letting the unshed tears flow into his shirt, as he did the same. Without looking, we heard the rest of the audience disperse. Leaving us alone together.

We stayed like that for several minutes. The only reason we broke apart was because my leg stated acting up. We sat down and just enjoyed our companiable silence for several more minutes. Reggie was getting ready to leave when we heard music come on over the speakers spread out through the room. Ne-Yo's 'Mad'. I gave a small smile as I realized who was playing it.

Without a word, Reggie rose and left the room. Nodding to Jameson as he entered. Jameson looked ashamed of himself, his head hung down as he rubbed his neck. He came over and sat down next to me.

"I'm sorry." He said.

"For what?" I crossed my arms and looked at him.

"For making you mad at me." he sounded sorry.

"Technically I'm mad at your mom. I am **upset** with you."

"Why?" he asked.

"Because you didn't say 'please' and seemed pissed that I had been about to slap her."

He nodded, "I wasn't so much as bealin, just surprised I guess."

I shrugged, "I don't like being called a thief. Especially not by someone who doesn't know or understand me."

"I can understand that."

"So how'd the talk go?" I asked.

"I gave her another ultimatum. Either she let me transfer, or I come anyway – on my own – and I disown her."

"Ouch." My tone conveyed that I thought it was overkill.

He shrugged, "I'm tired of it. I can't take anymore. She needs to except that I'm growing up and don't need her to always protect me."

"Did she accept your terms?" I asked. Trying to lighten the mood.

He chuckled, "Yes. Though she was gritting her teeth the entire time."

It was my turn to chuckle, "When do you head back?" he asked.

"The thirtieth. My flight leaves at nine a.m. You?"

"Not sure. My dad's been having some trouble with a few of the school requirements."

I raised my eyebrows, "Has he talked with Mr. McHaddish?"

"Don't know. I think he was trying to leave that to mum."

I nodded, "Well I hope everything gets figured out."

"Me too." He said with a small smile.

After that, we spent the rest of the day just talking in the library. At one point in our conversations he remembered to tell me that my school's trip had visited the estate on August 7th. So the teacher had been able to swing it after all. I was glad to hear it, and I felt a little funny realizing that my former classmates had been in school for most of the month now, and we had only a few days before ours started. I double checked my phone at one point. Mr. McHaddish had said the 5th of September. Next Tuesday, the day before the full moon.

As we walked down to dinner a few hours later, I asked if he'd gotten the chance to watch the movies I'd mentioned. He answered that he had, and he'd enjoyed both. He also said that his mom had almost caught him while he was watching 'The Last Days on Mars.' The only reason she hadn't was because he'd quickly turned the t.v. off.

We didn't get to talk much during dinner. He got deep in conversation with my brother while I began talking with Matilda and Gretchen. Mr. McHaddish joined us about halfway through and informed me that he would be joining me on my return flight, and acting as my guardian until Molly and Mr. Hydell returned home from Nepal. I didn't mind, honestly I was glad that arrangement had been made. I still wasn't feeling safe on my own.

I decided to skip dessert that night. I wasn't in the mood for cake and wanted to shower before getting some sleep. I wanted to wash off as much of Elizabeth's memory as possible.

Once I was done, I took a sleeping pill, pulled on my p.j.'s and climbed into bed. I took a few minutes to get comfortable before drifting off into yet another dreamless sleep.

Chapter 70

The next two days passed in a blur. I spent some time with my brother before he and Matilda began the long flight back to Costa Rica. I made sure Reggie still had his transport stone with him before they left though. Some instinct said he might need it soon. I really hoped it was wrong.

Jameson and I had a really hard time saying good-bye. Even though we both knew it was only temporary. We nearly missed my flight because we couldn't end our hug. Finally Mr. McHaddish succeeded in separating us and we boarded. I spotted Jameson in the terminal as the plane began its taxi. We waved at each other before the plane began to speed up.

I clenched the arm rest so hard nearby passengers heard the metal groaning. Once I was able to relax, I pulled Eragon out of my carry-on bag. I had finished it back in July and was starting it up again.

I then spent most of the sixteen hour flight in a daze. Barely paying attention to my book, a feeling of apprehension started to settle in my stomach. I had begun seeing California as a danger zone, now that I had spent time away from it. I tried to put it off as Scotland's departing cloudy weather staying with me, but it only worked for so long. Finally I just dozed off.

About an hour before landing, I felt my chair move. I woke up to find it had been leaned back by Mr. McHaddish and now the person behind me was kicking my seat, trying to put it back up. I tried to ignore it, but I finally had enough. I stood up to see that a thirty year old man was behaving like a child. He looked at me like he thought he'd won. Wrong-o dude.

I saw a flight attendant coming toward him with a bottle of champagne and a glass. I kneeled in my seat, Mr. McHaddish was nowhere to be seen. As the flight attendant passed him the glass I reached over and snatched the bottle from her.

The man chuckled, "Sorry sweetheart, your too young for that." He held out his hand. A shit eating grin on his face.

I growled. The flight attendant backed up a step as I met the man's eyes, "Stop kicking my chair fucktard, or this is what I'm going to do to you."

As lightly as possible, I flicked the bottle of champagne. Cracks immediately spider webbed across the entire bottle. He blanched as he fully realized what I was. He nodded and I gave him the bottle. Since the cracks went all the way through the glass, the bottle shattered in his lap. He immediately got up to go to the bathroom and nearly ran into Mr. McHaddish, on his way back from the bathroom. He took in the rushing man, the flight attendant coming back with a towel to clean up the glass, and simply smiled.

"Making friends, or pulling an Arnold Schwarzenegger?" he asked.

I chuckled, obviously he meant 'Kindergarten Cop', "Arnold."

He nodded and spoke to the flight attendant. I didn't catch that conversation though. By the time he sat back down, I was already fast asleep again.

I slept for the rest of the flight, the disembarking, and the departure from the airport. I didn't wake up until Mr. McHaddish was pulling into my buildings parking lot. I just barely managed to walk to the elevator and then to my door. I did manage to unlock the door and remember to sniff around. Thankfully all I smelled was staleness. No one had entered the apartment since we'd left. Fine by me.

Mr. McHaddish entered behind me and locked the door after closing it. He then steered me to my room. I took a deep breathe there too. Same staleness. Good. I dropped my bags on the floor and collapsed on my bed.

I woke up at about seven thirty the next morning. It felt weird to wake up in a more southern climate again. I stood up and stretched my limbs. My leg twinged as I went to stand up. I guess it wasn't happy about me being carried around at the airport. So, grabbing a fresh set of clothes, I stood and walked to the bathroom to shower.

I felt a little better afterwards. At least physically. I thought back to my evaluation with Ms. Hamper the day before we'd left. She had said I'd made excellent progress and could stop any further sessions if necessary. I'd decided not to of course. I wanted to play it safe until Kepner was officially dead. She was okay with that.

I came out to find Mr. McHaddish making pancakes. Chocolate chips pancakes at that. Yum! I came over and took three from the rather significant pile he'd created while I was bathing. He smiled as I added a small bit of butter to each and then the syrup. He then passed me a glass of chocolate milk before telling me that he'd gotten a call from Mr. Hydell shortly after we'd arrived. They'd finally gotten in the air right after I'd fallen back to sleep. We'd gotten back here at half past one in the morning so that meant – since Nepal was almost fourteen hours ahead of California – that they'd boarded the plane at two o'clock Nepal time.

I double checked my phone to be sure. Yep. That meant a twenty-two hour flight home. So they'd be home by one or two a.m. tonight. Mr. McHaddish then told me that he wanted me to have a packing plan in place before he went out to get boxes. I nodded past my mouthful and he simply smiled. I laid out my packing plan before he left.

Just before he left, Jim came up to tell me that a package had just been delivered and obviously was too big to put in the box. I knew what it was when I caught a glimpse of the paper used to wrap it. It was my dress from Emily and Amber. But how'd they know I was back from Scotland. I got my answer when I looked at Mr. McHaddish. His smile said it all. I returned his smile and took the box to my room. I made sure to smell it first to make sure it hadn't been tampered with in anyway. Emily and Amber were the only ones I could smell on it, other than a slight whiff from Jim.

I was still careful about opening it though. Thankfully my precautions were unnecessary. I opened the box the rest of the way, and found a note on top of the paper wrappings. 'Hope you enjoyed Scotland. Now we hope you enjoy the dress! Emily and Amber.' It said. I smiled and placed the note off to the side before removing the paper. It was just as Emily had drawn it. So beautiful. The almost delicate beading depicted perfect cherry blossom branches.

I grabbed it by the shoulders and gently pulled it from the box. Emily was true to her design, the bell sleeves ended just short of the floor, and the Chinese dragon embroidered on the skirt was equally perfect. They'd also thrown in some other colors to help the dragon and blossoms stand out a bit more. Even the zipper at the back blended in almost seamlessly. A button finished the neckline.

I laid the dress out on my bed covers, from there, I was able to spot the small belt like string of beads that would be the detaching mechanism for the skirt. Without wasting another minute, I closed my door and curtains, and removed my shirt and jeans to try the dress on.

It fit perfectly. I didn't need to adjust anything. Although I did test out the detaching cord. It worked like a charm, and the skirt was loose enough that I could wear a weapons belt and no one would be able to see it or the weapons it would be holding. I quickly double checked that before pulling out my spell equipment. I looked at my book of spells – which I had left here – to double check how to reword it so that it included tearing. The last thing I wanted was to damage it in any way.

My mom had given each of us a book to write spells in when we reached twelve years of age. Reggie's was almost full to the point of needing a new book. Amanda's had been half full. My wasn't very full. I preferred to do small stuff myself. Most of what was in my spell book were – of course – the protection spells, the instant transport spell, and a few minor glamour spells. I thought back to over the summer and added the spells I'd created.

I made the usual preparations, and began my spell. The telltale wind started out slowly this time, building as it got to the more important forms of protection. I even made sure to add in that only I could change the dress in anyway. Like a small repair. That way if anyone tried to destroy or sabotage it, they wouldn't succeed.

I'd been wearing the dress during the spell to make sure the whole thing was covered. Amanda had tried to perform a similar spell at sixteen and had the item of clothing on the floor. The spell for some reason had completely missed the very back of the item. She had been livid at the dry cleaning bill. She'd never done designer clothes ever again after that.

I returned everything to their proper places after performing small tests to make sure the spells had worked. Since this was fabric, I had left out water itself. I mean the thing would need to be washed, but anything else liquid related wouldn't be a problem. Not even blood.

I removed the dress and replaced it within its box. I listened as Mr. McHaddish returned with the boxes necessary for the move. I'd thought back over the plan while replacing the dress. All the books would go into one box, any clothing – minus new dress and kimono – would go straight into bags or if necessary could be used as padding for more fragile stuff.

Today was the 31st, and Mr. Hydell had told me that my stuff could be moved over on Saturday. That way I could kill two birds with one stone, I'd get my things to the school, and I'd get the official tour of the campus. Knowing Mr. Hydell, he'd go over the day before I did and look it over himself. So Friday the first of September. That gave me the whole weekend to acclimate to the school, and a day to spend with him and Molly before school started. Well then it was official, a plan was in place.

Chapter 71

The packing went well. Most of my clothes wasn't used for padding but a few things were. Like for my lamp and some keepsakes from trips in my childhood that had survived the explosion. I left my bedding on my bed for now, I'd pack that up when Mr. Hydell went to take a look at the campus. We ate leftover pancakes for lunch, then ordered pizza for dinner.

While eating, Mr. McHaddish gave me a surprise. He'd called and talked to Reggie – using a new phone – and had asked about my hobbies. He then pulled a medium sized box out from under the bar and passed it to me. Inside was an assortment of acrylic paints. Over three dozen different shades, along with several brushes in various sizes. At the bottom were mixing tools, a pallet, and a scrapper. Plus I found some charcoal pencils alongside a small sketch pad. I felt tears threaten and thanked Mr. McHaddish in a near choked voice.

His responding your welcome was a half dozen canvas packs in various sizes. I came around the bar and hugged him. Now that I was feeling more like myself, I could finally paint again.

He returned my hug and pointed to a pile of old newspapers. I took the hint and set up several along the floor. My back would be to my bedroom door and the windows to my front. I went to my room and pulled out my collapsible painting easel, as well as an old shirt of my dad's that I'd always used for painting. I didn't need to wear it anymore, but he'd been the one to teach me how to paint, so it had sentimental value.

I set up my easel so that I could sit and paint rather than semi stand. I grabbed the box of supplies, a chair, and went over to my little set up. I thought about what to paint. Finally I decided on Kilt Rock. I took out a standard lead pencil and sketched out a simple outline to start. Once I had it where I wanted it, I got to work.

Kilt Rock quickly came into being on the canvas. I took my time, but my dad had told me that I had a talent for it that he never did. I kept my strokes even and slow. Making sure to keep an eye on where the strokes needed to be either long or short. Mr. McHaddish turned on some of the lights when the dark got to almost too much. He never once stepped passed me to see my progress. I was glad for that. I didn't like people seeing my work before it was done.

Finally the landscape was finished, but it still seemed empty. I pulled back and thought, tapping the end of the brush against my lower lip as I did. I looked down at my shirt and made a decision.

Two hours later, with tears in my eyes, the painting was finished. A perfect rendering of my family stood along the top of Kilt Rock now. My mother near the pinnacle in her high priestess robes, them flowing in the wind and her staff held in her hand. A staff that had burned in the explosion. My father, myself, and my siblings all in dragon form behind her. It made me sad to see it. My father had insisted on never being in dragon form around us until my siblings' final finishing's. Obviously I would never get that opportunity, so it made my heart ache at the lost moment.

My dad hadn't been finished growing when he'd died, so my siblings and I were about shoulder height on him. Well, I should say they were about shoulder height. I only made mid humerus, and that was at the top of our heads. So needless to say our father had still been pretty tall in dragon form.

With a last bit of paint, I signed the bottom right hand corner with my signature. I let the tears flow as I admired my first painting in almost a year. It would take several hours to fully dry, so I got up, removed some of the newspapers so the easel wouldn't slip, and began cleaning my brushes.

While cleaning, Mr. McHaddish told me that he was heading to the airport to pick up Molly and Mr. Hydell. I looked at the oven clock. I hadn't realized the time. I nodded and said okay as he walked out the door. I went to the outdoor camera and turned it on.

I watched him walk down the hall and board the elevator. I went over and locked the door. I then played it safe and set up a chair so that I could watch the video screen. I'd wait to put everything away when they all returned.

Even though nothing happened while I watched, I was glad I had. I was there to open the door when the three adults returned to the apartment. Molly and Mr. Hydell went straight to bed. I followed suit after putting my things away and bidding good-night to Mr. McHaddish, who planned to stay the night for safety purposes.

The next morning I awoke to the sound of the adults moving about in the kitchen. I went to stand and nearly collapsed. Quickly, I snatched my brace from its place and slipped it on. I winced a little as I tightened it. I hadn't realized that I'd put on some muscle since last wearing it. That was only a few days ago but the difference was there. I'd last worn it when Jameson and I had camped the day before the trip to Drumnadrochit.

Once it was secure I stood and walked out to get food. They'd gone for simple breakfast today. Cereal and milk. I grabbed the Cocoa Pebbles and poured on some milk. Molly's hair was up in a towel and Mr. Hydell was making a quick phone call.

I look toward Mr. McHaddish. I could only guess that the papers in front of him were maps of the campus. He slip one of the papers my way. I pulled it the rest of the way. It was a lay out of the third floor. All of the vacant rooms were blank, and there were quite a few of vacant rooms available.

"Not a lot of flyers at the school?" I asked.

He shook his head, "The only ones are all half fae, and each of them has wings, so a room on the top floor was requested instead of required."

"Thirty rooms per floor," Molly started, "are all of them in use?" she asked.

"Most of them. Currently, there are 83 students. It'll be 85 when Maggie and Jameson officially start." Mr. McHaddish confirmed.

"What are the groupings?" Mr. Hydell asked, now that he was done with his call.

Mr. McHaddish double checked his notes, "Aside from the three half fae girls, there are seventeen full fae students, 28 witches and warlocks, another thirty-two shifters, one troll, one goblin, and one necromancer."

"Damn!" Mr. Hydell chuckled, "That's quite a group."

Mr. McHaddish nodded, "It certainly is. But I should amend my numbers, Maggie and Jameson won't be the only new students. Two other shifters are starting this year too, so 87 total. Hence why I wanted you to be the first to choose your room."

"Both dragons?" I asked. He nodded.

I examined the lay out. The rooms were perfect squares, 25 by 25 for most of them. There were two sets of stairs leading up to the third floor. The first one on the south side of the building, the second on the north side. The landing split the first ten rooms along the west wall, and most of that wall was one big window with chairs placed in front of it. The five northern rooms each had another room across from them while the southern rooms, only four of them had an adjacent room. I unfolded the lay out to find that the other eleven rooms were placed down hallways facing north and south. Six to the north and five to the south.

Thinking it out militarily, I immediately excluded those eleven rooms and refolded the paper. While eating, I looked at my options. I decided to exclude the rooms by the stairs and of course the already occupied rooms. That was seventeen rooms eliminated, only thirteen to go.

I decided I wanted to see sunset rather than sunrise, so I eliminated eight more. Five left to choose from. I looked them over. All the rooms were roughly the same size, so I narrowed it down by what I wanted. The biggest factor would by my wingspan, I'd need as much room as possible for takeoff from any of those rooms. Finally I made my choice.

"This one." I said, pointing to the room immediately north of the big window.

Mr. McHaddish took out a pen and marked the room. Not long after breakfast was finished, Mr. McHaddish left with Mr. Hydell for the forty minute long plane ride to the island. I didn't voice my suspicions, but it sounded like the school was amongst the Channel Islands. It was only a thirty minute flight to Santa Cruz Island from L.A.X., so it must be on one of the further out islands. Also in the past there have been rumors of a hidden island, so the possibilities weren't too outlandish.

While they did that, I gave Molly the necklace I'd bought. She loved it, and gave me the two things she'd gotten me from Australia and Nepal. From Australia she got me a travel mug with a design called 'dancing wombat' on it. Honestly I wondered why it was called that, the design looked like leaves to me. Mr. Hydell got me a 500 piece penguin puzzle. From Nepal, they got me seven different singing bowls – one for every chakra point, – a small piece of pottery shaped like an elephant – a plant holder she told me, – and a kukri.

For those of you who don't know, a kukri is a traditional Nepalese knife, and the one that Mr. Hydell and Molly got me had a dragon etched into the blade. I gave Molly a hug after she gave me everything and put them in their appropriate places amongst my now packed things. Each of them would come in handy.

Chapter 72

Mr. Hydell returned around noon from checking out the school, and Mr. McHaddish had given him permission to reveal the schools location to me. I had been correct in leaning toward the rumors of a hidden island. An extremely strong glamour spell protected it, plus of course a very specific distraction spell. Basically what that one did was cloud the mind and make it hard to focus on what you were looking for. I believe something similar was used in a book series called 'Fablehaven' by Brandon Mull.

I gave him the water bottle I'd bought before he gave us the update that he'd be starting work again soon. Neither of us was that surprised, we'd heard a bit of the original conversation earlier. He also had plans for the three of us to spend time in the city before I was officially shipped out as he put it.

As luck would have it, we did get to spend most of Friday together, but shortly after ten that evening, Molly got a call that one of her patients was in Seattle and needed an emergency session. We all were thinking 'good grief'. So Saturday morning, after seeing her off at the airport, the two of us went back to the apartment to load my stuff onto the van to take it to the airport. I'd packed my bedding before we'd left the first time.

Mr. McHaddish met us there with the private jet that would shuttle us there. Mr. Hydell had to get to work for an emergency meeting with a colleague of his. He wouldn't say what it was for, but he did give me a big hug good-bye.

He waved to us from the terminal once we were loaded and boarded. My ten boxes secured in the hold, we were ready for takeoff. Which thankfully was much smoother than the 747's in my opinion. I settled in with one of my other books and managed to read the whole way.

As we were coming in for a landing, Mr. McHaddish turned my attention to the island. Unlike the rest of the Channel Islands, this one was rather large and mostly forested. I was glad for that, and even happier about the amount of shoreline there was. I spotted the small airfield before we touched down and buckled my seatbelt. Mr. Hydell had asked me to call or text when we landed, so I sent a quick text. I figured it would probably be a few minutes till he answered though.

I was wrong, he answered back almost immediately, saying that his meeting went faster than expected. I sent back that I was glad to hear it. I then put my phone away and caught up to Mr. McHaddish for the official tour.

The main dormitory was bigger than I'd expected. From the north or south, the building would look like an L. Four stories, each floor twenty feet high, accept for the atrium, which took up the whole eighty feet. The atrium was done in a dark rose pink color, minus the linings, which were done in white. A large crystal chandelier was even with the third floor landing. Two sets of stairs started just opposite the front doors. These obviously would lead to the other staircases I'd seen on the lay outs.

Immediately to the right – or north – was a large dining room. Mr. McHaddish told me the kitchens were connected at the other end of the room, which we couldn't see from the atrium. To the left was a doorway to a green house. Inside was a menagerie of plant life. Both domestic and exotic. Between the stairs was a small hallway that lead outside to the rear garden.

He motioned some of the people who worked in the building to take my stuff up to the chosen room, which he'd marked with a spell. While they did that, he took me to the school building just south of the dormitory. He gave me my schedule and showed me which rooms I'd be in. While walking back, he pointed out a small cottage east of the school building. He said one of the human workers lived there with her three children. Two boys and a girl, as I saw when they came out to play in their small yard. We waved and moved on. The rest of the teachers lived in accommodations on the main land, except for his niece of course, who occupied a dwelling in amongst the trees on the west side of the island.

"Why don't we head up to your room and get everything situated?" he asked. I nodded.

It didn't take us very long to get everything set up. I even hung up my newest painting. The room was now how I liked it, so we began the walk back to the plane. Mr. McHaddish had decided that sense everything had gone so well, I could go ahead and spend the weekend with Mr. Hydell and Molly. I was okay with that. I did take a sec to admire the arched doorways as we left first.

While walking, I felt my phone buzz. I pulled it out and subsequently tripped over a fricking rock, dropping the phone. Mr. McHaddish had to help me up, thank you left leg. I picked up my phone. The call had been canceled. I checked caller i.d. Mr. Hydell. I immediately called back.

"Hey, we're heading back to the plane now. I'll be home in about forty minutes." I said.

"Good, I'm looking forward to it." He sounded funny.

Then, from the back ground, "NO! DON'T COME HOME MAGGIE! STAY AWAY!"

It clicked. Mr. Hydell had called the first time then hung up on purpose to keep Kepner from finding me. I had called back, and Kepner had answered. I dropped the phone. Mr. Hydell was in danger!

I began running, crushing my phone in the process. I ripped my brace from my leg and shifted mid run. I was faster than that damn plane by a long run. Unfortunately, the headwinds were against me. Even at top speed, it took me fifteen minutes to reach the mainland.

I was completely wiped out when I finally landed on our building's roof. I'd never received headwind flight training like my siblings had. But I didn't let that stop me. I wrenched open the roof door, tearing it fully away from its hinges. The sound of sirens didn't register until I hit my floor. I banged through the door to find Mrs. Tomasino crying into Jim's shoulder, his arms wrapped around her.

No. No! It couldn't be true! I ran forward, yanking myself from Mrs. Tomasino's grip when she reached out to grab me. I pushed past the cops between me and Mr. Hydell. I stopped in the kitchen, standing in the same spot where I had painted earlier. The smell of blood as overwhelming as it had been that night. Every single one of the cops on site recognized me from the murders, and they all tried to stop me from entering my room.

I stopped the second I passed the door. My former room had been turned into a blood bath. The mattress completely soaked in it, and written on the wall, using Mr. Hydell's blood, a single sentence, the same one he'd sent my brother. 'She belongs to me!'

My eyes finally landed on the body of Mr. Hydell. Strung out on the bed, his arms and legs tied to each bed post. His eyes still wide open in defiance, as he'd been skinned alive. I fainted dead away.

Chapter 73

"There's nothing else to say sir. She's suffered a complete relapse. All that work Ms. Hamper and you did, completely reversed. A full psychological breakdown shouldn't be too much of a surprise since it still hasn't been a year since her family was murdered." Someone said.

I was too busy staring off into the distance to pay any kind of attention. Mr. Hydell was dead, and it was all my fault.

"What did the police say?" someone else asked. I think Mr. McHaddish.

"Based on the screams Mrs. Tomasino heard, he never gave her up. He didn't say anything about where she was. He just kept saying 'fuck you' till the end." The first man said.

"I guess this makes me her official guardian." Mr. McHaddish stated.

"Since her brother can't do it, and Miss Jenkins is unable, now that she's entered protective custody." He paused, "Where will you take her?" the first man asked.

"School. It's isolated and hidden. She'll hopefully be able to heal again there." Mr. McHaddish answered.

I felt him walk up to me and lift me from the chair I was numbly sitting in. He hugged me to him as we walked to the hospital elevator doors. How long had it been? When had I been moved to the hospital?

Answers I didn't care to get, I was still too numb. More than ever, I wanted my brother and sister. To let them give me comfort now that the pain had returned tenfold. I leaned into Mr. McHaddish as we rode down to the main lobby. No, not the lobby, the parking lot. I soon found out why.

We were being smuggled out basically. Damn media vultures! We were loaded into a FedEx van and driven out of the parking lot that way. The reporters waiting at the front doors never even looked in our direction. I was glad for that, flashing my face over the news would only make Mr. McHaddish a target for Kepner. And tell him where to find me.

I barely registered the arrival at the airport. Or Mr. McHaddish carrying me into the same jet from before. He sat me in a chair and fastened my seatbelt. The t.v. was on so I heard how the media was disappointed that they couldn't get a comment from me. Too damn bad! I was in no mental state to do such a thing. Any more than I had been in November.

Mr. McHaddish turned off the t.v. and sat down next to me. I had my arms wrapped around myself, so I didn't bother grabbing the arm rests. He pulled a backpack from a cupboard once we were airborne.

"There's some better clothes in here if you want to change Maggie." He said.

I looked up and met his eyes. I gave an attempt at a smile, took the bag, and walked to the bathroom after unbuckling. I tried not to look at myself while there. But I did catch a glimpse of my face. I looked like I hadn't eaten in weeks. It felt like longer. I just couldn't get the image of Mr. Hydell's body out of my head. The sight of bare muscle showing where skin should be. The blood.

Needless to say the nightmares had started back up, and who knows how many more hours of therapy I was going to be put through. I could only imagine what my human friends and former classmates were thinking as they saw the news report. My friends were probably dying to know where I was as much as Kepner was and if I was okay.

I splashed some water over my face, trying to at least look a bit more decent for arrival at school. I somewhat succeeded. Emerging from the bathroom – my other clothing stuffed in the bag – I sat down next to Mr. McHaddish. He pulled out some candy.

"I know it won't help, but you should at least eat something before we arrive." He said.

I took the Butterfinger bar. Nothing about it registered as I chewed. I merely ate it and drank the juice I was given a few minutes later.

I was almost relieved when we finally landed. I decided to walk to the dorm. I picked up the backpack and followed Mr. McHaddish out. As we walked, one of the flight attendants passed him something. Saying it had been found in the cargo bay when it was cleaned. He passed it to me.

I was actually surprised. It was my wind crystal. How had that gotten out of my crystal bag? I simply nodded in thanks and continued following Mr. McHaddish to the dorm. I kept the crystal in my hand, as a kind of reassurance.

As we entered the building, the first thing that struck me was the amount of people inside. I'd only ever seen it empty. Now students roamed about, talking or staring at me. More staring than talking really. Just as we hit the stairs, one of the staff member called out to Mr. McHaddish. Apparently there was something that couldn't wait to be discussed. Mr. McHaddish told me to wait at the bottom of the stairs while he talked. So I did, sitting on the very first step. That was when the 'queen bee' decided to make her move.

"Look ladies. Mr. M's brought in a stray." Her friends laughed. I didn't react.

"What do you think she is?" one of them asked. Again, no reaction.

"Human." Another responded. Nothing.

I stood as Mr. McHaddish came back, "I'll bet she's that Kepner guys whore." The first one said. I saw Mr. McHaddish stop, and cringe. He knew what was coming.

I clenched the crystal in my hand as the memorized spell began going through my head. The rest of the snide remarks, drowned out by the roar of anger in my ears. The crystal was growing hot in my hand. Finally the first one who'd spoken came away from her friends to tap my shoulder. I took the opportunity that was given.

With a growl, I quickly turned and opened my fingers, using my thumb to hold the crystal in my palm. The wind I released was that of an F- 5 tornado. Concentrated down into the thin beam I now controlled, the force of it not only threw her into the wall, but indented her into it. The concentrated beam was as tall as her all the way around. As she struggled to breathe, her friends backed away in fear. As did the rest of the student body that was in the immediate area.

"Magenta!" Mr. McHaddish placed a hand on my shoulder.

He didn't shout my name, just said it loud enough for it to reach past the roar. Of both wind and anger. I dropped my arm, ending the small force of nature and releasing her from the wall. She gasped for breath without getting off her knees.

"You b-" another growl and partially raising my arm kept her from finishing. She coward in terror at the threat and wisely kept her mouth shut.

Mr. McHaddish came forward, and said, "Listen up! This is our new student Magenta Sharp. She is a dragon shifter gifted with magic. If anyone – and I mean ANYONE – bothers or angers Magenta in any way, I will not hesitate to punish the offenders severely. She is to be left alone until she deems herself as approachable. Is that understood?"

No one answered.

"I said, is that understood!!" he shouted now.

"YES, MR. MCHADDISH!" the students answered. Including the one I'd put in the wall.

"Good. Now go about your business." He turned back to me, and gently taking my shoulder, led me upstairs.

Told From the Eyes of Another.

I finished unpacking. Finally. Why I brought more stuff with me every year I had no idea. You'd think a male dragon shifter wouldn't need so many things. But I guess being a sports fanatic did have some drawbacks.

I went downstairs after I was done to check out the green house. I know the botany teacher didn't call it that, but it's what I called it. I liked being down here, in and amongst the plant life. My dad called me odd for that one. I didn't care, he'd never understood me anyway. I waved to a friend as I walked, and we met up at the orchids. I know that might sound weird coming from a guy, but it was the plant directly between our previous positions.

We were talking about summer vacation when I suddenly got a tingly feeling in my head. I tried to shake it away, but it refused to go away. My buddy asked if I was okay, before I could answer though, there was a loud boom from the main hall. We both took off at a run toward the doorway.

We both froze as we beheld the sight of Honey pinned to the wall by a massive blast of concentrated air. We both stared in amazement until the wind stopped and Honey fell to the floor. We were still staring as she lifted her head to speak. A deep growl from across the room stopped her, and drew my attention to the north staircase.

Something in my head clicked upon looking at her. Deep red hair that reached her knees, braided to perfection, tall for her age, and well-muscled. She wore jeans, a black t-shirt, a gray hoodie, and boots. Her eyes, I'd never seen magenta eyes before. Wait. Yes I had! That girl from t.v., what was her name? Magenta Sharp that's it! But what was she doing here six days after school had started?

I finally registered Mr. M speaking. She was to be left alone? Why? I mean, yes, I knew her guardian had been murdered nine days ago but this feeling in my soul was telling me she was my mate. Maybe I could help her.

"YES, MR. MCHADDISH!" I heard the other kids shout.

I watched as he took her gently by the shoulder and started up the stairs. I went to follow but was stopped by my friend. Apologizing, I pulled from his grip, walked across the hall, and promptly jumped to the fourth floor landing. It would take a minute for them to reach the top, so I hopped down from the railing and looked up and down the halls. Trying to figure out which one might be hers. There were four new students this year. Three dragon shifter and one bear shifter. The bear shifter wasn't here yet, and the other two dragons were already in their rooms. So several on our floor were free. I looked down to the south hall where my room was located. I was practically jumping with hope that her room was close to mine.

I heard them coming and quickly crossed to the lounge just across from the landing balcony. I took shelter behind the statue of Enlil, Mesopotamian god of air, wind, breath, and loft. He was the southern statue, the northern one was Ninlil, Mesopotamian goddess of wind and consort to Enlil. I should've hidden behind Ninlil, 'cause then I wouldn't have to turn up my hearing as they stopped at the door closest to Ninlil. Damn it!

"Just give it some time, Mag. Don't rush yourself." He said after she opened her door.

She didn't verbally respond. She just nodded, and hugged him. I could see the tears from here. I unintentionally let out a low growl. Apparently it wasn't low enough. I saw Mr. McHaddish look up and see me. She broke the hug and walking into her room, shutting the door and locking it. I came out from behind the statue and walked toward her door. Mr. McHaddish stopped me.

Hand on my chest he said, " Don't son."

I wasn't nearly as large as him, but I could almost meet his eyes, "But she needs me."

"What she needs is space and time."

"But she's my mate." I was getting angry now.

He growled. I cringed, I'd heard that one before, but never been on the receiving end of it, "Her mate is currently in Scotland, Andrew. Now get back downstairs."

Taking one last glance at the door, I nodded, "Yes sir."

I took the quick way down. Walking to the landing and jumping. I had heard and understood him saying her mate was in Scotland, but I hadn't missed the look of partial dismay in his eyes as I'd claimed her. Her whole family murdered, and now she had two mates. This was not going to be easy for her.

Back to Maggie

I didn't bother listening to the conversation Mr. McHaddish had with whomever that boy hiding behind the statue had been. Nothing registered beyond him being there. I'd even felt Mr. McHaddish's growl as he'd noticed him. I'd locked the door specifically to keep the boy from trying to enter behind me. Some instinct had said he would.

I picked up my tartan and wrapped it around me. I really wished Jameson was here, but Mr. McHaddish had told me on the way up that there had been a complication with his passport and he wouldn't be here till the end of the week. Great.

I sat on my bed and looked out my window. The dark rose pink of my room wasn't comforting in anyway. It was nowhere near blood red, but it was enough to remind me of my old room and house kitchen.

Finally I pulled my tartan over my head and just leaned over to lie down on my pillows. I let the silent tears flow. I didn't intend to sleep. There was just too many memories in there. Some I wish I didn't have. I shivered at the memory of Amanda dying in my arms. Not even the knowledge of her being alive gave me comfort. I thought about contacting Reggie, but shelved that thought for a later time. He would come rushing if I did, request or not.

Eventually I drifted off. I won't even describe the dream I had. It made me extremely sick to my stomach. In so many ways. I shook myself awake and let my tartan fall off my shoulders. I looked up and saw the moon had risen. I stood and walked to the door. There wasn't a curfew as far as I knew, so I opened the launch pad doors and stepped out. I made sure to close the doors behind me. The fall wouldn't kill me, but that wasn't what I had in mind. I grew my wings and jumped off. I turned my wings toward the north west shore.

Chapter 74

I stayed at the small beach most of the night. Just letting the waves speak to me. My general mood actually kept the seagulls away. I was glad for that, I really didn't want to deal with those rats with wings. I kept my legs bent despite my left leg protesting. I let the pain focus me. I needed to be at least a little bit functional for school tomorrow. Mr. McHaddish had said I could skip, but I needed the distraction. Sitting and moping in my room wouldn't help me.

Just before sunrise, I rose and regrew my wings. Take off hurt like hell but I didn't pay it much attention. The island was large, though not large enough to get lost. I landed on my launch pad to the sound of someone in my room. I checked the window. It was Mr. McHaddish with breakfast.

I came in the doors just before he left. He smiled knowingly at me, rather than chastise me for being out past dark. He closed the double doors and relocked them. I limped over to my bed and sat down. He'd brought me biscuits and gravy. I actually managed to smile at that. I picked up the plate and began eating. Wonder of wonders, I could actually taste it. It was really good.

I drank the milk he'd brought while I strapped my brace on. I was going to need it for the next few days. I finally looked at the calendar on my wall. It was the twelfth. Ten days since Mr. Hydell had been murdered. I tried not to think about where Molly was. I knew she was safe and that was all that mattered.

I stood and grabbed my backpack. Classes technically didn't start for twenty minutes, but I was going to need the extra time to walk there. I stacked the dishes and left them on my desk. If someone didn't come to get them, I'd take them down later.

I took the stairs as carefully as I could. It took me a little over five minutes to reach ground level. I pulled my schedule out to check my first class. Combat practice. Well that could go either way. I walked out the hallway between the stairs. I took my time getting to the gym area. All combat was done outside. I arrived among some of the students who'd watched me pin queen bee to the wall. Some pointed and said simple things like 'that's her' or 'don't look her in the eye.' I smiled internally at that one. Most just kept going like I was a common nobody you pass in school. I was fine with that one too.

I watched the other kids put their bags in spelled lockers. I did the same and followed the other students to the padded floor. I stood in line next to a muscular boy about a foot taller than me and – great – said queen bee. She tried to look intimidating, but gave up at my glare. Thankfully for both of us, a smaller boy pushed in between us. He smiled politely before we all turned our attention to the teacher. A tall woman with wild black hair, and a very Lara Croft get up.

"Hello class, for you new kids, my name is Mrs. Nakayama. I am the combat teacher." She began, "We will begin today with an assessment of skills. Mostly for you newbies, so that I can get a good estimate of what to teach you."

"Mrs. Nakayama?" oh great. What line did queen bee intend to cross today?

"Yes, Miss Hendricks."

"How's the cripple supposed to fight with a bad leg?" she asked. Her friends giggled.

I simply glanced at the boy between us. He got the message. He moved forward out of my reach, as did the boy to my left. Queen bee wasn't paying attention to me. I moved my left leg back in a low sweeping kick. I knocked her feet out from under her so hard she fell straight on her ass.

There were gasps of amazement all around. I'd moved so fast no one had caught it. I finished with my left foot flat to the ground, the rest of me perfectly balanced on my right foot. Queen bee looked up from where she'd fallen. Then she looked at her shoes, one had come off and was at Mrs. Nakayama's feet.

"I don't need magic to defend myself." I said to her. I stood back up and met the teachers eyes.

She chuckled softly and clapped her hands, "Well done Miss Sharp. A good, smart woman has an arsenal of techniques at her disposal."

With that note, she began the class. The two other new dragons demonstrated some of their fighting skills. Both had good form, but were lacking in power. They'd only ever sparred with humans so they were used to pulling their punches. Understandable.

When she had us do partner sparring, I was paired with the boy who'd been to my left. He introduced himself as Damian, a tiger shifter. That explained the height. I was glad he didn't go easy on me, but there were a few times when I had to pull my punches. He asked why and I explained the two incidents at my human school. He'd cringed a little, but didn't complain. I actually enjoyed sparring with him, even with the boy who'd hidden behind the statue staring daggers at us the whole time. I didn't care what that was about.

By the time class was over, only the non-shifter were sweating. Damian had told me that queen bee's name was Honey, and I was kinda glad that she stiffly walked to the showers. I grabbed my bag and walked with Damian up to the other classrooms. He'd insisted simply because he'd unintentionally hit my left leg harder than he'd intended.

I was glad he'd insisted. I almost didn't make it to the third floor for my next class. He made sure I got to geometry then went to his class. I pulled out my notebook and pencil as the rest of the class came in.

Geometry passed quickly. I even managed to answer a few questions for the teacher. So far so good. My next class was on the same floor so I only had to move a few doors down. Marine biology. I actually smiled as I walked in, which pleased the teacher. Mr. Gentry – who was a gator shifter – made the class fun.

After that was weapons training. Back to the gym, just the opposite side of it. I placed my bag in another of the spelled lockers and took a place in line. This time, the boy from the statue stood beside me. A little too close for me though. I moved away slightly, and before he could move closer, a medium sized girl came between us. She introduced herself as Kira Hashimoto. I shook the offered hand and asked her what she was.

"A Shinto witch." She answered with a smile.

My eyes widened. She giggled at my amazement. Then commented that she got that reaction a lot. I wasn't too surprised that she did, Shinto witches usually attended the Japanese school.

"Why here?" I asked.

She shrugged, "My parents immigrated here before I was born. It just made more sense."

I nodded. Ms. McHaddish came forward. And yes that was her name, she'd retaken her maiden name after her husband's death she explained. She got us started the same way Mrs. Nakayama did, with an assessment from the new students. I proved adept at wielding a sword, so she paired me with Kira. The other two new dragons got paired together. Neither of them had had sword training. Kira sure didn't go easy on me. She was relentless. Luckily for me, so was I. We both ended up with four tags on each other before the teacher called a pause.

"You're the young lady my uncle took in over the summer right?" she asked.

"Yes ma'am."

She nodded, "You're pretty good with that katana. Let's see how you handle a Scottish claymore."

I passed my katana to Kira and caught the claymore she'd tossed me. I got a feel for the sword and realized it felt more right than anything I'd ever held before. A quick flick of my finger and my brace fell to the floor. I twirled the sword in my hand to test its weight and took my position. I'll take the time now to say that these were not rubber practice swords, but real ones.

I stood opposite her and waited. She was good, I almost didn't see her make a move. I caught her sword and in one move pushed her back. She looked at me with a new light. She was impressed. This time I attacked. I took her by surprise, 'cause she barely got her sword up in time.

She held firm as I put my weight behind it. I saw her struggle, then get leverage and push me off. I got my footing back quick and caught her next attack. From there, we both executed a series of complicated maneuvers. Both taking and giving ground. Quite a few of my fellow students were watching with awe. Most were sitting watching the show. The fight seemed pretty even.

After a few more minutes of sparring, I noticed something. She was doing this on purpose. Giving me someone to vent at. But class was almost over and I needed to get my brace back on. I feinted, and as she got in close, I brought my sword up to block then in a lightning quick move, I disarmed her and had her on the ground. I placed my sword to her throat to several gasps. We both were breathing heavily. Then she threw back her head and laughed. I moved my sword away and helped her up.

"By the gods kiddo you can fight. I haven't been beaten in over a hundred years." She said, still smiling.

I smiled back in thanks as Kira handed me my brace and Ms. McHaddish took the claymore. I sat down with some help from Kira, she spent the whole time speaking in Japanese, in awe of my swordplay. I knew only a few words of Japanese, but I understood the tone.

"Can you teach me that disarming maneuver?" she asked, finally able to revert to English.

I nodded, "It'll have to wait till tomorrow, but yeah."

She made sure to walk with me to lunch, the boy from the statue not far behind. While walking, I'd asked Kira who he was. She'd told me his name was Andrew, he was a dragon shifter and a senior at the school. I resisted the urge to turn and look at him.

Thankfully he was grabbed by his friends as we entered the dining hall. Kira went to join her friends after I grabbed my food and sat down. I made sure to sit down where I was alone. I appreciated both Damian and Kira for their help, but I still wasn't ready to make new friends yet.

I looked back over my schedule. Basic Survival, Botany, and finally was Spells and Potions. I needed to get to the second floor for survival, then it was to the first floor for botany. Spells and

Potions was a door away from botany. That made sense, since you would need fresh herbs for certain spell or portions. While I ate my sandwich, I wondered if the spells teacher had been told – or had seen – my pinning Honey to wall yesterday. Maybe I'd bring it up as a poke at her. I would no doubt be seeing her in Spells and Potions.

Thirty minutes later, having finished lunch, I walked back to the school building by myself. One of the boys stopped me and passed me an elevator key, saying it was supposed to be given to me last night, but since I hadn't answered my door, he'd held on to it. He also apologized for not getting to me earlier that day. I told him it was okay and we both went to our classes.

The Basic Survival teacher – Mr. Memphis, one of the human teachers – had us put into teams to assess either progress or what knowledge we already had. I got paired with the two other new dragons. One was named Wilson, the other Javier. Both were from New Mexico. Javier even actually apologized for his cousin's behavior. At my questioning glance, he specified Nancy Lopez, one of Honey's friends. I simply said it wasn't something I couldn't handle.

Mr. Memphis passed us a sheet with instructions. Evaluate the movies listed and write down how each could've been either more survivable or faster. Ours consisted of Castaway, Quarantine, 2012, and Alien: Covenant. Well this was going to be interesting. We started with Castaway.

"Anyone seen it?" I asked. I had, but since it had come out in 2000, not everyone might have.

Both boys raised their hands, "It's been a while, but I remember most of it." Javier said.

"So where do we start?" Wilson asked, "Don't even mention that stupid ball."

"Hey psychologically that ball was good for him." I stated.

"Okay, point taken. But how would he have been rescued faster?" Wilson continued.

"Simple, build a raft from some of the trees. You can make a rudimentary axe if you know how." Javier said.

"Yes but a rudimentary axe is next to useless on palm trees. Their skin is too tough." I told him.

"Reeds then." He countered.

Wilson shook his head, "Not found on the island." The boys looked stumped.

I already knew what would have worked, "The HELP sign…."

Javier cut me off, "What plane or chopper is gonna see that?"

I glared at him, "If he had set the one he built from plant material on fire, he would have been rescued within hours."

They both slumped their shoulders as if it was the simplest answer in the world. And really it was. Even a large fire can be seen for miles during the night, black smoke is obvious against a blue sky.

"The smoke would attract a chopper to his location, they read the sign and he gets rescued." I finished.

"Rather than him wasting time on the island." Javier said.

We wrote it down, then moved on to Quarantine, "I've seen this one. Messed up." Javier said.

"I suppose you have a quick solution to this one too?" Wilson asked me.

"Have you seen it?" I asked him.

"Part of it. My sister freaked before we finished. You?" I nodded.

"To answer your questions, yes, I've seen it, and yes, just shoot all the infected people in the head, before the C.D.C. people even arrive. The cops had the ammo." I answered.

The two looked horrified, "Even Briana?"

I nodded, "At that point, it would be mercy, not murder."

They both reluctantly agreed, "She'd been infected the longest. The bronchitis just kept it at bay."

"No, technically the antibiotics she'd been on **for** the bronchitis had kept it at bay. Because those meds stopped, is why she turned." I stated.

"Right, because her dad got locked outside when it all started." Javier finished.

On that cheery note, we moved on, "2012. Oh so many ways." Wilson started, "Unless yet again, you have a quick solution."

"Don't approach the one jackass in the first place, and tell the world the truth once you have scientific proof of doom. Ignorance breeds chaos, not knowledge." I said.

"She's got a point. Anheuser was a major jackass, and the world only descended into chaos because the truth was withheld from the public for so long." Javier stated.

"I wouldn't even have let him on the boat." Wilson said.

"Ah then you'd be no better than him to most people." I stated.

He slumped again, "Dang it, you're right."

"Okay, so last but not least, Alien: Covenant. That movie was cool." Javier began.

They both looked at me, "I'll start by saying I wanted to strangle the replacement captain. You never send almost the entire team down, you first send a drone."

Raised eyebrows, "I like that idea. They would have learned from complete safety that the planet was uninhabited and left."

"Not so fast Javier," Wilson began, "they could still have gone down."

"Why?" Javier asked.

"Because the drone might not be programmed for air quality tests, and might not have audio capabilities."

"While you have a point Wilson," I interjected, "this is why you video scan the entire planet. Eventually they would have come across the necropolis, seen from that, that the planet in and of itself was a necro planet, and then left."

They both nodded, "No audio necessary."

I shook my head, "It would be simple enough to deduce that if that's what the humanoid species looks like, then most likely, any and all animal species."

We wrote down all our results, and handed in our paper. We sat down back at our table and started to look over the text book. We were about three chapters in when Mr. Memphis called us up to his desk, he sounded mildly impressed.

"These solutions are excellent," he started, "how did you reach these conclusions."

Both boys pointed at me, "My dad put me and my siblings through survival training most of our lives."

"Your father wouldn't happen to be Victor Sharp?" he asked.

I felt tears threaten, "You knew my dad?"

He looked at a picture on his desk, "We attended the same survival classes in college. Became very good friends." He turned to show me a picture of him and my dad. Dressed in hiking clothes, it was odd to see my dad in his late teens. I smiled despite the sadness building.

He turned the picture back to himself, "He saved my life on a hike once." He looked up at me, "We were attacked by a crazed bear shifter. That was the first time I'd seen him change, and of course how I learned of your kind. Sometimes I wish I was there the night they died, maybe I could have somehow repaid the favor."

"More than likely he would have asked you to protect me." I said with a sad smile.

He nodded, "Right, I'd actually forgotten you'd been trapped in the rubble."

Javier and Wilson gasped, "I know this might sound like an odd question, but, do you know why my parents didn't trust shifters?"

Amazingly enough, he nodded, "Come by after school and I'll tell you."

I nodded. Me and the boys went back to our table until the bell rang. They went up to the third floor while I went down. The botany class was held in one of the more open science class rooms, one of those old fashioned ones that have an attached greenhouse and lead straight outside. I spotted Andrew entering and tried to get a seat elsewhere, but no dice. Students were placed based on abilities, so the only two dragon shifters were placed together. Joy.

I sat down across from him. He tried to meet my eyes but I wasn't having any of it. I tried to enjoy botany, but I could barely focus with him staring at me the whole time. I was glad I managed to remember everything my mom taught me and turn in a full answer sheet. At the bell I made sure to high tail it to Spells and Potions.

I sat down next to one of the open windows. I could smell the ocean from here. That helped me regain my focus. Until Honey walked in. She looked surprised to see me. I just shrugged at her and opened the book I had brought with me.

I put it away when the teacher came in. Ms. Gravely, and yes she found that amusing, since she had a mildly foreboding demeanor about her. Of course, the first words out of her mouth, was to ask me what spell I had used to pin Honey to the wall. Everyone in the class looked at her. She tried not to look embarrassed.

"One that my mom had me memorize, amplified with a crystal." I said.

"But you don't necessarily need the crystal?" she asked. I shook my head.

With a gentle flick of her wrist, she cleared away the desks into a circle. And with the people still in them. She gave a gesture to demonstrate. That made Honey mad.

"Why her?!" she asked, whiningly, "I'm the best witch in class." She pouted. Ugh!

"Only because you let yourself think that miss Hendricks." Ms. Gravely started, "Please, Magenta."

I stood and walked forward. I stopped in the middle of the circle, turning this way and that to make sure nothing was out and loose on any of the desks. I didn't want debris flying around. I placed my feet together, spread my arms slightly, with palms facing forward, and began to speak.

"Earth to Sky, and Sun to Moon

Like a gentle breeze at noon

North to South, East to West

Here at your behest

Let the ties that bind

Here and now no longer combine

Let the wind be my guide

And lift me with pride."

This time, when the wind began, it kept going. Eventually reaching a concentrated force of over 124 miles an hour. That was fast enough to lift the human body. Of course it reached that speed within three seconds, so I was now hovering about three feet in the air. Ms. Gravely looked supremely impressed. She clapped and indicated for me to come down. I slowly let the spell go, and touched down gently.

"I have never seen such a simple and powerful spell. Most of mine require something from a bird." She said with the biggest smile of her face.

"Where did you learn that spell?!" Honey looked like she was about to explode.

"My mother taught it to me." I said again.

"That's impossible, that spell was lost centuries ago. When the Celtic population was converted."

"Bhiodh Fios agad, am biodh tu a-nis." I stated, not quite realizing that I'd shifted to Gaelic. Basically I said, 'you would know, would you now.'

Ms. Gravely threw back her head and laughed, "You speak wonderful Scottish Gaelic."

I thanked her and turned back to Honey, "Only my paternal grandma didn't hail from Scotland. My mother inherited dozens of old spell books from her ancestors. She made me and my siblings memorize it."

"And who was your mom?" she still looked ready to blow.

"Helen Sharp, formally Marcus." I said. The pencil she held snapped in two.

"That's impossible." Now she looked freaked out. And boy she liked to say that a lot.

"You got a phone?" I asked angrily.

She pulled it out and handed it to me. I pulled up the internet and typed in my family's murder. The front page picture was the first one up. I enlarged the picture and turned it toward her. Then zoomed in on my mom. Her eyes widened like saucers as she took her phone back. I guess my mom was famous amongst the witch community.

Honey didn't get to say anything after that though. Ms. Gravely got us started with – of course – an assessment of skill. I didn't have to do a spell, but she did have me make a small potion. A simple one I knew by heart as much as the wind spell. I combined the components to create an incense potion. I made my sister's favorite. A storm. Once it was done, not only could you smell the rain, but you could smell and feel the touch of electricity in the air from the lightning, and feel the slight change in pressure of the thunder blast.

I let a tear shed despite myself. I wiped it away as Ms. Gravely came over. She seemed fascinated about my potion. So I laid it out for her when she asked. It was simple, a small spell, some rainwater, a piece of lightning charred wood, and a small infusion of air to create the effect of a thunderstorm. She loved it.

I left class feeling a little bit lighter. The day had actually gone well. As I limped to the north staircase, a girl about my age barreled into me. I managed to keep my feet by grabbing the railing. She apologized profusely as she twitched her hands like some autistic people do. At first I thought she might be autistic, but then her scent hit me. I tilted my head slightly, she smelled like death. Finally she shook her head and her eyes focused. Then she focused on me.

"I'm sorry about running over you, but I have a message for you." She said.

"And you would be?" I asked.

"Oh, where are my manners. Sorry, my name is Andrea. I'm the necromancer." Well, that explained the goth outfit, short black hair, and smell of death.

"Okay, so a message from whom?"

"Your parents." She said.

I felt like the ground was spinning out from under me. A nauseous feeling came into my stomach as well. I really didn't want to puke here in the dorm. I composed myself and nodded to let her know she could continue.

"They said they're proud of you for being so strong these last few months, and that it is safe for you to trust both Mr. Memphis and Ms. McHaddish. Also that they want you to be careful. Even they cannot find Kepner." She had tears in her own eyes as she finished.

I nodded my thanks. She smiled and moved aside as I made my way back out the doors. She'd reminded me about my visit with Mr. Memphis. I unfortunately ran into Andrew as I went back out. He managed to catch me before I fell and I felt something jolt. I didn't pay it any attention at the time, I just thanked him and started moving back toward the school building.

I found Mr. Memphis in his office waiting for me. He seemed lost in thought, or maybe memory. He lifted the picture of him and my dad again as I sat down opposite him.

"Do you want me to tell it to you straight?" he asked.

I nodded, "I'd appreciate it sir."

He placed his hands under his chin, "The simple fact is, your parents didn't trust other shifters because some jealous females kidnapped your mother and nearly got her killed."

Okay, what?! "You're kidding?"

He chuckled, "I wish. Your dad was the most eligible bachelor in college. He was still mourning his parents and didn't want to settle down, but with how handsome he was, women just wouldn't leave him alone. Human or shifter. Even though he met your mom while in high school, after his parents death, he practically ignored her. When he finally bonded with your mother, the shifter girls became jealous and kidnapped her, with the intention of taking him for themselves."

"What happened to them?" I asked.

"Because of their gross misconduct, and the near death of a human – let alone a bonded human – they were sentenced to thirty years each of no shifting. A powerful spell was cast that would contain their animal halves inside them until the sentence was over."

"But the damage had been done, and my parents never trusted other shifters again." I surmised.

He nodded, "They didn't want to take the risk of their children coming to harm."

I nodded, "Thank you sir."

He smiled, "Your welcome."

Chapter 75

I managed to make it back to my room before collapsing. I also made it to the bed. I couldn't believe that my dad had so many females going hormone crazy back then. I mean sure, he'd been good looking, but oh my Gods. That didn't give anyone the right to try and kill my mom. In most cases the crime for harming a bonded human was more extreme than being bound. And thirty years was a long time. It made me wonder where those other females were.

I didn't let myself dwell on it too much though. One I had homework, and two, I wanted to try and contact Amanda. The token had remained around my neck even during my time in the hospital – which I had asked Mr. McHaddish about when he'd brought me up to my room – apparently, only I could remove it. A handy feature. Jameson's ring was there too. It had been removed, but it was intact. I'd have to remember to place a protection spell when I was done talking to Amanda.

I sat up and moved to my desk. I pulled my books and notebooks from my backpack and set them out. I'd get started on them once I was finished. I leaned back in my chair and let the late afternoon sun hit me. I didn't necessarily need all four elements to call her, and she could answer back easily.

It took several minutes, but eventually she answered, "I was wondering when you would contact me."

I ran forward and pulled her into a hug. She returned it with gusto. My guess was she'd watched as Kepner had tortured Mr. Hydell, wishing she could do something.

"I lessened his pain as best I could, but it wasn't enough to keep him from suffering." She said tearfully.

"So you embraced our name?" I asked. That was the only way she would've been able to do that.

"Yes. I'd seen Reggie do it with his mate. I figured it was time to complete the triangle."

"Was it bad?" I asked. Her arms tightened. That was answer enough.

"I'll probably have nightmares about that for the rest of my life." She said.

"I don't doubt it. I know I will."

"Have you spoken with Reggie?" she asked.

"No. I know he'll come running, and right now that's the last thing I want. Kepner was so close the last time that I want to wait at least a few weeks. Maybe you or I will get lucky."

"You really think it's time to let him find you?"

"Yes. He's crossed one line too many now, eventually he'll catch on to the fact that I'm not going to school in L.A., he'll start watching the airport. It won't take him long to see that one plane leaves at dawn and returns before sunset." I said.

"It could endanger the school."

"The barriers have a human alert charm worked in. I sensed it as we passed through it. If he gets within three miles, the barrier will let out an alarm. Much like the air raid sirens." I explained.

"So everyone will be inside if he succeeds in making land fall." She surmised.

I nodded, "I can apprehend him before he becomes a danger."

"Then make him pay." She finished vehemently.

"In full."

"In the meantime, I'll tell Reggie to be ready for your call, but only to come if you have Kepner."

"You can also tell him why mom and dad didn't trust other shifters." I said.

Her eyes widened. I took the time to tell her the story that Mr. Memphis had told me. She was totally surprised about it all. I expected that. I could only imagine how Reggie was gonna react.

We said our goodbyes as she felt her power begin to fade. We hugged once more first, then I returned to my desk. Only to find Andrew hovering over me. I punched him in the face as my chair fell backwards.

"Mother of the Gods you fucking idiot! Don't you knock!!?" I yelled as I stood up.

He was holding his nose as he sat up from where he'd fallen, "I did, but when you didn't answer, I got worried."

"So you just decided to walk in?!!" I was pissed.

He pulled his hand away from his face, "I admit, that was stupid."

"No shit Sherlock! So what the hell were you doing hovering over me!?" I stood with hands on hips.

"Your necklace was glowing and you looked to be in a trance. I thought you were in trouble." He rose from the floor still holding his nose. " What were you doing?" He began to tip his head back.

"Don't do that you idiot! You'll end up with blood in your lungs." I said. I pulled out two tissues and my ice crystal.

He looked confused, "How do you know that?" he grabbed two tissues himself and plugged his nostrils.

"Um, duh, you breathe through your nose, it has a direct line to your lungs. Even if you don't breath on purpose, the blood can reach them." I twirled the tissues into tubes, placed them on my desk and said a quick spell.

"Cats to Dogs, Rats to Mice

Make this crystal cold as Ice."

The white crystal began to feel cold. Carefully, I touched the two rolled up tissues lightly. I then set my crystal aside to warm back up, and handed the two chilled tissues to Andrew.

"What'll those do?" he asked unbelievingly, tossing his two bloodstained ones in my trash can.

"The cold will cause the veins and capillaries that have opened to close back up again. It's a much safer way to stop a nosebleed." I explained as he took them.

He gently put them in his nostrils, then shook as goosebumps appeared on his skin, "I'll believe you I guess."

"So why the hell were you knocking on my door? I thought Mr. McHaddish's orders were clear."

"They were, but I'll answer your question if you'll answer mine." He said.

I rolled my eyes, "Whatever."

"I wanted to ask if you wanted to come down to the lounge and get something to snack on while you did your homework." He answered. My turn.

"Yes, I was in a trance, but since I was told only to tell people I trusted, you don't get to know why."

"Fair enough."

"So where is this lounge?" I asked.

He pointed toward the big window, "Just down there."

I shrugged and started walking. He took the hint, left my room, and started down toward the window area. There was almost twenty students present at the small area. The coffee table I hadn't seen yesterday was laid out with muffins, fruit, sandwiches, mixed nuts, cakes, pretzels, and various drinks. I walked forward to choose when two boys started shouting.

"Just give up dude. You're never going to find them!" one said.

"NO! I won't give up. My mom hasn't, my grandpa didn't, so neither will I!" the smaller of the two replied.

"Shouldn't you two be downstairs?" Andrew asked, kinda rudely.

"Stuff it Longtooth, Jeremiah's just wiggen 'cause both of his last leads proved to be dead ends."

"I heard Mr. McHaddish was up here" Jeremiah said, "I wanted to ask him for help."

"Just forget it man, the Parthenian clan is finished. That shifter family your ancestors wiped out is just that. Long dead."

No way! This was him, "And you know this for certain do ya?" I crossed my arms.

"Stay out of it sister." He said.

"Excuse me?" my eyes went dragon.

He seemed to think a second, "Please stay out of it Magenta." He finished with a snide smile.

"The name, is Magenta Rose Regina Ferelith Sharpwingclaw."

Everyone stopped talking, the silence was palpable, "That's impossible." He said.

"Why does everyone keep saying that?! Is it too hard to believe that two young dragon shifter girls might have the knowledge to cross the river, get to the village and warn them of the crime committed."

Jeremiah came forward, "My grandpa said the two must have survived. The family was known for starting survival training early."

"Still is. My parents started when each of us reached three years of age." I said.

"How can we be sure you're not lying?" the big one asked.

"Ease off Paul." Jeremiah said.

My growl had everyone backing away. No one calls me a liar, "What was another thing the family was well known for?" I asked Jeremiah.

"Claws at the end of their wings. Excellent for climbing in Scotland's rugged terrain." He answered.

People had moved back quite a bit, but not enough for me to change. It needed to be a full change. I'd noticed the end claws didn't appear when I grew my wings in human form. I moved back till I was by the railing and shifted. Several people fell down trying to unnecessarily get out of my way. I stayed small, and gently unfolded my wings. Gasps all around, not just at their expanse – which didn't fit inside – but the six inch claws at the ends.

I lowered my head till it was even with Paul's, he looked nervous. Good, and for the first time ever, "That proof enough for ya?" I spoke vocally as a dragon.

Jeremiah collapsed to his knees, tears running down his face, "Please. My mom and I detest what our ancestors did to yours."

I could read not just his emotions, but with a little adjustment, I could read his aura better. He was truthful. He and his mom were truly devastated about my family's slaughter all those centuries ago. I looked deeper, and found the beginnings of a tumor in his brain.

At its rate of growth, he'd be dead before he could sire children. I was his only salvation. His and his mom's actually.

I stepped forward and touched my nose to his forehead, "I forgive you." I said sincerely.

There was a bright flash of light. Everyone closed their eyes until it faded. When I opened mine, I could see the tumor had completely disappeared. There was absolutely no trace of it. I smiled and shifted back. I offered him my hand. He took it and I helped him up.

"Thank you." He said once he was standing.

"Your welcome." I replied with a small smile.

He released my hand and booked it toward the south staircase. No doubt to check on his mom via phone call. I took the opportunity to grab an apple, a poppyseed muffin, a handful of the mixed nuts, and using my tail, an apple juice. This time, I made sure to lock my door after I entered. I had to use telekinesis to do it, but it was done. I put my snacking items on my desk and made a quick circle, I then removed my ring and performed my standard protection spell, making sure to add in impact and corrosion – from either me or earthly elements – that done, I plugged my mp3 into its speaker and started my homework.

Chapter 76

I had everything done by dinnertime. I decided not to bring a book as I went downstairs. I caught part of Jeremiah's phone conversation near the bottom.

"- and it was gone! All of it! She's going to live! Did you ask for a miracle?" someone asked.

I saw Jeremiah near the hall to outside, "No dad," he looked at me as I smiled at him, "I asked for forgiveness." He answered with a sniffle.

"You found them?" his dad asked.

"More like she found me." Jeremiah answered as he turned to his left.

I tuned out the rest as I walked into the dining hall. I made sure to spot a place for myself as I took a place in line. People were looking at me in awe now. I wasn't surprised that word had travelled fast. I grabbed a plate of beef stroganoff and took my seat near the windows.

I wasn't alone long, "I heard you've given someone something special." Mr. McHaddish said as he sat down opposite me.

I looked up and smiled, "You were right. He was repentant." I poked at my food.

"I'm proud of you. And I'm sure your ancestors are too." He said.

I looked toward Andrea, who gave me a nod and had the biggest grin on her face, "They are." I said.

"Was there a problem earlier?" he asked.

"Andrew came into my room while I was talking to Amanda." I made sure to answer quietly enough that no one but him would hear.

He grunted, "That explains the tissues sticking out of his nose earlier."

"Once a healer, always a healer."

"How hard did you hit him?"

"Full strength. I toppled over backwards as well, and I was in my desk chair." I answered.

"Do you want me to talk to him?"

I shook my head, "It only happened because I forgot to lock my door. I won't happen again."

"Alright." He placed his hand over mine, "Eat up kiddo."

He stood and walked out of the dining hall. I did manage to eat my food without crying. I then made sure to put my plate and fork in the baskets and went back up to my room.

I wasn't there for very long. I couldn't sleep. My pills had yet to be refilled, and I was angsty. I got up and walked back down to the kitchen. Maybe a midnight snack would help. I entered to find the kitchens empty. I turned one light on and started looking. I found everything I needed to make pecan pie. I know I should've just grabbed something and gone back up, but the need to bake just took over.

I gathered the ingredients and found a premade crust in the pantry. I chopped the pecans and mixed them with the other ingredients. My grandma had found a corn syrup free recipe once and it was the one she'd always used. I had it memorized. I poured the mix into the crust and stuck it in the oven. The oven was enchanted, so it cooked the pie to perfection inside of a few seconds. Handy when you have nearly a hundred kids to feed.

I pulled the pie out and cut myself a slice. I was about halfway through it when Mr. McHaddish came in. He didn't say anything, he just came over, cut himself a piece, and sat down to eat it. We had the pie completely gone before one o'clock. He tossed the tin and came up to me. He passed me a glass of milk and showed me the pill bottle I had heard moving in his pocket. My sleeping pills.

I took both, and he walked me back up to my room. I thanked him and he bade me goodnight. I locked the door and took the pill once I opened the bottle. He'd told me on the way up that it had been refilled that morning. He'd gotten it just after dinner. I finished the milk and laid down. I had the first dreamless sleep in days.

But there was another reason for this. Amanda made contact. I noticed two figures in the mist before they materialized. I guess Reggie wanted to see for himself that I was okay.

I hugged them both before Reggie said, "How you holden up?"

My expression said it all, "Could be better." I said anyway.

He closed his eyes to fight back tears, "I didn't even get to meet the guy. I should've been there."

"It wouldn't have changed anything." I said.

He nodded, "I know. But at least I would've been there for you."

"Can you still find him?" I asked Amanda.

She nodded, "Barely, but I can track him well enough to say he's started putting two and two together. Pretty soon he'll have the full puzzle."

Reggie shook his head, "I don't like it Maggie. I know Amanda explained everything, but what if something goes wrong."

"That only happens when someone says it bro." Amanda said.

"I'll be on guard the whole time Reg. He won't sneak up on me this time." I said.

"Just be careful then." He said.

I nodded and we hugged again as Amanda let the connection go again. I opened my eyes to see my clock say 6:15. Time to get up. I grabbed a towel and a change of clothes, and went down to the main floor, and out to the showers at the gym. They were less than fifteen feet from each building – or at least the gym of the school building. This way it could double as the gym showers and the regular showers. The bathrooms were attached by a small doorway. The school was old enough that the bathrooms were separate from the house. Not convenient, but I didn't care.

I finished my shower relatively quickly. I started hearing other people coming down, including Honey. Thankfully, she was still so tired and zombie like, she didn't even notice me. I was glad for that. I really didn't want to kick her ass again so early in the morning.

Once back in my room, I brushed my hair and braided it. My leg was feeling a bit more relaxed thanks to good sleep and a hot shower, but for safety's sake, I decided to wear my brace. I met Mr. McHaddish outside my door. I'd heard him come up. As we walked I asked why the teachers had done first day stuff on the technical 7th day of school. His answer was simple, he'd requested it. He wanted me to have as easy a start as possible, so the first few days had been the students reading back through their books, doing outdoor exercises, or finishing unpacking.

He continued with me to the gym. Apparently he had a demonstration planned or something. He met up with Mrs. Nakayama and they talked while the rest of the class showed.

Then said, "We're going to do something a little different today." He gestured to Mrs. Nakayama, "Leslie here will ask each of you to demonstrate one technique from your martial arts choice. Whether you know multiple," he gestured at me, "or just one." He pointedly looked at Honey on that one.

"I want each of you to then share how to do this move or set of moves to the rest of the class," Mrs. Nakayama started, "even if it's a simple move like the eye gouge."

Mr. McHaddish then left and we all got started. I knew four separate styles, so which to choose from. I paid attention as she started alphabetically. I narrowed it down to either wing chun or dragon style when it got to Honey. S.I.N.G., seriously. Anyone who'd seen Miss Congeniality knew that one. But for those of you who haven't, the acronym means solar plexus, instep, nose, groin. Works on both men and women.

Andrew was next. He seemed to be into wrestling, 'cause his chosen move was a headlock maneuver that got the opponent on the ground quick. Effective, but not always dependable. Then it was Wilson, Javier, and finally to me.

I came forward and Damian actually volunteered to be my dummy. I had chosen the straight blast technique from wing chun. We stood sideways from the class, and with relaxed arms, I punched straight in front of me, hitting Damian in the nose, throat, solar plexus, and other parts of his head. The technique was for protecting your center line, and therefore you struck the other person's center line as well. One throat punch I landed hit him straight in the Adam's apple. I hadn't meant to, but he was down from that one fast.

I covered my mouth with both hands as he fell backward. I stood still as the rest of the class watched him try to rise. Then he surprised everyone. As he leaned up, he started laughing. It was a raspy laugh, but he was laughing. Even Mrs. Nakayama was looking slightly concerned by that. Finally, still laughing, he gave a thumbs up.

"I'm fine." He chuckled to Mrs. Nakayama. The slight knot in my stomach loosened.

"I'm so sorry." I said as I breathed a sigh of relief.

He shook his head, "It was a good hit. Although I wonder if that was supposed to be part of the technique."

"Technically no it's not. That was just where I happened to hit. So I'm still sorry."

"You're forgiven." He said.

From there – once the school nurse said he was okay – the rest of the class did their demonstrations. Damian was one of the last ones. He chose to simply state that the Adam's apple shot not only could work, but if that didn't successfully take down an enemy, than go for the nose jab that sends the cartilage up into the brain. That would most definitely kill your attacker.

The rest of the day passed slowly for some reason after that. Something was distracting me. A gut feeling I think. I just couldn't stop looking out to sea. It wasn't until botany that things seemed to speed back up. I was sitting across from Andrew again, trying to put his stare out of my mind.

I was finally able to fully ignore him when Dr. Thorne came forward with a cart filled with several plants I had never seen. Each one was covered by a small glass dome. I listened while he called on certain people to identify the weird plants. I wrote them down as well, including the described smells when he lifted the domes off. He got to the second to last dome and looked toward me and Andrew with concern. As did the rest of the students.

"Any other day I would ask the two of you to hold your noses, but since it's better for you both to recognize this one, I won't." he paused as he lifted the dome, and held a lighter next to one of the leaves, "This, is dragon's bane." He lit the leaf.

Even from thirty feet away, the smell hit us both. Making us sneeze. Then I couldn't breathe, as the memory of my father's death came to the forefront. I started hyperventilating, as tears started streaming down my face, I stood fast enough to knock my chair down. The whole class was looking at me, but I couldn't take my eyes off that plant. The very monstrosity that allowed Kepner to kill my father.

Still breathing hard, I turned and ran out the back door of the classroom.

Chapter 77

I don't know how long I ran, I just knew I had to get away from the smell of that plant. Finally I made the beach, fell to my knees and once again, cried my eyes out. It wasn't until Mr. McHaddish showed up that I bothered to acknowledge the time. I didn't bother trying to shift. I knew all too well the plants power. I let Mr. McHaddish take me back to the school.

He took me straight up to my room after grabbing some food from the kitchen. He'd had my homework left out on my desk, including notes from Spells and Potions. Since it was only after eight, I had time to do it all.

The next morning came too quickly for me. I still wanted Jameson and my brother, but I was too mature to admit it beyond myself. Jameson had two more days till he got here. I'd just have to suck it up.

I'd left my pill bottle on my desk, I picked it up and returned it to the drawer I had been keeping it and my pain pills in. I'd taken it right after finishing my homework and my dinner. I was about to head down to breakfast when I noticed my Sherlock box had a light coming out of it.

I walked back to my nightstand and opened it up. I lifted out my book and watch, to find the dagger I'd hidden was glowing. Or more accurately, the gem in its hilt was glowing. I had placed the dagger in the box the day before Mr. Hydell had been killed. It had been my paternal grandmother's, I hadn't ever used it. I lifted it up, the glow didn't stop.

I pulled the dagger from its sheath, marveling at how light it was. On one side was the Gaelic symbol of protection near the hilt, while going down the blade, was an ancient protection spell, written in scottish Gaelic. On the opposite side, an ancient Hawaiian protection symbol, also near the hilt. Also going down the blade, another protection spell in Māori. My dad had said his mother had family from eastern Polynesia. Distant family, but still.

I held the dagger up to the light of my lamp, the glow from the gem intensified until I had to avert my eyes. I felt a weight appear on my neck. I looked down, now resting around my neck was the amulet I had seen in photos of my grandparents. The one my grandmother had worn before her death. My dad had told us it had been stolen when they'd died. I lifted it up to look at it. It was a small egg sized ruby, perfectly smooth. The gem was held by silver filigree that took the shape of a Hawaiian vine and flower. A Hawaiian hibiscus. It's petals delicately folded and painted to match its yellow and orange of nature. Holding it, I could sense the essence of my grandma. I closed my hand around it and held it to my chest.

I then retuned the dagger to its sheath, and stuck it into my extra pocket. There was no rule about carrying a weapon around the school here. I grabbed my bag and walked out of my room.

Thankfully the school day was uneventful. Well, at least until I walked into the atrium. There were several students milling about and arguing. I tried to walk past but got shoved by one of the boys who'd been pushed back. I was caught by Javier and another boy our age. There were two jolts that I put down to my grated nerves. I stood and looked at the other boy. Where Javier was distinctly Hispanic or Spanish, this other had Chinese features. Mixed really, his eyes didn't have a full Asian lift to them.

I looked back toward the rest of the group. I saw Honey was leaning up against the wall and had a bubble around her. And I mean a literal bubble. I turned to Javier and gestured.

"She's demonstrating a protection spell her mom taught her. Apparently it is literally impenetrable." He said.

I scoffed, "Yeah right." I made to finish going upstairs.

"Don't tell me the great Magenta Sharpwingclaw is scared to test it." She goaded.

I rolled my eyes, "If you honestly think I am going to waste my time proving that spell is obsolete, then you seriously need to get your head out of your ass."

I made to walk away, "Says the pooped out princess with lame taste in jewelry. And I mean the ruby."

"Don't Mason." I heard Javier say as I clenched my fist.

I heard the group lose interest in her display and begin to disperse. She'd pushed a new button now. I pulled my dagger from my pocket, flipped it so I had it by the tip, and threw it at her in a backhand. She'd been moving, so the dagger came to rest in the wall where her eyes would've been a second later. I turned to look. The spell of hers was still going, and my dagger had gone clean through it. The group was once again stunned into silence.

She was visibly sweating as I came forward, walked through the shield, and pulled my dagger from the wall. I looked her in the eyes, and gestured with my dagger at the bubble.

"Othinian Bubble shields were obsolete three centuries ago." I said.

I replaced my dagger and walked out of her bubble. I didn't pay anyone any mind as I climbed the stairs to my room.

I was coming back down for dinner when I noticed one of the other girls was looking at the spot my dagger had hit. Standing next to her was Kira. She was describing the disarming technique I'd shown her the second day of class. When she spotted me, they both came over.

"Hey, I was telling Mila what you did to Honey today." She said.

I quirked an eyebrow. There was no way this other girl's name was Mila. Her skin was almost as dark as obsidian. A deep, rich, earthly color. Beautiful along with her emerald, green eyes.

"I get that reaction a lot." She said. Her accent so thick I almost didn't catch her Tanzanian origins. She held out her hand, "My full name is Olufunmilayo Jelani. I am a spotted hyena shifter."

I was stunned as I shook her hand, "Uh, how's that?"

She laughed heartily, "Now you see why I go by Mila."

Kira and I joined her laughter, "Yes I do."

"I imagine you get the same problem with your third middle name." Kira said.

I nodded, "Only those who think it's not pronounced pretty much how it's spelled."

We finished walking to the dining hall. I decided to let them sit with me. Mila sat across from me with Kira beside her. Mila was very into how I'd managed to penetrate the shield spell. Apparently she was also into any and all protection spells because she was in hiding. Her clan had been ousted by a rival clan, and as heir, she'd been sent here for school to keep her safe. I could tell though, that the protection spells weren't for herself.

"Why?" I asked.

She knew what I meant, "My clan has several sacred gem mines on our land. Our rivals wanted it, and slaughtered several of my cousins to try and get it." Her eyes glazed with sadness.

I nearly crushed my fork in empathy, "So you're trying to get it back."

She nodded, "It's in our nature as hyenas and all but," she paused, "that land rightfully belongs to me and my family." To steal territory was their nature, but so was compromise.

"Can they enter or use these mines?" I asked.

She shook her head, "No. The magic that protects those mines only recognizes my bloodline. Because we took the time and effort to earn those gems." She looked out the window, "I am to inherit that queendom when my mother passes. How am I to do that when we have been forced out?"

I put my fork down and tapped my chin, "Can I borrow your phone Kira?"

She pulled it out and handed it to me, I quickly pulled up a map of Tanzania, "Where exactly is your territory?" I placed the phone between us. She moved her tray and looked.

"Here." She made a circle on the map, "and here, is theirs." She made a second circle.

"Do these gems only grow on your land?" I asked.

"No. My grandparents discovered veins in our rivals land as well, they just never shared it with them." She answered.

"There's your bargaining chip. They return what they stole from you for information on how to find their own veins."

She looked up at me, "I never thought of it that way. My people have seven sacred gems, but our land only produces four of them."

"Maybe your rivals have the other three." I stated.

She looked at me like I was genius, "I will have to check, but it is possible." she got up quickly, and made to leave, then remembering something, came back, and said, "Thank you."

Before I got a chance to reply, she was gone again. Kira and I finished our dinner, then separated to do homework.

I got my homework done in record time that night. I wasn't feeling great about tomorrow for some reason, and I wanted to have as much stuff ready as possible. It was bad enough Mr. McHaddish had showed up at my door to ask what Honey had said to piss me off. Obviously she had lied about it, and he wanted as many affirmations as possible before giving out punishments. I told him, and of course, he was less than happy. I went to bed that night with a pit of apprehension in my gut.

I was right. All shifter teens were gathered on the lawn beside the gym for first period. We were all told to shift, and then pick an opponent based on size. I saw that I was the smallest of the dragons – no surprise there really – while Andrew was the largest.

His scales a deep red color. I nearly put it down as blood red. Javier was chocolate brown, while Wilson was as white as snow. Figures I was the only female dragon shifter.

Looking down the ranks, I noticed Mason from yesterday. A wolf shifter, dark gray down his back with a white belly, legs, and most of his muzzle. Then of course, the bears – grizzly, black and polar, a few gators, one croc, Mila, several other wolves, quite a few cats – tigers, lions and cougars, plus one or two leopards and jaguars, even a few gorillas, and finally, one panda.

We were divided up according to weight. I was paired with a bear shifter named Tim who was almost as big as Jameson. Unfortunately, I was also paired with the jerk of the class. I heard several murmurs as we met up. Most said that it was hell waiting to break loose. I guess most of the class knew he was going to piss me off. In one way or the other.

I wish I could say I was wrong, but he didn't take being beat by a girl well. I never used my wings or tail during our spar, but he seemed to think I wasn't playing fair. He was the one not playing by the rules, he kept trying to bite me, or pin me down. I'd been pinned down enough.

Finally it escalated. I was forced to use my tail to deflect a blow, and he pulled out the big punch. He started insulting me. Bear shifters usually couldn't speak in bear form, but I guess he was gifted in that regard. Because he made the biggest mistake of anyone so far.

His final insult was, "Your weak. You let your family die!" I lost it.

I openly attacked him. All claws and teeth came into battle. I had just thrown him to the ground after shaking him violently, when Mr. McHaddish could finally get close enough to intervene. I placed my right paw over his throat and squeezed lightly. His blood was leaking out from several wounds, and there was genuine fear in his eyes. I was breathing heavily with his blood covering me as well. Mr. McHaddish was in lion form in case he needed to tackle me. Not that it would accomplish much in a rage. I outweighed him by quite a bit.

Thankfully he wasn't necessary. I managed to rein myself in, "Never say that again." I growled.

Tim nodded as best he could, and I healed his wounds. I then removed my paw and walked away from him. I shifted back, and threw the rest of my rage at a boulder. As a spell that is. The boulder disintegrated into several million pieces. Into the finest form of gravel.

I sat down where I was and stayed there until the period was over. I hadn't paid attention as Mr. McHaddish had removed Tim after I'd let him go. I assumed it was to give him a butt load of detention. For the rest of the first half of school, absolutely no one bothered me. Kira, Damian, Jeremiah, and Mila all asked if I was okay, but even they gave me my space. Andrew still stared daggers at Damian.

I was seated at a table poking at my lunch when I heard yet another commotion. I ignored it. I could hear most of the girls saying things like 'who's he' or 'he's cute', but I didn't pay attention. Not until I caught his scent as he sat down beside me. I turned to see Jameson sitting next to me.

I quickly pulled my legs from under the table, and we stood to hug. I practically crushed him in my relief to finally have him here with me. He let me cry quietly into his shoulder as everyone watched. I didn't care.

Until we were ripped apart. I spun so fast that I was face down on the rug, without any indication as to what had happened. Then I heard the growls. I looked to my left to find Jameson locked into a fight with Andrew, Javier, **and** Mason. What the Hell!?

I stood and putting all the authority I could into my voice, shouted, "ENOUGH!!"

All four boys froze. Not a one meeting my eyes. Their heads were bent in typical submissive gestures. Only Jameson looked up after a few seconds to meet my eyes. Then it clicked. There was only one reason that all four of them would have been that affected by my command.

"No. No way!!" I backed away as I talked. Then before any of them were fully upright, I bolted from the building.

Chapter 78

I ran through the woods to the opposite side of the island. There, I unleashed all my pent up emotions at my newest revelation. Four freaking mates! Why!? I was fine with just Jameson! Why the Hell did the universe decide I needed a freaking reverse harem of guys?! I wasn't even sure if I like Andrew! Yeah he was good looking, but good Gods that didn't mean I was interested. And why Mason?! I hadn't even known of his existence until yesterday! I was fine with Javier I guess, he was nice enough. But Jameson was the only one I could genuinely say I loved. We had spent the necessary amount of time together to form a bond. I know it wasn't a full bond since neither of us was over eighteen, but at least it was there.

Finally I sat down on a rock. I had actually used up what energy I'd had left for the day. I looked out to sea. I didn't know why at the time, but the pull was stronger than ever in that moment. I started to think about why, then moved off the rock to fully lie in the sand. My leg was starting to cramp up. I continued thinking until I drifted off.

Thankfully I didn't literally drift off the beach, since the tide had risen when I awoke. At moonrise. I leaned up and double checked the time by the stars. Ten to two a.m. on the fifteenth. So it was officially Friday. Great, that was another half of a school day gone. I would be surprised if I wasn't punished. Right then, holding my legs to my chest, I didn't give a damn.

I looked out to sea again, and came to a decision. I was going swimming. I stood, removed my hoodie, shoes, socks, and ripped my jeans off at the knees. I emptied my pockets, removed my necklaces, and finally ripped my sleeves off as well. I knew a sewing spell that would fix them all, I'd just do it later.

Leaving my stuff there, I walked into the water. Letting the semi warm water touch my skin felt like a release as I walked. I tilted my head back to enjoy it and the moonlight. Eyes closed, I breathed in the salty air, then opened them, took a breath, and did a dive into the waters of the Pacific. Even in shallow water the light of the crescent moon was insufficient, I didn't seem to mind at first. As I moved forward, I started to notice the nightly sea creatures. Rays and certain fish, including a few sharks. I had no fear of them though, they weren't bull sharks, and I wasn't bleeding.

I decided to swim out further. First though, I let my eyes go dragon, and I grew my tail. Thanks to my dragon abilities, I could hold my breath for several minutes. I noticed several minutes later though, that I was no longer holding my breath. I also noticed a peculiar feeling along my neck, just under my jaw. I lifted my hands, and honest to Gods found gills.

I started to freak out, and turned back to the beach. I made great time getting there. I hit the shallows and stood up. The gills disappeared as soon as my head was above the water. I dipped back down under and they came back. I stood and again, felt along my neck in confusion. That shouldn't have happened. I was about to shake it all off when I noticed some debris caught on my tail. I tried to shake it off, but apparently it was stuck good. So giving a sigh of frustration, I moved my tail around me to pull it off myself. I held my tail with my left hand, and yanked with my right.

"OWWW!!" I shouted.

I relooked at my tail. Okay, for real, this thing was attached to me! What the Hell! I let go of my tail and once it hit the water, I had a thought. My tail had never done that before, not until I'd grown it while under water. Maybe…?

I turned and ran back into the water. I dove again, and this time, fully shifted. Not only did the gills reappear, but my body became slightly more serpentine, my legs were longer and thinner with partial webbing between my fingers and toes, my wings didn't appear, and a few more flaps of skin grew along my tail. I was in sea dragon form.

I chuckled as best I could under the water. This was the most amazing experience of my life. Now I knew why some of my ancestors had failed to connect with our sea dragon blood. They hadn't shifted in the water, but before getting in. I swam in a circle, my eyesight a thousand times stronger down here than ever. It made sense, the dark of the ocean is deeper than above water. I was mesmerized by my transformation, and elated. Time to put myself to the test.

I shot through the water faster than I ever had before. The joy of it all couldn't be contained, as I gained momentum and shot to the surface. Like the great white sharks off seal island, I completely left the water, as I arched up, and back down. My shout of joy was consumed by the water as I went deeper. The pressure didn't bother me as I hit more than a hundred feet down. I marveled at the creatures down here. Each of them had a glow about them to my dragon eyes. Even the sea turtle that swam up to me. I bumped it with my nose and it swam off toward the beach.

That's when I realized how late it was. I looked up to where I knew the moon would be, and reluctantly turned back to shore. I did make the choice of one more bit of fun before heading back to the dorm. I gained momentum and shot out of the water again. This time, shifting in flight, to land on the beach, just short of my stuff.

I still felt elated. It had been my dream for so long to do that, and now I knew it was possible. This time my shout of joy went out across the waves and grass, to be swallowed by the distance. I gathered up my stuff after returning my necklaces to their place, grew my wings, and flew back to the dorm.

My elation evaporated when I opened my launchpad doors to find all four boys asleep in my room. I can't even begin to express my irritation at that. Jameson I didn't mind, he at least was the only one on the bed. The rest were in sleeping bags on the floor. I walked to my room doors and opened them with the intention of dragging the three on the floor outside and locking the doors. The note from Mr. McHaddish taped to my door stopped me.

'They insisted. They wanted to go after you and apologize, but Jameson talked them out of it. If you choose to, put them in the room next door.' -Mr. McHaddish.

I shrugged, I could live with that, the room next door was still vacant. Thanks to my leg, I decided against dragging them. So I opted for a levitation spell, my telekinesis wasn't quite up to snuff and I wanted the other three out in one go. I pulled out my pocket spell book and flipped to the appropriate page. Hand held out, I started.

> "Earth to Sun, Night to Day
>
> At my command, do as I say
>
> Lift with care
>
> Those I choose to bear
>
> Away from here."

There was no tell-tale wind this time, just all three boys on the floor gently rising up about three feet off the floor. I placed my book on my desk, opened my second door, and led the floating boys out and into the other room. I made sure the ride was smooth enough not to wake them.

I made sure the ride back down was gentle as well. The last thing I needed was one of them waking up and breaking my concentration. The sudden drop would for sure wake the rest. Once all three were settled, I quietly closed the doors, and went back to my room. Jameson was awake now, and made to leave.

"You, stay." I simply said.

He chuckled quietly as I closed and locked my doors. I made to walk to my bed, paused, and decided to add a locking spell to my doors. To the hall and outside. I grabbed my chalk, drew a symbol on both sets of doors, then the window – best to be safe – and began again.

> "Earth to Moon, Night to Day
>
> Remain locked until I say
>
> Or the mark is burned away."

The marks I'd made began to glow with a gentle light. That glow receding would be the indicator for how much longer the spell would last. Now completely exhausted, I didn't bother changing to pajamas, I just walked over to my desk, placed the chalk on top, then walked back around to the other side of the bed and climbed beneath the covers.

Jameson chose to stay on top of the covers, kinda like he had at the hotel in Drumnadrochit. I smiled as I remember back to that. That night seemed so far away now. I curled up into his side as he laid his arm under my head.

"I missed you mo ghaol." He said. I smiled at him saying 'my love' in Gaelic.

"I missed you too." I whispered, "Don't ever do that again."

He laughed lightly, knowing I meant how long it took for him to get here. Tomorrow I would ask what went wrong with his passport, and tell him about what I had discovered. But for now, we fell asleep to the sound of each other's heartbeats.

My dreamless sleep was only interrupted by an announcement made via magic to the whole dorm. It was made at six a.m., and was short. All morning classes were postponed and all students were to report to the gym at 8 o'clock. No questions asked. Fine by me, whatever was planned. I went back to sleep.

Chapter 78

I awoke to Jameson moving around at about seven. I rolled and stretched my limbs before rising to get up myself. I saw Jameson grab a bag from under my bed and move to the door.

"Where you goin?" I asked.

Still groggy, he answered, "The bathroom."

"Going out my launch doors is faster. Would you be able to make the jump back up?" I asked.

He walked over and looked out my window, and nodded, "I can make that."

He opened my doors outside, and stepped off. I smiled. I was glad he wouldn't have trouble. I stood and went to close the doors most of the way. I then changed my clothes. I put my torn jeans and shirt on my dresser to be fixed later. I ran a brush through my hair and looked through my homework, which someone had left on my desk. I had about forty minutes until classes started, so I got to work.

I had everything done when Jameson got back at 7:45. He came in and actually kissed me on the cheek. I smiled. I heard him close my launch doors fully as I put my things in my backpack. I put my shoes on and tied them.

I grabbed my hoodie and went to my door. I saw Jameson kneel to grab his backpack out of the corner of my eye as I opened my door. I heard him sneeze and turned to say, 'bless you', then promptly tripped over Andrew's legs. And because of how my arms were positioned, I landed full on my left hip. Which, of course, sent sudden and intense pain shooting down my whole leg.

I managed to bite back my shout, but it was unnecessary. As Mr. McHaddish was coming down my hall when I'd fallen. Also my falling had woken Andrew, and alerted Jameson. Gritting my teeth as Mr. McHaddish picked me up and carried me into my room, I couldn't keep myself from glowering at Andrew. By the time he got me to my bed, I was panting from the pain. I vaguely caught Mr. McHaddish asking Jameson to pass him my pocket spell book, but I was so focused on trying to get through the pain that it didn't fully register. I clenched my fist as my sides as I heard Mr. McHaddish begin to speak.

"Muscles as strong as an ancient drum

For today, make this leg go numb."

There was no wind, but his gentle touch to my leg did manage to activate the spell. I breathed a sigh of extreme relief as my leg did indeed go numb. I unclenched my fists, and relaxed.

Then heard Mr. McHaddish say, "Was her moving you into the next room not clue enough, Mr. Longtooth?!"

Andrew hung his head, "I'm sorry."

Mr. McHaddish stood with a growl, even I lowered my eyes, "That's not enough. She could've been seriously hurt, and that leg has already been through enough."

"Yes sir." Andrew said quietly.

Mr. McHaddish turned to me, "If you can, I need you down by the gym too."

I looked up, met his eyes, and nodded. He walked out of my room. I pulled myself up and realized he'd actually managed to make my entire leg numb. That meant my brace was going to be useless in helping me walk. I saw Jameson try not to chuckle. I actually did and told him to pass me my book.

I slipped on my brace and said the levitation spell. I touched my hand to my waist to give it a focus. I started to float off the bed. I only went up an inch, but it was enough for me to control the motion with my telekinesis. I pointedly ignored Andrew as I floated out my room doors. Jameson right behind me.

I stopped in my tracks when we got outside and I saw what had been erected in the gym area. It was a perfect spell replica of my old house. Before the explosion damage anyway. Jameson and I moved forward as the rest of the student body gathered around. I saw Mr. McHaddish gesture me over. I moved to meet him. He placed a hand on my shoulder as he steered me out of ear shot of the other shifters.

"This is a hard thing for me to request, but we don't have all the details." He said.

I swallowed. I understood what he was asking me. He wanted me to go inside and either correct, or add to the interior details of what happened that night.

"What is this for?" I asked.

"Disciplinary." He said, looking behind me.

I nodded in understanding, and walked in. I blinked a couple of times, since it felt weird to be back in this house. Magical replica or not. I saw the illusions of my grandparents and saw an immediate problem. The wound that had killed my grandpa was in the wrong spot. I quickly fixed it, checked for others, then moved on.

Most of the corrections were simple things. Like the placement of a decoration or furniture. I went up the stairs to check Amanda's death scene. Everything about that was fine. Then I went down to the garage.

Amazingly enough, that was where I hesitated. This was where I had been trapped and forced to watch as my parents died. The debris and everything was already in place, including an illusion of me looking out through a small hole. It was only then that I realized just how small my hole had been. Even with the good lighting from the sun, it didn't show I was hidden beneath it all. No wonder dad had had a tough time seeing me.

Finally I came back out and nodded to Mr. McHaddish. Everything was ready. He returned my nod, and I walked over to stand by Jameson. I rolled my eyes as I saw Honey trying to flirt with him. He saw me and we rubbed our foreheads together as she stared. She stalked off, and we heard her comment to her friends, 'why does she get all four of the hottest guys in school?' I saw Tim look at her incredulously. What that was for I didn't care.

Mr. McHaddish came forward and began, "The reason today's classes have been postponed, is because I decided to create this little demonstration for those of you who have found my orders to leave Magenta alone, hard to swallow." He pointedly looked at Honey and Tim.

Ms. Gravely came passed, "Everything's ready." She said.

Mr. McHaddish nodded, "I am also doing this so that you two," Honey and Tim, "don't receive the same treatment Magenta handed out to two of her human classmates last year. You both have already gotten your asses kicked, so the two of you are required to take a walk through." He gestured over his shoulder.

One of the other students raised a hand, "And the rest of us sir?"

"Voluntary. You may go through if you wish, but for the two of you, it is important."

"What will this prove sir?" Tim asked. Though he never took his eyes off the replica.

"That neither of you has a right to push Magenta the way you have been." he answered.

No one left. Not a single student walked away as the demonstration began. Jameson was actually one of the first to go through after Honey and Tim exited. Honey was visibly shaken and Tim looked like he was about to puke. Good. Let them both get the hint.

I was dismissed to go about my business. I chose to go talk to Ms. Gravely about my dagger. I was curious about the spell done in Māori. At least I was sure it was Māori. It had been a really long time since I had seen the language written down.

I got to her classroom to find her sitting behind her desk. I mentioned to her what I was curious about and she said to go ahead and show her the dagger. It was only as I pulled it out that I finally noticed that the hilt had changed. No longer was the handle a wraparound style, the leaves beneath the gem were gone, and the gem itself was no longer red. It was orange. I explained the changes.

She paused, and thought, "The necklace your wearing came out of it?" she asked.

"Yeah."

"What do you know about your paternal grandparents?"

"Not a lot." I answered, "Aside from their names, ages, origins, and shifter status, my dad never talked about them. I don't even know how they died. I have a few details that Mr. McHaddish gave me, but that's it."

She tapped her fingers against her lips, "I can tell you a little bit, but anything about them themselves will take some digging." She said.

"I'm okay with that." I said.

I passed her the dagger, and as she examined it, she said, "There was a heavy spell placed on this thing. And this is indeed an ancient pacific islander protection spell. I'm not 100% sure where from, since Hawaiian is closely related to about six other dialects, but I can do some research."

I nodded, "Thank you."

"Your welcome." She copied down the spell and gave me the dagger.

I walked out of the room feeling a little better. This was a good start for getting some possible answers. I hoped she got the answers soon though. I could only imagine what Reggie and Amanda would say when I told them.

I decided to head up to the library. Maybe they had some old spell books. I took the elevator instead of hovering the whole way up the stairs, I hadn't done this much movement by telekinesis in a long time. I had refused to do so after the murders. So it had been like, holy crap, more than a year. I hadn't done it since seven months before November. Were my folks still alive I'd get ripped a new one for that.

I did have to speed hover to the library 'cause I felt myself getting tired. I surprised the heck out of the librarian. I sat down before she actually got up and came over with a glass of water. I guess I should call it a paper cup of water. I told her what I was looking for, and she peeled off to find the spell books they had.

She came back with three carts worth of books. From over 17 different countries. About ten of them were from ancient Scotland. I recognized them immediately. My mom had had copies of each of them. And thankfully only three had been damaged in the explosion. Seventy percent of the books were actually ancient, but none of the ancient ones were pacific islander magic.

"There's a reason for that dear." The librarian said.

I looked up at her, "I didn't get your name ma'am." I said.

"Miss Turner dear."

"So let me guess. Most history was passed down orally."

"Correct. Just like most native American tribes and wicca."

I hung my head, "So I'm screwed for now."

"Not necessarily dear." She pulled the third cart over, and handed me one, "I assume you've heard of him."

The book she handed me was by Scott Cunningham, "Yeah. My mom had two of his books from before he died. She had planned on getting the rest but we never had the chance."

"I think he can help." She passed me the book. Cunningham's guide to Hawaiian Magic and Spirituality.

My eyes widened when I saw it, "I hadn't realized he'd done a Hawaiian one."

She nodded, "He wrote it, but I think his daughter published it back in 2009."

"Thank you." I said.

"Your welcome dear."

She left the carts just in case I needed anything else. I opened the book and got reading.

I was at the library for almost two hours. The book held a lot of great info. Lists of Gods, Goddesses, other kinds of spirits, and beings. All of it was fascinating! It didn't include any spells except for an ancient love spell – which was undoable in their culture – but I stay far away from those. I had just reached said chapter when I received a start.

"Maggie."

"Fuck a duck!!" I shouted.

Jameson started dying of laughter at his unintended success in startling me. I was surprised the librarian didn't come over to shush us. I was still breathing hard when Jameson came up for air.

"I'm sorry…" he chuckled, "I didn't mean to startle you." He laughed some more.

I shook my head and chuckled a little, "It's fine. This book was very useful."

He took a deep breath, the smile still plastered to his face, "What were you readin'?"

"A book about ancient Hawaiian culture and magic." I told him.

"Trying to connect with that side more." He sat down next to me.

I nodded, "And I was hoping there might be some spell in here. But most spells have been lost thanks to Christianity."

"So, it cannae help you." He said, seeming incredulous about the result.

"Not in the way I expected, but it gives me somewhere to start." I specified.

"Start with what?" said a voice. We looked up to see Andrew. I facepalmed.

Jameson stood, "Can I help yeh?" Oh great! More dumbass male dominance shit!

Andrew chuckled, "Cut the accent pal." They stood nose to nose.

"Hey!!" I said, they both froze, Jameson with his head turned to look behind him.

I stood, "You think this is bad for the four of you." I turned an angry stare at them, "Imagine what it's like for me." I shouldered my bag, and picked up the book.

My leg felt a little better so I walked passed the two of them and went to the front desk, I checked out the book and made my way to the dining hall. I heard Jameson and Andrew begin to follow me. I nearly stumbled on the way down the stairs, having decided not to take the elevator because I knew the two of them would join me. Andrew made to grab me, but Jameson grabbed him. I heard them growl at each other. This was going so well, I thought to myself sarcastically. I pulled myself straight and continued down.

"Why did you stop me?" Andrew growled as we got outside.

"Because she doesn't like to be helped without permission ya numpty." Jameson Growled back.

"And you know this how? And will you stop it with the accent!" Andrew tried not to shout.

"I'm from Scotland ya bampot! The accent is real. And two, Maggie and I spent the summer together so I think that makes me prequalified to know her habits and preferences."

"And why the hell should I believe that?" he asked.

"Because I was there too." We turned.

Mr. McHaddish was staring them down. None of us had heard him approach. Andrew respectfully lowered his eyes after a moment before raising them again. Jameson just smiled.

"Jameson, your mother called. She says your grounded for a month when you get back for 'forgetting' to call and tell her you'd safely arrived." He stated.

Jameson shrugged, "I had something else to worry about." He looked at me. I gave a small smile.

Mr. McHaddish nodded, "You two make a somewhat sad entourage following Maggie like that."

"Dominating wise?" Andrew asked.

"Arguing wise." Jameson told him.

"Like it or not, you both are two of her mates. I suggest you **all** get this straightened out before you spend the centuries together." He told them.

They meekly nodded, and we continued on our way to lunch.

Chapter 79

I didn't make it to the dining hall. I took one step inside the building and my leg screamed. I bit back my own as Jameson caught me before I hit the floor. He gently maneuvered me and lifted me up into his arms.

"I thought you said she didn't like help?" Andrew goaded.

"Zip it you." I said, "You're still in trouble so don't push it."

Andrew hung back a little. As if slightly embarrassed. Oh well. Jameson carried me into the dining hall, and like a gentlemen, went to get food for both of us after setting me down at the end of one of the benches. I spotted Javier and Mason come in and head to the line behind Andrew.

It didn't take Jameson long to get back with two trays. Sloppy Joes. Always good. A few minutes later Andrew, Javier, and Mason sat across from us. I was lucky to finish my food, since the three of them kept staring daggers at each other and Jameson. Finally when I was done eating, I'd had enough.

"Stop it." I said to the four of them.

They all looked at me. Jameson recognized my quiet angry and wisely didn't do anything. The others however looked back and forth between each other, like they hadn't known they were doing something wrong.

"Either all four of you get your shit together and butch up, or I will make you." I said.

None of them moved, then, "Jameson. Born in Glasgow Scotland. Officially recognized as Magenta's mate on August 20th." He stated. Okay a good start.

Andrew scoffed, "What the hell are we supposed to do with that."

"Oh for fuck sake." I stood and made to walk out.

All four boys stood, "Maggie!" Jameson said, trying to warn me I guess.

Andrew was right behind me, "Would you just.." he grabbed me and turned me around.

I growled loud enough that the whole room heard me. Andrew didn't even flinch. He just continued to meet my gaze until one of the others came forward. Then the rest made a small circle around us.

Andrew wisely let go, "Just answer me one question, and I'll cooperate."

"What?" I bit out.

"The bond is supposed to form on first sight. So why haven't you felt it? I did the second I saw you, so what's the deal?" he asked.

"Because I'm not eighteen yet you jackass! I only turned sixteen this last April!" I said.

The realization hit him like a ton of bricks. As did the next one. Of our little group, only he was fully physically mature. Only he was eighteen. He turned a little green at his sudden shame.

"I'm sorry." He lifted his head and met the others' eyes, "I guess we should sit and talk then."

Jameson, Javier, and Mason all nodded. They all looked at me one last time then returned to the table. Jameson came over with my bag and handed it to me.

"Good luck." I said as I shouldered it. He smiled and went back to talk it out with the others.

I hovered my way up to my room. I knew there was still a few hours of school left, but I wanted to try and contact Reggie and give him an update about the dagger and Grandma's necklace.

Turns out he beat me to it. I pulled my pearl out to see it was glowing. When did he get his hands on a diamond? I shrugged and sat down on my bed. Holding the pearl, I focused on him. He responded quickly.

"*Somethings been stolen!*" he shouted. Hurting my head.

I refocused, *"What has been?"*

"No one's telling, but the magic community is going ballistic. A human matching Kepner's description perfectly stole something powerful from Lady Nightingale."

I nearly came out of my trance, *"You have got to be shitting me!"*

"I wish." He replied.

Lady Nightingale was the most powerful sorceress of the century. Anyone who needed spelled amulets, glamour stones, love spells, transfiguration potions, you name it, they went to her. She demanded a high price, but her magical intervention was worth it for most people. The fact that someone had successfully stolen from **her**, was unbelievable.

"When was it stolen and how powerful was the item at least?" I asked.

"A few hours ago, and it came from her swamp vault." Again, I wish he'd been kidding. It was bad enough he'd stolen from her, the fact that he'd risked her swamp vault – which was guarded by well over three hundred gators and cotton mouths – was suicide!

"Do they know how he got in?"

"No! And that pisses her off more than the fact that he stole something from her." He answered. *"He'll be coming for you now."*

"I know. Keep your stone close." My anger and anticipation were matched by his.

We broke contact, and my resolve hardened. New Orleans was only a three and a half hour flight from L.A., so it was a good chance he was already back in L.A. That meant that he might just show his ugly face tonight.

I stood. My leg didn't make a single complaint. I walked out and launched myself over the railing to the ground floor. I landed amongst students going back to class. I radiated anger, so they moved away quickly. My fellow shifters began growling, including my boys. I turned as the doors behind me opened. Mr. McHaddish walked in. He saw me and tensed. Then he came forward and sensed what the other shifters already had.

"What is it?" he asked.

"He's coming." I said, "It's time."

Chapter 80

Preparations were made quickly. All students were released from class and told to get the school ready for war. I tried to insist otherwise. I wanted him to find me without trouble. It wasn't until Mr. McHaddish reminded me about one of my dad's war lessons that I agreed. If you don't put up a fight for the target of desire, then the villain will know something is wrong, and will retaliate in ways that would fuck up the winning plan. Like when Thanos collects the time stone in Avengers: Infinity Wars.

The teachers were told to create as many ward spells and potions as fast as they could without creating an explosion. I contributed there mostly. That ended up being the first time that Honey and I actually cooperated. We combined two of our strongest shield spells for a very effective deflector spell.

Jameson and the other boys started on any physical defensive measures they could come up with. Which was quite a lot. I decided to contact Amanda to see if she could give us any definitive information on his arrival. It took her some time to respond.

"That bastard has found a way to block me out!" Was the first thing she said.

"How?!" We were blind. I hate being blind.

She was pacing back and forth, if she could shift, she would have, "I have no idea. I took my eyes off him for one second – literally – and he was hidden."

That was **not** good, "Is there anything you can do?"

She shook her head, "No. I've tried, but whatever he's done aside from steal from Nightingale, it was not natural. He's officially coming for you. And the fact that I can't protect you, scares me the most." Her voice cracked for the last sentence.

I came forward and hugged her, "Don't worry about me," I pulled back and placed our foreheads together, "I'm not a little girl anymore." I smiled encouragingly at her.

She smiled back sadly, "I know, you haven't been since that night."

I chuckled lightly, then said what I'd been dying to say for weeks, "The next time we see each other, you'll be reborn. I promise."

She smiled, and gave a satisfactory growl, "Go kill that fucking son of a bitch. And make sure it's slow."

"That's the plan." We broke contact. Now came the hardest part. Waiting.

The waiting was agony. Much more than that damned tub. Night had fallen more than an hour ago. I had changed my clothes before coming outside, to give myself easier movement. I had also left my brace and grandma's necklace in my room, in case I needed to shift quickly.

Me and a few other shifters were on patrol along the island perimeter and along the interior, in case he got passed one of us. All non-shifters were inside, though not all of them were happy about that. The fae and half-fae students were on the roof, watching the sea for any signs of a boat.

That was literally the only thing we knew for sure other than he was coming. He had to come by boat. The only plane was still on the islands small tarmac. I could see it from here.

I passed several of the other shifters with whom I shared my patrol. Including Andrew and Jameson. Andrew told me as he passed that he and the others had talked and I could trust them not to fight anymore. I said that was good and we continued.

The patrols were planned so that no area of ground was unguarded for more than three seconds. Maybe enough time to slip passed a sloppy human but not shifters on high alert. I was about to perform my switch with one of the interior wolves when the fae students gave the alert. Someone was coming from the east.

I signaled to Mila via whistle – whom was in hyena form close by – that the call was made and to pull the other shifters back.

I turned and ran back to the side of the school building. As planned, the other shifters on border patrol hid, to wait and see if it was indeed Kepner. Though no one doubted it was him. As I made the side of the building, I shifted. I kept low so that I wouldn't be seen from shore. The distance was more than half a mile but better safe than sorry.

I heard the motor before I saw it. It was a small five person boat. He stood at the engine, maneuvering the boat to the shore carefully, and as quietly as he could. With my dragon eyes, I could see the large grapefruit sized amulet around his neck. It's glow told me all I needed to know. It was a glamour diffuser amulet, the most powerful in the world. That amulet was under the strictest guard, not just the gators and snakes, but dozens of different protection spells from over thirty countries. Each! So how the hell had he gotten it?!

He'd shaved off his beard and grown his hair out a little, he looked almost like he had all those months ago. I growled so low that anyone within fifty feet of me would have felt it instead of heard it. I stayed where I was as he beached the boat slightly and got out. I partially hoped his prosthetic leg would get stuck, but it didn't.

He started walking up the beach, not even bothering to remove the amulet. I had to steady my breathing as he moved further up the island. That's when everything went wrong.

The three children from the cottage became afraid, I saw them out of the corner of my eye, getting ready to leave the cottage and make a run for the dorm's main doors. I stayed low, hoping they wouldn't try it. But they did.

The youngest tripped when they were only fifteen feet from their little fence that surrounded the cottage. That put them withing a few feet of Kepner, and more than forty feet from me. The two older went back for their brother. Only then did they see Kepner. They instantly became even more afraid. He started to move toward them. I remembered what he'd done to his daughter, I would not let him hurt the three of them.

I covered the distance in a single bound. Carefully landing with the children underneath me. They all gasped, and covered their ears as I began to roar. If you've seen videos of mama bears giving that warning roar that can last several seconds, that gives you the best idea of what I did. He never even flinched. He just blinked. I stretch out my left wing, giving the children the cover they needed to get to the main doors. They took it. They ran so fast that Kepner didn't notice them again until the doors opened.

He made to follow them. I hissed and growled at him and took a step forward. He finally looked into my eyes, only then recognizing me.

"Maggie." He sounded so relieved. It disgusted me.

"Leave everyone on this island untouched, and I'll leave willingly." I said. I hated to, but it was necessary.

He nodded, "Of course." and threw a ball of dragon's bane in my face.

I shrieked. The smell was so much stronger as a dragon. I twisted and flapped my wings trying to disperse the damned powder, but it was no use. He'd used it once before to defeat my father, now it would be how he subdued me. I had no choice but to shift back to human form. Coughing on the ground, helpless, was when he came forward and finished the job. I don't know what he hit me with, all I know is that the world went black.

Chapter 81

I don't know how long I was out, the only thing I realized at first was the fact that my head was killing me. I went to rub my head, and came to the rest of the way. My hands were bound with thick rope. For some reason, my shirt was missing. I was clad only in my bra and the shorts I'd changed into before patrol. My shoes weren't too far away, and my hair had come loose, it now hung all over me like a veil. I was lying on a thin mattress in a cave. Some solar powered lanterns strategically placed around the cave gave it plenty of light. I could hear and smell the ocean, so we weren't far from the shore.

I looked around for my weapons. My gun and grandmother's dagger were directly across the cave from me. I felt my pocket and found my transport stone still there, of course he wouldn't deprive me of that, as far as he knew it was harmless. I reached in my pocket with some difficulty, and squeezed it, sending Reggie the signal he needed. It would take a few minutes for him to get here, but it was a start. I grabbed my shoes and socks, and put them back on. I tried to grow my tail, but apparently I was still under the effects of the dragon's bane. I could feel it dissipating, just not fast enough.

I started to get up and froze. I looked toward the cave entrance. Kepner was coming back, time to play for time. I leaned back down, like putting my socks and shoes back on had sapped me of my last dregs of energy. He fell for it. He came over with some water and helped me drink it. I only drank it 'cause my nose was working well enough to tell me it wasn't drugged in any way.

"I'm sorry about the dragon's bane. I wanted you to be unharmed." He said.

He stood and moved away, "How did you get the amulet?" he didn't catch my accusatory tone.

He smiled to himself, "I played it right, I bribed the right guard." Lady Nightingale was going to blow a gasket.

"And finding the island?"

"Old maps stolen from the Paris Museum of Natural History." He said. "Or was it the Archives?"

I rolled my eyes, there was a reason he was a science teacher, "Where are we?"

"Still on the island, the southwest side. I'm waiting for the creatures to calm down before leaving." He answered. Good, maybe I could signal Jameson and the others.

That's when I noticed the smaller amulet hanging from his belt line, "Did you steal that from Nightingale as well?"

He knew what I meant, "No. That I stole from the New Orleans Historic Voodoo Museum. They hadn't known they had an authentic soul concealer amulet in their collection."

A soul concealer amulet!? That was dark magic! A combination of voodoo – which counted as a neutral magic, just like elemental magic – and necromancy. The only true dark magic. I could tell from looking at it that it had deliberately been designed like a normal voodoo trinket, to hide it from misuse.

"How did you find that?" I asked. He once again missed the accusatory tone.

"I borrowed a bracelet from your mother's collection." He held up his wrist. Our mother's antique golden dragon bracelet that had been a gift from dad on their first anniversary was around his wrist. We'd thought it had been destroyed in the fire.

I was livid. That bracelet was a family heirloom! Our dad's three times great grandfather had handcrafted it himself for his mate all those centuries ago. When our mom had received it, she'd placed a few enchantments on it. One to protect the wearer from harm, the other to detect dark magic. He must've been wearing it since that night. The protection spell would've told him when the authorities were close, and that Amanda had been watching him. The bracelet would also have told him exactly what the soul concealer charm was.

"What do you plan to do with me?"

He misread my tone, "I'm not going to hurt you. I will take you from this evil place, I have a safe place in the Canadian mountains. That's where we'll go."

"This place is no more evil than Mr. Hydell was." I couldn't stop myself.

This seemed to confuse him, "He and this place were keeping you from me. As was your family."

My anger intensified, "Don't you mention my family!" I said quietly, standing as I did. I felt a pull.

He actually looked afraid. Good. I heard them before he did. My boys came charging into the cave at top speed, quickly surrounding him. Andrew actually knocked him to the floor. My strength was almost fully returned, so I yanked my wrists apart and shredded the rope. There was a bright flash of light, and sudden pain in my chest. The light was Reggie, finally arriving, he looked at me and froze, the pain, was my grandmother's dagger being imbedded in my chest up to the hilt. My boys felt the pain, but the biggest surprise was the look of confusion of Kepner's face. His arm was positioned in a throw and he'd managed to stand back up. So he'd done the same thing Elizabeth had. If he couldn't have me, no one could. It had pierced my heart, but with the duel protection spells, it wouldn't kill me.

I grabbed the hilt with one hand and pulled it out, then looked at Kepner, "Was that supposed to hurt?"

He seemed to only then understand that he was the only human there, 'cause he tripped over himself trying to get away from the two dragons, extra-large bear, and large wolf stalking toward him. Andrew and Javier had Jameson and Mason between them, but right now all I could see was my boys between me and my kill.

"No." I said with power.

They all turned slightly to look at my, Reggie passed me an extra shirt as well as a hair tie. I put the shirt on and pulled my hair back. And with Reggie at my side, walked between Jameson and Mason. Kepner looked relieved, like I was coming to save him. I raised my left hand to touch Jameson's head. He gave the equivalent of a smile and – giving Kepner one more hated look – began backing away.

"He's ours." Reggie said. The boys didn't argue, they backed away as well.

Kepner once again looked confused, "Maggie, I love you." His confusion was mixed with fear.

My eyes glowed, "And I want you dead."

I turned to my boys while Reggie moved forward, his eyes glowing as intensely as mine, "Head back to the school. I can handle myself from here. And let Mr. McHaddish know I'm fine.

They nodded, and went to leave the cave. I picked up my gun and placed it on the thin mattress, I wouldn't be using it. I placed my dagger next to it. Then stood and went to stand by my brother. That was the first and only time he took his eyes off Kepner. I gave him a wicked smile that Kepner couldn't see.

I was giving Reggie the first blow. He deserved it more, since he'd been absent from the murders. Reggie gave me a vengeful smile and returned his eyes to Kepner. He walked slowly toward him, and fast as lightning, ripped away his prosthetic leg – which apparently Kepner had had physically attached to his femur bone, because when I saw it hit the wall, the femur bone was with it, no muscles though. Reggie had yanked the bone clean out of the socket, leaving the muscles of his leg still attached and limp.

Kepner's scream of pure agony was pure joy to the two of us. And so our revenge began.

Chapter 82

An hour before dawn, Reggie and I were seated outside and above the cave entrance. We had taken our time with Kepner, making sure his death was excruciatingly painful. Making sure he took hours to die. He was now, had been for about half an hour. Ending him had been satisfying, as was our crying together afterwards. Crying in relief that he was dead, and that mom, dad, grandpa, and grandma could finally rest in peace.

I had my dagger in my hands and was twirling it between my fingers. Our mother's bracelet was safely around my wrist, where it belonged. I breathed the first sigh of freedom in months, and continued to sit in companionable silence with my brother. Soon we'd be leaving to provide proof of Kepner's death, I was just waiting for the call. I had already whispered that it was done, so while waiting for the coordinates, I'd returned to school to grab a cloth bag. I'd also taken the two amulets back, asking Mr. McHaddish to return them. I told him what was necessary for return and sent a message to Lady Nightingale about the bribe. The bag was next to me, empty for now.

Reggie broke our silence first, "So, who were the dragons and wolf?"

I smiled and cringed at the same time, "I would've thought it was obvious."

He leaned forward in disbelief, "Four mates?!"

I nodded, "And only one of them is over eighteen."

He laughed in sympathy, "Well at least I know how you feel."

It was my turn to be disbelieving, "What the heck are you talking about?"

"When me and Matilda passed through central America, we met three ladies, who also turned out to be my mates."

I covered my face with both hands and collapsed backwards into the grass, laughing, "You indeed know how I feel."

"All cats. One jaguar, two leopards, and one panther." He informed me.

"HA!!" I leaned back up, "Your officially screwed." I continued laughing.

He joined me, "Yes I am. And they would agree with you."

As the first rays of dawn began to lighten the sky, my necklace started to glow. I held it with my hand and closed my eyes. The coordinates formed in my head without trouble. 31.7537 degrees south, by 159.2512 degrees east. I knew the coordinates from a report I'd done last year for geography, the island of Ball's Pyramid, thirteen miles southeast of Lord Howe island in the south pacific. And well off the coast of Australia. One of the most secluded islands on the planet, and completely uninhabited by humans.

I turned to Reggie, "I know where to go." I grabbed my bag and dagger in hand, went back down into the cave to collect the evidence of death.

I'd spelled the bag on the way in, so as to one, keep it fresh, two keep it from getting wet, and three, to keep blood from seeping through and attracting predators. I met Reggie back where we'd been sitting.

"A hyena shifter stopped by. I told her you'd be leaving with me for a meeting." He said.

"Did Mila stop for a reason?" I asked.

"Yeah, to check on you. Mr. McHaddish was wondering."

I nodded, "Let's get going then." I tied the bag to my belt.

"Where're we goin'?"

"The island of Ball's Pyramid." I answered.

He was stunned, "That's off the coast of Australia."

"489 miles northeast of Sydney to be precise. Isolated and uninhabited by humans. That's where we are to meet Rowan."

"That's still several days flight from here." He said.

I got the biggest smile on my face, "Who said anything about flying." I gestured for him to follow me, and took off running at top speed.

I'd checked earlier, while the cliff was only thirty feet high, the water was deep, there was no beach below where we were jumping. I leaped over the edge with no hesitation, Reggie close behind. We hit the water at the same time. I felt the gills along my neck pop up immediately. I waved Reggie over. He got closer and noticed them, he recoiled in shock. I took a good look at his neck, and gestured to his.

He lifted his hand, and found gills of his own. His eyes widened. I didn't know if it was from fear or disgust, so I made a calming gesture, and gestured for him to watch me. He nodded and I moved a little further from the cliff wall. I looked back to make sure he was calm, and shifted.

I swear his eyes got so big I thought they'd pop out of his head. Then he smiled, it was a somewhat sad smile, like he was couldn't believe that the sea dragon gene was still strong. I gestured my head at him to try. He licked his lips, and moved out from the wall. Then he shifted as well.

I'd been right, he shifted into a sea dragon as well, his color still midnight blue, but he now had spots of light blue along his flank and legs. As well as feelers along his neck, and snout, the longer two by his nose making it look like he had a mustache. It made sense, since he was fully mature, unlike me. He looked at me with a playful gleam in his eyes that I hadn't seen in months. I returned it.

"*Race ya bro.*" I said, and we took off, swimming faster than ever.

Chapter 83

Swimming, it only took us two days to reach Ball's Pyramid. We'd have been there sooner, but we'd spotted some shark poachers and had given them incentive never to do it again. We hadn't hurt or killed them, but let's just say they'd have quite the story to tell when they got home.

We arrived just after noon. We actually lifted our heads up out of the water, marveling at its height and sheer cliffs. This island was *all* cliffs and sharp edges, a seven million year old volcano remnant that looked like a stone spire sticking out of the water. The only flat land was at the very southern end of the island, and it was small. The island itself was 562 meters in height – which of course translated to 1843.8 feet high.

Looking at it, I remembered that a scientific expedition was to take place here in November. I'd have to try to remember and try to apply for it. At the moment, I was trying to see where we were to meet Rowen. The island's coordinates were one thing, actually saying where to meet was another.

Finally I spotted him, he stood half way up the summit. His long hair was the best indicator. Reggie and I swam forward, and on the tiny piece of rocky shore, shifted back before shifting again into full dragon form to make the climb. This island was home to a rare form of stick insect, flying might disrupt their environment somehow, so we climbed.

We reached Rowen within a minute. For the last few feet, we climbed as humans with large wings. We retracted our wings once we were stable on solid ground. Seeing Rowen in person was weird, but I was glad our journey was nearly done.

He smiled, "May I see what you brought as proof?" he asked.

"Please, it's been killing me the whole way." Reggie commented.

I chuckled, and pulled the bag from my belt. I untied the top, reached in, and pulled out Kepner's head. His last moments of pain still on his frozen features.

Rowen nodded with an impressed expression, "That will do."

There was a blinding flash of light. We covered our eyes, and when we opened them, we stood in a room with the same golden glow from our talks with Amanda. Before us stood a table with Amanda's prone body on it. I couldn't stop the tears.

We walked forward, her body was in perfect condition, she seemed only asleep. There was no sign of her wounds, not even scars. Next to her table was a smaller one, on top was placed two small knives and a diffuser. Well, it looked like a diffuser, but our guess was that it was the magic item we had to bleed into. We had met all the criteria, we'd killed Kepner together, we were here with her body ready to offer blood, and we'd brought the proof of death.

Rowen and three other fae suddenly appeared on the other side of Amanda, "All is in order. Please give your blood."

We both grabbed a knife, "Does it matter from which hand?" Reggie asked.

They shook their heads. We were both right handed, so we cut into the meat of our thumbs, instantly releasing a strong flow of blood. We held our hands over the diffuser, and watched it fill to the brim. One of the fae healed our hands without touching us, added some other spell component to the blood, and lifted the diffuser.

I saw an apparition out the corner of my eye, Amanda's soul, answering the unspoken summons. Drops of blood were placed along Amanda's chakra points, the rest was poured down her unmoving throat and the fae began to chant. Neither of us paid attention to what they were saying, we were too busy watching Amanda's body start glowing.

The glow intensified as the spell reached its climax. We squinted a little, but we kept watching. Finally the glow died. The fae lowered their arms. At first, nothing happened, then almost imperceptibly, Amanda started breathing. I couldn't help but gasp in relief. I felt Reggie place his arms around me. Rowen was the only fae left in the room, as Amanda opened her eyes.

"Guys?" she whispered when she saw us.

We lost it. With a new found strength, Amanda rose and embraced us. We stood there, together for the first time in so long, that the tears didn't stop. Rowen sent us back to Ball's Pyramid without us seeing it, saying a quiet 'thank you and your welcome' to Amanda as he did.

Once we were done crying, hand in hand, we jumped from the mountain and showed Amanda our newest gift.

Chapter 84

We spent the next week swimming the Pacific together. Amanda told us stories of what she'd done while in limbo – most of which was pretty boring according to her. We gave her the details on Kepner's death, and everything else that had happened over the last year. I eventually got to the topic of grandma's necklace. They hadn't believed it as first, then I showed them the memory. That prompted a quick trip to Hawaii.

We'd tracked down a descendant of one of grandma's siblings. Our human cousin, Armand, was able to answer our questions about her death. Basically, she'd been blessed by the god Kanaloa, the god of magic. She'd been born a prophetess, but she specifically saw only one thing about a person's life. Their soulmate. Even shifters.

After our dad had been born, someone had spilled her gift to the shifter community. Hundreds of shifters had stormed the islands demanding to know whom their future mates were. Our grandparents had fled to the safety of Kilauea, Pele's domain where they asked for sanctuary. Pele had given it, but it hadn't lasted long. In a last ditch effort, the shifters had charged the barriers that protected them. Their charge is what caused the Pu'u 'O'o eruption of 1983. It's also what killed them. Their bodies were overwhelmed by the heat and they burned to death. An ironic death for two dragon shifter, especially one from Hawaii.

In the last moments of her life, she'd magically sent the dagger and necklace to her son – our father who was attending school on the mainland. Our dad had shown up a few days later to ask Armand's dad what had happened, and he'd been told what we'd just heard.

"How'd your dad find out?" Reggie had asked afterwards.

"My dad was watching from nearby. He has the ability to shape shift to a small bird at times, but he hasn't since that day. She may not have actually been his sister – his many times great aunt really – but that's how he saw her."

We thanked him and left shortly afterwards. Promising to stay in contact with him as well. We toured the islands for a few days before beginning the swim back to my school.

People went mad after we got back. A good kind of mad. There was a victory celebration for the three of us, held by Mr. McHaddish, who'd sent Kepner's dead body to the authorities. They'd been livid about what we'd done with him, and my taking his head, but he'd talked them down to the point that they dropped it.

He'd also sent word to my friends, Ms. Hamper and Molly, saying that it was safe to come out of hiding. They'd have figured it out after seeing the news, but he told us that he'd wanted to do it. He then explained that my shirt had been found, then subsequently burned. When I asked why he said that since it was saturated in dragon's bane, it was safer to get rid of it. I was fine with that.

Near the end of the celebration, me, Amanda, and Reggie got a chance to be alone. We talked about what our plans would be from there. Reggie would go back to school. He hadn't actually gotten permission for prolonged absence, so he needed to remedy that, but he planned to finish school. Only about five years left.

Amanda would take a gap year. She wanted to travel the world for real, and who knows, maybe find her mate. She'd contact MIT in the morning to confirm if her scholarship was still valid. We didn't know how Rowen was gonna make her return to life normal, but I at least hoped he'd just make it look like her death was staged and she'd been placed in an induced coma by an anonymous doctor after the murders. That's what I would've done. If the scholarship was still valid, she said she would look forward to the four years of college.

She even stated that she'd try and get me a recommendation at MIT for the marine biology department. I was shocked, I hadn't even known MIT had a marine biology option. That would be four years of college for me, plus 2-3 for a master degree, then if I went for a PhD, which would require an additional six years. I still had time to choose though, so I would use it.

The next day we said our good-byes. Reggie took the small plane to the main land with the staff. He'd return to his girls by another flight a day or so later. Matilda had chewed his ear off the night before for not contacting them. He then called the next day to say that he'd landed an internship at NASA, we'd both given him congrats and wished him luck. Amanda had called MIT, and had received the good news that now that she wasn't in hiding – apparently Rowen had done what I'd thought – her scholarship was still valid, and she was welcome to start when she was ready. She informed them about taking a gap year, and planned out where to go. Eventually she decided to start by visiting our parents graves in Michigan. Then she'd go to Scotland, it was only appropriate she'd said. From there, she'd figure it out.

I of course didn't get much choice. I had to finish up high school. But at least now I could enjoy it.

A few days into the next week, Lady Nightingale stopped by the school. She's wanted to personally thank me for returning her amulet and for giving her the tip about the bribe. She told us that after my message had been received, she'd done a full investigation into who the perp had been. Turns out her head guy had gone corrupt the year before. He was now nowhere to be found, but we all figured he'd probably been eaten by gators.

Amanda's travel plans were slightly waylaid. I saw a news report on the internet, apparently, her ex-boyfriend didn't believe that she'd been comatose, and called her resurrection, a work of the devil. I rolled my eyes, as did Amanda, she had looked so peeved at him. It wasn't until he finally stopped ranting that she slapped some sense into him. Literally.

She slapped him full across the face and said to ask one Dr. Hajima, from San Francisco, about her being comatose in his hospital, under his care. Later reports confirmed what she'd told her ex. And further inquiry done by Amanda, showed that the doctor had been given a similar cadaver by Rowen, and told to make it look real. Obviously, he'd done an awesome job! Now with her ex publicly humiliated, he apologized and asked if they could continue their past relationship. She'd given a hard no. She was done with him, it was obvious to her now, that he wasn't in anyway one of her future mates – or her only one if that was the case – and she intended to go through with her travel plans with new hope.

I received so many calls from my friends that the school had to limit them. Even Gretchen was amongst them. I reassured them that I was okay, and to my American friends, that I would be available over Thanksgiving break. Since Molly wanted me and my boys over for the holiday. I even heard from Emily and Amber. I was happy to tell them that I had gotten the dress and planned to wear it for the next school dance – which new students were required to attend. Dang it.

That was an interesting affair let me tell you. Barely a week before, Honey came to me for color coordination advise, stating that she'd actually spoken with Emily and Amber, and they'd pointed her to me as the go to person on color coordination. She wasn't an easy case, not a lot of colors go with Fuschia. But apparently that was her favorite shape of pink.

I ended up going through my entire stock of reds, blues, and purples before I finally found a workable combo. Plum purple. The dark shade toned down the pink beautifully. I sent the color choice to Emily and Amber before telling Honey the final result.

Obviously she'd been skeptical the whole week until it arrived. She took one look at that dress and melted. Not only did the plum work with the fuschia, but it complimented her skin tone very well.

I then heard from Mila, she'd been called away shortly before we'd returned to school. Her mother had taken my suggestion about the negotiations and Mila had needed to be present. Everything had gone perfectly, she'd said. The rival clan had gladly accepted the knowledge of the veins in their lands. Though of course they hadn't gotten the locations of them until they vacated Mila's queendom. Mila's family now had their home back, and she'd be going there over the summer.

Chapter 85

After that, everything quieted down. October was pretty normal. I had indeed worn my dress to the school dance – which had taken place on the 7th – and had actually made my own costume for the Halloween dance. I attended regular appointments with the campus doctor, not just for my leg, but to make sure my arm wasn't going to relapse. I'd had an incident in gym just before October began, so I was under surveillance for that.

I started some college classes as October turned to November. I'd finally decided that I wanted to major in actual biology for my marine biology degree, plus minors in volcanology and archaeology. I didn't succeed in getting a place in the Ball's Pyramid expedition, but I didn't mind.

As Thanksgiving approached, Andrew and the others started giving Jameson a little grief about never experiencing it. He didn't mind. He was more worried about me. The anniversary of the murders was coming up, and he wanted me as calm as possible. Luckily for me, the anniversary was on a Saturday. I spent the 18th quietly brooding in my room. I almost didn't eat anything, let alone talk to anyone. Jameson had other ideas though. He brought me cookies and milk, then an actual cake. I'd laughed, but accepted the food. I ate it slowly over the day. Then had fallen asleep as the moon rose.

We got a few extra days of break when it arrived. I had a backpack full of clothes with me as I got off the plane with my boys. They kept messing with each other as we approached the exits. I finally spotted Molly waving us down. As we got closer, my eyes widened and my jaw nearly hit the floor.

"You're pregnant!?" I asked happily.

She nodded with tears of joy, "A little over five months now."

I covered my mouth to keep from crying. It made me wonder if she'd known before Mr. Hydell had been killed, or if she'd found out afterwards.

She answered my unspoken question, "I found out the day he died. I'd planned on telling both of you when you'd gotten back from the tour." We hugged each other. "I also have another surprise for you. It's waiting back at my house."

I took the time to introduce her officially to Jameson and the rest, before doing the same for them. We were getting the rest of our baggage when things got a little interesting, and a lot messed up.

"Magenta Sharp?" someone behind me asked.

I turned to find myself face to face with a catholic preacher, "Who's asking?" I asked suspiciously.

He looked wistful, a bible clutched in his hands, "You look just like your mother."

Okay, now I was creeped out, "Uh, okay. Who the hell are you and how did you know my mom?"

He shook himself, "Sorry, uh, you don't know me, but then again, the last time I saw your mother, your brother was only a baby."

I raised an eyebrow, Jameson and the others moved a little closer, "Easy guys." I said. "That still doesn't answer my questions."

He fidgeted a little, "My name is William Marcus," I froze, "your mother was my younger sister."

"You're Uncle Bill?!" I asked. Mom had only mentioned him once, and that was to tell me to never ask about him again.

"So your mom did mention me." He smiled.

"Only as a snooping, super overprotecting jerk who stuck his nose where it didn't belong, and whom we were never to ask about – or even mention – ever again." I replied.

He seemed uncomfortable, "Yes, I admit I was wrong to try and get between your parents, but I felt the relationship was doomed. Although I never imagined how they would end up."

"And you think that absolves you?!" I crossed my arms. I felt smoke leave my nostrils.

"No, no. I know I can never atone for what I did to them, but I can still try and make it right." he stated.

Okay, now I was nervous. "How? It's not like you can apologize to my dad for threatening to cut off his wings and throw him to the sharks if he didn't stay away from my mom." I said. The boys sputtered in disbelief.

He cringed, "No I can't, and I regret my remark."

Molly decided that she'd had enough of him, "While I'm somewhat glad that Maggie has other family out there," she stated semi sarcastically, "we have to go if you don't mind."

"I do mind actually." He said. We all turned back to him.

"What the hell does that mean?" I asked.

"Do you mind not cursing." He said exasperatedly.

"You're not my dad!" I stated.

"No I'm not, but Mr. McHaddish and Miss Jenkins only have custody of you so long as a family member is unable to take you."

Molly turned green, "Excuse me!?" she sounded alarmed.

He pulled a document from his jacket and handed it to her, "I am applying for full custody of Maggie. That document is for a court hearing set for December 1st. You, Maggie, and Mr. McHaddish will be expected to attend."

I was hyperventilating. This could not be happening! I had only just gotten free of one man I didn't want in my life. This was the last thing I wanted or needed.

Molly crumpled the document in her fist and met his determined stare with her angry one, "Well get ready for a fight pal, 'cause you don't deserve her any more than Kepner did."

He leaned down and said, "You're on." And turned and walked out of the airport.

I put my arm around Molly, and made a silent promise. I was old enough to make my own decision, so when the judge asked, I would answer. I wasn't going to let anyone but me determine my fate from now on.